PRAISE FOR

CRIMSON LEAVES: DEATH OF AN EARL

"Dear Jane Austen, you'll be pleased to know that your beloved Regency Era is in the very capable hands of Jana Perkins. Master of witty, delightful banter, Perkins has weaved a mystery so clever and a plot so delightful to pull readers out of reality for hours.

Dear readers, please ensure you have a fan ready to cool your face. Perkins has crafted sweet romance at its swooniest."

—D.M. Tregaskis, author of
The Lonely Mortician
and Bake Wars

Crimson Leaves: Death of an Earl is a captivating story set in the 1800s. It has everything you could want in a regency romance novel from the dashing men, to the lovely ladies, an identity swap, a mysterious death, a villain (or two), and a bit of "magic." You won't want to put this book down until everything is resolved and your heart is content.

—Kim Golding, from
@kimsbooksandbites

CRIMSON SEASONS

BOOK I

CRIMSON LEAVES

DEATH OF AN EARL

JANA L. PERKINS

Copyright © 2024 by Jana L. Perkins

Second edition, 2025
Printed in the United States of America

ISBN 979-8-9999156-0-3

Created with Adobe indesign
Cover design by Jana L Perkins

*This book is dedicated to
the love of my life—
my husband,
who makes me whole*

Contents

HENRY

Wilton, England
October 10, 1801
Eight years old

It was autumn when I held the red leaf securely in my hand—it was delicate like Mother was. Panting, I rushed back inside, then squeezed past Katie and Doctor White to her bedside.

"I have it here, Mother, just as you asked." I lifted the leaf, hoping the small object that always brought her joy could somehow make all the difference.

Her breathing was labored and heavy when her eyes moved to me. Tears rolled down her cheeks as she reached her hand toward me and uttered, "My angel boy." Her words were a farewell that struck my heart with fear. I curled my fingers around her hand as she took her last breath.

"No," I whimpered. "No!" My voice cracked, emotion taking over.

No one stopped me or pulled me away as I lay next to Mother's still body, my arm wrapped securely around her, begging through inconsolable tears for her to come back. Tears continued to stream down my cheeks until I was convinced they'd run out completely.

Eventually, a light hand rested on my back.

I took in a shaky breath, grateful for Katie's presence. The smell of my leaf in hand clung to the air around me, reminding me of what I wanted to give my mother one last time. Sniffling, I opened my fingers and placed the leaf on the pillow near her face—the red ones had always been her favorite. I slowly stood before I touched her blonde hair, then turned away from where she lay, not caring to wipe the tears from my cheeks.

"How old are you, Henry?" Doctor White's voice echoed somewhere in my mind. I didn't want to speak—not when my mother was no longer with me.

"He's eight, sir," Katie, said at my side. She was my nursemaid, in her eighteenth year, and was the closest thing I had to a sister. The doctor knelt in front of me. I looked down at the floor, unwilling to meet his gaze.

"I know this is hard for you," he said with a kind voice. "I was about your age when I lost my own mother."

I glanced at him and he gave me a knowing look before his face lit up. "Oh, but we are in luck!" He quickly grabbed at the air, then cupped his hands together, eyes twinkling as he peeked inside. "I caught her last breath." He motioned with his head for me to come over. "Quick, grab the vial in my pocket, son, so we can trap it in."

I didn't move.

Katie obliged and reached her slender fingers into Doctor White's coat pocket, bringing out a small glass tube.

"Release the stopper, and bring it here," he said intently. She did so and held it underneath his clasped hands.

"Ready?" he asked.

She nodded.

He opened his palms just enough to carefully slide them around the narrow container, then eased the air into the vial. Once Katie capped the tube, Doctor White took it from her and opened my fingers, gently placing it inside.

"If you breathe it in, her soul will live in you, and so will her memory. Quick! Quick, breathe it in."

I sighed, turned around, and walked to the window. I didn't breathe it in. Any of it.

I held fast to the tiny bottle regardless.

Despite their hushed voices, I could hear them speaking behind me.

"Where is John?" the doctor asked Katie.

"Henry's father's in the parlor," she said with resentment. "We couldn't rouse him this morn'. Best he stays there for some time. He spent the night drinking and he's violent when he's been at it for a while. I wager he'll be murderous when he comes to." She let out a hesitant breath, then quieted her voice further, though it made no difference—I still heard every word. "He weren't always kind to the missus but he loved her fiercely. He blames Henry for her illness. Says she got the fever for lookin' after him all those nights when he turned real sick."

Doctor White gave a heavy sigh. "Look after Henry."

"I will, sir."

The doctor's footsteps fell slow and heavy until they were no longer heard.

Katie approached the window, standing just behind me. "Can I get you a bite to eat, Henry?" she asked softly.

I wasn't hungry, but I didn't say as much.

She waited for a time to see if I would speak before she finally walked away.

It was autumn when my world stopped. And as my world stopped, the trees continued to sway, the colorful leaves dancing on their limbs. It stopped while the vial weighed heavy in my hand. I looked down at the tiny glass that mocked my angel mother. It could never hold her smile and laugh, her tears or embrace. It could never hold her way of teasing or singing me to sleep. I unstopped the tube to release it, and raised it up to the window.

Then, just as quickly, I breathed it in. All of it.

November 7, 1801
Four weeks later

Doctor White lied. I felt none of Mother's soul in me, and she'd been buried for weeks now.

I stared at the plate of food Martha had placed in front of me, wondering if I'd ever feel happy again. Unlike the doctor, Katie's word could be counted on. Even at that moment she kept her promise to take care of me, watching to ensure I ate enough food to keep up my strength.

A maid rushed in, eyes frantic, finding Katie. A knowing look passed between them before Katie rushed over to where I sat. "Come Master Henry. You'll be much more comfortable eating in your room."

My father's slurred growls came from the other side of the door—drunk as always. She quickly pulled me away from the table and out of the dining room.

I was becoming used to this behavior from the staff. Only the day before, Martha had pulled me away from the entrance hall as boots sounded nearby, hiding me in a small room. "If you see your father, Master Henry, run the other way," she warned, eyes anxious.

Avoiding my father was nothing new—even before Mother's death. But since her passing, I hadn't exchanged a single word with him. It seemed as though the staff were holding their breath, waiting for the day my father would finally snap.

My toy soldiers were the only thing that seemed to pass the time. I carried them out to the back garden under my favorite tree in hopes of building a small barricade and finding some bugs as prisoners. Snapping a stick into small pieces, I wiggled the twigs into the dirt, and arranged them into a wall.

No sooner had I accomplished this than Katie approached, panic in her eyes. She whispered, "Go now, young master, near the stream until dark, and take your time about coming back, understand?"

My eyes narrowed in confusion. She looked back at the house quickly. I followed her gaze, then understood. My father could be heard shouting inside the house, accompanied by the sound of shattering glass. My eyes locked on the back door that Katie had left open.

I finally found my voice. "But I'm not allowed by the stream." I tried to sound calm, but my voice cracked.

My father's slurred shouting sounded through the house just then. "*Where* is that good-for-nothing *BOY*!" My heart filled with dread at the sound of his furious voice. It always surprised me how much of a gentleman he could actually sound when he was sober. Unfortunately it wasn't a frequent occurrence.

"Henry!" Katie snapped her fingers in front of me to get my attention and handed me a large sack of food. "Martha said this should be enough food for the day. You need to leave—now. RUN!"

I nodded and tried to do as she said, but my fear seemed to glue my legs in place.

"Henry, please!" Katie begged. My father's yells grew louder. Any second now he would appear at the back door.

Katie took one last look behind her, then let out a huge breath. "Come on!" With that, she grabbed my hand and started to run. A surge suddenly coursed through me, and I ran like death was at my heels. "Don't look back," Katie said, still grasping my hand tight. "Just keep running."

The back door slammed, and my father let out an angry yell in our direction just as Katie and I slipped out of his view into a copse of trees. I didn't look back, but I could hear his pursuit, boots striking hard against the ground.

My legs burned, but I knew I couldn't stop. He was slowly gaining on us.

"When I catch you, Katie!" he growled. I'd never seen Katie cry, but she gasped back a sob and heaved as we continued our furious pace. The smell of damp earth and moss filled the air as we approached the stream that I'd always been forbidden to go near.

"Thomases don't go near that filthy stream," Father had always said. "Lord Elliot will shoot you if you trespass, and that stream mixes with Elliot land. Anything that touches the Elliots' is scum. And we don't mix with scum, do we?" Despite his words echoing in my mind, we didn't slow our pace.

Our feet plunged into the pebbled stream, the frigid water reaching just above my ankles.

Those threats didn't matter anymore. Once Katie and I reached the other side, our legs continued their furious pace.

The moment our feet left the water, I heard the sickening splash of my father's boots hitting the stream's edge. He'd gained on us more than I had realized, and I couldn't help but look back. The glance over my shoulder was a mistake. Disoriented, I stumbled, taking Katie down to the earth with me.

I spat dirt from my mouth and wildly scrambled to get back up, completely covered in mud. My legs immediately buckled, quaking from exhaustion and terror.

Another glance backward brought fear into my very core as I realized it was too late. My father was already upon us. He grabbed Katie first, pulling her up by her long, brown hair. She shrieked out in pain.

"Please, sir," she begged, terror filling her eyes.

Hating myself for not having the courage to stop my father, I sat and cried. He slapped Katie hard across the face, throwing her to the ground.

"I'll deal with you later!" he growled before rounding on me. I thrashed and kicked as he yanked me up by the collar with both hands and jerked me close to his face. The rancid smell of his breath assailed me as he heaved from the exertion. "You know what I'm going to do to you, boy?" he snarled through clenched teeth. "I'll make sure you don't kill anybody ever again. You killed an angel! Now you get to live with the devil!"

Trembling uncontrollably, I took a deep breath as I felt his hands wrap around my neck. I closed my eyes and hoped my death wouldn't hurt.

Time slowed. Before his grip tightened, I thought of Mother.

Maybe what the doctor said was true after all. I felt her in that moment. I saw her smile, heard her song, welcomed her embrace, and felt her tears roll down my cheeks. Perhaps Katie would catch my last breath like the doctor had caught Mother's. . . .

BANG!

My eyes flew open as my father released me. I scrambled away from him, crawling to Katie. When she realized I was next to her, she wrapped me up in her arms, her whole body trembling.

Risking a glance at my father, I noticed his gaze was no longer fixed on us, but stared ahead in shock.

I followed his line of sight.

It was then that I first saw the man atop a large stallion. He was holding a rifle toward the sky in a cloud of smoke, furious.

Logically, I should have been afraid of him, but I couldn't help but be awestruck at his imposing, powerful figure. The newcomer dismounted his horse, not even minding to keep an eye on my father as he walked toward Katie and me.

"Can you stand?" he asked us.

My eyes widened as my father advanced on the stranger from behind. I wanted to yell out and warn the man that my father was dangerous—but just as my father pulled back his fist, the stranger, still facing us, shoved the back of his rifle into my father's gut. When my father doubled over onto his knees, the man turned quickly and knocked the end of his gun into my father's forehead. The blow put him on his back, and my father moaned, unmoving. It was clear to me that he wouldn't be getting back up again for some time.

"That's a warning, John," the man said, before turning his back on my father once more, approaching Katie and me with concern. "I'm afraid you're about to faint," he said to Katie. "Lie down a while. You are safe now. Help is on the way." Katie released me from her embrace that had gone rather limp and obliged without argument. Then the man turned to me. "Are you alright, son?"

I could only nod, but my tears betrayed me. When he spoke to me there was kindness and authority. "Do you think you can walk?"

"Yes, sir," was all my shaking voice could manage. But I found that once again, my legs would not bear weight, and it was impossible to stand. He extended his hand out to me.

"I'm James Elliot, Earl of Wiltshire." I took his hand and he helped me to my feet, steadying me until my legs cooperated.

I was not completely surprised at his name, since I was on Elliot property, but I was still wary of my father's echoing words that Lord Elliot would shoot me if ever I trespassed on his land. My eyes settled on his rifle before I shook myself from my daze, attempting to introduce myself the way Mother had taught me.

I dipped my head toward him. "I'm Henry Thomas, my lord."

He gave me a small grin. "Well, Henry Thomas, I have a decision to make. Your father trespassed on my property, and I have every right to shoot him."

I flinched at the words and he seemed to take note.

"Or, I can see to it that he stays where he belongs, and you and Miss—?"

"Katie," I volunteered.

"You and Miss Katie can clean yourselves up and take dinner with my family where we can talk things over. Would that be agreeable?"

I didn't know what to say, so I only nodded my head.

"Good. Then go and wait awhile with Miss Katie."

It was autumn when I made my first friend.

Lord Elliot escorted Katie and me back to his large estate where servants were waiting for us. A majestic stone edifice loomed overhead. I opened my mouth slightly as I walked beneath it and into the grand entry hall. Its tall marble pillars towered to the ceiling, a wide staircase curving as it trailed up the wall on the right side.

"Right this way," a servant said as he took hold of my wrist, attempting to lead me away from Katie. I clung to her muddy skirt as he did so. She looked so pale.

"Master Henry," Katie said, breathing out with exhaustion. "Go and get cleaned up. I can't even recognize you with all that dirt coverin' your face. I'll see you at dinner."

I wanted to discuss it further, but Katie looked like she could hardly stand. It seemed my best choice was to let them separate us without further argument.

After a bath and a good scrub, I was given some clothes that weren't mine.

"These are the young master's," the servant said as he handed them to me. "He is your age and size, and they should fit well enough for the time being."

After I dressed, a lady servant attended to my hair. She kept shaking her head and muttering to the other maid, "He looks just like him."

The other maid nodded her head. "I've never seen anything like it."

For dinner I was taken to an area with a smaller table. I was told that Lord Elliot's son would be introduced to me and keep me company while I waited.

A young lady servant with a tight bun and a thin, willowy frame approached me, someone following close behind. When she had a good look at me, her breath caught in surprise.

"As I live and breathe," she muttered. She quickly shook her head, remembering her station.

"Henry Thomas, this is Lord Elliot."

She stepped aside. Once the boy was in full view my eyes widened. Taking in his appearance was akin to staring at my own reflection. Almost every single detail, down to his dark hair and deep brown eyes, mirrored my own.

His mouth opened in surprise for a split second, our identical appearance startling him as much as it did me. He discarded his astonished look quickly and nodded his head toward me, as if he had practiced introductions a hundred times over.

"Lord Elliot," the young maid continued, addressing the boy behind her, "may I introduce you to Henry Thomas?"

I nodded my head but kept my eyes averted, feeling entirely out of place.

The young boy addressed me next. "I'm glad you could join us for dinner. It's very nice to make your acquaintance."

Mother had taught me my manners, but I had only ever practiced with her. I didn't want to mess up. I'd never had a friend my age, and the idea sounded nice. I did my very best to be polite and proper.

"Thank you, Lord Elliot for—er, your—hospitality. I am happy to make your acquaintance as well." I finished the last part quickly, as I felt odd speaking in such a formal way. Lord Elliot was all politeness and appeared to be completely in his element. We took our seats next to each other at a smaller table.

The young lady turned to the boy. "I'll be just over here if you need me, my lord."

He nodded and she walked off a few paces. Once she was out of earshot, he turned to me. "Call me Lord Elliot again and I'll slug you."

I was confused. It was a very respectable title and name. "Is that not your name?" I asked in concern.

"It is. But it's also my father's name. I'm Charles to you from now on, understand?"

I nodded. I thought it was disrespectful to do so, but I wasn't about to argue the point.

"Good. Now, do you want to see what I found earlier today?" Charles lost his proper demeanor entirely and put his hand in his pocket, fidgeting for a bit before looking around to make sure no one was watching. He carefully brought his hand under the table to slip something in my palm. It was cold and wet, and—a frog!

I jumped in surprise, then quickly recovered, smiling from ear to ear. "Where did you catch him?" I asked.

Charles grinned. "Down by the stream near the bridge. I had to sneak him in after lunch."

"I've always wanted to hold a frog," I said quietly.

"What do you mean you've always wanted to? Didn't you ever go to the stream and catch frogs?" Charles's eyebrows creased.

"No. My father said I should stay away from the stream because—"

I stopped talking. It wasn't a good time to tell Charles my father's thoughts.

10

"Probably because he thinks you can't swim," Charles said matter of factly. "It's alright. I can't swim either. Not yet. My father says I will learn soon, though. But you can't drown in the stream. You should tell your father so he will let you come catch frogs with me."

The thought of seeing my father again pulled me from my momentary state of ease. I wasn't about to confess my father's true nature to Charles. Thankfully he kept the conversation going.

"Then we could get a whole army of frogs and they could fight my soldiers!"

I couldn't help but light up at the idea. For the rest of the evening, we talked about soldiers, frogs, and times Charles nabbed food from the cook when she wasn't looking. We both agreed that green food was never meant to be discovered, and was only for horses and rabbits, and that pastries should be eaten all day. By the end of dinner, I felt another shift inside. For the first time in four weeks I felt a sense of peace—like I belonged.

Later that evening I was brought into a drawing room with elegant furnishings where the earl sat next to a beautiful woman he introduced as Lady Elliot. She wore an airy, white dress and had large, brown eyes that reminded me of my mother's. She didn't even try to hide her shock at mine and Charles's near identical appearance as she stood from her chair and walked over to me.

Her eyes widened in disbelief before she looked back at her husband. "You didn't tell me he is the very image of our son, James!" Turning back to face me, she studied my every feature, curious.

Lord Elliot chuckled. "I didn't know. He was completely covered in mud when I saw him." I fidgeted with my hands uncomfortably until the earl gave me a comforting wink.

Lady Elliot knelt in front of me, a light, floral scent drifting from her glossy brown hair, reminding me of summer. "Did you enjoy dinner, Henry?"

"I did, Your Ladyship." I tried to sound less awkward than I felt. I wasn't sure that I succeeded.

"I wish we could have been there when you were introduced to our son, but under the circumstances we felt we needed to help Katie arrange her affairs. I understand you both went through quite the ordeal today. We have offered your nursemaid a position at Wilton Manor, and—"

I looked down, tears already forming, as I realized Katie would be taken from me. Lady Elliot immediately noticed my distress and gently put her hands on either side of my arms. She waited until I looked at her eyes before she spoke again. "Lord Elliot and I have discussed the matter, and we will not send you anywhere you do not wish to go. If that means you want to stay here and never return home, so be it. But we'll not keep you here against your will."

I snuck a glance at Lord Elliot, who gave me a confident nod in agreement. Perhaps I should have been ashamed for the way I wrapped my arms around Lady Elliot and clung to her as I cried. Perhaps she should have been ashamed for holding me so tightly back. But I never was, and she didn't stop embracing me until I let go. When she breathed in, I must have breathed a little of Mother's last breath into her, for Mother's tears shone in her eyes. She felt like my mother had, and she was beautiful like her, too.

At that age, I never gave a thought to how incredible it was that the Elliots would keep me. I only knew that they said they would, and I believed them. I soon discovered that Lady Elliot was a distant cousin of my mother's. The relationship helped explain my permanence in the Elliot house and my near identical appearance to their son.

For months after I arrived at Wilton Manor, I worried about what my father might do. How would the Elliots respond if he demanded that I return home? Thankfully, my fears were in vain. My father never tried to reclaim me; I never missed him.

Servants from Wilton Manor claimed my belongings from home eventually—I wouldn't brave the trip back to my father's house for a long time yet. Lord and Lady Elliot had a room permanently made up for me right next to Charles's and we soon became inseparable, often up to some bit of mischief.

It was autumn when I made my first friend. His name was Charles Elliot and he liked frogs and soldiers. The doctor didn't lie, and Mother's soul lived in two people now: Lady Elliot and me. Shortly after that day, Charles became my brother; James Elliot, a father to me. And Lady Elliot became Mama.

And I breathed it in. All of it.

CHARLES

Wilton Manor
December 25, 1809
Eight years later
16 years old

There was no way Henry would be as tall as me. Our Christmas morning tradition began as usual.

"No, Charles! You can't stand on your tiptoes." Mama chuckled. "Henry, not you, too." We all laughed as she tried measuring us against the wall in the old nursery. She marked my height every year on Christmas Day, and she had added Henry too once he became a part of the family. For a few years now we had been too tall for her, making it necessary for her to use the extra height of a chair to complete her task.

"Hold still. If I fall and break my neck, I'll haunt you both for the rest of your lives."

I grinned. "Mama, why don't you have Papa or Lawrence do it so you don't have to stand on a chair?"

She put her hands on her hips and cocked an eyebrow. "I don't intend to stop this tradition. Ever."

"Even when you're too old to stand?" Henry teased.

"Even then." She swatted his stomach. "Besides, who else could pull off this masterpiece?" She smirked as she pointed at the wall. Every year, she used a piece of charred wood to make the marks, and then she'd use the bulky object to scrawl in our names as best she could. It was barely legible.

I finally gave in to her prodding and she marked my height on the wall. Thus far, Henry and I had grown exactly the same each year, give or take a hair. Each year we argued about who would be taller, and we always had to wait the entire year to find out—Mama wouldn't even let us measure ourselves back to back until Christmas Day. Since Henry was about two months older than me, he always stated that he should be at least slightly taller. I crossed my fingers that this would be the year I would finally beat him.

Regardless of who was taller, Henry and I kept slipping each other knowing grins: Our surprise for Mama was about to take place.

She finally marked Henry on the wall, and we stepped away, revealing our height on either side of her. From my point of view it looked as though we had grown the exact same amount once again. I handed her the large stick that we had propped up in the corner. It almost ran the entire height of the room from floor to ceiling. She put one end on the ground, then lined it up with Henry's marking and made a notch with the charred wood. Then she moved the stick over to my side and repeated the process. I helped her down from the chair and she showed us the results.

Mine and Henry's mouths dropped. There was an entire inch difference between the two marks.

"Who's taller?" we asked in unison.

She looked at us both. "Charles is," she said, giving me a nod and a smile before looking apologetically at Henry.

"Noooo!" Henry pantomimed a dagger to the heart, then fell to the floor dramatically. I raised my fists into the air and whooped and hollered. After seven years, I had finally won.

I bent down beside Henry and plastered the smuggest grin on my face. "I told you I was taller."

Now that we had discovered the long-awaited victor, it was time for Mama's surprise.

He continued playacting and then quickly punched my arm.

"Ow!" That hadn't been part of the plan. Regardless, I made it work. I rolled on the ground by the old bed, holding my arm, then snatched the present Henry and I had previously hidden underneath it, concealing it behind my back with one hand. I knocked my fist into Henry's arm with the other while I was at it.

"Maybe you have an inch on me," he said, sitting up, "but I hit harder than you do." He smiled.

"You do not!" I retorted.

Mama smirked. "I've seen the two of you spar. I do believe Henry's right."

I creased my eyebrows at her comment.

"You can't have every win, Charles," she said with a grin.

I rolled my eyes but quickly tucked my annoyance away. This moment wasn't about me. "Well, can I at least win a smile from you?" I raised my eyebrows at her, presenting the bonnet from behind my back.

"Charles!" she gasped, opening her eyes in surprise. She took the bonnet between her fingers and examined it. While she was admiring it, I nodded to Henry. He pulled the matching ribbons from his pocket and presented them. We had picked everything out before coming home from Cambridge for the holiday, from a little shop near the school.

Mama beamed and embraced us both. A grin bloomed from ear to ear on both Henry's and my faces—exactly as it happened every year.

Or was it exactly the same?

Somehow it felt different this time. It felt "one inch taller than Henry" different.

CHARLES

University of Cambridge
November 3, 1810
Almost two years later
17 years old

My quill scratched with precision across my parchment. I finally looked up as I realized a figure was standing over me.

"Why are you always in such a bad mood lately?" Henry asked.

"I'm not in a bad mood," I said while I wrote a third draft of my essay.

"Really, Charles? You haven't pranked Frederick or Jacob even once this semester, and you haven't stopped poring over your work for months." He frowned. "I've been working hard too, but you're overdoing it. It's time for a little break. Let's go catch some frogs for old times' sake and sneak them into Jacob's bed. It's been a couple years since we've done it."

I looked up at Henry, who used to be the "other me." I felt something inside that I could describe only as envy. Henry *did* work hard, and received excellent marks. But I was seventeen now, and more was required of me. I was the future Earl of Wiltshire.

Henry would be able to make a future for himself all while staying exactly as he was: carefree and the way I *used* to be. It was like seeing myself from another life that I couldn't go back to. A life that I missed but could no longer enjoy. When had it happened? The shift had been so slow and gradual I hadn't even noticed.

I looked at Henry's eager face. My essay was technically good enough the way it was. I contemplated his words and found that there was truth to them.

But I was determined to be better than just "good enough."

I shook my head. "Sorry, Henry. I can't today. There will be enough time for frivolity when the holiday is here." The moment I spoke the words I knew they were a lie. Henry shook his head and then left. I watched him walk off toward the pond while I put my quill back to my paper. A part of me walked off with him. I wondered if I'd ever get it back.

My reflection, Henry, still held on to the part of me that had been missing for almost two years now. He would have to hold enough of it for the both of us. I was still an inch taller. I would write on parchment, and he could still catch frogs.

Wilton
August 17, 1811
Nine months later
18 years old

Miss Ollerton had been trying to catch my attention the entire evening. I didn't even attempt to smile as she fanned herself coyly in my direction across the room. I bristled with annoyance as she made her way over to me.

"Good evening, Lord Elliot." She talked with a lilting voice that some men found attractive. It grated on my nerves. I looked down at her but still didn't smile. "Good evening, Miss Ollerton."

"Do you not plan to dance at all this evening, my lord?" She gave me a pretty little pout. It took everything in me not to roll my eyes.

"Not if I can help it."

She looked over my attire, including my black cravat and suit. "Of course. You're still in mourning." She looked up at me through her lashes before she continued. "It is two months past your mourning period. Surely one dance wouldn't hurt."

"I assure you, miss, it would." I didn't try too hard to hide my irritation.

She pursed her lips, then looked over at Henry, who was still wearing black and choosing not to dance, though he smiled at his company good-naturedly. She continued, "Your mourning period is over, Lord

Elliot. I think some dancing would do you good."

As if she could determine how long one should mourn. The very thought was offensive.

"I think you misunderstand me, Miss Ollerton. I choose not to dance because I do not wish to." I cocked an eyebrow. "Nor *will* I wish to."

She gave me a smile regardless. "Oh Lord Elliot, you're so droll." She fluttered her lashes. "How can I get you to dance?"

I stared at her, my mouth in a firm line, before I turned and walked away. I was accosted by two other women within moments, both of whom I quickly shrugged off.

I left Henry in the ballroom and found my father, who was talking in the billiard room with some gentlemen. I stood near him and was soon let into their conversation.

It wasn't that I hated women—I just had no patience for their antics. They all wanted me for the same things: my title and my wealth. Mama would have scolded me for the way I had just treated Miss Ollerton. I swallowed down the weight that rose to my throat as my mother's smile flashed in my mind.

I hadn't lied to Miss Ollerton; I truly didn't want to dance. Though my mourning was only an excuse now, it didn't mean I had stopped missing Mama. My mother was the only one who had seen through my hardened walls. She'd always assured me I would find someone who would catch my eye. So far, I wanted no part of it. I was fully convinced that I would forever remain a bachelor.

Henry could have them all.

The gentlemen in our circle laughed at some comment or another—All except Papa. He smiled out of courtesy, but it wasn't genuine. It had been that way for about eight months now. His eyes met mine for a moment and I understood the emptiness.

He needed these next years abroad as much as I did.

I

MISSIVE

Henry

Wilton Manor
September 6, 1816
Five years later
23 years old

The gray sky cast large beads of rain to the earth. As the water pounded against the estate, I stood behind the glass panes of Wilton Manor's library, untouched by the elements. My right thumb grazed over the surface of a small coin resting inside my palm: tuppence.

I continued tracing my thumb against the smooth piece of metal, then rubbed my other hand across my short beard, shifting my gaze once more to the ominous clouds looming overhead. The weather was reflecting my mood. The tuppence in my right hand was a reminder of both my gloom, and happier times. I finally transferred it to my other hand and deposited it into my left jacket pocket—my right pocket would forever remain empty.

"—Henry?"

My transfixed stare finally broke.

"Henry, did you hear a word I just said?" Charles's flat tone broke my strand of thoughts that were nowhere and everywhere at the same time.

Despite the gloom I felt, I smirked to myself. He'd caught me. And now I would use it to my advantage. I continued rubbing my beard, staring out the window. I hadn't heard the last minute or so of Charles's grumblings while he opened a stack of letters, each one inviting him to every high-class London event while parliament was in session.

My brother exhaled with annoyance. "Apparently all of London has been tipped off that we will be making an appearance after our five years abroad. It makes me want to flee the country."

I wanted to try Charles's patience just a little longer. I continued staring out the window as if I was still not listening. It was the only pastime that gave me some form of entertainment: a reaction from Charles other than sheer boredom and quiet melancholy.

I listened as he pushed his chair out and walked over to the settee. I tried to time this next part just right. Unfortunately, I was just a hair late—I felt the small decorative pillow hit my head right as I moved to duck.

I had only successfully dodged his throws a handful of times, but it was worth the attempt to see Charles's angry expression when he missed.

I slowly turned towards Charles. "You know, I do believe you're losing your touch. The last one had a lot more power behind it. How disappointing for us both."

"Don't worry," he said with a bored expression as he crossed the room back to the stack of letters. "I have asked Lawrence to hide a stash beneath my desk to help me get your attention when you find the window more interesting than this." He held up the letter in his hand. It wasn't much of a reaction, but it was more than . . . well, nothing.

I smirked. "Really, Charles, asking the butler to stash pillows beneath your desk. Whatever did Lawrence do to deserve such treatment?"

Footsteps approached the library, announcing the arrival of someone new. "It must be because I forgot to lock you in your room this morning, sir," came a voice from the doorway.

My eyes flicked up to see Lawrence, a graying gentleman. He returned my gaze with his usual wink before making his way towards Charles, a letter in hand. His walk was always steady and direct.

"This just came for you, my lord." He placed the envelope atop the desk. "Its carrier was somewhat unusual for this area. A young boy, no more than eight years old."

Charles looked up from his stack of letters inquisitively.

"That *is* unusual in Wilton," he agreed, glancing at the missive. "Thank you, Lawrence. I will notify you once I have read its contents. I'm sure you are just as curious as I am to find out what's inside."

"Very good, my lord," Lawrence said evenly as he excused himself with a bow of the head. Not only was Lawrence the butler of Wilton Manor, but he had been James Elliot's closest friend and a mentor to Charles and me.

Four months had passed since Papa's death. I missed the man I considered my father more than I could say. I feared there would never be joy in the house again.

For the past seven years it had been my job to bring laughter and smiles to the room. It hadn't always been that way. There was a time when I looked at Charles and felt that we were the same person. Not only was he my very reflection, but I had known his thoughts almost as well as I knew my own. We used to laugh at all the same things. Charles used to share a smile, a wink, a laugh, with anyone who passed his way. When we went to Cambridge, we made all sorts of mischief together. Then we turned sixteen, and he gained an inch on me. It never was the same after that.

I blame the inch. That, and our mama's passing. She left us just before our last year at Cambridge when we were almost eighteen.

The last words she spoke to me often found their way into my mind. She had taken my hand and said, "Promise me you won't give up on Charles. I hope you'll never stop teasing him. I want to see him smile and wink the way he used to, all the way from heaven."

I kissed her forehead, then said, "If it will ease your mind, Mama, I will be teasing Charles for the rest of his life, even if it's from the grave." She softly chuckled.

She died the next day.

A piece of Charles died even further with Mama. He pulled increasingly into himself, laughter no longer accompanying any of his moods. To pull a fleeting smile from him was no small feat, and a full grin no longer existed on his short list of expressions.

Her death seemed to have the opposite effect on me. When I wanted to crumble into a million pieces, I remembered the old doctor and caught her last breath. And just like I had done with Mother, I breathed it in. All of it. A desperation to make sure she stayed alive pulsed through my every fiber. Though tears had often been my companion in the late hours of night that first year, I never had a hard time sharing her smiles, mischief, and laughs.

That is, until Papa was put into the ground. Since his passing, I had attempted to lighten the mood for all of us. But my heart and mind felt much more like the storm pounding outside than I would let on. I looked once more to the window, brooding.

But I knew Mama was watching from heaven, next to my own mother. No doubt Papa was with them, being informed of my promise to never give up on my brother. So I would keep trying. I looked for the easiest distraction. *Ah yes, Charles's bad mood.* I felt better already. Walking over to the desk where Charles sat, I gestured to the stack of letters.

"Is Lady Morgan still trying to convince you to attend her annual ball to be introduced to her 'oh so eligible' daughter?" I asked with a mischievous grin.

"Naturally," Charles said flatly.

I cocked my brow facetiously. "What a burden it must be for you to have every mother trying to wed you to their daughters. Tell me, my lord, how ever will you survive?"'

"It may come as a shock to you, Henry, but people don't interest me. They aren't my hobby." He gave me an accusatory look. "I don't constantly think of ways to make them smile."

"Touché, old friend. You would first need to smile yourself to make others do it."

Charles exhaled, annoyed, then pushed his stack of papers aside, reaching for the curious missive Lawrence left on the table. I waited as Charles opened it. His expression was typical at first. A bored, flat demeanor crossed his eyes and lips. Then his brow started to crease as he leaned in close to the page.

"What is it?" I asked, suddenly alarmed.

Charles shook his head in angry disbelief. He put the letter down on the table only to immediately snatch it up again and reread it. This time he started pacing.

"Charles?" My concern grew as he completely ignored me. "Fine," I muttered, prowling to the pillow on the ground. I hurled it as hard as I could toward Charles's head. He had the audacity to step forward as it left my grip, leaving the pillow to hit the wall just beyond him. But it did the trick.

He flinched and looked up from the missive, staring at me with an unreadable expression before he finally spoke.

"Someone believes our father was murdered." He held out the letter for me to take. My heart lurched at his words, rendering me speechless. I took two large strides toward him and snatched the paper from his grip. It had no name or address.

Lord Elliot,

I am grieved at the loss of your father. He was a good man, and I knew him personally. I believe his death was no coincidence.

I have information if you would like to begin an investigation.

I do not feel comfortable at this time disclosing my identity. There is to be a grand ball hosted by the Duke and Duchess of Hastingwood at their estate in Westminster on the evening of November 1, in honor of the birthday of their son, Lord Fletcher.

At approximately half past nine I will be waiting

near the back-east garden, near the servants' quarters in a secluded area near the roses. If you would prefer to send a trusted representative in your place to receive the information, I will oblige.

I will begin our conversation by stating, "The weather is unusual for November." The code phrase I expect in return is, "Mother nature, like human nature, has no rules." If I receive no person by three quarters after nine, I will assume that you wish to let the matter rest.

I read it a few times over, rubbing my beard harder with each passing line, a tempest of questions and emotions swelling inside my chest, creating a raging storm of confusion, disbelief, and anger.

Papa's death had been so sudden. We'd received word that he had taken ill the day before his departure for home. He had stopped at an inn on the way back and died only hours after arriving. I'd never even considered the possibility that his death could have been anything other than natural.

Now that this letter was staring me in the face, I was angry that the idea of foul play hadn't even crossed my mind. The doctor's report stated that Papa had died of natural causes and that there wasn't anything unusual about his death. But he had been as healthy as ever when he left home. My chest tightened as I contemplated it all. The thought that Papa could still be alive if not for potential murder made all the wounds fresh.

I finally tossed the letter on the desk, exhaled slowly, and looked at Charles. "What should we do?"

Charles walked the length of the room again, but said nothing. It was torture watching Charles pace back and forth, saying, "No," to himself. Or, "That wouldn't work." After a minute or so, he finally stopped in place and looked up. I waited until I could stand it no longer.

"Well?" I demanded.

Charles gave me a small smirk and said, "I believe it's time for you to shave."

I reeled my head back in surprise. "It's been some time since you've had a lark, Charles."

He cocked an eyebrow, unamused. "I'm being serious, Henry."

I rubbed my thumb through my beard. "You're quite jealous, aren't you? Is it that you *can't* grow a beard, or that you *won't*?" We hadn't discussed my beard in over five years. As amusing as it was, I had no idea what it had to do with the information we had just received.

"Perhaps I'd like to see what's been growing under there all these years," Charles said flatly.

"I keep a very tidy beard and the ladies seem to like it." I knew full well that it wasn't the current fashion. "Perhaps you'd like to know, however, that I grew this beard to give you a sporting chance. My face would look so angular and masculine that you'd be left without a dance partner if it came off."

"Or perhaps," Charles notched an eyebrow, looking long and hard at me, "you would look exactly like *me*." He mirrored my posture. "Again."

"As a technical matter, *you* would look like *me*."

"I wasn't the one who grew the beard. You *will* look like me again." The way he emphasized "will" threw me off. It was rare that I gave up a row of banter, but this time . . .

"What is this about, Charles?" I finally asked.

"As amusing as you may find this conversation, I am being entirely serious. It's time for you to shave."

"I am not shav—"

"Just hear me out for a moment," he interrupted. "And please leave your jests for another time."

I gestured with my hand for him to proceed.

"How long would you say it's been since we've been mistaken for each other?"

"It's been some time," I admitted.

"I want a specific answer," he said flatly.

I exhaled slowly, thinking out loud. "I'd say the last time was when we were at Mr. Ollerton's ball. His daughter Olivia had been coyly smiling at me for a good quarter hour. I thought she was quite a rare beauty, and she appeared to be a sweet thing, so I asked her to dance.

By the end of the dance, I fancied myself completely smitten and intended to call on her the next day. When I asked if I could, she said, 'I can't believe the future Earl of Wiltshire would show any interest in *me*.' I clarified that I was *not* the future Earl of Wiltshire and that I was Mr. Thomas. She quickly hid her disappointment and laughed, saying, 'Oh, how silly of me. I am sorry, Mr. Thomas, but I'm otherwise engaged tomorrow.' Then she whisked herself off and found the real Lord Elliot."

Charles rolled his eyes. "Miss Ollerton was always a flirt and a trollop."

I chuckled. "Really, Charles, a trollop?"

"Fine. But she was absolutely a flirt and a title seeker."

"And what woman isn't a title seeker?"

Charles didn't look amused. "We are getting off topic. How old were we at the Ollertons' ball?"

"We had just turned eighteen, and I noticed I had to shave more often than you did. After the ball, I stopped."

"You grew your hair longer as well," Charles added.

I smirked. "Not by much, but I'm flattered you took notice."

"I always noticed when my other reflection started to change."

"As did I." My brother hadn't talked this way in a long time. "You were the traitor first, you know," I had to add.

"How so?"

"You gained an inch on me the winter we were sixteen."

"Ah, the legendary inch," Charles said, a corner of his mouth actually turning up. "You do look a little short compared to me, though you are still taller than most gentlemen. We may have to adjust your heel size for that anomaly."

"You still haven't explained what this is about."

"I think we should switch places for a time," he said abruptly.

My eyes opened wide, my head jerking back. A genuine grin spread across his face as he saw my expression. If I hadn't been completely taken off guard, I would have felt such a victory for getting him to smile. It had been months since I'd last seen one from him.

"Why would we switch places? And for how long?"

"It would only be for a fortnight, and only under very careful conditions. I have been invited to every social event in London. I believe there may be information circulating about these parties that could help us discover the truth. You have a gift for getting people to open up to you within a very short period of time. You know how people work. You can get in their circles easily."

I held back from rolling my eyes. Getting people to easily open up was one thing; being an earl was another entirely. The distinction certainly gave Charles special advantages.

I stroked my beard again, thoughtful. "You can get inside any circle you want, Charles."

"Not the way *you* could if people thought you were me. You have a way of making people trust you. They spill their secrets. I can't do that."

I had to admit it was true. I did have a way of easing people's minds until they told me things they hadn't intended to share.

Charles continued, "I am good with information. I will meet with the individual who wrote this letter while you gather the gossip you hear out of every mouth in London. Together, I believe we can get to the bottom of this. But I can't do it as Charles, and you can't do it as Henry."

I stared at him, taking in his words. "It's been five years since we were seen together in London. It could work. How long before we switch appearances?"

For the first time in years I saw excitement spark behind Charles's eyes. "We have a little over eight weeks before Duchess Hastingwood's party. I believe it can be done."

"You think you can master this perfection in eight weeks?" I gestured to my short beard.

Charles smirked. "I'll bring Lawrence in now. We will need his help."

"Will we need Jeremiah's help as well?" Jeremiah was expert at his job as valet.

"He can help me slowly shift my appearance to yours. But I don't want even him to know our plans. The fewer people that know about our disguise, the better. I will have him teach me exactly how to achieve my current hairstyle and dress so I can teach you. You won't make the switch until we arrive in London. The only one who can know of our plan is Lawrence."

I glanced again at the open letter on the desk, anger once again filling my core. "Who would kill Papa?"

"That's what we're going to find out." Charles looked at me, and for the first time in years I felt that our thoughts were the same: We wouldn't rest until the truth was uncovered and Papa was avenged.

I raised an eyebrow. "When do we start?"

2

DEEP-BLUE DRESS

Jane

London
November 1, 1816
Eight weeks later
20 years old

I studied my reflection in the full-length mirror as I held the light pink dress in front of me. My hand glided over the silky fabric as it gleamed and shifted. A dress stated everything about a lady: class, distinction, her intentions, whatever they may be. My intention this evening was to look exactly as I should—as society expected. Beautiful, but poised. Fetching, but dignified. It's what I always did. And it was this method that had attracted Lord Fletcher, the Duke of Hasting-wood's son.

My bedroom door opened suddenly. Lily entered the room carry-ing a silky, deep-blue dress. There was a determined look on her face that I recognized well. Being two years older than my sister gave me the advantage of stating that I'd seen her entire life from start to finish. As such, I knew exactly what she was thinking.

She cocked an eyebrow. "You promised, Jane." She looked down at the dress in her hands.

"I did *not* promise." I gave her an exasperated look.

"You said you would wear this dress to the duchess's ball."

"Yes, but I certainly didn't promise." I returned my gaze to my reflection in the mirror and the safe pink dress I was holding.

Lily laid the blue dress on my bed, then pursed her lips. "Perhaps we should really be asking what *Frederick* prefers."

"Lord Fletcher," I corrected.

She rolled her eyes. "I would never call him Frederick in public, Jane. But it becomes tedious calling him Lord Fletcher when we are in private. Besides, Lord Fletcher seems too lofty a name for flat, expressionless Frederick. I surmise that even you think of him by his Christian name in your mind."

"Only because your disgraceful behavior is rubbing off on me."

Lily gave me a sly smile. "It does make me feel rather rebellious thinking of a man's Christian name in my mind from time to time." She tilted her head at me. "There's a certain kind of thrill about it. And don't pretend that you're completely innocent. I've already caught you using Lord Fletcher's Christian name when we are speaking in private on numerous occasions."

I hated it when she was right. I did, indeed, think of him as Frederick, for I hoped to secure him as my future husband. I had to admit, unfortunately, that Lily was right: Lord Fletcher did seem too lofty a name for his bored character. But I'd never admit it to anyone, especially to Lily.

A knock came at the door and it cracked open before Alice popped her head inside, smiling. "Are you ready for your dress yet, miss?"

Lily grinned. "Perfect timing, Alice. We were just discussing which gown Jane should wear tonight."

Alice opened the door fully, eyes wide with excitement. "If I may be so bold, miss, all the ladies will be wearing light colors. I believe the blue would make you stand out more this evening." She gestured at the dress Lily had placed on the bed and smiled, lines marking her eyes. "Lord Fletcher won't be able to resist you, and I'll be surprised if you don't receive a proposal by the end of the month."

Lily would have to watch her use of Lord Fletcher's name now that someone else had joined the conversation. Lily smirked and grabbed the dress from off the bed, then held it up in front of me. The ladies in the dress shop had convinced me that it would be a crime if I didn't choose this fabric. They gushed about the way the color perfectly offset my auburn hair and accentuated my blue eyes. And Lily was right, I did say that I would wear it tonight. But now that it stared at me, it seemed bold.

I took a deep breath and nodded my head. "Alright, I'll wear the blue."

Alice smiled. "Let's get your hair in place first, miss. Then we can put you in your gown."

I sat at the dressing table while she went about pinning my curls on top of my head in a neat, orderly fashion, the way I always expected.

"Are you still trying to secure Lord Fletcher, then?" Lily asked.

"Yes," I said, without hesitating.

"I still don't understand what you see in him, but if you love him, then I'm happy for you."

I looked at her through the mirror. "I don't need to love him to be happy. He is not old, we have the same aspirations, and I find myself quite content that I don't mind his company."

Lily scoffed. "Content that you don't *mind* his company? What about your heart, Jane?"

"You know how I feel about this, Lily." We hadn't discussed matters of the heart for a number of years.

She shook her head in defiance. "Yes, I do. Your heart stopped beating a long time ago, and now I must keep my dreams to myself, as you'll never understand them."

"My heart beats as well as anyone else's. My mind works well too, and it tells me that Lord Fletcher is the best thing that has come along thus far. And—"

"You mean the most eligible with the highest-ranking title?" Lily interrupted, cocking her eyebrow.

"Why do you say that as if it's a bad thing?" I shook my head, unable to understand her. "You know as well as I do that we have not been accepted in our current circles. Marriage to Lord Fletcher would secure our future in high class society. It would ease my mind to know that any of us, Mama and Papa especially, could go anywhere we please and be respected."

"Mama and Papa are content." Lily fixed me with an even stare.

"They can't possibly be content when people mock them behind their backs." I was grateful that logic always seemed to yell louder than emotion in my mind. At least it had for the last several years.

There was a time, years ago, when I had romantic fancies like my younger sister. Lily and I used to run out to the field, lie beneath our favorite tree, and watch the clouds shift. We talked about how someday we would find a man who adored us, who would listen and be there during rain or shine. Back then, I felt I would be better off loved and poor than wealthy and lonely. But over time, I began to understand that I needed to change in order to find what would ultimately bring comfort and stability.

I met Lily's eyes once more through the mirror. "Do you truly think aspiring to secure a man with a high-ranking title is beneath you?"

Lily sighed. "I know it has been some years since you've talked about being swept off your feet, but have you never had your heart flutter, Jane? Or felt intoxicated by a man's presence?"

I had to laugh. "You are but eighteen. What do you know about such things?"

"I've never experienced it for myself, but I *have* heard stories, and I will wait until my heart is thoroughly snatched up. Which is why I will most likely live my life as an old spinster."

"You're better off an old spinster than a woman with a ruined reputation," I murmured under my breath.

"What is that supposed to mean?" Lily asked, irritated. "I have never been loose or given any impression that I am a light skirt!"

I could tell I hurt her feelings. And it was true that she was neither a naive flirt nor a woman easily turned for her morals. But she continued breaking the simplest rules that held up her reputation.

"Mrs. Allen said she saw you unchaperoned, wandering the gardens at her dinner party the other evening."

Lily's eyes sparked with understanding. "I see," she said. She walked to the window as she folded her arms. "So I'm not allowed a little fresh air from time to time without being seen as a woman of easy virtue?"

"Lily, we are not in Wilton. And even in Wilton you should not wander alone without a chaperone. We are under scrutiny at every turn. There are definitely some good people who would like to see us succeed. But there are others who would very much like to see us fail."

She held her rigid posture for a moment before it finally softened. She sighed. "I will be more careful. But the rules are unfair."

"The rules are for your own protection. I don't understand why you feel the need to break them. Are you really so bored of the London scene already? I know the season technically hasn't begun, but there has been enough entertainment to fill our time. You have never been without a dance partner and have received plenty of attention from the gentlemen. Have the ladies been so unkind?"

Lily turned her face from the window back to me, a defiant eyebrow raised. "Have the ladies been unkind indeed! I don't know how you survived your first season alone. But you are mistaken in thinking they are the cause. I rather enjoy their catty behavior. It gives me some sort of entertainment." She looked down at her hands. "I don't know that I could do it without you, though. It does give me comfort knowing that despite what the preening sphinxes think, my Jane will always be here for me."

"Yes, I will." I grinned. "As soon as you start taking a chaperone with you for your turns about the garden."

"I'll stop roaming the gardens alone when you give me a reason to like Lord Fletcher as my future brother-in-law."

Alice pinned up my last curl, then looked at my reflection in the mirror with me. "You'll be the talk of the evening, as always. Let's get you into your dress now." I stood from my dressing table and walked to the full-length mirror next to my wardrobe. She brought the deep-blue dress over to me and I stepped into it. The smooth fabric caressed my skin.

I took in my appearance as Alice buttoned up the dress. It was fluid and the color did something to me. It made me feel daring, like I wanted to taste something more. I had never experienced such a feeling. I didn't like it.

"Alice, I've changed my mind. I will go with the pink gown this evening." I was already trying to get myself out of the dress.

I could tell she was disappointed, but she hid it well. "Hold still, miss, so I can help you out of it."

I sighed with relief as Alice undid the back of my dress and helped me into the silky pink one. Lily looked at me with a smirk, clearly amused with my frantic display. I quickly deflected the conversation to her. "What will you be wearing tonight?"

"Whichever dress Alice thinks I should wear." She cocked an eyebrow. She knew me well enough to realize that I had backed down from the blue dress for more reasons than a simple preference to the color.

Alice smiled at Lily. "The green dress, miss. I'll fetch it from your room now."

"Thank you, Alice." Lily watched her leave the room. I knew the exact dress. It was the gown Lily was fitted for when I chose the fabric for my blue one.

"Are you really so unhappy here?" I asked again, hoping to avoid any questions about my sudden change in ball gown.

She looked down. "That is a difficult question to answer. It's not that I haven't enjoyed my time in London." She started pacing the room. "There is just such an air to the parties and balls. At first I found myself in love with the splendor of everything. I was flattered to find a compliment at every turn. At least, until I realized that a man's admiration is meant for any woman he finds mildly attractive, diverting, or wealthy. Women smile and compliment through their teeth all while they look down on one another like bugs to be rid of. I am restless for something more. And if I'm restless in London, I will be happy nowhere."

She stopped her pacing and faced me, then added, "I'm sure it will pass soon enough. I believe I may just be a little disappointed—and

I miss home. I miss sneaking sweets with Sterling and Oliver. I miss riding Stella, letting her run until I feel like we are flying."

I nodded. "I understand. I remember my first stay in London." And I did understand her, to an extent. I, too, missed everything she did. If only I could help Lily understand that a secure life was not a boring life—that men's easy compliments were the way the game was played. To me, there was no room for love or passion in place of logic.

As if in betrayal to the very thought, the image of the deep-blue dress and the craving for more flashed through my mind. I quickly banished it as Alice walked in with Lily's dark-green gown. She would be stunning in it with her dark-chocolate, wavy hair that always seemed to glisten when she moved. This evening she wore it mostly up with some ringlets cascading down the back and a few delicate curls at the sides.

Alice brought the gown forward, then turned to me, a letter in hand. "This just came for you, miss."

Once I took the envelope from her fingers, Alice turned her attention back to Lily and the dress she was carrying. She smiled. "I can't wait to see you in it. It's sure to bring out your green eyes."

Lily tried, but failed, to hide her smile at the compliment.

"Let's see you in it, then." As Alice helped her into the gown, part of me considered the blue dress again. Lily was always beautiful, but in this particular shade of green, she looked absolutely stunning. In the end, resolve won out and the pink dress stayed.

I grinned. "Matthew Johnson will not be able to resist you tonight."

Lily made a face of dread. "Ugh, perhaps I should wear my old brown gown this evening."

"You have complained about men being fake. But I do believe Matthew is quite devoted to you."

"Devoted, perhaps. But hopelessly dull and boring—and short."

"Don't be so harsh. You're only half a head taller than him."

Lily chuckled. "I could overlook such a "shortcoming" if he didn't make me feel uncomfortable. I can't quite put it into words, but there is something unhinged about him."

I shook my head. "Matthew Johnson is harmless."

"Well then, *you* can dance with him tonight," Lily said, raising her eyebrows. Her gaze fell to my hands. "Who is the letter from?"

My attention returned to the missive in question. "It's from home," I said, looking at the address.

Lily rushed over and reached for it. I snatched it back. "I am very capable of reading it aloud," I teased.

"Then read it."

I opened it slowly, intentionally trying her patience further. She rolled her eyes as I cleared my voice dramatically and read the words aloud.

Dear Jane and Lily,

I hope London finds you well. I have written to your aunt and uncle to see if they can spare you for our annual autumn celebration. It will take place the 13th of November, but we would love to receive you at your earliest convenience. I know it will momentarily take you away from your stay in London, so I leave the decision up to each of you. Sterling and Oliver would like me to include that if you don't come home, they will have all the pastries to themselves and most likely die of a stomachache.

All my love, Mama

Lily's face lit up. "You can decide what you will, Jane, but I am definitely going home for the autumn celebration. The sooner we leave, the better. It will be a blessed respite from the London scene."

"Of course I'm going home for the celebration," I said, already thinking through the events we would be missing in town. Naturally I wanted to go home and see my family, but there was always so much to look forward to in London.

I settled on a way to enjoy both. "I believe it would be ideal to return home the day after Lady Morgan's ball. That will be the ninth of

November. Leaving then will allow us to arrive home four days before the party."

Lily looked at me unconvinced. "It will take most of the day to arrive home."

"Yes, but we will still have a full three days before the celebration itself. And we can stay until the following Saturday, which will give us an entire week to be home. We will miss a musicale here in London, but it will be worth it." I looked at Lily. "Just because I love London doesn't mean I don't miss home too."

Lily gave me a small smile. "It's nice to hear you say it. I do wonder sometimes if you would ever choose to return if you weren't summoned. But your arrangement is fair. I suppose I can endure this next week if it means I will soon get a breath of home."

I smiled, grateful that things were finally as they should be. We would soon be on our way to one of the finest balls of the year, despite parliament being in session, Lily's spirits were back up—and she would not roam the gardens unaccompanied.

And I would wear the pink dress.

TUPPENCE

Charles

London
November 1, 1816
That same evening
23 years old

I stood alone in my bedchamber as I finished the last touches on my hair, the way my valet, Jeremiah, had taught me. I combed the front of my dark-chestnut hair back and then sideways so it was off my forehead, allowing a few strands to find their way back down near my temple. A slight wave remained on top. Then I combed the sides back. My beard wasn't quite as thick as Henry's was, but all things considered, I looked just like he did.

As I studied the man staring back at me, silence filled the space, with only my thoughts accompanying it. The still, quiet house was giving me too much time to think. It was easier to forget and pretend nothing had changed. And yet it was impossible to act like my father wasn't gone. I had relied on him for so long that his absence was hard to ignore, even six months later.

His personality had been magnetic. People had wanted to be around him—wanted to please him. I'd felt the same draw to his presence.

"Would you like to be wealthy, boys?" he had asked Henry and me one evening as we were playing. We were nine at the time. We ran over to him eagerly, full of anticipation. He held up a small, wooden button.

"How's that supposed to make us wealthy?" I asked, disappointed.

"I'll show you." He waved the button back and forth until it suddenly turned into tuppence. "If you can find the magic in everything, then you will always find success." Henry and I opened our mouths in amazement.

"Are you magic?" Henry asked in awe.

Papa chuckled. "Hold on to this, Henry." He placed the coin in Henry's right jacket pocket. "If you hold on to it long enough, perhaps you'll become magic too."

"What about me?" I asked.

He held up a small feather and folded his hand around it, rubbing his closed fist a few times. When he opened it back up, the feather was gone. He grinned at my shocked expression. "Now look in your right jacket pocket."

I reached into my pocket and pulled out a matching coin to Henry's. I opened my mouth in excitement. "Papa! I want to be magic too."

At first I really thought he was magic. But then he slowly started to share his tricks with us. It quickly became an unspoken challenge between Henry and me that one of us would become the best at "Papa's magic." Making objects vanish became a daily pastime, and eventually we all made a game of it. We would pick each other's pockets and later return the stolen items to a different pocket without the victim's notice. Whoever successfully moved the most items was named "victor of the thieves."

It was an entirely improper game, especially for an earl, so we kept it a family secret. I was always delighted that Mama, a much respected countess, loved watching us sneak around each other. She would laugh and smile when she saw one of us up to our tricks; then, just as quickly, she would swallow it down and put her most aired look on her face, daring anyone to ask what she was sniggering about.

Henry and I became quite proficient by the time we left for Cambridge. One of Papa's specialties was sneaking tuppence in our right jacket pockets for good luck without us noticing. By the time he passed, we were all so good at making things disappear and reappear that there was never a true victor—just items discovered in many pockets, different from the ones they were originally placed in, and tuppence from Papa. In reflection of the tradition, I placed my hand in my right jacket pocket. It was empty, of course.

I reflected on the time Papa and I caught so many fish we could barely carry them home. Cook was so angry when we threw them on her bread board in our excitement. She had actually chased Papa with a frying pan. It was the only time I'd ever seen him run away from anything. I grinned at the memory.

Then there were the moments I watched him steal a kiss from Mama when he thought no one was looking.

Mama—She'd been coming to my mind more and more as of late, though it had been six years since her passing. My father's passing made hers fresh once again. She'd always been able to read me like an open book.

"I haven't seen you smile for some time, Charles. Not really," she'd said. I was seventeen at the time, and Henry and I were back for the holiday.

"Nonsense, Mama. I was just barely smiling at your joke."

"As a courtesy, perhaps." She gave a flat smile of her own. "Has something happened to bring on such a change?" I remember feeling defensive, even annoyed at her question.

"I am as I've always been." I said the words, but they felt hollow even to me.

She pulled me into an embrace after that, hugging me tight. I'd been much taller than her at that point. She told me she loved me whether I chose to smile or not, then added that she still hoped to see it reemerge soon. I did my best to smile at her then, and it seemed to be enough for her, even though she knew it was empty.

It had been a strange sensation the last two months, letting my beard and hair grow out. I'd always set high expectations for myself: The way I carried myself, the way I acted and dressed. The way I was always perfectly clean-shaven and well groomed. In my mind it was because my parents and society expected it of me. But watching myself slowly change into Henry made me reevaluate that very thought.

Of course society had lofty expectations from the future Earl of Wiltshire. Even from my youth I intended to uphold the title of earl that came along with the Elliot name. It was a lot of pressure. And yet, there was not a single time I could remember my parents telling me to act or dress the way I did, let alone take the world in such a business-like manner.

My fingers tugged at the bottom of my vest, then moved to smooth the lapels of my suit coat to ensure that everything lay perfectly flat. I took in my full appearance, masked as Henry. Perhaps it was fitting that I already felt more carefree. Almost like I could feel the old Charles creeping back in—a Charles that had been locked away for a very long time. Trading places with Henry made me realize that I had been living years of my life in stifling boredom. Everyone always did exactly what I expected them to do . . . except for Henry. But even in Henry's company lately I never felt the urge to smile or laugh.

Now, as I stood on the precipice of the next two weeks, I felt a growing sense of anticipation. It was as though a string had been pulled tightly inside of me and would burst at any moment. I didn't know what would happen if it did.

Each of my footsteps down the stairs echoed loudly inside the deserted walls of the London house until my shoes found the rug inside the parlor. We had arranged for the town staff to be out of the house until tomorrow. We didn't want to take any chances of them discovering our change in identity. Though I was grateful for the privacy, I didn't appreciate the time it gave me to reflect.

As if in answer to my plaint, I heard footsteps approaching. I exhaled with relief knowing the thoughts would end.

Henry walked in, rubbing his fingers up and down his now smooth face. I could already detect the clean scent of my shaving soap from where I stood. He looked in the mirror above the mantel taking in his new look: my old look. He did his hair just as I showed him. With the help of Lawrence, who was very handy when a barber wasn't available, Henry's new hairstyle was still a decent length on the sides, but it was now cut shorter than mine currently was. The top of Henry's hair was full with thick waves that came to the side. It was amazing how the beard and the difference in our choice of hairstyles shifted our appearance from one another.

"I told you, Charles," Henry said, turning his face left, then right. "A face sculpted by the gods themselves." He turned toward me and leaned his back against the fireplace's mantel, a teasing grin tugging at the corner of his mouth.

I slowly walked toward him, readying the tuppence I carried in my palm. "I'll take that as a compliment, since that face is *my* face."

"I believe it is the other way around. *Your* face is *mine*."

"Only one inch taller," I said, unable to help myself.

He slugged my shoulder. As he did so, I quickly slipped the coin inside Henry's right jacket pocket without him noticing, the way Papa had always done. Lawrence entered the room just then. *Perfect timing, as usual.*

"Are the two of you finished?" he asked with mock censure.

"Just about." My fist returned a quick hit to Henry's arm. Lawrence held an envelope and a piece of parchment.

He walked toward us and handed the envelope to Henry. "This just arrived an hour ago for you," he said. "It appears to be from Katie."

Henry quickly opened the envelope and viewed its contents. A grin started to form as he read down the page. Lawrence tried to hold his patient look, but I could see anticipation brewing beneath the surface.

"Well?" Lawrence finally asked. He had a particular fondness for Katie; they had grown close when she worked at Wilton Manor, and Lawrence doted on her like a father would his own daughter.

Henry looked up at Lawrence. "Mother and baby are both healthy and well." Lawrence let out a small breath as if he had been holding it in.

Henry held his smile. "They've finally had a boy."

Lawrence smiled and chuckled. "I was hoping for a fourth girl.

When will they visit?"

Henry looked through the message. "In about a month. Katie says he has quite a mouth and cries all night like I did as a baby."

Lawrence chuckled, and Henry's smile turned reverential. "They've named him James."

As much as I enjoyed hearing the good news, I was feeling antsy to start the evening. The name "James" was exactly why we were here. I finally cleared my throat.

Henry looked at me. Lawrence gave me a nod, recognizing the need to move forward with tonight's plans. He placed the other piece of parchment he was holding on the small table near the sofa.

"I copied the items you relayed to me the other day, my lord."

"Will you read them aloud?" I asked.

Lawrence nodded as he picked it up again, straightened his back, and cleared his throat. "Item number one: For the next fortnight, Henry is to investigate as much as possible by way of all the social gatherings." He looked at Henry. "You are to collect any bits of gossip you may hear. You will set yourself up in as many circles as possible to leach out any information. However, it must be done in a way that when Charles returns to society, the switch won't be noticeable." He looked between Henry and me. "Is that suitable?"

Henry piped up. "Am I to understand that I'm to use my charms and gifts for getting information all while acting like *him*?" He pointed at me.

I cut in. "Precisely."

Henry turned his head in my direction. "Those are two very different people, Charles."

"Just don't overdo it, Henry. I don't want to have to act like you when I'm me again."

"Very well. But in that case, you must act like me as well." Henry grinned. "I'm excited to see such a performance."

I gave Henry a flat stare. "The fact that I will not be seen at any of the public events, alongside the fact that I will be working with men who won't know either of us personally, allows me to act however I please."

"I'm not amused," Henry said dryly, "but as we have limited time before the carriage is ready, I believe we should continue."

I rubbed my hand along the back of my neck, hesitant, before adding, "I will, however, do my best to act like you here at the house, as we must keep up appearances even amongst the staff. I'm not familiar with those employed at the London house, and I don't trust that they would keep something like this a secret. Not to mention they may have aided in, or even been the culprit of Papa's death. As such, I believe the only time it is safe for us to resume our usual roles is when we are inside the library with the doors shut. Are we in agreement?"

Henry sat still for a moment, contemplating the reality of what I was asking.

He finally nodded his head. "It will be hard to play a part in private as well as in public, but I will do my best."

I nodded. "Please continue, Lawrence."

Lawrence shifted the paper before reading. "Item number two: neither of you are to form any romantic attachments while pretending to be each other."

Henry chuckled. "We've been safe thus far. And we are practically bachelors at the ripe old age of twenty-three."

"You may laugh about it, Henry," I said flatly. "But London society is a very different game when you have the title of earl. Every mother will be concocting some way for you to fall in love with her daughter, all while her daughter is scheming on her own. You would be wise to remember Miss Ollerton."

Henry stared at me evenly. "I see that these rules were all made for me to follow, and not the other way around."

"I am confident that my heart is in no danger, since I will be working primarily with the Bow Street Runners and witnesses—if we get enough information to start an investigation."

"Your heart has never been in danger," Henry said with a smirk. "I'm relatively certain it fell out of your chest years ago."

It was true. My heart had not been open to the idea of marriage or winning a woman's heart since I was sixteen. But just to mock my brother, I put my hand over my heart. "Nevertheless, I promise to not fall in love while pretending to be you."

"With my face, it'll be a lot harder than you think." Henry flashed his most dashing smile.

"With this squirrel attached to my face," I said, rubbing my chin, "no one will actually *see* my face." In reality, Henry had very good taste in his choice of beard. I had even started to see the appeal, though I would shave it off the second I could. But I had to admit that it looked rugged and clean all at the same time.

I looked at Lawrence once more. "Now that we have that point established, if you could please continue."

He gave a nod. "Item number three: No getting shot, stabbed, or wounded. In short, no getting into any fights as each other."

Henry sucked in a quick breath. "I don't know, Lawrence. We are planning to go to the duchess's ball in honor of 'His Lordship, Frederick Fletcher.' And no doubt Charles's cousin Jacob will make his presence known as well."

He had a fair point.

I sent Henry a conspiratorial look. "So long as they don't get any punches in, I'm okay with a few throws." I grinned. "Our odds aren't bad. We did win the few fist fights we had with them, and we were only seventeen at the time."

"We were sixteen, Charles. It was our first year at Cambridge," Henry corrected.

I grinned. "Which further proves my point."

Frederick had put on airs since our first year at Cambridge. He'd been an arrogant, weaselly, whining boy with a poisonous, petty tongue, singling Henry out, and often me as well, since he got the two of us mixed up frequently.

A few months into our first year at Cambridge, Frederick said to Henry, "Your Mother *wanted* to die so she wouldn't have to see your stupid face again." Henry didn't hold back. His fist connected with Frederick's jaw, throwing him into the wall. Papa had been teaching us fisticuffs, and he'd been an excellent teacher. Later that same day, I had a fist fight with both Jacob and Frederick. They didn't get any punches in. Letters were sent home after that day, threatening expulsion for both

Henry and me.

"Do you remember the letters we each got from Papa?" Henry asked. Our minds had clearly wandered to the same thing.

"How could I forget? Your letter was nothing like the beratement I received," I mused.

"True. I always was the favorite son," Henry said with a wink. "But I do remember him asking me if I was prepared to throw away my entire future my first year at Cambridge."

I remembered my letter well. There was a fair bit of chastisement in the beginning; my father had even threatened to pull me from Cambridge himself if I didn't shape up. But then he wrote,

God's hand is powerful and just. With one wave he can crush the mighty. Yet he is merciful. Just because we can use a fist, doesn't always mean we should. God protected his people. Everything I teach you and Henry is to help protect. Not to plow down when offense has been taken. Be selective where your fists meet so they don't have to meet mine. You can find other ways to put people in their place.

So that's what we did. We found *many* other ways to put Frederick and Jacob in their place.

"Do you think Jacob is still afraid of frogs?" Henry asked.

"He always was a bag of moonshine," I said with a smirk. "We only put forty of them under his covers."

Henry smiled mischievously. "And poor Frederick could never quite figure out how to tell the professor that although he had placed his inkwell and quill on his desk, it had somehow magically ended up somewhere else." He folded his arms. "I do believe I'm rather excited to see our old rivals tonight. Perhaps I can make a few of Frederick's things disappear again."

"I'm almost envious of you." My mouth ticked up on one side.

"Almost."

We hadn't only used our "magic" for mischief though. We'd also used it to slip coins into poor pockets and to surprise Mama with gifts. By instinct, I put my hand in my right jacket pocket again, though I knew it would be empty.

My heart jumped as I felt a familiar coin housed there: tuppence. I looked at Henry. He gave me a knowing nod. But not one of jest. One of understanding for the way we both felt with his absence. He too pulled the matching coin from his pocket that I had just placed there. I returned the nod.

We all stood in silence for what seemed minutes until the clock chimed, breaking our reverie. I wasn't quite ready to speak. Henry quickly brushed away the moisture at the corners of his eyes.

Lawrence finally continued to read, though his voice was quieter.

"Item number four: It is imperative that in the fortnight you keep up this charade, the two of you are to be seen together as little as possible. It will be less suspicious and easier to make the switch back afterwards if you aren't seen together beforehand."

"Agreed," we both said in unison.

Lawrence came to the last rule. "Item number five: under no condition is Henry allowed to sing."

Henry's expression lifted slightly. "I wouldn't dream of it."

"You'd better not," I said sternly.

"Well now that you keep bringing it up, the idea is growing on me," he mused.

"Swear to me, Henry. I won't be able to show my face again if you sing in my place."

"What if I'm forced?" he asked, seeming almost hopeful.

I pointed my finger at him. "I don't want another incident like the time you sang at Cambridge, pretending to be me."

Henry laughed. "I forgot about that."

"I didn't," I said, still mortified at the memory. "With that rule in mind, do you still believe you can pretend to be Lord Elliot for an entire fortnight?"

A corner of Henry's mouth twitched upward and he folded his

arms. "I still believe it'll be harder for you to pull off being *me* for fourteen days."

I gave Henry a bored expression as I folded my arms in turn. "I guess we will see."

Lawrence turned to me. "Do you have your pocket watch, my lord?"

"Of course I—" I reached in my pocket to grab it, but my fingers felt nothing but empty space. I looked up to find Henry twirling it around his finger. I snatched it back.

"Remember, my lord, to be waiting in the designated spot at half past nine," Lawrence continued.

"I will be there so long as Henry behaves himself."

"Very good," Lawrence said, gesturing toward the door. "Then I believe it is time. The carriage has come around."

Henry took out the tuppence in his pocket and flipped it. "Good luck, *Henry.*" He emphasized the name I would be using for the next two weeks. It was going to take some getting used to.

"And to you, *Lord Elliot,*" I said, clasping the coin in my own pocket.

And with our coins in tow, rules in place, and agendas in mind, we set off for the Duke of Hastingwood's manor in Westminster, on the outskirts of London—to see old acquaintances, old rivals, new faces, and an unknown correspondent.

4

BENCH

Lily

Westminster
November 1, 1816
Later that evening
18 years old

The ballroom was breathtaking, with more flickering candles than
I'd ever seen in one place. The occasion was exciting and elaborate.
Sweet aromas trailed from wine glasses held by ladies and gentlemen.
Colorful dresses shifted between steps in time with the music, and
men followed to claim them. I stepped backwards and he followed. I
stepped to the side, and he mirrored. Our hands touched, his warmth
spreading beneath my silky white glove, then fell away. My younger
mind would have told me it was romantic. My present mind was trying
not to laugh at the man who was, at this very moment, my dance partner.

Alexander Campbell was handsome enough, but he was completely unaware of how pompous his demeanor was, and of how ridiculous
he looked. He held an eyebrow at an angle scrutinizing the entire room,

turning down his lips as if everything he saw was foul.

His cravat was so large and intricately woven that it made his head look small by comparison. And what was more, his lapels came to devastatingly high points in an overdone purple. I couldn't help but glance at his interesting choice of attire.

He notched his eyebrow further. "I can see that you have noticed the advantage of having me as your dance partner."

I did my best to maintain an even expression. "And why is that, Mr. Campbell?" I asked, unable to keep down one corner of my mouth.

"Come now, miss. It is hard to ignore perfection when it is right in front of you."

I couldn't help but play his game for at least some time.

"Indeed, sir. A creature of such perfection must be admired and adored."

His face showed pure endorsement of my statement. "My thoughts precisely," he said haughtily.

It was becoming very difficult to keep my face unaffected. But I had to keep going at least a little longer.

I grinned. "He certainly caught my attention from almost the moment I arrived."

"Naturally." His lips turned down. "The competition is underwhelming this evening."

"Indeed. But do you think he might return my notice?" I asked coyly.

He contemplated my question for some time before looking at me as if I was barely passable. He finally nodded his head once and said, "I believe I could make an exception for your appearance this evening."

I placed a hand to my heart, feigning sheer delight. "Mr. Campbell, I am truly flattered. Thank you for giving me the courage to approach the man who has captured my attention." I turned my head toward the oldest bachelor in the room, sitting near a table of refreshments. "Wouldn't you say there is no comparison for Mr. Reeves this evening? I must go speak to him at once." The dance ended at that moment, and I gave Mr. Campbell a quick curtsy before turning and taking myself off.

Before turning away, Mr. Campbell's expression showed absolute mortification at my statement. It was a very unladylike thing for me to do, and I knew Jane would scold me if she saw, but Mr. Campbell's reaction did not disappoint. He actually gasped in horror as I retreated from him and headed toward the old bachelor. Mr. Reeves was well into his fifties. He was very large, very severe looking, and very unfashionable.

I walked as near Mr. Reeves as I dared before sweeping past him and disappearing from Mr. Campbell's view into the sea of men and women. I caught a glimpse of Jane talking with Frederick. Most likely he would claim the next dance, even though I knew there was no real feeling between them.

Jane was truly the most beautiful woman I had ever seen. Thankfully, I felt pride instead of jealousy at having such a beautiful sister. Her eyes were pools of deep blue, always searching. Thick, dark lashes lined her eyes, giving off an air of mystery rivaled with poise. Her brow was marked with intelligence alongside a streak of rebellion, though it never manifested itself in her actions or behavior. She had a breathtaking smile when it was genuine—though at this particular moment, Jane wore her practiced smile. It was pretty, but false. Only I would have noticed.

I never did think the same way Jane did. She was always polite and proper, and, well, perfect. I seemed unable to be unaffected the way she was.

The crowd parted for a moment and my eyes met a familiar face.

"Oh please, no," I muttered to myself, looking frantically for a means of escape. Mr. Johnson began making his way towards me. I had already danced with him during the opening number. To refuse him would be extremely rude, but to dance a second time would not only be unbearable, but it would make a statement.

I looked around for my aunt, remembering Jane's words to bring a chaperone when leaving the ballroom. I couldn't find her anywhere in my brief sweep across the room, and Matthew was coming closer. I would have to find a secluded area somehow without anyone noticing.

Henry

I clasped the small coin in my palm as Charles and I stepped out of the carriage and walked toward the duke's estate.

Charles slapped me on the back. "Remember the rules."

I smirked. "Your confidence is overwhelming."

We parted ways before I walked up to the grand edifice. I wasn't one who normally felt nervous. At that moment, however, my stomach churned.

I also felt a fair amount of thrill at being someone else—almost like there were no rules. *Technically there are five rules*, I reminded myself. But in the end, I was Lord Elliot, Earl of Wiltshire, for 14 days. After that, I would be Henry again.

I smiled at the thought—then just as quickly pressed my lips into a bored, flat line, gave my eyes the cold, condescending stare I'd seen Charles wear to almost every social event since we were seventeen, and walked in.

Upon entering the ballroom, I was greeted by the hosts: the Duke and Duchess of Hastingwood. Despite my loathing for His Grace's son, Frederick, I didn't get the same impression about the duke himself during our past encounters.

"Good evening, Your Grace," I said, doing my best to sound like Charles, while giving him a nod.

He gave me a genuine smile. "Lord Elliot. So glad you could come."

The duchess turned her gaze on me. "It's a pleasure to see you in London once again, Lord Elliot, especially after such a long absence."

I acknowledged the duchess with a bow. "Indeed. It is truly a pleasure to indulge in such splendor this evening." I gestured to the magnificent room.

The duke extended his arm out toward a gentleman sporting a

cane and a lady with an exorbitant amount of feathers and ribbons in her hair. "And of course you remember my brother, Lord Edward Fletcher, and his wife, Lady Caroline." I remembered them being introduced years previous as the duke's brother and sister-in-law.

I gave them an affable smile. "Certainly. How do you do?"

"Very well, Lord Elliot, thank you," said Lady Caroline, returning a smile of her own. "Should you wish it, we would be delighted to introduce you to our guests this evening."

I nodded. "I would be most obliged."

As we made our way around the ballroom, I created a list in my mind of the people I was introduced to, including their connections and influence. Surely someone at this event knew something about Papa's murder.

As I glanced across the space, candles illuminating even the farthest corners, I was met with women's gazes in every direction. Older women stared at me, then whispered to younger women—their daughters, no doubt. Other ladies would make eye contact, smile demurely, sometimes fanning themselves, and then walk up to other women, who would join in the whispering and staring.

I always made fun of Charles for his paranoia and bad humor during such events. I was beginning to sympathize with him. It had been five years since Charles and I participated in the London scene. He—or I, in this case—would surely be the talk of the evening. I was tempted to walk right back out and join Charles with his investigation.

Then I got a glimpse of Frederick. He was dancing with an absolute beauty in a pink dress. Suddenly, I had a renewed sense of determination. The evening was young, and there was no reason I couldn't collect my information while enjoying myself at the same time. Besides, it had been far too long since I had made something of Frederick's disappear.

I glanced at his person to decide what best to take. His pocket watch, perhaps? Then my eyes settled on the lovely creature in his arms, and I had an even better idea of what I would be taking from him this evening.

Charles

The evening air was exceptional. It was cool, crisp, and refreshing without the bite or sting that winter air brought. I inhaled it eagerly, clearing my head. I was grateful that I did not have Henry's role tonight. Having to tolerate the preening peacocks was something I could not endure at present. The ladies' practiced smiles leaking through carefully crafted compliments, breathy laughs, and covert hints would have been agonizing.

The moon was bright enough that I could see the time on my pocket watch. It was only two minutes past the arranged time, but I was already feeling irritable at the tardiness of my unknown correspondent. Just as I wondered if this might be a setup and had a mind to leave, I heard rustling nearby.

A silhouette appeared at the opening of the little path, then quietly moved toward me. "Good evening, sir. The weather is unusual for November," a low, hushed voice muttered.

My suspicions eased and I responded with the code. "Mother nature, like human nature, has no rules." There was a small pause of silence before the man spoke again.

"Thank you for meeting me here tonight." He glanced behind his shoulder. "I will make this brief as I must return presently."

I nodded my head in agreement.

"I am Arthur Brown. I run a shop here in London." He extended his hand toward me.

"Yes, I am familiar with your shop, Mr. Brown. I am Henry Thomas." Surprisingly, introducing myself as Henry didn't feel as odd as I thought it would. I brought my hand forward, gripped his palm firmly, and gave it a good shake before our hands returned to our sides.

"Henry Thomas," he said, recognition entering his tone. "I know that name. Aren't you the young man who lives with . . . " He abruptly halted his words and looked around, deciding against what he was about to say. "Well, never mind that."

I got right to the point. "I believe you may have information about Lord El—"

Mr. Brown quickly raised his hands, cutting me off. "I believe," he said quietly, "that we should not use the name for the individual we are discussing this evening. It is amazing what the household staff may hear in passing, regardless of how careful we are. I suggest we refer to him as 'David' for the time being."

I did not want my father's murder circulating every gathering in London, so I readily agreed. "Very well, sir. I believe you may have information about 'David' for me."

"That I do," he whispered, waiting silently for a time, before looking over his shoulder once more and continuing.

Lily

It really was Mr. Johnson's fault. I would have stayed put if it weren't for him. Even in November, the gardens were beautiful. The frost had not yet claimed the petals from the flowers. I inspected the roses and other blooms as I walked through the neatly manicured hedges, making sure to stay in areas where I would not be seen.

To my delight, I found a pathway that led to a secluded area near the back-east side of the house. After walking the small perimeter, I noticed that one of the bushes had a narrow opening that I'd almost missed. I poked my head through to get a better look and was absolutely enchanted to find another space, slightly larger, opening up beyond it. I glanced around to make sure no one was looking.

I was completely alone.

After examining the bottom of my dress and the narrow fit I would need to make, I gathered my skirt and carefully stepped through the pinched opening. I was gratified, and perhaps a little proud, that I did not snag a single twig or leaf on my gown. Upon further inspection of this second little haven, I found that it was designed in a circular shape, and completely surrounded by tall hedges. On one side, a bench awaited me.

Perfect.

I took a seat and leaned back, looking up at the stars, taking in soothing breaths. I stayed in that attitude for several minutes until eventually, sighing with disappointment, I stood, acknowledging the need to return before someone noticed my disappearance.

I silently thanked the bench, the shrubs, the stars—

My breath caught when I suddenly heard faint voices. I stilled myself, listening intently to ensure they weren't approaching my hiding place. I inched forward until I was just on the other side of the hedge from the hushed exchange. It was two men speaking. I shook my head in chastisement. This was exactly the sort of bind Jane would never find herself in.

I cursed my heartbeat and breathing for being so tremendously loud while I prayed I wouldn't be discovered.

"I believe you may have information about David for me," I heard one of the men say.

"That I do," came the response of the other man, who sounded older. It suddenly became silent and I feared that perhaps my pounding heart and quickened breath had actually given me away. I waited for what felt like an eternity. Each breath I took in and out was torturous, unbearable. I contemplated making my presence known, but it was out of the question.

The older man's voice finally broke the silence. "About two weeks before his death, I was taking some items out of my shop through the back. A heated argument was taking place, and I recognized one of those voices as, er—David's."

"And to whom was David speaking?" a deep voice rumbled.

It was silent for a moment, and I could hear one of them shuffling slightly.

"I don't know, sir. It was dark and I only recognized—er, David for his voice."

It seemed to me as though the older gentleman wasn't being entirely truthful.

"And what were they discussing?" the younger man asked.

"I don't know the full extent of it, but I did hear David say, 'I will give you a week to come clean. If you haven't done so by then, I'll do it for you.' Then the other man said, 'You keep your nose where it belongs, or I'll make sure it never finds itself where it isn't wanted.' "

"He threatened him?" The younger man sounded furious.

"He did, sir."

"Would you be able to identify this man if you heard his voice again?"

"Not sure that I could or that I couldn't."

"This is not enough information to start an investigation, Mr. Brown."

Despite my pounding heart, my interest was piqued. I listened carefully as the gentlemen continued. The man identified as Mr. Brown spoke next.

"I'm aware of that, sir. But there is a servant girl who comes to my shop from time to time to buy things for the duke and duchess. The duke has recently tasked her to pick out a gift for Her Grace, and this servant told me confidentially that she may have evidence that points to Lo—er, David's death. She usually comes to my shop around two in the afternoon. She is expected to pick up the gift tomorrow. If you would like to see what insights she has, it may fill in the gaps of my story and give you enough information to start an investigation."

"Very well. I will bring a Bow Street Runner with me tomorrow when I come."

"No, sir! I beg you to come alone." He sounded frantic. "I do not wish to make a scene at my shop. It's bad for business."

"And why is it that you would go out of your way to share this information in the first place? Do you expect compensation?" the deep voice asked curtly.

"I do not expect compensation. I wouldn't take it even if you offered." The older man sounded sincere. "And besides, it wasn't out of my way. I just finished delivering a large order of goods from my shop for the Duke of Hastingwood before coming to meet with you. But more than that, David was a friend of mine. He was always kind to me and even helped me out when I found myself in a bind a time or two. My family was very sad to hear about his sudden death."

"We have all felt his loss," said the younger man.

"I will do what I can," said the man called Mr. Brown. "I would, however, appreciate confidentiality for the time being."

"I agree. You have my word of confidence, and I will be at your shop tomorrow as described."

"Very good. When you arrive, be sure to come through my front door as a regular customer and ask to see my penknives. I keep them stored in the back. That way I have a legitimate reason to bring you to the back of the shop. And now I must be going."

"Very well, Mr. Brown. Until tomorrow."

I heard them shuffling around and leaned my ear even closer to see if their footsteps were retreating. I could hear at least one pair of footsteps leaving, but wasn't quite certain about the other. I waited for a bit longer, listening for any movement, before I decided to dare a peek around the hedge. I inched forward, readied my dress, and—*SMACK!*

5

HEIRLOOM

Lily

I was knocked backward, hitting my head on the ground. Bewildered, I looked around me, so shocked that I didn't even cry out in the throbbing pain that followed.

A deep, angry voice cursed, making my breath hitch. All I could make out was a tall silhouette standing over me.

"Have you been here all this time?" he seethed.

My head was swimming in pain, and his words seemed to blur together.

"What is your name?" His tone was clipped.

I held up a hand to make him stop talking while I gathered my wits. He either didn't understand the gesture or didn't care.

"Were you sent here by someone to spy?"

Once his questions sank in fully, I found that my anger was kindled, and I was thoroughly irritated.

He hadn't even apologized for plowing me over or helped me up. Now he was throwing questions and accusations my way before I even had a chance to collect myself. His accusatory words drilled holes in my composure. If he was a smart man, he would stop talking now and leave.

His next words were laced with condescension. "And to think they would send a young lady. Tell me, do they pay you well?"

I'd heard enough. "My business is none of your concern!" Unfortunately my wits had not yet returned, and it was the only thing I could think of to say.

"Tell me, does your father approve of such behavior from his daught—"

"My father would give you such an earful if he saw the way you have just treated me." I clenched my jaw, not caring that I interrupted him. "I doubt you would survive such an encounter. Clearly you have never learned how to treat a lady! I feel sorry for your wife." I glared up at him, though I couldn't make out his features in the shadowed darkness. Even so, I could feel his anger brewing at my comment.

"I have been taught how to treat a lady," he said in an angry, hushed voice. "But you are no lady. And I am glad I don't have a wife— but if I did, she certainly would not be out here, unchaperoned, spying on conversations that don't concern her."

His venomous words fueled my own fury, but before I could retort, he let out a frustrated breath, and took my hand, helping me to my feet. He still made no effort to apologize, the infuriating man.

I immediately turned from him and stalked to the opposite end of the plot, fully intending to leave. Unfortunately, he was standing near the only exit. I looked at the shrubs that trapped us together, grateful for a moment of silence to collect my thoughts. I gingerly touched the back of my head, and though it was tender, I was grateful to find that my hair, for the most part, remained undisturbed.

I took in another deep breath, trying to calm my aching head as well as my building rage toward this arrogant man. Surely he would give me at least a few more moments of silence before he continued his interrogation. Unfortunately, my hope was in vain. He wasted no time.

"Who are you?" he demanded again, dissolving what little patience I had left.

"Who are *you*?" I snapped back, turning around to face his direction. "Clearly no gentleman!" He had pushed me over the edge, and I was beyond checking myself. "You have all but thrown me to the ground with no attempt at an apology! You have tossed accusations and snide remarks at me without so much as a kind gesture or form of greeting. So, you tell me. What is *your* name?" My voice was sharp, and I felt a moment of pride that he took a step back, my words clearly startling him.

"I'm—er, sor—" he stumbled over his words. "I'm Ch—Henry," he said quickly.

Thankfully the dull pounding in my head was no longer clouding my judgment. It gave me enough clarity to recognize that he had given me a false name.

"You are not Henry," I said coolly. I still could not see his features well, but I saw his face reel back at my accusation.

"You asked my name, *miss*." He was annoyed again. "Are you set on contradicting me after censuring me as well?"

"Well, *Ch—Henry*," I spat, matching his poisonous tone, "you are either truly no gentleman, or you are certainly not Henry. For if you *were* a gentleman, you would have never introduced yourself by your Christian name. So which is it?" I folded my arms. "Are you a gentleman? Or are you Henry?" He took a couple steps toward me, and though I still could not see his face well, his tall broad figure reminded me that I would do well to hold my tongue.

"Or perhaps," he said, folding his arms in turn, "your fiery tantrum scared my Christian name out of me."

I scoffed, but he continued.

"And you, miss, are clearly no lady if you are out here unaccompanied. I have given you my name. Now it is your turn." He made a fair point, but I would not relent so easily.

"But you have *not* given me your name. I will give no information until you speak the truth." It was a bold claim. And my accusation of him not being a gentleman was most likely a far cry. His voice and speech were refined, so unfortunately I did believe him to be a gentleman—though I would never admit as much.

He stepped toward me slowly until he was only a couple feet away. His face slowly came into view beneath the moonlight. To my dismay, he didn't appear to only be a gentleman, but an exceptionally handsome one at that. He had dark features and a rugged but clean look about him, with a solid jaw beneath a short, well-kept beard. I decided his appearance would help me further disdain him. He was most likely self-absorbed, something else I could add to my list of reasons to despise this man.

I must have been staring at him for a moment longer than was proper, for he smirked and cocked an eyebrow as if he could read my thoughts. We continued staring at one another, each of us calculating how to proceed.

He finally broke the silence. "You want me to speak the truth?" he asked. "The truth is that I have never met someone quite like you. You are just about as stubborn as I am. My name may not be Henry," he admitted, "but it is not your business to know my true name. You have stated nothing about yourself and have been caught lurking near a sensitive conversation. So I will ask you again." His tone was softer than before, but there was still an air of command to his words. "Who are you, and were you intentionally listening to the information that was passed?"

We were at an impasse. Neither of us would give information until the other surrendered first. *Fine*, I thought. *If he wants to play that way, so be it.*

"Very well, you have found me out," I said, feigning defeat. A brief look of surprise entered his features and I felt victorious. "I am working undercover for the Prince Regent himself, to recover a most prized memento that has mysteriously disappeared." I stared at him as seriously as I could, daring him to contradict me. I expected to see anger return to his countenance at my outrageous claim, but he surprised me with a look of amusement.

"The Prince Regent himself. You don't say." He shook his head in mock disbelief. "How honored I feel that you would seek out my private conversation in hopes of discovering this 'missing memento.'"

So, he intended to toy with me. Part of me wanted to drop the charade, but the look on his face stated that he expected me to do just that. I wasn't about to give him what he wanted.

"Indeed," I said with a smirk. "I was most grateful for the opportunity. It has led me straight to the object I've been seeking." I discreetly slid an old family ring off my gloved finger and bent down to the earth, pretending to pick it up off the ground.

"Behold," I said dramatically, bringing it in front of his face. "Here she is. The royal family's ancestral treasure." Though the ring was special to me, it had no monetary value. It was made of no precious metals and was very plain. I raised an eyebrow. Surely he would end the charade now. He carefully took the ring between his finger and thumb and dropped it into his palm, examining it by the moon's light.

"I can see it has been made of the finest materials," he said, a small corner of his mouth twitching up, as if he couldn't quite manage to hold it down. Apparently he had no intention of quitting our little game. How unfortunate. I was having a hard time keeping my own smile at bay.

I continued, "Of the finest material, to be sure."

"And such intricate designs and detail." It was the most plain ring imaginable. Just a simple metal band with absolutely no detail, and even slightly warped. The corners of my mouth were no longer obeying my commands to keep down.

"Fashioned by a true craftsman." I bit back a laugh.

"Truly masterful," he said, cocking an eyebrow. "It would not surprise me if Michelangelo himself crafted it."

It was too much. My laugh had just begun to bubble up when the bushes began rustling. My heart skipped a beat, eyes scrambling to find a place to hide. Apparently "Henry" had the same idea. We both glanced at the bench at the same time and attempted to cram beneath it. It wasn't big enough for the two of us. If I was caught out here alone with this man, my reputation would be ruined. I tried to communicate to him with my hands to find another place to hide. He clearly was much too big to hide under it anyway.

We looked at each other with panic as we realized someone was about to come through the clearing. I held my breath as the leaves parted, a shadow emerging. It ran through the center of our secluded area, sleek and shiny, then meowed.

It was a cat.

I looked at Henry and his large frame stuffed under the bench and couldn't help the laugh that escaped me. To my surprise, he joined in. We laughed loudly together before he put a finger up to his mouth and started laughing under his breath, reminding me that we didn't want to be discovered. For whatever reason, we both found this even funnier.

The cat took one look at us and bolted. We laughed as silently as we could until my stomach hurt. I crawled out from under the bench with some effort. Our quiet laughter finally dissipated. I took in some air and let it fall around me, wiping at a tear or two that had actually escaped my eyes. We collected ourselves before he finally spoke.

"I didn't realize how much I needed that. May we start over? Call a truce?" He asked with real sincerity. I saw it in his eyes and softened posture. I was surprised at how easily I wanted to agree with him now that his words and demeanor were no longer hostile.

I smiled, taking in another deep breath. "I would like that very much. Real names included."

He returned my smile, then extended his hand forward, my ring clasped inside his closed fist. I opened my hand and felt the ring hit my gloved palm.

He inhaled slowly, then let it out again. "I hope you will believe me when I say that at this time I cannot give my real name. For now, Henry will have to suffice."

I sighed. "Very well. But I can't simply call you Henry."

He smirked. "And why can't you call me Henry?"

I was at a loss for words. For all my claims of his ungentlemanly behavior, his impropriety surprised me. "Because I don't even know you, sir."

"Let's rectify that at once." He dipped his head slightly and said, "Good evening, madam. I would be exceedingly gratified to make your acquaintance. Whom do I have the privilege of addressing?"

My mouth twitched mischievously. Two could play at this game. "Lily—just Lily."

He raised an eyebrow and hitched the side of his mouth. It was hard to focus on my objective when he looked at me like that. It felt like whiplash trying to adjust to this man compared to the one I had first encountered.

He leaned slightly closer and said, "Lily," locking my eyes to his. A tingle moved up my arms at hearing my given name on his lips. "It is very nice to meet you." Heat rose to my cheeks and I was grateful for the cover of the night sky.

"On second thought," I said, trying to keep my voice level, "I believe I would prefer Miss Mason." I was quickly losing my nerve.

Henry chuckled. "I keep waiting for you to do something that doesn't surprise me. You have got to be the only woman I have met that sticks with a challenge of interrogation with a gentleman, yet blushes at hearing her Christian name."

"It isn't proper." I sounded like Jane.

"I do believe, thanks to you, that nothing about our meeting this evening has been proper. Wouldn't you agree—Lily?" He dangled something in front of my face. My ring. But how was that possible? I was holding my ring in my—I opened my clamped hand to find tuppence, not my ring, inside. My mouth fell open. I couldn't help it.

He smiled delightedly back. "Won't the royal family be so proud of me for recovering their missing memento?"

I quickly grabbed for it, but he must have read my thoughts. He snatched it out of the way just in time. I tried once more but he moved his hand behind his back as mine followed. In my haste to retrieve it, I grabbed his wrist. I pulled away quickly.

He shook his head while the corner of his mouth turned up facetiously. "Here I am trying to make a proper introduction, and you're trying to hold my hand."

I gasped. The wicked man!

He chuckled. It was then that I noticed he was much too close. Or was I too close to him? He studied my eyes, then slowly took my hand and placed it between us, turning my palm skyward. This time I watched carefully as he placed my ring inside and let our hands fall. We stood silent for a time.

"Now, Lily," he said seriously. "Why are you out here unaccompanied?"

I sighed. "I was trying to escape from Mr. Matthew Johnson."

"And who exactly is Matthew Johnson?"

"He is quite dashing, coming all the way up to my nose," I said, raising my eyebrows. "But his appearance does not quite rival his charm and wit—for he is extremely well versed on birds. To this topic he will always cling and never leave. His charm leaves me speechless. Just tonight he likened me to a magpie."

Henry clasped his lips together, biting down a smile. "Such poetry."

"Indeed," I grimaced.

"I understand the need for you to flee from an unwanted suitor, but you should not be out here alone."

"I know it to be true. Yet it is unfair that if I wish to have a reprieve or moment's peace, I cannot simply do so. I must find someone else to accompany me, which completely defeats the purpose of finding solitude. You, sir, came out alone. And yet there is no question about your respectability. Have you never sought for peace from a ballroom? Or from people in general?"

A look of understanding passed his features at my question.

I sighed, then continued. "In truth, I hadn't planned to come out to the gardens at all. I was on my way back from hiding from Mr. Johnson when I figured just one glance at the gardens wouldn't hurt. But after I glanced, as you can see, it wasn't enough. How lucky I was to happen upon this little haven." I gestured at the plot around us. "Until I heard voices intruding on my solitude."

"You should have made your presence known. I wouldn't have trampled you if you had done so."

"I was not about to give my position away to two men I didn't know. Especially when I was alone." I felt self-conscious as he examined my face.

"I see your point," he said.

For the first time since meeting this man, I actually felt sorry for causing him so much trouble. His new humility and politeness won me over so easily. It was disconcerting, really, that it had been so effortless. Especially when I'd been so content to despise him only moments ago.

I looked down at my hands, unable to face his penetrating gaze. It was my turn to feel some humility now.

"And *I* see *your* point," I said quietly. "I'm sorry I was privy to your conversation. It was not intentionally done." Why did our newfound honesty make it so much harder to look at him? I could feel his eyes on me.

"I would like to believe you at present." He paused, waiting for me to meet his gaze again. I finally raised my eyes to his. "So I will," he concluded.

"And are you an investigator, sir? Working undercover? Is that why you won't disclose your true name?" I knew it was an impertinent question and that I had no place asking it, but my curiosity had the better of me.

He grinned. "I am not an investigator. But I *am* investigating a murder, as you well know."

"Whose murder?" I asked, unable to stop myself. I clapped my hands over my mouth. What was wrong with me? I wasn't usually so nosy.

Henry chuckled. "I have to keep some of my secrets, Lily."

The word "secrets" sparked a thought I'd had earlier when overhearing the conversation. "He was keeping something from you," I said, caution edging my tone. "The shopkeeper," I added. I didn't want to remind him why he had been angry with me at our first encounter, but I felt it was important for him to know.

"Why do you say that?" He studied me intently.

"When he told you he didn't know the identity of the other gentleman arguing with David, I believe he wasn't being completely truthful."

"And why would he come to give me information but lie about something like that?" He was clearly unconvinced.

"I'm not sure. But his voice changed when he said he wasn't sure who the other man was. He also appeared to be afraid of a Bow Street Runner, or of drawing any sort of attention to his shop."

"True. But he did have good reason for not wanting to draw that sort of attention."

"I suppose." I put a hand behind my head in thought. Pain quickly surfaced as my hand made contact. "Ouch!" I pulled my hand away. I had momentarily forgotten the bump on the back of my head.

"Did you hit your head when I walked into you?" Henry asked, alarmed. "Why didn't you tell me?"

"It's nothing," I said. He disregarded my words and walked towards my back until he was directly behind me.

"Let's have a look," he said. I was too aware of him facing my back.

"It's nothing, really. I—" I turned to face him. I hadn't anticipated how close he would be standing to me; otherwise I would have stayed put. I couldn't remember what I was about to say. He appeared to be momentarily struck with the same curse, for he said nothing, studying my eyes for a time before he found his voice.

"Lily," he said, quietly. "I would like to make sure there was no serious injury done. Especially since I was the cause. Head trauma is not something to take lightly. I hadn't realized you hit your head."

I breathed in slowly, then nodded in agreement as I turned around again. It was hard to breathe normally while he stood so close behind me.

"No retort or argument this time?" he mused as his fingers slowly and carefully brushed against the back of my head a few times. His light touch sent whispering currents down my neck and a tingle through my spine. I found it both soothing and distracting.

He let out a frustrated breath. "I'm glad that you appear to have no concussion. At least, you seem to have your wits about you. You do, however, have quite a bump, and I surmise it will be very sore for a few days." He came back around to face me. "I really am sorry. My behavior was unforgivable, and I'm thoroughly ashamed of myself."

"As was my behavior," I said, remembering my own outburst. "I believe it was exactly the type of spectacle that all of London's eyes and ears are constantly seeking." My words sparked a thought.

"Publicity." I muttered to myself.

"Publicity?" Henry asked.

"Yes, publicity. The shopkeeper said he was afraid of a scandal. But a Bow Street Runner simply coming to the premises would not bring scandal to his shop, but curiosity—and as a byproduct, people. It is actually the exact kind of publicity a shop would not usually turn down.

"Suddenly all of London would be about your shop trying to

discreetly squeeze information out, then they would purchase goods to appear as though they hadn't simply come for gossip. It is very good for business. I have seen my own aunt go into a shop a time or two to glean some little bit of gossip.

"The shop owners eat it up, even if they pretend not to. It would be in any shopkeeper's interest to welcome such a thing. Unless," I said, pointing my finger at nothing in particular, "there was something else going on that made him wary of drawing attention to himself or his shop."

My mind flooded with thoughts all at once. "He sounded truly afraid of a Bow Street Runner coming. Perhaps there is something untoward about his goods or the way he does business."

"I have known of Arthur Brown and his shop for many years, and I can say, with some confidence, that there is nothing scandalous about the way he does business."

I bit my bottom lip in thought. "I still can't help but feel that he was frantic for a reason other than the chance of a scandal at his shop. He is being cautious. He stated that it was no inconvenience meeting you here tonight, as he was already here. He was very careful not to break his routine." I began pacing.

"And he stated that he would need to be brief this evening at the very beginning of our meeting," Henry interjected.

"Did he?" I asked eagerly. "Do you think there is a possibility that he is afraid of being discovered divulging information? He has asked that you enter through the front door and that you seek out an item in the back. Is it possible he is being watched? Or at least, that he believes he's being watched and potentially even followed?"

Henry drew his fingers to his chin in thought. I couldn't help but watch his movements. I tried not to think about how striking he was as he moved his fingers away from his chin, and folded his arms. It was impossible not to notice the strain of the fabric against his arms and chest as he did so. Or how broad his shoulders were.

I shook my head. How had my thoughts wandered there? I thought back to the conversation between Henry and Mr. Brown.

"Your shopkeeper isn't very good at working covertly. It was very clear to me that he was not truly discussing a man named David. "

"He wasn't quite hitting the mark there, was he?" Henry agreed with a smile. "Do you believe he may be trying to set me up?"

"I'm not sure." I put a finger to my mouth in thought. "He very well could be. But I believe his intentions are noble. He sounded very sincere when speaking about his friendship with 'David.' He may just be afraid. Perhaps he has even been threatened," I suggested.

"Then why would he risk telling me anything?"

"If his aspirations are truly noble, then perhaps his conscience demands that he give some information in hopes that it can lead you to discovering the truth by other means that wouldn't point to him if it doesn't turn out well."

"I'm impressed, Lily. I never would have thought of any of the things you've just stated." He grinned. "Are you sure you're not a secret investigator?"

I laughed. "It does sound rather exciting. Perhaps I will become one after tonight."

"Very well, you're hired."

"Very well, sir, I will begin immediately."

"For one, you've already slipped once and called me 'Henry.' You might as well stop calling me 'sir.' For another, I'm being entirely serious about including you in this investigation."

"I did not slip already," I protested, avoiding his other proposal, though I was deeply intrigued and flattered.

"You did. Albeit you were quite snippy when you said it. I'd like to hear a good-natured Lily say my name."

"It's not your name."

"Ah yes, well, I'd like to hear a good-natured Lily say my *fake* name, then."

I placed my hands on my hips. "I don't know how to take you, sir."

"I hope you'll take me up on my offer."

"If I could trust you entirely, then I just might." The thought of this man wanting my assistance was more than exhilarating. But I was not about to accept it. How could I? I hated how much he already affected me. It would be one thing if I knew who he was. But I was truly in the dark.

"What can I say to convince you?" he asked, stepping toward me until we were an arm's length apart. "I confess that I don't read people as well as you just did. I am exceptional with facts, ledgers, books, information. You, however, knew *my* name was false, knew *David's* name was false, and have now brought things to my attention that I would never have considered."

My gaze drifted to the ground. His compliments were making my cheeks warm.

"Lily," he said with amusement, waiting for me to look at him. What a frustrating man. I finally looked up. "Will you meet me at the shop tomorrow afternoon to hear what this servant girl has to say?" His eyes held me there. They were testing me. Seeing whether I would take the leap or take the expected path and reject his offer. I wanted to say yes. I wanted to keep surprising him and do what he thought I wouldn't. But there in my desire was my answer. I could not. How could I go unaccompanied to a shop in London? My eyes gave me away and I saw a wave of disappointment enter his.

I opened my mouth to speak, already feeling regret toward my decision. "I . . . " I couldn't finish.

"I understand." He looked down, trying to hide his disappointment.

"I'll do it," I said, shocking myself.

Henry's look of surprise was worth it. "Are you in earnest?" he asked suspiciously. "Because I tell you Lily, if you're teasing me just now—"

"I am, sir."

He chuckled. "That's vague. Do you mean you are teasing me? Or are you in earnest?"

"I will do it," I said. "I'm not sure how to come unaccompanied. I have already put my reputation in enough danger this evening. My sis—"

"I said nothing about coming unaccompanied," he interjected.

"And how exactly would I explain to my chaperone that you and I already know each other? Or that we would be listening to a servant girl's statement of evidence for a potential murder?"

"I have no intention of putting your reputation at risk. Come to the shop with a chaperone. If I cannot find a way to get you in the back to hear her statement without raising suspicion, then I won't. You have my word." There was no hint of teasing. For whatever reason, I trusted him. A stupid thing to do.

"And where do I find this shop?" I asked.

"It's 15 King Street, Covent Garden. Arthur & Co." He had me repeat the location a few times back to him. "Remember to be there no later than two o'clock."

"I'll be there," I said, more to myself than to him.

"Oh, and one more thing," he said, leaning a little closer. "I don't want to find you alone unaccompanied again. You could find yourself in worse company than mine." He dipped his head and looked at me a moment longer before saying, "Goodnight, Lily. Until next time."

Before I had time to say anything in return, he vanished behind the bushes. I took in a deep breath and exhaled quickly. What had just happened? I couldn't help but smile as I discreetly made my way back up to the ballroom from the gardens. How long had I been gone? The encounter with Henry felt lengthy and fleeting at the same time. I felt as though I had passed an entire evening with him, but in reality, it had most likely been only three quarters of an hour.

For all my longing to return home, I was inclined to think that London wouldn't disappoint me after all. I touched the back of my head again, recalling the sensation of Henry's light touch. My stomach leapt at the recollection. And to think it was all thanks to Mr. Johnson. Perhaps I *did* owe him a second dance after all.

6

HANDKERCHIEF

Jane

The evening was going according to plan. Frederick had asked me to dance a second time. It was exactly what one would hope for when courting a man. True, he didn't seem interested in my company necessarily, and we were nearing the end of our waltz, but that was just the way he was. He was rarely ruffled, rarely excited. I looked up at him for a moment, hoping he would glance my way. He didn't have an unpleasant-looking face, and his hair was a rich brown. But I did have to admit that when he wore his current bored expression, he looked so severe.

I looked out at the crowd, realizing Frederick was most likely not going to meet my gaze. That's when I first noticed him. A man I had never seen was looking at Frederick, wearing a calculated grin. The man's eyes then moved to mine. He raised an eyebrow, along with one side of his mouth. I quickly looked away as heat rose up the back of my neck.

My eyes moved back to Frederick's "Lord Fletcher?"

"Yes," he answered flatly.

"Do you know the gentleman accompanying your aunt and uncle? I don't recognize him, but he appears to know you."

The gentleman staring in our direction had a look of mischief about him, and I made a point not to glance his way again. Frederick turned his head to the man in question, a look of sheer loathing creeping into his features.

"I didn't realize the devil himself was invited. I'm only surprised his shadow isn't tailing him," he sneered. "My father knows I don't approve. He must have extended the invitation just to spite me." It was the most animated and vulgar I'd ever seen him. He seemed to notice my shock. "You'll have to excuse my lack of decorum, Miss Mason. Charles and I met at Cambridge and he was always bent on making Mr. Hughes and me look bad in front of our professors. Not to mention he's violent and uses fists to solve his problems."

It surprised me that Frederick hadn't even attempted to refer to this new gentleman by his proper name when in my presence. He was worse than Lily. Clearly this "Charles" ruffled Frederick more than usual. He shook his head in disdain. "His greatest delight is to make me miserable. He hasn't shown his face in London for five years, and it's been a blessed respite. No doubt he will be the talk of the evening."

"I see." And I certainly did see, for this newcomer had stolen most of the room's attention. Though I didn't dare look at him for more than a moment, what little I could make out with my sweeping glances was a tall, striking man. It was hard not to pick him out of the crowd, and I had to do my best not to stare at him the way everyone else was.

I watched out of the corner of my eye as the gentleman and Frederick's relatives slowly made their way toward my Aunt Mary. As they drew near, she smiled graciously, pointing in our direction as she spoke. Smile lines seemed to be permanently etched next to her mouth. My aunt was an easy soul to love. She trusted without reserve and gave most people the benefit of the doubt, though her eyes and ears were always open for the latest scandal or bit of gossip.

Frederick and I made our last steps through our waltz before he led me off the floor for my aunt to reclaim me. He grew stiff as we neared his aunt and uncle and this man he called Charles. The tall, unknown man had his back to us as we approached, and Aunt Mary was laughing at something he said.

As we neared the group, I looked in every direction to avoid the man's eyes. Lady Fletcher, addressed her nephew. "Lord Fletcher, I believe you are already acquainted with—"

"Yes we are acquainted." Frederick scowled, interrupting his aunt.

If she was surprised by her nephew's ill manners, she certainly didn't show it. Instead, Lady Fletcher simply smiled. "Of course you are."

In that moment, I couldn't help but look up at the man Frederick so clearly despised. Now that I was at liberty to get a good look at him, I found that he was even more striking than I had previously deduced. It was impossible not to notice his penetrating eyes and charming smile. He seemed to hold a grin in place, permanently.

Lady Fletcher looked at me next. "Miss Mason. May I introduce Lord Elliot, Earl of Wiltshire?" He nodded in my direction, grin still in place. "Lord Elliot, this is Miss Mason." I dipped a curtsy as my mind suddenly buzzed. His name sparked an old familiar cadence. Growing up in Wilton, Lily and I lightheartedly fantasized about owning Wilton Manor every time we passed the beautiful estate. My father had occasionally done business with the late Earl of Wiltshire, James Elliot. But I had never had as much as a glimpse of him or his son, since they had been abroad many years, and before that we hadn't run in the same social circles. Now I was finally meeting him. Frederick's opinion of Lord Elliot was very clear, and it was Frederick's heart I sought to secure.

Lord Elliot smiled at me fully. There was something in his look that unnerved me, as if he had a secret that I had not yet discovered—a secret that somehow involved me.

We all talked for a time, though Lord Elliot mostly kept to smiling with enthusiasm at Aunt Mary's and Lady Fletcher's comments. Eventually couples began to gather at the dance floor again.

Lord Elliot turned to my aunt with a dazzling smile. "Madam, would you permit me the privilege of claiming your niece for the next dance?"

Aunt Mary smiled with delight. "Indeed you may, Lord Elliot. And once we have spotted our Lily, and have made the proper introductions, you may stand up with her as well."

"It would be my pleasure," he said politely. He turned toward me. Frederick had not yet relinquished my hand from his arm.

Lord Elliot cocked an eyebrow at him. "Lord Fletcher," he said, holding his grin in place. Frederick looked daggers at Lord Elliot, then reluctantly handed me over to him. I glanced back at Frederick, hoping to see something comforting in his look, but he had already turned away.

Panic surged through me as I contemplated the mess I may have gotten myself into by accepting a dance with this man Frederick so fully despised. And yet, how could I have done otherwise without appearing entirely improper or rude?

I was suddenly very conscious of Lord Elliot's close presence as he led me towards the other couples. He waited for me to meet his gaze, still grinning, and took his place across from me. I wasn't sure what to do in this situation. For the first time in years, I felt entirely out of my element. I worried that employing my regular practiced smile toward Lord Elliot could be seen as an insult to Frederick—and yet to refuse to meet his gaze at all would be ill mannered of me.

I opted for a pleasant look, though not my usual smile, for Frederick's sake. The music started and our eyes met for a moment as our hands came together. Something stirred inside me as he studied my face. I quickly averted my eyes, nervous. I was thankful that my gloves separated his fingers from mine.

"I must say, Miss Mason, that thus far, you are the only lady in this room who refuses to meet my gaze." I couldn't believe his frankness.

I raised an eyebrow, finally daring to look at him. "Really, my lord, I don't believe you can claim the entire room. I see plenty whose attentions lie elsewhere." My statement was hardly true. Most of the room was, indeed, looking in our direction. I even received a few acid smiles from some of the ladies.

"Perhaps. And yet, I am seeking *your* attention at present." He smiled at me, then immediately glanced Frederick's way. Frederick glared back. What was this man about? I hoped he wasn't dancing with me simply to annoy Frederick—If he was, it appeared to be working.

"And why would that be, Lord Elliot?" I asked, hoping he would prove my theory wrong.

His eyes softened, giving me a look that would have melted any woman's heart. "If you are not aware of the way you stand out in a room full of people, I would be astonished. I hardly need to tell you of your striking beauty, for I am sure you are already aware."

His endearing words and charm may have worked on me if I hadn't seen through his charade. Unfortunately his next actions proved my suspicions, for as soon as the flattery fell from his lips, he looked once again to Frederick's rage-filled face and flashed a delighted smile.

It was absolutely clear to me that he had no interest in me other than trying to get a rise out of Frederick . . . at my expense. Another woman with less sense may have been beyond flattered by his compliments. But I was livid. I could see that Frederick's estimation of Lord Elliot was accurate after all.

A feeling of disappointment came over me, a feeling I was not accustomed to. I had taught myself to expect this sort of pettiness from everyone, and was therefore always ready when it came. But the curiosity from my younger years had always led me to believe that Lord Elliot would be as pleasant and charming as his estate.

This man was the appearance of all things pleasant and charming, to be sure, but inside lived an impostor. He came to his first social event after a five-year absence solely to patronize a man who was being celebrated that evening.

Livid or not, decorum told me to hold my tongue, and I always listened to that voice.

"Have you nothing to say to me in turn, Miss Mason?" His words brought me back to the present, and when our eyes met again he must have been able to read at least some of my thoughts, for he looked confused. I decided to steer the conversation to a safer topic.

"It's a beautiful room, is it not?" I said without emotion.

He reclaimed his usual grin and said, "Really, madam, the room? Surely you have more on your mind than that." He tried his charming smile again, but it was wasted on me.

"I assure you that I do," I said, meeting his eyes for only a moment before looking away. I shouldn't have said the words, but I found it impossible not to do so.

He raised an eyebrow and gave me a conspiratorial look. "Please do share," he said, amused.

"I dare not speak my mind at present, my lord, as I doubt you will like what I have to say."

His eyebrows knit in what appeared to be concern, but he couldn't fool me. I knew who he was now; he could only disappoint me further. I would prefer him to be unkind and inattentive over feigning decency.

"And why would that be?" he asked, his grin dimming but not leaving him altogether.

"We have an audience at present. I believe we should remain cordial." I continued to hold my pleasant demeanor, though I felt anything but.

"I see," he said, somewhat coolly, changing his face to one that would look agreeable enough to onlookers but was quite a notch down from his previous grin. "So you have formed your opinion of me based on the comments of others." He cocked his head in Frederick's direction.

"You have made it impossible for me to do otherwise, my lord." My pleasant expression wanted to slip, but I did my best to hold it in place. We stepped through the dance, meeting each other's eyes only when necessary. We were silent for some time, which I preferred. I could tell he was brooding under the surface. He finally broke the silence.

"And what exactly, madam, have I done to make you despise me in such little time?"

"Do you really want to know?" I asked, raising an eyebrow. A foreign rebel was at the helm just now. I didn't know her, but I decided to let her take over—just this once.

For the first time since I'd seen him, he looked unsure of himself, as if he wasn't entirely sure he *did* want to know.

I didn't wait for a response. "You have come here with no desire to enjoy company or woo a lady. You have no objective to play by the rules that society dictates, though you pretend to do just that through your smiles and charm."

"So you *do* admit I'm charming." He said the words, but his grin was no longer in place.

"You have come here with only one objective in mind: to berate a man who is being celebrated this very evening." My face remained polite, but my voice held a sting I was not used to hearing. He opened his mouth as if to speak, but my words came out first.

"I could perhaps forgive you this arrogant conduct if it were not done at the expense of others. You have given no thought to my feelings or to how I would respond to your practiced charm. You have flattered me and have said such endearing words, but only in jest. You expected to toy with Lord Fletcher tonight without giving a thought or care to how I could possibly feel in the process. You cared only that you would succeed."

His countenance fell completely and he truly looked remorseful.

I didn't trust it. I found myself unable to maintain my pleasant look any further. My facade dropped completely.

"You will not succeed tonight, Lord Elliot. I have found you out, and there can now be room for nothing other than disappointment. You should know I have always prided myself in claiming Wilton as my home." My words brought a brief look of surprise to his countenance. "I always hoped and believed that when I finally met the Earl of Wiltshire, it would further my pride of that claim."

How was it that I felt I could look down at him in this moment when he was so tall? And why was my breath quickening and all of my practiced poise leaving me entirely? I needed to put this new Jane away. I promised myself I would, as soon as she was finished.

"I feel no added pride or joy at the association, my lord. Quite the opposite, I assure you."

He looked at me with something I could not quite define. But all his composure had fled with mine.

My heart was pounding, but I had one more thing to add. "Contradict my assertions if you dare, Lord Elliot. But I promise you will not find yourself more to my liking if you try."

Taking a slow breath, I put this foreign Jane back where she belonged and assumed my pleasant facade once more. Lord Elliot said nothing. He didn't glue his grin back in place. He didn't even try to look pleasant afterwards. In fact, he refused to look at me at all. We passed through the majority of our dance in silence after that. It startled me when he finally spoke.

"I will not contradict you," he said, finally meeting my gaze. "Your assertions are correct, and you have thoroughly put me in my place." His eyes held mine for a moment longer. "I will not try to right my wrongs tonight, as I know it will do no good."

We remained silent for the rest of the dance, which felt as though it would never end. I was relieved when the music finally concluded and he returned me to my aunt. Lord Elliot looked at me once more and nodded. "Thank you, Miss Mason," he said solemnly. Then he left me to my own thoughts.

"Jane!" Aunt Mary exclaimed, perplexed. "What ever have you said to Lord Elliot? He looks as though he's had a royal beating."

"Nonsense, Aunt Mary." I placed my perfect smile back on. "Perhaps he is only tired from dancing and the heat of the room. He hasn't been to London for some time."

She raised her eyebrows and gave me a look, contemplating whether or not to believe my story. She watched Lord Elliot as he approached a group he'd been introduced to. His repressed look slowly regained some confidence.

"I suppose so." She smiled back at me. "Hopefully he will be right again quickly. He is so charming and pleasant to look at. You must try to revive him, Jane."

"I do believe he is quite taken care of." A sea of people swarmed Lord Elliot, his charming smile back in place already, though it was slightly subdued.

Breaking my gaze from him, I stood next to Aunt Mary, joining in a conversation with some of her friends. It was a welcome distraction at first, but after a time it became tedious. I found it hard *not* to watch Lord Elliot as he was introduced to new people. The ladies were practically swooning. I shook my head to myself. He could have them all—

His eyes suddenly found mine across the room. He smirked as if he'd caught me doing something naughty. Heat rose to my cheeks, and I quickly looked away, embarrassed and frustrated that I'd looked in the first place.

The women prattled on for another quarter hour before I dared peek at Lord Elliot again. This time, thankfully, he was nowhere to be seen.

I sighed with relief. It was only then that I noticed I hadn't seen Uncle Francis for some time, nor had I seen Lily return from her dance with Mr. Campbell, for that matter.

"Aunt Mary, where is Uncle Francis?" I asked, expecting to hear that he and Lily had wandered off somewhere together. Uncle Francis was a kind man and was generally in high spirits, though he wasn't normally keen on company outside of close relatives.

"Uncle Francis is playing cards with the gentlemen this evening," Aunt Mary said casually.

Alarm pounded through my chest when I realized Lily was un-chaperoned . . . again. It had been nearly three quarters of an hour since I had seen her. I talked quietly to Aunt Mary so only she could hear. "I believe we should find Lily." I gave her a knowing look.

She swept the room with her gaze. "Yes," she said, pressing her lips together in a line of worry. "I believe you are right."

We walked in opposite directions to find her quicker. I surveyed my side of the ballroom. But she was nowhere to be seen. If she had gone out to the gardens after she promised—

I turned and headed to the garden doors. I was near the edge, where people were scarce, and still there was no sign of her. I was about to go back to help Aunt Mary when I spotted Lily near the refreshment table, talking to Mr. Johnson. She glanced my way and gave me a weak smile with a grimace. I smiled back, then watched as Aunt Mary approached from the other side, speaking to Lily and Mr. Johnson. After a brief exchange, Mr. Johnson led her off toward the dance floor.

Poor Lily. He had already found a way to secure a second dance. I was about to turn back toward the way I came when a familiar face appeared in front of me: Mr. Hughes. Despite my plans to catch Frederick, I did not care for the company he kept in the way of friends. Mr. Hughes was a man that hinted at everything vile, while saying very little.

"Miss Mason," he said, daring a glance at my entire frame, then putting on a suggestive face. "Would you do me the honor of the next dance?" He dropped his eyes to my lips. We were on the very edge of the ballroom, where prying eyes weren't as much of a concern. It was a bad time to be caught in such a predicament.

"Excuse me, Mr. Hughes, but I am otherwise engaged." I tried to get around him, but he stepped in front of me again.

"I don't believe you are, Jane." I had never given him permission to use my Christian name. He leaned closer to me, and I stepped back. A look of amusement danced in his eyes as if he enjoyed the feeling of trapping me further.

"People are approaching us." I prayed it would be true. He looked over his shoulder briefly, but to my dismay, no one was coming our way or even looking in our direction. I tried to walk past him again but he stopped me, grabbing my wrist. This was a bold move, even for Mr. Hughes. He raised his eyebrows, calling my bluff.

"Don't touch me, Mr. Hughes, or I will cause such a scene," I said venomously. It was only then that I realized how drunk he was. His breath reeked of brandy.

He smiled but didn't let go. "I know you secretly watch me," he smirked, looking at my lips again. "But I don't mind. I won't tell Lord Fletcher if you don't."

How could he claim such a thing? The only time I ever 'watched him' was if I wanted to ensure I was on the opposite side of the room. I pulled away from him as discreetly as I could. I really didn't want to make a scene, but I would if I needed to. He chuckled and started pulling me closer. I pushed with my other hand at his wrist and was about to yell out when I felt someone grab Mr. Hughes from the other side.

"Let her go, Jacob, or I'll knock you so flat you'll never stand again," a deep, angry voice commanded. I was shocked to see that the face belonged to Lord Elliot. He was absolutely furious.

Mr. Hughes let go of me, but Lord Elliot did not let go of him. Instead, he squeezed Mr. Hughes' wrist until he couldn't help but grunt in pain.

"If I find you near a lady again in such a way," Lord Elliot seethed,

"I swear you'll wish you had never been born."

Mr. Hughes looked furious. "Understood, Cousin," he spat.

Lord Elliot released him forcefully, and the very drunk Mr. Hughes stalked off.

The shock of the moment hit me suddenly. Tears threatened to take over, but I held firm.

"Are you alright, Miss Mason?" Lord Elliot asked, sounding truly concerned. I didn't trust it. Why did it have to be Lord Elliot that intervened? His question made it harder to hold back the tears. All I could do was nod my head. Unfortunately a tear slipped out despite my strict orders to stay back.

I quickly turned away from him.

He discreetly pulled a handkerchief from his pocket and handed it to me.

I dabbed at my eyes, then turned toward him and returned his handkerchief. "Thank you, Lord Elliot." I refused to meet his gaze.

"Miss Mason." Silence followed.

I kept my eyes averted.

He talked quietly. "I do not wish to repeat our previous conversation, as I believe it would accomplish nothing." He took in a slow breath. "I would, however, be grateful to state a few things. I did not come here solely to berate and bite at Lord Fletcher."

I looked up at him and opened my mouth, ready to contradict his statement, but he put up a hand.

"Please let me finish." He waited until he was sure I would listen. "I have not been in London society for some time, and I will admit that my plastered smiles and charm are not to fool young ladies and their mothers, but rather to fool my own feelings of being entirely out of place. That . . . and the fact that I simply can't help but be absolutely charming." He smirked before he continued.

"Will you at least consider forgiving me for my poor behavior earlier, Miss Mason?" His eyes were sincere. I wanted to take him at his word, but I knew I needed to tread carefully. He threatened everything I was working for. He was a man that had no thought for social graces, because he was ranked above the rules. My hard-earned climb into high-class society meant nothing to him. My years of waiting for someone like Frederick could be ruined if this man continued to pay me heed.

"Lord Elliot." I felt nervous holding his gaze, but stayed firm. "I believe there is a difference between forgiveness and trust." I hesitated, finding my next words. "I can forgive you . . . but trust you . . . " I lifted an eyebrow. "Certainly not."

Despite the fact that I did *not* trust him, I couldn't help but be drawn to his eyes. They were dark and rich, holding mystery and depth.

He gave me a look of challenge. "And yet you would trust someone like Lord Fletcher?"

"Why wouldn't I trust Lord Fletcher? He is exactly as he appears to be," I countered.

"Are you referring to the fact that he is predictable, flat, and gloomy? Or the fact that he has no heart?"

Once again, I couldn't believe his frankness. "Lord Elliot, if you are trying to gain my forgiveness, you're doing a very poor job of it."

He raised an eyebrow and gave me a tight, forced smile. "I can see that we are at an impasse, Miss Mason. You don't want my charm or my good humor, which leaves only my honesty." He studied my face. "And that I cannot give without offending you, for I will always think poorly of Lord Fletcher."

Lord Elliot's expression surprised me. It was not charming or teasing or even angry. It was a look of frustration mixed with something else. His eyes held mine for a moment longer before he spoke again.

"I believe we will agree on only one matter this evening." He stepped closer so prying ears wouldn't hear. "Don't find yourself alone with Jacob Hughes again."

A shiver went through me. Whether it was due to the memory of Mr. Hughes' unwanted attention or Lord Elliot's close proximity, I was not sure. But it agitated me and I wanted to escape.

Before I could do so, he bowed briefly and walked away into the sea of men and women. He quickly reclaimed his charming smile, drawing everyone to him.

Something boiled within me.

I couldn't define exactly what it was or why it was there.

I had never experienced such an emotion. All I knew was that it stemmed from Lord Elliot.

7

GREEN RIBBON

Jane

London
November 2, 1816
The next day
13 days of disguise remaining

Dreams never came when I finally sank beneath the covers after the duchess' ball. Nevermind that exhaustion seeped through every pore in my body, including heavy eyelids and aching feet. Deep eyes and a smooth voice continued stirring my thoughts until I was sure I would go mad.

Sun filled my room, making me conclude that there was no point pretending to sleep any longer. Letting out an exasperated breath, I sat up and decided to greet the day.

To my delight, I discovered that Lily was planning a small shopping venture, though neither of us had rested for more than five hours. Regardless, I was ready for a distraction.

Lily and Alice were just ahead of me, peering through a large window showcasing elegant parasols and laced gloves. The other side of the window exhibited an array of pocket watches and canes. The large glass pane was edged with a fine, gold trim. Whoever owned this shop took care with its appearance; it was quaint and enchanting.

I looked over at Lily, smirking. "And this is really the only shop in London that carries dark-green ribbon?" She had been so adamant that we visit this particular shop.

She returned my look with a grin. "According to Marianne Morgan, this is the only place with the exact shade of green I'm looking for."

I arched my head back and stared at the wood paneling above, which was covered in well-kept forest-green paint. A large sign hung above the door. It read:

Arthur & Co

I was surprised that no bell chimed as we stepped through the entrance—It seemed the only thing missing in this perfect little shop. It was just as lovely on the inside as it appeared on the outside. Small displays were set up throughout the entire storefront. In the center of the shop, towards the back, was a large counter. An archway was fixed on the back wall near the right corner, leading to an interior room. I stopped at a display of colorful fans while Lily made her way to the ribbons displayed near the back-left corner. Alice sat on a bench by a small window near the entrance, making herself comfortable while we perused.

I carefully draped open a light-blue fan with gold markings. It was exquisite. My fingers brushed against the beautiful pattern before I carefully closed it and returned it to its place. The ribbons called to me next as I watched Lily look down at a table displaying an assortment of colors. I made my way to her and began browsing.

Lily beamed, looking down at a beautiful dark-green ribbon that peeked through an assortment of colors. Lily's fingers moved to it, picking up the silky strand.

"It's perfect," she said with a smile, moving her fingers down her find.

She nudged me, then cocked an eyebrow, mischief dancing in her eyes. "Now, let's find you a deep-blue one." Apparently she was in the mood to bring up my sudden change in ball gown the night before.

I sighed. "I don't know why I chose that fabric. I—"

"Good afternoon, Miss Mason." My words were cut off by a smooth, deep voice behind me. It was the very one that I'd been replaying in my mind ever since we returned from the ball, when sleep should have taken me. I turned to see Lord Elliot, his charming grin in tow.

"Good afternoon," I said, my practiced smile covering my apprehension. Perhaps I needed to speak to the shop owner about putting a bell up. Had one been in place, I would have heard Lord Elliot's arrival.

We stared at each other in silence before I realized he was most likely waiting for me to make an introduction. It caught me off guard, making heat rise to my cheeks. This never usually happened to me. Why was this gentleman so masterful at putting me on edge? Thankfully, I held my practiced poise, though I didn't feel entirely in control of myself.

Swallowing my irritation, I gestured to Lily. "I don't believe you have yet made my sister's acquaintance."

"I have not had the pleasure," Lord Elliot said, smiling.

"This is my younger sister, Miss Lily Mason." My sister dipped a curtsy, then looked at me, a curious grin teasing the corner of her mouth. Why was she looking at me in such a way—?

I was introducing them in the wrong order. I wanted to walk out of the shop and cover my cheeks that had, no doubt, turned deep red. I never made mistakes like this.

What was wrong with me?

Nothing could be done about it now. I maintained my practiced smile and continued. "Lily, may I introduce Lord Elliot, Earl of Wiltshire?" Lord Elliot nodded just as Lily's face lit up with recognition.

"Lord Elliot!" she exclaimed. "Jane and I are from Wilton. We have often talked about what a pleasure it would be to finally meet you. It's truly an honor."

Lord Elliot smiled fully at her kind words. "Thank you, Miss Mason. I'm very pleased to make your acquaintance as well. It is truly a delight to meet someone else from Wilton." His expression was genuine. I would do well to be wary of it. It was clear to me from observing him last night that Lord Elliot was a master of making people feel the way he wanted them to.

He glanced in my direction briefly before he looked back at Lily. "And where are you residing during your stay in London?"

"With our aunt and uncle." Lily handed him our calling card. "Please call on us sometime soon. Tomorrow if you can spare the time."

"I certainly will, as long as your sis—"

"Excuse me," Lily said abruptly, cutting off Lord Elliot. "I must purchase my ribbon before I lose it." She held it up, emphasizing her point. "But I hope we will all become better acquainted while we are here in London. And don't forget to visit tomorrow." She made her way to the counter.

Lily

I excused myself to purchase my ribbon the moment Henry walked in. There was no mistaking his tall, broad figure and deep, brooding eyes as he entered the shop. I was dismayed to find that he was even more alluring in full light. His dark chestnut hair was thick and wavy, framing his deep brown eyes and chiseled jaw beneath his short beard. I almost gasped as I realized how much he looked like Lord Elliot.

It was uncanny.

Lord Elliot had no other siblings that I was aware of. But if I hadn't known any better, I would have believed they were, at the very least, brothers. I was surprised that neither Jane nor Lord Elliot had noticed his arrival through the shop door. Thank goodness Mr. Brown had no bell to signal someone's entry.

It must have been fate that Arthur & Co actually carried a ribbon just like the one I had described to Jane. Marianne Morgan, in truth, had not told me about the ribbon, though I *had* met her at the ball, and she had indeed been kind to me. I was genuinely grateful to have finally made a friend. So the story wasn't entirely a falsehood. I hoped Jane's and Alice's presence wouldn't complicate matters.

Upon seeing me, Henry's mouth turned up on one side and he gave me the smallest nod in recognition. My heart pounded at the sight of him. It took effort to force my thoughts back to my current objective. As I made my way to the counter, a man came out from the back room. I couldn't help but smile. This man must belong to the other voice I heard last night. Mr. Arthur Brown. He was a middle aged man, portly, and well dressed, with a kind look about him.

He greeted me with a smile. "Hello, Miss. How can I assist you?"

I smiled back. It was odd, feeling as though I had already met this man when he was unaware that I had happened upon Henry's and his secret encounter.

I held up my find. "I would like to purchase this lovely ribbon." I dangled it between my fingers.

I was suddenly very aware that someone stood just behind me, waiting. It could only be Henry. My heart thudded when I felt my other hand, at my side, fill with something cold and metallic: tuppence from the night before.

Definitely Henry.

It was hard to concentrate when Mr. Brown told me the sum for my ribbons. I was proud of myself for appearing unaffected as I pulled out my small money purse and paid the appropriate amount. I felt another item come into my hand when I returned it to my side—a small piece of parchment, if I wasn't mistaken. I thanked the shopkeeper and, without turning to face Henry, walked off a few paces near the bonnets on the opposite side of the room from Jane and Lord Elliot. I had to remember that, to the general public, Henry and I had never been introduced; I was, therefore, not at liberty to speak with him.

"Good afternoon, Mr. Brown. I am in search of a penknife." Henry's unmistakable voice filled the space.

"Very good, sir," came Mr. Brown's reply. "They are stored in the back. If you will come this way, I will show you what we have."

"Thank you," Henry's deep voice resounded. My eyes followed his retreating figure, trying not to stare at him. He looked back, catching my eyes, just before he walked through the back of the shop and out of my view. I discreetly opened the small piece of paper featuring elegant, neat handwriting. It read,

You will recognize your moment when it presents itself. Be ready.

I swallowed, excitement mixed with apprehension making my heart hammer. All reason was screaming that this was a bad idea.

I looked down at my ribbon, realizing thus far my story added up. No one ever had to know that I'd snuck out to those gardens. I could leave with Jane, together making our way to other shops, and I could be safe from whatever this was. My chest rose and fell as I debated whether I should stay or go.

Thinking through my choices, I glanced at Jane and Lord Elliot. My sister seemed agitated, though she was hiding it well. Her shoulders were stiffer than usual and her practiced smile was tight. I hadn't had a chance to really talk to her since the ball, but by the looks of it, something significant had passed between the two of them last night. I would have to ask her about it later.

I looked back down at the note in my hand. I needed to make a decision, and it needed to be made quickly.

Jane

I didn't know where to put my hands as I stood alone with Lord Elliot. Looking down at nothing in particular, I was about to excuse myself and join Lily to purchase her ribbon, but he spoke before I had the chance.

"How are you this afternoon, Miss Mason?" I looked up. His expression gave nothing away.

I wanted to flee but held firm. At least he decided to begin our exchange with polite conversation. This was something I could always navigate.

"I am well, Lord Elliot. Thank you. And how are you this afternoon?" I said the words evenly.

He watched me carefully as I spoke, eyes still unreadable. Why did his gaze make me so self-conscious?

"I'm well enough. I trust you enjoyed the remainder of your evening last night?" he added.

"Indeed," I said mechanically. "I trust you did as well?"

"I did." He paused, smirking ever so slightly. "Though it was dampened somewhat by a certain lady's distrust in me." I couldn't tell if he was mocking me or trying to hold back frustration.

"Is this your attempt to gain my trust?" I tried to speak with an even tone.

"I believe it is impossible to gain your trust when you choose to trust a man like Lord Fletcher." I let out a breath of frustration. Just when I thought he would stick to safe topics he proved me wrong.

"Lord Elliot," I said with some impatience. "Do you have a purpose in being here?"

For a moment he looked unsure of how to answer, turning his eyes down to the ribbons displayed in front of him. But as soon as his look of discomfort came, it left, leaving a mischievous smile instead. "I am ribbon shopping, of course." His eyes returned to mine and he raised an eyebrow.

I stared at him flatly, surprised to find that I wanted to smile at his ridiculous statement. Studying the ribbons, my eye caught the most hideous ribbon I'd ever encountered. I grinned and reached down, slowly picking it up. It was a brownish yellow with a hint of green. It was frayed at the ends and crinkled. I held it up to him. "In that case, I really do believe this is your color."

He chuckled and posed in a dramatic fashion. "It really does bring out my eyes, wouldn't you agree?" His smile was back in place, and this time, I couldn't help but mirror it with my own.

His smile deepened. "Be careful, Miss Mason. You are actually smiling in my presence. I might begin to think you don't loathe me entirely."

I opened my mouth at his bluntness. "Be careful, Lord Elliot, or one of these days I might actually take you seriously."

"Where would we be if that were the case?" He said it under his breath as he extended his hand forward slowly and picked up the other end of the ribbon I was holding up.

His eyes returned to mine, gauging my reaction. "I do believe this now belongs to me," he said. I let go of my end, and he slowly lowered it into his pocket. As he did so, he pulled a different-colored ribbon out of the same pocket with his other hand. It looked like the ribbon was changing color, though I knew that was not possible.

"And I believe," he said, extending it completely, "this one belongs to you." It was deep-blue in color. I could only stare at it. Did he know what that color meant for me? I took it from him, and something stirred within me, my mind flashing to the stranger in the deep blue dress, looking back at me in the mirror, craving something more. I glanced at him, his eyes drawing me in once again.

A gaggle of women's voices suddenly entered the shop. Turning to see who the approaching party was, I quietly let out a sigh of dread as Edith Barton and Amelia Elwell walked our way, accompanied by Amelia's mother. They were debatably the cattiest gossips I'd met since entering London society, and they never tried to hide their disdain for me.

Amelia's mother glanced in my direction with a haughty expression, then walked over to a display of parasols.

Amelia and Edith glanced at me with pursed lips, then looked past me to Lord Elliot. They exchanged excited looks with one another as they further made their way to us. I placed my practiced smile on my face and greeted them.

"Miss Barton, Miss Elwell. Have you come to browse for ribbons as well?"

They didn't even attempt to make small talk. They ran straight for the meat. "And are you alone, Miss Mason?" Edith asked with an overly sweet voice.

"Certainly not." I smiled as I gestured to Alice, who was now looking our way. She always gave us enough space to have private conversations but made her presence known when it mattered. Their faces soured, annoyed that their plan to ruin my reputation had been thwarted.

Amelia pursed her lips. "Miss Mason, will you introduce us?"

Lord Elliot cleared his throat behind me, almost making me jump. I recovered quickly, realizing that, once again, it was up to me to perform an introduction.

"Miss Barton, Miss Elwell, this is Lord Elliot, Earl of Wiltshire?" I gestured my hand toward him but didn't look at him directly. Edith and Amelia tried for subdued expressions, but it was easy to detect their eagerness at hearing his name. I gestured next to Edith and Amelia. "Lord Elliot, this is Miss Barton and Miss Elwell."

Amelia spoke next with a velvety tone that had been perfected by years of practice, no doubt. "It is truly an honor." She looked at him demurely through her dark lashes in a way that set me on edge.

Edith tittered, her sickly sweet voice joining in. "Are you enjoying your time in London, Lord Elliot?" Her blonde curls bounced as she tilted her head. She didn't even attempt to hide her look of captivation as she took him in.

He grinned. "Indeed I am. I plan to attend the Morgans' ball this weekend. Will I have the pleasure of seeing you there as well?" He looked at each of them in turn.

"We are attending," Amelia purred. Her dark, glossy locks shined perfectly, not a single hair out of place.

"Delightful," he said with his easy charm. "You must each save a dance for me."

Their faces lit up.

"I would be honored," Edith said. I rolled my eyes at her breathy tone.

"As would I," Amelia said, smooth as silk. She looked at me triumphantly, clearly pleased that Lord Elliot had not asked me to dance as well.

Edith spoke next. "And what brings you into the shop this afternoon, Lord Elliot?" She eyed me, then returned her focus to him.

His mouth turned upward. "I was intending to look at some pocket watches, as I have misplaced mine somehow. Upon entering the store, however, I noticed Miss Mason picking out ribbons. I had to step in when I discovered that she," he started pulling the hideous ribbon from his pocket, "has the worst taste in ribbons I've seen yet." Dread washed over me as he extended the ribbon out to them. I knew Edith and Amelia would use any chance they could to make me look inferior.

They stared at the ribbon, then Lord Elliot, who couldn't help but be charming. They smiled at him, clearly smitten, then looked at me, their smiles turning almost imperceptibly to sneers.

"It is such a pity she does not have a more refined taste," Amelia said with her velvety tone. "Those who were not born into wealth simply don't know how to use it, I suppose." She eyed me derisively, then turned an adoring eye back to Lord Elliot.

I usually knew how to handle these women. It was not the first time I'd received a petty barb. But at that moment, I was at a loss for words. I felt vulnerable and unsure of what to say. Lord Elliot was making me the target of ridicule, and I didn't see how to get myself out of it. This whole experience added further to my list of reasons why I should stay as far away from him as possible.

I needed to escape.

I bobbed a quick curtsy. "If you'll excuse me, I must be going." I turned to leave, but Lord Elliot took my arm. Something lurched inside me at his touch.

"Just a brief moment of your time before you leave, Miss Mason." He said it as if he wouldn't take no for an answer. "You see, I have a conscience, though a very small one, and I won't be able to sleep to-night unless you know the full extent of my treachery."

What game was he playing at now? If he intended to make me look even more ridiculous, I didn't know if I could bear it. The looks on Edith's and Amelia's faces were sheer condescension.

Lord Elliot proceeded. "I believe you misunderstand me, Miss Elwell," he said, looking at her, keeping his charming smile in place but adding a foppish stance to his entire demeanor. He raised his eyebrow. "You see, I believe Miss Mason has the ability to make even this hideous ribbon look fetching. She is quite a genius, really. If you shine in the ugliest attire, you are sure to make a statement. And where would that put me, if she were to outshine me?"

The look on Amelia's and Edith's faces was priceless. They tried to hold their smiles, but they were framed by sour pouts. Lord Elliot continued his dramatized charade.

"See, I am incredibly vain, and need to prove absolutely that I can look just as handsome with this ribbon in tow as Miss Mason does. I convinced her to trade the blue one for this," he confessed, dangling the hideous ribbon. "My plan had worked, but now my conscience is wracked with guilt. I do believe you have found me out, Miss Mason. But if you will now be as generous as you are genius, I'd be grateful if you would still allow me to move forward with my plan."

It was difficult not to laugh at the look on Edith's and Amelia's faces. I couldn't help but feel grateful that Lord Elliot had come to my aid. Normally, I wouldn't play along with such a far-fetched story, but I couldn't pass up this chance.

"Very well, Lord Elliot. I will regretfully relinquish my ribbon," I said with feigned reluctance. I watched as Lily began making her way to us from a display of bonnets in another corner of the store. Our eyes met, and she puckered her lips as if she had eaten something sour upon seeing Edith and Amelia. Then she straightened her shoulders and leaned back dramatically, gliding over, mocking Amelia's walk. I held down my laugh. They didn't notice her approach.

"Good afternoon, Miss Barton, Miss Elwell," she said behind them. Her voice gave away none of her feelings. She lifted her purchase in the air. "Unfortunately, the best ribbon has been spoken for."

Amelia and Edith looked at each other, a wave of annoyance spreading between them. Lily wrapped her arm through mine, noticing my deep-blue ribbon in hand. She gave me a curious look and a smirk. "And now," she said, gazing sidelong at the gossips, "I do believe I need to get my sister to purchase her ribbon before it gets away from her." She nodded to both ladies and Lord Elliot. "Please excuse us."

She walked me over to the counter to purchase my ribbon. I glanced back at Lord Elliot as she did so. He grinned and lifted his hideous ribbon up slightly. I nodded back with a timid smile, hoping he would recognize my gesture of thanks.

Perhaps he understood exactly who Amelia and Edith were and he wouldn't give them the time of day. If so, Lord Elliot would gain a few points in my book.

Within no time, however, Lord Elliot was smiling and laughing with them. I just could not trust this man. He was clearly a flirt who didn't mind whose attention he captured. I had watched him smile and charm all the ladies at the ball last night. I watched him do so again with Amelia and Edith.

As I was paying for my ribbons, Amelia's mother reclaimed the two scheming ladies and they left the shop.

"Thank goodness they're gone," Lily muttered near my ear.

"Are you ready to leave now?" I asked, needing to escape from the shop as soon as possible.

"In a moment," she said quietly. "I would like to speak to Lord Elliot before we leave. We won't be long."

"I would rather continue our shopp—"

She pulled me over near Lord Elliot and I bit my tongue. He was now browsing pocket watches.

He glanced up at our approach, reclaiming his smile.

"Lord Elliot, I hope you'll forgive me for stepping away so abruptly earlier," Lily said with a smile.

He shook his head. "Think nothing of it."

Lily's smile mellowed. "I was sorry to hear about your father's passing." Her words were conveyed with real sincerity. His smile became subdued as she said the words. "I'm sure you miss him very much."

He looked down, his countenance endorsing her statement.

Lily allowed silence to pass for a moment before she continued. "I know this is very little comfort in a time such as this, but you have friends by way of the Mason family. My father spoke highly of your father. If ever you need anything, only ask."

My stomach wrenched as Lily spoke the words. I realized I had never offered my condolences for his father's passing. Recognizing my own mistakes never sat well with me.

"Thank you," he said to Lily. "His loss has been keenly felt. I am grateful for your kind words and appreciate your offer of friendship. I, too, extend the same offer to you and your sister." He looked at me as he said the last word. In this kind and serious manner, Lord Elliot pulled on me. A sliver of guilt and remorse edged its way inside of me.

It didn't help that his eyes lingered on mine—magnifying that buried desire for more. As he held my gaze, I felt my defenses begin to lower.

My thoughts were interrupted by a female voice coming from behind the counter.

"Excuse me," she said, "but would one of you ladies mind helping me choose a gift for Duchess Hastingwood? I'm to pick out something that's to be given as a gift from the duke, and I'd be right grateful for another woman's eye."

"I would be happy to assist!" Lily volunteered almost immediately. I didn't even have time to register what she was asking before Lily whisked herself away and followed the servant to the back.

I could feel that Lord Elliot was looking at me again. My gaze moved to the floor, feeling vulnerable under his scrutiny. I also felt conflicted. Though I didn't trust Lord Elliot, I truly felt ashamed that I had not considered his recent loss.

"Miss Mason," he said. "Have I done something else to offend you?"

I looked up quickly to contradict him. "No, Lord Elliot—" I tried to find the right words to apologize. His awareness of my every move made me feel nervous.

After my first encounter with Lord Elliot, I had convinced myself that he was a very singular gentleman. I had found him to be handsome, charming, and eager to find amusement at the expense of others. I'd assumed those traits made up his entire personality until he intervened with Mr. Hughes. He had been an entirely different man in that moment. Watching him now as he observed me only made him more unpredictable; I didn't like unpredictable.

"You are not at ease," he said perceptively.

I fidgeted with my hands. "I'm always at ease." I never fidgeted. What was wrong with me?

His eyes flicked down to my hands, noticing my agitation, before he raised an eyebrow, along with the corner of his mouth. "Miss Mason, am I making you uncomfortable?" Once again, I couldn't tell if he was taking pleasure at my discomfort or if he was hiding his frustration.

I had never been asked such a blunt question by a man. How was I to answer?

"How exactly do you intend for me to answer that question?" I tried to keep my emotions under control but they weren't obeying. My words came out short.

"I intended for you to be honest." He hid his frustration well. I could almost believe it wasn't there at all. But I recognized a fellow master of impressions when I saw one.

It appeared as though our one moment of camaraderie was over. Perhaps it was fate that Lord Elliot and I would never be able to have a civil conversation for any extended period of time.

I finally looked down. "Tell me truthfully. Are you intending to make me uncomfortable?"

"So I *do* make you uncomfortable," He didn't pose it as a question.

"Lord Elliot," I said with exasperation. "I am trying to find a way to apologize, but I believe it would no longer carry value." The air was tense.

He stepped closer to me. "And why is that?"

My breath hitched at his unexpected move. "Because at this point, my lord, an apology would be overshadowed by discord."

He watched me carefully. "What need would you have to apologize to me?" There was no sarcasm in his question.

Holding my breath, I watched for any indicator that he was teasing me. I wouldn't be able to bear it if he made light of my apology—if I did, in fact, end up giving it. I decided to take my chances. "Lord Elliot, I'm sorry that I did not consider your recent loss last night when I chastised you. I hope you will forgive me."

His eyes searched mine. "Miss Mason, I do not wish for you to apologize for putting me in my place last night. Losing a loved one does not excuse bad behavior, especially when it is at the expense of another."

"Then I would like to echo Lily's words. I am truly sorry for your loss . . . and . . . " My words faltered. I looked down. "I wanted to thank you for helping me out of a difficult place yesterday. I don't know what would have happened had you not intervened with Mr. Hughes. I'm truly grateful, and I wouldn't want you to think otherwise." Silence followed for a moment.

Then he grinned. "It appears as though you are in my debt, Miss Mason."

I tried to return my practiced smile to its place, but it didn't seem to work. Recognizing that I was in Lord Elliot's debt was bad enough. It was ungentlemanly for *him* to acknowledge it openly, and it made me feel even more vulnerable than before. The look on my face must have shown more than I intended.

Lord Elliot shook his head. "Why is it that my attempts to pull a smile from you seem only to do the opposite?" He sighed. "I can see that I'm making you uncomfortable again. Despite what you may think, I do not delight in your discomfort, Miss Mason. Nor would I wish for you to believe that I find amusement in being the cause of it." He appeared to be sincere. I could see that he was waiting for a response, but once again I was at a loss for words. "Do you wish for me to leave you alone?" he finally asked.

His expression was difficult to read, his question once again bold, direct, and impossible to answer. My life would certainly be easier if he left me alone. But there was also something that stirred inside me when he was near, reminding me of silky, deep-blue fabric and a hunger for more.

He inhaled slowly. "I can see by your silence that you are too modest to tell me you wish to be left alone. I will respect your wishes, Miss Mason. I'll not bother you further."

"Lord Elliot, I didn't ask you to leave me alone."

"You didn't need to." He tried putting on a polite face, but I could see that he was conflicted beneath the surface. "Good day," he said, dipping his head. He walked out of the shop.

Frustration coursed through me as I questioned whether or not I handled the situation appropriately. Lord Elliot was proving to be an even bigger challenge than I had originally anticipated.

8

GIFT

Lily

The lady's maid walked swiftly through a doorway to the back of the shop, making my heart tick even faster as I followed. Her dark brown hair, almost black, was a stark contrast to her white apron and cap, ringlets trickling out the side.

When Henry came into view, my heart pounded through my chest, a sense of thrill growing inside me. I reminded myself, for what felt like the hundredth time, that I didn't really know him, and that for now, I needed to be careful.

It was difficult to breathe normally when he kept finding my eyes, ticking up the corner of his mouth as though we shared a secret, then just as quickly looking away. We formed something of a circle, and then the servant girl spoke, looking at Mr. Brown.

"And you are sure they are trustworthy, sir?"

Mr. Brown nodded his head. "I trust Mr. Thomas. If Mr. Thomas trusts this lady—" he gestured to me— "then I trust her as well."

Henry spoke next. "As it stands, miss, we all have an interest in this case. We have no intention of revealing anyone's identity. It would put our own reputations at risk as much as it would yours. We have all agreed to be here in hopes of uncovering truths that have been buried."

His deep rumbling voice asserted such an air of certainty that there was no room for questioning or doubting him. I made my way to stand between Henry and Mr. Brown so the maid wouldn't feel the need to move her head in three different directions while speaking.

She clasped her fingers together, apprehensive.

Henry broke the silence. "What is your name, miss?"

"Molly Black, sir. I serve as lady's maid to Her Grace, Duchess Fletcher. I must make this meeting brief since I'm expected back within a few hours and I still have some other tasks to perform before I return."

Henry nodded. "I understand. Please tell us what information you have so you can be on your way."

She nodded and gave a coy smile in Henry's direction, as if she couldn't help it in the presence of such a man. Coming out of her momentary stupor, she straightened up and cleared her throat.

"I am loyal to the Fletcher family and am right grateful to have such a position in their household. The duke and duchess are highly respected, as I'm sure you're aware, and conduct themselves in such a way that truly makes me feel honored to serve them. Their son, Lord Fletcher, has my loyalty as well. I believe that when the time requires it, he will become a great man like his father." She hesitated for a moment. "The company Lord Fletcher keeps, on the other hand, is something I don't approve of. Especially in regards to his friend, Mr. Hughes."

I sensed Henry stiffen at the mention of Mr. Hughes. I was only slightly acquainted with the man being discussed. The little I had seen of him proved that he was suggestive enough to make me feel uncomfortable but discreet enough that I couldn't call him out in public. I was extremely grateful that the one time he'd asked for a dance it had been toward the end of the evening and I had the rest of the night already spoken for.

Henry spoke next. "And does the information you've brought here today point to Jacob Hughes as the culprit of this potential murder?" His voice came out level as he spoke, though I could hear a hint of strain, as if he was trying to sound unaltered.

"It does, sir," Molly said. "About six and a half months ago, I overheard Mr. Hughes talking to Lord Fletcher. I say talking, though there was more slur than speech present. He was drunk as a mule on this particular occasion. I am usually with Her Ladyship, so I had never previously encountered Mr. Hughes in such a state.

"But the lady servants talk, and they say he's best not to be around when he's been at the drink for some time, as he becomes brash and doesn't mind forcing himself upon a lady."

I dared a glance at Henry. His composure was starting to slip.

"I'm getting off the point," she said apologetically. "I was tasked to seek out a book of poetry for the duchess. I started in the library, but it wasn't in its usual place. They have a large library, so checking all the shelves was no simple task. It was as I was searching that I overheard Mr. Hughes talking with Lord Fletcher in the lounge across from the library. The doors were wide open and he hadn't a care to keep his voice down. I heard Mr. Hughes slur, 'If it weren't—for that arrogant—stuffy Charles—I'd have the entire Elliot Legacy.' " She mimicked a heavily drunk Mr. Hughes. "I'll save you the drunk impressions further, sir, as I assume you can envision the rest."

I smiled at her impersonation. It was rather impressive. I assumed Henry would take on the same look of amusement—but I couldn't have been more wrong. He stared flatly at the wall behind Molly and was completely rigid. Molly noticed as well. She began to fidget and had a look of discomfort about her, as if she'd done something wrong. The moment lasted longer than I felt was natural. I needed to somehow pull him out of the cloud that had such a firm hold of him. I found myself fidgeting with my ring—my ring.

I took it off, then discreetly slipped it into Henry's hand at my side without anyone noticing. I hoped he would understand its meaning; I liked to think of it as a memento of our truce and secret friendship. The gesture surprised him and broke his look of intensity. His eyes flicked over to mine briefly, portraying gratitude and new strength.

"Forgive me, Miss Black," he said to her. "I have a complicated history with Mr. Hughes. Hearing his name and the circumstances you have described struck a chord. You have in no way angered or upset me yourself. I will be more amicable from here on. You have my word."

She still looked uncomfortable.

Henry gave her an encouraging look. "And I must say you do a very good impersonation of a drunk Mr. Hughes." Her face lit up significantly at his compliment. "Now, I believe you stated your apprehension at lingering here for too long. Let's hear the rest of what you wanted to say."

She nodded her head. "Yes, sir. As I was saying, Mr. Hughes is often drunk, and he has often been overheard talking about the Elliot legacy and inheritance; he has talked about little else the past year. He claims multiple relatives have passed within the last ten months, leaving him next in line to inherit if the current Lord Elliot dies."

Molly continued. "On this particular occasion, Mr. Hughes said, 'I'll kill them all. Then I won't have to wait for the old man to die, and I don't ever have to see that smug look on Charles's face again. I can get it all over with. I'd put his money to far better use anyway.' "

She stopped speaking and looked from Mr. Brown, to me, to Henry. "That is all the information I have. I admit that I've been reluctant to share it with anyone. It is likely to put a taint on the Fletcher name if anything were to come of it, since Lord Fletcher is well acquainted with Mr. Hughes. But I feel it's my duty to be forthcoming, since the information is true."

She pressed her lips in a firm line. "I also don't mind telling you that I don't like Mr. Hughes lurking about the house. It would ease my mind to see him out of the Fletcher house for good. I can't get the thought out of my head that if he did in fact have something to do with the late earl's death, he may try to take his son next. I believe I would feel somewhat responsible for his death, if ever it happened, had I said nothing.

"That being said, I believe I would lose my position if it were discovered that I revealed such information. It could be seen that I am spreading gossip about the Fletchers' close friend, and by association, the Fletchers themselves."

"I understand," Henry said. "We have no intention of bringing this information out into the open for the time being. We will keep your identity a secret. If ever we need you to make a formal statement, would you be willing to do so if it was done with discretion with a bow street runner?" His voice bore a confidence that would have been hard to refuse.

She looked at Henry for a moment, then grinned softly. "If you wish me to, sir. I will do it as long as you are there to ensure that everything is done just so." Her grin turned to a warm smile. I held back the urge to shake my head and roll my eyes. Of course she was taken with Henry in such a short time. She added, "And might I inquire your address to inform you if anything new arises?"

My stomach plunged as I envisioned this maiden visiting Henry in private. The other part of me listened eagerly. His address could give me more information about his identity.

Henry shook his head. "If there is to be any further correspondence, we will use our current method: Inform Mr. Brown, and I can find a time to meet you here again." He nodded. "Miss Black, thank you for your time. The information you have brought us today is valuable. I understand the risk you are taking in divulging this information, and I am grateful for your honesty." His expression was genuine but professional. "I know where to find you should the occasion arise for an official statement."

Mr. Brown spoke next. "Now Molly, let's see about that gift for the duchess." She nodded, offering one last smile in Henry's direction before following Mr. Brown. My gaze followed their retreating steps until they were hidden from my view.

I was suddenly aware of Henry's presence just behind me.

"I didn't think you would really come." Henry's words came out deep and hushed. The sound sent a tingling sensation throughout me. His voice was even richer than I remembered from the moments I had replayed in my mind since our first meeting.

I turned to look at him, doing my best to put on a playful grin. "And what kind of investigator would I be if I didn't show up today?"

He returned my grin. "You'd be a smart one."

"Are you warning me to stay away? If so, you're doing a poor job of convincing me to keep this position," I teased, tapping my finger to my chin in thought.

"Will this help make up your mind?" He held up the ring I had slipped into his hand.

I cocked an eyebrow. "That depends on your intentions. Do you intend to keep it? I believe I'm less likely to work with men who make off with valuables."

His mouth curved up on one side. "It's not stealing if it was given. But I will return it to you if that's what you wish."

I held out my hand to receive my ring.

"I didn't say I would return it immediately." He still held the ring in front of me, taunting me to grab for it. "I do need something to ensure you'll show up the next time I need your expertise." His eyes sparked with challenge.

I half-heartedly grabbed at my ring, knowing he would be quicker than me. As I made the attempt, he flicked my ring in the air. It spun up and over us until he caught it with his other hand. Lifting an eyebrow, he opened his hand. My ring had vanished.

I couldn't help but smile. "Sir, your skills of persuasion are unparalleled."

"Good," he said with a grin. His rugged but clean appearance was enticing, his proximity giving off faint scents of wood and leather. I was disconcerted to find that I loved it . . . and wanted to inch even closer to him to breathe it in.

"Henry." It was time for me to put my thoughts elsewhere. "How are you connected—"

I was cut off by the sudden change in Henry's expression. He raised his eyebrows in surprise and grinned so fully that I couldn't continue speaking. I was captivated by his smile and by the way his eyes ignited. It was a lot harder to concentrate when I didn't have the night's sky to dim his striking features. In that moment, I realized just how difficult it was going to be to continue working with this man without being completely snared.

"What do you find so amusing?" I demanded, though I couldn't help but smile at his expression.

"You just called me Henry."

"I—I believe you are mistaken," I lied.

"Am I really?" he mused.

He had caught me. His "name" had finally slipped from my mouth. "It's really your fault," I protested. "Your disregard for the rules is rubbing off on me."

He held his smile and leaned in, lowering his voice so only I could hear his next comment. "I really can't take all the credit. You did disregard the rules first when you went out in the gardens unaccompanied last night."

I shook my head, trying to ignore the tingles that shot down my neck. "It was your fault for entering my little garden of solitude."

Henry looked at me for a moment with a guarded expression. "Solitude," he muttered so quietly I wasn't entirely sure that I heard him correctly. "You have completely upended mine." A small glimpse of the man I'd first met entered his features. So much mystery surrounded him.

"Henry, who are you, really?" I did my best not to sound like I was pleading.

He searched my eyes as though he was actually considering my question. Eventually he softly shook his head. "You know I can't answer that right now, Lily."

It was too much to hope for. "Then what is your connection to the Elliots?"

He shook his head again. "I can't answer that either." His expression was becoming more shielded. "I suggest we stick with the information Miss Black has given to us for the time being."

I couldn't help the sigh of exasperation that escaped me. "Very well. You admitted to Miss Black that you have a history with Mr. Hughes. It is very obvious that you dislike him. What is your history with Mr. Hughes?" I smirked, folding my arms. "Or is that confidential as well?"

"Are *you* acquainted with Mr. Hughes?" he asked, turning the question back to me.

"I am." I said without emotion, giving away none of my own feelings toward the vulgar man we were discussing. It was clear that Henry despised this man—we both agreed on that matter—but I didn't need to let him know that right away. If he wouldn't let me know certain things about him, I would at least prolong his curiosity for a time.

His eyebrows furrowed. "And what is your opinion of him?"

"I'm sorry, Henry. I can't share that information." I smirked. "It's confidential." He actually looked irritated. How satisfying.

"Point taken," he said flatly before sighing. "I understand your frustration at my secrecy, but it is necessary for me at this time."

"But it is not necessary for you to hide all of your thoughts about every topic we discuss, such as Mr. Hughes in this case. You can share parts of your history without divulging information about your identity. *I* will cooperate when *you* do."

We stared at each other. Henry seemed to be debating whether or not to let me have my way.

"What am I going to do with you, Lily?" Henry said under his breath before he finally spoke. "I have known of Jacob Hughes since before I can remember, though I wasn't well acquainted with him until I was about sixteen. I have never encountered him without feeling that I would prefer he was unconscious. I am not surprised at him being excessively drunken or stating that he would like to finish off all the Elliots, as he tends to be brazen and irascible on even his finest days. I was aware that he is a relative of the Elliot family, though to my recent knowledge, he was not next in line to inherit. That information does leave me suspicious." He folded his arms, a corner of his mouth hitching up. "Does that satisfy you?"

I grinned. "It does." He gave me a look indicating it was my turn now. I couldn't help but pretend I didn't understand. I held my grin. His eyes moved to it, then returned to my eyes.

"It's your turn to share now."

I sighed. "Very well. Mr. Hughes is a disgusting flirt and a rake."

"And?" He gestured with his hand that he wanted me to expound.

"And weaselly."

"And?"

"And sloppy."

"I'm not looking for character traits anymore, Lily. How are you acquainted with him?"

I laughed lightly. "Oh, that. I still had a few more traits on my list. But I will oblige."

He grinned. "That's a relief."

"I am only slightly acquainted with Mr. Hughes." I thought about bringing up Jane's connection with Frederick, but at the moment I didn't want to reveal my sister's hopes to secure him. It felt like a betrayal of trust.

"I am more familiar with his friend, Lord Fletcher." Henry bristled at the mention of Frederick's name.

"How familiar?"

"My aunt, uncle, sister, and I have been invited to most events he has attended since our stay in London. I have danced with him on occasion and we have engaged in some very basic conversations. My sister is even better acquainted with him."

He was silent.

"Henry, I can't help but notice the way you change when these two men are brought up. Despite the fact that I don't really know you, I am on your side in this. I gave you my ring in hopes that you would understand that I'm here in whatever way I can be. I absolutely detest being anywhere near Mr. Hughes and I find Lord Fletcher extremely dull and suffocatingly arrogant. What's more, I take pride in my Wilton origins. If this is a murder case for the late Earl of Wiltshire, I would like to do what I can to help."

"You are from Wilton?" A look passed across Henry's face. At the forefront was understanding and appreciation. When he finally found his voice, it was quiet. "Thank you, Lily." His eyes found mine and all hints of teasing were gone. His sincerity pulled me so thoroughly. "I appreciate that sentiment more than I can explain."

We stood there for a moment longer until the back door to the shop opened and closed, announcing Molly Black's exit. Mr. Brown could still be heard rummaging around, most likely rearranging the display that now featured one less item. Henry reclaimed a hint of his amused look and lowered his voice further. "I applaud you for recognizing Mr. Hughes and Lord Fletcher for the imps they are."

I smiled. "It really is impossible to miss. It makes me wonder how someone like Mr. Hughes could be elusive enough to commit murder."

"He really was never very bright," Henry agreed.

"Yet people can surprise you." I gave him a pointed look. "You are certainly not the man I assumed you to be when we first met."

"I believe that's because I'm Henry to you. To everyone else I am someone very different."

"Do many people know you, then, when you aren't Henry?"

"I believe we are straying from our topic."

"One day I will discover your secrets. Why prolong the inevitable?"

"I hope you *will* discover them some day. But for now, I want to ask if you believe Jacob Hughes could have been the man Mr. Brown heard arguing with Lord Elliot behind this shop those months ago."

I shrugged my shoulders. "It's entirely possible. Especially if the late earl knew something about Mr. Hughes that would discredit his ability to inherit. And knowing the kind of man he is, it wouldn't surprise me if it were true." I tapped a finger to my lip. "And yet I still can't see him being bold enough to stand up to another man in that sort of way. Taking advantage of a lady is one thing, since he would most likely feel that he has the upper hand. But in a man's world, I assume Jacob to be a coward."

"You are entirely right on that score." He inhaled slowly, then blew the air out as he pushed a hand through his hair, deep in thought. He let his hand fall to his side. "Unfortunately I don't think it's enough information to prove anything."

"Though you can't prove anything yet, If Mr. Hughes is truly next in line to inherit, I do believe you have enough evidence to at least start an investigation."

He nodded his head. "That's where I will start, then." He opened a piece of parchment and found a quill on a nearby table. "Find out if he truly is next in line to inherit," he read aloud as his quill etched letters on the parchment.

I stepped up next to him and leaned in toward his ear, lowering my voice barely above a whisper so Mr. Brown wouldn't overhear my next thought. Henry held perfectly still, almost rigid, as I uttered the words, "You may also want to find a way to watch the surroundings of this shop to see if Arthur Brown is being watched or not."

Henry didn't breathe until I stepped away from him. His eyes found mine and he gave me a look that made my stomach flip. There was no humor behind it, but instead a serious expression, as though my unexpected closeness had brought to the surface an intense desire he was trying to bury. I felt the need to swallow at such a look.

He looked back down at his notes, allowing me a moment to breathe. "Agreed." He finally said as he continued to write. "It is also very unlikely that Mr. Hughes would have committed a murder on his own. I will keep my eyes and ears out for anyone who is connected to him inside and outside of his daily interactions."

I waited for Henry to stop writing, then shared one last thought.

"Is there anyone else you know of that has a tainted history with the late earl? Anyone who has ever threatened him or hated him?"

He looked up at me and breathed in slowly. He only nodded and wrote something else down, then fanned his hand back and forth just above the page, ensuring the ink was dry, before folding up his piece of parchment and securing it in his pocket. His gaze returned to mine again.

"Thank you for coming here today, Lily. I know it must have been difficult finding a way here without divulging why." Part of me dreaded this moment. It meant our work was coming to a close. I didn't want to always wonder about this man. What if I never saw him again?

"It wasn't so very difficult," I lied. "When will I get my ring back?" I remembered the one hope I had at meeting him again. I also took courage in the fact that he had attended the duchess's ball, even if it was from the gardens. Perhaps he had been invited to the Morgan's ball. "Have you received an invitation to Lady Morgan's ball?" I tried not to sound as desperate as I felt.

"I have," he said.

"And will you be attending? We could keep our eyes and ears open for anything we hear and keep a careful watch on Mr. Hughes, then collaborate afterward." The idea of seeing Henry at a formal occasion was so entertaining to me. I could be properly introduced to him and we would have to pretend we didn't know each other. It would also be a relief to be allowed to speak in public.

He gave me a sly grin. "It almost sounds like you want me there."

"You will have to find out," I said, returning a grin of my own.

He studied my eyes, then stepped toward me, leaning forward. "Until next time, Lily." He was close enough that I was able to detect his inviting scent again. My breath hitched as I felt him slip something small and metallic into my hand just before he walked past my shoulder in the opposite direction.

I closed my fingers around the familiar form of tuppence resting inside my palm. By the time I turned around to bid him farewell, the back door of the shop was closing and he was gone—with my ring. I exhaled. Henry was so easily drawing me to him, making me want more with each interaction. Perhaps Jane was right; I never should have ventured out into the gardens alone.

9

BLACK BOX

Lawrence

London House
November 2, 1816
Later that day

The smooth wood finish of the black box always brought memories with it. Glancing once more at the bolt on my door, ensuring it was secure, I set the box on my bed and cracked the lid open slowly. The smell of old paper and nostalgia filled my senses almost immediately as I peered inside. I removed the newspaper clipping that rested on top, my eyes finding the name "Etienne Dupont" in the article.

The corners of my mouth turned up as I placed the article aside and viewed the contents within the box. Thankfully I hadn't needed to use it yet, but I carried it with me just in case. It reminded me of younger days, when life held a certain thrill. Gently moving the items around, I found an old letter from inside. The wax seal was broken but remained intact on the top half of the parchment. I lightly traced my finger over the small image pressed into the wax: a goldfinch.

A passing noise outside my door brought me to the present, most likely a member of the staff. I quickly put the letter and newspaper clipping back inside, shut the lid, and locked it. The box was then carefully returned to its current hiding place beneath my bed.

I pulled out my pocket watch, then opened my door and made my way to my usual post. Charles and Henry would be back soon from their excursion to Arthur & Co.

I was butler of Wilton Manor. This meant I would wait calmly for the information. I'd perfected my ability to patiently bide my time and be agreeable. Nothing ever ruffled me—yet here I was, downright irritated at being left in the dark. I justified my behavior by reminding myself that it came as a shock to all of us that James had been murdered; he had been like a brother to me.

Carriage wheels approached. I hurried to the window and shifted the curtains aside, hoping my suspense could finally reach its end. Alas, my hope was in vain. The carriage passed by without even slowing. I grumbled, letting the curtain fall back into place. My patience would have to hold out a while longer. Making my way, once again, to my customary spot to greet the gentlemen, I sat in my chair and waited. I most certainly would not doze off.

I woke with a start, footsteps approaching the front door. I jumped to my feet and tried to appear as I always was: perfectly at attention every moment of the day. Never mind that I felt off-kilter.

Standing with my shoulders straight, I opened the door.

"Welcome home, my lord." I said to Henry. "I hope your outing was agreeable this afternoon." I took his coat and did my best to act as I usually did when addressing "Lord Elliot." I had never addressed Henry as "my lord," but I agreed with Charles's plan to keep the pretense up even to the staff here at the London house.

"Thank you, Lawrence." Henry grinned knowingly. Charles followed close behind Henry and gave me a nod and a smile of his own.

He was playing the part of Henry very well. It warmed me to see him in, what appeared to be, a cheerful mood. He did not carry his usual no-nonsense greeting. I addressed Charles as I typically would have addressed Henry.

"Good afternoon, sir. I hope your afternoon was to your liking." I helped him out of his coat.

"Indeed, it was." He nodded to me, his smile holding.

I wanted to ask if he had received any information about James right then, but I knew better than to ask when prying ears could be lurking in a nearby room.

Charles spoke next to me. "We will need refreshments brought to us in the library. We have much to discuss."

"Very good, sir," I said, pushing down my smile. Henry was supposed to give the orders to keep up appearances, not Charles. Charles was the one so set on keeping to the rules—but it appeared he would be the first to break them. He caught his blunder and turned to Henry.

"Is that agreeable, Charles?"

Henry adopted a serious pretense, mimicking Charles's usual expression. "So long as you don't eat all the cake like you did last time," he said dryly.

I waited for Charles to retort in his cynical, bored way, but he surprised me by smiling and saying, "I'm glad you reminded me. I've gone this long doing just that—I'll not stop now." If I didn't know any better, I would have believed Charles was indeed Henry.

Henry turned to me in a lord-like manner. "Lawrence, if you would please give the word, then meet us in the library, I would be most appreciative. We won't begin without you."

"Yes, my lord," I said, bowing. I hurried to the kitchen as quickly as a proper butler could to alert Mrs. Caldwell of "Lord Elliot's" request.

As I approached the library, I could hear Charles and Henry speaking. The library door was cracked open and they were no longer assuming their pretend roles—already breaking the rules. As I listened, I was gratified to hear that they were having a lively conversation, something I had not witnessed for years. Not wanting to end their sport just yet, I waited quietly just outside the open door.

Henry chuckled. "I'm being completely serious. She intentionally tripped over me so I would catch her after I led her off the dance floor."

"I told you they are all title seekers," Charles said, without his usual bored tone. "I once had a woman pretend to faint while we were nearing the end of a dance so I would have to escort her off the dance floor and attend to her for the next half hour."

"Elizabeth Kensington was not pretending," Henry chuckled. "I remember. She was white as a sheet that night and later came down with a fever."

"She was a title seeker," Charles said. But his tone had humor behind it. Was he jesting? He hadn't jested in . . . well, I couldn't think of the last time.

"Miss Barton and Miss Elwell are title seekers," Henry said, sounding annoyed.

"You haven't fallen for London's 'Miss Ollerton,' then? Bravo." The sound of Charles applauding Henry made me smile. Perhaps the investigation was bringing some life back into him after all these years.

I quietly took a few steps backward so I could create some noise to make my presence known before I reached the doorway. As I did so, their voices quieted, anticipating my arrival. They each sat up a little straighter as I entered.

"Would you like me to close the door, my lord?" I asked, already closing it.

Charles nodded. "Thank you, Lawrence."

They were seated in a corner near a window and fireplace. Flickers of light danced over the logs placed inside. Charles and Henry occupied two of the three cushioned chairs surrounding a small table.

I took my seat. "Mrs. Caldwell said refreshments will be ready in fifteen minutes."

Charles tapped his armrest. "Let's discuss what we can before we are interrupted."

Henry piped up. "I believe you should begin, Charles, since Lawrence and I have both been waiting in suspense to hear what you discovered last night." Henry clapped his palms together then rubbed his hands in anticipation. "Tell us what you found out."

Charles leaned forward. "The short story is that Arthur Brown, owner of Arthur & Co., heard Papa arguing with a man in the dark behind his shop weeks before his death. This unknown man threatened Papa. In addition, a servant girl divulged information about my cousin, Jacob Hughes. Jacob believes he is next in line to inherit after me and was heard stating that he would kill Papa and me to that point."

"What?" Henry asked with disgust. "He isn't even closely related. How could that be possible? Please tell me it isn't true, Lawrence."

They both looked at me next.

I let out a long breath. "It's true. Your father informed me of the details almost nine months ago when he received word of two untimely deaths in the family. James told me he would change his will to make sure Jacob could never inherit. He was in the process of having it altered when he passed."

"I hope this servant girl gave you enough information to convict Jacob," Henry said venomously.

"That's where it gets tricky." Charles exhaled. "It may be enough evidence to start an investigation. But it's not enough to put him away. I don't want him to catch wind of our scent until we have everything we need." He shook his head. "Then there remains the fact that it might not be Jacob alone. He isn't smart enough to murder someone with his own genius. Whoever poisoned my father knew what they were doing."

"Are you sure the cause of death was poison?" I asked.

Charles rubbed his beard. "No. But there were no marks or wounds on my father's body. The only other thing I can think of that would have made him ill is poison."

Henry nodded in agreement, and I had to admit that Charles' reasons were sound.

"Charles." Henry looked over at his brother. "Are you not afraid for your own life at this point?"

I cleared my throat and looked between the two of them. "In this case, it is *your* safety that's on the line, Henry. Everyone believes you to be the Earl of Wiltshire presently."

Charles nodded his head. "Lawrence brings up a good point. We will need to end our charade." He looked mournful but resolved at the statement.

"Absolutely not," Henry said firmly. "I did not shave all my hard work off for nothing. Besides—" He smirked. "I still haven't proven how much better I am at your role than you are." Charles opened his mouth to object—

"Might I make a suggestion?" I asked before they kept arguing. They both looked at me. "We continue as planned for now. We continue gathering evidence. We find a way to merge the two pieces of information we've been given and see if we can prove Jacob's guilt beyond doubt. We take extra care with Henry.

"I will see to it that the three of us only drink from glasses provided by myself when we are here at the London house. When dining with other families, I recommend that you bring a spare flask with your own liquid inside. I think you will be able to find creative ways to drink from it without being noticed. If drinks are being filled from one bottle to all of the company in your presence, then it should be safe to consume; I doubt someone would stoop to poisoning the entire dinner party. Aside from that, we should have Henry guarded at a distance when attending social events."

Henry grinned. "What do you say, Charles? Will you be my bodyguard from afar? You can stalk me at all the balls and soirees from an outside window."

Charles cocked an eyebrow. "Better to view it from a window than have to endure the company inside." He grinned, then lowered the expression, exhaling. "Henry, if you are sincere in wanting to continue as planned, then let's see if we can further uncover the truth. If we come up empty-handed in two weeks, we will give the information we have to the Bow Street Runners." He pulled some parchment from his jacket pocket and unfolded it, reading over some notes. I couldn't help but smile at how much the gesture reminded me of his father: always keeping some sort of list.

"Now." Charles tapped his finger near the top of the page. "I believe Mr. Brown's shop is being watched. He seemed paranoid when he was relaying his information to me last night. And when I left his shop this afternoon, a man was standing outside. It appeared as though he was keeping track of who was coming and going. If Mr. Brown is being watched or threatened, he may be in danger. I want to ensure he has some form of protection.

"Aside from that, I would like to have Jacob followed. I want to be informed of who is coming and who is going from his place. Who is he acquainted with? Is he acting secretive or suspicious? I need it to be done discreetly."

My mind turned to the letter inside my box. "I have a contact here in London who I believe can help. I will make the necessary arrangements."

Henry spoke with a grin. "Or *I* could follow him closely and put him out of his misery."

"After these two weeks are over, I will do it myself," Charles countered.

"Not if I beat you to the punch," Henry mused.

"Speaking of punch," I interrupted. "How was last night's party? Were you able to obtain any useful gossip?"

"Gossip, yes," Henry chuckled. "Useful? Absolutely not. I was introduced to several people though. I have a list of those I hope to become better acquainted with. Hopefully I'll be privy to some sort of information to help our cause."

Charles and I nodded our heads in agreement with Henry's plan before I continued my questions. "Was there anyone at the celebration last night that stood out?"

Henry's eyes turned in my direction while he put his hands behind his head and leaned back in his chair. "I don't believe I can say 'His Lordship, Frederick' was too happy to see me. Nor was Jacob." He smirked. "I will attend the ball Lady Morgan is hosting." Henry looked from Charles to me. "I will watch Jacob closely and dance with as many women as I can to see if I find any helpful information. I have already asked two of London's biggest gossips to save a dance for me. I hope to glean what I can from them and see if it amounts to anything useful."

I nodded my head. "It's a good plan."

Charles repeated my sentiment. "It *is* a good plan." His tone was even agreeable. It was as though an old piece of Charles had somehow dug its way out.

Henry cocked an eyebrow and folded his arms. "Will you come inside the ballroom if my dancing puts you to shame?"

"Only if you're singing while you do it."

A rapping noise suddenly came at the door, and we fell silent as the door opened. Two young servant girls entered. One carried a large tray filled with cured meats, cheeses, apples, and biscuits. The other carried some port and glasses.

They placed their offerings carefully on the table between us.

"Is there anythin' else I can get you, m'lord?" the girl who carried the tray asked.

"No. Thank you," Henry said, nodding toward her, assuming the role of Lord Elliot once again.

They both bobbed a curtsy and exited the room, shutting the door behind them.

Before Charles or Henry had a chance to pour themselves a drink, I took the port in hand, walked over to the window, opened it quietly, then uncorked the bottle and poured its contents outside.

The locked desk was my next destination. My keys clinked as I brought them forward and unlocked the deep drawer. I slowly pulled it open, then looked up at Charles and Henry.

"I did have the forethought to hide a few bottles of port in the library earlier while you were away, as a precaution." The four slender glass bottles I had prepared earlier were still inside, undisturbed.

I pulled one of them out and replaced it with the empty bottle in my hand, then returned to the table and uncorked it, pouring a glass for each of us. "I poured this myself from the large cask in the kitchen while Mrs. Caldwell was out. I highly doubt someone would contaminate the entire barrel with poison. It would be too risky."

We sipped at our drinks and picked at the food. Charles seemed to be preoccupied in thought by something as he kept looking over at Henry.

He finally spoke. "Have you broken any rules yet?"

Henry looked back at Charles and cocked a corner of his mouth. "I wouldn't say I've broken any—" He faltered. "Bent a little, perhaps."

"What do you mean?" Charles asked, impatient. "Please don't tell me that you've waited this long to tell me that you did, in fact, sing."

Henry chuckled. "No." His fingers strummed against his leg. "You may, however, have a harder time coming back into your role as Lord Elliot than you would appreciate. As much as I find it entertaining to act like you for ten minutes at a time, it does get awfully dull while attending social events. Thus far, Charles, the public has seen you smile dashingly in a room full of people, make polite conversation, laugh easily, and . . . "

"What?" Alarm edged Charles's voice.

"Act like a complete fop in Mr. Brown's shop."

Charles glared. "And what exactly did I do to act like a complete fop?"

Henry pulled out a hideous piece of ribbon from one of his jacket pockets. "You, my friend, were seen ribbon shopping today."

My exterior remained calm, though I was biting back a smile at Charles's look of mortification.

"Are you intentionally trying to make me forfeit our plans?" Charles retorted.

Henry's hands raised in defense. "I swear that from now on I will not find myself in a similar position."

"This isn't a joke, Henry," Charles said flatly.

"I am aware." Henry's tone turned serious. "I will be more careful from now on."

Charles grabbed a fistful of his hair. "You have one more chance, Henry. Don't break any more rules. The smiling and socializing I can handle. But no more acting like a fop . . . and I don't ever want to see you pull a ribbon out of your pocket again."

"Agreed," Henry said with a grin, an awkward silence following. "And what about you, Charles? Have you broken any rules?"

Charles averted his eyes to his glass. "I assure you, Henry, that becoming you is not as difficult as becoming Lord Elliot. Thus far I have stuck to dark corners and talked only with people who are helping with the case—and I have certainly purchased no ribbon."

Henry seemed to take that answer as a no. But Charles usually answered a question outright. My brows knit as I watched him. Had he just side-stepped the question? After his response, he looked down into his drink and followed it with a hard swallow of the remaining liquid. Though I found his behavior strange indeed, I would have to simply wait and watch.

The conversation shifted to altogether more agreeable topics and the food began to disappear at a quicker rate as Charles and Henry continued their friendly banter. An overwhelming sense of contentment washed over me at seeing Charles behave in a way I hadn't witnessed in years.

Henry brightened more and more at his brother's long-awaited return. If only James and Elizabeth could have witnessed it. We talked and reminisced about old times until it grew dark. I felt younger and lighter.

Henry eventually stood, and I mirrored his gesture before he spoke. "It's been a long two days. I'll bid you both goodnight." As he walked past me toward the door, he gave me his usual light slap on the back. "Thank you, Lawrence."

"You're welcome, sir. Goodnight." He slowly walked out of the room, closing the door behind him.

Charles yawned, then stood, taking a step in my direction. "Best I get some sleep as well." He put a hand on my shoulder and gripped it lightly. "Thank you for your help with everything the last two days, Lawrence."

I nodded. "Certainly, my lord."

Charles then left the library, leaving the door open just a crack. I returned to my seat for a moment longer, basking in the warmth of the moments that had just passed. The fire danced around the logs until eventually the flicker of light died down, leaving black coals that shifted with red and orange embers. Deeply satisfied, I stood and exhaled.

I placed my hand inside my right jacket pocket to get my keys, but they were not there. I was used to this charade when James was alive. He always switched my keys to my other pocket and replaced them with tuppence. This time they were replaced with two coins. Charles and Henry must have worked their magic just now when they'd bid me goodnight.

I smiled to myself and quickly brushed a tear away that somehow found its way onto my cheek. James and Elizabeth were still here after all. I checked my left pocket and found my keys inside.

Making my rounds, I made sure the appropriate cupboards and doors were locked. As I entered the parlor, I almost jumped in surprise. Henry was staring out the window, deep in thought.

"My lord?" I asked, keeping up the pretense. "Aren't you rather tired?"

Henry turned. "I am." He said it as if he was tired for more than sleep. I nodded my head and took a step forward so I was standing directly next to him.

"Is there anything I can get you to make your sleep more comfortable?"

He stared out the window solemnly before he looked at me. "I need more than one comfortable night of sleep." He folded his arms and returned his view to the window before he spoke again. "The Elliots have been my family in every way but blood. And now only Charles is left. Up until today I felt as though he'd mostly died with them. Tonight I watched him return to life more than I have seen in years. You know better than anyone how much I owe the Elliots. And now I can't ignore a feeling that I have been pushing away for some time: The older I get, the more indebted I feel to them. I can offer no monetary means. I help Charles where I can, but everything is ultimately his responsibility.

"The only thing I have to offer Charles is my friendship. But if he no longer needs someone to try and pull him out of his moods, what good am I to anyone? I don't know that I could bear feeling useless. Now that Papa is gone, Charles pays for everything. He pays for my food, my clothes—everything."

My next words came out quiet in case anyone was listening. "Do you truly believe that if Charles has finally returned to his old self he will have no use for you anymore? For a man he considers his brother?"

Henry shook his head. "It isn't as simple as you make it sound, Lawrence. I am my own man, and I can't live off Charles forever. I have no legacy to claim unless I face my father. Even then, I have no idea if there would *be* anything to claim. I own no property, no home to raise a family in. I am an Elliot in every way at heart. But in the end, I'm still Henry Thomas."

I looked at Henry, considering his plight. "What do you intend to do?" I asked.

"For now I intend to wait and watch. I would like to feed this transformation within Charles. If we can find the cause, we can try to make sure it continues. Once I feel he's here to stay, I will take my first steps to becoming independent. I will confront my father."

Our eyes looked out to the street below as we stood in silence for a time.

"I will support you in whatever way I can. I know James and Elizabeth would have wanted to do the same. I do believe Charles will take some convincing, though. He may be offended that you feel the need to make your own way, since he sees you as a brother."

Henry grinned mischievously and turned toward me. "Do you think he might change his mind if I told him I broke rule number two?"

I furrowed my brow. "You've already formed an attachment with a young lady?"

His grin stayed in place, but it was forced. "An attachment generally refers to both people regarding one another. I assure you, if there was an attachment, this one would be very one-sided."

He looked back out toward the street. "But let's pretend for a moment that I had formed an attachment." He inhaled slowly. "She would be under the impression that I am Lord Elliot, Earl of Wiltshire. And if I *did* somehow miraculously win her over, she would fall for a man that she believes would give her a title and great wealth, only to discover that I am actually a man with absolutely nothing to my name. I would be a fraud of the worst sort."

I narrowed my eyes with concern. "You can't woo a lady under false pretenses. Tread carefully, Henry. It's a tricky business you're in even without adding your heart in the mix."

Henry nodded and looked at me, trying his best to put a grin on his face. "As much as I agree with the sentiment, Lawrence, what if I miss my chance with her?" He said it quietly.

"There will be other young ladies."

I expected Henry to agree with me. Instead, he returned his stare to the street below, his mouth slanting downward, until eventually, he turned away. "Good night, Lawrence."

He exited the room.

I decided to check the library once more to verify that I'd locked the desk containing the bottles of port. Upon entering, I saw Charles seated at his writing desk, quill etching quickly and quietly.

"Sir?" I asked, confused at his behavior. He jumped ever so slightly in his chair.

"Are you always so quiet, Lawrence?" he asked flatly, condescension lining his words. Apparently Charles's usual coldness had returned. How would Henry feel about it?

He looked up at me, relaxing his tense expression. "I didn't mean to speak so forcefully. I was startled."

I nodded my head. "I apologize, my lord. I did not expect you to return to the library."

He lowered his voice. "That may be because I didn't want my presence known." The quill returned to its position, Charles scratching a few more words into the page before signing it in elegant, swooping motions.

I was unsure of how to respond.

He looked up at me again, then exhaled. "Lawrence, I feel it necessary to inquire about John Thomas's whereabouts at the time of my father's death. It is my hope that Henry will remain unaware of this inquiry."

"I see." I thought about the conversation I'd just had with Henry. If he found out his father was a suspect for the murder of James, he might feel even more conflicted about being a burden. It would destroy him.

"Do you have reason to suspect John Thomas?" I asked.

He looked up at me. "You know that I do."

I nodded my head, hating to admit that he was right. "Henry will take it very hard if his father is, in fact, guilty."

"Indeed. Can I solicit your discretion with these inquiries for now?"

"Of course, my lord." I let out a hesitant breath. "Let's pray, for Henry's sake, that John Thomas has an alibi."

Charles nodded solemnly.

It was time to excuse myself, but I didn't know if I'd find Charles in such a mood again. Before I could think too much about it, I spoke.

"My lord, you seem different tonight." I placed my hands in my pockets, a gesture I often did when I felt I was treading unknown waters. "Might I ask what has brought on such a change?"

Charles looked up at me and rubbed his finger across his beard, considering my question. "Do you have any idea what it is like to be introduced as Lord Elliot, Earl of Wiltshire, wherever you go?"

I chuckled. "Certainly not, my lord."

"Do you know what it's like to wonder whether the women who smile your way, or the friends you make, and the businessmen that surround you, do so simply because of your wealth, title, and social standing?"

"I can't say that I do." It was the first time I had ever had a glimpse inside Charles's mind. Suddenly I found it easier to understand him.

"As Henry Thomas, when someone treats me with respect, I know it's sincere. If someone slanders me, I can fight back knowing the odds are fair. If I won a lady's heart . . . " He looked down at his hands. "I would know it was something real."

"And what happens when you are no longer Henry?"

Charles gave a mirthless smirk. "Eat, drink, and be merry, for tomorrow we die."

"Forgive me for being so bold, but are you suggesting that you plan to live without a care as Henry this next fortnight but then intend to go back to living your life as before? With another piece of you left behind with him?"

Charles exhaled, replacing his cynical look for something serious. "I don't know, Lawrence. Being back feels like such a relief. I don't believe I've been living as much as just existing for years. And yet I don't know how to be Lord Elliot, Earl of Wiltshire any other way."

My eyebrows pinched together, looking down at the man who had been a boy not so long ago. "And there is truly no way that you can be both?"

Charles didn't answer for a time until his mouth turned up on one side. "Perhaps there is one way."

"And what way is that?"

Charles gave me an amused grin. "I will keep that to myself for the time being."

I notched an eyebrow. "Just don't be too reckless, my lord. Henry will have to eventually resume his role again."

"When have I ever been reckless?" he asked flatly.

I smirked. "Remember, Charles, I have known you your whole life. Perhaps you don't remember the mischief you got yourself into as a boy, but I certainly do." I feigned a stern look, then gave him a nod and a wink. "Goodnight, my lord."

"Goodnight, Lawrence."

10

SPIDER

Jane

London
November 4, 1816
Two days later
11 days of disguise remaining

I looked at my reflection as Alice finished pinning up my last curl. Frederick would be picking me up soon for a ride through Hyde Park.

"There, miss. You look lovely, as always." She smiled at me through the mirror. "Which dress would you like to wear?" Alice walked toward my wardrobe.

"I'll wear my yellow muslin this morning," I said as I continued to study my face. The reflection that peered back looked exactly as I expected: perfectly arranged, poised. Affected by no one and no thing. But underneath, I was beginning to feel more and more like an imposter.

If I thought on it long enough, I was sure I would discover why, though I didn't want to find the reason just now.

I looked to the window, forcing my mind somewhere new. Sunlight danced on the changing leaves, filling my heart with warmth.

Alice brought my dress over. "How was Duchess Fletcher's ball?" she asked.

"It was lovely—elaborately done." I couldn't help but smile. "They used more candles than I believed possible."

Alice's eyes twinkled at my response as I stepped into my dress. "And how was the company, miss? Did Lord Fletcher dance with you?"

"He did. Twice." A corner of my mouth pulled up in a grin.

Alice's face lit up. "That's a good sign! And now he's taking you for a ride today."

"It is definitely encouraging."

"I heard that Lord Elliot made an appearance at the ball," Alice exclaimed with enthusiasm. "It was a delight seeing him in the shop the other day. It appeared as though the two of you were already acquainted. Did you meet him at the ball?"

"I did." I wouldn't include the fact that he also asked me to dance.

I tried to look as natural as possible about the gentleman we were discussing—and the name I'd been trying to forget.

"And what is your opinion of him? He *is* very handsome, of course."

"He is handsome," I agreed mechanically, evaluating the tone of each syllable I uttered to ensure it sounded as though I was discussing the weather.

To state that Lord Elliot was simply handsome was a gross understatement. The women in attendance at the ball couldn't keep their eyes off of him, for good reason. At first glance, his tall, broad frame made him an easy target for any woman's wandering eye.

Unfortunately, his appearance grew in magnetism with each interaction. To my dismay, I had spent more time the last few days trying *not* to think about his charming and inviting smile. Or his dark, wavy hair framing his deep-brown eyes. Eyes that held mystery, and depth, and laughter, and affection. No man had a right to be so alluring. I shook my thoughts from their drift.

"What is he like?" Alice asked. I didn't know how to respond.

Admitting he was handsome was one thing, but to put Lord Elliot into words was another entirely. He could be flirtatious one moment, then serious the next. He was charming and then suddenly interrogative. I thought of the way he boldly questioned my trust in Frederick. He could play the fop, yet be absolutely masculine and powerful. I replayed the two opposing scenes in my mind of Lord Elliot in the shop with the ribbon, compared to his fury at Mr. Hughes's unwanted attention toward me. He was an absolute puzzle.

"He's frustrating," I said under my breath before I could stop myself. I almost clapped my hand over my mouth the way I had seen Lily do on occasion. I hadn't intended to say it aloud.

Alice tried to appear casual by my statement but I saw a smile bubbling beneath the surface. She quickly buried it down.

"And why would you describe him that way, miss?" My door flew open and Lily appeared.

"Alice, have you seen my shawl? I was wearing it the day before yesterday, when we were out and about the shops. I can't seem to find it." I inwardly sighed in relief for the interruption.

Lily's eyes took in my hair and outdoor morning dress. "And where are you going, Jane?"

I realized I hadn't informed Lily of my outing with Frederick. It was odd that we hadn't really talked in depth about anything since before the ball. "Lord Fletcher is taking me for a ride this afternoon," I said, placing a smile on my face.

"I see." Lily leaned against my bed post. "And are you excited?"

"Of course I am."

Lily smirked and raised an eyebrow. She clearly wasn't convinced.

Alice broke the silence. "Miss Lily, I was just asking Miss Jane what she thinks of Lord Elliot. What are your thoughts about him? Did you find him to be very handsome as well?"

"Yes." She smiled. "I would say he is very handsome."

"And do you find him as frustrating as Miss Jane finds him?" Alice added.

My heart began to hammer as Lily raised her eyebrows at Alice then gave me a surprised look. "I can't say that I do," she mused. "But I suppose

I didn't meet him at the ball or have a . . . " She paused to find the right words. "Tête-à-tête with him in the shop."

Heat rose up the back of my neck. "It was nothing like that. Lord Elliot and I don't seem to agree on most things."

Lily grinned. "I'm beginning to like the earl more and more."

Alice chuckled but turned to me. "Miss Jane, Lord Fletcher will be here soon. Best we get ourselves to the parlor."

I nodded, then turned to Lily, remembering that I'd wanted to discover how her evening fared at Duchess Hastingwood's ball. "I was hoping you and I might have some time to talk about how the ball went for you the other night. It feels odd that we've not had any time for conversation. I know you weren't keen on going—I hope you had a pleasant time regardless."

I thought back to all that had happened since then, wondering if anything eventful had happened to her as well. "I'd love to hear more about Marianne Morgan. Perhaps we could call on her soon after their ball this Friday. It would be such a comfort for us both to have a friend."

Lily nodded, a warm smile in tow. "I would like that very much."

I turned to leave—

"And Jane." Lily called me back. "I do hope you have a pleasant outing with Lord Fletcher. Though he isn't a gentleman I would personally wish to court, it doesn't mean he isn't who someone else would choose. If you are truly happy with him, then I will do my best to respect it."

"Thank you, Lily." Relief filled my heart. Though I would never state it aloud, I cared more about my sister's opinion than arguably any other living soul. "We can talk more when I return."

"Very well. Go have your jaunt around Hyde Park. Don't worry about me. I will just sit here and be bored . . . all afternoon." She fell back onto my bed dramatically. I knew she was teasing, but I still felt a twinge of guilt for leaving her here to do who-knows-what with no company other than my aunt and uncle.

At that moment, she reminded me of the little sister I played with years ago. Smiling, I committed the image to memory, then left my room.

The crisp smell of autumn brought a small smile to my lips as Frederick escorted me toward his carriage. The cool air excited my heart and smelled like fond memories of the past. Autumn had always been my favorite, ever since I was a little girl.

Frederick took my hand to help me into his landau. Up to this point, I had danced many times with him, and had even taken his arm. But this was the first time I felt his hand support mine in this way.

I glanced at our fingers for a moment as I stepped up into the carriage. It felt no different than when Uncle Francis or a coachman assisted me. Though I knew it to be a girlish fancy, I was hoping I would feel at least *something*. Banishing the silly thought from my mind, I situated myself on the smooth leather upholstery, nearest the side of the open carriage. Alice sat next to me but moved to the opposite end of the seat.

Frederick stepped up and sat across from me. Soon enough, the conveyance was rolling along the cobblestones. It was a perfect day for a ride through Hyde Park. The colorful leaves were at their peak and the sun kept its appearance. It was an enchanting sight that brought to mind thoughts of change. Perhaps today there would be a change to Frederick's and my relationship.

Alice sat as close to the other side of the carriage as possible and looked out the side, allowing Frederick and me space to talk.

Though I was grateful for her aloofness for the first minute or so, after a time, I wished she would make her presence more engaging. Perhaps it was due to Frederick's interest in the grass of Hyde Park over making conversation with me. Albeit, he *did* ask how I slept the night before and if I enjoyed the ball the other evening. We commented briefly on the weather . . . but then we had nothing else to talk about. The silence wore on. I searched for something engaging to say.

"How is Lady Eve?" I asked.

"My sister is well." His bored expression stated that he was done with the current topic. Lady Eve had not yet entered society. But she was kind and elegant and absolutely stunning. I'd had the pleasure of crossing paths with her on multiple occasions while shopping in London. A rare sort of fate indeed. During our few encounters, we'd gotten on swimmingly. I imagined we would get along very well if ever we became sisters-in-law.

"Will you be attending Lady Morgan's ball this weekend?" I asked, trying for a new topic.

"I hadn't made up my mind. But if you're going I'll consider it," he said flatly.

I should have been flattered, but his comment felt so bland. There was no flutter in my stomach or race of my pulse. I reminded myself that I wasn't disappointed—I was comfortable and satisfied. I opened my mouth to inform him of my plans to attend the ball, but it was unnecessary: His attention was once more diverted to the ground.

I decided to follow suit, and we passed a considerable amount of our ride in silence. In the beginning I found the silence awkward. But after a time, I found it ideal. I could look at the beauty around me without interruption and be content.

That is, until my mind drifted to deep eyes.

I was not usually one to daydream. Indulging in such distractions was silly and did no good. So why did I find that I couldn't pull myself from this one? Lord Elliot's eyes kept flashing through my mind. My pulse quickened as I remembered him stepping toward me in the shop.

"Miss Mason." I blinked and shook my head. Frederick was looking at me expectantly.

"Yes?" I asked, trying to appear as though I hadn't been caught off guard.

"Well, what are your thoughts?" His tone was still bland, but I felt frantic regardless. Had he really just asked me a question and I hadn't heard a word of it due to my daydreaming?

"I'm sorry, I believe my mind was with the trees and the sound of the carriage. Could you please repeat the question?" I hoped he wouldn't be annoyed at my distraction.

He stared at me, a blank slate, impossible to read. "What is your opinion of Charles Elliot?" I knew he wouldn't be satisfied with every thought I had regarding Lord Elliot. In truth, I still didn't know exactly how I felt about him. I had no opinion I could yet voice. In that thought, I found my safe answer.

"I haven't an opinion of him." I said it as evenly as I could manage. It appeared to be the right response.

"That's because there is no opinion to be had." He grinned ever so slightly. "He was the talk of the evening at the ball because he is new. In no time he will be old news and of very little consequence to anyone. I relish what that will do for his ego."

I knew Lord Elliot would always be a man of great consequence, but I didn't say as much.

"You mentioned that you went to school with him." I tried to keep my voice as bored as Frederick's always was.

"Unfortunately it's true. He never did understand the meaning of respect. Neither he nor his pathetic little shadow. They were constantly plotting to antagonize me. They would hide my inkwell and quill and trade mine and Mr. Hughes's assignments. I'm still irritated that they weren't expelled from Cambridge that first year."

It was the most Frederick had said since the carriage ride began. I tried imagining Lord Elliot in such a way. It was difficult and easy to picture all at the same time. I managed to keep my expression exactly as it had been: calm and serene. I tried to think of something to say in response.

"I hope his presence doesn't truly grieve you."

He gave a disgusted look toward the open park and curled his lip. "It does grieve me," he said, clearly annoyed. "The devil himself rides this way even now."

I shifted my gaze toward the open field and was transfixed at the sight before me. Lord Elliot sat atop a large, black stallion, riding toward us. His tall, powerful frame astride his muscular horse could only be described as formidable.

He hadn't yet noticed our gradual approach. He appeared to be deep in thought, eyes averted to the ground. His usual grin was replaced with a firm expression.

I remembered my company and looked at Frederick. He continued to glare out at the field.

I didn't know if I dared another look at Lord Elliot. I didn't want to give the wrong idea to the man I was trying to secure, but Frederick didn't appear to notice what I was doing at the moment, as he only seemed keen on staring daggers at the approaching man.

I decided to brave one more glance in Lord Elliot's direction. His gaze was still averted while he rode, leaving me to feel like an intruder, scrutinizing him in a moment when he was vulnerable and unaware of my presence. His entire being, from his slumped shoulders to his forlorn eyes, displayed a hopeless sense of melancholy. How was it that this small glimpse of a man I hardly knew weighed so heavily on every conscious part of my mind? I should have looked away—I wouldn't have wanted to be caught in such a moment. And yet I couldn't pry my eyes from him. What was it that weighed him down so fully? It gave me a glimpse inside of the man that always wore a smile.

I still didn't entirely trust Lord Elliot, but he was slowly proving that perhaps he wasn't who I assumed he was at our first meeting. I was still dissecting our most recent encounter in the shop. He had walked away from me so abruptly when he assumed I wanted to be left alone. Adding to that was the fact that he stepped in with Mr. Hughes at the ball, and with Amelia and Edith, when I needed help.

His very presence seemed to disrupt everything inside of me. I didn't like the way he wreaked havoc on my usual perfect stronghold. Unlike Frederick, he pulled my feelings every which way.

He continued to look down as we drew closer. Despite our complicated acquaintance, I wanted nothing more than to see his smile reignite. As if in answer to my silent wish, his eyes suddenly drifted up, finding mine. My breath caught as he studied me before offering a small smile and nod in my direction, though it didn't fully mask his despondency. His eyes found Frederick next.

A firm expression replaced Lord Elliot's smile as he took in my company. He looked back at me for another brief moment before he passed out of my view. It took some control to stay put and not crane my head to watch him retreat.

Frederick finally spoke. "I'm glad you aren't taken with him, Miss

Mason. The way the other ladies were behaving toward him the other night made me want to set fire to the entire place. I overheard a circle of women claiming to have fallen in love with him after just one dance." He rolled his eyes.

I wasn't surprised at his comment. It was fated that women would easily fall for such a gentleman. My eyes turned up at Frederick and his bland expression.

"Have you ever fallen in love?" I surprised myself by asking such a forward question. His face maintained its bored exterior, with no shift whatsoever.

"No," came his even response. "Only idiots fall in love. They make irrational decisions and often throw away their future. Such feelings are for impulsive people who have no self-control. I'm glad I can claim to have a regular head on my shoulders."

"I agree," I said mechanically. I did agree with Frederick. At least I had a few days ago. I found, however, that his words held a sting. Had I hoped for a declaration of love? What would I have thought if he had made such a statement? I didn't love *him*. The remainder of the carriage ride was spent in silence.

Lily

I was still laying on Jane's bed, not even a half hour since her departure, certain I would die of boredom.

"There is a letter here for you, Lily!" Aunt Mary exclaimed as she entered Jane's room. Excitement buzzed through me, making my stomach lurch at her announcement. I sat up quickly and eagerly grabbed the folded parchment from her hand. She sat on the edge of the bed and watched me expectantly as I turned it over. There was no name on the front. Holding my breath, I opened it, hoping it would be from Henry.

Miss Mason,
I think of you as often as the birds sing in the trees and fly overhead. I do not make my identity known yet, but I intend to soon.
Your secret love

"Is it from Mr. Johnson again?" Aunt Mary asked, wincing. It was indeed. Not only did I recognize his handwriting, but he referenced his favorite winged creature . . . again.

I held the letter toward her. She hesitantly took it from my grasp and read its contents, then looked up at me, eyes portraying sympathy.

"His words are more bold this time," she muttered. "What do you intend to do?"

"What am I to do? He hasn't made his intentions known in a way that allows me to dissuade him vocally. He only writes these covert letters," I pointed at the paper my aunt was now holding, "making it impossible for me to call him out. He could just as easily deny that he is the sender. He has never brought me flowers or asked to take me for a ride through Hyde Park. He has danced with me twice at one ball, but that is the most I can claim. It isn't as if he is courting me. So how am I to dissuade him?"

She nodded. "I assume he will try his hand at courtship very soon. I am surprised he is sending these letters before he has even sent flowers. Perhaps he knows you will turn him down once he tries, and assumes this will give him the upper hand."

I fell back on the bed again and looked up at the ceiling. "Perhaps I can just challenge him to a duel with pistols and have it over with."

Aunt Mary chuckled. "You always have such wild ideas." She stood with my letter in hand and walked out the door.

I sighed, disappointed that the letter wasn't from Henry.

The wooden boards that made up Jane's ceiling only held my interest for so long. After finding the fifth oddly shaped knot in the wood's pattern, I was done.

Slowly sitting up, I lazily found my way out of Jane's room, down the stairs, and into the library. My eyes drifted to the clock above the fireplace, cueing a dramatic exhale of irritation—the half-hour mark had barely passed since Jane had left with Frederick. I eyed the book-shelves, contemplating if I should try to pass the time curled up on a chair with a book in hand. Grabbing a book at random, I sat in a big chair next to the window and turned the book over. It was a book of poetry by William Wordsworth. I flipped to a page and started reading.

> *I wandered lonely as a cloud*
> *That floats on high o'er vales and hills,*

I snapped the book shut. Certainly not. I breathed out restlessly and leaned my head against the wing of the chair. It was then that I noticed a slight breeze. Looking over at the window next to my chair, I realized it was cracked open, as if someone had intended to shut it earlier but hadn't finished the task.

Odd.

As I stood to close the window, I spotted it. My lost shawl was on the floor between the writing desk and the wall. It must have fallen off the wooden tabletop. As I picked it up, a coin and a small piece of parchment fell to the floor. I quickly picked them up, my heart picking up speed. I recognized that handwriting.

> *You will recognize your moment when it*
> *presents itself. Be ready.*

My excitement was quickly doused as I realized it was only the note Henry gave me in the shop the other day. I let out another exasperated breath.

Curse it all, I'd never sighed so much in my entire life.

"No better time to start than today," I muttered, annoyed.

If memory served me right, however, I hadn't placed my shawl here. I was also surprised I'd been so careless to leave the note and tuppence inside.

Then again, my brain had been fully occupied the last couple days. Since we had returned home from Arthur & Co the day before last, I remembered very few details about my days other than moping about the place. I looked at the paper again and put the handwriting to memory, revisiting the images of Henry in my mind for probably the hundredth time.

My eyes scaled the books on the shelf once more, wondering if there was anything that could truly distract me from my current state of agitation. Convinced nothing would, I bundled up my shawl and made my way toward the door, already planning where to hide my little note.

As I exited the library, I flipped the small piece of parchment over, then halted, my breath catching. There was writing on the other side. I examined it more closely. Only three words appeared in Henry's elegant writing.

You left this.

My mind reeled with excitement, wondering how he had gotten it into the library. He clearly didn't deliver it at the front door, or it would have been brought to me.

The open window came to mind. I threw my shawl around my shoulders as I raced back into the library. My fingers pried the window back up as quietly as they could muster.

How disappointing that I didn't catch him in the act. I smiled, picturing multiple different scenes in my mind. I imagined Henry climbing through the window and getting stuck. I pictured him then trying to throw my shawl onto the desk, since he couldn't get through, and I imagined the annoyed look on his face as it fell off the side of the desk and landed on the floor. I chuckled at the thought.

More scenarios ran through my head, each a little more far-fetched than the previous one. Once I had the window open fully, I poked my head out and looked toward the small back garden. Henry was nowhere to be seen, but I still wasn't satisfied. Not wanting to lose a single second, I left the library window wide open and sped out to the back garden.

It was small but provided a few places to hide. Vines grew on lat-
ticed archways near the back wall, hiding the view of a bench beneath
its foliage from where I stood. Tall shrubs grew in hedges that lined the
stone walls on both sides—another potential hiding place.

I walked to the back of the garden, hoping he would be on the
bench. But as the bench came into view, it held nothing but empty
disappointment.

Looking at the left side of the garden, I calculated that there was
more likely a space between the foliage and the stone wall compared to
the right side. I peeked behind the thicket, my hopes shrinking. It was a
tight fit, even for me. Henry would have to be determined, indeed, to fit
in such a space with his broad shoulders and height.

Regardless, I slowly pressed forward. "Henry?" I whispered,
branches scratching against my arm.

I was crestfallen once more as I searched behind the first tall bush.
Nothing. Though the shrubs appeared to be one long hedgerow connected from the front, in the back they widened and narrowed individ-
ually with winding curves. I couldn't see in between each one until it
was right in front of me.

"Henry?" I whispered again as I made my way past another shrub.
I passed a third bush and started for the fourth when I felt my dress
pull me back.

My heart raced. I looked behind me, expecting to see Henry—
but found instead that I was hooked by a branch. I let out an irritated
breath, then tried reaching from behind to unhook myself. It was no
use. I couldn't reach far enough to undo the snare. I tried turning to the
side but found that the attempt only hooked another branch to another
part of my dress.

Great. Now I'm stuck in two places. If I continued to pull or turn my
body in any way, I would ruin my dress. I let out an exasperated sigh.

I didn't know what was more frustrating: the fact that Henry wasn't
out here, or the fact that I had no way of getting back inside without
ruining my dress. I had no idea how I would explain it to my aunt. Now
facing the way I came in, I could see a long stick almost in reach. If I
could just grab it, perhaps I could use it to unhook the branch behind

me. I carefully leaned toward the stick. I was so close.

A tickling sensation traveled up my wrist just as I was about to wrap my fingers around the long piece of wood. A very unladylike, garbled yell escaped from my mouth. It was a spider! I flung my hand back and slapped it off.

A low chuckle sounded behind me.

II

SHRIKE

Lily

Igasped and jerked my head toward the sound. Unfortunately, the quick movement hooked another branch into my hair, which Alice had so nicely arranged, and I was now stuck in three places. I quickly reached up and unhooked my hair. It pulled parts of my curls from their pins and snagged other pieces with it. I cringed inwardly at the thought of how I must look just now. I decided I had better pull the rest of the pins out. My fingers extracted each one as fast as they could, letting my loose curls fall where they pleased. I was thankful Henry was still nowhere to be seen.

"Lily, would you like some help?" His amused voice came from behind one of the shrubs just ahead.

I froze with embarrassment. "At what point were you planning on making your presence known?" I chided.

"I didn't think it was necessary, since you clearly have everything under control." I could hear the smile in his voice. He emerged from behind a bush a few paces off, but kept his distance. I swallowed down my mortification at being caught in such a moment.

"Tell me, Henry, do you often find yourself hidden in the foliage of people's private gardens?"

He eased toward me, sideways, his back against the stone wall so his suit wouldn't be snagged like my dress. "I might start making it a habit if it's always this . . . " He paused, glancing at the vice I was in, then finished with, "amusing." One side of his mouth turned up. It was hard to pretend I was angry with him. I was so happy to see him that I almost didn't care that I was stuck. Almost.

"Lily, what are you doing out here?" He had the audacity to chuckle.

"I could ask you the same question." I folded my arms. It was difficult while I was stuck, but I managed.

"I thought that was fairly obvious, since you clearly found your shawl." He gestured at the ground. My shawl must have fallen when I slapped the spider off. Heat rose to my cheeks at the memory.

His eyes found mine again. "Your turn to answer now." He probably wanted me to state that I was looking for him so he could tease me about it. I would see how he liked his own words.

"I thought that was fairly obvious." I smirked back.

He grinned. "Which part? Is it that you enjoy being tangled up in the hedges? Or do you enjoy things that crawl?" He looked near my skirt. "You have another friend."

My smirk faded.

"Get it off! Right now!" I said frantically.

He chuckled and bent down, grabbing something near the hem of my skirt. He held it up to show me.

A caterpillar.

I narrowed my eyes at him. "Henry, do you think that at any point you might actually help me out of this?"

"I might."

I opened my mouth in exasperation.

"I might, if you tell me why you are out here." He folded his arms.

"Henry, you know why I'm out here. Must I spell it out?"

He smiled smugly. "That would definitely help your odds."

I rolled my eyes. "Are you always this difficult?"

"Are you?" Henry raised an eyebrow, then looked past my ear. "There is another spider on a nearby branch. I suggest you talk." He was most likely bluffing, but I wasn't willing to find out.

"I was looking for you," I finally blurted out.

"Was that so hard to say?" Henry mused. "And why were you looking for me?" His amused expression fell away slowly. "Do you have more information for me?" His features became more serious.

"No, I—" Embarrassment ran through me until it burned in my cheeks. I had no reason to try and find him other than to see him. I decided to change the subject.

"Henry, could you please help me out of this? I don't plan on reaching for that stick again." I shuddered as I remembered the spider. "And I really don't want to ruin my dress."

Aside from that, I was feeling vulnerable facing his question without the ability to flee.

Henry looked behind me at the sticks holding me hostage and resumed his amused smile. But as he stepped closer to me, his amusement fell away. His eyes took in my hair cascading over my shoulders in loose curls. My heart tripped at his expression.

"First," he said, "I believe this is yours." He stooped down, careful not to become prey to the many vices surrounding us, and picked up my shawl, draping it over his arm. "And so is this." My ring suddenly appeared between his thumb and finger. He carefully took my left hand and loosely placed the ring on my index finger before letting go.

"Now." He tried skirting to the side to get around me, but there was no room between me and the wall. He gave me an apologetic look. "I'm going to have to unhook you from here," he said, facing me.

He watched me as he slowly moved his hand behind my back and found the culprit. He wasn't able to release me from my snare with only one hand at work. He stepped closer and carefully wrapped his other arm around my back until it joined his other fingers behind me.

My arms rested on his while my heart pounded with force. I was certain he could hear it. He watched me with no hint of levity as his fingers moved slowly and gently. One by one, the snags were undone from my dress until I was free. We stood in silence but he didn't release me. His eyes studied mine. I reminded myself he wasn't really Henry. I found that at the moment, I didn't care. Not right now, when all I wanted was to be exactly where I was. His arms slowly tightened around me, making my stomach leap.

"Lily." His deep voice came out so soft it was almost a whisper. It sent a tremor throughout my entire being.

"Lily!" Aunt Mary's voice called from inside the house, somewhere near the open window. My breath hitched and I suddenly had more clarity.

Henry breathed in slowly, deeply. As he exhaled, he hesitantly released me until my arms fell away from his. Disappointment seeped in next from his new distance.

"You weren't supposed to find me," he said with resignation. I had no words. The entirety of the moment hit me like a tidal wave.

He continued to speak quietly. "I only wanted to return your shawl but couldn't bring it to the front door, as it would have raised suspicion."

I felt humiliated for getting carried away so easily and for searching for him in the first place. What if he hadn't intended to see me again, and now I was putting him in a precarious position?

"I understand," I said, guarding my tone. "I'm sorry to have put you through so much trouble." I hoped he didn't hear the hurt in my voice as I turned to leave.

Henry caught my arm before I could walk away, then let go, pulling his hand back. "I believe it is the other way around. I have already put you in one convoluted scheme. I'm trying to keep you out of it. And I don't want you looking for trouble."

"And are you trouble, Henry?" I asked before I could stop myself.

"Lily!" my aunt called again.

"You need to go." Henry's voice became even quieter.

I was anxious about getting caught, but my apprehension was outweighed by the letdown of not knowing when, or if, I would see him again. I wouldn't stoop so low as to ask, though I wanted to. There was nothing left for me to say. I turned to leave once more without a word.

"Wait," he whispered, carefully pulling me back by my hand again. If he was intentionally trying to torture me by prolonging my departure, it was working. My heart was already too far in, despite my best efforts to guard myself and tread carefully.

My pulse quickened as he slowly led me back in front of him.

"Lily, I—" He paused, then shook his head slowly. "I have a mind to tell you that we should not meet like this anymore." He raised an eyebrow. "But I am incapable of saying the words just now. So I think instead we should set some rules.

"First." His eyes found my hair undone. He took a small strand and held it between his thumb and finger, then carefully glided his fingers down it until my hair fell away. "I think *I* will behave better if your hair does." He grinned. "And second, it might be best if you avoid branches when we meet." Heat rose to my cheeks once more as I was reminded of the embarrassing scene Henry found me in.

"Lily?" Aunt Mary was calling out the library window now. The reality of my situation began to sink in.

"My aunt will disown me if she finds me out here with you." It might not have been true, but I wasn't willing to find out.

Henry took my shawl from his arm and slowly wrapped it around my shoulders. Then he took my hand one last time and placed tuppence inside.

"For luck," he said, closing my fingers over the coin.

I turned to leave, then looked back once more. "How will I notify you if I discover new information?" It was the best way for me to find an excuse to see him again without stating it directly.

"I will find you," he said quietly as he backed away into his hiding place.

"When?"

"Soon."

His answer would have to suffice. Now I needed to get back into the house without my aunt knowing, and think of a really good excuse as to why my hair was undone and why I didn't come when she called. As I neared the exit of the surrounding hedgerow, I had an idea.

I darted behind another tall bush and made my way to the lattices until I was underneath the small archway of vines that concealed the bench from the house. I had been discovered dozing off on it on more than one occasion. I quickly arranged myself as if I'd been sleeping. Not long after I assumed my role, I heard Aunt Mary open the back door and call my name again. I held my position until she walked over and was in full sight of me "sleeping" on the bench.

"Lily!" she said with exasperation.

I quickly shot up from the bench as if startled. I looked around me and blinked, making my lids appear heavy.

"I see you have fallen asleep out here again." She shook her head.

I gave her my usual answer. "Certainly not. I was simply resting my eyes."

She chuckled. "And your ears as well. I've been calling your name for some time." She took in my appearance. "Whatever has happened to your hair?"

"Do you usually sleep with pins in your hair, Aunt?"

"So you *do* admit to falling asleep." She smiled, but it quickly turned to a look of alarm, eyes widening. "But we have company." Her hand flew to my arm, pulling me upward. "Young Lady Morgan has just called on us. I'm not sure there is much we can do with your hair." She looked flustered at the state of my disheveled appearance.

"Marianne is a friend," I said reassuringly.

Aunt Mary took in a slow breath, trying to calm herself. "I'm just grateful her mother didn't come along. I can only imagine what a baroness would think if she saw you in such a state." She finally chuckled. "Come on."

My lips tugged into a grin. "Very well. I will join you in my atrocious state, but only because you're my favorite."

"I should hope so," she teased. It took everything in me not to look back at the shrubs where I knew Henry was waiting.

Marianne's chaperone was an elegantly dressed, cross-looking old woman with a bent spine. She was already seated in a chair near the fireplace when we entered. Aunt Mary took a seat on the opposite side of the mantle, looking flustered again. Marianne was positioned on the sofa against the wall, situated farthest from her chaperone. I joined her on the cushions, giving her a warm smile.

From our time together at the duchess' ball, I gathered that Marianne was a rare sort. For someone who was raised by a baron and baroness and who spent her entire life amongst wealth and expectations, she certainly had her own ideas about how she would conduct herself.

While most ladies of the *ton* held a bored expression, Marianne's face lit up and showed genuine emotion. When the other ladies smiled with acid, she smiled with kindness or not at all.

It seemed you knew exactly what you were getting with her. She was frank, and she loved to talk about the latest gossip. Above all, Marianne was a romantic, and had spent the majority of our time at the ball talking about men and suitors.

Once we were settled, Marianne smiled cordially, looking at Aunt Mary. "Mama insists that you and your nieces join us for afternoon tea tomorrow."

Aunt Mary's eyes opened wide. "We would be delighted."

"Wonderful!" Marianne beamed. "It will give us something to look forward to."

Her chaperone piped up with a scratchy, forceful tone. "Sit up straighter, Marianne. You're sure to disgrace us all."

Marianne rolled her eyes playfully. "Really, Grandmother, we can't all have perfect posture like you."

I bit back my smile as I looked at her grandmother's crooked frame.

"Hold your tongue, child," the old woman said crossly.

"Very well." Marianne smiled warmly at the prickly old woman.

I looked at Aunt Mary, unsure of how to respond. My aunt looked at my hair again and bit her lip in apprehension, worried the woman might call me out for my appearance. I shrugged and gave her an apologetic look.

As if the old woman could read our minds, she looked at my hair and gave a stern look. She opened her mouth to speak but Marianne jumped in first.

"Lily, I really do love your hair. I do believe it is the latest fashion, though only the bravest of us are daring enough to wear it," she winked at me.

"I think it's atrocious." The old woman gave me a cold stare.

"You think all the newest fashions are atrocious. But I also know that you have a keen eye for such things, Grandmother. You have to admit that Miss Mason has a natural grace that makes this new fashion very becoming."

The crumpled old lady pursed her lips and narrowed her eyes before she finally lifted her chin. "I suppose so, my dear. I do have a keen eye for such things, as you say, and I do believe you are right."

Marianne smiled at me, raising her eyebrows and shrugging her shoulders before addressing her grandmother once more. "Mrs. Mason is splendid company. I do believe the two of you must become better acquainted."

Aunt Mary did her best not to look alarmed at having this woman's full attention drawn in her direction. Marianne watched for a time as they exchanged a few words until they fell into what appeared to be an easy conversation.

Marianne finally turned her attention to me. "Grandmother is all prickles and thorns at first. But underneath she's sweet as can be. Just don't tell her I said so." She grinned. "Now, did you enjoy the duchess's ball?"

"Of course." I said with a smile. "I've never seen such splendor."

"Indeed," Marianne agreed. "The Duchess of Hastingwood knows how to host a proper ball."

"How are the preparations coming along for your mother's ball?"

Marianne beamed. "Mama is overdoing it. No one seems to be able to stop her when she has her mind truly fixed on something. And I'm delighted about the new ball gown Mama had me fitted for."

I smiled at her excitement.

"But enough talk about that," she said, waving her hand dismissively. She raised her eyebrows conspiratorially. "Grandmother and Mama always chide me for asking such direct questions—But as I feel we are friends now, I have to ask." Marianne looked over at her grandmother to confirm she wasn't listening, then leaned closer. "Are there any gentlemen in particular that have caught your interest?" She exuded such innocent excitement that I couldn't help but smile. I could not relate details about Henry, so I decided on an altogether different approach.

I raised one side of my lips along with an eyebrow. "Marianne, my first three dances of the evening were with Mr. Johnson twice, and Mr. Campbell once in between."

She winced. "That is rather bad luck. Mr. Johnson is not a bad sort, though he is very odd. Mr. Campbell, however, is detestable and deplorable." She lowered her voice. "Not to mention the rumors."

"What rumors?"

Marianne leaned in so her voice wouldn't carry past my ears. "This is old news, but according to some men, Mr. Campbell and the late Lord Elliot had quite the disagreement at White's gentlemen's club. It all happened only a month before the late Lord Elliot died." Her eyes widened as she said it.

My heart stopped at hearing Lord Elliot's name. I held my breath as I listened to Marianne. Perhaps she knew something useful I could give to Henry.

She continued. "About seven months ago, the late earl was seen approaching Mr. Campbell. They were speaking quietly at first, so no one knows exactly what was said in the beginning. But apparently Mr. Campbell owes money to several gentlemen there at the club and Lord Elliot was attempting to help settle the debts." I hung on to her every word.

She leaned in, lowering her voice further. "Some gentlemen even overheard Lord Elliot offer to help pay some of Mr. Campbell's debt if he promised to stop gambling in the future. Mr. Campbell loudly stated that the earl was a coward and never took any risks with his money." Marianne tilted her head in thought, then tucked a small, blonde strand of hair behind her ear. "It's true that Lord Elliot was not a gambling man. For whatever reason, he made an exception this time. Lord Elliot set the terms. If Mr. Campbell won, the earl would pay five hundred pounds of Mr. Campbell's debt and say nothing more about Mr. Campbell's gambling addiction. If Lord Elliot won, Mr. Campbell wasn't allowed to gamble at White's again." My eyes were wide, glued to hers as she continued. I had to remind myself to breathe as she laid out the details.

"The entire club gathered for the game of whist between the two gentlemen. They wouldn't let anyone else join, since so much was on the line. Apparently it was a close game. I won't bother giving you all the little details. In the end, Lord Elliot won.

"Mr. Campbell only ever appears aware of himself and is unaffected by anyone or anything surrounding him. He's always bored to death unless he is talking about himself. After he lost, however, he threw his cards to the floor and hurled his chair out from behind him before pointing a finger at Lord Elliot and yelling that he was a cheating man and that he'd better watch his step."

I couldn't help the small gasp that escaped my lips. "Marianne, do you mean to tell me that Mr. Campbell threatened Lord Elliot openly at a gentlemen's club only weeks before he was murdered?"

"Murdered?" Marianne whispered, aghast. "I'm not suggesting that he was murdered." She put a hand to her chest in shock. "Lord Elliot passed from a sudden illness while traveling. I am simply pointing out how despicable Mr. Campbell's behavior was. And the rumors of his gambling addiction are on almost everybody's ears in London. He is not exactly the type of man you would want to associate with."

I was alarmed at my own carelessness. The general public had no idea of the late Lord Elliot's death being a potential murder.

"Of course you're not suggesting such a thing," I said, doing my best to sound lighthearted. "I was so consumed by your story that my imagination ran away with extra details." I would need to be much more careful with my conversations.

Marianne's expression took on one of understanding. "I daresay I have imagined such things as well. I was all speculation when we first received word of the late earl's death. If he had in fact been murdered, Mr. Campbell would be the first person I would suspect."

A scratchy voice interrupted our conversation. "What are you two whispering about?"

"We are discussing Lord Elliot, of course," Marianne said, leaving out which Lord Elliot we were discussing.

"But why are you *whispering* about him?" Her grandmother gave us a stern look.

"He is rather handsome, grandmother. Wouldn't you whisper about him too, if you were younger?"

The old woman actually chuckled. "I suppose I would." She bent forward and slowly found her feet. "It's time we leave, Marianne. But I look forward to getting to know you better, Mrs. Mason, Miss Mason." She looked at each of us in turn and nodded.

"Likewise," Aunt Mary said as she rose from her chair. I stood as well, and Marianne followed suit. She gave me an excited smile and lowered her voice.

"Until tomorrow. I look forward to meeting your sister. And then we can really talk about Lord Elliot." She grinned. Clearly she was taken with him, just like all the other ladies from the duchess' ball. They'd all been whispering about him that night.

I smiled. "Perhaps you can pry from my sister what she thinks of the earl."

She chuckled quietly. "Has she fallen for Lord Elliot like we all have?"

"That's what I would like to find out."

"Leave it to me," she winked, crossing the room to join her grandmother. We all curtsied to one another before Marianne gave the old woman her arm for support, and they walked out.

Aunt Mary collapsed into her chair once the front door closed, as if the experience had left her completely exhausted. "Upon my word, Lily. I thought I might faint."

I chuckled. "Marianne seems to understand her grandmother."

"She certainly does."

George suddenly entered the room. "Mr. Johnson to see you, madam," he said, dipping his head.

Aunt Mary and I looked at one another with anxious eyes before Mr. Johnson walked through the threshold.

I had to endure Mr. Johnson's company for almost an hour. He sat in the armchair near the fire on the very edge of the cushion so his feet could reach the floor.

"Miss Mason," he said near the end of our visit, "last time we spoke, I likened you to a magpie. Further contemplation, however, has led me to realize that it is not a true likeness. The species has dark wings, which is indeed comparable to your dark locks. A magpie, however, has an iridescent blue that shimmers off its wings. I do not believe you have a similar quality." I bit down the grin that was threatening to find its way to the surface. Aunt Mary was faring worse than I was. She was barely holding back a laugh.

"I believe you are correct, Mr. Johnson. I do not have a blue sheen to my hair."

"Precisely. So we must find your true fowl likeness."

I couldn't help the chuckle that came next. "You have hit the mark, Mr. Johnson. Sometimes my likeness is indeed foul."

Aunt Mary broke and laughed before quickly stifling it. She gave me a look that said I had better behave, but followed it with a look of shared sympathy and humor at the situation.

"You may laugh, Miss Mason. But fowls are among some of the most clever and beautiful creatures on this earth."

"Tell me, then, Mr. Johnson. What fowl should I be likened to?"

He stared at me, unblinking. His prolonged study of me was uncomfortable.

"I daresay, Miss Mason, that you are superior among your sex. You are intelligent, graceful, and beautiful. Truly a rare creature." The way he looked at me was unsettling—like he was sizing me up for a bug collection, and I was the centerpiece.

He continued, "I could compare you only to a Golden Eagle. I have only ever read about them. But they have dark feathers with golden markings. They are beautiful and exquisite, powerful and superior to any of their species. They are intelligent and rare."

He gave me a smile I had never seen from him—like he might catch me and put me in a cage for safekeeping. I wanted to escape—preferably to the back garden behind the shrubs where Henry hid.

Aunt Mary must have sensed my discomfort. She spoke before he could continue.

"And what bird would you choose as your likeness, Mr. Johnson?" she asked.

"An appropriate question, Mrs. Mason. As you can imagine, I have studied this very question for a number of years. And in all of my research, I believe—"

He was suddenly interrupted by the butler walking in and nodding his head. "Lord Elliot, Earl of Wiltshire, is calling."

Aunt Mary's mouth turned up at the announcement.

"Thank you, George. Please show him in."

"Very good," he said, excusing himself.

Lord Elliot walked in with a pleasant smile in tow, and we all stood. "Good afternoon, Mrs. Mason, Miss Mason." He dipped his head to each of us, then noticed Mr. Johnson. He addressed Aunt Mary. "I was out for a ride and remembered I had promised Miss Mason that I would call on my Wilton friends. But I see you already have company. I'll not impose upon you." He turned to leave.

"Nonsense, Lord Elliot," Aunt Mary said. "We do love company. The more the merrier. I'll think it rude if you leave now when you've only just arrived." She smiled warmly as he turned back around, then looked at Mr. Johnson and extended her hand toward the earl. "Mr. Johnson, meet Lord Elliot, Earl of Wiltshire."

Lord Elliot dipped his head in Matthew's direction.

"And may I introduce our friend? Aunt Mary asked.

"Certainly." Lord Elliot smiled.

"This is Mr. Johnson."

"It's a pleasure, Mr. Johnson." Lord Elliot was all politeness. Mr. Johnson, however, didn't even bow as was customary.

A crease formed between Aunt Mary's eyebrows at his rude conduct, but she continued the conversation, turning to Lord Elliot. "It is a pity Jane is not here at the moment, though I anticipate her return shortly now."

Lord Elliot nodded with an easy smile. "And what were you all discussing before I rudely interrupted?"

Matthew spoke. "We were discussing fowl and our likenesses to them."

"I see." Lord Elliot seemed genuinely intrigued. "And what likenesses have been surmised thus far?" I appreciated Lord Elliot's enthusiasm, but I did not want to be compared to an eagle again.

I prepared myself as Matthew opened his mouth to speak. "We have found only Miss Mason's likeness thus far," he said with some haughtiness.

"And what likeness did you all choose for Miss Mason?" Lord Elliot asked, turning to me.

"A Golden Eagle," I said, before Mr. Johnson had the chance to expound. I took a seat once more along with Aunt Mary and the bird lover. "But I think you misunderstand, Lord Elliot. Mr. Johnson alone has been finding our likenesses."

Lord Elliot raised his brows in understanding. "I see."

"He was just about to tell us what his own likeness is," I added.

"Very well. Don't let me stop the fun." Lord Elliot took a seat next to Matthew before adding, "Though I must insist on being evaluated myself before I take my leave." Mr. Johnson did not look pleased. He stared at me for a long moment, then eyed the earl.

"I assume you are not as well educated on fowl friends as I am, Your Lordship, so I don't expect you to keep up." His tone was condescending. Aunt Mary narrowed her eyes at Mr. Johnson's behavior once more.

Lord Elliot smiled with amusement. "I believe you are correct. I try to avoid the company of foul friends. The less educated I am about them, the better."

I couldn't help but grin at his comment. I could tell Lord Elliot would be a kindred spirit.

Mr. Johnson's mouth turned down with displeasure. "I believe you find yourself most amusing, my lord."

"Certainly not, good fellow. Forgive my base sense of humor. Sometimes I find that I simply can't help myself." He gave Mr. Johnson an apologetic look. "Please continue. It is true that I may not be as educated about birds as you are. I'll do my best to keep up."

Mr. Johnson looked from Lord Elliot, to me, then back again. His eyes narrowed and his mouth formed into a hard line, a look of jealousy marking his features. Did he think Lord Elliot was pursuing me? Or that I regarded Lord Elliot as a suitor?

Though I certainly would prefer him to Mr. Johnson, the only contender for my heart was back in the hedges. I had never seen Mr. Johnson wear the angry, meditative expression he was wearing just now. It did not suit him. He glanced at Lord Elliot once more before he spoke.

"I am a shrike," he said, coolly. "It is a small, handsome bird. I, too, am small but able to contend with birds that are my size and larger." His petite frame was swallowed up by the chair he occupied, making him look even smaller than usual in contrast to Lord Elliot.

He eyed Lord Elliot's tall frame. "I may not fly as well as my competition, but I am more patient and wait for the right moment to conquer."

Lord Elliot nodded his head. "Very interesting choice." He paused for a moment. "And what would my likeness be?" he asked with interest.

Mr. Johnson gave Lord Elliot a twisted smile. "A cuckoo."

Lord Elliot made no reaction.

A corner of Mr. Johnson's lips twitched. "I can see by your expression that you are not familiar with the species," he said victoriously. "Let me enlighten you. Cuckoo eggs are laid by their mother in a nest that belongs to another bird. The mother searches for a nest that already has a few eggs occupying it so that when the baby hatches, it will be fed by a bird other than its own mother. The cuckoo is bigger than the other babies, so naturally, once the baby cuckoo hatches, it kicks all the other eggs or hatchlings out of the nest until it is the only one monopolizing the home. The mother of the other chicks continues to feed the baby cuckoo, unaware of its deceit—never considering the fact that the entire system is a sham."

Aunt Mary gasped. "Mr. Johnson! I will not have you speak to my guests in such a way!"

Matthew looked to her, then did his best to put on a repentant smile. "Forgive me, Mrs. Mason. Perhaps you don't quite understand," he said as if she were a child. "He who is titled, wealthy, and strong feeds off of those beneath him. Society supports him while he does nothing but kick everyone else out of the nest."

Silence followed. Mr. Johnson didn't even attempt to hide his dislike for Lord Elliot. I was shocked at such an offhanded comment, especially from someone who usually did his best to blend in.

"Defend it how you will, Mr. Johnson," Aunt Mary said firmly. "It's an insult. If you aren't more careful with my guests, then George will show you out immediately."

Lord Elliot spoke next. "Please madam, think nothing of it." He turned to Matthew. "You flatter me, Mr. Johnson. I must say, I applaud your brilliance in finding a bird that depicts so well the issues within society, though I must also add that the German ornithologist, Johann Bechstein, had an altogether different idea in regard to the cuckoo.

"For example, he theorized that the reason a crow allows a Great Spotted Cuckoo to lay an egg in its nest is because its offspring will benefit—the cuckoo omits a smelly, sticky substance that serves as a defense mechanism against predators. In short, the cuckoo can protect its hosts." He let his words sink in before he continued. "As much as I would like to take credit for such a bird, I don't believe I can. I thank you for the compliment all the same."

Mr. Johnson opened his mouth to speak, a sour expression forming on his face, but Lord Elliot beat him to it.

"I do have one more thing to point out, Mr. Johnson. You have likened yourself to a shrike. One might note that shrikes are unassuming songbirds that wait above their victims to strike whilst the prey is unaware of its attacker. If their prey is not killed by the initial impact, shrikes will use swift tactics to sever the vertebrae. And I believe it is important to consider that they impale their victims on spikes for safekeeping and sometimes even hang them upside down. As you are the expert, I'm certain you are aware of these attributes."

Lord Elliot's voice was calm as he watched Mr. Johnson and concluded, "Therefore, I find it interesting that you would choose a shrike for yourself."

The imagery was disturbing. Mr. Johnson had clearly underestimated Lord Elliot. The earl had beaten him at his own game, which surely did not occur often, if ever.

Mr. Johnson's bad mood was palpable. He stood tensely before he spoke.

"I thank you madam, Miss Mason, for your hospitality." He dipped his head to both of us. "I must be going now." He didn't acknowledge Lord Elliot as he stiffly walked out.

Aunt Mary gave me a look of astonishment. Once Mr. Johnson left the house, she put a hand to her chest.

"Upon my word, Lord Elliot, I have never seen him insult another living soul. I assure you I wouldn't have introduced you had I known how he would behave."

Lord Elliot gave Aunt Mary an easy smile. "Please, think nothing of it. His words have not injured me. There is no harm done."

She let out a shaky breath. "Thank you, my lord."

I smiled. "Lord Elliot, I hope you will visit us often." I couldn't help but like him. Not in the way I craved Henry; I just thoroughly enjoyed his company. On top of that, he was genuine, intelligent, and titled—in short, everything Jane needed.

Perhaps it was selfish of me, but I couldn't bear the thought of Jane with Frederick, nor the idea of him being my brother-in-law. I knew Jane had her sights set on the bored, flat Lord, but nothing was official until she accepted a proposal. I prayed I wasn't already too late. I looked at Lord Elliot. She would change her mind about Frederick if I could help it.

Jane

Frederick's carriage rolled to a stop in front of the house. I held back a sigh of relief. Alice exited the carriage first, followed by Frederick. He helped me down, then took both my hands in his. The gesture was intimate, but I felt nothing stir inside me.

"Thank you for your company this afternoon," he said in his usual flat tone.

"The pleasure was mine," I said, matching his.

"May I take you for another ride Monday next?" he asked.

"Certainly." I placed my smile exactly where it should go.

"Very well. Until then." He dipped his head and I curtsied. As he ascended his carriage, Alice walked inside. I was grateful she left me to myself and refrained from hounding me with questions about what I thought of the dull afternoon. Frederick's carriage pulled onto the street. I finally exhaled as I reflected on the ride, feeling absolutely exhausted from our time together.

It seemed the entirety of our outing consisted of me trying to gauge whether I should continue to stare out the carriage in silence or strike up a conversation that went nowhere.

Before today, I had only ever spent time with Frederick at public events. We usually had conversations in groups or were dancing or being entertained in some fashion or another. Would life with Frederick be like the carriage ride? Suffocating and dull? I let myself inside the house. George was not at his usual post. I was grateful for his absence, since I didn't feel myself at present and didn't want to have to put on a show any longer.

"Lily?" I called as I dashed up the stairs. I knew it was very unladylike for me to run about the house yelling for my sister, but for whatever reason, I didn't care.

"Lily?" I called again as I opened my door, expecting her to be lying on my bed still. My bed was empty, the covers disheveled. I walked into Lily's room to find it empty as well. Then I heard Lily's voice coming from the parlor. Lifting my dress, I rushed down the stairs, calling her name again as I approached. I rounded the corner and rushed in.

"Lily, I'm in desperate need of some fresh air and—" I stopped abruptly. Lord Elliot was in the parlor with Aunt Mary and Lily. He stood as I entered the room. They were all staring at me. Of course; it was calling hours. What was wrong with me?

Aunt Mary furrowed her brow, "Jane, is anything the matter?"

Silence followed. I didn't know what to say to justify my unladylike conduct. I opened my mouth to say something and floundered until I couldn't help but blush in embarrassment at the ridiculousness of my manners.

I finally found my words. "It's just such a lovely day. I am simply overeager to be out walking in it." I could feel Lord Elliot's eyes on me as I spoke to Aunt Mary. I dared a small glance in his direction. His mouth turned up into a soft, welcoming smile.

"I think a walk is a lovely idea," Aunt Mary said. "Come sit and talk with us and I'll have someone fetch your uncle. He's been avoiding callers this afternoon, but I'm sure a walk would bring him out of hiding," she said with a chuckle. "And Lord Elliot, you must join us," she added enthusiastically.

I took a seat next to Lily on the sofa. Lord Elliot sat after I did, smiling at my aunt's invitation.

"I should decline your offer in fear that I've already overstayed my welcome—but then I'd have to beg you to let me along afterward, and that would be most ill mannered of me. So I will gratefully accept your invitation, Mrs. Mason, and hope that you truly haven't tired of me yet." He winked. He was clearly restored to his usual self since I had last seen him during my ride.

Aunt Mary swatted the air. "Oh, how you flatter us. As if we could tire of your company." Aunt Mary turned to me. "You missed all the excitement, Jane. Mr. Johnson was here moments before you arrived. He was so ill mannered toward Lord Elliot that I almost dismissed him from the house."

Lily spoke next. "Lord Elliot, was this truly the first time you have met Mr. Johnson? Or is there a history between you?"

"I have certainly never met the fellow." He grinned. "I would definitely remember meeting such a man."

Lily smirked. "I have never seen anyone use his love of his precious birds against him. How is it you know so much about them?" The way Lily was making Lord Elliot's eyes light up was turning my stomach for a reason I couldn't understand.

He leaned back in his chair. "I was abroad for a number of years before my father passed. Studying the native animals of the various places we visited was a fascination of ours. I came upon a book solely dedicated to birds while on my travels. It was most thorough and the pictures were magnificent. I read details about many different species of birds and their behaviors. I must admit that I found it fascinating." He exchanged his exuberant look with something serious and turned to Lily. "Mr. Johnson, however, displays an obsession with the species that unsettles me—especially when he likens himself to a shrike. I would be surprised if he was not aware of its disturbing habits before today. I would be wary of him, Miss Mason."

It appeared as though I had missed an exciting afternoon, indeed. I wanted to hear the story in its entirety, but I also found that I didn't enjoy watching Lily and Lord Elliot talk in such a friendly manner. I certainly wasn't jealous, I told myself. I simply had endured a dull ride and wanted to be included in a conversation that I hadn't missed all the details for.

Aunt Mary nodded her head. "Lily, if accepting a dance from Mr. Johnson makes you feel uncomfortable, at this point, you may decline his invitation."

Lily opened her mouth, and her eyes widened as if she had just inherited a large sum. "Lord Elliot," she beamed, "you must visit us regularly if this is the type of luck you bring!"

"Consider it done," he said, smiling. He was clearly in his element with Lily and Aunt Mary. I turned my gaze to the floor, feeling insecure in the one place I was hoping to find refuge. I didn't know how to behave normally. My practiced poise was futile in this company. I needed to leave. I needed some fresh air. Perhaps I could find Uncle Francis after I changed my shoes and we could sneak out.

I stood. "Excuse me." I tried to sound as natural as possible, making a point not to look at Lily or Aunt Mary, lest they discover something amiss, before I quickly left the parlor and headed for the stairs.

12

LEAF

Jane

I heard Lord Elliot excuse himself as I left the room. The staircase was in my reach when I felt his presence behind me.

"Miss Mason." I froze on the first step, his voice echoing inside me.

"Miss Mason," he repeated, walking in my direction. I slowly turned around to face him, placing my hand on the rail as I did so, as if it could somehow keep me grounded from this man that disrupted everything.

I wasn't ready to talk with him when I had just endured such a disappointing ride with Frederick. Lord Elliot stood at the base of the steps, bringing our eyes almost level. He glanced at my hand on the railing, then back at my eyes.

"I know that you wish for me to leave you alone. I'll not impose on your solitude any longer. I only wished to state that you shouldn't leave the room on my account. I intended to leave before you returned from your ride, but your aunt and sister were such splendid company that I lost track of time. I will leave now so you don't have to retreat." He turned to exit.

"Lord Elliot, you are putting words in my mouth. I never stated my wishes to be left alone."

He turned back around. "It was heavily implied." His tone was even, eyes watching mine as he said it.

"And how is that?" I asked, trying to keep my voice level.

"It is still implied, even now." He glanced at my hand clasped tightly to the railing. I stared at it as well. He raised an eyebrow. "You clearly want to escape."

"You cannot claim such a thing without knowing my thoughts," I defended.

"Then why are you so determined to leave?" He was too observant.

"I simply need some air," I countered. He looked at me as if he was gauging whether to take me at my word or not.

"Then please answer me once and for all: Do you welcome my company?" It was hard to breathe when his eyes moved between mine, studying my expression.

I couldn't speak. What a frustrating man. Why couldn't he just leave things be? Why couldn't he converse with me the way he did with Lily and Aunt Mary? Perhaps it was my fault. I didn't know how to behave in the presence of such a gentleman.

His eyes held disappointment beneath the surface. "In some cases, Miss Mason, silence states more than words ever could." He turned to leave again.

I grabbed his arm with my free hand. "Lord Elliot, please don't pretend to know my thoughts simply because I am silent." My boldness surprised me. He looked down at my hand on his arm, then turned to face me again, closer than before. My heart sped up and my breath quickened. I went to take a step back but felt the next stair against my heels. I held my position, frozen. He too held perfectly still, taking in my eyes. Realizing my hand was still on his arm, I quickly pulled it away.

"What should I take your silence to mean, then?" he asked quietly. I collected my thoughts.

"Would it be acceptable if my silence means that I'm still deciding?"

His eyes searched mine for a time as he contemplated my response.

"That depends on what you ultimately decide," he finally said, lifting a corner of his mouth.

"I believe that depends on you," I countered.

"Then we are certainly in trouble," he said, grinning.

"Are you planning your next maneuver to antagonize me already, Lord Elliot?" I couldn't help but grin back.

"It seems that I can't help but antagonize you, even when I have the best intentions. For instance, I wish to ask how your ride with Lord Fletcher went today. And yet, I know that you and I would not be able to breach the subject without discord."

He was indeed correct. I didn't want to talk about Frederick just now. I didn't want to think about the suffocating carriage ride I had just endured, all while trying *not* to think about the man standing in front of me.

He continued, "But I can't help but ask regardless. How was your ride with Lord Fletcher?"

I hesitated as I contemplated whether or not I should be truthful. "It was suitable," I finally said.

He smiled. "I'm impressed that it was suitable. However, I can assure you that if *I* were to take you for a carriage ride it would be more than suitable."

"You are very confident. Lord Fletcher has the finest of carriages and I found it only suitable," I teased. "What makes you think you'll have better luck?"

"What a snob you are," he said with a grin.

I lifted an eyebrow. "Indeed. I'm impossible to please."

"Be that as it may, you are forgetting one small thing. *Lord Fletcher* was riding in his carriage"—he put on his most charming smile—"and *I* will be riding in mine." I couldn't help but grin at his gesture. His smile dimmed. "There is still one thing I have not been able to understand. Why do you keep Lord Fletcher's company?"

I should have been used to the directness of his questions by now, but they still seemed to take me by surprise each time.

"If we are to ever get along, Lord Elliot, you cannot berate me for having an interest in Lord Fletcher."

"So you not only keep his company, but you encourage it?" he asked, unable to hide his displeasure.

"And why is that wrong?" I asked. "I would be a fool not to encourage his attention toward me."

His mouth formed a line. "And why is that, exactly? Is it because he is the son of a duke?"

"You say that as if it's a bad thing," I said defensively. Lord Elliot pushed his fingers through his hair in frustration. My eyes couldn't help but follow the gesture.

He dropped his hands and looked at me. "Lord Fletcher has no soul. He has no passion except to hate. He's petty and thoughtless and thankless. Have you truly felt a spark in any way for him? Or is it only about his title and wealth?"

I was left with nothing substantial to say. "Lord Fletcher is predictable. He has never been unkind to me." I hoped my words would somehow contradict his statement enough for him to leave the subject alone.

He shook his head slowly. "For some that may be enough. But not for you. There is a restlessness I sense in you."

"You paint me in such an exciting light. I assure you, my lord, I am exactly as I appear."

He studied me. "You *are* exactly as you appear, . . . and you appear restless."

Why was there nowhere to escape? How could he possibly see a restlessness in me when I buried it so deep? I turned his words against him.

"Perhaps you see in me only what you see in yourself." I said the words as evenly as I could manage while my breath picked up speed.

His eyes held mine. "Perhaps. But we will never know unless you prove me wrong. Allow me to take you for a carriage ride tomorrow morning. I guarantee you it will be more than suitable."

"I don't believe it would help your cause, Lord Elliot. It is no secret that you despise Lord Fletcher. I could never be sure your offer wasn't just an act of using me to spite him."

He stiffened. "I promised I would never use you again in that way."

"And yet I cannot see into your mind. How am I to know if you are being truthful? Your word alone guarantees nothing."

"Have I proven myself so untrustworthy?" His words were etched with frustration and betrayal.

I thought of the way he came to my aid with Mr. Hughes, Amelia, and Edith. I looked away from him. "No, Lord Elliot, you have not proven yourself untrustworthy." I let out a conflicted breath. "I just need time."

"What if I don't have time?" he muttered under his breath. Silence filled the space around us.

His next words were quiet. "Is Lord Fletcher truly enough for you?" His eyes held me captive, making me want more. I said nothing. I could have easily answered his question even two days ago. Frederick was enough. He was suitable, comfortable, and consistent. I reminded myself of my creed: my head ruled my heart. I found, however, that I couldn't speak the words when Lord Elliot looked at me that way.

"Lord Elliot—" I finally said.

"Charles," he said, correcting my choice of name. He stepped up next to me. "If we are to get along, you must call me Charles." Why did his request and his nearness make me so nervous?

"It isn't proper, Lord Elliot." I was surprised at his forwardness.

He didn't grin like I expected him to. His eyes moved between each of mine before he spoke again. "And why isn't it proper? Our fathers have done business. We both claim Wilton as our home. We have practically known each other our entire lives." His grin finally emerged. What he was claiming was a far stretch from the truth and he knew it.

"I can't call you Charles."

He grinned. "You *can* call me Charles." Then he shot me a challenging smirk. "The real question is, *will* you call me Charles? Perhaps in private so we can get along."

I shook my head at him.

He continued, "And since we are practically old friends, may I call you Jane?"

I opened my mouth slightly at his audacity. I didn't know what to say. I finally looked at him with mild irritation. "If you insist, my lord."

"I do insist." He gave me a grin as he raised an eyebrow. I wanted to trust him, but he was making it so difficult.

"And since we have decided to tolerate one another," he added, "will you not shake hands with me?"

I looked at his hand for a moment with trepidation before I slowly offered my free hand to him. He carefully took it in his and coaxed me toward him. My heart lurched at the contact and continued to hammer inside of me. My other hand was still secured to the rail of the stairway. I needed to go upstairs to clear my head. But my hand let go of its own accord, and I allowed him to guide me in front of him, his eyes following mine. He slowly released my hand, then spoke quietly. "And are you upset about anything else?"

It took me a moment to collect my thoughts. I wanted to ask him about the sadness I had seen in him when he was out riding, but I knew it had been a private moment.

"No. I'm not upset." My heart sped up as I said the words. I turned and stepped up, ready to retreat. His hand wrapped around my wrist. Startled, I looked back.

"Very well. Then will you come back to the parlor?" His eagerness drew me in. I needed to retreat to my room for at least a small moment to clear my head before returning.

"I will once I've changed," I said, trying to place a calm smile on my face. I felt anything but calm. "These shoes are much better suited for carriage rides than they are for walking."

"You could wear mine and save yourself the trouble," he winked.

I looked down at his large feet and chuckled. "If I fit in your shoes I would never go out in public again."

"In that case, I rescind my offer." He smiled. I looked at his hand around my wrist. I expected to feel his release so I could withdraw. Instead he slowly moved his fingers from my wrist to my hand. He softly traced the top of my hand with his thumb. A current of tingles spread throughout me until they met at my heart. I pulled my hand away quickly at the intimate gesture.

"Forgive me," Charles said as he watched my reaction. My heart was going haywire. "Now," he said, returning his usual smile to his face.

"I will leave you to change. Best not keep our company waiting." He dipped his head, then turned from the stairs and made his way toward the parlor. Before he turned the corner he looked back at me, his smile no longer in place. His eyes held a hundred unspoken words and questions. Then he disappeared from my view.

Slowly making my way up the stairs, I brushed my fingers across the place on my hand where he had lightly touched. I had never felt such a sensation. I couldn't help but think about the difference I felt when Frederick took my hand compared to what just transpired.

Lord Elliot—Charles—was proving more and more of a disruption to my perfect plans. I changed my shoes as quickly as I could then made my way down once more to the parlor. Uncle Francis was seated comfortably next to Charles and they appeared to be having a light-hearted conversation.

Uncle Francis gave me a smile as I entered. "Now that we are all here, let's make our way outside before anyone else decides to call." He offered his arm to Aunt Mary.

Lily and I walked arm in arm a few yards ahead of Lord Elliot, who was entertaining our aunt and uncle. Though I would have loved to be privy to whatever they kept chuckling about, I was grateful for the fresh air and my sister's company. We finally had a chance to talk.

Lily's eyes lit up. "You'll be so excited, Jane. We've been invited to have tea with Marianne Morgan and her mother tomorrow afternoon."

"The baroness has invited us to tea?" I beamed.

"She has."

"Perhaps we might finally make a friend in London after all," I said with a grin. "And how was your time at the duchess's ball? Did you dance with anyone worth mentioning?" I was hoping one of the men would eventually excite her.

"If you count Mr. Campbell, then absolutely," she said with a smirk.

"That ridiculous dandy?" I looked at her face to make sure she was joking.

She held an unreadable expression for only a moment longer before she finally laughed. "I said he was worth mentioning, not that I was taken with him. He did offer me a fair share of amusement though." She scrunched her face into a look of snobbery, then said in a mocking tone, "I can see that you have noticed the advantage of having me as your dance partner."

I opened my mouth in disbelief. "Did he honestly say that, Lily?"

She continued her impression of Mr. Campbell. "Come now, miss. It is hard to ignore perfection when it is right in front of you."

We both laughed.

I grinned. "You can certainly do better than Mr. Campbell."

She chuckled. "I should hope so." Her voice grew quiet. "And what about you, Jane? Was there anyone worth mentioning that you danced with? It is clear to me that you met Lord Elliot that night. Did he dance with you?"

"He did," I said evenly. I wasn't ready to have this conversation, especially when he was so close behind us. I thought quickly for a way to change the subject. "In fact," I said, cocking an eyebrow, "we couldn't find you when he was being introduced. Where were you?"

Lily gave an apologetic look. "Well, I was perhaps a little improper." She hesitated. "I led myself away from the dance with Mr. Campbell instead of allowing him to escort me back to Aunt Mary. I couldn't help myself, Jane. He was so pompous and I put him so thoroughly in his place. But then Mr. Johnson started making his way towards me and I had to find a place to hide. The little good it did. He did, in fact, snatch me for a second dance later."

This was exactly the type of thing I was trying to help her understand. I was grateful she hadn't gone to the gardens, but hiding when she should have found our party was dangerous for her reputation too—Especially when people were watching and waiting for us to make even the smallest mistakes.

"Lily," I said, exasperated.

"I know. I'm a truant pupil. You have taught me well and I keep abandoning my post."

"This isn't a game, Lily! Your reputation is at stake when you don't follow the rules, and so is mine."

"In truth Jane, I care little for my reputation in a society such as London's, especially when I know that my character is better than that of many who follow the rules but are despicable behind closed doors. But—"

"Don't say such things!" I scolded.

"Let me finish," she snapped. She waited to make sure I wouldn't interrupt again before she proceeded. "I care little for my reputation in London society, but I do care about yours. I really am trying. I recognize that I am impulsive and used to the countryside's rules. I am sorry that I hid from Mr. Johnson when I should have found our party. I will do better."

I sighed. "I don't wish to be cross with you, Lily."

She didn't answer immediately. "I don't wish to make things difficult," she finally offered, averting her eyes to the ground.

We said nothing for a time.

Lily finally broke the silence but left her usual teasing tone behind. "So you danced with Lord Elliot?"

"I did."

"And what is your opinion of him?"

I hesitated, unsure of what to say. "He is a good dance partner," I finally said.

Lily laughed, but there was reservation behind it. "That's all you have to say about him?"

"What would you like me to say about him?" I asked quietly.

"Perhaps that he is handsome," she said quietly. "And easy to talk to . . . unlike Frederick." She struck a chord. She had no idea how much her words rang true. Then she added, "I find Lord Elliot to be genuine and kind."

I could hear his deep voice behind us bringing laughs from our relatives. My heart warmed at the sound. Lily remained silent for the next few minutes. I didn't realize my chastisement would bring such a change in her mood.

She slowed our pace until the remainder of our party caught up to us. It was apparent she no longer wanted my company alone. She began a conversation with Aunt Mary and Uncle Francis. The path was not wide enough for us all; I had no other choice but to walk next to Charles. I found that I was both wanting and wary of his company. We walked in silence, at an easy pace, taking in the trees and their changing leaves. It was a comfortable silence. I took in a soothing breath of the autumn air and let it out contentedly. I glanced at Charles briefly and found that he was watching me, a thoughtful look on his face. His expression changed upon being caught and he actually broke our gaze, looking ahead.

"If you don't tell me what that look was for, then I'll simply have to guess," I said, feeling brave at his sudden reserve.

He grinned. "What look?" He met my eyes again, raising his brows. His confidence was already back. I decided I would remain silent and see if it helped loosen his tongue. This time I redirected *my* eyes forward, returning them to the path ahead. Only a moment went by before he gave up the fight and decided to illuminate me.

"You love autumn." He said it as a statement, not a question, reading my thoughts again.

I smiled. "Of course I do. How could I feel otherwise?"

"It *is* possible to feel otherwise." A fragment of the solemnity I saw from earlier today returned. "Why do you love autumn?"

"I believe I will disappoint you. My answer is quite straightforward. I love autumn for the same reasons most people do."

"I am not asking most people."

I was grateful that this topic was safe. I took in another breath, instantly reminded of the first thing I loved.

I exhaled slowly, grinning. "That's the first thing I love about autumn. It smells like something is around the corner—like adventure. It's cool, clean, crisp, and inviting. When Lily and I were little girls, we would chase each other out into a little thicket of trees and play. During the autumn season, we would run out to those trees and have adventures in far-away places. We would be captured by gypsies and turn into magical beings like fairies or goblins. We could be anything and everything.

"When the leaves turn colors it feels like change is coming—like luck. Some people wish to their gods and their stars. Not Lily and me. We would lay under our favorite tree, talk about our hopes and dreams, and then find the prettiest leaf above us and wish on it. And if it fell while we watched, our wishes were sure to come true. Lily always wished to be a pirate," I said, laughing. "I always wished for a palace and as many dresses as I could think of." I raised my eyebrows mysteriously. "We never did see our favorite leaf fall, but Lily may yet become a pirate."

Charles laughed softly. "Please, keep going." He appeared to be truly engaged in my silly childhood stories. A sense of happiness and peace came over me at the retelling of my adventures with my sister. I felt whole in a way I hadn't felt for a long time. I knew it was unladylike to bore one's company with long stories, but once I started, it was impossible to stop.

"Every year, Lily, my two younger brothers, and I would try to sneak Cook's apple pie during our harvest party. Later that night we would sit around a large fire wrapped in blankets. My brother, Sterling, loved starting the fire with my father. Papa shared stories, both heartwarming and scary, and he taught us old songs. Oftentimes neighbors joined in the festivities."

Charles was ever the engaged listener. He laughed with me and smiled with real delight. I was struck by his attentiveness. It was very different from being in Frederick's company. I found it odd that I really didn't know much about Lord Elliot, even though I had heard about him my entire life. It was his turn to do the talking.

"Charles," I said quietly, speaking his given name aloud for the first time. He smiled at my choice of name before I continued. "Am I to understand that you don't enjoy autumn?" I was definitely curious. It was deeply puzzling if it were true.

Charles breathed in. "I find that I rather enjoy your version of autumn."

"And what is your version?" I asked.

"I can see the beauty in the changing leaves, and in the fresh air as you've described it." He looked ahead at the path. "They just mean different things to me. My mother died in autumn. But when she died, the season continued to move. The leaves kept changing, even when my world stopped completely. And as the leaves fell, they withered to dust, never to return again. In its place, something new grew instead. They would never be the same ones that lived while she breathed."

I was moved by his sentiment for his mother.

He looked over at me. "I won't pretend at being miserable every autumn since her passing. There were years when we too gathered with friends for parties. But the beautiful things of autumn seem to cast solemnity in my mind from time to time. This year has made all the wounds fresh since my father's passing." I waited for him to continue but he was silent.

I bit my lip, mustering my courage to ask a personal question. "And are you unhappy?"

His eyes stayed on the trail ahead. "Do I appear unhappy?"

"In truth, I have only ever seen you appear full of life. I can't recall a time that you weren't bringing smiles to your company." I thought back to his downcast solitude earlier that day. "But when no one else is around, are you happy?"

Charles looked at me. "I believe there is more to it than simply being happy or unhappy." His eyes moved between mine before he asked, "Are *you* happy?"

"I have no earthly reason why I shouldn't be happy. I want for nothing. I have been very fortunate in having a loving family that has not yet faced loss." I thought of the tragedies Charles had faced.

"Being grateful is not necessarily the same thing as being happy." He raised an eyebrow at me. "And you have an uncanny way of saying one thing while altogether avoiding the question. You state that you have no earthly reason why you shouldn't be happy, yet you brush off the real question. Are you happy?"

"Perhaps there is wisdom in what you say—there is more to it than simply being happy or unhappy." I didn't expect Lord Elliot and me to manage a conversation for so long without it ending with conflict, let alone one that meant so much to me. I was drawn to this side of him more than I cared to admit. I wanted him to let me see into these parts of his vulnerable soul. I didn't know if my next question would ruin what progress we had just made. But I rallied my courage and decided to try.

"So why are you unhappy?" I met his eyes briefly, then looked back down to the ground. His pace slowed and I followed suit until we were no longer walking.

"Jane." Hearing him say my given name aloud sent tingles through me. But his voice sounded conflicted. He appeared to be deciding whether or not to share his thoughts. "Have you ever longed for more? Been unsettled with no hope of rest?" When our eyes met, I could see his restlessness. The torment for something more. It mirrored my very own.

He looked down, cutting off my view into his soul. I found that I wanted to soothe his turmoil. I had never seen this side of Lord Elliot.

I could tell he wanted to say more but was holding back. He began moving forward once more. I stayed at his side as he spoke.

"You ask if I'm unhappy. I have never considered myself unhappy before. Lonely at times, perhaps, but never unhappy. And yet, I've never wanted something before that couldn't be mine . . . until now." He looked from the trail up to me.

"May I ask what it is you want?" I wondered what the Earl of Wiltshire could possibly want and not obtain.

He looked back down, grinning. "You may ask, Jane, but that doesn't mean I'll tell you."

I grinned but narrowed my eyes. "Very well. Then you will have to wish for it." I put my finger to my lips in thought, then scanned the trees around us and found a large, yellow leaf that was absolute perfection. "That one there," I said, pointing to it.

"Which one?" Charles asked, following my gaze.

"The big yellow one."

He chuckled. "I see more than a few that meet that description. Could you be a little more specific?"

I brought myself closer to him and pointed again so he could see my line of sight. He shifted until he was right behind me and brought his face level with mine, aligning his view. My heart quickened at his nearness. I continued as if it was the most natural thing in the world.

"See, right there," I said, pointing very specifically. "The one that stands out among all the others." I felt his eyes shift to me.

"I see it." He was so close to me—too close.

I tried to act normal as I stepped to the side, giving us more distance. "Then make your wish," I said, doing my best to control my breathing.

Charles smiled. "I thought you said this method wasn't very effective, unless your sister is secretly a pirate."

"Perhaps you will have better luck than we did," I said with a grin.

"Perhaps."

I dared a look in his direction, our eyes meeting. A breeze rolled around us, sending dancing leaves around my ankles. The whispering wind rose until it touched my face, loosening a strand of my hair from its perfect position. It felt as if a part of me had been set free—a small piece beginning to unravel. I wasn't sure what it meant.

Charles finally broke our silence.

"And what would you wish for now, Jane? Are you still waiting for your palace and fine dresses?" His words brought to mind only one dress: The deep blue one that made me feel bold, that made me crave more.

"Just one dress, actually."

He gave me a quizzical look. "And does this dress have all the diamonds and jewels one could ask for?"

The corner of my lips ticked up, as if they couldn't help it. "I have to keep some things to myself." I began walking again and he followed my lead.

Charles grinned. "Very well. You may leave me in suspense for now." He notched an eyebrow. "But I do believe you are still in my debt."

"Must you always ruin a good conversation?" I sighed, but wasn't truly upset.

"Must you always find my faults?" he teased back.

"That depends on whether or not you tax your subjects heavily when they are in your debt."

He looked at me with his signature grin. "Only when I want something desperately."

"And do you want something desperately now?" I knew I shouldn't encourage his teasing, but I couldn't help it. He waited for me to look at him. When I did, his expression no longer held humor.

"I do want something." He studied my face. "I want a chance, Jane. A chance to prove to you that I'm not as terrible as you think I am. I am asking you to put aside your opinions of me for now and trust that I'm not your enemy."

It was a dangerous thing he wanted from me. Being in Charles's presence alone threatened everything I'd been working for. He stirred me and made me feel things I had never felt before. Aside from that, being on friendly terms with Charles would surely make Frederick furious and could end all my hopes of making a match that would ultimately bring my family into a place of respect and influence.

In short, Lord Elliot had the power to take away everything in a matter of moments. And yet he'd come to my aid when I had needed it, twice.

"And what exactly would you like to be, Lord Elliot, if not my enemy? My friend, perhaps?"

His eyes held unspoken words. I watched as he buried them deep and settled on something else. "Perhaps an ally."

I considered his offer. "And if we are allies, will you try to use me against your enemies? Namely Lord Fletcher?"

He stopped walking and faced me. "Jane, I can promise you that I will never change how I feel about Frederick. I believe we are destined to loathe one another indefinitely. But I will do my best to respect your decisions, whether I agree with them or not. I can promise you that I will not use you as a means to attack Frederick. And perhaps you could grant me some leniency, allowing me to dislike him without it getting in the way of your opinion of me."

His terms were not only fair but clear. "Very well, I accept." A side of my mouth turned up without my permission.

Charles smiled fully. "Excellent."

13

ENVELOPE

Jane

London
November 6, 1816
Two days later
Nine days of disguise remaining

Alice helped me step into my evening dress for Aunt Mary's small dinner party. She had already arranged my hair like usual: curls perfectly pinned in place near the top and back of my head so they wouldn't budge. She fastened my dress, then excused herself.

My stomach was already in knots. Aunt Mary had invited both Charles and Frederick to her dinner party, and both men had accepted her invitation. How could I possibly uphold my new agreement with Charles while not upsetting Frederick?

"Jane! You look positively ill." Lily's face peeked in through my door. "Whatever is that look for? Are you lovesick for Frederick?" She grinned, but I could see concern behind her eyes.

"Please, Lily, I'm in no state for your teasing at present." She walked over to me, real concern etching her face now.

"Are you truly ill, Jane?"

"I'm well enough," I said with a sigh. "May I solicit your help this evening, though?"

"Of course." Lily sat on my bed and watched me expectantly as I began to pace.

"I just really need this evening to go well with Frederick." I dropped his formal name as Lily was the only one around.

"Has something happened?" Her expression was unreadable. "A quarrel, perhaps?"

"No, nothing like that."

"Is he showing his regard for another woman?"

"No—I just—" I exhaled. "Lily, I need to secure Frederick sooner than later. More now than ever before." I was beginning to worry that if he didn't propose soon, I would choose to forfeit my hard work altogether. Something was changing in me and it was not part of my plans.

Lily narrowed her eyes, then just as quickly softened them, giving me a reassuring smile. "I know just the thing," she said, smoothing her skirt. "I will do my best to have Frederick seated across from you at the table this evening so you can see each other easily."

"That would be helpful, Lily. Thank you." I bit my lip. "Could you do one other thing for me?"

"Of course."

"Will you keep Lord Elliot distracted?"

"If you wish me to." She gave me a quizzical look. "Might I ask why?"

"Frederick and Lord Elliot have a difficult history. If Frederick sees me talking with Lord Elliot and there is any sort of friendliness between us, he may see it as a betrayal. It could upend everything I've been working for."

"If Frederick would truly toss you away for something so petty, he's not worth having."

"Lily, I don't expect you to understand. I'm just asking for your help."

"And what of Lord Elliot?" She raised an eyebrow.

"What do you mean?" I asked evenly.

"Would he not be a safer man to secure?" Her expression held no teasing. "If Frederick is truly so easily swayed, why not try for Lord Elliot instead?"

I laughed. "Lily, Lord Elliot will have his pick of any woman he wishes for. He flirts with every woman he meets; he uses his charm on every single one of them. Furthermore, they are all besotted with him. I would never feel safe pursuing such a match. Frederick at least pursues only me."

"And do you have feelings for Lord Elliot?" Lily watched me carefully.

"You know how I feel about this, Lily." My heart pounded.

"That doesn't answer my question." She looked at me with anticipation. "Do you have feelings for him or not?"

I didn't know how to answer. I didn't even dare ask myself the question she was posing, for I feared what I would find. I needed her to stop prodding.

I exhaled with frustration. "He and I have only just begun to tolerate one another. We have recently agreed to put our differences aside, and although I don't want to lose Frederick, I do value Lord Elliot's company and friendship. I would very much like to keep it that way."

Lily smirked. "You still didn't answer my question, Jane. But—" She studied me. "I will help you tonight as best I can."

"Thank you." My shoulders relaxed. "I feel better knowing that someone understands me and is willing to help."

"Understands you? Not quite," Lily said with a grin. "Willing to help? Always." She walked to my door. "I'll be ready to find a way to get Frederick to sit across from you tonight, . . . and I'll do my best to distract Lord Elliot for you." She closed the door as she left, leaving nothing but my own thoughts to keep me company.

Lily was true to her word. She managed to keep Charles occupied before we were seated for dinner. I talked with Frederick and a small group of guests. He kept looking over at Charles with annoyance.

I reminded myself, again, that I wanted to be near Frederick. Pretending Charles was *not* across the room, charming smile in tow, was something I could manage, I lied to myself, glancing his way. His eyes were already on mine, as if he had been waiting for me to simply look over. He gave me a warm smile. I returned it, then quickly looked away, returning my attention to Frederick, afraid he would notice.

Dinner was finally announced and as we walked into the dining room, the chairs gradually filled. I glanced at Lily, who gave me a reassuring look. She would help me. I slowly walked around to the other side of the table and took my seat near the far end. It would be easier that way for Lily to strategically place Frederick and herself. If everything went according to plan, he would sit across from me, and Lily would sit at my side.

I breathed out a sigh of relief when Charles took his seat near Uncle Francis toward the head of the table. Lily quickly directed her attention to Frederick. She talked with him as she made her way toward the end of the table across from me, navigating a path for him to be seated. He took his seat where I hoped he would and I felt part of my tension dissipate as Lily walked around the back corner, taking a seat next to me.

"Thank you, Lily," I whispered.

"I'm glad I could help," she whispered back. "Though it was a headache to try and pull more than two words from Lord Fletcher. I can't understand how you can bear him."

"He's better with conversation once you get to know him," I lied.

She shook her head. "Don't lie to me, Jane. You put on a good face to the public and hide your emotions well, but you've always been a terrible liar. I would prefer you to be truthful about Lord Fletcher and tell me he is as dull as ever and that you are somehow fine with it. But if you lie to me, I will start to worry about why you are lying." Her curt whispers were starting to draw attention.

"Do I get to be in on the secret?" a deep voice said on my other side.

My breath hitched. His voice was committed to memory. Without needing to look, I knew that Charles was sitting next to me on my other side. I looked toward Uncle Francis and found that Mrs. Bagley, an elderly widow, was now seated in Charles's original place. Frederick looked furious as I made eye contact with him. I didn't know what to say.

Frederick gave Charles an icy look. "Mrs. Bagley may be charmed by your chivalry, but I know you never do anything unless it benefits yourself somehow." He said it quietly so only those nearest him could hear.

Charles smirked. "A selfish being only sees others as selfish. Therefore, it only makes sense that you would view it that way." It looked as though Frederick was trying to burn a hole through Charles with his glare. I looked down at my plate, unsure of what to do.

I was touched that Charles gave his seat up for Mrs. Bagley. She was a kind lady, and attention from Lord Elliot was sure to make her entire evening. I looked over at Mrs. Bagley, who appeared to be in high spirits indeed. I glanced once more at Frederick, who was staring at me flatly. This time, however, there was a question behind it. A wave of panic came knocking. Was he questioning my loyalty? I tried to give him a look of reassurance but he looked away from me and began talking with the gentleman seated next to him. My stomach began twisting in knots again.

"Jane?" Charles's voice came out quietly so only I would hear. I finally dared a glance in his direction. Concern marked his features. "What is it?" he asked.

His sincerity was palpable. Why did he have to make it so difficult? It was his fault I was in this mess. I wanted him near me, and yet his nearness made it impossible for me to succeed. "Jane, please don't look at me like that unless you tell me exactly how to fix whatever is the matter." He spoke so quietly, so gently.

I couldn't help but glance at Frederick again to see if he was watching me. He looked my way one more time, then at Charles with a flat, icy stare, before he looked away. My stomach completely dropped.

I hardly noticed when the first course was served.

Charles watched my agitation as I looked at Frederick. "Why?" His tone was quiet.

His question confused me. As I looked up at him, his eyes searched mine. "Why Lord Fletcher?" His tone did not carry censure like it had in the past. "I don't wish to cause you further distress. I just need to understand why." He talked with a quiet, soothing voice. "I know you don't trust me fully, and I'm not asking you to. But will you at least trust me with this?"

I looked back at my plate and moved the food around.

"Do you really love him?" His voice was guarded.

"Charles, please," I whispered as I continued to move my food around on my plate without eating any of it. "Not right now."

Charles watched my movements with amusement. His mouth twitched into a small grin. "That's an unusual way to eat."

I looked up at him and his attempt to lighten my mood.

Charles changed his look to one of camaraderie. "If Lord Fletcher has hurt you, I can always make him pay for it." He raised an eyebrow. "I won't even charge you."

I couldn't help but grin. "What a relief. I can't imagine what you might ask for as payment the next time I'm in your debt."

"The next time? Do you plan to make a habit of it?"

"Certainly not. But you have a knack for getting me out of tight spots. It appears as though I can't escape it."

"I'm glad to hear it. I'll be thinking of your next payment so we don't waste any time. Would you like to make payments in advance?"

"And what could you possibly want from me now?" I asked.

He looked at me intently. "A smile, Jane." I felt Charles's hand carefully brush mine beneath the table where nobody could see. My breath caught as tingles ran up my arm. He slowly turned my palm upward, then placed something in my hand before his retreated back in place.

I looked down at my hand and saw a large, yellow leaf. I looked back at Charles in confusion, and then understanding dawned. "This couldn't possibly be the one that—"

"Does this mean I get my wish?" he said with a grin.

"Are you telling me you actually watched it fall?" I asked skeptically.

"I did," he said with a smile. "It fell this afternoon. And now I've brought it to you so you can make your wish."

I couldn't help the smile that overtook me. I was so touched by Lord Elliot's gesture. The most beautiful arrangement of flowers wouldn't mean as much to me as this one leaf.

"I'm glad you pay your debts quickly." Charles glanced from my eyes to my smile. "But your payment won't count if your smile retreats again this evening. Will it be staying?"

As I looked at Charles once more, I realized I was standing on the precipice of something dangerous. Something that called me from just beyond its edge. If I got too close, I would surely fall in. I knew there would be no returning once I did.

I looked at Frederick again, renewing my plans. I wouldn't fall in. I would be careful. I wouldn't stand on the very edge, but skirt its safer ledges with care, for just this one evening. Tonight I would enjoy Charles's company, his smiles and charm. Tomorrow I would return to my stronghold of predictability and comfort. Tomorrow I would keep Charles at a distance.

I brought myself back to his question and smiled as I examined the leaf under the table. It was beautiful. "My smile will be staying," I said, continuing to keep my eyes averted downward. "And this wish is perfect." I spoke quietly so only he could hear. I could feel Charles's eyes on me once again. As I glanced up at him, something passed between us that I couldn't put into words. All I knew was I couldn't pull my eyes from his.

"Keep it safe for the both of us," he finally said, looking down at my hands.

"I will."

Lily

I watched as Jane and Lord Elliot had a quiet conversation. Jane's look of dread slowly turned until eventually, she was smiling. Frederick periodically looked at them with his unreadable expression. Things were running more smoothly than I'd anticipated. We moved through the courses of the meal, and I spoke with a gentleman seated next to me named Mr. Graves. He was handsome and kind, but I found that our conversation made me miss Henry's company even more.

A servant appeared by my side and extended his arm until I could see a letter resting on a silver plate. "This just arrived for you, miss," he said quietly.

Jane looked over at me, questioning.

There was no name on the outside. My heart pounded as I discreetly opened it up, trying to remain calm. I anticipated what Henry might say—my heart faltered. I knew the handwriting. It wasn't Henry's; it was from Mr. Johnson.

Miss Mason,
I wish to speak to you about a private matter alone. I will call on you tomorrow afternoon.
I will think of you until then, my Golden Eagle.
Matthew Johnson

Panic took control as I read his letter over again. "A private matter alone" could mean only one thing: he planned to propose tomorrow. Jane looked at my face with concern.

"Lily, now *you* look ill. What ever is the matter?"

"Mr. Johnson," I whispered, handing her the letter.

She read its contents. "Eventually you will have to face him, Lily. Better to have it over with sooner rather than later."

"I'm not ready, Jane. I don't wish to hurt or offend him, but I could never accept his proposal. I need more time to think about how I can kindly refuse his offer. I will write to him immediately and explain that I will be away tomorrow afternoon."

"If you believe that is truly the best course—"

"I do." Excusing myself as discreetly as I could manage, I made my way to the library, sat at Uncle Francis' desk, snatched a piece of parchment and quill, and quickly wrote my letter.

Mr. Johnson,
I will be away tomorrow afternoon. I apologize for the inconvenience.
Miss Mason

I walked into the entryway where George waited. "Could you please have this delivered promptly, George?"

"Certainly, miss." He took the missive from my hand, then placed another small envelope in my palm. "And this just arrived for you as well."

"Thank you, George." I returned to the library, turning it over to look at the sender—There was none. My heart quickened again, despite my efforts to talk it down. I opened the envelope, faltering. There was no message inside. But it still held weight, so I turned it upside down and something small fell out, hitting the table below me with a small 'ping.'

I smiled as I picked it up: tuppence.

I quietly left the house and tiptoed to the back garden, hoping Henry would be there again. When I arrived at the opening of the shrubs where we had met last time, I inched forward, feeling my way through the darkness of the evening. It took only a brief moment before someone took my hand and carefully led me inside. My heart thudded as I followed blindly. It had to be Henry.

After a few paces, I felt him step close to me and whisper quietly near my ear. "Don't speak for a moment." His light breath on my neck sent a tingling sensation throughout my body. I held my breath and listened. It was then that I could faintly detect two men speaking somewhere on the street behind the garden.

A voice full of frustration said, "No, Fairhurst, I don't agree with your practices."

"Do you truly believe you could do better?" a cold voice asked.

"I'm not as practiced as you, perhaps, but at least I'm honest."

"What makes you think you can cast judgment of that magnitude on me?"

"Because I've seen it more than once now. I saw it just now when you turned a blind eye to that woman who was beaten, but wrote the report as though she was drunk and fell down a flight of stairs. And I saw it when you claimed that a death was from natural causes when there were clearly signs of poison. Are you receiving compensation for writing these false reports?"

A slight scuffle was heard. "You keep your nose out of my business," the man named Fairhurst said. "You have a good future ahead of you as my apprentice. Don't ruin your chances."

As my eyes adjusted to the darkness, I looked at Henry, realizing his gaze was already on me. He put a finger up to his lips to indicate I should continue to remain silent. I nodded. The sound of footsteps retreated, and the two men's voices slowly faded.

Henry slowly took my hand and led me farther into the shrubs. He guided me toward him until we were close enough to hear each other's hushed whispers.

"If we could hear those men speaking, then there is a chance others will hear us," Henry said near my ear.

I turned my lips towards his ear, grinning. "Isn't it interesting how one can be minding one's own business only to accidentally overhear sensitive information?"

"We could have made some noise to alert them that they had an audience," he whispered with a smile. His nearness was making it difficult to think clearly.

In the darkness I saw the faint outline of his smile fade. "The information we just overheard was troubling, don't you think?"

"Indeed. Do you know who those gentlemen were?" I asked.

"I have an idea. We will discuss it later."

"I have new information for you," I said, leaning in again.

"Already?" He sounded impressed. "Unfortunately, I think it may have to wait."

"Then why did you summon me?"

"Because I have some new information for you as well. There is a guest at your dinner party tonight. Robert Graves."

That was the name of the gentleman who was seated next to me. "Yes. I met Mr. Graves at dinner."

"I noticed," he whispered.

I grinned. "Are you watching me, Henry?"

"It's hard not to watch you when you are attending the same party as the subject of my investigation. Especially when he sits right next to you and you smile at him." He notched an eyebrow.

"And why wouldn't I smile at him?" I teased. "He is kind and handsome."

"And are you willing to fall for any man that meets that description?" He leaned in even closer. I couldn't see his expression in the dark but I could hear his teasing tone behind his words. I had only been cordial to Mr. Graves, and my smile had been one reserved for polite conversation and nothing more.

I turned to his ear again. "What do you think?"

"I think that perhaps I enjoy it better when you are out here helping me."

"Then how can I help you?"

"Unfortunately, it involves you going back inside to talk with Mr. Graves."

"You could always come with me," I countered, lifting a corner of my mouth.

"Don't tempt me, Lily." He regarded me, considering. "Mr. Graves was seen doing business with Jacob Hughes recently, though no one knows what type of business it was. There are no descriptions on his ledgers."

"How do you know what his ledgers look like?" I asked, raising an eyebrow.

"I have my ways," he said with a grin. "And I know you have your ways as well. Could you ask Mr. Graves about what type of business he conducts?"

"Am I allowed to use my smile?" I teased.

"Sparingly." His lips twitched as he tried to suppress a smile. Holding his position, he laced his fingers around mine, making my stomach flutter, then carefully brought my hand closer to his chest, using his other fingers to gently remove my ring from the place he had put it last. "Meet me here again before the evening ends," he whispered, making my ring disappear.

I smiled as my heart raced. "If you insist."

14

WHIST

Jane

The knots in my stomach finally settled and I was able to enjoy the dinner courses. Frederick stopped looking my way and I found that I didn't mind. I could try and smooth things over later. It wasn't my fault that Charles sat by me, and it wasn't Charles's fault that Mrs. Bagley needed a seat closer to the door.

"Jane, do you miss Wilton?" Charles asked quietly, ensuring no one else could hear.

I looked up from my plate. "I do miss Wilton."

"And what is it that you miss the most?"

"My family." I smiled. "My brothers, Sterling and Oliver, are usually up to some bit of mischief."

"How old are they?"

"Sterling will be thirteen next year and Oliver is almost eleven. My parents plan to send Sterling to Eton soon. Oliver will be absolutely miserable without him."

"I can understand that sentiment," Charles said with fondness.

"Lily and I used to bribe them to steal pastries from the kitchen for us," I said, smirking. "Sometimes we joined in on the fun too."

"Did you ever get caught?" Charles grinned.

I chuckled. "Every time I helped. They usually wanted me to distract Cook. But Cook would take one look at me and know I was up to no good. Eventually Sterling and Oliver said I couldn't help anymore."

Charles laughed quietly and looked down at my hand beneath the table that was twirling the yellow leaf through my fingers. "Perhaps you should wish to restore your honor as a pastry thief."

"Together, Lily and I would make a fierce team," I said with a smile. "The pirate and the pastry thief."

"I am a professional kitchen thief myself." Charles wagged his eyebrows conspiratorially. "If you let me join your crew, you won't regret it. I come in handy in a pinch." Holding his fork beneath the table so only I could see, he rotated it through his fingers, then suddenly made it disappear. He then returned the fork to its original position.

I smiled in sheer delight, trying to bite it down, but failed miserably. "Lord Elliot, you may certainly join our crew."

He grinned. "What a relief." He looked at my smile for a moment before looking at my eyes again. My stomach fluttered at the gesture, reminding me that we weren't the only ones in the room. I looked up at Frederick, praying he wouldn't be paying attention—he wasn't looking at me. Hopefully he hadn't noticed what had just transpired between Charles and me. Thankfully, everyone else seemed busy with their own conversations. I returned my focus to the food in front of me.

"Jane." Lord Elliot's smooth voice resonated throughout me. I couldn't help but be drawn to him—just like every other woman in London.

I finally looked at him. "Yes?"

"May I see you tomorrow? If I'm not mistaken, you still owe me a carriage ride."

I hadn't expected those words to come next. I looked at Frederick once more. He still didn't meet my gaze. I was treading dangerous waters already; accepting a carriage ride from Charles would surely make things worse.

Charles followed my line of sight, landing on Frederick. "He doesn't own you," he said quietly.

"If I go with you, he will see it as a betrayal." I didn't mean to say the words, but they came out anyway.

"Let him see it that way, then. Let him fight for you."

"He doesn't love me. He would never fight for me. It's beneath him."

"And do you love him?" His eyes held mine, silence following.

"Our connection is not about love." Apparently I couldn't keep my mouth shut. "He knows I don't love him, just as I know he doesn't love me."

"Then what is it about?"

"My family is not well liked in many social circles, Lord Elliot." I felt myself stiffen as the words escaped me. It was painful bringing up old wounds. It made me feel vulnerable. How had I let down so many walls? I quickly started throwing them all back up. I grabbed my poise, my decorum. I snatched logic, my practiced smile in tow. I pulled them close to me. I clung to my list of reasons why I couldn't be around Charles—

My heart suddenly pitched as I felt Charles's fingers brush across my hand and take the leaf. It was then that I noticed I was crushing it with my fingers. My breath caught as I looked at the perfect wish I'd ruined.

"Don't retreat, Jane." He said it so quietly I wondered if he had even said it at all. When I found his gaze again, his eyes willed me to stay, to let my walls fall. It wasn't fair. My stronghold was no match for his ability to tear it down piece by piece. I felt helpless. The worst part was that in this moment, as much as I wanted to be safe and weld my fortress back together, I wanted him to find a way to pull it down.

He slowly pulled his hand away, still holding the leaf that was now crinkled. "You can trust me," he said quietly." Don't think that just because I take life with smiles and humor I can't be serious. Tell me what you were going to say about your family. I will keep it safe."

I had never wanted to confide in anyone other than Lily before. How strange that now I wanted to confide in this man I'd considered my foe mere days ago. I took in a slow breath and waited in silence for a moment before I finally spoke.

"My family, my parents specifically, have been laughed at, mocked, and disrespected since we entered high-class society. We grew up with little money, though we never went completely without. What money my parents did have went towards our education.

"Though I was very happy, and loved my childhood, I always wanted more. I wanted just one more dress than my old, worn-out one. I wanted ribbons for my bonnet and new gloves. Then suddenly my father came into a large sum of money. All the things I wanted were suddenly at my fingertips.

"I was so excited to go to my first ball. I was only sixteen then. My parents were being introduced to some new circles and decided to bring me along. I had a lovely new ball gown, new gloves, and jewels in my hair. I'd never felt so beautiful." I gave a soft smile at the memory. Charles's eyes hadn't left me once while I relayed the details. Once I started, I was unable to hold back the rest of my story.

"A girl named Margaret was introduced to me," I said quietly.

"Margaret Talbot?" Charles asked, creasing his brows.

I nodded my head. "Yes, Margaret Talbot."

Charles shook his head and quirked an eyebrow. "I'm sure she was all sweetness," he said facetiously.

The corner of my mouth turned up. "Oh, yes. She certainly was. At first she said, 'Aren't you such a pretty little thing?' Of course I was flattered by her kind words." I could see by Charles's expression that he knew where the conversation was going.

I looked down at my plate. "She proceeded to introduce me to her friends. Among her friends was a 'dashing young man.' "

Charles smirked. "You only thought he was dashing because you hadn't met me yet."

I chuckled. "Phillip Wood most likely disagrees."

"Yes, I suppose he would. His face reeks of arrogance, and he certainly appears to think he's swoonworthy." He hit the nail right on the head.

I nodded. "The first time I met him, he flattered me, speaking of my beauty. Of course I was taken by his words. Margaret then looked at my parents across the room and said to all of her friends, 'I can see that our hosts have invited the entertainment for the evening. I could practically smell the pigs as they entered. I wonder if they even know how to hold a conversation? Perhaps if I bring a chicken next time they'll feel more at home.' "

I stopped talking. It was a painful memory to relive. Charles's hand moved over mine once more. When I looked up at him, there was no teasing in his look.

"Keep going," he said quietly before he removed his fingers.

I let out a breath. "All her friends laughed at my parents then looked at me. I was suddenly filled with embarrassment. I assumed she hadn't been aware that they were my parents—otherwise she wouldn't have been so openly rude. I wanted to shrink away, but I also wanted to defend Mama and Papa. They were nothing to be embarrassed by and I wanted them to succeed in society.

"At first I tried to handle it diplomatically. I spoke quietly to her and stated that she must not have been aware that they were my parents, and that she wouldn't say such things if she knew them. She laughed at me with mock pity, then said loudly, 'Of course I knew they were your parents. How else could you explain your gown that must be from two seasons ago?' She gave me the prettiest little pout, then finished by saying, 'You may be wealthy now, Miss Mason, but money isn't everything. You can buy as many pretty ball gowns as you want, but you will always stand out as an intruder in high-class society. You are not well connected, nor do you have a title.' The rest of the group held looks of haughtiness and condescension after she spoke, and then Mr. Wood said, ''Tis a shame, Miss Mason. You really are a beauty.' "

I stared at my plate as I finished the last part of my unpleasant memory. I could feel Lord Elliot's eyes on me.

I dared a glance at him. He held an expression that was a mixture of understanding and frustration. It looked like he was holding back. Like he wanted to reach out and touch me. His next words came out barely above a whisper.

"And now you think Lord Fletcher will save you from it all." He didn't pose it as a question.

I nodded. "After that occurrence, I had a hard time making friends. But it only fueled my desire to protect my family and my own station.

I have decided to climb the social ladder high enough that no one can touch my name or my family. My mother is an angel and my father is more worthy of praise than any man I know, yet they are ridiculed. I, too, am often treated with coldness from the upper class. Marriage to Lord Fletcher would change all of it. I could breathe easily knowing my parents would be respected—that my mother would be treated with the kindness she deserves. I myself would no longer be met with hostility."

"And would you be happy then, Jane?" he asked. "Society is not kind. To be accepted among those you describe is to become one of them. Do your parents expect you to make this alliance for your family's sake?"

"No. They have encouraged me to pursue whatever course makes me happy. But seeing them treated well *would* make me happy."

"You have a pure heart." He glanced at me, then looked down at his plate. "I loathe the idea of it being tarnished by Frederick."

"He is not so terrible."

Charles raised an eyebrow, clearly disagreeing.

I sighed. "I need him to secure my family's future."

"Do you believe that Frederick will truly do all of that for you? That he will be kind to your family? Treat them with the love and respect you are looking for? If your parents are as you've described, I believe they would much prefer to be loved and cherished rather than raised up on a pedestal by hypocrites. Society tears down each of us in some fashion or another."

"They don't tear *you* down," I said resolutely. "Society loves you; you appear to love society."

"I assure you, they try to tear me down. Frederick has been trying to do it this very evening." He grinned. "But I've been playing this game for a long time. I love people, Jane, not society. Yet people are what make up society. To say that I love society would be akin to stating I love every single person in it. I assure you that is not the case.

"When I find the people who are worth keeping around, I keep them around. When I find those who tear down others, I keep them at a distance. It is true that there are those who would esteem your family as more valuable if you formed an alliance with Frederick. But are those truly the people you want your family to associate with?"

It sounded so simple when he put it that way. But I was already in too deep with Frederick. There were still rules and reputations to uphold. No gentlemen had even attempted pursuing me since he had. Perhaps it was because they felt it was futile going up against the son of a duke. In either case, the ton acted as though Frederick had already claimed me. If I decided to leave that safety net now and turn down his attention toward me, I was sure to be seen as fickle and foolhardy. No man would dare pursue me after that. And yet I couldn't help but hear the truth in what Charles was saying. Although I didn't believe Frederick would disrespect my family, he would never love or cherish them either. At best, he would tolerate them.

Charles gave me a look of unrepentant mischief. "What do you say, Jane? May I claim you tomorrow morning?"

"What if I say no?" I teased.

"I will just keep pestering you until you say yes . . . or until George has me thrown from the house. Besides, you won't be able to eat unless you agree." A look of amusement touched his eyes.

I looked down at my plate and found that all my utensils were missing. I bit down my laugh. "I see I have no choice."

"That's what happens when you let a thief join your crew."

"How could I resist?"

"I am hard to resist," he said with his most charming smile. "May I collect you tomorrow morning?"

I smiled. "I'll be ready."

"So will I." He handed my utensils back under the table. "And I guarantee that it will be more than just suitable."

Lily

Upon reentering the dining room, I noticed that the window at the far end of the table was cracked open slightly. I smiled at it, knowing

Henry was most likely on the other side gleaning what he could from the conversations in the room. He would have a fairly good view of Mr. Graves and me. I pulled my chair out and took my place again next to the gentleman. We fell into easy conversation. In truth, he appeared to be anything but sinister. Thus far he had talked about his home life, upcoming inventions, and horses.

"I'm a bit of a horse racer myself," he said with enthusiasm. "Nothing serious, of course. But I do love to compete now and again in local events. Do you ride, Miss Mason?"

I lit up. "I love riding. I would definitely be a poor competitor in a race, but there is such a feeling of freedom and exhilaration being astride a horse in full run."

He smiled at me, a dimple forming. "I couldn't agree more. Do you enjoy any other sports, Miss Mason?" He truly seemed interested.

"If you include climbing trees, then yes."

He laughed at my response. "And are you quite proficient?"

I grinned. "Absolutely." I couldn't be certain, but in my periphery I thought I saw the window push up ever so slightly. I decided to try and get to the meat of our conversation. "Mr. Graves, what sort of employ do you undertake?" I gave him a warm smile.

He smiled in return, looking at my smile for a prolonged moment, and then flinched suddenly.

"What is it?" I asked, noticing his shock.

He looked down at his lap and picked up a tiny rounded stone, clearly surprised. "I believe this pebble just hit me."

I looked at his face. A small red mark appeared near his cheek bone. I looked to the cracked window and raised an eyebrow. Henry was toying with Mr. Graves.

"Are you hurt?" I asked.

"No, it's nothing." He smiled at me again. He was kind and attentive . . . and handsome. In essence, exactly the type of gentleman that would have turned my head before I'd met Henry—but I *had* met Henry, and now it was hard to think of little else.

"Where were we?" Mr. Graves asked.

I resumed my task at hand. "I was just asking what type of business you undertake."

"It is quite interesting, actually," he said with some excitement. "I am an apothecary of sorts. I mostly specialize in using herbs for medicines, draughts, and remedies for a variety of ailments and infirmities. But I have also recently made a hobby of blending fragrances for perfumes with my herbs. It has been more successful than I anticipated."

"How did you come to be an apothecary?"

"I have an uncle here in London who is in the trade. He took me on as a student and I have since made it my living."

"And do you find satisfaction in your work?"

"Indeed, I do." He smiled.

"Mr. Hughes finds satisfaction in your work as well," I said matter of factly.

"Mr. Hughes?" A crease formed between Mr. Graves's eyes.

"Yes. I believe it was you that he recommended."

"Jacob Hughes recommended me?" he asked skeptically. "And was he open about why he solicited my services?"

"I believe so. Perhaps I'm mistaken. Are you not familiar with Mr. Hughes?"

Mr. Graves focused on his fork. "I am familiar with the man you are referring to, though I cannot fathom why a lady such as yourself would be. I'm further surprised that he confided in you the details of his foot odor condition, as he seemed very embarrassed by it and wanted to ensure it remained a secret."

I tried to bite down a grin. "I am not as familiar with the gentleman as you may think. I was talking amongst a group of people at a party, and he did not share with us the exact details of why he recommended you. Just that you were a miracle worker."

"I see." His features formed into a look of embarrassment. "Miss Mason, I was not supposed to volunteer Mr. Hughes's condition. Do I have your word to keep it a secret?"

"Certainly," I said. It was good to know that Mr. Hughes was embarrassed about something. I looked toward the open window and gave a slight nod. Hopefully Henry understood my meaning. I had received the information from Mr. Graves, and I would be out again shortly.

Once dinner was finished, the men made their way to a separate room for some port while the ladies gathered in the sitting room with a pianoforte and some tables for playing cards. I found Jane and we took a seat on one of the sofas.

"I'm sorry things didn't go according to plan," I said to Jane quietly. "I hadn't the faintest idea that Lord Elliot would end up sitting by you when he had already found a seat." It was the truth. Though I had been scheming up a way to get Lord Elliot to somehow sit by Jane, it appeared as though my plotting was unnecessary.

"Thank you for trying to help me, Lily."

"Will you be alright? Frederick seemed more cold than usual."

"I admit that I dread facing him now. I believe he thinks me a traitor."

"It'll smooth over in no time." I gave her a reassuring look.

I prayed it would not, in fact, smooth over. Watching Lord Elliot and Jane at dinner was very telling. He brought something out in her that I hadn't seen in a long time.

My gaze shifted to the window. I found that I continued glancing at it, looking for Henry, which was silly since we were no longer on the base level and there was no way he could watch any longer.

"You were gone for a while at dinner, Lily. Was your response to Mr. Johnson long?"

I already felt guilty about keeping my secrets from Jane. I didn't want to blatantly lie to her as well. "No. My response was short. I needed a quick breath of fresh air before I returned." I looked at Jane. "And don't you dare scold me for taking a turn about our own, very small, private garden."

Jane smiled. "I won't. I could use a good turn about the garden myself."

I felt panic at the thought of Jane going out to the garden when Henry was out there. "I believe it might rain," I lied.

"I didn't mean tonight, Lily." She said with a chuckle. Then, grinning, she added, "You and Mr. Graves appeared deep in conversation."

"Yes. I enjoyed his company."

She raised her eyebrows. "And what is your opinion of him?"

"He is everything a gentleman should be." I knew what she was implying, but it was no use.

"And?" She looked at me expectantly.

"I'm sorry, Jane, but that's all I have to say about him. I believe he and I would get along well, and he is handsome. But I don't have feelings for him more than that."

"Oh." Jane looked surprised. "Do you believe you could develop feelings for him?"

"I really don't think I could." I needed to turn the conversation. "And what of you and Lord Elliot?"

"What do you mean?" Jane asked quietly.

"Can you honestly tell me that you would prefer to be in Frederick's company over Lord Elliot's?" I whispered.

Jane opened her mouth, but said nothing.

Aunt Mary suddenly spoke from across the room. "And what are the two of you whispering about? Some bit of gossip, I hope."

"No gossip this time, Aunt Mary." I gave her an apologetic smile. "Sorry to disappoint you."

"Then what are you both looking so secretive about?"

"Nothing of consequence," Jane said evenly.

"If it's nothing of consequence, then you won't mind sharing it." Aunt Mary was ever persistent.

Jane looked at me expectantly.

"We were speaking of Mr. Graves's herbal perfumes," I said, grasping for straws.

"And why would you be secretive about that?" she asked.

"Because," Jane stepped in, "Lily and I were debating which scent was most likely to attract men."

"Oh heavens!" She put a hand to her chest. "That is an interesting debate. I'm sure we would all like to participate."

A wave of relief washed over Jane's face as the women in the room began discussing what they believed would be the most alluring scent for a man. The debate slowly turned into a conversation about London's latest fashion, then lulled into easy talk about nothing in particular. It was the perfect time for me to excuse myself to "use the privy."

It took everything in me not to run to the garden. I walked as quickly as I could without drawing attention to myself. This time I found Henry waiting for me on the secluded bench. His figure in the dark was mysterious and inviting. He stood and extended his hand out to the bench, offering me a seat. I smiled and sat. There was no backrest to the bench, so he sat in the opposite direction so we could face each other.

He leaned close to my ear, speaking so quietly I had to listen carefully. "What did you discover other than the fact that Robert Graves is clearly smitten with you?"

I rolled my eyes, then whispered back, "Mr. Graves is an herbal apothecary. He makes remedies and perfumes." I then added, "And I did not find him to be smitten."

"And does his business seem to be untoward? Secretive?"

"No, actually. His business seems very honest and straightforward. Someone else's business, however, was to try and ruin my progress by hurling rocks at him from an open window." I leaned back slightly and gave Henry an accusatory look before I leaned forward to my original position.

"It was clear he was straying from the topic you were trying to discuss. . . . " He leaned in close to my ear, grinning. "And I didn't like the way he was looking at you."

"He was only being polite," I argued.

He cocked an eyebrow and gave me a look that told me he didn't buy it. "I don't trust him. He appeared secretive to me."

"He was very open about his business. And when I stated that Mr. Hughes recommended him, he seemed surprised that I would associate with such a man. Anyone who doesn't like Mr. Hughes gets at least a few mentions in their favor, wouldn't you agree? On top of that, he accidentally let it slip that Mr. Hughes has a foot condition. Apparently he is quite embarrassed about it."

I sensed Henry smile near my ear. "It would explain why Jacob has always smelled foul."

I laughed quietly. "How fitting."

"Indeed." He rested his hand on the bench next to mine. "You said you have information for me, but I believe you must get back before people notice you are missing."

"Will you meet me here tomorrow?" I asked, trying not to sound as desperate as I felt.

"Not tomorrow," he whispered in my ear. "Meet me on the north terrace at the Morgans' ball."

"I will try to come alone."

"No," he said quietly, but firmly. "Come with a chaperone. Walk along the west side of the path. If I can't think of a way to talk with you alone, we will figure something else out." He looked down at our hands, almost touching. "This is the last time I can meet you here in this garden. We are putting too much at risk if we continue to do so."

My stomach plummeted. "I am careful, Henry."

He looked at me, considering. But he slowly shook his head. "It's not up for negotiation."

I sighed quietly.

He leaned closer to me. "I didn't know you like to ride, Lily." His nearness sent tingles down my neck, spreading throughout my entire being. It took me a moment to realize he was referring to the conversation I'd had with Mr. Graves about riding horseback.

I quieted my breathing. "I love riding. It's one of the things I miss most about Wilton."

Henry gave me a look of satisfaction. "One day I will take you riding and show you the best places on horseback in Wilton." A thought planted itself in my mind. If Henry knew all the best places in Wilton, he must either be from Wilton himself or have visited frequently. Maybe he really was related to Lord Elliot; it would certainly explain their uncanny similarities in appearance.

"And what do you love most about Wilton?" I asked quietly in his ear.

He was silent for a moment. "The past." He said the words so quietly I almost didn't hear them.

"What do you miss about the past?" I held my breath, hoping he would reveal something about his identity.

I sensed him grin. "Nice try, Lily."

I sighed in mild frustration.

"I have something else to discuss," he said quietly. "Those two gentlemen we overheard earlier. It seemed to be a physician and the man studying under him to eventually take his place." I nodded my head in agreement. He continued, "If Lord Elliot was murdered, the most likely cause would have been poison. The apprentice stated that the physician falsely reported signs of poison at some point. I believe it's time for me to pay a visit to this apprentice."

"Just be careful, Henry." I meant to hide the concern in my voice, but it was all too obvious as the words came out.

He grinned, lips close to my ear. I could practically feel them against my skin, making me shudder with pleasure. His next words came out low and gravelly. "I'll be careful when you admit that Robert Graves isn't well suited for you."

"I never said he was well suited for me," I said breathlessly. I couldn't think straight. His face was close to mine.

He reached over and lifted my hand. He made my ring appear in his other hand, then let it fall loosely on my pinky. "Good," he whispered with a grin. "Until next time."

He was gone before I had time or sense to form a complete sentence.

Jane

Lily had been gone too long. I was getting dreadfully bored, and was about to excuse myself when she finally reentered the room, flushed, a reserved smile brewing beneath her calm exterior.

She glanced at the other door the men would eventually be coming through as she approached me. "I see the men are still enjoying their port," she said casually. As if in answer to her comment, the door opened. Uncle Francis entered first, followed by Mr. Graves. They shared a look of amusement as they found their way into the room. The rest of the gentlemen filed in, Charles and Frederick emerging last.

They were speaking back and forth in clipped tones. "You may have everyone else fooled, but I know exactly who you are," Frederick said bitterly. "You're a pompous coward. "

"What's this?" Aunt Mary asked, aghast.

"Nothing of consequence," Charles said reassuringly to Aunt Mary. "I confronted Lord Fletcher for personal reasons, and he challenged me to a duel this very moment. I take no issue with this, save for the fact that there are ladies present, and it would do his Lordship's ego no good to be bested by his foe."

I put my fingers to my mouth in surprise as I imagined them dueling. I hated the very thought.

"Come now," Aunt Mary said with shock. "Might we handle this with a little more civility?" She looked at Lily and me for help. "Perhaps a game of whist. The loser must undertake a form of punishment and admit defeat," she finished.

Charles gave Aunt Mary his winning smile. "An excellent plan, Mrs. Mason. And as you are the hostess, it is only fitting that you should select the form of punishment."

"Very well, Lord Elliot. I accept," she said with a smile.

Charles looked over to Frederick with a look of mischief. "What do you say?"

Frederick gave his usual flat stare. "It appears I have no choice." I quietly breathed a sigh of relief.

The room gathered for the game of whist. I didn't know whether I wanted Charles to win or lose. I was trying to find reasons to stay away from him. He was too . . . everything. Too charming, too handsome, too observant, too intriguing, too magnetic. It would be nice to add "too unlucky" to that list so there could be just one thing he wasn't good at. On the other hand, I wanted to see Charles win. I wanted to see him smile and laugh and, ironically enough, pester Frederick.

It was beginning to amuse me the way Charles handled him. Everyone else I met thus far tended to skirt around Frederick and do his every bidding because he was the son of a duke. Charles had no rules in that regard; it was refreshing.

Lily

Jane hadn't been exaggerating. Lord Elliot and Frederick clearly had a history of rivalry. Lord Elliot hid it well; Frederick was an open book. The game began and Frederick quickly took the lead. He wore a smug expression as he consistently took the hand. Lord Elliot appeared unfazed.

He occasionally glanced at Jane, who was standing behind Frederick. She appeared to be trying her hardest *not* to look at Lord Elliot. I caught her glancing his way several times, then quickly looking down. At one point their eyes met when Lord Elliot was supposed to play his card and it delayed his momentum of laying his hand.

"You're throwing the game," Frederick sneered. "You might have more luck if you actually focused on your cards instead of a pretty face." His comment was loud enough for most of the room to hear. Jane's cheeks flushed, and I didn't catch her looking at Lord Elliot again after that. The game ended quickly with Frederick as the victor. Lord Elliot nodded to Frederick and offered his hand to shake. Frederick looked at the earl with loathing, then shifted his gaze elsewhere.

His gesture was as good as a cut.

Unphased, Lord Elliot turned to Aunt Mary, feigning a look of submission. "Mrs. Mason, I admit my defeat. What is my punishment?" He acted the part of a contrite groveler. "Should I be thrown from the steps? Beaten with a frying pan? Be relieved of my shoes and coat?"

"Heavens, no!" Aunt Mary chuckled. "What ideas. A song will

suffice."

A look of surprise, even panic, crossed his features. "A song, madam?"

"Yes. I believe it's punishment enough if you have a fear of performing for an audience. And if you do, in fact, have a lovely voice, then we will all benefit. And I've heard rumors, Lord Elliot, that you have a pleasing voice." I had never seen Lord Elliot more agitated. I glanced at Jane, her expression unreadable.

"Certainly it isn't severe enough a punishment, Mrs. Mason," Lord Elliot said, trying to remain calm. "I'm sure something else would suit our company more."

"No, I insist. Unless you're not up for the challenge and you would rather forfeit." He looked as though he might perhaps forfeit the challenge after all. Then he looked at Frederick's cold, smug face and appeared to take courage.

"Certainly, madam. Indeed, it is most fitting, for it is a lethal and deadly punishment for all. The rumors you have heard surely must be about some other Lord Elliot."

"Oh, I'm sure you are being overly modest!" Aunt Mary said, swatting the air with her hand. Lord Elliot looked as though he would be sick as he slowly walked toward the pianoforte. He looked over at Frederick once more, sharing the same look as his competitor: Sheer loathing.

Lord Elliot cleared his throat and looked as though death was truly upon him. I was so curious to see what his voice sounded like. I, too, had heard that Lord Elliot had a very rich, pleasing voice. He glanced in Jane's direction briefly before he looked at the floor and began to sing.

"Loud roar'd the dreadful thunnnder!
The rain a deluge show'rs!"

After only the first two lines of Lord Elliot's song, I could confidently say I had never heard anything so terrible. The words were that of "The Bay of Biscay." If not for the lyrics, I'd not have

recognized it. Not only was he unable to carry a tune, but he sang loudly with no ability to keep a rhythm. I was mortified for him. It took everything in me not to cover my
mouth . . . and my ears.

"The clouds are re–nt asuunnnder!"

His deep voice cracked on the word "rent." Our company averted their eyes, or tried to hide their smiles. Frederick wore a calculating stare as he watched.

"By lightning's vivid pow'rs;
The night was drear and daaark!"

When I glanced at Jane I almost did a double take. She was smiling from ear to ear, holding nothing back.

"Our poor devoted barK!"

He accentuated the "k" at the end.

" 'Till next day, there she lay,
In the Bay of Biscay, O!"

Jane

I had never heard anything so dreadful in all my life. Charles Elliot was finally terrible at something. He could not sing to save his life. I found, however, that it did not make him less appealing to me; it only made him more endearing. I had thought he was perhaps being modest about his poor ability to sing. I, too, had heard that Lord Elliot had a beautiful voice.

But as I watched him struggle through the song I could not help but smile, though he wouldn't look at me. After his song ended we all clapped politely. Charles tried to hide his embarrassment by pasting his usual smile on, but I could tell he was squirming underneath.

He avoided my gaze for the rest of the night, doing exactly what I had hoped he would do before the evening started—he left me alone completely. Except now all I wanted was his company. This was the one day I was allowing myself to enjoy him without reserve. If I couldn't enjoy it fully, I would have to allow myself just one more moment, one more careful dance along the edge of the precipice. Surely I could manage it once more without falling in completely.

15

POST

Lawrence

London
November 6, 1816
Later that night
Nine days of disguise remaining

"You did what!"

I could hear Charles's horrified yells all the way down the hall. The door to the library was wide open and his words were carrying through the house. I shook my head, dashing through the hall until I sped into the room. Charles and Henry looked at me as I entered. Charles was glaring and gritting his teeth while his fist clenched. Henry held an amused look on his face. Beneath the surface, however, I detected embarrassment.

I quickly shut the door. "My lord," I said with an even tone. "I could hear you all the way down the hall."

Charles fumed, then paced. "I told you." He pointed his finger at Henry, tightening his jaw. "We are close to getting to the bottom of this. Are you truly so reckless that you would be willing to put our entire operation on the line? Do you care nothing for uncovering the truth about our father?"

Henry gave Charles an even look himself. "That's a low blow even for you, Charles. I told you it couldn't be helped."

"And explain to Lawrence how it couldn't be helped," he seethed.

Henry gave a flat smile. "Frederick and I had a disagreement tonight at the Masons' dinner party. He was prepared to challenge me to a duel. Remembering our rule about avoiding fights, I attempted to smooth things over. The hostess suggested a game of whist instead, and we agreed. The loser would be issued a challenge. When I lost the game, she declared that I must sing."

Charles shook his head. "And instead of throwing yourself from the steps like a good boy, you made it so that I can never show my face in London again."

"I thought you hated London society," Henry said with a smirk.

"And yet I still have to appear from time to time," Charles snapped.

"It was only a small handful of people," Henry countered. "Besides, it was I who sang and not you. *I* have to live with the mortification."

Charles mirrored Henry's flat smile. "And yet, everyone present saw 'Lord Elliot' singing. Not Henry Thomas."

"You've made your point, Charles." Henry didn't seem to be in his usual teasing mood. "Are you demanding that we switch back now?" Henry gave none of his feelings away.

I found that in rare moments, such as this, when tension was high, it was best to let the two brothers sort out their frustration without getting involved. Therefore, I kept my mouth shut.

Silence filled the room before Charles finally spoke. "You want me to deal with the humiliation of tonight's performance while it's fresh?" He raised an eyebrow. "Certainly not. I'll leave that to you for the next nine days."

Charles continued to pace, rubbing his fingers across his forehead, wearing a mortified expression. "You've already broken two rules that will make my life harder once I return. How much more damage could you possibly do?" He let out an irritated huff. "No, we will resume as planned." He let his words sink in before adding, "But Henry, you're not to break any more rules."

Henry's mouth, now formed into a line of annoyance, stated that he was done being chided and done with the conversation altogether. "What have you discovered with your investigation, Charles?"

Charles rubbed his beard. Henry smirked at the motion, it being a gesture he himself had employed mere days ago. Charles finally stopped. "I overheard a physician named Doctor Fairhurst and his apprentice speaking. The apprentice didn't seem to approve of some of the doctor's recent practices."

It was time for me to pipe in. "What practices, my lord?"

Charles looked over at me. "The apprentice claimed that, at least twice, Doctor Fairhurst has falsified reports—one of those being a death that clearly showed signs of poison but was written up as natural causes." The room went silent. Henry took a seat. I followed suit.

"What else did you hear?" I asked.

"The apprentice asked if Doctor Fairhurst was being compensated for his lies. The physician didn't take kindly to his words. I would like to investigate this further and pay the apprentice a visit once I discover his identity."

I turned my attention from Charles to Henry. "Were you able to speak with Robert Graves about his business?"

Henry looked over at me and nodded. "I was able to get to know him better towards the end of the evening."

Charles raised an eyebrow. "Yes. You seemed particularly distracted at dinner. You couldn't stop smiling at an auburn-haired lady."

"Is it not my job to smile at all the ladies and get inside their inner circles?" Henry countered.

Charles rested his finger over his chin and gave Henry a long stare. "So long as that's where you draw the line." His face held no hint of teasing as he stared at his brother.

After a pause, Henry finally said, "If at any point you feel I'm crossing a line, we can switch back immediately."

This response seemed to satisfy Charles—at least for now.

I spoke next to Henry. "And what did you find out about Robert

Graves?"

"Yes. What did you find out?" Charles interjected. "Does his business appear to be secretive?"

"I'm sorry to disappoint you, Charles, but his business seems very straightforward to me. He is passionate about his work. Everything he shared with me was based on improving overall health. He told me about some research and inventions he has been looking into to improve the overall quality of his herbal remedies. He practically gushes when talking about helping others. If he is a criminal, Charles, he is a very good actor."

"I still don't trust him," Charles grumbled.

Henry shook his head and rolled his eyes at his brother's comment, then said, "Aside from that, there is only one gentleman who appears to entirely loathe me. His name is Matthew Johnson. I'm not sure if it is something we should look into, but there you have it."

Charles's eyes narrowed slightly in thought at the name. "Did you say Matthew Johnson?"

"I did," Henry said, somewhat confused. "I assure you, we don't know the fellow, Charles."

"Indeed, I'm not acquainted with Matthew Johnson," Charles agreed. "But I have heard his name." He made some notes on a piece of parchment. "I'll follow him to see if I can find out more".

Henry turned to me. "Lawrence, have your contacts discovered anything new?"

I was eager to share my findings. "They have discovered some interesting details," I nodded. "Arthur Brown's shop does indeed appear to be under watch during all hours of the day, and even sometimes at night. Mr. Brown himself is being loosely tailed from one place to another. If he goes to deliver goods, or anywhere, for that matter, he is followed at a distance. Even his mail is being read. So yes, Arthur Brown is, indeed, being closely watched."

"Thank you, Lawrence," Charles said. "That is very helpful." He made more notes. "And what is your plan for tomorrow, Henry?" Charles asked.

"I will be taking a lady out for a carriage ride to see if she may have any information. I will then call on a few other women I met at Duchess Hastingwood's ball and see if I can glean any more."

Charles nodded his head. "Good—as long as you don't sing again." He smiled grudgingly at the end of his statement.

Henry grinned back. "We could always switch places permanently so you don't have to live with the shame."

"Don't tempt me." Charles said, smirking.

Henry stood. "If I'm not needed anymore, I must put my affairs in order for tomorrow and bid you both goodnight." Henry put his hands in his pockets as he walked toward the door.

"Good luck tomorrow," Charles said.

"And to you." Henry exited the room.

I waited until I heard Henry's footsteps fade in the distance before I spoke.

"My lord, a letter arrived in response to your inquiries of Henry's father's whereabouts at the time of your father's death."

Charles looked at me. "Do you have it with you now?"

"I do." I reached inside my coat and pulled from it a letter, then handed it to Charles. He stared at it for a moment before breaking the seal. I held my breath as he read its contents. He breathed in slowly as he looked up from the letter.

"Well, my lord?" I asked with anticipation.

Charles let out his breath. "John Thomas had not been seen in London for nearly ten years . . . until the week before my father's death."

16

BASKET

Jane

London
November 7, 1816
One day later
Eight days of disguise remaining

I waited with Alice in the parlor. I had never felt so nervous. Charles would be here to claim me at any moment now. Ever since accepting his invitation, I'd gone back and forth on whether or not I should have done so. It took everything in me not to stand up and pace the room.

The sound of wheels against cobblestones filled the space, then slowed to a stop. I stood and walked to the window as casually as I could manage and parted the curtain. The carriage that waited in front of the house was elegant and open. My heart sped up as I saw Charles. I quickly let the drapes fall and came away from the window before he had the chance to spot me looking out. I attempted to take calming breaths, though it did very little to slow the rapid pulse of my heart. I heard the door open. Lord Elliot's voice couldn't be mistaken. George walked into the parlor and announced, "Lord Elliot to see you, Miss

Mason."

Charles walked in with his hands behind his back. He dipped his head toward Alice and me before he took several steps in my direction.

"Good morning, Miss Mason," he said, smiling softly. It was strange to hear him use my formal name, but with Alice present, it came as no surprise. "Since we are allies now, I thought it only natural to bring you this." He brought a bouquet of flowers forward from behind his back. Large, colorful leaves surrounded the outer edge of the flowers—I'd never seen anything like it.

"I love it, Lord Elliot, thank you." I smiled as I turned it slowly, examining each leaf.

He grinned. "I probably should have left the arrangement alone, but I couldn't help myself as I continued finding the most splendid leaves during my early morning walk."

"You added these?"

"I thought you might like them," he said.

"They're perfect." I had received flowers many times since my first debut in London, but this arrangement made me smile the most by far. Upon further inspection, I started noticing more and more about it. "Is that—?" I pointed to the ribbon binding the flowers together.

Charles grinned. "The legendary hideous ribbon? Indeed it is. Alas, I don't think it suited me after all. I decided to return it to you with much wounded pride."

I smiled, and then a quick laugh escaped me as I noticed a fork and spoon in the center of the arrangement. They looked identical to my aunt and uncle's set. "Did you steal these off my plate last night, my lord?" I tried hard to keep a straight face.

"I told you, I'm a kitchen thief."

I chuckled, continuing my examination. The thought he put into this bouquet made me feel cherished.

"Will you give me a moment to put these in my room?" I couldn't push my smile down.

"As long as you don't run away." He returned my smile. I wondered what Alice thought of our unusual conversation. She held her face as if it were the most natural discussion in the world, but I could detect a smile brewing beneath the surface. "I'll be back in just a moment."

Keeping the bouquet in my bedroom would allow me to admire it later without an audience. As I walked to my room, I couldn't stop smiling at the hidden gems in the arrangement. Alice appeared in no time with a container of water for my treasure, and I did my best not to disturb a single part of it.

It was perfect.

Charles's open carriage rolled on as we enjoyed the sun and autumn air. He was seated next to me, with Alice sitting across from us at the far end of her seat, looking out the side as usual.

"Miss Mason, how would you feel if we took a small detour on foot?"

"What will we be doing on foot?" I asked, intrigued.

"You'll have to wait and find out," he said cryptically.

I gave him a teasing grin. "It seems I have no choice."

He lifted a corner of his mouth and gave me a look that made my heart skip at least two beats.

It was getting more and more difficult to be in Charles's presence without wanting more. The longer our "alliance" carried on, the harder it would be to walk away from it all.

"Lord Elliot, I know you were abroad for some years." I looked at him. "It's one of the reasons we have never met until now. What did you love most about your travels?"

He smiled. "It's hard to choose only one thing I loved most. Venice is magical. In the early morning we would watch the sun rise until it danced on the water. It's absolutely breathtaking." His eyes trailed over my face as he smiled softly. "You would love it."

I wanted to hear more. "Please, keep going," I said.

He looked at me thoughtfully. "Do you really wish for me to?"

"Absolutely."

His lips turned up in a grateful smile before he continued speaking. His voice soothed me while his arm brushed against mine, talking with his hands, painting enchanting pictures in my mind of France and Spain.

Places I had dreamed of visiting had never felt more tangible than when he described them. His eyes lit up when he talked, and I hung on his every word, convinced I could listen to him talk this way forever. Eventually, Charles looked ahead. "Are you ready, Jane?" he asked quietly with a smile.

The coachman suddenly deviated off the path until he brought the horses to a stop under some trees. The area was hidden from the main path.

Charles descended the carriage, helped Alice and me down, then held out his arm. "Shall we?"

Lacing my arm through his, we walked at an easy pace. I would let myself enjoy all of Charles today, for it would be my last. Tomorrow I would be disciplined and return to my original plan, though I would replay these moments of him in my mind forever. "What is it that you miss most about your travels?" I asked, wanting to hear his voice as much as possible.

"My father." He gave me a soft smile. "He made all of our travels an adventure, even if it was for business. Once Mama died, he had a hard time being in Wilton. It was no longer home for him. So we would travel for fun, then return to Wilton. Within the next week, he would already be melancholy, so we would travel for business. We continued this pattern until . . . " He trailed off, looking at the ground before he continued, "until he passed. Despite the fact that he never was the same after Mama's passing, he always saw the beauty in the simple things. He made every new place magical, somehow.

"Ironically, he always missed Wilton when he was away. We all did. My favorite part of our journeys was returning home. Each time, our return gave me a renewed sense of purpose and breathed some of my mother back into me."

His words made my heart ache. I put my hand on his arm. "And what do you plan to do now?"

His eyes glanced at my hand, and then he studied my eyes. "That all depends."

"On what?" I asked, unable to pull my eyes from his.

"On the next eight days." His eyes held secrets and questions.

"What happens in eight days?" I knew I was overstepping my bounds by asking, but I couldn't seem to help myself.

A flutter ran through my stomach as I felt Charles's hand rest on top of mine. "Let's just enjoy today." We walked around a small thicket of trees and a small area opened up to a blanket spread out in the sun, right on the edge of some trees shading a basket. My mouth opened in surprise. He smiled at my reaction and motioned with his hand toward the blanket. Finding a seat, I crossed my ankles and leaned back on my hands. The sun felt wonderful against the chill air. Alice took a seat a small distance off on a tree stump.

Charles brought the basket over and placed it next to him, then removed his coat, revealing his white shirt and vest beneath. It was hard not to stare as the sun exposed his strong form beneath his shirt. He opened the basket, pulled out a bottle of grape juice and two glasses, and handed one to me. As I wrapped my fingers around its smooth surface, he didn't release it immediately.

His eyes settled on mine. "Thank you for allowing me to have your company today."

I was enjoying his company far too much. "I'm afraid, Lord Elliot, that you are spoiling me. I'll never be able to deem another carriage ride as suitable after this." I felt the need to swallow as his eyes searched mine. He finally withdrew his hand from the glass.

"Good." His mouth turned up on one side before he brought some plates forward. He pulled a napkin out of thin air next and handed it to me.

"How do you do that?" I smiled, feeling like a child.

"Magic," he winked.

I grinned. "A magical thief."

"A *charming* magical thief."

I smiled. "I would have hired nothing less."

He poured juice into my glass, then filled his own before raising it in the air with a smile. "To us. A thieving crew built on a leaf, a hideous ribbon, and some stolen utensils."

"To us." I laughed as I lifted my glass to his. We both took a sip, the sweetness of my drink accenting the sweetness of the moment. I was touched by all of Charles's efforts to make this occasion 'more than just suitable.' His attentiveness made me feel esteemed. Frederick had never done anything even remotely as thoughtful.

Next, Charles brought a few platters out of the basket that carried sliced apples and pears, cheeses, cured meats, and biscuits. He put a bit of everything on a plate, then handed it to me before dishing up his own plate and joining me on the blanket. His nearness made me feel alive—enraptured. We sat quietly for a moment as we looked at the trees and ate.

"Jane?" He looked over at me, eyes brimming with questions. It seemed he was debating whether or not to say something. I wanted him to trust me, to say whatever was on his mind.

He exhaled and the questions left his eyes. "Tell me more about your family."

Disappointment came as I watched him retreat from what he really wanted to say. "What do you want to know?" I asked.

"Tell me more about your parents." He turned on his side towards me and rested on his elbow.

"Neither of them had money when they married, though they were both well educated. They met at a public ball. Papa danced with my mother one time and claims he was in love by the end of it." I grinned. "Mama was already engaged to another man—Oliver. But Papa was persistent, and after some time, he won my mother's heart."

"Was Oliver wealthy?" he asked. "Did your mother choose love over money?"

"No. Papa and Oliver were equally matched in wealth and class."

Charles nodded his head. "Was Oliver a cold man?"

"Actually, no. He was a good man with a good heart. He was absolutely in love with Mama, but he noticed that her heart had turned to my father. She wouldn't break off their engagement—she had already made a commitment and she didn't want to hurt anyone. But in the end, Oliver gave her up so she would be happy. My parents named my youngest brother after him."

"And what ever happened to Oliver?" Charles asked.

"No one knows. He moved away shortly after my parents were married, and they never heard from him afterwards."

Charles was quiet. "And did your mother ever regret her decision?"

"No. She felt bad for hurting Oliver, but she knows she would have been miserable, always longing for Papa. Despite the financial burdens my parents faced in the past, they have loved each other through it all. But about four years ago my father inherited a large sum from an uncle. A few months before that, he struck gold with a trading venture. He has done very well with his business ever since that time."

"And is your mother even happier now that she has wealth?" Charles asked.

"Why wouldn't she be? She has love *and* wealth now. Her children want for nothing, and she doesn't have to worry about the future."

"Is that you speaking, or her speaking?" He looked at me, the unspoken questions returning to his eyes.

"I believe it is both," I said.

"And what about you, Jane?" His eyes held me captive. "Would you rather be loved and penniless? Or would you rather be wealthy and lonely?"

My heart pounded at the way he looked at me. His question brought back to my mind what I had been working for these last four years. I wasn't destined to find love. I was destined to do what was hard, logical.

"As much as the idea of love excites me," I said, turning to face him while I leaned back further on my hands, "it doesn't feed hungry mouths. It wouldn't buy shoes and clothes, or an education for my children." I looked at the trees, then back at Charles. I found his question odd, since he had more wealth than most people could dream of. His expression was unreadable.

"And you?" I finally asked. "Would you rather be loved and penniless? Or wealthy and lonely?"

He sat up slightly and turned toward me, the movement putting his face close to mine. I held my breath, my heart tripping.

"I can't answer that at present." His look of restlessness from a few days ago returned. "What you say is true. Love is meaningless if two people can't afford to eat or be clothed or take shelter." He looked at my hair, my lips, my eyes. "And yet," his voice came out quiet, "I don't think it would be living, Jane, to have a constant ache in my heart, with no end in sight. A yearning for the one who makes me whole, without the hope of holding her in my arms. To dream of the one I love by night, knowing I can never have her when I wake. To have her haunt my every waking thought just to know I would still never imagine her eyes exactly right."

I couldn't breathe. I was drowning in his words, his eyes, his heart. I wanted to be swallowed up by it. I no longer wanted to stand on the very edge of the precipice; I wanted to jump off and be taken completely.

My thoughts awakened me, startled me. I finally pulled my eyes from his and looked down, my chest rising an falling as I tried to breathe normally. I was so easily sucked in.

Charles breathed in slowly as I broke contact, then gave us more distance before he spoke again. "I believe what I'm trying to say is although I could never live truly penniless, I could never be wealthy and lonely."

I could say nothing. I was planning my future to be exactly that—wealthy and lonely. All the while, my heart had awakened, yearning for more. After we watched the leaves dance through the park for a time, we picked at our food.

"It's time for me to get you back," Charles finally said next to me. I didn't want this moment to end. I didn't want to give up Charles tomorrow; it was all going too fast.

He collected the dishes and placed them back in the basket, then stood and offered me his hand. I contemplated just staying put until I felt his hand carefully take mine. "We've already been gone too long," he said as he tried coaxing me up. "Your aunt and uncle will never let me see you again if I don't get you back soon."

"I don't want to leave yet," I said, refusing to move.

He grinned. "Are you admitting that our outing together has been more than suitable?"

I grinned back. "You have completely spoiled me. How could it not be?"

He smiled and gently tugged at my hand again until I finally allowed him to help me up. He folded the blanket and placed it in the basket, then laced my arm through his. The coachman took the basket and led the way, with Alice walking a fair distance behind us.

"Thank you for today, Lord Elliot. I can't recall having such a splendid morning."

He looked at me with a mischievous grin. "Are you saying I'm not so terrible after all?"

"I'm saying no such thing," I teased. "I believe every morning should be spent just like this one, but I know that's impossible. So you are indeed terrible for making this morning perfect."

He smiled. "You really mustn't flatter me, Jane. I'll start getting ideas."

"You're not allowed any more ideas. It's why we are in this mess in the first place." We arrived at the carriage, a reminder that our time together was almost gone. Tomorrow would start the renewal of my plans. As Charles took my hand, I wondered if my heart would ever get used to his touch. Charles assisted me up into the carriage and I had to stop myself from sighing, melancholy already setting in.

Once again we were rolling through Hyde Park. And once again I was next to the man I wouldn't be able to stop thinking about. I would have to say goodbye to him, shut him out again, all while wishing I could spend my days like I had spent this morning.

Before I knew it, the carriage pulled in front of my aunt and uncle's house. Charles turned to me. "Jane, may I see you again, the day after the Morgans' ball?"

He was making it even more difficult to say goodbye. I tried to think of all the ways I could justify having just one more outing with him. A reminder of how easily I'd been convinced to jump off the edge into the void earlier made me pause. I couldn't be trusted around Charles.

And yet, I wanted what he was asking for more than anything. I couldn't say no when his eyes invited me in like that. I couldn't say no when I knew I would always wonder what another one of these perfect days would look like. "What did you have in mind this time?" I finally asked.

"You will just have to wait and see." He smiled at me, then stood, helping me up. He carefully handed me down, then descended. Alice waited a few paces off as we said our goodbyes.

"Thank you again." Nothing I uttered could truly convey how much this outing meant to me.

"Thank you for your cooperation this morning. Before I arrived, I was certain I would find you locked in your room." He grinned. "I was prepared to climb through your window, of course, but I believe George himself would have thrown me from the steps at that point."

I laughed. "I would like to see that."

"Which one?" he asked with a wicked grin. "Me climbing through your window? Or being thrown from the steps for doing so?"

I knew he was teasing, but I couldn't help but watch his lips when he looked at me in that rakish way. I shook myself from my wandering thoughts, then smirked. "Both. As long as you don't try to serenade me from the window."

Charles made a face of pure mortification. "I was hoping we would never speak of that moment. That we could pretend it never happened."

"And why would we ever do that?" I laughed.

"Jane, I'm in earnest," he laughed back. "I'm trying to forget what transpired last night. It was hard for me to swallow my pride and actually pick you up this morning after such a spectacle." He looked down, truly embarrassed.

"In that case, I will say nothing about the subject again."

He gave me a relieved smile. "May I pick you up in the afternoon this Saturday for our next outing?"

My smile fell as I recognized my blunder. "I've just remembered that Lily and I are to travel home the day after Lady Morgan's ball. We will be gone seven days."

Charles's expression fell. I suddenly remembered him mentioning how something was dependent on the next eight days.

"Charles, are you leaving in eight days?" The thought of being away from him for seven days was hard enough. The thought of returning from Wilton without Lord Elliot's presence for who knows how long was torment. Panic filled me as I contemplated how long he had been abroad. Five years. What if I never saw him again after Marianne's ball?

"I will be leaving in eight days on business, and I don't know how long I will be gone." An ache formed in my heart, and he hadn't even left yet. The thought alone was painful. "It appears that tomorrow is our last day," he said evenly. We studied each other. "May I claim your first dance, Jane?" I had so many questions, but my words didn't seem to work. I could only nod my head. I didn't want him to leave yet. I wanted to reach out and take his hand and ask for him to stay for the remainder of the day. I wasn't ready to say goodbye.

"Goodbye, Jane," he said, quietly.

I tried to say goodbye, but the words were lost. "Until tomorrow," I finally managed.

He nodded his head to me, giving me a conflicted look before turning and stepping up into his carriage. His eyes were facing mine as his conveyance pulled away. We watched each other until it was no longer possible.

It had been the most splendid morning I could recall—It would be the most melancholy afternoon.

17

NEST

Lily

London
November 7, 1816
Later that day
Eight days of disguise remaining

O nce Jane returned from her outing with Lord Elliot, I begged her to join me for a bit of shopping so I could be away for the afternoon, in case Mr. Johnson still called on me. But Jane said she wasn't feeling well and immediately went up to her room.

I gathered my money purse and in no time Alice and I were in the carriage heading for the shops. I felt more relieved the farther we got from the house. I would face Mr. Johnson eventually when I knew what to say to him. Today was not that day.

Alice and I spent the afternoon walking through the shops. I purchased a pair of gloves and a new bonnet for my ribbons. We walked at a leisurely pace with no particular agenda in mind, then headed back for the house once calling hours were over.

Despite the fact that Mr. Johnson made me feel unsettled, I took no delight in the idea of refusing his proposal. How could I convey to him that we were not well suited without wounding him? It was certainly a dilemma. Jane would have an answer for me, I was sure of it. Alice and I stepped down from the carriage once we arrived at the house, a crowd of men walking by.

"Good afternoon, Miss Mason," a familiar voice said once the group dispersed. My stomach dropped. I looked up from the cobblestones to find Mr. Johnson waiting.

"Mr. Johnson! Did you not receive my letter that I would be away this afternoon?"

"I did receive your message. I decided I would wait for you to return. If you remember, Miss Mason, I am a shrike: patient and clever."

My chest tightened as I realized he was determined to see this through. I decided to test my luck regardless. "Mr. Johnson, I will go speak to my aunt to see if she will make an exception to receive a caller at this time. Excuse me a moment while I—"

He took my hand. "Miss Mason, I wish to speak with you alone."

A weight thudded in my stomach. I slowly pulled my hand from his grip and bobbed a curtsy. "Very well, Mr. Johnson." I looked at Alice, trying to hide my panic. "Alice, will you please have George show Mr. Johnson into the library? I need to speak with Jane. I'll be with you shortly."

He bowed to me. "I will wait as long as needed." The words were kind and gentlemanly, but his countenance was predatory. I excused myself and all but ran to Jane's room.

I opened her door and found her facing the window. "Jane! You have to help me," I said frantically.

She turned, a look of concern lining her features. "What is it?"

"Matthew Johnson is here to propose. Please tell me what to say."

She walked away from the window toward me. "Lily, I could never do that. The words must be your own. You must be honest and firm, but kind." She turned her eyes on me. "More than anything, you need to stop making him wait."

I took a deep breath. "Honest and firm, but kind. . . . Jane, couldn't you at least come with me?" I felt sick with dread.

Jane put her hands firmly on my shoulders. "No, Lily. You must do this alone." She gave me a sympathetic look. "I'm not suggesting that what you have to do is easy. But you alone must do it." She turned me around and started moving me out the door. "And you must do it right now." I turned around to argue as she shut the door in my face. I put my hands on my hips and sighed. Unfortunately, Jane was right . . . as usual.

I steeled myself as I walked through the library door. Passing the threshold, I left the door open intentionally. Mr. Johnson was standing near the desk. I didn't know where to look or what to do with my hands; eventually I settled on staring at the floor. My heart was pounding from nervousness and my cheeks burned. I was grateful for the open window that brought a slight breeze through the room.

He walked past me and shut the door, then came to stand in front of me. I adjusted my gaze to meet his eyes, which were more than a few inches below my own. I knew he intended to have out what he would say. The longer I prolonged it, the longer it would take.

"Miss Mason." He took my hand. "Lily." I looked at his small hand around mine. "I'm sure it is no surprise that you have won my affection. It is only natural that a creature as rare as yourself would capture my interest. Only a Golden Eagle could truly tempt me."

The look on his face made it hard not to quickly pull my hand from his. But I did need to be honest like Jane advised. "Mr. Johnson." I took my hand from his as gently as I could, then began pacing the room. "I am not a rare creature, nor am I a bird. I am flattered that you think so well of me, but I must stop you before you go any further."

"I will not be rebuffed, Miss Mason. I am in earnest and intend to make you my wife. I intend to build a nest with you, and in it, raise children of our own." He followed me as I continued to pace. It took everything in me not to bolt from the library.

"Mr. Johnson—"

"Matthew," he interrupted as he took my hand again and stopped me from pacing.

I was beginning to lose my poise. He was making this more difficult than I expected. I took in a breath. "Mr. Johnson," I again pulled my hand from his, "I don't wish to use forceful language or be unkind, but you and I are not well suited for one another. Please leave it at that and allow us to part ways as friends."

"Perhaps you will come to feel differently about the situation with time."

"No, Mr. Johnson, I will not." I tried to use a sympathetic tone.

"Is this due to your regard for another man?" he asked with a chilling, possessive look.

I let out an exasperated huff. "Whether or not I have a regard for another man has nothing to do with the fact that you and I are not well suited for one another."

"Is it Lord Elliot?" He watched my reaction as he spoke the name.

"Mr. Johnson! I have given you my answer. My decision is not based upon another man. If I do have feelings for another man, it would have no sway on the fact that my answer is no. Please take my answer as final." I was quickly losing my patience.

Mr. Johnson looked at me through narrowed eyes. "I know you regard Lord Elliot. How could you not?"

"You know nothing, Mr. Johnson."

"He truly is a cuckoo." He stared at me with a calculating look. "I know you would not refuse me if not for him."

I shook my head with disbelief. There was no way to let Mr. Johnson down gently. He would not take no for an answer, and his calculating stare was making my skin crawl.

"Mr. Johnson, if you will not take me at my word, then we have nothing further to discuss." I walked over to the door and opened it. "You may leave now."

He slowly walked up to me and gave me a bow, his mouth pressed in a firm line. His eyes watched mine once more, the shadow of possessiveness returning. "I'll not give up, Miss Mason. I'll be back. Lord Elliot will regret this."

Before I had the chance to say another word he took himself away. I shut the library door forcefully, disgusted at his arrogance and possessiveness. Had he truly just threatened Lord Elliott? I had never given Mr. Johnson any reason to suspect I had feelings for either him or

Lord Elliot.

Perhaps Jane should have reconsidered being here with me after all. I was sure she would have smoothed it over. Walking near the window, I all but fell into the chair.

Another knock came at the door and I thought I might scream. If Mr. Johnson had come back to say something else, I might just challenge him to a duel myself. I was sure I could beat him in a sword fight for my own honor, even if I hadn't any experience.

George walked in. "There is a man to see you on a matter of business, miss." *A matter of business, indeed.* Mr. Johnson was ever persistent.

"I'm not interested in speaking with Mr. Johnson further, George. In fact, I don't ever want that man to be permitted to call on me again."

"Very good, miss. And should I send the other gentleman away as well? He claims to know your father and would like you to relay some business matters to your father on his behalf."

This happened on occasion ever since my father struck gold with trade. A man would come to the London house to speak with Jane or me briefly with a business letter and information to solicit my father's advice, or to try and convince him to take them on as a partner. Although a lady didn't usually carry out such tasks, my father prided Jane's and my knowledge and skills and encouraged us to take part in his business.

I sighed, "Very well, you may show him in."

George dipped his head, then disappeared. I sat at the desk and rubbed my temples, still tense.

Footsteps entered the library. "Please state your name, sir, so we may begin." I said the words without enthusiasm as I found a quill and a blank piece of parchment. I wanted to get this over with as soon as possible so I could check the garden. I knew Henry said he wouldn't meet me out there again, but I couldn't help but search regardless.

"Henry Thomas," a deep voice said at the other end of the desk.

I gasped in surprise and looked up. Henry was biting back a laugh. He held up a finger and cocked his head toward the door, reminding me it was open. I realized he'd just given me his last name—or a fake last name at the very least.

I tried to act as normal as possible as my heart picked up speed. "And what business proposition would you like me to relay today, Henry Thomas?" I walked toward the door and closed it as I spoke.

He was biting back an amused grin when I turned around to face him. "I would like to propose—" His eyes glanced at the open window.

I opened my mouth in embarrassment as I realized that Henry had likely heard the entire altercation between Mr. Johnson and me. I put my hands to my cheeks as I felt them burn again. "Henry!" I said, mortified.

Turning from him, I walked away, hands still pressing at my burning face. He slowly stepped toward me from behind until I could feel him at my back. Slowly lifting my left hand from my cheek, his fingers moved over mine until they found my ring still loosely placed on my pinky. He didn't take it off, but spun it around the base of my finger, setting off a flutter in my stomach at his touch.

"As amusing as I found his proposal, Lily," he said near my ear, still from behind. Tingles ran down my neck. "I can't say that I enjoyed it. It's a good thing I wasn't in here. He didn't seem to take no for an answer." Henry gently coaxed me around to face him. Would my heart ever stop hammering at his nearness? "And is he right in assuming that you have fallen for Lord Elliot? Lord Elliot is wealthy and titled, and is rumored to be very handsome." I could feel his eyes on me while his fingers gently lifted my chin until I was looking at him.

I reminded myself to breathe before I spoke. "And yet, when I look at Lord Elliot, all I can think about is—" I stopped myself before I finished my sentence. I couldn't divulge just how often I thought about him. I wanted Henry more than I could say. Every fiber of my being wanted to be with him. And it appeared that he wanted me too, to some extent. But I would never know if he desired me but was otherwise engaged, or if he was just toying with me—at least not until I knew exactly who he was. His fingers slowly fell away from my chin.

"Henry Thomas," I finally said. "Who is Henry Thomas?"

"Eight days, Lily. Eight days." He brought my hand to his lips and lightly brushed the top of it. "If I can wait that long," he muttered. A current ran the length of my arm until it pulsed in my heart. He took the ring off my pinky. I knew it would disappear before it happened. "Unfortunately for now, I need to leave."

Grasping for anything to say to make him stay longer, I blurted, "I thought you came here with a business proposition."

"Ah, yes," he said, putting some distance between us. "May I have full permission to take Mr. Johnson off immediately, assuming he walks through your door again?"

I laughed. "I was planning on challenging him to a duel. I believe I might stand a chance."

Henry chuckled. "No one is a match for you, Lily."

I bit my bottom lip mischievously and moved just in front of him. "I'm certain you're equal to the task."

He appeared to be holding his breath at my closeness. "I've stayed too long," he said, finally letting out his breath. "I need to go now before—" He looked at my eyes, then my lips. It was my turn for my breath to come up short as he studied me. "Do you remember where to meet me tomorrow?" he asked quietly. I nodded. "Remember, bring a chaperone." He lifted my hand to his lips once more. "Until tomorrow."

As he released my hand, I felt the familiar shape of tuppence placed in the palm of my hand. This time I didn't even turn around as he walked past me. I knew he would be gone by the time I did. Instead, I held my hand close to my heart and traced the top of it with my other hand, where his lips had claimed a part of me.

18

TERRACE

Jane

London
November 8, 1816
One day later
Seven days of disguise remaining

The full-length mirror was once again my companion as two dresses looked back at me. It was intentional that I was without an audience for now; I wanted to make my decision alone. I held up a new cream gown, then the deep blue. Sighing, I put the blue dress back inside my wardrobe and laid out the cream.

My eyes flicked to the small clock on my wall. It was still one hour too early to start getting ready, but I had been restless ever since returning from my morning outing with Charles the day before. Since that time, I had been counting my breaths, the beats of my heart, the minutes on the clock that stood still no matter how much I urged time to pass.

I had promised myself to keep Charles at a distance after our outing the day before. But now that I was faced with the thought of never seeing him again after tonight, I told myself I could enjoy his company one last time.

I walked to my dressing table and sat in front of the mirror. I did not, however, look into its reflection again. I was worried what I might find if I did. Instead, I looked at the bouquet of flowers Charles gave me. Rather than bringing a smile to my face like they did the day before, they brought a deep sadness.

Opening a small drawer, I pulled out the deep blue ribbon from Arthur & Co. I wrapped it around my index finger a few times before letting it fall away, repeating this gesture over and over. Then I stared at it and sighed, winding it once, reminding myself that I wanted to secure Frederick. I wound it twice; I ruled with my head. I wound it again; love was an illusion. I held it there for a moment longer, then wrapped the entire ribbon around my finger. Reaching the end, a renewal of my convictions slowly trickled back to where they belonged. It was bound and structured, exactly as it should be…until my fingers slipped off the end and the entire thing unraveled, falling to the table. I stared at it as if it would give me some insight to my own mind and the pieces that were quickly unraveling.

My door quietly swung inward. I turned around and saw Lily peeking inside.

"Are you as restless as I am?" she asked, eyeing the dress I had already laid out. I put the ribbon back in the small drawer and closed it.

"That depends on how restless you are." A corner of my mouth turned up, but it was forced.

"How improper would it be if we showed up a few hours early to Marianne's estate?" she asked with a grin.

I gave her a questioning look. "If I didn't know any better, Lily, I'd say you were eager for this ball. Why the sudden change since Duchess Hastingwood's event?"

"This one will be different because it's Lady Morgan's ball." She said it as though it should explain the change and make all the difference.

I smirked. "All the same people will be in attendance. Will Mr. Graves be attending?" I raised my brow.

She narrowed her eyes. "I don't believe an apothecary would be invited to Lady Morgan's ball. In either case, I feel the same about Mr. Graves now as when we spoke last. But I'm looking forward to the festivities nonetheless." She gave me a sly look. "And what are your plans for this evening? Are you going to secure Frederick once and for all?"

"You act as though it is up to me."

"And if Frederick asked for your hand today, would you accept?" Lily's voice held no humor.

"Why would you ask that question?" I was taken off guard. "It's not as if he would propose tonight. I would be surprised if anything of that magnitude occurred within the next month even."

"It's a simple question, Jane. He has clearly shown an interest in you. Marriage, inevitably, is the next step." I had been working towards this match, of course, but when Lily put it so plainly, I was terrified.

As knots of dread twisted in my stomach, I attempted to act normal. "Yes, I believe I would accept his hand if he asked me tonight." The words were hollow even as I said them. I felt nothing—worse than nothing. I felt empty.

"Then we must make you look as fetching as possible tonight," Lily said with a mischievous smile.

"Lily …" I said hesitantly. "Are you trying to imply that Frederick will propose tonight? Is there something you know that I'm unaware of?" The very idea shot panic throughout me.

"Certainly not," she grinned. "I just want you to look your best this evening."

As she smiled, I narrowed my eyes, unsure what to think of her behavior. "You're acting odd."

Lily gave me an errant look. "Am I?"

Once again, Alice was working her magic on my hair. Thus far, I looked exactly as I always did before a ball—Perfectly put together. Lily came in halfway through the process, wearing a maroon dress. She looked absolutely stunning. Her hair had loose curls piled and pinned on top of her head, with a few cascading down the back. She would certainly be the talk of the evening. On occasion, she preferred to do her own hair for balls or parties. She certainly had a special touch, and tonight she used it to her advantage. She watched me as Alice placed the finishing touches to my curls and helped me into my gown.

"Is there anything else you need, miss?" Alice asked.

"No. Thank you."

Alice curtsied, then left the room. Lily walked over as I stood in front of the full-length mirror.

"Breathtaking, as always," she said with a smile. "I have an idea though." She ushered me over to sit at my mirror, then looked at my hair, curled and pinned to perfection. "May I try something new?" She bit her lip. "I promise I can put it back exactly as it is if you don't like it."

"Very well. We do have quite a bit of extra time. We might as well pass it somehow."

Her face lit up. "I couldn't agree more." She began carefully pulling out selective pins and replacing them until about half the curls were piled and pinned to one side. Then she arranged the other half to trail down my shoulder on the same side. She added some hair jewels to the pinned curls, then smiled. "What do you think? Can we keep it? I daresay no man will be able to resist you tonight."

I'd never had such a hairstyle. It was elegant, daring, and free. I couldn't help but smile. "It's beautiful, Lily. You truly have a gift."

She smiled slyly. "If Frederick wasn't planning on proposing by the end of the week, I'm sure he will now." A rush of dread and excitement flooded through me at her words. Tonight would be eventful, I could feel it. It would turn the tide one way or another. It reminded me of autumn: change was coming. But if I was being honest, I *was* hoping one particular gentleman wouldn't be able to resist me tonight, . . . and it wasn't Frederick.

I looked at my reflection once more. It was time to be bold, daring. I walked over to my wardrobe and opened it, bringing out the deep blue dress. "Lily, will you help me?"

She nodded, leaving her teasing behind, then walked over and helped me out of my cream dress and into the deep blue one. "It's perfect," she said as she looked at me in the full-length mirror. "I'll meet you downstairs. There are a few things I want to freshen up before we leave." She shut the door behind her.

I faced the mirror in my deep blue—This time I was ready. It still felt bold and daring. But now . . . I embraced it.

Upon entering the Morgans' ballroom, we were greeted by the baron, the baroness, and Marianne. Her grandmother sat in a corner looking displeased at everything.

Marianne smiled delightedly at Lily and me, looking lovely in her pink ball gown. "I'll come find you both later once I'm done greeting guests." We exchanged a few more words and then were ushered away from the entrance.

"And look just there," Lily said near my ear, motioning with her eyes to a corner in the room. "Frederick has already noticed you." She gave me an excited smile. I glanced in his direction and found that he was, indeed, looking my way. I gave him a timid smile in acknowledgment but found that I wanted to turn away. I was grateful when Aunt Mary led our party to a different area of the ballroom. I tried my best not to immediately look for Charles, but it was no use. Whether I admitted it or not, I had been looking for him the moment we exited the carriage.

We congregated as a group and Aunt Mary found someone to prattle with about the latest gossip. I stood on my toes next to Lily to get a better look around. Lily was also scanning the room as if she was searching for someone. Perhaps she did, in fact, have feelings for a gentleman but was too reserved to talk about it.

I looked at her curiously. It wasn't like Lily to be reserved about anything. I would pester her later about her peculiar behavior. At present, I just felt a pulling need to find Charles in the crowd. I stood on my toes once more to see if I could get a better look around.

"Are you looking for someone?"

I turned around quickly, unable to help the smile already forming on my lips.

Charles's charming smile greeted me until it shifted into something deep and full of desire. He looked at my eyes before he took in my hair and the loose curls Lily had draped down one side of my shoulder.

I felt breathless as he studied me. I collected my thoughts. "I *was* looking for someone."

"And are you still searching, Jane?" His words had so many meanings. A corner of his mouth turned up slowly. "I believe it is time for me to claim this first dance." Couples began making their way to the floor. He offered me his arm and a flutter went through me as I took hold of it with my gloved fingers.

I smiled. "Only if you promise to—"

"I believe this dance is mine." I inwardly gasped as I heard Frederick's voice behind me. I felt a pull on my hand from behind and was led away from Charles before I had the chance to say anything. I kept my eyes on Charles, my heart tearing at the look on his face. I wanted to reach out for him. I wanted him to claim me from Frederick, but I knew it was out of the question. If Lord Elliot was seen making a scene by taking me from Frederick, it would be as good as a declaration of love. I knew Charles would never make such a public statement. Especially when he could have any woman he wanted. The reminder was a sting as I watched Charles fade into the crowd.

I was suddenly aware of Frederick's presence. He was actually studying me. It was the most attentive he had ever been.

"You look exceptionally beautiful this evening, Miss Mason," he said, complimenting me for once. It didn't make my heart flutter or quicken. It made me feel claustrophobic and hollow inside all at the same time.

I didn't know what to say. I searched my mind frantically. Old Jane finally took over. "You are too kind," I said without emotion.

"No doubt I saved you from enduring a dance with that tiresome flirt?" Frederick watched my face carefully as he said the words. His usual flat demeanor was replaced with a cold, questioning look. I had absolutely nothing to say. My mouth felt dry and I wanted to flee. I felt Charles's eyes on me but I knew I couldn't look at him just now under Frederick's scrutiny. I needed to say something.

I decided to try for ignorance. "Who exactly are we speaking of?" I asked with my practiced smile. This seemed to appease him.

"Yes, precisely. He is no one to be speaking of." He misinterpreted my meaning, but his cold look dissipated slightly and he resumed his usual bored expression. The dance continued without much conversation. At one point, when it was appropriate, I tried to seek out Charles. He was no longer in the place I had left him. A feeling of disappointment claimed me. I searched the sea of men and women, and my heart wrenched as I finally spotted Charles dancing with Lily. They were smiling and clearly enjoying one another's company. I certainly wasn't jealous, I reminded myself as I looked away.

It felt deceitful even as I thought the words to myself. I could lie to myself no longer. I wanted to be where Lily was. I wanted to be the one that Charles held in his arms. I returned my gaze to Frederick. He was watching me again, almost making me jump.

"I look forward to our carriage ride on Monday," he said evenly.

I tried to bring myself back to the conversation. When I recollected his words I realized my blunder. "Oh. Lord Fletcher, I hope you will beg my pardon. I forgot that I am due home for a dinner party. Lily and I leave for Wilton tomorrow."

"I see," he said with a hint of challenge in his voice. He looked over at Charles as he said it. "In that case, I wish to see you the moment you return."

"Of course." I did my best to keep my practiced smile in place. I should have been flattered by his words. Instead, I was filled with dread.

Lily

Jane looked positively miserable dancing with Frederick. I couldn't have been more thrilled. Lord Elliot was truly the best dance partner I'd ever had up to that point. He was spectacular at leading and his conversation was witty and lighthearted, but genuine. He was perfect for Jane. I felt very satisfied with my choice of potential brother-in-law.

Now I needed to ready myself for an outing on the north terrace . . . accompanied.

I found Uncle Francis sitting near Aunt Mary as she gossiped with her friends, looking positively miserable. He noticed my approach and lent me a flat smile, then pointed in the direction of the gossiping ladies and gave a gesture as if he was hanging himself.

I chuckled as I approached. "Don't show your excitement too much, Uncle. People will begin to think you actually enjoy these spectacles."

"I do enjoy them . . . " He paused for dramatic emphasis, then added, "when we leave."

I gave him an apologetic smile. "Well I can't offer you the solace of leaving just yet. Aunt Mary would surely roast us alive."

Uncle Francis chuckled. "I daresay she would."

"But . . . I *can* offer you a walk around the terrace so you can escape for a time." I gave him a conspiratorial look.

A look of relief came over his features. "Bless you, Lily." He stood up and walked over to Aunt Mary, informing her of our plans. She gave Uncle Francis a smile and a nod, then returned to my side. "Shall we?" He offered me his arm, and I took it with a smile.

My heart hammered. How would this work with my uncle accompanying me? As we walked towards the terrace, I thought of ways to somehow evade Uncle Francis for a short time. Each option seemed impossible. I sighed inwardly with frustration. We had already passed the open doors leading out to the garden and I hadn't thought of a single way to see Henry alone.

I made sure to walk along the right edge of the path, as Henry had instructed. It was lined with tall hedges and was beautifully manicured. If I wasn't so distracted about seeing Henry, I would have been able to appreciate its beauty fully. Walking slowly, I pretended to soak up the freedom of being outside.

"You're just like me." My uncle chuckled. "Just waiting to escape company and have a moment's peace."

I stopped walking and did my best to give him a genuine smile. Normally this would have been an easy conversation, but I was so distracted.

"That's not true," I said with a smirk. "I love *your* company, and Aunt Mary's company. I love the company of these bushes, and that splendid-looking bench over there that is calling our names." I pointed as I saw a bench with a backrest tucked close to the tall hedges. If Henry were to hide something, I was sure it would be there.

Uncle Francis smiled. "I daresay you are right." He led us over to the bench and we sat in silence, taking in the night sky and the beauty around us. I liked that Uncle Francis could pass the time without a word. It gave me more time to think. I continued pondering ways to be alone with Henry, with my uncle still close. Perhaps I could tell my uncle I would just roam the gardens nearby. . . . But no, he would simply insist on joining me.

Something small fell into my hair. I held back a shriek as I swatted at whatever it was until it fell in front of my face and into my lap. Sighing with relief, I realized it was just a small, oddly shaped leaf. I brushed it off my lap—it felt like parchment. Removing my gloves, I quickly picked it off the ground to get a better look, heart racing with excitement.

Uncle Francis looked at me curiously as I bent down. "Have you lost something?" he asked.

I had to think of something quick. "Pardon my unladylike manner, Uncle. I do believe a pebble is stuck in my shoe." I proceeded to act as though I was fishing through my shoe until he looked away.

Straightening back up, I held the small, skinny piece of parchment at my side, farthest from where my uncle sat. I glanced at him, noticing his drooping eyes. He wasn't focused on me at all, clearly tired. I turned my body slightly away from him in case he decided to look in my direction, then lifted the small piece of paper up in the moonlight and read the small words from Henry:

Don't leave your chaperone.

I opened my mouth in disbelief and annoyance. Henry knew exactly what I was planning. I wanted to throw his little paper on the ground, bury it up, and see what he thought of that.

And where was he now? I couldn't exactly search for him without raising suspicion from Uncle Francis. I looked at my uncle again, his eyes now at half-mast. An idea came to me. Uncle Francis could fall asleep anywhere and in any position; he could fall asleep sitting on this very bench resting up against its back if he was comfortable enough. And when he fell asleep, he might as well have been made of stone with deaf ears. Nothing could rouse him.

"Uncle Francis," I said quietly.

He quickly opened his eyes fully and turned his attention to me, as if he hadn't been sleepy in the slightest. "Yes?" He tried to sound natural. It was hard not to chuckle at his attempt.

I tried to make my own eyes look tired. "I was wondering if I could just rest my eyes here on this bench for a few minutes. I'm rather tired and I believe a small nap will rejuvenate me."

Based on the way he smiled and relaxed his shoulders, I'd clearly suggested the best idea in the world. He nodded. "Certainly. I might rest my own eyes for a minute as well."

"I'll wake you when I'm ready to go back inside," I said, already beginning to close my eyes and lean back on the bench in a leisurely manner.

"Take all the time you need," he said with relief. Within a minute I could hear him breathing in and out, slowly and rhythmically.

"Uncle Francis?" I asked quietly.

He didn't respond.

I closed my eyes and waited another minute or so just to be extra sure. I opened my eyes, hoping to see Henry there, only to be disappointed that he was not. Standing quietly, I placed my gloves on the bench, deciding to take matters into my own hands. I was about to walk forward when I felt a hand on my arm from behind the bench.

My stomach lurched with anticipation.

I slowly turned without making a sound, only able to make out a tall silhouette, blending in with the shrubs. It had to be Henry. He put a finger up to his lips for me to be quiet. I nodded, then followed as he vanished through the bushes.

There was a break in the tall hedgerow a few steps away from my uncle. I slipped between and felt Henry's hand take mine, guiding me to the other side. The shrubs were no longer shading his features from the moonlight. His entire being enticed me, reminding me of our first meeting.

He slowly brought me close and spoke in my ear. "I thought I told you not to leave your chaperone." A tingle went through me as his breath grazed my neck.

"I didn't leave my chaperone," I whispered back. "He's still right there on the other side."

Henry pulled back from my ear until his face was close to mine. "Lily," he said quietly, with a hint of frustration. "If your chaperone is over there, he's going to have a very hard time keeping me in line." He found my eyes. "You said you have new information." Even his intoxicating presence couldn't stop the excitement I felt about bringing him new information.

"I do," I breathed enthusiastically. "Are you familiar with Mr. Alexander Campbell?"

"I am not," was all Henry obliged me with.

"He is a gentleman who used to frequent White's." Henry's eyes stayed on mine as I spoke, and then they slowly moved to my hair and the loose curls that rested on my shoulders.

"And you are familiar with this gentleman?" he finally asked.

"I am," I said, volunteering no further information.

He cocked an eyebrow. "How familiar?"

I smirked. This was one of my favorite moods to find him in. It made me want to hold out just a moment longer. I should have known that wasn't a smart move.

"Are you aware, Lily, that when you smirk like that, a dimple forms right by the corner of your mouth?" His eyes found the spot he was describing. "I find it maddening."

I dropped my smirk immediately. Heat rose up my neck and burned through my cheeks as my pulse quickened.

"And your blush is lovely," he added, grinning.

I put my hands up to my cheeks as if it would somehow stop them from acting up. A victorious smile erupted on Henry's face, and he chuckled lightly. I turned away from him, feeling self-conscious. He took my hand and slowly turned me back toward him. "Will you please tell me how you know Mr. Campbell?"

I shook my head at his flirting, despite the fact that I loved every minute of it. "The last time I danced with him . . . " I paused, "was right before I met you for the first time at Hastingwood's ball." One side of my mouth turned up. I didn't add the fact that it was the first and only time I'd danced with Mr. Campbell.

"And do you enjoy his company?" he asked.

"His company is very entertaining, to be sure." I smirked. If Henry was jealous, I would play this card for as long as I could.

Henry grinned. "Don't toy with me right now, Lily. You're smirking again, and your uncle isn't being a very good chaperone. Be honest with me, who is Alexander Campbell? Do you enjoy his company? And what does he have to do with Lord Elliot's death?"

"I'll answer your questions if you answer one for me in return," I said, hopeful.

"Very well. I'll answer a question once you've answered mine." Hope tickled at the back of my mind. Was it possible that he would divulge his real name? I wasted no time answering his questions.

I told him about the altercation between Lord Elliot and Mr. Campbell at White's. I explained Mr. Campbell's gambling debts and how he accused Lord Elliot of cheating, and threatened him afterward.

Henry rubbed his finger over his short beard as he listened, distracting me each time it grazed his bottom lip. I finished relating the details Marianne gave me, then waited in silence for his response.

"And in what way do you find this gentleman entertaining?" He used my exact words from earlier.

"The first . . . and last time I danced with him, he was dressed so ridiculously that it was hard to take him seriously. Towards the end of our dance I glanced at his absurd dress attire. In response to my poorly timed glance, he said, 'I can see that you have noticed the advantage of having me as your partner.' "

Henry smirked. "How modest of him."

I grinned. "Truly a gentleman of humility. When I asked him what his advantages were, he said, 'Come now, miss. It is hard to ignore perfection when it is right in front of you.' "

Henry scoffed.

I gave him an amused grin. "He even said he could make an exception for my appearance that evening. As you can imagine, I was beyond flattered."

Henry's face was suddenly angry. "Did he really say that to you, Lily?" He inhaled slowly.

I didn't expect this reaction. I thought he would find it as humorous as I did. I didn't know what to say in response.

"If I see him dancing with you again, I don't believe he will walk out of the ballroom in one piece."

I gave him a mischievous smile to lessen his fury. "Perhaps I will ask *him* to dance, in that case. However, I don't believe there will be a next time." I bit my lip. "I humiliated him at the very end of the dance. He wanted me to swoon over him so I played along for a time. He believed I was talking about him when I stated that there was a gentleman that had certainly caught my eye that evening—"

"Were you referring to Lord Elliot?" Henry raised a brow. "I couldn't help but notice the way you were dancing with him a moment ago."

"Let me finish," I interjected. "You're interrupting the best part."

Henry smirked but waited for me to continue.

"Right when he thought I was about to confess my undying love for him, I stated that I must go and speak to the gentleman who had caught my attention and tell him of my feelings." I paused for dramatic effect. "Then I confessed that the man who had caught my attention was none other than Mr. Reeves."

A corner of Henry's mouth twitched as if he was doing his best to suppress a smile.

"If you aren't aware," I continued. "Mr. Reeves is the oldest bachelor in London. He is also very beefy, very severe looking, and very unfashionable."

Henry finally broke, chuckling. He shook his head as he laughed softly. "I should have expected nothing less. No blow to the face would have hurt his ego as much as being regarded below Mr. Reeves."

I grinned. "I'll take that as a compliment." We stood there for a moment in silence before I suddenly remembered that it was my turn to ask Henry a question. I stepped in closer and reached out, touching his arm. "Henry." He held perfectly still as I looked up at him. "It's your turn to answer a question now."

"What would you like to ask me, Lily?" He asked the question gently but with reserve.

"Who are you really?"

19

COAT

Lily

Henry looked at my fingers resting on his arm and eased my hand into his, tracing his finger along each of mine. My heart pounded at the intimate gesture. "What will you do if I don't answer your question?" He continued tracing my hand until my ring appeared in his fingers. He let it fall on my thumb.

My eyes fell away from his. I'd been so hopeful that he would tell me what I wanted to know . . . what I needed to know.

I answered him truthfully. "I don't know what I'll do. Eventually I'll have to learn the truth, or . . . " I trailed off. The thought of never seeing Henry again was too painful. I found I couldn't state the words aloud. Henry brought my hand up, then brushed his lips gently across my fingers, making me breathless. I was well past falling for this man. My head had submerged below the water and there was no chance of coming up for air without Henry.

I should have left him right then and there, but it was as if he knew I couldn't.

It was in that thought that I somehow mustered the will to do just that. I wanted to be able to discover him fully. I didn't want to hold back anymore. My heart ached as I pulled my hand from his and turned to walk away. I was about to walk through the opening in the hedge near my uncle when I felt Henry take my hand, stopping me.

Though I hated to admit it, I wanted him to stop me. I wanted him to follow me and tell me why I should stay. At the same time, I wanted him to let me go. Every moment I spent with him would be more heartache if I found out I couldn't be with him once his identity was revealed. I still faced forward as he held my hand from behind.

"Lily." He spoke so quietly, I wondered if it was my imagination.

I finally turned to face him.

"I can't tell you who I am just yet. But if you can wait just one more week, I promise, you will have your answers. All of them." It wasn't what I wanted. But when he looked at me with his determined eyes, desperation hidden beneath his gaze, I couldn't stay away—at least not for now.

"Can you at least come inside the ballroom and join the party?" I asked. "You could ask me to dance if we were introduced. I don't even mind if you give your false name." I smiled encouragingly.

He lifted an eyebrow. "Are you sure you wouldn't rather just dance with Lord Elliot?"

I opened my mouth and smiled. "If I didn't know any better, sir, I would think you were jealous."

He slowly pulled me toward him. "And what if I were jealous?" he whispered in my ear.

I tried to speak, but nothing came out. We stayed suspended like this for a time. I could feel his breath near my ear. I wanted to stay this way forever. The only thing that stood between us was the truth. Music swelled from the open terrace doors; another dance was starting.

Henry smiled softly, then quietly spoke. "It appears I am in luck." He stepped backward and bowed. "Lily, might I have this dance?"

I smiled. "Only if you promise not to plow me over like you did the first time we met."

Henry chuckled. "I will if you promise to bring a better chaperone with you next time."

The music was slow. We moved through the dance steps. Despite knowing the moves well, I felt as though it was a foreign dance. It was far more intimate than I ever remembered. Henry slowly pulled me closer every time we came together. His strong arms held me tenderly while he led me through the steps with confidence. I would forever be ruined by the way he moved me.

No other man could snare me like he did. It was disheartening to realize I would have to spend the rest of the evening dancing with men that weren't him. His eyes watched mine as we moved together. It felt as though time stood still and moved all too quickly at the same time. I didn't want the music to stop—didn't want to leave.

My wishes were in vain. The music's end echoed in the space between my heart and Henry's.

He slowly wrapped his arms around me and held me close. "I'm afraid I must leave you now," he whispered. I knew this moment would have to come eventually, but it was harder than I anticipated. "I won't see you for some time."

My eyes shot to his. "How long—?"

"I'm not sure. I believe it will be a few days at least. I don't know how else to see you without getting caught eventually." He let out a breath of frustration, then carefully took a lock of my hair between his fingers. He gave me a look that could only be described as desire.

"Lily." His voice came out low and gravelly. He put the side of his head against mine. "It's getting harder and harder for me to leave you." I felt his lips brush near my temple. I trembled at the contact. He pulled me in even closer and breathed in. "Perhaps I can call on you again tomorrow as a matter of business." He grinned.

"Tomorrow," I muttered, realizing I had completely lost track of the days since I met Henry. "Henry, I'm leaving for Wilton tomorrow and won't return to London for seven days." My voice was filled with dread. I had never felt so reluctant to go home.

"You can't leave me for seven days, Lily. I hired you." He grinned. "What would you do without all that tuppence?"

"Seven days." The words sounded like a death sentence as I said them again.

"I could always hold your carriage up at gunpoint as a highwayman and smuggle you back." He gave me a wicked look.

I would never admit it out loud, but it was a very tempting option.

"My sister, Jane, would certainly die of a heart attack, and then I'd have to challenge you to a duel for killing her."

Henry chuckled. "I know when I'm beaten."

I had been waiting so long to find out Henry's true identity. But the thought of never meeting him like this again made me feel desperate in a way I hadn't expected. What if the next time I saw him I realized I could never be with him again?

"Will you still be Henry when I see you next?" I asked.

He exhaled slowly. I felt his arms slowly release me. "That remains to be seen." I recognized his cue. He would walk away soon. I wanted to beg him to stay but I knew I couldn't.

I reached for him regardless, my hand gripping his arm before he had a chance to leave. "Henry, when will I see you again?"

He looked at me with an unreadable expression. "I'm not sure."

I drank in his eyes until eventually I released his arm. He breathed in deeply one last time, giving me a tortured look, then walked away. It was only after he disappeared that I noticed tuppence in my palm. I couldn't recall him placing it there. Sighing, I ran my fingers over my temple, in the place Henry's lips had found my skin. My stomach flipped at the recollection. I wasn't ready to go back inside just yet. I needed time to get my heart to behave normally again. Perhaps Uncle Francis and I would take a long walk through the gardens after all.

Jane

I did my best not to feel completely despondent. From the time Frederick stole me away, Charles had danced with two other women aside from his dance with Lily. I was hoping he would ask me for the next dance, but I watched as Edith and Amelia crossed to the other side of the room together and found him. They smiled demurely at him and laughed as they talked.

He actually smiled back. I couldn't stay in the room any longer. I needed an escape. I needed to find Lily and Uncle Francis—I knew they would gratefully accept such a venture. I searched, but found no sign of them. Aunt Mary was talking excitedly with her friends in a corner near an exit to a garden terrace.

"Aunt Mary," I finally interjected.

She turned to smile at me, then looked concerned. "Jane, are you well? You look flushed."

"I believe some air will put me right." I tried my best to smile.

"Of course. Francis and Lily are just out on the terrace if you would like to join them. Mind you, they've been away far too long. Tell them to come in when you're ready."

"Yes, of course." I excused myself, then walked swiftly toward the garden. I looked back once more to find Charles. He was still talking with the gossips, his charming smile in tow. I sighed. I wanted nothing more than to be near him. I wanted—

He suddenly looked up and found my eyes from across the room.

My heart thudded, unable to look away. I wanted him to come to me—to pretend he wanted to be near me as much as I wanted to be near him.

But his eyes turned away from mine and found Amelia's. She was touching his arm. My heart tore. I was falling to pieces so quickly.

Turning away, I fled the ballroom to ensure I wouldn't be tempted to look back again. My lungs filled with the cool air of November and I found that I wanted to cry in relief for its familiarity. I wanted it to wrap itself around my entire existence and swallow me whole.

After walking a few paces, I closed my eyes and let it take me completely—

My eyes shot open when I felt a hand take my wrist, hopeful anticipation brewing. Perhaps Charles wanted some fresh air himself. I gasped as my eyes landed on Mr. Hughes.

He was watching me curiously. "You're early," he said.

My chest rose and fell in dread as I looked around for Lily and Uncle Francis. They were nowhere to be seen. I snatched my hand away from him.

"I came out here to find my sister and uncle. Are they here?"

He smirked, then slowly walked toward me. "There is no one here but us." He was blocking the entrance back into the ballroom. If someone else decided to come outside and discovered me alone with Mr. Hughes, my reputation would certainly be ruined.

I walked backward towards the gardens, hoping to find Lily and Uncle Francis, all while keeping my eyes on him. "What do you want, Mr. Hughes?"

"You know exactly what I want," he said in a suggestive tone.

I knew that reasoning with him would never work. I grasped for straws. Threats were my best option. "Lord Fletcher would never forgive you." I backed up faster, but it was hard to do as I kept my eyes on him.

He easily kept pace with me. "He doesn't have to find out. Besides, Frederick and I are at odds at the moment. He doesn't think my character is worthy enough for his 'highly esteemed' reputation. At least, not during public events." He grabbed for my arm but I yanked it away.

Mr. Hughes smiled as if he enjoyed the challenge. "Don't pretend you don't want this, Jane. I know you came out here for this very purpose. I enjoy your teasing, but enough is enough. I promise after one good kiss you'll beg for more." There was no way I could outrun him. Looking around me frantically, I found a stick on the ground. I quickly snatched it up but he jerked it away before I could use it and grabbed both of my wrists, chuckling as he forced both of my arms around him.

"Please let me go," I begged, my voice shaking. I knew pleading was futile, but I couldn't help it. I struggled to get free, but tears came instead as I realized he was stronger than me. I shut my eyes and prayed for an escape. I heard him snigger at my helplessness—

THWAM! A sickening thud sounded in my ears as I was thrown toward the ground. My eyes flew open just in time for me to catch myself. Legs shaking, I tried to right myself and flee, but my arm was seized again. I turned quickly to slap Mr. Hughes with my free hand, but he caught it as I was about to make contact.

252

Except it wasn't Mr. Hughes.

Charles held my hand suspended as if the force of my arm was nothing more than a passing breeze. What did he think of me? I couldn't help the tears that followed. I turned away from him.

"Jane." His voice was tender.

I looked down to find Mr. Hughes unconscious on the ground.

Charles carefully took my shoulders and turned me around to face him. "Jane, are you hurt?" he asked quietly.

I shook my head.

"What happened?" His tone was comforting.

"I—" My voice quavered. I couldn't get anything else out.

"You're shaking."

I tried to take a calming breath but I shook even more.

He shrugged out of his coat and put it around my arms. It smelled like wood and soap, its warmth enveloping me.

"Thank you," was all I could get out. I continued to shiver despite the warmth, but forced myself to breathe deeply.

He waited patiently. "Take your time."

We stood silent for what felt like minutes. Just as I felt I might be able to speak, I detected voices somewhere near us. We looked at each other. He must have realized as much as I did that our reputations were at risk. Charles took my wrist and led me through some tall hedges with a narrow opening to escape the main path.

I came willingly.

It opened up to a small space, barely big enough for the both of us to take a step in each direction, surrounded by tall bushes on all sides. I quieted my breathing as best I could, though my shivering continued. Charles was already close to me, watching me shiver, a tortured expression marking his eyes.

The look on his face reminded me of how much I wanted him. I tried not to think about how much it would hurt when he no longer looked at me that way—when he found the woman that would secure his heart. He inched forward, then slowly took my hand. The warmth of his fingers pulsed through me and sent a surge straight to my heart.

"Your hands are freezing," he whispered near my ear before taking both of my hands in his. He appeared to be at war with himself, trying to hold himself back from something. I tried not to think about how my heart was racing as I looked at him without his coat. His inward battle continued until he finally cursed under his breath and threaded his arms around me beneath his coat. My hands rested on his chest, warmth radiating through his shirt while his heart beat strong and fast. He eased me in, holding me closer with each breath.

"Jane," he said in a low, agonizing breath. My heart pounded with his as he released one of his hands from my waist but held me just as secure with the other. He laced his other hand through the back of my hair where it fell in loose curls. I was ensnared. I was completely breathless. I wanted more.

His fingers entwined themselves in my hair and I felt him gently pull my head back until I could see nothing but him. I watched his eyes as they led me to their depths. I watched them as they moved from my eyes to my lips. My hands slowly made their way up until they found his shoulders. He leaned in slowly, wrestling with himself until we were a breath apart. My hands entwined around his neck of their own accord. I was no longer in control. I wanted to pull him to me completely. I didn't want to think about what came after. I didn't care if my heart bled later.

"Jane." Charles's voice came out low and breathy. "You are not making this easy for me." I felt his breath on my lips.

I shuddered. "You aren't making this easy for *me*."

We didn't move. Just as I was sure he would close the distance between us, the voices grew louder. Charles continued to hold me close, but sighed as he slowly moved his face away, eyes not leaving mine as the voices came closer. He reluctantly removed his fingers from my hair and slid them around my back.

Disappointed, I removed my hands from around his neck and let them fall to his arms around me. He pulled me closer as I rested my head on his chest, exhaling with contentment as he held me close. I opened one ear to the approaching people, Charles's heartbeat filling the other. I felt safe and whole, surrounded in his embrace.

As the voices neared I noticed they were distinctly female. It sounded like two of them.

"I don't like this," one of the ladies hissed.

"You're never any fun," said the other. I couldn't distinguish who they were from their voices.

"If anyone catches us out here—"

"No one will," came the flippant voice. "Besides, if you want the rakes you have to be willing to break a few rules. And rakes are worth the risk. They know how to handle a woman." My stomach twisted at her words as I realized these ladies had been seeking out Mr. Hughes.

"What if he gives us up to the wolves and tells the public what we're up to?"

Her friend scoffed. "And ruin his own reputation in the process?"

"Where is he, then?"

"He will be around here somewhere." The voices were just beyond our hiding place. Charles pulled me even closer.

It was then that I remembered Mr. Hughes's unconscious body on the ground near the area we were hiding. My heart pounded with Charles's as we held perfectly still. I heard their footsteps slow until one of them gasped.

"Is he dead?" the more cautious lady asked.

"No. But it appears he took a blow to the face."

"What if someone knows we were meeting him here?"

"Not even *he* knew who he would be meeting tonight. It was all arranged very carefully," she said, annoyed, before sighing. "So disappointing. We'd better go back in before we are discovered."

"Indeed." She sounded relieved. Their footsteps slowly fell away in the distance. We waited a few more minutes in silence.

Charles continued to hold me close. "Jane," he said softly.

I didn't want to move.

He slowly lifted my chin until I was looking up at him. "Did Mr. Hughes think you came out here intentionally to meet him?"

I nodded. "I didn't understand what he was talking about in the moment, but yes, he said I was early when I first came out." My stomach twisted at the reminder.

"I came out here to find Lily and my uncle. Mr. Hughes blocked the entrance back into the ballroom, and . . . "

I exhaled. "How did you know I was in trouble?"

He tensed. "I didn't. But I watched you leave the ballroom, and I had a nagging feeling to find out where you'd gone." His jaw tightened before he spoke. "When I saw Jacob force your arms around him I thought I might actually kill him. I don't want that disgusting creature near you again."

"That makes two of us," I said quietly. Charles breathed in slowly, then spoke close to my ear in a quiet voice.

"Promise me you'll have someone already with you when you take a walk around next time." He lifted my hand and put it against the side of his face, closing his eyes. "For your sake and for mine." My eyes followed his every move as he deliberately brushed the back of my fingers across his cheek, down over his jaw and across his lips on the way down. A tremor pulsed through me. When he opened his eyes he looked at me and slowly shook his head.

"You've always been breathtaking, Jane. Tonight, you've been torture. And I have no chance of surviving this if you keep looking at me like that. I've already stayed out here far too long."

I didn't know what to say. I didn't want him to leave. When he was here with me, I could convince myself that he felt for me as much as I felt for him—that he was falling for me too—that he would be here when I returned from Wilton and stay for me. But once he left, I would have to face reality again.

Charles sighed. "Frederick is probably wondering where you've gone." He slowly began to release me. "If he notices I'm missing too, he may become suspicious." My heart already began to ache as he put distance between us.

I understood what Lily meant about wanting to be thoroughly snatched up, about wanting to fall in love rather than marrying for status. If only I hadn't fallen in love with the most sought-after bachelor in all of London.

Charles spoke again. "I want you to stay hidden near the hedgerows as you make your way back up to the ballroom from the back entrance. I will follow you from behind at a safe distance to ensure you don't end up in another situation like earlier."

He glanced at my lips again. "Whatever you do, don't look back at me. I don't know how much more self-control I have tonight." His eyes burned.

"Charles, I'm not ready," I whispered. Tears threatened to escape their stronghold, but I kept them in.

"Neither am I. But you need to leave now."

"You said you would dance with me," I said, almost pleading.

"I can't, Jane. I must leave once I've seen you safely inside."

Tears fell from my eyes. I could no longer hold them back. It was possible that I'd never see him again.

He let out a breath of anguish as he looked at me. "Please don't cry, Jane," he whispered.

"I can't help it."

"Tell me what to do." His voice was little more than a whisper. "Tell me how to make it better."

"Don't leave. Stay until . . . " I faltered. Until when? Eventually he would have to leave.

He took my hands in both of his. "For as long as it takes." I could tell he wanted to say more but held back. He stepped close to me again and placed my hands to his shirt as he slowly wrapped his arms around me. I rested my head on his chest as he pulled me even closer.

"What will you do in Wilton?" he finally asked. "Will you restore your honor as a pastry thief?" I sensed him smile, his fingers lightly tracing up and down my back.

A small laugh escaped me. "Cook is a fierce woman. I wouldn't dare set foot in her kitchen without all of my crew and a plan."

Charles's finger slowly coaxed my face towards his as I smiled. His eyes found my upturned lips. "What am I to do without your smile these next several days?"

I lifted my hand and touched his face, unable to help myself. He closed his eyes as I did so, breathing in deeply. Releasing one of his arms from around my waist, he took my hand in his, softly pressing his lips to each of my fingers. My entire being pulsed and thrummed.

As my fingers were released, they found his chest. The pounding of his heart mirrored my own strong pulse. We looked at one another until his eyes closed in defeat. "I'm afraid it's time."

My heart already ached at the thought, but I knew I couldn't argue again. He'd already stayed longer for me than he should have.

I carefully took off his coat and handed it back to him, immediately missing the smell and the warmth. "Thank you," was all I could muster as I turned away from him.

"Wait." He didn't touch me again, but waited for me to look at him. "I believe, more than ever, you are in my debt." He gave me a small grin. His attempt to lighten the mood warmed me, even if I knew he may never have the chance to claim his payment.

"I'm counting on it." I would hold onto that thought for the next seven days. As I walked away from Charles, the ache in my heart grew. I had fallen off the edge of the precipice completely. I would have to crawl my way out, forever changed. Never whole again. Forever wanting him.

20

CUCKOO

Lawrence

London
November 8, 1816
Later that evening
Seven days of disguise remaining

Charles and Henry both arrived home from the Morgans' ball early, wearing somber expressions.

"Would you like anything brought to you in the library, my lord?" I asked Henry, maintaining our act.

"No, Lawrence, thank you," he said without any emotion. "But your company would be appreciated."

Charles and Henry walked to the library in silence. Their teasing and banter from the first evening was non-existent. It was as if a cloud loomed above each of them.

I was nervous about what their silence and flat expressions could mean. What if they'd hit a dead end? Once we entered the library, I shut the door, taking a moment to listen, ensuring no one else lurked close by. "Is something amiss?" I asked when I was certain we were alone.

"No," Charles said flatly. "We simply obtained our information early and had no reason to stay."

"I see," I said with some confusion. "And what did you discover?"

Charles started. "I learned that a gentleman named Alexander Campbell was witnessed arguing with Papa at White's only weeks before his death. Apparently Mr. Campbell owes a fair amount of money and my father put him in his place with a wager. He won, and Mr. Campbell made a scene, yelling that Papa was a cheater, and that he'd better watch his step."

Henry shook his head, a frustrated exhale following close behind. "That means we have two likely suspects now. I was hoping we could point it all at Jacob and have it over with."

"Jacob may have been working with Mr. Campbell," I piped up, drawing Charles's and Henry's eyes to me. "My contacts here in London have been following Jacob. Yesterday they spotted a gentleman talking with him on a street corner late at night. They followed the other gentleman home at a distance and discovered that the name of the man belonged to a Mr. Alexander Campbell."

"That detail may help clear up a few things I overheard tonight," Henry said.

"You never did tell me what it was you discovered," Charles said.

"I wanted to wait for Lawrence." There was still little expression in the way either of them spoke. Then Henry smirked slightly. "Because I might need him to protect me."

"What rule did you break this time?" Charles folded his arms, already annoyed.

"Let's just say that Jacob Hughes may have lost consciousness at some point this evening."

"Is there a reason you felt the need to render him unconscious?" I asked.

"Does he need a reason?" Charles smirked. "I'm only disappointed I wasn't there to help." Charles looked over at Henry. "Lawrence does bring up a good point, though. Is there a specific reason it was done tonight and not sooner?"

Henry smirked. "I guess I finally found him away from prying eyes. I don't think he even saw me before he was on the ground. I heard voices immediately afterwards and hid in a small opening of shrubs nearby—it was two women speaking. I couldn't see who they were, and I didn't recognize their voices, but it was clear that they had come out to intentionally meet Jacob. They said it was arranged by someone else, and that Jacob didn't even know their identities. This was no casual meeting.

"One of the ladies was worried about being caught. When they discovered Jacob unconscious they were nervous about being caught and went back inside. I wasn't able to follow them to discover their identities, unfortunately."

I looked from Henry to Charles, a thought forming. "Is it possible that Mr. Campbell is the one who arranged the meeting?"

"Perhaps," Charles said. "And it is entirely possible that Papa found out about similar dealings with Jacob and was about to exploit him. He would have been able to easily justify taking Jacob out of the lineup to inherit if such details were brought to light."

"What about our duke-to-be? The honorable Frederick Fletcher?" Henry asked sarcastically. "Do you think he could be involved?" His face didn't hold emotion, but underneath his flat exterior he sounded hopeful, as though he would love nothing more than to see his old rival guilty for such a thing.

"Perhaps," Charles said. "I wouldn't put it past him to participate in anything dishonorable, especially if Jacob is involved. I think it's important to note, however, that I observed Frederick having a clipped conversation with Jacob at the beginning of the Morgans' ball tonight. It appears as though they are not on friendly terms at present."

Henry looked disappointed. "Now what do we do?"

A knock sounded at the door, quieting each of us. A young man walked in. "This just arrived at the door," he said, holding a square package wrapped in brown paper, about the size of a shoe box.

"Thank you." I nodded, taking it from his hands. After he exited the library, I waited until his footsteps faded before I examined the package. "Henry Thomas" was written along the top. I narrowed my eyes, then looked at Henry and handed it to him. "Who is it from?" I asked.

Henry took it, looking perplexed. "Your guess is as good as mine." He slowly unwrapped the packaging, a wooden box inside. Curious, he slowly removed the lid—

Henry jolted in surprise, the box clattering to the ground, landing upside down.

"What is it?" Charles asked, eyes uneasy.

I walked over to the box and carefully lifted it. Splayed wings, lifeless eyes, and a large, thornlike spike protruded from the chest of a bird. Horrified, I covered the disturbing sight before me.

Charles walked over to view the box's contents. His eyes shot to Henry. "What is this?"

Henry slowly turned the underside of the lid over. There was a small piece of parchment glued to it. His brow raised in understanding as his eyes moved over it, then he placed it on the table for us to see. The paper had been ripped from a book. A snippet of poetry, as it appeared.

TO THE CUCKOO.

O blithe New-comer! I have heard,
I hear thee and rejoice:
O Cuckoo! shall I call thee Bird,
Or but a wandering Voice?

I know the truth—Henry Thomas. I could easily let it slip.

Charles looked furious as he read. He picked up the lid with the message attached and the box holding the dead bird and threw them in the cold fireplace. He uncapped a lantern and threw the oil over it all, then grabbed the tinderbox and struck it forcefully, sending sparks into the hearth. Flames engulfed the contents within.

Whether Charles was angry that someone had discovered their switch in identities or that someone would send such an unhinged message to the man he considered his brother, I could not tell.

"Who would send something like this to you?" he asked Henry.

"I'm sorry, Charles. I've not done anything to give myself away."

"Never mind that," Charles said angrily. "Who would send you this sort of disgusting message!"

Henry looked exhausted. "I have an idea."

Charles raised an eyebrow. "Please. Do share." His tone was clipped.

"I told you about the gentleman, Matthew Johnson, who has acquired a severe dislike for me. I made a social call on some acquaintances I met at the duchess's ball. Mr. Johnson was already there visiting. I believe he was intending to woo a young lady and saw my presence as a threat. He was choosing each person's bird likeness, and when he described himself, he chose a shrike."

Charles narrowed his eyes. "That's unsettling."

"Precisely. He watches the younger Miss Mason as if he owns her already. He's possessive, even though she shows no interest in him. He treated me as if I was pursuing her in earnest when we were all having a lively conversation equally."

"*Do* you pursue her?" Charles's voice was even but I detected tension beneath the surface.

Henry gave Charles a flat stare. "Really, Charles, that's what you ask me after what I just explained?"

"You've broken three rules already. It's a simple question, Henry. Are you pursuing Lily Mason?"

Henry narrowed his eyes at Charles for a moment, clearly suspicious. "I didn't state that her name was Lily. How do you know her name?"

Charles's expression was flat. "The last time we spoke, you told me that Matthew Johnson had taken a particular dislike to you. So I followed him the other afternoon. He waited outside a house for three hours. It was the same house where you attended the dinner party the other evening. Mr. Johnson practically forced his way inside after a young lady arrived, even though calling hours were over.

"I hid beneath a window that was cracked open and listened while he proposed to this young lady. He called her Lily Mason. I'm assuming this is the same Miss Mason you speak of? I only ask because when she refused him, he stated to her that he knew it was because of her regard towards Lord Elliot. So I feel it is only natural that I ask."

Henry's look of suspicion slowly retreated. "I have no regard for Lily, other than respect and friendship. I have not pursued her, nor have I shown more interest in her than the rest of the women of the *ton*. If I am accused of doing so, then I should also be accused of doing so with practically every lady in London. You have asked me to dance with and charm as many women as I can.—call on them, and try to get into as many circles as possible. And you're missing the point, Charles. The point is that Matthew Johnson is unhinged. He saw me as a threat when I showed no more than polite manners to Miss Mason."

Charles's tension dissipated. "I believe you misunderstand my questions. I agree with you that he is certainly unhinged. His *thoughtful* package is evidence of that. I was simply trying to understand the situation better." He looked at the blazing fire. "Did that specific bird have any significance?"

"The bird inside that box is technically a sparrowhawk. Cuckoos are not native to England. A sparrowhawk's appearance, however, is very much like a cuckoo's. When Matthew was giving all of our likenesses, he likened me to a cuckoo. He claimed it was because of my title—that I feed off those below me. Clearly he knew my identity all along. And as much as I hate to admit it, I *am* a cuckoo. I was raised by parents other than my own. I was placed in a different nest. A nest where I was fed, clothed, and treated as their own. And as much as I want to be an Elliot, I will forever be Henry Thomas."

"I don't see it that way," Charles protested.

I wanted to stop Henry from speaking further. I didn't think Charles was ready to hear Henry's new plan to leave us once their disguise ended, in order to make his own way. But I couldn't stop him. It didn't matter that I disliked the idea of Henry leaving . . . he needed this.

"You don't see it that way because you *are* an Elliot," Henry said. "You have no idea what it feels like to live off of someone else's money."

"I give you full access to any money you would ever want or need," Charles said defensively.

"Exactly. You give me money. I don't make my own money."

"You help me with my business ventures," Charles argued.

Henry shook his head. "It isn't the same. You are Lord Elliot, Earl of Wiltshire. I may help in my own way, but ultimately it is your money, your business ventures. When you finally find a lady that you would like to bring home, you have a home to call your own. You have money that is yours—that will offer stability. I—I have nothing."

"You are my brother, Henry. You have claim to this money as much as I do." Charles looked as though he had been betrayed.

"I *am* your brother—in every way except blood. And I won't steal from my brother. I will not someday bring a woman I love to my brother's house and ask for permission to raise my family in his home. I need to start making my own way. I know you have never thought of it in those terms, which is why I have been able to turn a blind eye for so long. But it's time for me to begin anew. I have plans to do just that once we have officially uncovered the truth about Papa's death."

Charles pressed his lips together before he looked at Henry. "I've never considered that this is how you would feel. I imagined it would always be as it has always been. But you're right. I would feel exactly as you do. What do you plan to do?"

Henry let out a long breath. "I'm working that part out. I believe I may need to confront my father after all these years, to begin with. Then I will use the schooling I was given to make something of myself."

"If I may be so bold," I interjected, "the two of you work well together. You may both consider doing business with Mr. Lucas Mason. He, too, is from Wilton and has had much success in trade. Your father did business with him from time to time and always spoke favorably of the man and his capability at his trade."

Henry actually smiled. "Lawrence, I believe that is truly a brilliant idea."

"I do have rare moments of genius occasionally." I held my lips straight, but I could feel my smile peeking through.

Charles and Henry both smiled in return before Charles rested his chin on his fist, looking over at his brother.

"Now Henry, what are we going to do about Matthew Johnson? Nobody sends dead birds to my little brother and gets away with it."

Henry's mouth turned up. "Technically, Charles, you're *my* little brother."

Charles smirked. "I wasn't talking about age, Henry. You have been my 'little brother' by one inch since we were sixteen."

Henry rolled his eyes. "Technically, we haven't measured for a few years. You may have shrunk."

"With Charles's big head?" I grinned. "It's very unlikely." A small laugh finally escaped both Henry and Charles. My heart lightened at hearing the sound.

I reflected on everything the evening brought to my mind. We had been as careful as possible since arriving in London and had uncovered a lot of information. I looked at the fireplace as it consumed the wooden box. I didn't know what the next seven days would bring, but one thing I knew for certain: Charles and Henry were no longer safe, and needed to leave London as soon as possible.

21

HORSE

Jane

London
November 9, 1816
One day later
Six days of disguise remaining

Only the noise of the carriage wheels sounded between Lily and me. Whether or not she wished to speak, I could only guess. I stared out the window, watching everything and nothing. The ache in my heart was tangible, a pain I could have never predicted. The logical part of my brain told me I was overreacting, that I'd always known I'd have to give Charles up and there was no sense in longing for him now.

But to shut him out of my mind was impossible.

Despite my heartache, I couldn't bring myself to regret our time together. The pain and torment of being without him would help me remember each moment we shared—the hunger I saw in his eyes, as if he wanted my nearness just as much as I wanted his. More than anything, I would relive in my mind the way he held me, my heart beating with his.

Sighing, I closed my eyes, hoping that eventually slumber would take me. I doubted that I would ever truly sleep again. Not when Lord Elliot took up all the space in my mind and left no room for dreams.

Sterling and Oliver ran to the carriage as we pulled up. When my father inherited his money, my parents decided to expand our current house instead of purchasing another one far from home; they didn't want to leave Wilton. So they modified our old home into an estate, complete with a ballroom. I smiled as I took it in.

We were home.

Lily jumped from the carriage and ran to my brothers, embracing them with a crushing hug, followed by a special handshake. The corners of my mouth tugged upward, remembering the moment I'd taught those same handshakes to Lily. When did I stop doing them? I swallowed back my tears as I watched Lily put her hands out and twirl with Oliver. Why had I been trying so hard to tame her free spirit?

As I watched the scene of my brothers and sister unfold, I felt ashamed for wanting more for my family than what was right in front of me. It had been so long since I had embraced Sterling and Oliver the way Lily did. When was the last time I closed my eyes and ran through the meadow?

I slowly stepped down from the carriage, feeling as though I hadn't truly been home in years. My first few steps were timid as I drew towards my siblings. Then my feet began treading faster with each step until I was running. Sterling saw me first. His eyebrows knit in confusion just as I all but plowed him over with my hug.

He was so much bigger than he had been the last time I embraced him this way. After Sterling overcame his initial shock, I felt his arms wrap around my back, holding me tight. I laughed and a tear escaped. Oliver came from behind, crushing me as hard as he could with Sterling. Lily joined at the side and pulled us all in until we started tipping. I laughed harder and more tears came.

Mama came through the door just then, beaming. She smiled as she saw all of us embracing, quickly brushing at the corners of her eyes before walking to us with open arms. Lily and I finally pried ourselves from Sterling and Oliver, then embraced Mama together.

"You're home," she sighed with relief.

I was home.

Lily

My heart was full as we sat at the table for dinner. Watching Jane, it seemed as though she were returning home for the first time in years. I hadn't seen her act this way since before we were wealthy.

I was sitting next to Sterling as the courses were brought in. He watched my hand curiously as I took a spoonful of soup.

"Why is your ring on your thumb?" he asked suddenly. I looked at the place where Henry had last placed my ring and nervously noticed that his question seemed to attract the entire family's attention. I thought quickly of a way to blow it off.

I grinned. "I'm waiting to see if it will become the newest fashion in London. I suspect every young lady will be wearing her ring this way in no time."

Sterling gave me a funny look. "Is that all women think about? Being fashionable?"

"Absolutely," I teased.

"Fashion and men." Papa said, winking.

"And money," Sterling added.

"And dolls," Oliver said, looking like he couldn't believe everyone had overlooked the most obvious thing. Mama tried to bite down her smile.

"How could we have forgotten to mention dolls," she said, smiling at Oliver.

"Girls just always want to play with dolls," Oliver said, as if the very idea was taxing. The conversation continued to flow in a similar fashion. When I was sure no one was watching, I looked at the ring again, touching it with my fingers.

I didn't know what I would find when I returned to London. Would Henry still be Henry? If not, who would he be, and would the mystery surrounding the late Lord Elliot already be solved? I tried to shove thoughts of Henry out of my mind and simply enjoy my family's company—but it was futile.

It wasn't only that Henry was full of mystery and made my heart race: He felt like freedom. He didn't judge me for my need to find solitude at the duchess's ball or for my outbursts at our first meeting. He didn't simply tolerate my opinion—he actually sought it. I felt important to Henry.

I sighed. If only women *did* just think of fashion. Life would be so much simpler.

"Tell us about London," Mama said with enthusiasm. "Any gentlemen worth mentioning?"

"Bluugh!" Oliver said, sticking out his tongue in disgust.

Jane chuckled at him. "One of these days, a lady will strike your fancy and then you'll wish you'd paid better attention to this conversation." She winked at him.

I looked at Mama and grinned. "There are a few gentlemen worth mentioning, though not for the right reasons." I looked over at Sterling. "Promise me that when you start dressing for London society, you won't wear flamboyant purple, and promise me you won't tell a lady that you suppose her looks are acceptable for the evening."

Sterling shook his head. "I'm not a complete idiot."

"Did a man truly say such a thing to you, Lily?" Papa asked with a firm expression.

"He did," I said, grinning. "But I daresay I put Mr. Campbell in his place, Papa. You needn't worry."

"Well if you change your mind, I believe a hunt for London pigs would suit me very well." He gave me a smile before continuing, "It's no secret that I have the most beautiful daughters in all of England." When Jane grinned and shook her head at his comment, he notched an eyebrow, a resolute look on his face. "It's the truth, Jane, and don't let anyone tell you otherwise." He smiled at us both. "You got your good looks from me. That's why your mother still has hers." He winked at Mama across the table.

Oliver stuck his tongue out again and thumped his head on the table. "Can we be done talking about this now?" he grumbled. "I really want to tell Lily and Jane about how I fell out of that really tall tree the other day and didn't even get hurt."

"You just told it," Sterling said, rolling his eyes. "And you pretend to hate all this mushy stuff, but I saw you watching Isabelle Kensington the other day and you were practically drooling."

Oliver punched Sterling's shoulder. "I was not!" He knit his eyebrows together. "*You're* the one who's always spying on her."

Sterling's face turned red. "I am not!" He slugged Oliver back.

We laughed. It was exactly the type of day I had missed while in London. Now I just needed to find ways to distract myself until I could see Henry again.

Lily

Wilton
November 10, 1816
One day later
Five days of disguise remaining

It was only an hour past noon and I was sure I would die of boredom. I went to the stables, but Stella had thrown a shoe and I was told she wasn't ready to ride. Disheartened, I donned my coat and headed toward mine and Jane's favorite copse of trees for memory's sake.

I walked through the meadow, the sun touching my face, and breathed in the crisp air, grateful for the way it cleared my mind.

As I neared the trees, I broke into a run until they surrounded me, welcoming me back. I found my usual spot and looked up into the branches, the image a collection of memories.

Laughter bubbled up inside me as I remembered my girlish dream of becoming a pirate. I found the prettiest leaf like Jane and I used to do, then wished for Henry. As I watched the perfect leaf dance in the breeze, I leaned back against the tree and sat down, eyes suddenly feeling heavy. Mesmerized by the light playing with the leaf, I began drifting off to sleep.

I woke on the bench in my aunt and uncle's garden. It was hazed in a thick fog from the ground to the sky. Through the mist I saw a figure coming toward me; I knew his tall, broad silhouette anywhere.

"Henry," I said, standing to follow him. The shadowed figure turned away from me then started walking in the opposite direction. I pursued as swiftly as I could in the fog, getting closer to him—but as soon as he was in my reach, my legs froze in place and Henry faded into the mist. I called out for him again, but he was no longer in sight. I spun around, startled. Swirling white met my view at every turn, ensuing panic; I couldn't breathe. The fog was consuming me and I gasped, afraid it would swallow me whole.

A hand suddenly reached out for me. I knew it was Henry's. Relieved, I took it, and he immediately pulled me close.

I was safe.

With the swirling mist distorting his face, Henry held my head in his hands and bent his face towards me, lips inches from mine . . . when he finally came into focus.

I reeled back as Mr. Hughes's face appeared. Desperate, I tried to scream out, but the thick fog choked me into silence. My hands flew in front of me, pushing against him until I was free. But as I turned to run, Mr. Johnson materialized in front of me with a twisted grin. He held out his hand, a lifeless bird inside.

I panted and backed away, feeling something press against my back. Hands grabbed my arms and forced me to turn around.

Mr. Campbell's eyes met mine. "You shouldn't have refused me, Miss Mason," his voice echoed in the fog. He held my arms down as

I squirmed, then pushed me backwards. I stumbled, meeting a metal floor. A sickening sound clanged, iron meeting iron. When I frantically found my footing, I gasped—Mr. Johnson's eyes peered at me through metal bars.

"I have you now, my Golden Eagle." I turned in circles, horror-struck as I took in my prison: A giant birdcage. My arm was suddenly seized from between the bars. My screams were still muted, the white mist choking me—

"Lily, wake up!!" I sucked in a full breath, air filling my lungs. My eyes flew open next, Jane's look of worry flooding my vision as she knelt in front of me, shaking my arm.

"Are you alright?" she asked, bewildered. "You were holding your breath for so long."

My mind began to clear as I took in the view of the meadow. I finally nodded my head but wrapped my arms around her in relief. "I haven't had a dream so terrible in all my life." She reciprocated my embrace, rubbing my back, until I let go of her, leaning against the tree. She shuffled over next to me and sat against the tree as well.

"I remember when you used to have nightmares as a little girl." Her expression turned wistful. "You would come to my bed and ask if you could get in."

I grinned. "You were always too nice to tell me no."

"How could I have refused? You had these adorable little curls and your big eyes would fill up with tears before I'd even given you my answer. You were afraid of gargoyles and goblins coming out of the shadows."

I chuckled. "I remember."

"And what are your gargoyles and goblins now?" Jane asked.

How could I even explain my dream to her without revealing my meetings with Henry and the mystery around Lord Elliot's murder? I missed confiding in my sister. It felt as though Henry had formed a small wedge between us. But I knew Jane would put a stop to me seeing him further if she knew the truth.

I looked at Jane and notched an eyebrow. "*Men* are my gargoyles and goblins."

She shook her head. "Be serious for once. What was your dream about? I've never seen you so afraid."

I sighed, "I'll do my best to explain it." I fidgeted with my skirt, feeling nervous under Jane's scrutiny. "In my dream, I woke on the bench in Aunt and Uncle's garden. Thick fog surrounded me on every side. It didn't cling low to the ground but shrouded everything in sight. I saw a figure in the fog that I felt was a friend, and I followed it. I kept losing the shadowed figure until it finally reached out for me and pulled me close." I stopped talking, feeling a shiver creep down my spine at the recollection. "The shadow brought me close, revealing Mr. Hughes's face."

I felt Jane put her hand on my arm. When I looked in her direction, her eyes were turned down and she wore a grim expression.

"What is it?" I asked.

She met my eyes and gave me a fixed look. "Lily, has Mr. Hughes ever tried to force himself upon you?" Her question and guarded countenance surprised me.

"No. But his reputation precedes him," I said, thinking about Molly Black's description of his way with the servants. I studied Jane, reservation written across her face. A sickening realization crossed my mind.

"Has he ever tried to force himself upon *you*, Jane?" I finally asked. Her eyes said it all. He had.

I put a hand up to my mouth as I contemplated the possibilities. "What happened?" I asked, hoping it wasn't the worst.

Jane let out a heavy sigh then finally spoke. "It has happened twice. The first time was at the duchess's ball. He was heavily drunk and he found me in an area where people were scarce. He was trying to pull me into him and claimed he wanted a dance. I was in no real danger at that moment, other than causing a big scene. If I'd have screamed or yelled, others would have come to my aid, but it certainly would have put me in a very uncomfortable position."

"How did you get out of it?" I asked, on the edge of my seat.

"Lord Elliot came upon us from a back entrance—and he intervened." I felt relief at her words until I remembered that she stated he had forced himself upon her twice.

"And the second time?" I was already afraid of what the answer might hold. She stared out at the meadow, fidgeting with her skirt. Would she keep it a secret?

She finally spoke. "At Marianne's ball I tried to follow you and Uncle Francis out to the terrace. I don't know what I was thinking. You had already been gone for some time and I hadn't considered the fact that you were most likely exploring."

"Oh Jane." Guilt found its way into my stomach—especially since I had been thinking only about Henry that night. Apprehension lurked in the silence.

"It isn't your fault, Lily." She looked at me. "There are more reasons than one that I hound you about having a chaperone. I have heard stories of innocent women losing their virtue whilst being unaccompanied in such a way. I wasn't in my right mind."

I prayed she wasn't suggesting that a similar fate found her that night.

"What happened when you came to look for us on the terrace?" I finally asked. "I hope you will confide in me. I'm here for you no matter what has taken place."

She gave me an appreciative look. "It could have been the absolute worst," she said. "Mr. Hughes found me as soon as I exited the ballroom. He blocked off my way to get back inside. I hoped I would be able to find you and Uncle Francis, so I walked further into the garden. He followed me and claimed that I intentionally came out to meet him. I attempted to defend myself with a stick, but he easily ripped it from my grasp. He was forcing my arms around him when—" Her voice trailed off.

"When what?" I thought I would go mad in the silence that followed.

She finally took a breath. "When Lord Elliot stepped in—again."

I let out a breath I'd been holding as relief entered my heart. The look on Jane's face intrigued me.

"What did Lord Elliot think of you being alone with Mr. Hughes?" I asked.

She actually grinned. "I'm not sure. Lord Elliot knocked him unconscious before asking any questions."

I mirrored her grin.

Her smile turned to a look of care. "Just promise me you'll take a chaperone with you from now on, Lily. And don't ever find yourself alone with Mr. Hughes."

I nodded, then put an arm around Jane and embraced her from the side. "Thank you for trusting me with this."

"I'm glad you know. I have been meaning to tell you, but I couldn't find the words. I'm grateful there are no secrets between us."

Guilt twisted my stomach. I looked at her and considered opening up about Henry. But right as I was about to open my mouth to confess, she smiled and pointed toward the sky.

"There," she said. "I've found the perfect leaf."

I looked to where she was pointing and mirrored her expression. "Perhaps it's not too late for me to become a pirate after all."

Jane

Wilton
November 11, 1816
One day later
Four days of disguise remaining

It had been some time since I'd visited the stables; Lily was the one who usually rode—at least that's how it had been the past four years. Before our climb in society, I'd lived for my time with Winnie.

I knew right where to find her though it had almost been a year since I'd visited. When I came upon the stall, her back was facing me and she was munching on a helping of hay. I made a clicking sound and smiled as her ear twitched, head turning toward me. She eagerly clopped in my direction then rubbed her head against my arm like she'd always done.

Regret etched my heart as she greeted me like an old friend. I had neglected her, but she hadn't forgotten me. I rubbed her forehead and put my head to hers, my eyes pricking with moisture at the familiar gesture.

She snorted and I laughed, grateful for her timing. I put my mouth next to her ear and talked soothingly to her as I slowly stroked her muzzle.

"Do you want to go for a ride?"

She snorted again then nudged me with her nose. I smiled as I rested against her.

A stable hand approached. "Would yeh like me to get 'er ready for yeh, miss?"

"Please," I said.

He smiled and nodded, then led Winnie from the stall. After she was saddled, he helped me mount. I could feel her excitement as we neared the meadow. I leaned near her ear again.

"Do you want to fly?" I said the words she knew so well.

She whinnied, and I flicked the reins, sending her into a run until we were soaring through the long grass, the cool air whipping at my cheeks and hair. I could sense Winnie's joy as she ran with the breeze, leaves falling at the meadows border, her breath coming out in heavy puffs.

As we flew past a line of trees, a yellow leaf came free from one of the branches and sailed in the breeze. My mind flashed to the moment Charles placed a similar perfect leaf into my hands, asking for a smile. I replayed it in my mind until my face broke out into a grin. I held my arms out like I was flying, the way I used to.

I was free—completely alive.

In that moment, I relished the ache in my heart for Charles, and I loved him more and more for bringing me back to life. I couldn't accept the fact that I would never see him again.

I held onto the hope that I would find myself in his company at least one more time when I returned to London.

22

GRASS

Lily

Wilton
November 12, 1816
One day later
Three days of disguise remaining

It was only ten in the morning, and I already needed a distraction. I made my way to the meadow once more.

I found it difficult to be in my own company; it gave me time to think, which immediately led to thoughts of Henry. It hadn't even been four days since I'd seen him. I touched my ring, still on my thumb. Since I'd arrived in Wilton, I had been daydreaming that he would mysteriously emerge from corners of the rooms, his brooding eyes in tow, and steal me away to a place where he could wrap me in his arms. I imagined how he would whisper in my ear, tell me his real name, tease me, and—I stroked the place Henry's lips had touched near my temple.

Upon arriving at mine and Jane's copse of trees, I shivered at the memory of the dream I had the last time I visited. I was grateful, however, for the time I'd spent talking with Jane afterward. Sitting in the same place as before, I was satisfied to discover that the perfect leaf from yesterday was still attached to its branch.

Perhaps my wish for Henry wasn't impossible after all. I wished for him with everything I had as I sat and leaned my back against the tree, watching the leaf flutter in the breeze. I would watch it until it fell this time, even if it meant I had to be out here all day. At least, that was my last thought before my eyelids drooped and darkness overtook me.

A light breeze rustled the few strands of my hair that came loose from their pins. It roused me from my sleep enough to remind me where I was. I didn't know how long I'd dozed off, but I kept my eyes closed, unwilling to wake fully for anyone or anything—

My eyes flew open as I felt something crawl up my arm. I jumped up to my feet and slapped it as I yelled, taking a few steps away from the tree. As I turned to see where the spider landed, my breath caught. Henry was sitting next to where I'd been sleeping, holding a long blade of grass, wearing an unrepentant look of amusement.

I felt as though I was dreaming again. I was questioning the very thought, in fact, of whether or not I was truly awake. How could Henry possibly be here? My senses focused on the things that set reality apart from a dream: the breeze in real time, the clarity of detail. I took in his clean, rugged appearance. I couldn't have imagined his every detail so perfectly in a dream. I knew I would be able to distinguish the difference if only he spoke to me, or reached out and touched me.

"Henry?" I finally asked, my heart still pounding as I waited for him to respond.

He stood and walked toward me, smiling mischievously. "Did you have pleasant dreams?" He touched the blade of grass to my arm again. There was no way this was a dream. A hundred different questions poured into my mind.

I was trying to decide which to ask first when he put the blade of grass near my ear, sending an unbearable tickle down my neck.

My hand lunged toward his, trying to snatch the blade, but he was too quick. He wiggled it above my head and smiled as I tried to grab it again, attempting to rid him of his torture device. I almost succeeded, but his arm came back down to his side—and no sooner had I reached for it at his side than he hid it behind his back.

I put my hands on my hips. "That isn't fair."

He chuckled then brought his hand back in front of him. He was no longer holding a blade of grass but a bouquet of wildflowers.

I opened my mouth in surprise then smiled. "Are magic tricks a requirement to becoming an investigator? Or," I grinned, "are you simply magic and can find me whenever I wish for it?"

"Only the wickedly handsome ones are magic," he winked. "And were you wishing for me, Lily?" He gave me a satisfied look as he raised his eyebrow, then handed me the flowers. I blushed, realizing what I had just said. I grasped for a way to evade his question.

"Will you teach me to be magic?" I asked.

"If I teach you, Lily, you won't be impressed anymore."

"Then I must seek out your teacher and beg that he teaches me. I'll bribe him with tuppence as you do, and he won't be able to refuse."

Henry smiled but there was sadness behind it. "My father taught me."

I grinned. "And do you think he will teach me too, if I beg?"

"Unfortunately, he is no longer with us."

My heart pricked. I chided myself for speaking before thinking. "I'm sorry, Henry. I didn't realize I was bringing up an old wound." I placed a hand on his arm. "He must have been a great man." I dimmed my eyes apo logetically. "How long has he been gone?"

"Nearly six months." He looked at my hand on his arm, then took it in his and met my gaze. "He would have loved you." He eased the bouquet from my fingers, pulling a small flower from the middle, then placed the rest of the flowers in the crook of a large tree. He took my hand again and guided me closer to him.

"My father taught me to find the magic in everything." He lifted the small flower near my face and placed it behind my ear, his fingers softly brushing my neck as they came away. Tingles spread down my back at his touch. He brought his thumb and finger forward in front of my face, gripping tuppence as if he'd pulled it from thin air, then opened my hand and placed the coin inside. His fingers then moved to my thumb where he had placed my ring last. Slipping it off, he made it disappear as usual.

He cocked an eyebrow. "We still have a case to solve. You can't just run away from a job. Especially when I pay you so well."

I grinned. "You could just as easily say you missed me."

"And did you miss *me*, Lily?" He held my fingers to his lips and lingered there for a time before lowering my hand and entwining our fingers. My stomach fluttered at the gesture. If he only knew how much I had truly missed him.

"How is it possible that you are here?" I finally asked.

Henry smiled, clearly delighted that I was so surprised to see him.

"I was taking a long walk to clear my head, and I happened upon this beautiful little copse." He pointed to the trees as he still held my hand. "As I came closer, I discovered that this tree also works as a pleasant resting place." He bit back a teasing grin.

"And why is it that you are taking long walks in Wilton instead of London?" I asked, still afraid that at any moment he would disappear and I would wake. "How long do you plan to stay?"

"My business has brought me here to Wilton for the next few days or so. And I didn't even have to hold your carriage up at gunpoint to get your help."

"I'm a little disappointed," I teased. "I was looking forward to the performance." I bit my lip. "And why does your business bring you to Wilton?"

I tried to breathe normally as his fingers traced the top of my hand.

"A few reasons." He looked at me. "First, there is a suspect here in Wilton who hadn't been to London for almost ten years until the week before James Elliot's death. It is no secret that he despised the late earl. I intend to find out more information about his whereabouts and business in London.

"And second . . . " He studied my eyes, the side of his mouth ticking up. "There is a certain lady who is stirring up a bit of trouble. She has been accused of falling for Lord Elliot, but a particular bird lover is quite sure *he* will capture her instead. Lord Elliot has now been threatened, it seems. He was recently sent a very charming gift—a dead bird that looks like a cuckoo, impaled with a very large spike."

My breath hitched in horror, and I put a hand to my chest at Henry's words. A shiver ran through me at the disturbing scene Henry just described. My terrifying dream from the other day flashed through my mind. "Is Lord Elliot—?"

"Lord Elliot is whole and well. We have decided, however, that for the time being, it is no longer safe for him in London."

"I'm relieved to hear it," I said, sighing. I would have been sick if harm came to anyone due to Mr. Johnson's possessive jealousy—but especially if it were to the man my sister was falling in love with. "Are you working closely with Lord Elliot?" I asked, remembering him being at Arthur & Co. when we spoke with Molly Black.

"Since I am investigating the case of James Elliot's death, naturally I am working with Charles Elliot." Henry watched my reaction as he said the words. "Lily . . . I know we have teased and skirted around this question more than once, but I need a straight answer from you." He took both of my hands in his. "Are you in love with Lord Elliot? Is there anything between the two of you?"

"I will answer your question, Henry, if you answer one for me as well."

"Assuming it's not to discover my true identity, I accept."

I nodded my head. "I have no feelings for Lord Elliot, other than respect. He *is* kind, handsome, genuine, and titled, as you have stated in the past . . . but my heart does not call for Lord Elliot."

"And who does your heart call for?"

I shook my head as my heart and breath quickened. "It's your turn to answer my question first."

Henry looked at me intently. "Very well, what do you want to know?"

I bolstered my courage. "When you aren't Henry, do you have an intended? Is there someone waiting for you when you return? A lady with whom you are in love?" I held my breath in anticipation.

"Technically that's three questions," he said with a grin, "but . . . " He slowly lifted my chin, then threaded his other arm slowly around my waist. "I am not engaged, or in any other way obligated to another lady. The other questions I will answer at another time."

"That's not fair," I teased.

"You're smirking again." He brushed the dimple at the corner of my mouth with his thumb, his eyes drifting to my lips. "I need your help, Lily, but we're not going to get anywhere if you keep that expression on your face." His voice was little more than a whisper.

"What do you need my help with?" I asked, feeling breathless. I couldn't help but glance at his lips as he held me close. He was making it hard to think clearly. His eyes returned to mine. They were inviting me to come closer, to close the space. I wanted to— more than anything. But I stayed frozen, still needing to know exactly who he was before I could fully jump.

He exhaled and closed his eyes, resting his forehead against mine, easing me even closer. "You'll be the death of me," he murmured. My breath caught as I felt his lips lightly press against the side of my face. "I'd better go." He turned to leave.

"Wait," I said, grabbing his hand. "You said you need my help."

I wasn't willing to let him leave so soon. The last few days away from Henry made me realize how quickly things could change. It felt as though every moment we spent together could be our last.

"Please, Henry. Don't leave just yet."

He turned and looked at me as my eyes begged him to stay.

He let out a breath. "If I stay, Lily, you'll have to put that expression away."

I smiled with relief. "I'll be on my best behavior."

"No teasing?"

I raised my hand as if to promise. "None whatsoever."

He glanced up at the large tree we were standing beneath then looked at the trunk where I had fallen asleep. He gestured with his hand for me to take a seat. We sat against the tree side by side in silence for some time before he finally spoke. When he did, his voice was quiet and unsure.

"I'm afraid I won't find the truth." He leaned his head back against the tree and looked over at me. I saw his vulnerability, making it nearly impossible not to reach for him.

"You'll find it, Henry. Tell me everything you've discovered thus far, including what I already know."

Henry breathed in slowly then let it out. "First, a shop owner, Arthur Brown, claims to have overheard a heated conversation between James Elliot and an unknown man just before Lord Elliot's death. We've had men observe Mr. Brown and his shop, and he is indeed being followed and watched almost constantly by men we have not yet identified. Even his mail is being intercepted."

"Do you believe he is in danger?"

"I can't say for certain, but it appears as though he is being very careful. And you were right, Lily—it seems he has been threatened."

I nodded my head. "What else do you have?"

He held up two fingers. "Second, Jacob Hughes was overheard by Molly Black stating that he would 'kill them all,' referring to James Elliot and his son, Charles. In addition, Lord Elliot found Jacob Hughes waiting out on the garden terrace at the Morgans' ball."

I remembered Jane's story of Mr. Hughes and felt odd discussing this moment. I wanted to tell Henry that Jane had been out there as well, but I kept her secret. It appeared as though Lord Elliot hadn't told Henry about Jane's presence either. I was grateful for his discretion for the sake of her reputation.

"Jacob Hughes took a blow to the head because Lord Elliot felt it was deserved and Jacob lost consciousness." I held a smile back, knowing the real reason Lord Elliot had rendered him unconscious. "Afterward, Lord Elliot heard voices and hid himself. The voices belonged to two women who were planning to meet Jacob. They said it was arranged by a third party and that even Jacob didn't know their identities."

I narrowed my eyes. Jane didn't include this part of her story. Had she gone back inside at that point or had she still been with Lord Elliot when it happened?

"Third," Henry held up three fingers, "Alexander Campbell was publicly humiliated by James Elliot weeks before his death, then proceeded to threaten the earl openly." He looked over at me again.

"Adding to that fact, we had Jacob Hughes followed and discovered that he met Mr. Campbell on a secluded street at night." My thoughts strained, trying to put together the puzzle of how or why Mr. Hughes and Mr. Campbell could be connected.

Henry held up four fingers. "Fourth, Matthew Johnson took an instant disliking to the current Lord Elliot, despite the fact that they have no history that we are aware of."

A shiver went up my spine as I remembered my dream and the dead bird in Mr. Johnson's hand. I couldn't believe that he'd sent Lord Elliot such a disturbing package. Henry continued with a hint of anger to his voice. "Mr. Johnson has now sent a threatening 'gift' to Lord Elliot. We have discovered from some gentlemen at White's that Mr. Johnson has been known to loathe anyone who is titled. According to some gentlemen I spoke with, he feels that titles should be done away with." He looked over at me and raised his brows. "I have more, Lily. Are you still with me?"

"I am," I said. "Though I feel the need to write everything down to keep it straight."

Henry reached into his pocket and pulled out a piece of parchment, handing it to me. "I've already written everything down. You can look it over as I talk through it. May I keep going?"

I nodded my head. "Please."

He held up five fingers. "You and I overheard a physician and his apprentice on the street discussing that the physician has falsified at least two reports, one of which evidenced signs of poison. James Elliot was in perfect health when he left for London. The physician that inspected James at his time of death wrote it off as a natural cause.

"Sixth, when searching for an apothecary to find a source of poison, we found record of a man working with Jacob Hughes: Robert Graves, in this case. Unfortunately, he appears to have a very straightforward business with no record of carrying anything that would be even remotely poisonous. I believe it would help our case to find the source of poison, but I have no idea where to even start if Robert Graves does, in fact, run an honest business."

I raised a finger, a thought coming to mind. "Mr. Graves studied under his uncle in London. Perhaps his uncle could give you some information about who would concoct such a thing."

Henry smiled. "Your mind's already at work."

"You don't pay me for nothing," I said with a smirk.

"You're doing it again," Henry said, looking at the corner of my mouth.

I dropped my grin as quickly as I could. "It was an accident," I said, innocently raising my eyebrows. "Please continue."

Henry chuckled at my attempt. "Last," he held up seven fingers, "a man who has loathed James Elliot for many years was seen in London a week before his death when he hadn't been to London for almost ten years prior to that."

"Is that all?" I teased. Henry sighed and pushed his hands through his hair. It was a lot of information to take in.

I looked over his notes. "Henry, you have uncovered so much in such a small amount of time. This is encouraging."

"I have you to thank for many of my finds," he said, looking over at me again. I was flattered by his words. They made me feel needed, important, instilling in me the desire to continue finding more evidence for him.

"I have only a few thoughts based on your evidence." I handed back his notes. "It is possible that Mr. Campbell and Mr. Hughes are working together to arrange meetings between men and women in high-class society with the most immoral intentions in mind. If James Elliot discovered this information, he may have blackmailed Mr. Hughes in order to displace him from inheriting."

"Yes, I've thought about that," Henry said. " But what if we're wrong?" He rubbed his forehead. "What if it is someone else?

"It sounds to me as though you need to find out three more pieces of information." I looked over at him and held up one finger the way he had. "First, why was James Elliot's enemy, a man who normally resides in Wilton, visiting London?" I held up two fingers. "Second, who would have access to poison?" I held up a third finger. "And last, who was the other man speaking to Lord Elliot behind Arthur Brown's shop? You need to find a way to guarantee Mr. Brown's safety before you ask him again. I know he wasn't being truthful with you when he stated that he didn't recognize the other man's voice."

Henry looked over at me again as we sat side by side. He nudged my arm softly. "Thank you, Lily."

"For what?" My heart warmed at his look of appreciation.

"For everything. For helping me solve so many of the things I never would have discovered on my own with this case."

I softly leaned my head on his shoulder. He breathed out in satisfaction, then put his arm around me.

"But more than that—Thank you for bringing back a part of me that has been missing for a very long time." Warmth filled me as I sat with him.

"Henry?" I asked quietly. "What's going to happen when you are no longer—Henry?"

He gently leaned his head on mine and took my hand in his. "I don't know. Right now I just want to be here with you and not think about tomorrow."

My heart pounded at his words. I looked up at the tree we were sitting beneath and found the prettiest leaf I could find and wished to have Henry forever. We stayed that way for a long time, but the leaf never fell, and before long, it was time for both of us to retire.

Henry helped me up and handed me the bouquet held in the crook of the tree. I already missed his nearness.

"Next time, Lily, we will ride."

My heart soared at the thought. "Promise?"

"Promise."

"When?" I asked, already smiling.

"The day after your parent's autumn celebration. Same time as today."

"Where will I find you?"

"I'll find you." He stepped close to me and slowly lifted my chin. "Three days, Lily," he breathed as he slowly brushed the corner of my lips with his thumb. "Three days until . . . " His eyes glanced at the place he touched. "Until this torture ends."

My heart pounded. His eyes searched mine.

"Three days." I repeated. His hand slowly fell away from my chin, signaling his cue to leave.

"Until next—"

"Henry," I interrupted. "Will you come to the autumn celebration?" I held my breath in hope.

"I don't know how I would be able to attend without an invitation."

"I could invite you," I countered.

He smirked. "We've technically never met each other."

I sighed in frustration. "We can break the rules just this once."

He smiled wickedly. "That's what we've been doing all along." He was certainly a different man from the one I first encountered.

I looked at the flowers in my hand and smiled as I stepped close to him. I knew we needed to leave—the longer we stayed, the harder it was to go. But I couldn't stand to watch him walk away again. This time it was my turn. "Thank you for everything," I said quietly next to his ear. He held perfectly still as I pressed my lips lightly on his cheek, his breath catching as I did so. "Until next time," I said, stealing his usual line. Then, before he could utter another word, I left.

23

WOODEN SPOON

Jane

Wilton
November 12, 1816
Later that day
Three days of disguise remaining

A light pink shawl was draped about my shoulders when I ventured out to the garden. I wore my hair mostly down, letting it dance lightly around me in the breeze. Breathing in the November air, I was once again reminded of Charles. It seemed I could scarcely look at anything and not be brought to thoughts of him: A leaf, a flower, a spoon and fork, a ribbon, a carriage; even the color of deep blue. It had only been four days since I'd seen Charles, yet it felt as though weeks had passed—and there were still four days remaining until we would return to London. The time seemed to move slower and slower with each hour.

Since my arrival home, I felt as though I was consistently teetering between feeling hopeful and alive and feeling discouraged and fearful for what I would find upon my return to London. Either way, I found that tears were often my companion. It felt as though they were making up for lost time. Now I almost regretted that it had been so long since I'd welcomed them.

I walked the garden's perimeter until the edge of a large stone, engulfed in sunlight, became my resting place. Closing my eyes, I let the warmth of the sun and my emotions fill me without shame. I felt more at peace with myself and my family than I had in a long time.

I was free.

The emotions threatened tears of relief to spill over. Those tears of relief were rivaled with tears of longing and heartache. Charles had opened my heart. At the same time, he was the cause of the pain I carried inside. I continued to close my eyes and allowed myself to feel it all. I didn't chastise myself when the tears escaped and I saw him in my mind.

I spent the remainder of the afternoon with Lily and Mama, proving myself less than useful.

"You seem rather distracted, Jane," Mama said when Lily left the room. She looked at me perceptively. "Is anything the matter?"

"Perhaps I'm still a little tired from the journey. And I didn't sleep well last night. I don't feel myself at present." I averted my eyes from her gaze.

She studied me. "You seem different. I feel that I have a piece of my old Jane back. I like this change, though there is a sense of melancholy about it as well. Would you like to talk about it?" Mama missed nothing.

"I don't know that I'm ready to talk about it just yet. But when I am, you'll be the first I come to."

She nodded then slowly pulled me into a hug, giving me a comforting smile. "You'll figure it out soon enough, I'm sure."

"Thank you." I returned her embrace, feeling a small weight lift from my shoulders, knowing that I could turn to Mama if I needed. I was also grateful that she took me as I was, without badgering me with further questions.

I just needed to pass the time until I saw Lord Elliot again.

I changed into a cream evening gown for dinner and Alice pinned parts of my hair up.

Mama found me on the stairs as I was coming down. "Your papa has invited a guest for dinner this evening, Jane. He says he is acquainted with you and Lily."

My eyes found hers and she gave me a smile. "He is very handsome. Why did you not tell me you were finally introduced to Lord Elliot?"

My pulse quickened. "Lord Elliot is joining us for dinner?"

"Yes," she smiled. "He speaks very highly of you, Jane."

"You spoke with him?"

"I did." A corner of her lips turned up in a small grin. "And I can see why you have been so melancholy if you are pining after him."

"Mama, I'm not pining after—"

"I'll not badger you further," she interrupted. "You'll talk to me when you're ready. But I know that look in your eyes." She gave me a sympathetic look. "Now, I'll not scheme or hope. You are a grown woman and you will make your own choices. But I do expect that we will all have a very enjoyable time with Lord Elliot this evening. And now I must go fetch Lily." She smiled once more before walking past me.

Charles Elliot was in my house. I couldn't believe it. My feet found their way back upstairs and into my room. As I stood in front of the mirror one more time to make sure I was presentable enough, the woman that reflected my image greeted me with nervous eyes. The prospect of seeing him so suddenly was one thing; having Charles surrounded by the people I loved most was another entirely. My stomach flipped over and over again until I finally rallied my courage and exited my room.

Upon entering the dining room, my heart warmed at the sight before my eyes. Papa, Sterling, and Oliver were laughing with Charles. They all looked so leisurely and comfortable standing in a group together. Charles's eyes found mine. They spoke a hundred words. At the forefront, I saw eagerness. His presence made it impossible to think straight, engulfing me entirely.

Breathe, I reminded myself.

Lily and Mama walked in shortly after my arrival and we took our seats. Sterling and Oliver both hovered by Charles as he neared the dining table. They weren't going to let him sit anywhere unless they were seated on either side. He took his place and the two boys quickly slid their chairs out, stationing themselves on his right and left before anyone had a chance to say otherwise.

A smile made its way across Charles's lips at the boys' enthusiasm to have his attention. I sat across from all three of them while Mama and Lily took a seat on either side of me. As the food was served, Charles was engrossed in a secret conversation with Oliver and Sterling. They discreetly whispered to one another, Oliver laughing a few times until Charles looked up at me and gave me a mischievous grin—followed by a sign I hadn't seen in years.

I almost laughed. He laced his fingers together, clasping his hands, then slowly put his fingers up against each other one by one. It was the secret sign that Sterling and Oliver used to give to Lily and me when they wanted to steal more pastries from the kitchen after dinner. Oliver and Sterling looked at me, sending the sign as well. I smiled then covertly sent it back. I noticed Sterling giving the sign to Lily. She grinned and discreetly sent it back as well.

Lily nudged me softly. "It's good to have you back, Jane."

"It's good to be back," I returned. My lips twitched up as I observed my brother's smiles. It appeared as though Charles was showing Sterling and Oliver something beneath the table. Their eyes grew with excitement. I could only guess that he was making something disappear. I couldn't take my eyes off him. I smiled, my heart pulsing with warmth, feeling completely whole. The moment was so perfect; If it were possible, I would freeze it forever in my mind.

Charles looked up at me just then. Something significant passed between us in that moment, as if our souls were created to move together—to call for the other. I could no longer ignore the truth that was knocking so loudly at my door: I had fallen completely and hopelessly in love with Charles Elliot.

At the conclusion of dinner, we retired to the drawing room and listened to Papa read poetry. He stood in front of the fireplace, flames slowly burning within its hearth. He cleared his voice.

> "She walks in beauty, like the night
> Of cloudless climes and starry skies;"

As I watched Papa read, I saw his passion, his fire. I imagined him as a younger man trying to win Mama's heart and grinned, looking over at Mama, who was smiling contentedly as she watched him.

I dared a glance at Charles, who was seated across from me in a chair. His eyes were already on me, filled with a sense of desire. As Papa continued, Charles held my gaze and softly recited the remainder of the poem under his breath so quietly that I wouldn't have heard his voice if I hadn't been looking at him. Breath forsook me as he studied my eyes .

> "And all that's best of dark and bright
> Meet in her aspect and her eyes:
> Thus mellowed to that tender light
> Which heaven to gaudy day denies.

> "One shade the more, one ray the less,
> Had half impaired the nameless grace
> Which waves in every raven tress,
> Or softly lightens o'er her face;
> Where thoughts serenely sweet express
> How pure, how dear their dwelling-place.

> "And on that cheek, and o'er that brow,
> So soft, so calm, yet eloquent,
> The smiles that win, the tints that glow,
> But tell of days in goodness spent,
> A mind at peace with all below,

A heart whose love is innocent!"

I was pulled from my trance when the poem ended and everyone clapped for Papa. Everyone was smiling except for Oliver, who looked bored out of his mind. He walked past me and discreetly slipped a small piece of paper in my hand. He dropped a similar item in Lily's lap.

I opened the note.

Thievery begins now. Meet in the wine cellar.

I looked at Oliver, who looked back at me expectantly. I gave him a nod and he smiled. From the corner of my eye I watched as Lily nodded to Oliver as well. Charles was already looking at me when my eyes searched for his. He gave me a grin with a look of challenge behind it.

Challenge accepted. I sent the secret code again to Charles. It was now or never.

"Excuse me Mama, Papa," I said, making my voice sound worn, "but I'm feeling rather tired. May I retire, please?" If I didn't act now I was sure to back down from this silly little charade.

Mama gave me a questioning look. I smiled at her reassuringly.

"If you are indeed feeling tired, then you may be excused. But I am surprised. We have a guest and it's not yet late. You're accustomed to staying up all hours of the night in London."

Papa placed a hand on Mama's arm, as if to prompt her to let me go. She looked at his hand then to me and nodded. "I hope you get some rest, Jane."

I stood and bobbed a curtsy to Charles. "It's good to see you again, Lord Elliot. I hope you will visit again shortly." Charles stood and dipped his head. "It's always a pleasure." He gave me a small wink and a corner of his mouth lifted up into a mischievous grin. I did my best to hold a natural look, but couldn't keep it in place completely. I left the room, turning out of the doorway, then quickly put my back against the wall, listening to the conversation within the drawing room.

"I believe I'm tired myself," I heard Lily say without reserve. "Excuse me, Mama, Papa, Lord Elliot." She didn't even wait for a reply. I chuckled at her boldness as she walked out the door and found me. We smiled at each other.

"Welcome aboard, Pirate Lily," I whispered with a laugh.

"Goodnight Mama, Papa, Lord Elliot," I heard the boys say. Sterling and Oliver exited the room, practically running to join Lily and me. We all made our way to the wine cellar as quietly as we could. Sterling walked ahead of us and peeked through the doors to make sure we wouldn't be seen by any servants. Then he nodded his head to us and motioned with his hand that we should come forward.

I couldn't help but smile. Memories of our many attempts to sneak food came flooding back to me. We arrived in the wine cellar and waited for Charles. It was mostly dark inside and we hadn't thought to bring a lantern.

"I think Lord Elliot is really magic," I heard Oliver whisper to Sterling.

"It's a trick, Oliver. But a really good one. I wonder if he will teach it to me," Sterling whispered back.

"You just want to impress Isabelle Kensington," Oliver jeered. I heard a thud near Oliver's arm, then, "Ouch!"

A light suddenly appeared at the entrance of the cellar, a lantern dimly illuminating Charles's features. He looked wickedly handsome as he grinned with the light flickering off his face.

"Welcome, thieving crew." He cocked an eyebrow and spoke with an air of mystery. It was hard not to laugh. "Tonight will determine our honor as fellow pastry thieves." He gave each of us a conspiratorial look. Oliver was hanging onto his every word. Sterling shook his head but was smiling. "I hear that Cook is a fierce woman. But tonight, we will liberate the pastries and prove that England should fear us." I laughed quietly.

Charles took my hand and lead me to the center of our small group before he released me. "Miss Mason has explained to me that she wishes to be the best pastry thief in all of Europe." Oliver and Sterling sniggered. "Tonight, she will prove herself . . . or suffer the wrath of the kitchen staff."

"Hear, hear!" Lily raised her hand as if she was holding a goblet, raising a toast.

We all grinned as we raised our hands in a similar fashion. "Hear, hear!" we all said together.

The voting commenced and Charles was dubbed our captain. He found a roll of linen and draped it over a table in the wine cellar then placed his lantern on top. He grabbed a few wine bottles and placed them over the linen.

"Now, Sterling, show us the layout of the kitchen."

Sterling grabbed a bottle and placed it on one end of the table. "Here is the main door to the kitchen," he said, making his voice sound important. He took another one and placed it on the opposite end of the table, positioned lower than the first. "This is the back door that leads outside." He carefully placed another wine bottle on its side. "This is Cook's main bread board that she guards like a hawk." Placing another bottle close to the one representing the bread board he said, "Cook has a scullery maid who is usually working near the stove. Between the two of them," Sterling grabbed a small wine glass and placed it right next to the wine bottle on its side, "they always have eyes on the target." He tapped the wine glass.

"Very thorough, Commander Sterling," Charles nodded with dramatized seriousness.

"Captain," Sterling nodded, playing along.

"Lieutenant Oliver, how good are you at being invisible?" Charles asked.

Oliver drifted away from the lantern until he disappeared in the darkness. I tried to find him in the shadows—

"I do a decent job." He suddenly appeared next to Charles and me. I jumped in surprise and Oliver grinned in delight at his achievement.

"Impressive," Charles said with pride, before facing Lily. "Miss Lily, I have a feeling you are exceptional with a blade."

Lily laughed. "You would be correct, Captain, though I've never wielded one."

He handed Lily a penknife. "Guard it with your life," he said as if it were a precious sword. Sterling and Oliver both snickered.

"Now, Miss Mason," he said, facing me, "if you are ever to be an honored pastry thief, you must first learn the art of deception. You will accompany me and see how a true master works." He gave me an enticing grin, making my pulse race. I found that I wanted nothing more than to kiss his smile.

I raised an eyebrow. "Very well, Captain. But I should warn you that Cook sees through even the best imposters."

"Even if they have a silver tongue?" he winked.

"I guess we will find out," I said with a smirk.

"So we shall," he said confidently. "Sterling will secure an escape route once we have accomplished our goal. He will be in charge of noting any casualties along the way."

Sterling smiled. "Aye, Captain."

"Oliver, you will sneak past the scullery maid once Miss Mason and I have her and Cook fully distracted, and then you will slip our prize to Sterling." Charles looked at Lily. "You will stand guard at the entrance and use any means necessary for us to achieve our goal, in case all goes awry."

"Aye!" Lily said theatrically.

We all laughed.

Sterling went around back, stating that he would sneak in from outside. The rest of us walked noiselessly to the kitchen. Charles took my hand, giving it a squeeze.

"We're up," he said near my ear. When he guided me into the kitchen, we were immediately faced with a severe glare from Cook. She was truly a cross old lady with no nonsense about her. I tried to look as though it was the most normal thing in the world to be about the kitchen after dinner with a man she had never met. It was hard not to laugh.

"Hello, Cook," I said with a smile. Her name was Ann, but she had always insisted that we call her Cook. If ever we called her Ann, she immediately chased us from the kitchen. "Did you miss me while I was away?" I asked, already knowing what her answer would be.

"I can't say that I did, miss," she said flatly. I didn't look at the pastries on the board, as I knew it would immediately give me away. The scullery maid was nowhere to be seen.

Charles stepped forward. "Are you the lady who is to thank for the delicious dinner this evening?" He gave her a dashing smile. "Upon my word, miss, I haven't had such delectable food even in London. I fear I have been spoiled and will never want to eat again." In my periphery, Oliver knelt down and began to crawl behind the board.

Cook gave Charles a scowl. "I'm no miss, sir, and my food is nothing that wouldn't be served in any other kitchen."

Charles grinned charmingly. "It must be the love you put into it." Oliver eased forward.

"I don't like the cut of your jib," Cook said, narrowing her eyes at Charles. "I can smell mischief a mile away and you stink of it."

Charles beamed. "How perceptive you are, for I have truly come with mischief in mind." The back door from outside slowly opened and Sterling's head appeared from behind it.

Charles continued, smiling. "I have come to see if I can buy your secrets." Oliver was slowly reaching for the pastry platter from behind the board.

Cook glared at Charles and walked to the wall, grabbing a wooden spoon. "More like you're up to no good, attempting to steal pastries from my board with the rest of the lot." She swatted at Charles and he dodged.

"The jig is up!" Charles hollered as he grabbed my hand. I laughed as he pulled me toward the outside door, Oliver quickly jumping up and snatching a pastry in each hand. He tossed one to Sterling and ran for the back door. Lily darted through the kitchen door and stabbed two pastries with her penknife. They clung to it and she giggled and screamed as she rushed to the outside door.

Cook chased after us, swinging her wooden spoon, but we were too quick. Running out the door and into the meadow, we laughed, my brothers holding their stomachs from the effort. Charles never let go of my hand.

We finally slowed our pace and sat in the grass, looking to the sky as it darkened, the sun already hidden behind the horizon. Charles and I sat next to Oliver, Sterling, and Lily. They ate their pastries and laughed.

"I'm sorry you didn't get any," Oliver said to Charles and me.

"Why didn't you warn me that Cook is such a stiff?" Charles teased.

"Jane *did* try to warn you," Sterling said with a smile.

"Not near enough," Charles chuckled.

"I thought your silver tongue might win her over," I said, biting back a laugh. "Her pastries are worth all the trouble though. Maybe some other time you and I will be successful." I watched my brothers and sister eat their stolen goods.

"Jane," Charles said smoothly, "just because my silver tongue doesn't work on stone, doesn't mean I don't still come in handy in a pinch." He presented a pastry to me and smiled as my face lit up.

"Told you he's magic," Oliver said to Sterling as he stood up and wiped the pastry crumbs from his hands and pants.

Sterling stood as well and mirrored Oliver's actions. "Will you teach me your tricks someday, Lord Elliot?"

Charles smiled. "Certainly."

Lily stood as well. "I will see you inside, Jane. I really am rather tired, and I don't want Mama and Papa to scold me if I'm found out of bed." She handed Charles the penknife. "I may have sullied your blade, Captain," she said with a grin.

Charles chuckled. "You used it well."

Lily turned to me with a sparkle in her eye. "Don't stay out too long, Jane."

"I'll be in once we've eaten our reward." I smiled. "Don't get caught, Lily."

"I won't," she called back. As Lily and the boys walked towards the house, Charles held the pastry out for me.

I grinned. "I want you to have it, Charles."

He took a bite and savored it for a moment, then nodded in

approval. "It appears there is something sweet about Cook after all." He handed me the rest. "I took it for you, Jane. I want you to have it."

I took a bite and smiled as the sweet, flaky outside and soft center reminded me of Cook's special touch. "We may all be scolded severely by Mama and Papa for sneaking around after dark once Cook tells them of our mischief."

Charles turned to me. "They already know."

"What?" I said in alarm.

"I wasn't about to put your reputation at risk, along with Lily's, all for the sake of a few pastries. After you all left the drawing room, I told your parents of the plan that Sterling and Oliver were so bent on. They readily agreed and are most likely watching us from the house as we speak so we are 'chaperoned.'" He smiled then nudged me. "Your family is enchanting, Jane. I can see why you want to protect them."

He was quiet for a time before he spoke again. "Don't hand them over to the wolves. They will be far happier without Lord Fletcher and his company."

When I turned my gaze from the meadow to Charles's eyes, he was already studying me. I was lured by the moonlight reflecting in his eyes. As much as I was grateful that Charles told my parents of our plans this evening, I wished we could be alone. I wanted to pull him away to my favorite tree. I wanted to taste his lips as he held me in his arms.

"Jane," he whispered, tracing his finger along my jaw. I held perfectly still. "Forfeit your plans with Lord Fletcher. He plans to propose when you return. I can't bear the thought—"

"How do you know Lord Fletcher plans to propose?" I asked, feeling a sense of dread.

"I have my ways." He looked at my hair. A strand had come loose from all of the excitement. He gently tucked it behind my ear.

I took his hand and held it close. "I can't accept him," I said quietly. "Someone has brought me back to life, and I think I would suffocate if I spent my life with Lord Fletcher now."

Charles let out a breath of relief. "I can't bear the thought of him tainting your goodness—your purity and passion. He could never deserve you."

His words echoed within me. Eventually he leaned near my ear. I knew it was dark enough that my parents wouldn't be able to see our exact movements.

"Your father has invited me to the autumn celebration tomorrow evening. May I claim your first dance?" His lips grazed my ear. Tingles spread throughout me, my breath catching as his lips brushed my jaw. He pressed a light kiss to my cheek. "I insist." His voice was low and husky.

I looked at him, his face close to mine. I wanted to pull him to me, to be taken completely in his kiss. But knowing my parents were watching, even though they likely couldn't see in the darkness, made me pause. He took my hand and held it to his heart. It pulsed hard and fast, mirroring mine.

"Jane," he said as if he no longer had restraint. "I should leave you now, but I find that I am incapable." His face was still close to mine, eyes glancing down at my hand against his chest. "Make it stop so I can leave." His voice was little more than a whisper.

My hand stayed where it was. When I spoke, my voice came out as a quiet entreaty. "I don't want you to leave."

"That isn't helping," he said, a corner of his mouth twisting up. "And you still owe me some form of payment for my heroic actions against Mr. Hughes."

"And what do you want this time?" I asked, unable to look away from his grin that pulled me in.

"Will you save your first dance for me?"

I smiled. "Is that all you want as payment?"

He smiled wickedly. "No, I want that for free. I have something else in mind for payment." He stroked his finger below my chin and looked at me. We stayed frozen for what felt like an eternity. He gently brushed his thumb across my bottom lip. "It'll have to wait for now," he said quietly. "But Jane, may I have your first dance?"

"And another after that," I said, completely consumed by his intoxicating presence.

He breathed out, content. "Then I will have you again tomorrow."

He slowly took my hand at his heart and raised it to his lips. I stayed frozen in place, wondering if my heart might hammer out of my chest. My feelings were mirrored in his eyes.

He let out an afflicted breath then slowly made his way to his feet, helping me up in the process. He threaded my arm through his and walked me back toward the house until we were at the back door. "This is where I leave you."

I turned to face him and stood on my toes, lightly pressing a kiss of my own to his cheek. He held perfectly still.

"Good night, Charles," I said in his ear. "Thank you for tonight."

He looked at me with a tantalizing expression. "You'd better go in now, Jane," he said, notching an eyebrow, clearly being pushed over the edge.

"Don't be late tomorrow," I smiled, opening the door and letting myself in. I quietly shut it and rested my back against the solid wooden frame, knowing it was the only thing between Lord Elliot and me. I breathed in deeply, smiling as I exhaled, then held my hands to my heart, a strong pulse echoing inside. I wondered if my heart would ever stop emanating these overwhelming waves of fire and warmth.

I would find a way to convince him to stay. He could put his business on hold or take me with him . . . forever.

24

LANTERN

Lily

The window in my bedroom granted a singular view: complete darkness. Clouds covered the moon and stars. From the moment my head hit my pillow, I tossed and turned, images of Henry flashing through my mind. I sighed and placed my fingers on the corner of my lips where Henry's fingers had touched, my cheeks warming at the memory. My heart had been on fire since our time in the meadow. The more time I spent with Henry, the harder it was becoming to hold back. The two days until I would see him again would surely feel like an eternity. Exasperated, I threw my covers off and placed my feet on the cold wood floor.

A small table next to my bed held a lantern. I lit the wick then lifted the handle. Shadows leapt to life, moving and dancing around me. I always hated lighting a lantern in the black of night for this reason. The thought of something lurking behind me always crept into my mind—something waiting for the right moment to snatch me away. My eerie dream from the other day certainly wasn't helping. Though I had grown more sensible over the years, I still couldn't help a few glances over my shoulder as I made my way to the library. A book of poetry would help pass the time.

Quietly opening the library door, I tiptoed to a shelf, setting the lantern down. I began perusing when a creak sounded near the door. Holding perfectly still, I rallied my courage to shine the lantern toward the door. I found however, despite reasoning with myself that I had no need to worry, I seemed to be glued in place with fear.

James Elliot's murder circled in my mind, along with the image of a lifeless bird in Mr. Johnson's hand. A whisper of noises continued to sound and then stopped. Heart pounding with trepidation, I eased a book from the shelf at random. If I needed to throw it, I would. Leaving my lantern glowing dimly behind the shelf, I slowly crept toward the door. An intake of breath sounded behind me. I spun around and hurled my book.

A ghostly figure of white clutched its chest.

"Lily!" Jane's voice cried out in the darkness. "Did you just throw a book at me?" She bent down and picked it up.

I clutched my chest in return. "I thought you were a ghost." Lifting my lantern, I came closer to her.

Jane chuckled in the darkness. "You've had some bad luck with hauntings the last few days, have you not?"

I shook my head, rolling my eyes.

"Did you venture out tonight to test your courage?" Jane asked.

"If only," I mused. "As it stands, I am currently suffering from something far worse. I have been cursed with the inability to sleep."

"Sleep is eluding me as well," she seemed to glow, a far away smile lining her lips. As I considered her, Lord Elliot came to my mind. He had certainly made the evening special and exciting for all of us. I would be forever grateful for the way he brought Jane back to life. She was clearly smitten. I'd seen the way they looked at each other while Papa was reading poetry.

I grinned. "No doubt you couldn't sleep in fear that we will never eat another pastry again, if Cook has anything to say about it."

"Precisely." Jane laughed. "I'm sure Lord Elliot isn't sleeping either, for fear of Cook haunting his dreams with a wooden spoon."

I smiled. "He definitely made our evening enjoyable. I do believe

Sterling and Oliver have found a new idol. They believe he is magic." The only other person I knew that was "magic" was Henry. Since hearing my brothers' remarks, I was curious about how closely Henry and Lord Elliot were really working.

"Sometimes it's hard to believe otherwise," Jane said. "He makes things disappear and reappear so effortlessly, it seems it's as natural as breathing for him."

My mind buzzed with the possibilities of their connection. Perhaps Lord Elliot himself was an investigator working covertly as well, and Henry's father, whoever he had been, taught them both the skills needed to get information, including making things appear and disappear. When I finally discovered Henry's true identity, I would push to discover the truth behind their connection as well.

I brought myself back to the conversation and smiled. "He appears to have worked some magic on you as well, Jane."

She couldn't help but grin. "I daresay he has."

"And do you still plan to continue your plans with Frederick?"

Jane put her hands over her cheeks, distressed. "Lily. I don't know what has come over me, but I cannot marry Frederick. I don't know what to do. I know I will have to face him, but I believe he will be very angry that I led him on to think—"

"You have done nothing of the sort," I interjected. "You have done nothing but be agreeable. Yes, you have accepted his attention towards you, but you can hardly be accused of intentionally trapping him. It's the way courting works. You *can* refuse Frederick and you *must* if you feel this way. And I will even be there in the room when you do it if you feel you need my support—even if you weren't there for me when Mr. Johnson proposed."

She gave me an apologetic smile. "How was I to know he wouldn't take no for an answer?" She didn't even know the half of it. I wondered what Jane would think if she found out that Mr. Johnson had sent Lord Elliot a bird with a spike through its chest. But for the time being, I wanted to see if she would admit her feelings for Lord Elliot. She seemed to be in a state of ease; it felt a good time to try and get her to open up.

"Jane?" I asked, without any teasing or lightheartedness. "What has brought on this sudden change? Is it possible that Lord Elliot has turned your head?"

Jane tried to hold back a smile. "And my heart." She wrapped her arms around the book I'd thrown and hugged it, then looked to me with a furrowed brow. "And don't you dare make fun of me," she scolded. "I know I'm just like every other lady in London now, smitten by his very presence. But I believe he feels for me too."

"I believe you're right, Jane. I know he is a flirt with everyone he meets, but he is different around you."

"And what about you, Lily?" She looked closely at me. "There is something different about you lately. I can't quite place my finger on it, but I know something has happened. Have you fallen in love with a man but feel the need to keep it to yourself?"

My heart quickened at her direct question. I had been wanting to confide in her ever since I met Henry. I could feel the change taking place within her—but would she understand, or would she try to put an end to it? I decided to tell only partial truths for now.

"There *is* someone who has caught my attention, but I'd rather keep it to myself for now."

"That is very unlike you," Jane said, knitting her eyebrows.

"Perhaps. I would just like a little more time before I talk about it. There are so many unknowns when the heart is involved."

"I know what you mean," Jane said. "I'll not push you further for now. I'm just glad you have finally admitted that there is, in fact, a gentleman who has caught your interest."

"And I'm happy you have chosen to forfeit your plans with Frederick." I smiled. "You were never well suited."

"You just don't want him for a brother-in-law," Jane teased.

I grinned. "Indeed, I do not. I don't believe Frederick would ever steal pastries from the kitchen."

Jane laughed. "That would surely be a sight. Perhaps Frederick and Cook would understand one another."

I raised an eyebrow. "They are both made of stone. Do you think Cook might take Frederick, since you are giving him up?" We both laughed quietly until it slowly fell away, bringing a peaceful silence. I breathed in with contentment as I looked at Jane. It felt so nice to have her back.

Jane looked out the window then sighed. "We should probably return to our beds. I don't want to wake the house, and we really should try to get more sleep before the festivities tomorrow."

I nodded. "It is rather late."

Jane took my lantern in hand and led the way out of the library. We walked side by side until we reached our adjacent rooms. Handing me my lantern, as well as the book I had thrown, she opened her door at the same time I did.

"Goodnight, Lily," she said with a smile.

"Goodnight." I passed through my door and silently closed it behind me, happy that Jane had finally confided in me. When I was ready, I would entrust my secret to her—perhaps in three days. My conversation with Jane brought a feeling of peace with it, drowsiness thankfully being the byproduct. I would finally be able to sleep. Putting out the lantern, I soaked up the warmth of my bed and closed my eyes, dreaming of Henry.

Lily

Wilton
November 13, 1816
The morning after
Two days of disguise remaining

The sun's rays peeked through my window, bringing with it the excitement of our autumn celebration. Not only did I love the merriment, but it also meant I only needed to wait out the events of the day and last one more night before Henry would take me riding.

I slowly sat up. Despite my few hours of rest from the night before, I knew there would be no point in attempting to sleep longer.

Alice helped me change and arrange my hair for the morning. As she walked out, I carefully pulled a few more curls out in various places to accentuate my face.

Sterling, Oliver, and Mama were already at the table as I walked into the dining room.

"I hope you slept well, Lily. I would like to get an early start on our plans," Mama said with an excited smile.

"Where are Papa and Jane?" I asked.

"I believe Jane is still sleeping. Your father has accepted a business call this morning and I'm not supposed to be angry about it, but I am." She folded her arms. "I was hoping he could put his business aside for this one day and help me oversee the last minute details for this evening. But alas, this gentleman, Henry Thomas, arrived not ten minutes ago and your father agreed to see him."

I almost jumped at hearing Henry's name.

"You say this gentleman is here speaking with Papa right now?" I asked, narrowing my eyebrows. "On a matter of business?"

She sighed. "Indeed. I hope it will not take long." It took everything in me not to immediately excuse myself.

"Mama, I would like to help with your arrangements as soon as possible. What can I assist with this morning?"

Her smile lit up at my offer. "Thank you, Lily. I need someone to talk with Cook to ensure she prepares Papa's steak the way he likes it. Can I put you up to the task?"

I almost laughed. Cook was more likely to poison the food if I said anything about it after the act we pulled last night. But I wasn't about to say anything about it to Mama.

"Very well, Mama. But you know Cook has never been very fond of me."

Mama smirked. "She isn't fond of anyone." She then eyed me. "But she *does* have a special dislike for thieves." Her smirk grew into a sly grin as my eyes widened.

"Did she snitch on us already?"

"No." Mama smiled. "Lord Elliot told Papa and me of your treacherous plans when you left the drawing room. He didn't want you all to be scolded."

I opened my mouth. "Traitor!"

"Yes. And it's a very good thing he was a traitor."

"Did he warn Cook ahead of time as well?"

Mama chuckled. "I should think not. She would have skinned him before he took more than a step inside her kitchen if she knew what he was up to."

"Yes, I daresay she would have." I raised my brows. "And since you know about our little ruse last night, do you still think it wise for me to advise Cook on preparing Papa's meat? Or do you think she would be more likely to poison it?"

Mama grinned. "Leave Cook to me. I want you to see to the flower arrangements as they come in, which shouldn't be for another hour or so. It should give you enough time to eat." As if in response to her remark, breakfast was brought into the dining room.

Were the servants walking slower than usual this morning simply because Henry was here? I fidgeted with anticipation as they put the trays on the table. I wanted to run to the table the second they were put down, dish up my plate, and run off with my utensils in tow.

Patience won out and I waited until it was appropriate for me to dish up my food, though I filled my plate with only a small amount. I wanted to finish quickly so I could spy on Henry and Papa.

Mama looked surprised when I excused myself so soon from the breakfast table. "I'll ensure the flowers are splendid," I said as I kissed her on the cheek and walked out.

I made my way down a hallway toward Papa's study. It was located in a secluded area, in the old part of the house's structure, and designed in such a way that a small sitting area shared a wall with the study. We had discovered as children that if we put our ear to a specific spot on the wall, we could hear the conversation taking place inside.

Unfortunately, reaching the spot included standing on top of a tall, narrow console table to get high enough. I carefully hoisted myself up on the table, noting that it had been easier to manage when I was smaller. I righted myself as I stood, then pressed my ear to the wall. Thankfully I would hear the door open on the other side of the wall before I was caught, though I would have to be quick and quiet at getting down and then either hide or pretend I was just walking through.

I quieted my breathing as I tried to listen. It was difficult to hear anything.

"Lily?" my father's voice sounded behind me. Gasping, I wobbled, my hand splaying out . . . I was going to tip over and there was nothing I could do about it.

A strong hand steadied me. I looked over, mortified to see Henry standing next to my father, biting back an amused grin.

"What on earth are you doing up there?" Papa looked at me as if I was mad. My cheeks burned, and I quickly snatched my hand out of Henry's grip.

Henry smirked then pointed. "I recall seeing a spider on the wall earlier, just there, sir." He eyed the place on the wall that I had just been pressing my ear to. "She must have been intending to find it a new home." Henry looked at me, holding back a laugh.

"My daughter is terrified of anything that creeps and crawls." Papa chuckled then gave me a quizzical look. "Do you need help down, my dear?"

"I believe I can manage on my own." My cheeks still burned.

"Please, I insist," Henry said as he offered a hand. It felt so odd acting as though we had never met. I finally took his hand and he helped me down carefully. It was hard not to stare at him for too long. As he released my hand, the familiar shape of tuppence was felt in my palm.

Papa cleared his throat. "Lily, may I introduce you to Mr. Thomas?" My father pointed to Henry then continued. "Mr. Thomas, this my younger daughter, Miss Mason."

"How do you do, Miss Mason?" Henry dipped his head in my direction and I curtsied as if we were meeting for the first time. I had always imagined we would be introduced at a public, formal affair.

"I am well, Mr. Thomas, thank you," I tried placing a normal look on my face, finding it difficult to procure the right expression. Despite the oddity of the moment, there was something exciting about the challenge. "I am happy to make your acquaintance," I added, "though I hope your business with my father won't take up too much time. My mother is quite put out that Papa is doing business today when there are so many things to oversee."

Papa gave me a stern look to leave it be.

Henry leant me a grin. "Our business has already concluded, Miss Mason; have no fear."

I did my best to swallow my disappointment. I hadn't been able to overhear what they discussed.

"I see." I placed a pleasant look on my face then added, "Mama will be so pleased." I bobbed a curtsy. "Good day, Mr. Thomas, Papa."

Curtsying, I turned away from them and walked down the hall, slipping into a nearby alcove—It would allow me to hear the remainder of their conversation. No sound met my ears.

I waited . . . and waited . . . until eventually, I pressed my back against the wall and slid toward the opening, hoping it would allow me to hear more clearly. Muffled voices could be made out, but it wasn't enough to decipher exactly what was being said.

I sighed in frustration. If Henry's name was *not* in fact "Henry Thomas," then why would he come to my father with a business proposition using that name? The entire thing was befuddling. A sudden thought came to mind, bringing panic with it. What if Henry suspected my father of murdering James Elliot? Henry had stated that there was a suspect from Wilton. I knew my father had done business with the late earl from time to time, but never had my father been his enemy. He had never even said an ill word about the late earl. He certainly couldn't be the man Henry had referred to. My stomach twisted at the very thought. I would set Henry straight immediately.

Voices were no longer detected. How long had it been since they stopped? I waited a moment longer to ensure it was completely silent. Holding my breath, I quietly stepped forward.

"Eavesdropping again, are we, Miss Mason?"

I gasped as I met Henry's eyes just around the corner. He leaned against the wall, face angled toward mine. He gave me a most amused grin. I quickly pulled back and resumed my position on the other side of the alcove, absolutely mortified that he had caught me . . . again.

He chuckled. "There is no sense in hiding, Lily. And your father is gone, if you're worried about him discovering you." He rounded the corner so he was directly facing me.

My cheeks flushed and I angled my eyes down so I wouldn't meet his gaze. His hand gently coaxed my chin up until I had no option but to look at him. "And why, might I ask, are you eavesdropping today?" The corner of his mouth turned up, clearly holding back a snicker.

"Why are you meeting with my father?" I asked, already dreading his response. "He plays no part in the late earl's death, I assure you." My voice came out in a pleading tone.

"Do you truly think that is why I have come to speak with your father?"

"Why else, if not that? You have given him your false name as well. I don't believe you would be inclined to conduct business as Henry Thomas if you plan to reclaim your true identity in two days."

Henry breathed in and looked at me with satisfaction. "You never miss a detail, do you?" He shook his head. "Although what you say is true, I did, in fact, bring a business proposition to your father. I assure you, my change in identity will not affect our arrangement in any way. And to put your mind at ease, I do not suspect your father of anything other than being a gentleman of high character with competent skills in his trade."

The corner of his mouth notched up in a mischievous grin. "I also suspect him of raising a daughter who is absolute trouble." He looked at my eyes and hair, then slowly shook his head and gave me a restless look. His next words were quiet but rumbled. "Every day I tell myself I will have more restraint, and every day it gets harder and harder. I promised myself I wouldn't see you today, and yet here we are." His eyes studied mine. "How am I to stay away from you?"

It took everything in me not to reach for him. I tried to steady my heart but it was futile. As my back rested against the wall, his fingers moved upward, finding the side of my neck. They softly glided over my skin then traced a small curl near my ear. He slowly leaned in, his lips only a whisper from mine. I held my breath as he looked at my lips. "I don't know if I can wait two days," he whispered.

"Then tell me your name," I breathed. His lips lightly kissed the dimple that formed at the corner of my mouth. I shuddered and closed my eyes. "Henry, please."

"Not Henry," he said in a low, husky voice, then placed a light kiss on my cheek. My heart hammered and he let out a tortured breath, slowly releasing me as if it was a tremendous task. He pushed his fingers through his hair as he looked at me.

"Lily," he said in anguish, "have you any idea how much I long to hear my real name cross your lips? How immensely I crave your company and your presence? I believe you have cast a spell on me." I was consumed by his every word. "I don't know that I can wait. And yet, I have made a promise."

He slowly put his arms around my waist. I brought my fingers up and rested them against his cheek. He closed his eyes as I did so and breathed out.

"Can you tell me tomorrow?" I whispered.

"How about we get through today and cross that path when it comes?"

"Very well, 'not Henry,' let's just get through today."

He smiled at my comment. "I might need help letting you go right now." He looked at me as if I was the very air he breathed—

Footsteps sounded in the hallway. My eyes widened in alarm.

"What will happen if you are caught alone with me?" he asked under his breath.

"Most likely my father will shoot you first and ask questions later," I said frantically. "At least that's what he always told Jane and me when we were little girls."

"He'll go that easy on me?" He grinned then quietly backed as far away from me as he could.

The footsteps grew louder and louder. There was no way we wouldn't be discovered unless the intruder decided to suddenly turn around and walk the other way. I prayed for a miracle then held my breath as the figure walked past the alcove. He saw Henry first and stopped in his tracks.

Then the youthful figure turned around to face me. My heart pounded as Oliver narrowed his eyebrows at me, then looked at Henry on the other side of the alcove.

Oliver folded his arms. "What's the meaning of this?"

25

SLEEVES

Lily

Oliver looked from Henry to me, then back again. My breath quickened. "This is Henry Thomas, the man Papa was just doing business with," I did my best to sound natural.

"And why, exactly, is he having a private conversation with you, Lily?" He glared at Henry.

"Might you be Oliver?" Henry asked. I was surprised that he knew Oliver's name. "Your father tells me you are quite handy."

Oliver gave Henry a flat stare. "I am quite handy, sir, when I feel someone is coming onto my sister." He rolled his sleeves up and balled his fists in front of him, ready to fight. I had never seen Oliver be so protective. My heart warmed at the way he was ready to defend me, but I really didn't want him to cause a scene.

"Oliver, that isn't necessary," I interjected.

"You are mistaken, Miss Mason. It is absolutely necessary," Henry said, looking at my little brother. "Oliver is wise to defend you against any man who finds you alone."

Henry took off his coat and draped it over a small table inside the alcove. My stomach flipped as I noticed his muscular build beneath his white shirt and vest. He nodded to Oliver. "Now, show me what you've got."

Oliver punched at Henry but Henry blocked it without so much as flinching.

"Again," Henry said.

Oliver looked angry and punched harder. This time Henry put his entire hand over Oliver's fist and stopped him short. "You're punching out your elbows," he said. Henry bent Oliver's elbow slightly. "Stop your punch here."

Oliver yanked his hand away, eyebrows pinched in annoyance.

"Again," Henry said.

Oliver swung at Henry from the outside but Henry easily deflected it then tapped Oliver's chest and stomach with the back of his hand in one swift movement. "Don't leave yourself open to your opponent. Hold your arms here." Henry moved Oliver's arms into place.

Oliver still looked annoyed, but it appeared as though Oliver was beginning to forget his original goal of defending my honor and began focusing on Henry's tips.

I was touched by Henry's care in teaching Oliver, and consumed by the way Henry moved. "Now," Henry said, with a voice of authority, "guard your face with your fists." Henry raised them slightly higher. "Good," Henry nodded. He held his hand out toward Oliver. "Now punch." Oliver punched Henry's hand. "Lean with it." Oliver tried again. "Good," Henry said. "Again."

Oliver punched his hand over and over again. Sometimes he tried to get an extra punch in. Each time, Henry deflected it easily.

I wasn't prepared for the gravity Henry's movements would have on me. I found it impossible to take my eyes away from his powerful build and athletic ease. Thankfully he was focused on teaching Oliver. I was able to watch him without reserve. Henry showed Oliver how to block a few punches. He had Oliver punch and block over and over again until Oliver was completely out of breath and smiling.

"Good!" Henry said with a smile and a nod. Then he glanced at me for a moment and raised an eyebrow. Apparently my face said it all. He had found me gawking at him, and there was no way to hide it. He grinned at me . . . until Oliver punched him in the stomach.

Oliver was grinning from ear to ear. "That's what happens when you look at my sister that way." He folded his arms.

"I believe I've been bested," Henry said with a grimace, one hand rubbing his stomach. "What would you like me to do to make up for my ungentlemanly behavior towards your sister?" he asked.

Oliver smiled with pure mischief then looked over at me. "Let's see how *he* handles Cook."

We poked our eyes through the entrance of the kitchen. Both Cook and the scullery maid were present this time. Henry would be lucky if he got one step inside the kitchen, especially since Cook was already fired up from the night before. I didn't want her to hurl a frying pan at Henry.

"You really don't have to do this," I muttered to Henry as he assessed the situation.

"Yes, I do," he said with a smirk.

Oliver looked at Henry doubtfully. "Good luck," he said, wagging his eyebrows. "Cook has skewered even the sweetest of talkers."

"Good thing I don't intend to sweet-talk her." He winked at Oliver and walked in.

Cook immediately noticed his presence and narrowed her eyes. "I don't like the looks of you, sir. You best take yourself out of my kitchen." She didn't even wait a moment before she went straight to the wall, unhooking a frying pan. I covered my mouth in anticipation. Henry collected a frying pan for himself next to the entrance.

"I don't like the looks of you either." He gave Cook a look that would have scared even a grown man. She looked surprised for a moment and lowered her frying pan for a second before she raised it again.

"No doubt you have those Mason brats about you, causing mischief." She raised her frying pan higher. "I won't be sweet-talked, ya hear."

"I don't—talk—sweet." Henry gave her a flat stare. "You've hoarded your pastries long enough. Oliver, Miss Mason, and I intend to take your entire platter of pastries off the board, and there is nothing you can say to dissuade us. I am wicked with a frying pan, and I promise you don't want to cross me, madam."

"Don't you madam me!" she raged as she walked right up to Henry's face.

"I'll madam you if I please."

I opened my mouth in absolute shock as they bantered back and forth. The scullery maid watched them, face aghast. Henry and Cook locked eyes in a glaring contest for what felt an eternity.

Then Cook did something I'd never seen her do. She smiled and chuckled, putting her frying pan down, then patted his cheek. "I like the cut of your jib."

"Don't sweet-talk me, madam," Henry winked, lifting a corner of his mouth.

"Oh, off with ya," she said as she handed him the entire platter of pastries and some pudding to go along with it. "And come back for seconds when you're ready."

He smirked. "I intend to." Henry made eye contact with me and Oliver and nodded his head for us to follow him out the back door. Cook gave both Oliver and me a glare as we walked through behind Henry, but there was a grin behind it. Once we were out of earshot, Oliver opened his mouth in sheer surprise.

"That was AMAZING!" he gasped as he stuffed a pastry in his mouth. "Sterling will never believe this."

Henry smiled at Oliver. "Have I made up for my misdeeds?"

"Only if you promise to keep coming back to the kitchen for seconds."

Henry looked over at me and winked. My heart warmed at the entire scene.

Oliver narrowed his eyes. "And so long as you stop looking at Lily that way." I blushed in embarrassment.

Henry gave Oliver an even stare. "Oliver, I believe your sister is a witch. She has cast a spell on me, and I can't help but look at her that way."

Oliver rolled his eyes. Henry chuckled at Oliver's antics then gave him a nod and softly punched his shoulder. "Promise me you won't stop looking after your sister. And now, I must be leaving." My heart sank. His departure always came too soon.

"You're leaving already?" Oliver asked. He actually looked disappointed.

"I have some business I must attend to."

"But you'll come back for the celebration this evening?" Oliver asked.

"I don't believe I'm able to tonight, but your invitation is appreciated," Henry said with a smile. "Does this mean we are friends now?"

Oliver grinned. "Yeah, I guess you're not too bad."

Henry's mouth turned up on one side. "Good."

He moved to the platter of pastries and took one in each hand, then walked to me with his back toward Oliver. "This is for you," he said quietly, placing a pastry in the center of my palm. His eyes moved to mine. "I'm glad Oliver can keep me in line." He smiled then dipped his head. "Two days, Lily," he said under his breath.

Then Henry looked at Oliver and said, "Give my best to Madam Cook."

Oliver saluted, smirking. "Aye aye, Captain."

Henry looked back at me once more then walked away. My heart was calling for him to come back even before he was out of sight. My eyes turned down to the pastry in my hand before I took a bite. It was then that I noticed a small piece of parchment beneath it. I discreetly moved the pastry so Oliver wouldn't notice. The note read:

Meet me on horseback tomorrow beneath the tree an hour past noon. Bring a chaperone.

My heart raced at the thought.

Oliver eyed me suspiciously. "Lily, how can you bewitch a man you only met today?"

I quickly hid the message. "He was simply paying me a compliment," I said, unsure of what else to say.

"I don't think so," Oliver replied. He was silent for a moment. "I think Isabelle Kensington has bewitched Sterling."

I raised an eyebrow, trying not to smile. "And has she bewitched you as well?"

Oliver grinned, "Maybe a little." After a short pause, he added, "But don't tell anyone."

I raised my hand as if to promise. "Not a soul."

Jane

I looked in the mirror and couldn't help but smile. I would enjoy Charles's company this evening without reserve. I wanted to be more beautiful than ever. Unfortunately, I hadn't packed my deep-blue ball gown; the only formal dress I brought was a light champagne color. Though I longed to feel bold in my dark blue, this dress was, without a doubt, exquisite—a delicate lace ruffle, peeking up around the fabric of the neckline and shoulders.

I had already asked Lily if she would arrange my hair for the evening once she was finished with her own. As if in response to the thought, Lily entered my room. She looked beautiful in a lovely pink dress that contrasted with her green eyes. Her hair was mostly up with only a few curls down, framing her face.

She smiled at me with excitement. "Let's see what magic we can concoct with your hair this evening." Walking over to where I sat, she looked at my reflection in the mirror, tilting her head as she examine me…then she got to work.

She loosely curled the front of my hair, strategically pinning it away from my face. Then she did something similar to what she had done for Marianne's ball, curling my hair and pinning it to one side.

This time, however, she left more of it trailing down the side and onto my shoulder. She pinned pearls in my hair as a finishing touch then smiled. "I must say, I believe I've outdone myself." She stood back and looked at me from all angles.

I couldn't help but smile as I admired her work. I felt absolutely radiant.

I didn't think it was possible to feel more exquisite than I had at Marianne's ball. But somehow, Lily had pulled it off. This evening would make all the difference. It was tonight or never. I would convince Charles to stay and abandon his business travels for now. I would find a way to be with him.

The celebration began as we gathered in a large waiting area. Charles hadn't arrived yet. My eyes continually found the door each time a new party entered. Desperation became my companion when I realized the dinner portion of the evening would begin at any minute and Charles had not yet made an appearance. Lily came to my side.

"For someone with so many practiced faces, Jane, I'm surprised you are deciding to wear despair this evening." She lent me a look of sympathy. "Don't worry, he will be here."

I gave her a censuring look. "I'm not wearing a look of despair."

She cocked an eyebrow. "That's a relief, because Lord Elliot has just arrived." She gave me a smile then turned her eyes toward the door. It wasn't fair how he monopolized an entire space without so much as a word; the entire room seemed to notice his presence. Charles was beyond handsome. I wouldn't have been able to pry my eyes from him even if I tried.

His eyes found mine almost immediately and he gave me a look that made my heart skip. He didn't wear his usual grin—he looked determined, with blazing eyes and a look of intensity that made my mouth run dry. I had to remind myself to breathe. His long strides were elegant as he entered, taking him first to my parents. He smiled, greeting them, then said something that made both my parents smile. Mama made eye contact with me briefly, giving me an approving grin, then returned her attention to him.

They spoke for a minute longer before he dipped his head and began walking toward me. I barely noticed when Lily excused herself at my side and walked away. When he came close, his smile changed again to something deep and unyielding as he took in every piece of me. From my hair and eyes, down to my dress. He leaned towards me, then softly said,

"You look beautiful." The look in his eyes mixed with his low, velvety tone sent tingles down my spine.

"I was afraid you wouldn't come," I said, dipping a small curtsy. I did my best to make my voice behave. I wanted to reach out and take his hand. I wanted him to pull me close. Unfortunately, we had an audience. Men and women began flocking to Charles; no doubt they were surprised and excited about Lord Elliot attending, and wanted to meet him since he had been abroad these last five years. His attention was soon claimed and I felt awkward standing in the middle of it all.

I bowed out of the circle and reminded myself I could have his company later. I walked to where Mama stood.

"I believe Lord Elliot is quite taken with you, Jane," she said quietly to me. I looked over at Charles conversing with our party.

"I'm afraid to hope, Mama. And yet I can't help but hope." I looked over at her.

She nodded, giving me a look of understanding. "I know." We watched the group around Charles until eventually, Mama patted my hand and joined Lily.

Dinner was announced and Papa offered his arm to Mama. They entered first, followed by the guests. I entered last, and by the time I walked through the door, Charles was already seated next to Papa, no doubt at Papa's request. A young lady sat on Charles's other side, doing her best to claim his attention. I swallowed down the lump in my throat and took my own seat next to Lily. Another gentleman, William Ashby, sat next to me on my other side. We were well acquainted. He was a handsome gentleman, though I had eyes only for Lord Elliot.

Mr. Ashby smiled. "Miss Mason, I can't help but state that you are more beautiful than ever this evening. I have missed your presence here in Wilton."

I smiled back at him. "Thank you, Mr. Ashby. It is good to be back for a short time."

"How long do you intend to stay?" he asked.

"Lily and I return to London on Saturday."

"That isn't very much time," he said, looking disappointed. "Will you permit me to take you riding sometime before you leave?"

"I would be delighted." I was flattered by his words and attention, but I felt nothing stir inside me at his attentiveness. I tried my best not to look in Charles's direction but it was futile. I glanced toward him. He was watching Mr. Ashby and me.

A side of his mouth turned up as our eyes met, but as he looked to Mr. Ashby, his mouth formed in a straight line. The lady at Charles's side began talking to him, wearing a besotted smile all the while. He reluctantly looked away from me and gave her his attention, though his eyes continued straying to mine.

"May I visit you tomorrow morning?" Mr. Ashby's voice brought me back to the present conversation. I felt a sense of hesitation agreeing to see him during any of my stay in Wilton in case Charles also thought to call on me then. I needed as much time as possible to convince him to forfeit his plans to travel for business.

And yet, Mr. Ashby was a long standing acquaintance. I couldn't deny him if Lord Elliot had not yet claimed my time.

I nodded and did my best to place a smile on my face. "Very well, Mr. Ashby. I look forward to seeing you."

He smiled earnestly. "Thank you, Miss Mason. May I claim your first dance as well?" He gave me a hopeful smile. I could feel Charles's eyes on me. I didn't know if he could hear our conversation or not.

"I beg your pardon, Mr. Ashby, but I've already promised my first dance to Lord Elliot."

He looked over at Charles and I couldn't help but look as well. Charles gave Mr. Ashby a smirk and raised his glass before putting it to his lips.

Mr. Ashby nodded his head. "I see. Then may I claim at least one dance this evening?"

"Indeed, you may," I responded cordially.

He gave me a satisfied smile. "Thank you, Miss Mason. I look forward to it." Mr. Ashby looked at Charles again and cocked an eyebrow, raising his own glass, then took a small sip. I looked at Charles with amusement. This silent game he had begun with Mr. Ashby was entertaining.

Charles returned my gaze, but this time he gave me a look of mischief, discreetly clasping his hands together then lifting his fingers one by one. I swallowed down the laugh that was threatening to escape. When I was sure no one was paying attention, I sent the sign back. I was sure he had no intentions of raiding the kitchen after the party tonight, but it felt exciting trying to send the signal without getting caught.

I suddenly felt Mr. Ashby's presence close to me, as if he was telling me a secret. "Miss Mason, is Lord Elliot a close family friend?"

I backed away slightly from his position. "No, sir. He has only recently become acquainted with my family." I glanced over at Charles and had to bite down a laugh as he took out the penknife he had lent to Lily as a sword and stabbed a piece of meat, giving Mr. Ashby a challenging grin.

Mr. Ashby narrowed his eyes at Charles's odd behavior, then added, "I fear Lord Elliot believes to have some claim upon you, then. Is there an understanding between the two of you?"

I opened my mouth, trying to best form my words. "There is no understanding between us. We have, however, become well acquainted in London and I do enjoy his company." I bit back my smile as Charles put the meat in his mouth with the pen knife and began to chew while staring at Mr. Ashby. "I have found that Lord Elliot loves to fully charm or annoy his company," I added.

"I see." Mr. Ashby looked over at me. "In that case, Miss Mason, challenge accepted." He gave me a grin.

I wanted to tell him I hoped he hadn't accepted a challenge to win me over. But to do so would be to claim that I believed he had taken an interest in me, which would be unladylike indeed.

After dinner concluded, we made our way to the ballroom. As I entered, Charles was waiting for me at the door. He smiled and offered his arm, which I took happily, my light colored gloves a rich contrast with his black suitcoat. He walked me towards my parents, lowering his voice so only I would hear.

"Should I run him straight through the heart with my blade, Jane? Or should I have Cook deal with him?" He looked at Mr. Ashby as he said the last words.

"And what exactly is Mr. Ashby's crime?"

"For one," he looked at me with a wicked grin, "I had intended to take up all of your dances this evening, and now he has claimed one." I laughed at the thought of him taking every single one of my dances. It was highly improper, and yet I could see him somehow getting away with it.

I laughed. "You never were one for the rules."

"Precisely," he said. "Which leads me to my other accusations." He looked over at me. "I intend to have as much time with you as possible before I leave. If he calls on you tomorrow morning, and if he takes you riding, it will take away some of the time I planned to have with you." He apparently overheard most of our conversation. I hung on his words about wanting to spend as much time with me as possible. My heart faltered, however, at his mention of leaving.

"Then I suggest you claim the remainder of my time now," I said.

His grin slowly softened and he looked at me intently, leaning close to my ear. "I want all of your time, Jane." My heart thudded at what his words implied. We stopped walking a few paces away from my parents and he faced me.

I lowered my voice. "It will be difficult for you to have all my time if you leave."

"And yet I have to leave if I'm to ever have what I want," he said grimly.

"And what is it that you want?" I asked.

"I think you know what I want, Jane," he said quietly. His eyes said everything: he wanted me. But why would he need to leave in order to have me? It made me worry that perhaps I misunderstood his desires.

Charles shook his head. "Just when you have decided to give Lord Fletcher up, I have Mr. Ashby to worry about."

I decided to be bold and ask just one question. "Why must you leave to have what you desire?"

He took in a steady breath then let it out. "What would you think if you knew?" he muttered softly. His question etched my mind with uncertainty. I was about to ask more, but Charles looked out to the middle of the room.

"I believe it's time." He offered his arm to me once more as couples made their way to the dance floor. I put my hand on his arm then looked up as I felt his eyes on me. "And this time, Jane, I'll not let you be taken from me." I thought back to when Lord Fletcher had taken me from him as we were about to make our way to the dance floor.

"Promise?" I asked, turning my lips into a smile.

"Always."

26

HAIRPIN

Jane

As we made our way to the dance floor, I thought back to the last time Charles and I had danced. So much had changed since that time. I had changed. I looked at him standing across from me and felt nervous.

The music began, and I wasn't prepared for the way he would dance with me. Each touch was a caress. When our hands met, his thumb gently traced the back of my gloved hand. When his arm came behind my back it felt intimate and tender. Each movement was intentional.

Coming together once more, he didn't passively go through the motions. No. Instead, his eyes drank me in as if I was something he craved. My heart pounded and it felt as though Charles and I were the only two people in the world.

We separated all while his eyes followed me almost hopelessly. We came back together and he brought me close. This happened over and over again until he finally let out a heartbreaking sigh next to my ear.

"Jane," he breathed. "I want you so much it hurts." His eyes found mine, burning with longing. "I want you to be mine, forever." He said it in anguish, as if he thought I could never be his. My breath picked up as he watched me and held me tenderly through the steps. I couldn't speak. I didn't know what he was saying.

Was he proposing or simply stating his desire for me? We separated again and just like before, his eyes followed mine with intensity until we came together again.

"Then why are you leaving?" It was the only thing I could ask.

"I have to," he said.

I shook my head. "But you don't. You are Lord Elliot. You can do whatever you want."

His face fell. "Lord Elliot," he said quietly, as if it left a bad taste in his mouth. His eyes turned melancholy before he put some distance between us. I felt an ache as he did so, dread filling me. Was I in some kind of blissful dream that was turning sideways? Dropping me into the hole of a nightmare?

"Loved and penniless," Charles said quietly, looking at me. "Wealthy and lonely… penniless and lonely." His eyes went back and forth between mine, his expression despondent. What had I done? I couldn't fathom why these words were coming from his lips.

My eyes searched his, seeking some sort of explanation. "I don't understand." I breathed, desperate to end the twisting knots in my stomach.

"I know," he said with a sad smile. "It's not your fault, Jane." He brought me back in a little closer, though not as close as before. I felt a small sense of relief, but something nagged in the back of my mind. For the last third of the dance we were silent. Charles still danced with me in a way that made me feel breathless, but it was overshadowed by a pit in my stomach.

And then my breath suddenly caught as I noticed a pair of eyes watching me that I had never seen before. They looked like Charles's eyes, but belonged to a man with a short beard and longer hair. Charles Elliot had no brother that I was aware of. This gentleman watched us dance, eyebrow notched, a firm expression on his face. This stranger's eyes met mine briefly and he tilted his head, giving me a curious look. Now I was sure I was having a nightmare. The dance ended and Charles escorted me back to my parents. When Charles looked at me, his eyes held so many questions.

He dipped his head. "Thank you for the dance, Miss Mason." Before I could speak, he walked away. Everything was moving too fast. I looked back again to find Charles's look-alike, but he was no longer there. I felt like I was hallucinating. I needed to clear my head. I slipped out of the room while no one was paying attention and headed for the garden.

Lily

Jane walked off the dance floor with Lord Elliot. She seemed off-kilter, and the earl looked melancholy as he walked away from her. I felt sick with worry for my sister as I wondered what could have transpired between them. She had been so content the night before when I found her in the library.

I gasped quietly as I felt something enter the palm of my gloved hand. I quickly turned around.

"Henr—Mr. Thomas!" I said in shock. I felt as though I was dreaming. He was actually here, at a public event. He was well dressed and looked intoxicatingly handsome.

"Good evening, Miss Mason." He grinned. "Your father invited me to attend the festivities, and I'm only sorry I'm late." I didn't know what to say. His formality felt unnatural, but exciting.

"I'm pleased you decided to come," I said, feeling awkward with the way we were speaking.

He smiled. "As am I. May I have this next dance?" He offered me his arm.

"You may," I said with a grin, lacing my arm through his as he escorted me to the center of the room where all the couples were lining up.

I realized I'd only ever danced with Henry in the dark. I thought about the way he had pulled me close to him. I didn't know what would happen when he danced with me now.

Henry had already gained some attention from the ladies of our party. It was clear we would have an audience.

Henry watched me. It was as if he was barely able to hold his formal expression in place when our eyes met. The music started and I was filled with anticipation for how this would all work. Our hands met in the middle then fell away.

I stepped to the side and he mirrored. His hand went about my waist while the other took my hand. He turned me into him and his hand that was about my waist took my other hand. I suddenly recognized it as the same dance I had done with Mr. Campbell the night I met Henry. The way Henry moved through the steps made it feel like a completely different dance.

He kept me at a proper distance but his arms held me tenderly, and he deftly swept me through the steps. His eyes held me captive as usual, but they pulled me into their depths more than ever. It was as though he was holding himself back to the point of torture. Raw passion simmered in his eyes.

"Henry," I said quietly, so only he would hear. "Why didn't you tell me my father invited you?" He continued to look at me as our hands came to the center again. This time, he held my ring between his fingers as he took my gloved hand. Before our hands fell away, he placed it on my middle finger. His trick never got old and it always felt like an intimate gesture the way he placed it on a different finger each time—claiming each of them.

When he was close enough to me that he could speak quietly he finally said, "I am not supposed to be here, Lily."

"Will you stay?" I asked, hoping I would like the answer.

"I can't," he said. He was slowly pulling me closer through the moves. I could feel the way he tried to hold back. I felt how he was slowly slipping. Most onlookers wouldn't notice, but I certainly did.

"Why did you come if you plan to immediately leave?" I asked, hoping I would be able to talk him out of it.

"I had to see you," he said before he grinned. "And I'm much better behaved when I'm chaperoned by an entire room full of people."

I smiled, then looked at him with pleading eyes. "How can I convince you to stay?"

"You can't look at me like that, Lily." He appeared to be at war with himself. Maybe I could sway his decision.

"Then what am I allowed to do?" I smirked just as he brought me around to face him.

His voice got quiet. "Lily, do you want me to kiss you in front of all of these people?" He looked at the dimple by the corner of my mouth. I opened my mouth in shock at his comment. He chuckled. "I suggest you put that expression away for another time."

I smiled mischievously. "If you kiss me then you'll have to stay. My father will insist so he can shoot you on sight." I pursed my lips in a way that would hopefully drive him crazy. "Perhaps I'll keep it up just to keep you around."

Henry put his lips in a firm line. But I saw them twitch at the corners. He was trying not to smile at my comment.

I dropped my teasing. "Henry, I'll behave. Please stay."

He sighed and pulled me slightly closer. "I'll stay for as long as I can." It was better than nothing.

We danced through the remainder of the song in silence. Henry was giving in slowly. Each time we came together, he brought me just a little closer. At one point I noticed Lord Elliot watching us closely. He wore a smirk. When mine and Lord Elliot's eyes met, he nodded in my direction and grinned while he raised an eyebrow.

His eyes held questions. I remembered that Lord Elliot had no idea of Henry and me being at all acquainted. I wanted to ask Henry about whether or not it would make trouble, but I didn't want to chase him away. The music came to an end and Henry escorted me back to where Papa was standing. Papa introduced Henry to Mama.

"I'm sorry, Mrs. Mason, for taking your husband's time this morning," Henry said with an apologetic smile. "If I had known your wishes against it, I wouldn't have come."

She smiled in return. "That is very kind of you, Mr. Thomas. It's no trouble at all, and I'm glad you could make it this evening for the celebration."

"I was grateful for the invitation." He smiled politely at Papa. "And thank you, Miss Mason, for the dance." He nodded to each of us then walked in the opposite direction of Lord Elliot.

"You appeared to enjoy that dance, Lily," Mama said with a grin.

I smiled. "I don't mind stating that I *did* enjoy it."

Mama chuckled. "Why do I sense trouble brewing?"

She had no idea.

Henry made himself as invisible as possible in the crowd of people. It was hard not to watch him constantly—I feared he would disappear when I wasn't looking. I was hoping he would ask me to dance again, even though I knew it would be suspicious for us to dance twice when it appeared as though we'd only just met. Doing my best to seem natural, I found a small group of people to talk with, continually sweeping glances over Henry, who stood across the room. Eventually their company became tedious and I left their group, joining Mama and Papa. As I found Henry's eyes once more, he gave me a warm smile in return while speaking with a gentleman. My heart fluttered and when I looked away, my gaze was met with Lord Elliot's. He was watching me again. I felt as though I was under inspection.

He began walking toward me and I suddenly felt conscious of my every move. Where my eyes landed, what I did with my hands.

I thought about fleeing, but he looked determined. No doubt he would seek me out regardless of where I fled to. I tried to appear natural, peering into the crowd as if I was observing the guests generally. Lord Elliot came to stand next to me, looking out at the ladies and gentlemen in my view.

"I wondered if I might have this next dance," he said with his usual grin in place. I felt panic at the prospect. He had just witnessed me dancing with, and watching Henry in a crowd full of people. What would happen if he found out that we had been seeing each other secretly? If I refused to dance with him, it could just as well confirm his suspicions.

"Certainly," I said, trying to sound at ease.

"Splendid." He gave me his arm and I took it hesitantly. As he led me out to the dance floor, I searched for Henry and found that he was already watching us. The music started and we made our way through the first few steps before Lord Elliot decided to speak.

"It appears as though you've met my friend, Henry Thomas," he said with a smile.

"Indeed," I said, hoping my voice was steady.

"What is your opinion of him?"

His question made my heart pound. My throat went dry, making me swallow.

"I hardly know," I said, trying to sound at ease. "I was just introduced to him this morning when he called on my father as a matter of business." It technically was the truth. I hadn't been formally introduced until this morning.

Lord Elliot's grin turned into a full smile. "Very well put. But you forget that I know well-crafted words when I hear them. I will rephrase my question. How long has my friend been in love with you?"

"What do you mean, my lord?" I tried to sound confident, but I heard my voice shake beneath the surface.

"Would you like to confess, Miss Mason, or would you like me to spell it out for you?" He looked at me with amusement. I wouldn't give in until he stated that he knew absolutely.

"I believe you will have to spell it out, because I have no idea what you are referring to." I tried to return his gaze with a confident look.

Lord Elliot cocked an eyebrow and gave me a suspicious look. "Very well. Since you insist. I have known my friend for a very long time. I have seen him dance a hundred times over and I have seen the way he behaves around young ladies. I have never seen him dance with anyone the way he just danced with you. What's more, I have never seen him *look* at someone the way he looks at you. He is not even supposed to be here this evening, but it appears as though he couldn't help himself."

My legs began to feel wobbly. I didn't know how to get out of this.

There was no way for me to contradict him without my shaking voice giving me away.

He continued, "If I were a betting man, which I'm generally not, I would wager you have known each other since Duchess Hastingwood's ball."

My breath started picking up speed. He was guessing everything.

He narrowed his eyes at me for a moment. "Is that why you and your sister were at the shop that next afternoon?"

I was feeling disoriented. I looked frantically for Henry. When our eyes met, concern etched his eyes as he watched Lord Elliot and me dance. Everything around me started turning into a haze of white.

"Lord Elliot—please stop." My voice felt detached from my body as it came out.

"Miss Mason?" He sounded alarmed. It came out muffled. A ringing filled my ears. Lord Elliot attempted to lead me away from the dance floor but my legs weren't working. It felt as though the world was coming up to meet me.

I closed my eyes, but before blackness took me I felt an arm around my waist and I was lifted into strong arms. I didn't need to see to know it was Henry. I knew his smell, his arms.

"What happened?" he asked in an angry tone. I wanted to tell him not to be angry with me, but the words wouldn't come.

"I don't know." Lord Elliot's voice was concerned.

"She's white as a sheet," Henry barked. "What did you say to her?" I felt him lay me down on something soft then take my hand. The ringing in my ears began to fade.

Lord Elliot's voice came next. "I asked her how long she's known you—how long you've been in love with her." There was no levity or jest in his tone. There was silence. I wanted to see Henry's reaction, but my vision was still hazy.

"Lily," Henry said quietly. "Are you coming around?"

"Yes," I said, but my voice sounded strange. I wanted to tell him not to leave me.

"What has happened?" Mama's voice approached, heavy with concern. Henry released my hand.

"She nearly fainted," Lord Elliot said.

"Thank you for assisting her. I can take it from here." I wanted to reach out for Henry and tell him to stay, but it was out of the question.

I could finally see more clearly. Henry looked at me with concern then looked at Mama. She was looking at me too. My eyes finally focused on her.

"I'll stay here with you while you rest for some time," she said.

"Thank you, Mama." I looked back at Henry who gave Lord Elliot a hard stare.

"A word outside," Henry said.

Lord Elliot set his jaw. "You took the words right out of my mouth."

Jane

Things made no more sense out in the garden than they had in the ballroom. Had I truly seen a man that so closely resembled Charles or was it a trick of the mind? And what did it mean either way? Charles's cryptic words and manner towards me near the end of our dance was putting knots in my stomach. I couldn't make sense of any of it. I paced around until my arms shivered.

It was time to go back inside. And perhaps it was time for me to ask Charles direct questions. What did he desire? Did he love me? Why did he need to leave? The very thought made me tense. I took in a breath to calm my nerves.

Walking back towards the house, I halted in my tracks—a clipped exchange between two deep voices was coming my way and I was unchaperoned. Looking about me, I found a tree with low-hanging branches that Lily and I used as a fort when we were young. Its branches touched the ground on one side, concealing me from view. I prayed I wouldn't dirty my dress as I crouched low and hid behind the branches. The voices were too muffled for me to hear for a time until they moved even closer.

"That's ironic coming from you after the way you just danced with the eldest Miss Mason." It was a deep, rumbling voice I didn't recognize. I couldn't see who was on the other side of the leaves and branches. "When did you start forming an attachment to her?" There was silence on the other end. My heart pounded as I realized they were discussing me.

"From the moment she put me in my place for behaving poorly at Duchess Hastingwood's ball." Charles's unmistakable voice filled the air. My heart swelled at hearing the confession.

"It looks to me as though more than an attachment has been formed. Do you love her?"

Charles took in a breath and let it out quickly. "I'm not here to answer obvious questions."

"Then let me be clear," the other voice said with a clipped tone. "I just saw Lord Elliot dancing with a woman that he appears to be deeply in love with. So in love, in fact, that it seems as though she is the very air he breathes." My heart pounded. It wasn't only me who saw it.

"Then it would appear as though you and I have fallen under the same curse," Charles said, matching his clipped tone. Silence followed for a time.

"And yet, how do you believe Miss Mason will feel in a few days when she sees that Lord Elliot suddenly prefers another? When he proposes to the woman who is truly intended for him?"

My heart plummeted. It felt as though all my breath had been sucked away.

"I will tell her the truth," Charles's voice said quietly. "I can't lose her right now."

"You will say nothing for another few days, and not until everything is settled. We have to see this through." The man's voice paused. "And how do you think she will feel when she discovers the truth? You couldn't have stopped at breaking just a few rules, now could you? You had to break them all." There was silence for a moment. "I can't save you from this one," the deep voice said, sounding frustrated.

My nightmare was becoming reality. If only I could wake from these treacherous words.

"And yet you are free to break the rules without any recompense," Charles said furiously.

"I won't be potentially breaking a woman's heart in the process," the man said. Then his tone of frustration tempered slightly. "I really am sorry for your plight. I don't believe we could have foreseen what a mess this would be. And I won't push all the blame in your corner—I know I am just as guilty as you are. But you really have created a mess. I'm not sure how this will mend itself."

Charles let out a frustrated breath. "What do we do? If you ask me to leave Jane alone, I will refuse."

"Believe it or not, I understand that sentiment," the other man said. "For now, return to the party and act as though nothing is amiss, though I must ask that you temper your outward passion for her. I don't want you to completely ruin the reputation of Lord Elliot in one evening. Do you think you can do that?"

Charles let out a breath. "I will do my best."

"I need better than your best now. You have broken every single rule at this point."

"Technically, I only broke four of the five. And you've broken two rules now as well," Charles said with a hint of humor.

"Ah, yes. What ever will Lawrence say?" Their footsteps retreated away from the garden, but I couldn't move. I felt as though my entire world had been flipped upside down.

Charles did love me. But he was intended for another woman and would be announcing his engagement in only a few days.

I slowly made my way out from beneath the tree, clutching my heart as it ached. My breath shook in anguish as I attempted to walk back inside. I wanted to fall to a million pieces—I wanted to cry out in agony. I leaned my hand against the wall for a moment to steady myself.

I couldn't cry now. I would wait. I was Jane Mason, and there was nothing I couldn't do. I heaved a painful breath and grasped my poise. I held it close and reclaimed my unaffected smile. I pulled decorum next, straightening my back, holding my head high. I steadied my breathing and chastised the tears that threatened to fall. Then I walked inside.

I didn't want Charles to realize I had been in the garden. I would not let him see the truth in me. If I couldn't have him, there was no point in drawing out this torture. I would be an impenetrable stronghold again.

I entered the opposite doors from the ones that led to the garden. No one was looking my way as I walked in and mixed amongst our guests. Mr. Ashby smiled at me from across the room and I returned it with my practiced smile as he walked in my direction until he stood in front of me.

"I believe this next dance is mine, Miss Mason." He grinned, and though it was charming, it was nothing like Charles's alluring expression.

"I believe it is," I said, holding the smile on my face. It was fake, but it was my only hope of getting through this.

It was then that I noticed Charles standing in the crowd, looking at me. My eyes went to his of their own accord. My entire stronghold nearly collapsed in one glance. He loved me. I could see it in his entire being.

But it wasn't enough for him.

I looked away from Charles and turned my attention back to Mr. Ashby as he offered me his arm. It took everything in me not to look back at Charles as I was led to the floor. Mr. Ashby danced like any other gentleman: straightforward. I forced myself to look at him and hold a typical conversation. I promised myself I would not turn my head to look for Charles. By the end of the dance, I was exhausted but proud that I had managed to keep that promise to myself.

Mr. Ashby returned me to Mama. She smiled then saw my expression. Her smile fell and she gave me a questioning look.

"Are you alright, Jane?" She put a hand on my arm. The gesture made my eyes well.

"Mama, may I please retire? I know it is terrible manners, but—" I took a breath. Tears threatened to spill over once more.

"Will you talk to me about it tomorrow?" Mama asked. I nodded.

"Very well. Lily has retired early to her room as well—she almost fainted. I can't leave our guests right this moment, and I've asked Alice to watch over Lily. Will you be alright on your own?"

"Yes," I said with relief. I turned and headed for the door that would best lead to my room, parting the guests as I made my way to the other side.

I was almost there.

Charles suddenly appeared in the way of my route. I did not look at him directly. I shifted my course slightly but it made no difference. He was there again, this time even closer to me.

"May I claim a second dance, Jane?" he said near my ear. I chastised the tingles that went through my entire body.

I breathed in, gathering all my strength. I concocted a look reserved for acquaintances. "I don't believe that is a good idea," I said as evenly as I could manage. His posture tensed.

"What is this, Jane?" His eyes narrowed, searching mine, making it increasingly difficult to stay strong.

"Excuse me," I finally said, unable to muster anything else. I pushed past him, away from prying eyes. I didn't want everyone to see me if I could no longer hold up this charade. I was about to leave the ballroom when Charles grabbed my hand.

"Where are you going?" he asked, worry etching his tone. "Have I offended you?"

I tried to plaster on a practiced face but nothing came. I couldn't speak when he looked at me as if I was everything to him.

"I need to leave," was all that came out. I tore my hand away from his and ran. But instead of going to my room, I went for the back door towards the meadow. I couldn't stand the thought of being in the house now that I knew the truth. I wasn't strong enough to stay away from Charles tonight if I knew he was simply downstairs.

The meadow was the only place I could think to go where I would be entirely alone. I needed a place to give all of my sorrow to. A place to cry out in the despair I felt without a soul to hear.

I finally stopped running when I reached the trees. The meadow was dark except for the moon. My breath came out in heaves from running and from the pain etched in my heart. I tore my gloves from my hands, threw them to the ground, and found my wishing tree. Leaning my palm against it, I rested my forehead on the back of my hand. Tears pricked my eyes, one tear falling after another.

"Jane?"

I gasped then turned. Charles was approaching. I thought about running again but my heart wouldn't let me. As he came to stand in front of me, I cast my eyes to the ground.

"What has happened?" he asked, quiet, uneasy.

"Nothing." I still didn't look at him.

"Nothing?" His question held a sting. Silence passed and I could feel his eyes on me. "Will you not even look at me?" My heart tore at the defeat I heard in his voice. It was almost too much.

After a few more moments of silence, he said, "You may as well start talking, Jane. I have no intention of leaving until I understand what this is about. I'll wait for as long as it takes."

If only it were true. I would have him wait forever if he would truly stay.

His fingers slowly lifted my chin. I wasn't ready for his eyes. I knew I wouldn't be able to stay strong if I—my eyes found his. Logic was futile and resolve left me completely. It would be impossible to flee now. We looked at each other in the darkness for a time before he spoke quietly.

"What is this about? Why have you retreated again?" He took my hand in his and held it against his heart. My own heart pulsed with pleasure and warmth, quickly replaced by betrayal and an aching throb.

"Please, stop," I breathed out. A tear escaped me. Charles looked in agony at my expression. He watched as another tear escaped, then gently brushed it away.

"I have waited longer than I can bear," he said, in torment. "I have refrained from asking, but I can ignore the question no longer." He looked at me hesitantly. "Do you love me, Jane?"

His eyes sparked with desperation. I wasn't ready for his question. His every breath, heartbeat, movement ensnared me.

"Why?" I said with an aching breath. "Why would you have me say it when you know we will never be together?" I had already said too much, but I couldn't help it.

"What do you mean?" Charles looked guarded.

How could he have deceived me without a single word when he was to be engaged? How could he have held me so close? Lured me to him, without holding back? The pain kindled a spark of anger inside me.

"I know of your deceit," I finally said with bitterness. Charles looked at me, dread filling his expression. "How could you deceive me so fully?" I cried. "I trusted you. I opened my heart and you held nothing back. You tore down every single one of my walls, and all for what?" My voice broke. "So you could break my heart with your lies?"

Charles gave me a tormented expression. "Are you saying you will never have me now that you know the truth?" His fingers traced along my jaw and then trailed down my neck. His eyes held such despair. How could he imply such a thing? Did he believe I would be his mistress once he was married?

"Don't turn this on me." My voice cracked. "You should know me better than to think you could lure me into such a trap."

His eyes became unreadable. "I *should* know." His voice was pained. "You would rather be wealthy and lonely than loved and penniless."

"What does that have to do with your deception?"

He stepped closer to me. "Is it my deceit alone that makes it so we can't be together? Or is it the truth it reveals?"

My heart tore at the reminder. "Both," I said, barely above a whisper. It wasn't fair. Even now when I knew of his deception I wanted him. I could never see him again after this moment. I knew that if I allowed him to try, he could lead me to anything.

"This is the last time I can see you," I said, feeling a stab in my heart as the words left my mouth.

Charles shook his head slowly and his eyes pled with mine. "Jane, don't say that." He looked at me as if it was a death sentence.

"I have no other choice," I whispered. I needed to leave before I changed my mind. I tried to slip between Charles and the tree but he put an arm in front of me, blocking my escape. I tried not to look at him as he did so but it was no use. I glanced at him and realized immediately that it was a mistake.

"Not without one thing, Jane." His eyes were determined as he spoke. He put his hands on either side of me, resting them on the tree against my back. "You still owe me something, and it appears as though you're giving me no other option than to claim it now." Dread filled me as I contemplated what he might ask for.

"What do you want?" I asked hesitantly. He looked at my hair falling down my shoulder, then at my eyes. His fingers gently lifted my chin again, his eyes settling on my lips. I couldn't breathe. His eyes finally returned to mine.

"You know what I want, Jane." My heart pounded as I realized what he was asking for. "Tell me you don't want this and I will walk away." His voice was barely above a whisper. His eyes begged me to stay, to want him. I was silent. I couldn't deny how much I wanted what he asked for, even though I knew my heart would bleed more for it.

"You claim that I am breaking your heart," he said in a low, quiet tone. "But you have no idea the agony I already feel knowing you will leave me. It won't be living with this constant ache in my heart." My back pressed against the tree as he moved in even closer. "I will yearn for you, the one who makes me whole, without an end in sight. And you . . . " He looked back and forth at my eyes. "You will haunt my every waking thought, just to know I will still never imagine your eyes exactly right. I will dream of you by night, realizing I can never have you when I wake."

His words pierced my soul to the very depths.

He placed the side of his face to mine, lips close to my cheek. "So I will meet you in my dreams," he whispered. My breath caught as he placed a kiss below my ear. "And in my dreams I will relive this moment every night." His voice came out raw and husky. His fingers traced my neck and jaw then moved through my hair at the back of my neck. His lips brushed against my jaw as he entwined his fingers in my hair, his lips inching toward mine until we were a breath apart.

He held me suspended like this, then finally closed the distance.

His lips brushed against mine slowly, my breath quivering at the touch. Then his lips moved tenderly against mine. My heart exploded. I knew I should stop him, but my lips were already moving of their own accord. I pressed my hands to his chest to push him away, but it was no use. My fingers clung to his shirt as if it was a lifeline. His hands moved my head gently as he tenderly kissed me at every possible angle.

He loved me. I felt it in his every movement. A tear streamed down my cheek, knowing I could never have this again. My hands moved up until they found his hair, my fingers clinging to it as I kissed him back.

"Jane," he groaned in agony. His breath came out ragged, tortured. "Why do you insist on tormenting me?"

My heart hammered against his as he pulled me in closer. His kiss deepened and he tasted of passion. I was lost in the hunger of it, clinging to him as I kissed him back. His fingers twisted in my hair and he gently pulled it until my head tipped back, resting in his hands. His lips moved to my cheek then softly trailed down my neck. My breath came out in tortured sighs. "Tell me you don't love me," he said in my ear. His voice was low and husky.

"Tell me you don't feel for me as I feel for you." His fingers clung to my hair and he looked into my eyes. "Tell me your heart doesn't call out for mine even now." He kissed a tear that trailed down my cheek.

It was too much. *He* was too much. And I wanted him more than anything. I had to leave now or I might never escape this. I heaved in a breath.

"Stop," I cried. I tried to push him away but my heart wouldn't let me. My hands pressed to his chest as it pounded against my fingers. Taking my hands in his, he kissed them softly. My knees became weak and I suddenly felt as though I hadn't the strength to stand. He steadied me and held me to him as I began to weep, resting my head on his shoulder. He gently stroked my back as he held me.

"I'm sorry, Jane," he whispered. "Please don't cry. I don't know if I can bear it."

"I don't want to leave you." I clung to him.

"Then don't leave me," he said, sounding hopeful. He pressed a light kiss to my forehead as he held me close. I wanted to pretend that

I hadn't heard what was said in the garden. I wanted to stay with him here under my tree forever. I wanted him to kiss me and hold me and make me feel undone. I didn't know if I had the strength to walk home, to leave him beneath the tree.

"I have to leave," I said, trying to hold back the tears.

My knees buckled completely. Charles held me up. "Sit with me a while," he said in my ear. He helped me to sit against the trunk. I was incapable of leaving despite the fact that I knew I should. He sat next to me, placing his back against the tree as well, then he slowly pulled me to him. His arms wrapped around my waist as my back rested against his chest.

I felt his every breath. One of his arms pulled away from my waist and I felt a piece of my hair fall away from its pin. His hand moved in front of me and he rotated my hair pin around in the moonlight examining it. He pressed his face close to my neck and breathed slowly, as if he was committing my scent to memory. He pressed a light kiss to my neck.

I closed my eyes at his touch. When I opened them I watched him hold my hairpin between his thumb and finger until it disappeared.

"To remind myself that tonight was not a dream," he whispered in my ear before he pressed a soft kiss on my cheek.

The despair swept through me again, but this time it gave me the ability to do what needed to be done. I held the tears back for now. I would let them come again when I was alone in my room. My heart cried out as I took his hand and unwrapped it from my waist.

"Not yet, Jane," he whispered desperately. "I'm not ready."

I leaned forward, away from him, and stood. My legs shook but I steeled them enough to make it to my feet. Everything inside of me protested as I took a step away from him and then another. I heard him stand behind me and take a step after me. I would never be able to leave if he wouldn't let me. I turned to face him one last time. He was already close. I knew he would reach for me if I didn't leave.

"This is where I leave you," I said, barely above a whisper. I touched his face with my fingers, committing him to memory.

"Not yet," he pleaded.

"Please don't follow me," I whispered, trying to hold back the tears. I pressed a light kiss to his cheek and heard his breath come out in a painful exhale. "Goodbye," I said in his ear.

I watched the muscles in his arms contract as if he was straining to keep himself from pulling me back towards him. He was doing his best to respect my wishes.

I could no longer prolong our agony. With every effort, I turned and left. My legs moved of their own will. My heart screamed and railed against me. My mind kept me moving home.

I didn't make it to my room before the tears came. They streamed down my cheeks before I reached the back door. I flung it open and hurried to the stairs, then ran up each step, hoping I could make it to my bed before I completely fell apart. Wrenching my door open, I slammed it shut before I stumbled into my bed. I wrapped myself in my covers, taking no mind for my dress or remaining hairpins. I didn't hold back. I cried bitterly, weeping into my pillow until I was sure I had no more tears left in me. I was wrong. More came and then more came again, until finally, the darkness took me and I felt nothing.

27

KEYS

Lawrence

Wilton Manor
November 13, 1816
Later that night
Two days of disguise remaining

Though I washed my hands well, I could always smell the silver polish on my fingers. This time was no different as I folded one arm and let the finger of my other hand rest above my lip, deep in contemplation. Both Charles and Henry had been acting unlike themselves since the duchess's ball.

Charles seemed more carefree and light-spirited, as if he was truly becoming Henry. Henry was more weighed down than usual. It was almost as if they had truly traded places.

I quickly glanced at the front door as a soft knock came out in a specific rhythm. Long, short, short, long. I quickly stood and opened the door. As usual, it was a mail carrier in disguise. I nodded my head to him and handed him tuppence. He exchanged it for a letter then walked off without speaking. I looked left, then right, to make sure no one was around to witness the exchange, then closed the door. I ran my finger over the wax seal of the goldfinch.

Before I broke the seal, I walked to the nearby rooms and peeked my head in, watching for any lurking staff. Once certain there was no one close by, I sat at my usual chair again and opened the smooth parchment, glancing at the top of the letter.

Greetings brother,

The front door abruptly flew open. I quickly folded the letter back up and stashed it inside my pocket, standing at the ready.

Charles walked in alone. It didn't surprise me, since both Henry and Charles left at different times. Due to Charles's last rule, not being seen in public with Henry while in disguise, Charles hadn't originally planned to attend the festivities. About an hour after Henry left, however, Charles came downstairs dressed in formal attire. He said it would be ill-mannered of him *not* to make an appearance, especially since Mr. Mason invited him personally.

"Back so soon, my lord?" I asked, grateful that we no longer had to keep up the pretense at Wilton Manor. Charles appeared to be deep in thought. He didn't answer my question right away. Rather, he looked at me, fingers rubbing his chin.

"I will have you know, Lawrence, that between the two of us, Henry and I have broken every single rule."

"I see." I didn't know how else to respond to his comment. "And at this point do you plan to continue your disguise?"

Charles stood in contemplation. "We will need to wait for Henry to decide that." He inhaled slowly then let it out quickly. "Let's have something to eat while we wait in the library. I will change and then I will be down shortly." I nodded my head in agreement then headed to the kitchen.

Once inside the library, we settled into some comfortable chairs. I was grateful for the fire's warmth.

"Have you any idea what time Henry plans to return?" I asked.

"I don't. But I'm worried for him, Lawrence. I've never seen him look at or dance with someone the way he did with the eldest Miss

Mason this evening. And she appears to be as besotted with him as he is with her. But she believes he is Lord Elliot." Charles shook his head. "I don't personally know the young lady, but I have observed her generally at the parties in London and she certainly has her sights set high. It is rumored that Frederick plans to propose once she returns to London. I believe her heart is completely ensnared with Henry, but I don't know if she will feel the same way when she discovers that Henry is a gentleman of no means or property. I will offer him all that I can, but I don't know if he will accept it."

"The Masons are very well off," I said. "Her dowry should be more than enough for the both of them."

"But will she see Henry as a fortune hunter once she discovers the truth?" he asked. "It's all very bad timing. I believe her heart will break with his and that she will choose Frederick in the end. I don't know how Henry will bear it."

I nodded my head. "He will grieve for a time. But then he will find someone else," I said confidently. "There will always be other women."

Charles raised an eyebrow. "I may have agreed with you two weeks ago. But if you told me I would eventually find someone other than Lily, you may find yourself unconscious. Tonight I saw in Henry everything I feel myself for Lily."

I narrowed my eyes. "Lily, my lord?"

"Ah, yes," he said, smiling ironically. "Henry isn't the only one who has been breaking the rules. And it would just so happen that Lily is Miss Mason's sister."

"Do either of the ladies know of your true identities?" I asked.

"Not that I'm aware of."

"And how long have you known . . . Miss Lily Mason?"

Charles's lips twitched up as if he couldn't help but smile at hearing her name. "I met her at the duchess's ball. She was roaming the gardens outside, and I—ran into her, quite literally." Clearly there was a bit of a story that he chose to keep to himself.

"I see. And what do we do now?" I asked. "When do you plan to speak with Henry's father?"

Charles rubbed his forehead. "I don't want Henry to know where

I've gone. I will speak to John in two days."

"Speak to him about what, exactly?" Henry's voice came from the door. There was no humor or levity in his tone. He leaned against the door frame and held his mouth in a firm line. He looked more like Charles than ever before.

"Oh, I'm sorry," he said flatly. "Should I have knocked?" Charles and Henry stared at each other with rigid expressions. The silence stretched for an uncomfortable amount of time.

I looked between the two brothers then finally spoke. "Come sit down, Henry, and we will talk it through."

"Or you can both start talking now, and I will decide if I want to stay," Henry said in a clipped tone, then added, "I have a right to know."

Charles looked at me, questioning how to proceed. I finally gave Charles a nod.

"Very well, if you insist," Charles said, mellowing his tone and his stare. "But I don't think you will like what you hear."

"We are talking about my father," Henry said wryly. "I expect nothing less."

Charles hesitated, folding his arms, then looked over at the fireplace, prolonging the silence. "John Thomas was seen in London a week before Papa's death, and he hadn't been seen in London for nearly a decade before that week," he finally confessed.

Henry's expression shifted to weariness before he looked down, absorbing the information.

"You must despise me," Henry finally said, drained of any emotion. He continued to stare at the floor.

Charles knit his brows together and leaned back in his chair. "Why would I despise you?"

"I am the product of that despicable monster. If he did kill Papa, I will constantly be a reminder to you."

Charles rolled his eyes. "Don't be daft, Henry. You are more Elliot than I have ever been. You are not John Thomas. You're my brother. If your face would be a constant reminder of his death, then my own reflection would be as well."

Henry's mouth twitched into a small grin of appreciation before he slowly made his way into the library from the doorway and sat in a chair facing Charles and me.

"Thank goodness blood alone doesn't determine one's family," Henry said quietly. "One thing is certain. *I* will be speaking to my father. It's time I face John Thomas."

Charles held perfectly still for a time before he finally nodded. "Very well. When do you intend to speak with him?"

"I will leave tomorrow morning."

It was a disconcerting sight to see Henry so expressionless. It appeared as though the world had finally defeated him.

"What about Miss Mason?" Charles asked.

"Which one are you referring to?" Henry asked with a masked tone.

"Your Miss Mason," Charles said.

Henry looked at Charles with hollow eyes. "She will never be *my* Miss Mason."

Charles gave Henry a questioning look. Henry let out a breath. "She knows the truth."

Charles reeled back. "You promised you wouldn't say anything until—"

"I didn't say anything," Henry interrupted in a defeated tone.

"Then how could she possibly know?" Charles argued.

"How did Matthew Johnson know?" Henry muttered. "Perhaps we weren't as careful as we thought we were."

I looked at each of them then cleared my throat. "How do you know she will never be yours?"

Henry looked at me, completely despondent. "She said she could never be lured into such a trap. That both my deceit and the truth it has revealed make it impossible for her to be with me. I should have known better. She did tell me she would rather be lonely and wealthy than loved and penniless. She refuses to see me again."

"Then it appears that she really is a title seeker," Charles said.

Henry shook his head. "I'll not hear a word against her. She is goodness personified. She is selfless and loving and honest. She is beautiful in every form. I believe I truly broke her heart along with mine."

"Surely you will move on soon enough," I said, curious to see his reaction.

Henry's eyes flickered with anger. "Surely you have never fallen in love with Jane Mason."

I smiled. "Very true, Henry. I wonder how you would feel if I had." I let silence take the space for a moment before I added, "And it appears as though you are more like your father than you would think."

Henry's eyes narrowed. "I hope I'm nothing like my father."

"I thought you *wanted* to be like James," I said with an easy tone. My comment took him by surprise.

I continued, "James loved Elizabeth to no end. He would have never stopped fighting for her. Are you willing to fight for her, Henry?"

Henry exhaled. "Not if it would make her feel trapped to a penniless man."

"If Jane is truly as admirable as you say she is," I continued, "then I believe there is something that goes beyond the surface. Together you would not live penniless on her dowry, I'm sure of it."

Charles chimed in. "Is it possible that she believes you are after her money? Perhaps she isn't sure if you won her over simply so you could gain her wealth."

Henry looked down. "I've not thought of that. Perhaps it is possible. But I would not feel worthy of her if we did have to live on her dowry alone."

"Then confront your father," I said. "Find out if there is something left in the name of Thomas and whether you are still able to inherit his property and house. Whether or not he has left you anything, you will use the schooling you've had and that brain of yours to make something of yourself."

"I will lend you any money you need to get started," Charles added with a nod. "Lawrence is right about the fact that we work well together. We will use our minds to expand both of our wealth."

Henry looked truly touched. "Thank you," he said quietly. "You have given me hope." He dropped his head into his hands. "And yet I'm afraid to hope. What if I do all of this and I'm still not enough for her?"

The room was silent.

"Then your heart would truly be better off elsewhere," I said. Henry held perfectly still, his eyes looking toward the fire. Silence filled the space for several minutes.

"It appears I have a big day ahead of me," Henry eventually said, a sliver of hope showing through his countenance. "Charles, may I beg a favor?" he asked as his lips twitched up.

"That depends on what it is," Charles said smugly.

"Mr. Ashby," Henry said, smirking. "I can't blame the fellow, but I do believe he intends to pursue Jane. He is not titled or exceptionally wealthy, but he *is* handsome and does have some money, not to mention the fact that he is the master of his own house. I believe he intends to snatch her from me. And if her heart is as broken as mine is, she may want to be comforted. He could use it to his advantage."

"What exactly are you suggesting?" Charles asked.

"Mr. Ashby intends to call on Jane tomorrow morning. If you were to sabotage their time together, I would be most appreciative."

Charles chuckled. "Leave it to me."

Henry grinned. "I'm only sorry I won't be there to witness it." He leaned back in his chair. "And once you are done sabotaging his visit, what do you intend to do for the remainder of your time in Wilton?"

"I believe that will largely depend on what you discover when you speak with your father tomorrow," Charles said. "I still need to talk with the physician's apprentice in London. I would like to maintain my disguise while speaking with him, which means I may have to travel back early and stay at an inn. I don't believe the London house is safe, nor is 'Lord Elliot' for that matter, until we get to the bottom of this. I was hoping to stay in Wilton while we make the switch back." The corner of Charles's mouth twitched up. "I, too, have plans to secure my own Miss Mason. I may have to reveal my identity to Lily before I return to London."

Henry smiled. "Then I wish you the best of luck." Charles seemed to understand his meaning and reached into his right jacket pocket. He pulled out the familiar form of tuppence that must have been placed during the celebration.

"And to you," Charles nodded. Henry pulled an identical coin from his pocket.

I knew there would be two coins in my own pocket before I put my hand inside. Sure enough, at some point before they'd left for the Mason's party they had switched my keys into my left pocket and replaced them with two coins.

28

FRYING PAN

Jane

Wilton
November 14, 1816
Early the next morning
One day of disguise remaining

Numbness settled in as I opened my eyes. The sun had not yet risen. I didn't move, didn't cry. My shoulders felt the chill of the morning but I didn't pull my blankets around me, instead staring blankly beyond the window at the dark sky slowly being taken by the dawn. I hardly blinked as the sky gradually shifted to a hazy blue.

Eventually I would have to rise. Mama would be waiting for me, expecting me to explain my behavior from the night before.

To explain it would be to relive it. I wasn't ready, couldn't face the truth—again. Maybe eventually I would be able to breathe when I remembered the look in Charles's eyes as I left him. With time, perhaps my heart wouldn't ache so deeply when I recalled the way he'd held me so tenderly and kissed me so longingly.

Last night I relived those moments a hundred times over as I poured my sorrows into the night. This morning only brought numbness. I didn't know what I preferred. To feel the anguish? Or to feel nothing but emptiness? Logic told me I preferred the numbness; at least I could breathe. My heart told me to hold on to the pain—To hold him in my mind until he found me there. I could drift to him in my waking thoughts and dreams as he would meet me in his.

More time passed and I still didn't rise. Eventually my door opened, footsteps sounding until a figure emerged in front of me. I stared without blinking. The figure bent down in front of me; Mama's eyes came into focus. She lightly stroked my hair.

"I have asked that your breakfast be brought to your room this morning," she said in a quiet, soothing voice. She waited in silence for a moment before she sat on the end of my bed. "Will you confide in me now, Jane?"

I didn't move. Perhaps she would eventually leave if I said nothing. She didn't.

I finally took in a heavy breath. "Lord Elliot—" Even as I said his name the pain began again. "He is intended for someone else. I believe he will announce his engagement within the week." Tears pricked at my eyes again. Mama was silent for a while before she spoke.

Her words came out hushed. "Even though he loves you." She said it as a statement. Her eyes mirrored my hurt, as if the pain of her child, no matter the age, was her pain as well. "Oh Jane, I'm so sorry."

Her eyes welled with tears as mine did and she pulled me into her embrace. Clinging to her, I wept. She continued to hold me to her as she spoke, her voice quiet and sympathetic. "Would you like me to tell Lily?"

More tears came as I shook my head in defeat. "It makes no difference either way.

Henry

I stood in front of my father's house. It was nowhere near the size of Wilton Manor, but it was large and respectable. It had been fifteen years since I'd seen the structure that was once my home. I felt no reverence or nostalgia for the edifice itself; only the memories of Mother held any sort of affinity for me. I knocked loudly before I had the chance to back down, then waited. I was about to knock again when the door opened up to a man I didn't recognize.

"Hello, sir," came the man's voice. He looked at me, waiting for me to speak, then asked, "Are you here to see Mr. Thomas?"

"I am."

"Very good, sir. Please come this way." He led me through the entryway toward the library. Though decorated exactly the same as when Mother arranged it, the house was in better condition than I expected. It was dusted, the walls were in good repair, and it was clean.

The butler extended his arm out to a chair once we were inside the library. "Please make yourself comfortable while you wait."

I didn't sit.

He looked at me with curiosity. "Might I get your name, sir?"

"Lord Elliot, Earl of Wiltshire," I said with an authoritative tone. I had been running through how to approach this since the night before. The butler's countenance changed briefly, showing his surprise, before he quickly put his even expression back in place.

"And what is your business this morning, my lord?"

I looked at the butler with a flat look, reflecting Charles's stare. "I will keep my business to myself."

He bowed. "Very well, Lord Elliot. Please wait here." My heart pounded as I waited.

I knew I had no real reason to fear John Thomas; I was fairly certain I could handle myself against him if it came down to it. Yet in the darkest recesses of my mind, he was the tallest, strongest man of my recollection. I remembered him as a man who was only ever angry and drunk, or passed out somewhere, disheveled and unkempt.

I paced the small library as my heart raced faster and my hands began to tingle, footsteps approaching. I stopped moving and took a deep breath as the library door swung open. The man who entered had the same face as the man I recalled from my memory, but everything else about him contradicted the images therein.

Though he was by no means short, I was at least half a head taller. He was not nearly as broad as me, and he was clean, groomed, and well dressed.

He stared at me for a moment before nodding his head in my direction. "Lord Elliot."

He shut the door behind him then walked to his desk, gesturing toward a chair across from him, offering me a seat. I looked at it for a brief moment then finally sat. He followed suit, taking the chair on the opposite side.

I had a hard time believing this was the same man who tried to kill me fifteen years earlier.

"You've grown to be a strong young man, my lord," he said. "Just like your father."

I nodded my head. "Thank you." It was the strangest experience to have my father say these words—especially when I knew how he had loathed James. We locked eyes for a moment and I was gratified to find that I didn't feel the need to look away.

"I was sorry to hear about your father's passing," he said. I was surprised that his words sounded sincere. "Your father and I didn't see eye to eye, but he was a good man." He fidgeted in his seat for a moment.

I decided to get to the meat of the conversation. There was no reason to stand on ceremony.

"My father is the exact topic I would like to discuss today, Mr. Thomas." My speech held no warmth or congeniality.

"Is that so?" John looked at me with an unreadable expression. "Very well, what is it you would like to discuss?"

As I watched him, his expression slowly turned, various emotions crossing his face: guilt, shame, and regret were at the forefront. My stomach writhed at what it could possibly mean. I held even more contempt than before for this man who had only ever brought me pain and disgrace.

"We have recently received evidence that my father was murdered." I followed my words with silence, watching John's response. At first his face was immovable, holding perfectly still. His expression slowly shifted to one of understanding.

"You believe I'm responsible," he stated. He gave a mirthless laugh. "Though it has been over fifteen years since I have spoken with James, I am not surprised."

"You had not been seen in London for nearly a decade until the week before he was murdered," I said, trying to keep my words even.

He nodded his head. "It's true. I don't usually do business in London."

"And what business were you seeing to this time, Mr. Thomas?" I asked with a clipped tone.

"That of a legal nature. I was making adjustments to my will and investing some money I had recently acquired."

"And are there people who can vouch for this claim?" I asked.

"There are. I can give you all the people I worked with and the places I stayed." He looked at me. "Do you truly believe he was murdered?"

"I do," I said with finality. If I hadn't known any better, I would have believed him to be grieved by the information.

"It might as well have been me," he said. "I know I wished it many times over, though that was many years ago. I always believed him to be invincible." He looked down, seemingly ashamed.

His next words were quiet and took me by surprise. "How is my son? Does he miss James?" He continued to stare at the ground, as if he couldn't bear to face the answer to his own question.

I felt as though I was speaking with a stranger who bore my father's features, but in every other aspect, was not him. I was grateful that I would be able to relate my feelings to this man in a way that allowed me to be honest while hiding behind the guise of Lord Elliot. It made me feel less vulnerable. I finally spoke.

"My father's absence has been very hard for Henry. He considers James to be his father." I didn't stop looking at John as I said the words. I felt no shame in stating them. They were true.

John nodded his head. "As he should." He looked back up at me. "I've heard it rumored that you and my son look very similar." He paused, smiling subtly. "Is it true?"

Our conversation was taking us on strange paths at every turn. I had prepared myself for a shouting match and fists—possibly even swords.

I nodded. "It's true."

He smiled and chuckled. "Serves me right that my boy would look just like James Elliot's son."

In all my eight years of living among these walls, I could not recall such a pleasant expression ever crossing my father's face.

"And what's Henry like?" he asked eagerly. "Like his mother, I hope."

"He would like to think so," I said. "He was frightened of you, Mr. Thomas. But he loved his mother dearly. He still remembers her, and thinks of her often. He has made it very clear that he will be nothing like you."

"Good," John said, resolutely. "And he's not a drunk?"

"No," I said firmly.

John looked to the floor again. "I know what you must think of me, Lord Elliot. It's nothing more than I already know. I'm sure you know the details of my shameful, disgusting behavior." His voice was quiet.

"To what, exactly, are you referring?" I asked. "The fact that you blamed Henry for his mother's death when he was already grieving? Or the fact that you tried to kill him because of it?"

John held perfectly still, eyes averted. He didn't speak for a time. He wouldn't look at me. His eyes shifted to the desk in front of him and I could see that moisture was building inside them. I wouldn't have believed it possible if I hadn't seen it with my own eyes. He finally cleared his throat, attempting to hold his emotion back before he spoke with a strained voice.

"I feel pressed to talk about this, my lord, if you will let me. I have wanted to speak these words for many years, and I feel that it is no coincidence that you are now here. I wish I could say these words to Henry, but I can't face him. If you would be willing to relay this information, I would be much obliged." He still didn't look directly at me, but waited for my response.

I finally nodded.

"Thank you, Lord Elliot." He took in a heavy breath and quickly brushed at his eyes. "I'm not usually a man for tears, but the more time passes, the more I find myself incapable of casting them away when I recall my wretched choices. I hope you will bear with me."

He collected himself, taking in a slow breath, then exhaled. "My wife, Rachel, was an angel. Despite the fact that I'm a wretch, I somehow convinced her to marry me. She saw something in me that didn't actually exist." He closed his eyes. "Rachel was the only goodness in my life, and I was so afraid of losing her that I didn't even let her leave the house. I wanted her to myself, so I never let anyone call on her. She still loved me somehow, but I broke her spirit."

I thought of Jane. In a twisted way I understood his sentiment. I wanted Jane all to myself. I wanted her so much that everything inside of me was torn up and lit on fire. I could never imagine trapping her, though. It was disturbing to realize that this man, my own father, had truly locked my mother away.

He went on. "I hated myself for it and yet I continued to do it. I was convinced that she would never return home if she saw what else was out there—that if people visited, she would finally see what real goodness was. She cried so much at first when she had no friends. I whispered sweet words and promises that I would let her go someday— that I would show her the world. She all too easily let me hold her every night despite the fact that she lived in a prison. And she always told me I was a good man and that she loved me despite it all.

"Somehow she believed in me. She trusted me, and I . . . " His mouth formed into a firm line. "I was a monster. I knew I was never good enough for her and I always liked my drink. But I found myself drinking more and more to drown out the inadequacies I saw so clearly in myself.

When I finally came around, I would see the disappointment in her eyes. But she still curled up next to me at night and kissed me, telling me she believed in me . . . and the next day I was drunk again . . . and the next, and the next, until I began to hate myself to the point of bitterness.

"I always tried to justify my bitterness, as if it was all someone else's fault. And then Henry was born. I held him in my arms for the first time as I sat next to Rachel. It was the first time I had cried in years. Rachel cried with me and kept saying, 'He's an angel.' I looked at him and knew there had to be something good in me if I had helped make him. I thought I would change for him . . . and I did for a time. I stopped drinking. I started taking Rachel out to social events occasionally.

"I slowly started to believe that I could be the good man she somehow saw. But the more we went out, the more I saw what good people looked like. I watched Rachel's eyes light up around other people and I became afraid again. My inadequacies slowly started whispering in my ear over and over that she would leave me. I pushed them away for a time, however.

"We went on this way for about four years, though my demons never stopped their pursuit of dragging me down. She eventually became acquainted with your mother, Lady Elliot, or Elizabeth, as my wife called her."

John stopped talking and finally looked at me. "Henry was four at that time, and he was still an angel boy. Rachel and Elizabeth discovered that they were distant cousins and became fast friends. They looked alike too." He gave me a look of appreciation before he said, "Your mother was truly an angel to my wife. Rachel told me that she felt as though she'd known Elizabeth her whole life after their first meeting."

Moisture pricked my own eyes at the thought of both my mothers being friends. It made me miss them even more.

John continued, "Your father, James, insisted that we get to know each other better for the sake of our wives, and I agreed. Despite the insecurities that constantly whispered in my ears, I loved seeing Rachel blossom. Your parents invited us over for some social events once or twice, and eventually James and I made a business arrangement of sorts. I looked forward to the prospect of working with a gentleman such as your father, and Rachel looked forward to her time with Elizabeth.

"But it couldn't last because of my treacherous mind. Your mother invited Rachel over for tea one afternoon. Up to that point, I had only ever let Rachel go anywhere with me. She asked if she could go, 'just this once,' and my inadequacies crept in again. I reluctantly let her leave. She was so excited. It was the first time since we had been married that I allowed her to go anywhere without me. She smiled at me so sweetly, hugged me and kissed me as if I'd given her something truly precious." He said the words with shame, shaking his head.

"The moment she left the house, my mind filled with the worst ideas imaginable. I was consumed with thoughts of your father and my wife. It was no secret that all the ladies thought him to be very handsome. He was strong and powerful all while being humble and kind. He was the best husband to Elizabeth. I noticed how he treated her. How he gave her free reign to do what she pleased. How he stole kisses when he thought no one was looking. How he made her smile and how she made him light up. I began to imagine Rachel in Elizabeth's place and before an hour had passed I was sure I would go mad.

"I hadn't had a drop of wine since Henry's birth up to that point, but I didn't even last two hours before I had a bottle in my hand. I drank and drank until I was the devil himself." He pressed his lips together, no longer able to speak. "This next memory of my actions disgusts me to the point of revulsion, even twenty years later.

"I arrived at your father's house heavily drunk and angry. I stormed inside without being let in—I was so convinced I would find your father and Rachel alone. I threw the drawing room doors open and found Elizabeth and Rachel talking and laughing. It was only the two of them. It's disturbing to me that even then, when it should have been perfectly clear that there was nothing untoward happening, I still suspected the worst.

"When Rachel saw me in my drunken state, her expression fell. At the time I thought it was because she no longer loved me. I was enraged and walked to her, grabbing her arm and yanking her to her feet."

He stopped talking, a tear escaping his eye, and then another. His next words came out hoarse. "I slapped her across the face and called her a whore." He raised a fist to his mouth and clenched his jaw. It was clearly painful for him to relive.

"I—" His voice broke. More tears escaped his eyes. "I truly broke her heart in that moment. She looked up at me in such despair and fear. I took no care while I dragged her toward the door. She cried out that I was hurting her, and I felt justified." John shook his head, wearing a look of disgust.

"Your mother, Elizabeth, was in tears. She ran to Rachel's aid and slapped me in the face, giving me a look I'll never forget. She did not shy away from me as I released Rachel. Even as I raised my fist, Elizabeth looked at me with unyielding fury. She had no fear.

"I thank the heavens that James intervened just then. I had every intention of striking Elizabeth. James grabbed my arm from behind just in time and jerked me around so fast I didn't know what was happening. When his eyes met mine, I saw pure rage. I tried to jerk my arm back but he held my fist firmly in place. I still didn't relent and attempted to swing from the side, but he blocked me easily, then punched me in the stomach so hard I couldn't breathe. He put Elizabeth behind him to protect her from me then noticed Rachel on the floor in tears.

"James looked at me with sheer disgust. Elizabeth helped my wife to her feet and hugged her as Rachel cried. When my wife dared a glance at me, a red mark across her face from my own hand, I knew she finally saw me for the monster I was. She no longer saw the 'good man.'"

More tears streamed from John's eyes. "To this day, I don't know why Rachel returned home with me. Your mother even offered to let her stay at Wilton Manor with Henry, but she declined Elizabeth's offer.

Instead, Rachel helped me up and walked me to the carriage. But she never did look at me again as if she believed I was good deep down.

Her eyes never lit up again unless she looked at Henry—" His words choked on my name and he was silent for a time.

"I received a letter from your father stating that I was to never set foot on his property again unless I intended to be shot where I stood. He pulled out of our business arrangement, stating that he could never do business with a man who threatened Elizabeth, or that struck a woman. When I saw letters arrive for my wife, from Elizabeth, Rachel refused to open them. She just tucked them away and silently cried. She knew she couldn't trust me with any of her friends again so she pretended they no longer existed.

"Rachel never asked to leave again after that. Slowly her spirit broke entirely and the only thing she loved was Henry. I didn't even try after that day. Most of the time I was too ashamed of myself to even look at her. I returned to my drinking habits worse than before. The few rare times I wasn't drunk, I spent the time loathing myself. Eventually my loathing turned to Henry. I watched his goodness, his kindness, his strength. He got none of it from me.

"He was something I could never be and I hated him for it." John's tears no longer held back. They flowed freely. "I hated my angel boy. I hated the way he collected Rachel's favorite leaves and flowers in the meadow just because he knew they would make her smile. Or the way he lived just to play the games they made up together. He always looked at me as if I was letting Rachel down. He escorted his mother in for meals. I hated that one evening as I came out of my drunken state, I overheard Henry say to Rachel as she was crying, 'Don't worry, I'll always take care of you.' "

John stopped talking again, his voice choking up. "My young boy, feeling the need to take care of his mother, because she wasn't being taken care of." John shook his head as he tried to collect himself.

"The more Henry grew, the more he acted like your father. I hated him even more for it. Rachel and I became strangers to one another. She never let Henry near me, and when she looked at me, which was rare, she had a look of emptiness in her eyes. It ate me to the core. So I used the bottle to drown it out. I never tried to make it better because I knew I would just disappoint her further."

He stopped talking and finally looked up at me. "I have wanted to speak to your father about all of this for many years and never had the courage. If there is one thing I have always been, Lord Elliot, it's a coward. And now I no longer have the chance to speak with James or Elizabeth and apologize for my actions against them both. I no longer have the chance to thank them for taking Henry.

"I don't know that I can speak about the next part of this story. As much as I've hated myself in the past, it's nothing compared to how I feel about this next part of my miserable, loathsome heart. But I fear if I don't speak of it now, I will never have the chance again. It is the greatest of all my disgraces. The more time that passes, the more I feel the need to unburden myself." He closed his eyes for a moment, as if he was finding the courage to speak the words that weighed heavy on him. When he opened his eyes, fresh tears brimmed the surface.

"Henry turned—" He couldn't finish the words. He gathered his composure. "Henry turned ill, very ill. The doctor didn't know if he would make it. I was grateful that he might die. I even hoped for it." The tears began again. "I thought that if he died, I wouldn't be reminded of the terrible wretch I was each day when I looked at him. I could comfort Rachel in her grief and she would somehow love me again. I could make it right again." He shook his head.

"Even as I say the words aloud I can't believe them. They are words that only a fiend would think. But it's how I felt, and no amount of shame now can change it. I watched Rachel toil over him. She was haggard and exhausted and fraught with worry for our son. I didn't even offer to help her watch after him. I watched in hope as he worsened. For once I didn't drink, in case she needed my shoulder to cry on when the time finally came.

"But it never did. Instead, she contracted his illness just as he made a turn for the better. For days she was sick. I finally visited her the night before she turned real bad. I could no longer stay away from her. She was fevering, but not so much that she was delirious. She looked at me with such loneliness. I gently pulled her to me the way I used to and she kissed me, lips hot while her body shivered. She began to cry and asked, 'Why did you stop holding me this way? I've stayed here for you all this time, and yet you don't even see me.'

"She clung to me and cried. I told her that I knew she could no longer love me, so there was no point. She sobbed and said she'd loved me even when I broke her heart."

He stopped speaking again, swallowing down his pain. "I told her I loved her more than anything the world had to offer. I told her I hated myself and that she deserved better than me. She held tight to me that night and made me promise not to leave her.

"I told her I would change again. I told her I would stop drinking again and that I would be better. She looked at me and smiled. Her eyes regained a small spark and she told me that she believed me. Then she fell asleep in my arms. I marveled that she was there once again, and I held her all night. For a moment, I was grateful she was sick.

"I thought that perhaps I could stop hating Henry, and that one day I would thank him for passing his illness onto Rachel. That is, until I woke the next day to find her symptoms worse. I ran for the doctor and by the time evening came, she was so delirious that she was unresponsive. He told me to prepare myself for the worst. My entire being was wracked with fear and grief and anger. I couldn't be in the same room as her. I couldn't watch her die. In my mind, if I wasn't there to watch, it wouldn't happen.

"I didn't even hesitate before I began to drown my sorrow. I drank until I passed out, hating Henry even more. It was all his fault that she was sick, I told myself. I convinced myself, as I drank relentlessly, that Rachel wouldn't die without me. That I would wake and find her mending. That I would start over again and pull her close to me every night. I would become the man she deserved.

"When I woke the next day, she was gone. She died while I was passed out, drunk, on the couch. She died while Henry, my eight-year-old boy, stayed with her until the end."

This time, a tear rolled down my cheek, mirroring my father's, as I relived the memory.

"When I finally came to, I was fierce. The servants and staff made sure to vanish if ever they saw me. I raged and railed against anything and everything. Most of all, I wanted to make Henry pay. I justified my anger by telling myself it was all his fault. But deep down I knew the truth. It was all *my* fault. If I had taken care of her or helped her with Henry, she might have pulled through.

"As the weeks passed, I hated Henry more and more. In my eyes, I'd almost had Rachel back and he took her from me . . . " John heaved a sorrowful breath. "And my angel boy was hidden from my view by Martha and the staff. He grieved without a soul to comfort him other than Katie, his nursemaid.

"And yet I still saw glimpses of him. And every time I saw him, I saw Rachel. I saw her goodness; I saw her kindness and compassion. It angered me more and more until I could stand it no longer. About a month after Rachel's passing, I completely snapped. I finally decided Henry could no longer breathe if Rachel didn't."

John looked up at me. "I believe you know the rest, Lord Elliot. I was the devil himself. Just before I attempted to take Henry's life, I saw Rachel's fear in his eyes. I saw her tears roll down his cheeks and still I wouldn't yield. I have never been more grateful than when your father saved my boy. I hated him then, but it didn't take long for me to be swallowed up by my own demons and see the truth.

"Your father had some men return me to my house after the incident. Later that same day, James himself came over. I had no idea of any of this, since I was unconscious on the couch. He told my household staff of what transpired, including what I had attempted to do to both my son and Katie. He offered each of my staff a position at his own estate or elsewhere.

"When I finally came to, I immediately went for a bottle of wine. There was none that I could find. I went to the wine cellar, and it was then that I realized I had shattered every bottle in my crazed state the day before. I yelled for my staff to assist me but no one came. They had all abandoned me for James. Only my cook, Martha, stayed. She was once friends with my own mother and had known me since I was a child. She felt she couldn't leave me."

Martha's face came into my mind, though it had been years. My father looked down as he continued to speak.

"The first few days, I raged and yelled and thought I might die from want of drink. Martha stayed out of my way, though I found food left on the table during mealtimes. The house was in such a state and there was no one but me to clean it. Each time I picked up glass or washed the wine-stained floor I hated James Elliot more and more. I hated the Elliots' very existence. In my mind, they took everything from me: my wife, my son, my staff—everything.

"A short time later, Lord Elliot and some of his men returned to claim Henry's belongings. I wasn't drunk with wine when he came, but I was drunk with hatred. When he approached my door, he carried a rifle in his hand, along with a sword at his hip. He told me that he was here to collect Henry's things and that if I put up a fight, he would too. I didn't attack because I'm a coward. But I seethed with enough hatred that I'm sure I would have tried had I thought I stood a chance.

"A day passed, and then another. I felt as though I was in purgatory. I hadn't a thought to live or breathe, nor strength to leave my house even to buy wine. My very existence was to hate and be hated. The food and drink that Martha left out for me was scarcely touched until I became a shell of a man. I hated my very existence, and teetered between loathing no one more than myself, and loathing Lord Elliot even more. I was certain I would waste away into nothing and finally be taken by my maker, whom I believed at that time was the devil himself.

"Then Martha finally emerged. It had been weeks since I'd seen another living soul. I had all but forgotten that she was living under the same roof as I was. By the time she came to me, she was confident that I had no strength left in me if I decided to rail against her. She was a patient woman. When she did finally speak to me, she didn't skirt about anything. She was as blunt as a hilt and she didn't sweeten her words. She gave me the full blast of God's wrath.

" 'Your mother would be ashamed of you,' she said to me. 'I'm ashamed of you.' I could hardly speak, so fatigued and frail I was. I hoped I would soon depart from my existence. But Martha didn't let me. She bullied me into eating and taking water that night.

" 'Rachel will never have you in this state,' she said. In my delirium I drank the soup and water she held up to my mouth with thoughts of pleasing Rachel. I don't know how many days Martha nursed me this way. It felt so long and yet so fleeting. I dreamed of Rachel in my unconsciousness, and for a time I thought that perhaps I had died and somehow cheated my way into heaven, into her embrace, finally feeling peace . . . until I was ripped from her once more and brought to Martha's face. It was the first time I cried since . . . since Rachel died.

"Martha didn't pity me. She made me eat more food, drink more water, until I overcame the struggle of teetering between life and death.

"After my wrestle with death, I had a small amount of strength. The first time I ate at the table, Martha joined me. I didn't ask her to; she just did as she pleased. As I ate and drank, I felt my senses slowly invigorate. My anger and hatred rekindled for Lord Elliot tenfold. I muttered that I would kill Lord Elliot once and for all under my breath, and I meant it.

"Martha looked over at me with such piercing eyes. Her hand suddenly moved to her glass and she threw its full contents over my face, followed by a hard slap. She gave me a look of such scolding, the kind that only a mother can give to her child. She then lifted a frying pan from the side of her chair, and pointed it between my eyes, practically touching my skin, as if it were a crossbow.

" 'You are a wretched man, John Thomas,' she said furiously. 'You killed your wife and you almost killed the only good thing you have left.' Her words hit me so hard that I felt as though I was standing before my true Maker at judgment day. She looked at me with fierce eyes and said, 'You will never be able to look Rachel in the eyes, or feel peace, until you face your demons. Lord Elliot has only ever saved you and those you love from your own despicable actions. You were making something of yourself until you killed Rachel's spirit. She loved you so perfectly, and you destroyed her. She waited for you day after day, night after night, to come out of your drunken stupor, only to be disappointed again and again. At night she cried herself to sleep, wrapping her arms around herself as if all she wanted was for you to notice her again.'

"Her words cut me so deep. I cried out for her to stop, but she wouldn't hear of it. 'I'll stop when you stop pretending that this hatred is for Lord Elliot, and when you face the fact that it's only ever been for your own self.'

"I felt as though I couldn't breathe as she said the words. I was taken with such torment and grief that I thought it might choke me to death. Then she took my own glass of water and threw it into my face. I sobbed like a child after that. She stood as I wept, frying pan in hand, and knelt beside me. I wouldn't meet her eyes.

" 'You're a wretched man,' she said again. 'But you haven't always been.' It was the first kind thing she'd said to me. It gave me pause and I finally looked at her. She didn't look at me with sympathy or even pity. She looked at me with determination. 'You were a good lad when you were young. You can be good again, but not until you rid yourself once and for all of your demons.

" 'Make it right, John. Make it right for your Mother's sake. Make it right by your wife, and for Henry. Only God can save you. Give your life to Him. Only then will you be able to face Him and Rachel.'

"She shook that frying pan at me and instilled a fear into my soul that I remember to this day. If Martha made me quake about my wrongdoings, I couldn't imagine the shame and anguish I would feel when finally meeting Rachel and God if I did nothing to right my wrongs. I finally nodded to Martha and it was then that she slowly embraced me." He gave a look of remembered gratitude. "Her embrace was motherly and supportive. I knew she would help me. From then on, she became my one friend and mentor.

"She took every meal with me and scolded me when my temper wasn't in check. She carried a frying pan wherever she went and reminded me of what I wanted if ever I was behaving ungratefully.

"The more I acknowledged my faults and my sins, the more of them I saw. It was a very slow, painful process. One slow month at a time I began to change. My heart finally opened and I was faced with the despicable things I was, and had been, from the time I married Rachel.

"But instead of ignoring or justifying them, I faced them. Each time I wanted to give up, Martha was there with some food and a Bible in tow to remind me whose hands my life was now in, never forgetting her frying pan in case she needed to use it. About nine months into my reformation, I wanted Henry back. I was so desirous to have the one thing of Rachel that still lived. I wanted to right my wrongs and do right by Henry. I dressed in my nicest attire, groomed my hair and beard so that I looked like a gentleman again.

"I rehearsed my apology over and over again, knowing the exact words I would say. Surely James would allow me on his property if I approached with honor.

"I walked to the stream that connects our two lands and was reminded of that horrendous day. Nearing a small bridge, I heard voices coming from the other side. I hid myself then quickly recognized one of the voices to be your father's." He looked at me with a nod. "He was laughing with two young voices in tow then said, 'Henry, you've got to quickly seal your hands together once you've got him or he'll just jump right back out.' He was helping Henry catch a frog. Something I had never done in his entire life."

The moment my father described could have been one of many. James often took Charles and me out to the stream for little adventures.

My father fidgeted with his hands before he spoke again. "Henry's voice echoed next amongst the trees. He said, 'I'm trying, but he's just too quick.' My heart stopped as I heard my angel boy laugh for the first time in what felt like years. I heard another boy's voice next. I assume it was yours, my lord." John looked at me with a smile.

"The boy laughed and said, 'Are you finally going to do it this time? Or are you still afraid you'll accidentally hurt it?' I heard them splashing around, laughing in the water until I heard Henry's voice say, 'Look! I finally caught one by myself. Papa! Charles! Look!' He was so thrilled. He laughed with such delight.

"I couldn't help but notice what he called James. I decided to sneak a peek from my hiding spot. I could see only your father and my son. You were hidden from my view. But Henry smiled down at his hands. James put a hand on his head and tousled his hair. When Henry finally looked up at James there was no disappointment in his eyes. There was only pure admiration and a desire to emulate the man that stood before him.

"In that moment I realized I could never be seen in Henry's eyes that way. No matter how much I made up for my transgressions, I still had the horrors of my past. My heart sank, and for a moment I felt angry again. I felt angry at James for taking my son from me. I felt angry that Henry could look up to the very man that tore us all apart. I sat in those old feelings of hate for only a moment before Martha's piercing words came back into my mind.

"I banished my thoughts of hatred and remembered my own wretched nature before I watched James and Henry again. And this time, I saw Lord Elliot in a new light. He was the man who had saved me from my worst choices in life. He had taken a boy that wasn't his, without so much as a question. He appeared to be just as fond of Henry as he was of his own boy. Henry was well dressed, well taken care of, and clearly loved.

"In that moment, I knew I would never be good enough for Henry. What would happen if I took Henry back and Martha was no longer around to haunt me with her frying pan and Bible? What if I turned back to my drinking again? I couldn't take him from this place that made him so happy.

"I heard him run after the other boy before long and say, 'Charles, let's go show Mama!' I thought of Elizabeth, the woman who was so good to my wife. I thought of this boy, Charles, who would become Henry's brother. It was clear to me that the kindest thing I could do for my boy was to let him live with his new family in peace, and let him forget about me as quickly as possible.

"They left the stream and I made my way home, defeated. Martha took one look at me when I entered the house and knew what happened.

" 'You couldn't do it, could you?' she asked. I only shook my head. 'Good,' she said. 'Means your heart's actually changin'. You care more about Henry, and what he needs, than you do about what you want.'

" 'What do I do now?' I asked.

" 'You let Henry grow up as an Elliot. He will become an Elliot in every way but blood and name.'

"So that's what I did." My father looked up from his desk towards the window. "It was hard at first, but it got easier with time. I don't expect Henry to forgive me."

His eyes returned to his desk, fresh tears forming again. "I just hope he will know—" he paused, his voice breaking, "that I am so sorry. That I'm sorry I broke his mother's heart. I'm sorry I disappointed him. I'm sorry I blamed him and hated him when I really only blamed and hated myself."

His words brought emotions to the surface that I didn't realize existed. They were buried deep. Tears ran from my own eyes as I felt a sense of relief at hearing these confessions. My mother's death wasn't my fault. My father regretted his actions, and never tried to claim me from the Elliots because I deserved better than what he had to offer. I'd never wanted him to claim me, but it was a comfort knowing he did care.

He glanced up at me through his tears. "Lord Elliot, if you could tell Henry of my shame and sorrow, I would be willing to do anything. I believe Rachel would sing from heaven."

I looked at my father, seeing the change in him. I felt his love for my mother and me, and I sympathized with his broken heart, relating with my own feelings of torment for Jane, the woman I couldn't have, and couldn't live without.

It was finally time for me to speak with my father. I reflected on his comment about Mother singing from heaven.

"Mother always did love to sing," I said as I looked at him. My words were full of emotion. He froze and looked at me for a long moment, deciding if he heard me right. "She sang like an angel," I added, unable to keep back the tears.

My father couldn't speak for a moment. He finally stood, examining my face while he walked over to me. I raised up from my own chair, feeling taller than ever before.

He looked at me with pride and shook his head. "Henry?" He looked in my eyes as if he was searching for his young boy inside, then clasped both his hands about my arms. "My boy!" he cried. "My son."

I nodded my head as more tears came. I didn't know if he embraced me or if I embraced him first.

He held me in a tight grip and continued to weep. "I'm sorry, son.

I'm so sorry."

I couldn't speak. I could only nod my head as the tears flowed. I was taller and stronger than him—but in that moment, I was an eight-year-old boy once again.

After our embrace, my father and I took our seats once more. We had a lot that needed to be discussed.

"You've turned out tall and handsome, Henry." My father gave me a look of pride. "I'd be surprised if ladies weren't lining up, waiting for you to notice them."

My thoughts immediately turned to Jane. "I'm not sure about a line of waiting women." I exhaled. "But if there was one, I would only care about one woman standing in it."

"It appears that in this regard, we are alike," John nodded. I couldn't deny his loyalty to my mother. Even after all his disgraceful behavior, his love for her was obvious. "Can I expect to hear of your engagement soon?" he asked.

The ache in my heart for Jane pressed more acutely at his question. I tried to find the right words, and my emotions were already raw from just having faced this man while reliving my early childhood trauma.

"It would just so happen that the woman I love will not have me."

My father creased his brow. "Then she's not worth having."

How could I explain it to him? I trusted that my father was being truthful with his information. I didn't believe that he was responsible for James's death. But could I explain mine and Charles's disguise to him without speaking to Charles about it first? I decided I could explain it without giving away what Charles and I had been up to.

"You stated that you have heard rumors that Charles and I look similar. We don't just look *similar*; we basically look identical. When Miss Jane Mason met me—"

"The woman you speak of is Miss Jane Mason?" my father asked expectantly.

"Yes, are you acquainted with her?" I was intrigued.

"I wouldn't go as far as claiming we are acquainted. I have done business with her father from time to time, and both of his daughters have acted as scribe. They are both very kind, very capable, and very beautiful." It felt odd and natural all at the same time, speaking to my father about something like this.

"She is all those things and more," I said. Silence passed between us before I spoke again. "As I said, Lord Elliot and I are nearly identical in appearance. The first time Miss Mason met me, she believed me to be Lord Elliot."

Recognition dawned on my father's face. "She believed you to be titled and wealthy."

"Yes."

"Is that the reason she tried to steal your heart? She wanted your title?"

I couldn't help but grin, thinking back on how much I had aggravated her in the beginning.

"No, actually. She is being courted by Lord Fletcher, the Duke of Hastingwood's son. She wanted nothing to do with me, because I enjoy nothing more than ruffling Lord Fletcher's feathers. I did it at her expense the first evening I met her and she put me in my place."

"I like her already." My father grinned.

I nodded. "It's impossible not to love her. She believed me to be Lord Elliot, and I didn't correct her. In fact, I pursued her, knowing full well that I should leave her be. I couldn't seem to help myself. I wanted to be in her company. I wanted to draw out her smile and I wanted that smile to be aimed at me. She stole my heart almost immediately and I justified every action I took, telling myself it was for her benefit, if only she didn't marry that tyrant, Frederick.

"Her family lived without money for most of her life, and though they are wealthy now, she has this idea that if she marries a title and someone with influence, her family will be treated with less hostility in society. Slowly I lured her away from Frederick, and I believe I even won her heart until—"

I stopped speaking.

"Until she learned of your deceit," my father finished.

I nodded. "She won't have me now. She won't have me because I deceived her, and because I am a penniless man who can offer her nothing. I have no home to claim as mine. Charles states that I am always welcome to live with him, even if I were to bring home a bride, but in the end, it's still not my house. I have no money that is not given to me by Charles. He insists that I'm not a burden, and that his money is just as much mine as it is his, but—"

The library door slowly creaked open. I looked over and found the familiar face of an elderly woman carrying a plate of food, a frying pan in tow, and a Bible under her arm.

"In the end, you're still Henry Thomas," she said with a grin. "Sorry, I couldn't help but overhear your conversation. I had my ear to the door." She gave an errant smile.

I chuckled. "Hello, Martha."

My father rolled his eyes as he looked down at her hands. "She still insists on carrying this blasted frying pan around, even though it's too heavy for her now." He walked over and carefully took it from her grip, placing it on the table.

"Gotta keep him in line." She winked at me. "And look how you've turned out, Master Henry. You're a handsome thing, I'll give you that, and you're tall too." She gave me a proud smile. "So you want to win the fair lady, but haven't tuppence to rub together, is that right?" she asked.

I nodded. "It's another reason I've come here today. I will do anything I can to secure Miss Mason. I plan to work to make money, but I fear I haven't much time. Lord Fletcher plans to propose when she returns to London. And now another man here in Wilton, Mr. Ashby, is pursuing her as well.

"Mr. Ashby's a good man," my father said. "Many of the young ladies around here are after him."

"That's not helping." I gave my father a flat look.

He chuckled. "No, I daresay it's not."

Martha looked at me with a satisfied expression. "It's my turn to tell a story now," she said as she handed my father a plate of food and some water. "After your father returned home defeated, wondering what to do next if he couldn't bring you back home, he said to me, 'What now, Martha? Henry has everything. What can I possibly offer him now that Lord Elliot won't already give him?' And I told him. I said, " 'You will let him become an Elliot in every way but blood and name. As he grows into the man he deserves to become, you will work hard to give him something to claim when he finally returns home. As much as he will *want* to be an Elliot, he will always be Henry Thomas. You will work to give him a legacy to be proud of.'

"So that's what he's been doing these last fifteen years. This good man has been saving money for you and has slowly repaired the house." She looked at John with pride. "The house is fully staffed again, and has been for a few years now. He intended to send word to you when you turned eighteen, but he was too much of a lily-livered coward to face you." She winked at my father who looked down.

He shook his head. "All the silver and gold in the world will never make up for my sins, Henry. I felt shameful asking forgiveness for the sake of the money I have saved for you. But I do want you to know that you have a home and money to claim whenever you're ready. You will never be as wealthy as Lord Elliot, but you have a large sum that most people would be proud of."

I felt as though I could cry for joy—cry in gratitude for the way this man, my father, had worked so hard to give me something to call my own.

"My recent business in London was to write all of my assets, including my money and this house, over to you. I have saved some little money of my own. If you wish for me to leave this house, I will do so immediately. I have found a small cottage nearby that will allow me to take care of Martha."

"Don't you mean I'll be taking care of you?" She grinned with fondness. "You're practically worthless."

He smiled. "I'm the product of your own making, Martha. If I'm worthless, it's because you made me that way." She swatted the air. I couldn't help but smile.

"Father,"—it had been so many years since I'd called him that—"I wouldn't dream of throwing you and Martha from this house. And I will gratefully accept everything you have offered me."

Relief marked my father's eyes, as if he believed I would have thrown his hard work back in his face and not accepted it.

"I do feel pressed to claim this money as soon as possible. I can't bear the thought of living life without Miss Mason, especially if she were to accept Lord Fletcher in the end. But I'll not ask for her hand without first being able to offer her a house and some form of financial stability. Neither will I be a burden to her and take her money to establish myself."

My father looked at me with respect. "And this is why James was meant to raise you. You are good, noble, and honorable, just like him."

He cleared his throat. "It appears as though you haven't much time if you are to accomplish this. If you leave for London immediately, you can sign all the necessary documents, and everything will be yours by this time tomorrow." He opened a drawer and removed a stack of papers. "Everything you need is in here, including the addresses and contacts of the people you need to see to make it official." He walked around the desk to where I sat, and I stood. He placed the papers on top of the desk.

"Martha will give you some food for the journey. Do you have everything else you need?"

"I may need a small amount of money to stay at an inn. I am currently not safe in London as Henry Thomas or Lord Elliot. I will need to keep my presence as hidden as possible."

"I have some contacts in London. I will come with you to ensure your safety," he said eagerly.

"I appreciate your offer, but I believe you would only draw more attention to me. I must do this next part on my own."

"Very well." My father nodded reluctantly.

"Thank you for everything." Immense gratitude for this man returned once again. "Thank you for letting me grow up as an Elliot even when you wanted me back. Thank you for changing your heart, and thank you for giving me what I need to hopefully secure the woman I love." I let my words settle in the silence. "It is true that gold and silver can't buy forgiveness. It isn't what has softened my heart towards you."

I couldn't speak for a moment because of the emotion I felt. New moisture found its way into my eyes.

"It's your heart that has made all the difference. Your heart is good, and I not only forgive you for the past," I looked into his eyes, "but I'm proud to call you my father. I'm proud to be Henry Thomas."

It's been said that grown men don't cry. But my father and I cried as much that day as any woman or child. We cried for the pain and the sorrow of the past and the present. We cried for the joy and the mercy of change and renewal, and we cried for the goodness life brings with its many unexpected turns.

29

FROG

Jane

Wilton
November 14, 1816
That same day
One day of disguise remaining

Breakfast was brought to my room. I tried to eat but hadn't the stomach for it. Mama finally left me to my own thoughts.

Eventually Alice entered. "What an evening we had last night," she said, unable to hold back her bewilderment. "First with Miss Lily nearly fainting, then you retiring so early." She looked at me with concern. "I hope you're feeling better this morning, miss."

"Thank you, Alice," I said, trying not to sound as empty as I felt.

"Let's get you ready for the morning, then," she said enthusiastically. "Though you and Miss Lily made an appearance for only a short time last night, I daresay you will receive callers this morning."

I barely understood what she was saying. She drew a bath for me then led me over to change. A dull headache thrummed at the base of my head, reminding me that the pearled pins were still in my hair from the night before, and I still wore my gown.

Alice said nothing about it but went to work, pulling out the pearls and helping me out of my dress. She left me, and I mechanically finished undressing, lowering myself into the water. I was grateful for the soothing warmth that helped release part of the tension I was holding onto. I thought about the next few days ahead of me and put my hands to my eyes as tears threatened to return once again.

I had already cried too much. I needed to force myself to keep going today. I would take it one breath at a time until those breaths turned to minutes, hours, days . . . and event
ually years. Today's breaths would lead me to other callers. I remembered Mr. Ashby. He planned to call on me this morning. I inhaled shakily and wondered if I could bear it.

I would have to bear it.

Once I was clean and dressed, Alice led me over to my mirror and had me sit, deftly working on my hair. I watched my eyes as they stared back at me. I felt nothing; they felt nothing. For once we understood one another perfectly. Once Alice was finished, she left my room.

I didn't move.

Eventually a knock came at my door, opening a sliver. Lily's head slowly poked in through the reflection. She eased toward me until her eyes found mine in the mirror.

"It isn't fair, Jane," she said quietly.

I looked down, unable to speak.

"He deceived us all." Lily shook her head.

"I don't think he meant to." I couldn't help but defend him, even if she was right.

"Well I can't bear it. I'll get to the bottom of it. I will ask him outright what he means by all of it."

"Please don't, Lily. What's done is done."

She folded her arms. "I don't know how you can stand it." She looked at me with frustration. "He loves you. It is so clear to anyone with eyes. How could he do this?"

"Please, say no more." I didn't know if I could keep the tears back any longer, and I needed to be presentable when Mr. Ashby called.

"I *will* say more," Lily said defiantly. "I don't want to lose you again. I just got you back. I don't want you to slip right back into the shell you just came out of."

"Please don't make this harder for me than it already is," I said quietly. She looked as though she was about to argue further then stopped herself.

"I'm sorry," she said quietly. "I just want to make it better somehow. I feel powerless."

"I know." I gave her hand a grateful squeeze.

"What will you do now?"

I swallowed, holding the tears back, then spoke with a shaky voice. "I will go down to the drawing room. I will put a smile on my face for Mr. Ashby and hope that perhaps he can distract me."

Lily's mouth formed a straight line then nodded. "Whatever you need."

"Thank you," I whispered.

Henry

I pushed Spartan hard. He ran like the name he was given: fast and furious. When I reached Wilton Manor, I darted inside, immediately finding Lawrence.

"Is everything alright?" Lawrence asked, breaking his usual practiced calm.

"More than alright." I heaved a sigh of relief as I caught my breath.

"Then your father is not responsible for James's death?" he asked.

"No, he is not. What's more, he regrets his actions towards the Elliots and me. He's changed." I felt so unlike myself. I had nothing to joke about, nothing to bury down. I had just cried with my father and embraced him. And now I was hopeful I could win Jane back.

I felt an urgency to make my journey back to London. Even as

I spoke, Mr. Ashby was most likely visiting Jane, or would be soon. I could only pray that Charles's sabotaging would work. I needed to have a plan in place before she returned to London in the next two days. On top of that, I wanted justice for Papa, and I wanted it soon. I wanted to bring Jacob to his knees and put him behind bars once and for all.

"Lawrence, I must leave immediately. My father's business in London was to sign all of his money and his house over to my name. All I need to do now is claim it. I don't have much time before Jane returns to London. I must secure my affairs."

Lawrence looked at me cautiously. "Are you sure it isn't a trap to lure you and Charles to London?"

I shook my head. "It's not a trap. But I will be careful. Once I have my affairs in order, we will put Jacob and Mr. Cambell behind bars. Then I can propose to Jane. And if she still refuses me—"

I couldn't think of life without Jane. It was torment staying away from her for even one day. I couldn't bear the thought of another man's arms around her. Her kiss would truly haunt me forever if I could never have it again. If she refused me, I would have to go somewhere far away—somewhere that wouldn't constantly remind me of her and the way she made everything magical.

She was, in a word, enchanting. I saw her in everything. I saw her spirit in the young girl that passed me in the London streets days ago with a tattered dress, skipping happily with her little sister at her arm. She was in the genuine heart of the kind lady I watched give money to a beggar on that same street. I saw Jane in the sparrow that clung to the safety of the branches against the wind and rain before jumping into the storm, wings wide open. Jane's heart had drawn me in almost from the start. Her goodness was palpable. From the way she sacrificed for her family, to the way her eyes and smile lit up when she was excited. A leaf brought her more joy than an extravagant ball. Autumn was now a balm to my heart because of Jane, instead of a season of solemnity.

I remembered Lawrence's presence. "I won't be able to stay here in Wilton if Jane won't have me," I finally said.

He nodded. "I know. Why do you think James could never stay in Wilton once Elizabeth passed?" He gave me a knowing look. "I took the liberty of preparing trunks for both you and Charles in case you needed to make a hasty departure. We can take the smaller carriage. It will be less conspicuous."

"We?" I asked.

"Yes, I will be coming with you," Lawrence said resolutely, as if there was no question about it.

"I won't be staying at the London house. I will be staying at an inn."

"I would hope so, sir. The London house isn't safe." He looked up at me, resolute. "I am coming along."

I stared at him for a moment, taking in a breath and letting it go. My throat tightened with emotion for this man that had been a mentor for me and a dear friend to Papa. I could only nod my head for a moment before I cleared my throat and finally found my voice.

"Perhaps if we are lucky, we can uncover the last pieces of Papa's murder. Charles will be furious about being left behind, but—"

"Actually, it was Charles that suggested I leave with you if at any point there was a chance of you winning Miss Mason back. And I agreed with him, of course."

I didn't know what to say. Seeing the efforts that Charles and Lawrence were willing to go through touched me.

I finally smiled, feeling more and more like myself. "Lawrence, you really shouldn't leave Charles to fend for himself. He's practically worthless without you." I grinned, but gave him a look of gratitude, then added, "We all are."

"It'll be good for him to remember it," he said, winking. "I'll meet you downstairs in ten minutes. My bags have been prepared ahead of time as well. I will write to Charles, indicating our plans, and then we will depart."

Before Lawrence turned to leave, I placed a firm hand on his shoulder. "Thank you, Lawrence." I wished I could fully convey the gratitude I felt for everything he had done for me. My thanks would have to be enough for now.

Lawrence returned the gesture, placing a firm grip on my shoulder. "It's what family does."

Jane

Mr. Ashby called on us near eleven o'clock. He smiled as he walked in and dipped his head politely.

"Mrs. Mason; Miss Mason; Miss Lily." He looked at each of us as he said our names then presented a bouquet of flowers to me. I took them and did my best to place a smile on my face.

"Thank you, Mr. Ashby." The gesture was truly kind, but it immediately turned my mind to Charles and his bouquet with hidden gems.

We took our seats; I sat next to Lily and Mama on the sofa, and Mr. Ashby sat in a chair near the window, facing us.

"I was sorry to hear that you weren't feeling well last night. I hope that, if you are feeling up to it, you might allow me to accompany you on a ride tomorrow afternoon." He looked over at Lily. "And of course you should come as well, Miss Lily."

I attempted a smile. "I think it's a lovely idea." I did my best to sound sincere.

As I looked at Mr. Ashby, I noticed his coat pocket begin to wiggle and move. I narrowed my eyes and looked at it closer. Mr. Ashby noticed my gaze and turned his own eyes down, looking startled as his pocket moved again.

He stood quickly. "What the devil?" He reached inside his pocket.

It was then that I noticed Oliver lurking near the door watching from an inconspicuous place. Glancing at Mama and Lily, I saw them look over at Oliver as well. I shook my head then watched as Mr. Ashby pulled a frog from his pocket. To my surprise, he laughed.

"Now how did you get in there?" he asked the frog, holding it up to his face to get a better look. His other coat pocket began to move around as well. Mr. Ashby chuckled. "I believe you have a friend," he said to the frog. Mama looked mortified as Mr. Ashby lifted another two frogs out of his other pocket.

"Excuse me, Mr. Ashby," Mama said, "I believe I need to speak with my son."

Oliver quickly slipped his head away from view as Mama stood and took the frogs from Mr. Ashby. She walked as swiftly as was ladylike in Oliver's direction. Once she turned the corner, her footfalls could be heard picking up speed.

"Forgive Oliver, Mr. Ashby," Lily said. "He is always into some bit of mischief."

Mr. Ashby chuckled. "It's no trouble." He sat down once more. "I'm sure I'm only being given a taste of my own medicine. When I was young, I would sneak frogs and snakes into guest's beds. One time I even snuck a snake into one of their pockets before dinner," he said, chagrined. "I believe your brother and I are more similar than you might think."

I still felt numb even when he smiled at me. I did my best to return his smile, but it made the emptiness that much more apparent. I hoped he wouldn't see through it.

He truly was a man that would easily turn a woman's head. He was handsome, with honey-colored hair and rich-blue eyes. There was an easy air about him. Perhaps if Charles hadn't captured my heart so thoroughly, I could have felt something for Mr. Ashby. With time, perhaps there was a chance that I could one day open my heart again.

Mr. Ashby looked at me with one of his warm smiles. "Did you ever like catching frogs, Miss Mason?"

"Believe it or not, Mr. Ashby," Lily interjected, "my sister was the master of catching frogs, bugs, and snakes. Where do you think Oliver learned the art?"

Mr. Ashby's face lit up. "Is it true?"

I did my best to give a genuine smile and prayed that I hit the mark. "I would like to believe so." The window behind Mr. Ashby slowly raised up. Lily noticed it too and gave me a look of exasperation. Surely Oliver didn't have Sterling in on the prank as well.

Lily suddenly stood. "Please forgive me, Mr. Ashby, I have just remembered something I must immediately attend to." She dipped her head and walked out briskly toward where Sterling was most likely hiding.

"Is there more mischief behind me?" he asked, grinning. Apparently he missed nothing. A pebble shot through the window, barely missing Mr. Ashby's head. He noticed too.

"I believe my chair is no longer safe," he mused as he raised his brow. "Perhaps a seat next to you would be safer." He grinned as he sat near me. Neither my pulse nor my breath quickened. I tried to feel flattered by his attention, but it wouldn't come.

He looked at me, then gestured to the flowers I was still holding. "Let me put those somewhere for you." I hadn't even realized they were still in my hands. He took them from me and stood to place them on a small table near the center of the room. When he sat down a second time, he was even closer to me than before.

The window suddenly shut. He chuckled. "It appears as though your brothers have been caught. I hope your mother and sister will go easy on them."

"Most likely they'll be handed off to Cook for some good, hard cleaning." I smiled back and it felt mostly real. Not because Mr. Ashby made my heart flutter, but because he was kind and genuine.

"A harsh punishment indeed," he said with a wink. He was teasing, but he hadn't met Cook. Charles's attempt to sweet-talk Cook entered my mind. I tried to push it out as quickly as it came.

I could feel Mr. Ashby's eyes on me. When I looked up he gave me an intent look. "I must tell you, Miss Mason, that you look lovely this morning, as you always do."

"Thank you, Mr. Ashby." The words felt forced when they left my mouth. He smiled, however, so it must have been convincing.

He stood. "I believe I must be going now, but I look forward to our ride tomorrow afternoon."

I nodded. "As do I."

He dipped his head. "Good day, Miss Mason." He turned and left the drawing room. I hoped Mr. Ashby would prove a distraction.

Lily

I walked briskly out of the drawing room. Normally I would have thought Oliver's and Sterling's antics toward Mr. Ashby were funny. But not today. Jane needed a handsome gentleman such as Mr. Ashby to cheer her up from Lord Elliot's deceit, and they were sabotaging it.

I was so angry with Lord Elliot I could hardly think. I was furious at him for breaking Jane's heart and fuming about the way he interrogated me at the dance.

I wouldn't admit it to myself just now, but I was also deeply disappointed that Lord Elliot was engaged. He fit so well with all of us and made Jane light up. Even Oliver and Sterling liked him. He was full of life, and it was so clear that he loved Jane by the way he looked at her. It made no sense. He had no family alive to expect him to marry for a title, and we were a family of great wealth now.

Perhaps he had been secretly engaged before he met Jane, and my sister stole his heart by surprise. Perhaps he felt honor bound to keep his previous arrangement. I knew how easily it was to lose one's heart without meaning to. I thought of Henry. If I had been engaged, then met Henry shortly after, I wouldn't know what to do. He had stolen my heart so easily, and I had so little control over the entire thing.

I was about to turn the corner, where I would find Sterling beneath the window, when I heard it slam shut, followed by the noises of him scampering around and the rustling of bushes. He had clearly heard my approach and was now hiding. I smiled victoriously as I rounded the corner.

Only bushes faced me.

I put my hands on my hips. "I know you're in there, Sterling. You might as well come out."

Silence followed.

"If you make me come in there after you, I promise you'll regret it."

The bush was completely still.

I let out an exasperated breath and neared it. I didn't really want to have to skirt between the tall bushes and the house, but I was determined to put Sterling in his place.

I moved a branch out of the way so I could get through. "Sterling, I'll have Cook deal with you if you don't—"

A hand grabbed mine and pulled me in quickly. I tripped over a root and started to fall—until strong arms caught me. My breath hitched as Henry's face suddenly appeared close to mine.

"Not Sterling," he said, grinning.

"Henry!"

He smirked, shaking his head. "Not Henry either. But I'm sure you'll guess it eventually. And your punishment doesn't hold weight— Cook and I seem to understand one another." Henry held me steady as I righted myself before he released me.

"Henry? What are you—"

"Not Henry," he teased again.

"What are you doing?" I persisted. I was so confused. Why were Henry and Oliver trying to sabotage Jane's time with Mr. Ashby? "Did Oliver put you up to this?" I asked.

Henry gave me a repentant look before admitting, "It was actually the other way around."

"Why?" I knit my eyebrows together.

"I'm observing Mr. Ashby," Henry said.

I gave him a questioning look. "Are you implying that William Ashby is the man you are investigating from Wilton? That you suspect him to have potentially murdered James Elliot?"

"I said I was observing him, Lily, not that he is under investigation."

My face must have given away my confusion, because he continued, "Perhaps Oliver and I wanted to make sure you didn't use your magical abilities to cast a spell over Mr. Ashby."

I narrowed my eyes. "Mr. Ashby is pursuing my sister, Jane, not me."

"Well, how was I to know?" He grinned, unabashed.

I wanted to smile back, but I was reminded of Jane's grief. "Your friend Lord Elliot has made quite a mess of things." I said the words before I could stop myself. "He has thoroughly broken my sister's heart."

Henry looked at me for a moment before he spoke. "Your sister has broken his heart," he countered.

How could Henry take Lord Elliot's side in this? I opened my mouth to express my anger, but Henry put a finger to his lips, bidding me to be quiet. I felt further fury at his gesture until I heard someone approaching—most likely Mr. Ashby. We waited until the footsteps retreated then Henry leaned close to my ear, talking quietly.

"Please don't let this come between us. I know Lord Elliot has made a mess of things, but I don't know how he could have helped it. I know both of their hearts are broken right now. It will be hard for me, however, if you despise him. He's like a brother to me, and has a better heart than any man I know."

That confirmed my suspicions. Lord Elliot must have lost his heart to Jane but had too great a conscience to break off his previous engagement.

It was telling that Charles and Henry were close—close enough that he would consider him to be like a brother. I was still angry with Lord Elliot, but I could understand Henry's desire for me to forgive him.

"I'll not let it come between us," I finally said. "And I don't despise Lord Elliot. My heart just hurts for Jane right now."

"For them both," Henry said.

Folding my arms, I nodded reluctantly. "For them both."

Henry looked at me. "I must ready my horse for our ride. Bring a chaperone, Lily, and meet me under the tree in an hour."

He didn't wait for me to respond this time, nor did he say his usual line before he left. I waited a few minutes before I left the seclusion of the bushes and immediately ran upstairs to change for my ride. Henry would be upset, but this time I didn't intend to bring a chaperone.

Today, I would come alone. I needed to ask him questions without a chaperone to hear. Besides, we would be riding. What was the worst that could happen?

I led Stella out to the meadow. She was already itching to run. I leaned down so she could hear me and I stroked her neck. "I missed you, girl." She chuffed in response. I smiled, "Shall we?" This was the phrase I usually said to her right before I let her run without holding back. I could feel her excitement growing, hooves dancing with anticipation, until I finally flicked the reins and yelled, "Hah!"

She took off and soon our movements were one. She ran smooth and fast and before I knew it, we were gliding through the meadow. The wind whipped my hair and pulled small pieces from their pins until they danced around my face. I smiled and breathed in deeply before I let out a happy call. It was something I did every time I rode with Stella. She ran faster and whinnied in the breeze, making me laugh contentedly.

Stella's pace slowed when I steered her towards the trees. As I neared the meeting place, I could see a broad figure atop a tall horse. When Henry came into full view, my mouth went dry. His hair was windswept and he wore only a white shirt and breeches beneath his coat. I committed the image to memory.

He looked at me in a way that made my breath catch and my stomach flip. His eyes said it all. He desired me . . . and I didn't bring my chaperone.

He directed his horse toward mine until our horses were side by side.

"Where is your chaperone, Lily?" His voice was exasperated.

"I don't have one," I said, feeling stupid now that I thought about how hard it had already been for Henry and me to behave.

"I can see that." He raised an eyebrow at me and shook his head as if he was debating whether or not to continue our little adventure.

"Perhaps we should postpone this until tomorrow." He said it as if it took everything in him to suggest such a thing.

"Henry, I'm sorry. Please don't make me wait until tomorrow." I felt anxious at the very thought. "I'll behave. I'll not smirk and I'll not tease you." I raised my hand as if to promise.

He studied my eyes for a moment, clearly wanting this outing as much as I did; I could see it in every part of him.

I bit my lip as I waited in his silence until it was unbearable. "Please?" I said again, quietly.

Henry cursed under his breath. "That's not fair, Lily. You know I can't refuse you when you ask like that."

I tried not to smile.

"But you aren't allowed to cast a spell on me. Nor are you allowed to look at me . . . or speak to me . . . and what are you thinking, biting your lip that way?" he finished with a teasing grin.

"So what, exactly, *am* I allowed to do?" I asked.

He raised an eyebrow. "My question exactly. Do you see why we need a chaperone today?"

I was quiet as we stared at one another. "Fine," I finally said. "After this moment I won't speak or look at you. I will hold my expression perfectly level so that you will believe me to be a statue. You can lead the way, and I will follow."

He tried to hold back his laugh but wasn't able to, chuckling. "I would love to see you try."

I said nothing in response. Without giving him any expression whatsoever, I flicked my hand in front of me and gestured for him to lead on.

I didn't look at him but I heard him laugh. We rode for about thirty seconds with him in the lead before he stopped and turned back toward me. I averted my gaze so that I wasn't looking at him directly. "At least ride by me, Lily. When you ride behind me I can't see if you are casting spells." I could hear the smile in his voice.

I rolled my eyes.

"Technically, rolling your eyes is an expression," he dead panned.

I shook my head at his taunts.

"And so is that."

I couldn't help but look over at him and give him a look of scolding with one of my eyebrows raised.

The corner of his mouth twitched up as if he was trying not to smile. "I'll behave, Miss Mason, lest you take a switch to me. Now come ride next to me."

I did as he asked, riding silently by his side. After a time, we crossed over the Mason property line and entered new territory.

Henry cleared his throat then spoke as if he was announcing for a group touring abroad. He pointed to his left. "And now, if you look to your left, you will see one of England's rarer sights . . . " He paused for dramatic emphasis. "Trees amongst a meadow. Try not to blink or you might miss it." He was trying to get me to laugh. It wouldn't work. I tried to keep my lips steady—one traitorous side was already threatening to turn up. Henry continued. "Directly ahead of us—dare I believe it?—is yet more trees and a meadow. What fortune we have to see such diversity this afternoon." I pressed my lips together and refused to be taken by the laugh that was trying to escape. He looked to his right and pointed, making his next words sound reverential, as if he'd seen the most spectacular sight in all the world. "Upon my soul." He placed a hand to his heart. "You won't believe until you've seen it for yourself. But to our right we have, yet again . . . more trees and a meadow."

Laughter finally bubbled up, escaping me. I couldn't help it. He laughed with me. "Henry!" I scolded. "I'm trying so hard!"

I finally looked at him, his eyes already fixed on mine, smiling. "I know. And I'm being downright wicked. And now—we fly."

He flicked his reins and his horse lurched into a run. I smiled excitedly and followed suit. I kept up with him, but I could tell his horse was holding back. He looked at me, impressed, then pushed his horse faster. I breathed in and called out to Stella like I had earlier. Stella whinnied and pushed herself even faster until we were neck and neck. Henry looked at me with satisfaction before his horse ran even faster. I knew I couldn't push Stella or myself any faster. I pulled her back to a slower run as I watched Henry fly ahead of me. I couldn't help but take in every bit of him as he flew through the grass.

I craved everything about him—his hunger for the truth, his perseverance; the way he left no stone unturned to find answers. I had never felt that my opinion was so esteemed than when I was in his company. When I spoke, he hung on my every word . . . and I his. And now, watching him astride his horse, I was reminded that I had no hope of coming away from this unscathed. If everything turned sideways, my heart would bleed out . . . just like Jane's.

By the time I finally caught up to Henry, he had entered a thicket of trees. I could hear the small stream before I saw it. Henry had already dismounted and was letting his horse drink from the shallow water steadily trickling over smooth pebbles. Henry's gaze turned to me as I approached before I pulled Stella to a stop. I needed help dismounting. Henry understood my need without any words being exchanged. Putting his hands about my waist, he eased me down, looking at me as if he was holding everything back. He held his breath, taking in my hair and eyes, before reluctantly reaching for Stella's reins, turning, and leading her to the stream.

Taking in the view before me, I was absolutely enchanted. Sun filtered through the leaves. There was a small bridge a ways off, and the water was the perfect depth for catching frogs and playing in. It would have been any child's haven.

"Is this where you got a hold of your frogs for Mr. Ashby's pockets?" I grinned, turning to face him.

Henry made his way toward me, removing his coat, looking even more windswept than before. My pulse was on fire. I felt the need to swallow as he neared me.

A corner of his mouth turned up. "What would give you that idea?" My mind went blank. I couldn't remember what we were even talking about. "You're looking at me again." Henry grinned, but I saw restraint in his eyes.

"*You're* looking at *me*," I countered, barely keeping my voice even.

He stepped closer. "You're speaking too." His eyebrow raised.

"So are you."

"So I am."

"Henry," I said quietly.

He closed his eyes as I said his name, then let out a breath. "Not Henry."

When he opened his eyes, I could see the war he was having within himself. I was having one of my own. He finally reached for me with just one hand, as if he could grant himself this one small thing. He moved his fingers to the front of my hair where it had escaped in the wind, tucking it behind my ear. I cupped my hand over his and rested my cheek against it. He maintained the same distance until his hand fell away and he wrapped his arm around my waist, slowly inching me in closer and closer.

His other hand reached out, fingers trailing my neck until they moved slowly from my neck to my cheek, before gliding to my lips. He lightly traced the corner of my mouth with his thumb like he had done the previous day. I could see the fire in his eyes as he watched the place his thumb traced. My breath shuddered as his other fingers slid back behind my neck, lowering his face to mine until our lips were a whisper apart. His strong hands gently held my face close to his.

"Tomorrow, Lily," his low voice rumbled. "I can wait until tomorrow."

"Tomorrow," I repeated, heart hammering.

"You really should have brought your chaperone." He placed a gentle kiss by the corner of my lips. Fire spread through me. I couldn't wait for tomorrow.

Fortunately, neither could he.

He lowered his lips to mine until they tasted mine completely, holding me tenderly. His hands supported my head as he kissed me softly, leaving my hands to fall to his chest as he pulled me in closer. His hands moved down my back, pressing me to him until my hands had no room but to lace around his neck.

His kiss turned deep and passionate until his breath came out in exhales of longing. He suddenly pulled his lips from mine and took a step back, raking his hands through his hair. I tried to calm my breathing but it was no use.

"Lily," he breathed with intensity, his chest rising and falling. "We need to get you home."

Heat rose to my cheeks and I suddenly felt embarrassed for getting carried away so easily. I put my cool fingers to my burning cheeks and turned away from him.

He gently pulled one of my hands from my cheek. "Please don't be angry with me." He slowly kissed my hand then wrapped his arms around me from behind.

"I'm not angry." My heart was still pounding, making my words come out breathy and quiet. "I'm afraid I may have taken things too far."

"*You* took things too far?" he asked quietly. "I believe it's the other way around." I heard him smile. "Though perhaps you *are* to blame. You are a witch, after all." Then he dropped his teasing tone and let out a breath. "I just don't trust myself to be alone with you right now. If anything, I am to blame." He exhaled as he held me close.

I knew he was right, that we couldn't trust ourselves to be alone, but I wanted him to kiss me and hold me like this forever. Tomorrow I would learn the truth. What if I didn't like what I found? My stomach fluttered as his arms tightened around me even further, the warmth of his chest at my back.

I sighed. "Henry, will everything change tomorrow?" I felt him lean forward, resting his face to the side of mine.

"I believe it will." His words were even. His hand found mine as he kept me wrapped in his arms from behind, his fingers tracing mine until they landed on my ring, which resided on my middle finger. He smoothed his finger around it until he slowly pulled it from its place.

It disappeared.

"I'm afraid you will eventually disappear, just like my ring." I whispered, not caring to hide the vulnerability in my voice.

"That would mean I would have to stay away from you, which I seem incapable of doing. If I were to call on you again tomorrow afternoon would you promise to bring a chaperone? Preferably one who can keep a good eye on us while giving us enough distance to speak in private?"

His words assuaged my worries. "Just to be clear, are you stating that you will tell me who you really are tomorrow afternoon?"

"Yes." He lightly kissed my cheek. "Now, I'm going to let go of you, and I'm going to be a perfect gentleman and walk away from you and retrieve our horses. And I'll not kiss you for the remainder of the day . . . even if you work your spells on me."

"Are you giving me permission to tempt you?"

"No." He chuckled. "Don't you dare."

I smiled at his words. I was grateful that he didn't release me immediately; he stayed there for a time, breathing in deeply. It was a perfect moment. My heart felt full and loved. I would find out who Henry was tomorrow, and I would tell him I loved him once I knew the truth.

He slowly released me, inducing a regretful sigh from deep within me. I immediately missed the feeling of being wrapped in his arms. As I heard his footsteps retreat behind me, I put my fingers to my lips where Henry's lips had been. My heart pulsed as the reality of it sank in. My fingers then found the place where he had taken my ring, right along with every piece of my heart.

Completely undone, I turned, watching him retreat towards the horses. I wanted to spend every day like this: with Henry. I wanted to ride with him while he made me smile and laugh. I wanted to hear his thoughts and help him solve the impossibilities he faced. And I wanted him to hold me close and kiss me until I was completely unraveled. What if it was all an impossibility when he was no longer Henry?

He helped me mount Stella and was true to his word: he didn't pull me in before he helped me up, though I could sense his inward battle any time he was remotely close to me. We rode side by side and took in the scenery.

Henry finally spoke. "Tell me about your family, Lily."

I looked over at him with a smile. "It's impossible not to love them. Watching Mama and Papa over the years has been something I take pride in. They adore each other. Their fondness for one another has only grown with time."

Henry smiled warmly. "I understand that sentiment more than you know."

"Jane is pure goodness. She has always watched out for me and loved me. When I was little, she would hold me on her lap and read to me even though I was too big for her." I laughed at the memory. "She would sit me in front of our mirror before we had money and she would braid my hair, telling me that I was a lost fairy and that someday I would find my wings." Henry smiled.

I felt emotion brim to the surface, recalling childhood with my sister. "Jane taught me handshakes and poetry. And when I had nightmares, she would let me sneak into her covers without question."

My smile slowly faded. "Once we came into wealth, Jane made up her mind that she needed to sacrifice her own happiness to secure ours." I shook my head. "Ever dutiful Jane. I slowly lost her. She was still sweet and kind, and we still had fun together, but she wasn't the same Jane I grew up with." I had never expressed these feelings aloud. "I don't understand why she felt the need to change when we all loved her exactly as she was. If we didn't expect her to do it, then why did she?" I was surprised to find that my eyes were welling with tears.

Henry gave me a look of sympathy. "I understand your sister better than I care to admit."

I took in a deep breath and let it out. "I finally got Jane back when Lord Elliot opened her heart again. And now I will most likely lose her once more now that he plans to marry another woman."

Henry suddenly pulled back on the reins. I stopped Stella as well.

"Do you mean to tell me that your sister believes that Hen—Lord Elliot is intended for another woman?"

"Is he not?" I asked, scared to hope.

His eyes looked back and forth between mine until he finally smiled with what looked like understanding. "*Lord Elliot* is most certainly intended for another woman."

He looked as if he had just received the most splendid news. My hopes dashed for Jane once more, and I was beyond irritated that Henry looked so pleased about it.

"Lily, I'm sorry. But I must leave immediately. I'll see you tomorrow afternoon. I'll explain everything then." He didn't even wait for my response. He turned his horse and took off at a run.

I looked after his fading figure, confused and angry, and at the forefront, disappointed that he would leave me so suddenly.

30

CHAISE

Charles

Wilton
November 14, 1816
That same day
One day of disguise remaining

Ipushed Apollo hard, racing home to give Henry the good news. The eldest Miss Mason must have overheard us in the garden—apparently she and Lily shared the same propensity to eavesdrop. Or perhaps I needed to be better about checking my surroundings before I talked freely. Regardless, I couldn't wait to tell Henry.

I hated leaving Lily the way I did. But if her words about Miss Mason were any indicator, she would thank me if it meant her sister would find happiness.

Lily was driving me to madness. I was consumed by thoughts of her. Since meeting her that first night, I had constantly been plotting ways to see her or involve her in the mystery surrounding my father's murder. I owed her my thanks for uncovering so many aspects of his death, and I paid with my heart.

She had drawn me to her almost instantly with the way she'd held her ground. She was intelligent, with a kind, free, untainted spirit. Now I could hardly be in her presence without . . . well, I wasn't even strong enough to wait to kiss her before she found out my true identity. She was so stubborn. It made me smile just thinking about it.

I wouldn't trust myself to be alone with her anymore. I would require a chaperone from now on until I asked her to have me . . . which I intended to do as soon as possible.

Hopefully she wouldn't be angry when she discovered my true identity. It was so refreshing to know that my title and wealth had nothing to do with Lily's feelings for me. At first I hadn't wanted her to learn the truth. I'd enjoyed the fact that she only knew me as Henry Thomas. Now I wanted her always, to have and to hold, in sickness and in health.

When I arrived at Wilton Manor, Lawrence didn't meet me at the door, which meant he must be in the library talking with Henry. But when I briskly strode through the doorway, it was vacant. Checking the drawing room and the stables only produced the same outcome: Henry and Lawrence were nowhere to be found. I returned to the library and let out an annoyed huff when I spotted a letter in the center of the desk. I would have saved a lot of time if I'd just looked instead of tearing all over the estate. I tore it open.

> My lord,
> Henry believes he may be able to secure Miss Mason.
> John Thomas has an alibi that I trust.
> I believe we must complete our investigation as soon as possible so that we can finally have peace, and ensure Henry's and your safety in London.
> I have attached the address of the inn we will be staying at once we reach London.
> I know you wish to secure your own Miss Mason as soon as possible. I believe the sooner

we bring everything to light, the sooner your wishes will be possible.

Please be careful if you decide to travel alone. There is a traveling trunk already packed with your things. We took the small carriage.

Be smart, be safe, and good luck.

Tuppence was placed inside with an address. I let out an exasperated sigh, realizing I must have missed them by just an hour or two.

I rubbed my forehead, considering. Lawrence was right: We needed to resolve this sooner than later. I couldn't take a wife if my name was being threatened. What if I was murdered only a short time after we were married, leaving Lily a young widow? Or what if some form of harm came to her because of it? I wouldn't stand for it. I hated the very thought of leaving Lily just now, especially when I had told her I would reveal everything the next day. But the sooner the murderer was uncovered, the sooner we could have peace about Papa's passing— the sooner I could be with Lily. I would have to be Henry Thomas for just a little while longer.

Immediately after scrawling a letter to Lily, I placed it inside an envelope, tuppence accompanying it, and gave my orders for it to be delivered. Now . . . I stared down the old open chaise, rubbing my beard—wondering how I would make it to London unseen in such a conveyance. Adding to that dilemma—it was better suited for taking leisurely rides—Not a long trip. I also wanted to bring my father's pistol and dueling swords for protection, but it would not be ideal to store the swords in the chaise. The more I looked at the state of the old conveyance, the more I considered taking the new carriage—but people would recognize it when they saw it.

While contemplating this, I heard a coach roll in front of Wilton Manor. As I approached the entrance, a modest but sturdy covered carriage came to a halt, and a man emerged that I had never seen before. He didn't notice me at first. He arched his head back, taking in Wilton Manor's grand stone edifice, a look about his eyes conveying a mixture of shame and nostalgia.

"May I ask what your business is?" I asked.

The man started, turning his view to me, eyes widening in surprise. "Henry wasn't exaggerating," he said. "You must be Lord Elliot."

I gave a curt nod. "And who might you be?"

He looked at me with some hesitation. "I'm John Thomas, my lord."

I gave him a cold stare, trying to grasp the fact that this was the man who had tried to take Henry's life when he was a young boy.

"I don't mean to intrude," he added, watching me cautiously. "Has Henry left for London yet?" he asked when I didn't respond. "I meant to give him his soldiers from when he was a boy. I had them stored and—" he turned toward his carriage and pulled a box from the inside, "I wanted him to have them." He put the box into my hands. "I know he doesn't have a use for them now, but I just thought he might want them back." He shuffled his shoe around in the dirt as he spoke. Was that embarrassment I sensed?

"You're Henry's father?" I finally asked, still wearing a cold stare.

He opened his mouth for a bit before he closed it again. "I know your father raised Henry. I won't discount that or try to pretend that I've been a father to him. But yes, I am his father."

"Henry has already left for London," I said curtly.

He nodded. "I hoped I might be useful to him on his next journey, but he insisted I would only draw more attention."

"Forgive my frankness, Mr. Thomas, but I don't trust you." I let my words sink in. "I assume you know now that my father was murdered. I have only received word from my butler that you have an alibi. I have not talked with Henry since he has seen you. Therefore, I do not appreciate your presence here."

John nodded his head. "I understand." He looked hesitant before speaking again. "Regardless, I want to help, whether you trust me or not. Is there anything you can think of that I can do in London where you can either keep an eye on me or put me out of the way?"

I rubbed my beard as I contemplated. He posed an interesting question. If he was, in fact, the murderer, I could keep a close eye on him in London. If I could prove it was him, he would be exactly where I wanted him to be. I could possibly even catch him in the act of trying to murder Henry or me, and then everything would be over. If he wasn't the murderer, and truly wanted to help, he could come in handy.

I glanced at his carriage, considering. I would be able to transport my trunk, pistol, and dueling swords easily if we took Mr. Thomas's conveyance. Furthermore, in a covered carriage, my presence would be undetected by passersby.

Looking over at John, I sized him up. I would easily be able to defend myself against him. Adding to that, I would have my pistol and my sword with me. I wasn't worried for my immediate safety in the slightest.

I finally nodded. "Very well, Mr. Thomas. If you wish to help, I will find something useful for you to do. To begin with, I believe we should take your carriage. Mine is too conspicuous."

Mr. Thomas gave me a look of surprise. "Thank you, Lord Elliot. We can leave immediately. I have everything packed and ready to go. I made up my mind to go to London to assist Henry, even if he insisted against it. But if you can tell me what to do, I believe I could actually be of some use. I have waited so long to be helpful to Henry. I feel as though I should go mad if I sit at home and do nothing now that I've seen him. Especially knowing your father's death was the result of murder, and that you and Henry are no longer safe in London."

He gave me an amused grin. "I just spent an hour talking with a man who I thought was you. I poured my entire heart out to 'Lord Elliot' only to discover it wasn't you after all. It feels strange knowing I had an entire conversation with you . . . and yet, you have never met me until now." He shook his head. "And in reality, I have never met *you* until now."

I scrutinized him, unsure what to think of his comment.

"It's strange that even when I was acquainted with your parents, I never met you, the boy who looks identical to my son."

He was rambling. I wasn't willing to be friendly with this man until I knew exactly what I was up against.

I gave him a flat stare. "There will be time enough for that in the carriage."

I made sure to maintain eye contact with Mr. Thomas as we stood just outside the conveyance, the coachman loading my trunk and belongings onto the carriage. I lifted one corner of my mouth as Henry's father watched them load my father's rifle and dueling swords in the interior. The pistol I concealed inside my coat.

I gestured my hand towards the weapons then looked at Mr. Thomas, cocking an eyebrow. "In case I run into any trouble," I said, making sure he understood my meaning.

He actually grinned back at me. "I have no doubt that you know how to use each of them well and can handle yourself against any threat." He pulled a pistol from his coat and held it out to me. "You had better take this too, my lord. I think you would be a better shot if we were held up by a highwayman."

His gesture surprised me. I held a flat expression as I took it from him.

"I decided to bring my knife as well, in case Henry needs defending. I will let you hold onto it for our travels, but I insist that you give both weapons to my son once we arrive in London." He held his coat open and took a sheathed knife out, handing it over to me. He clearly knew I didn't trust him. I didn't know if his actions made me trust him more or less.

"Are there any other weapons I should be aware of?" I asked sarcastically. He patted at his coat then opened each side, revealing pockets within. He pulled a penknife out of one of the inner pockets and handed it to me. It was the most bizarre experience.

"That should be it," he said with a confident nod.

I raised an eyebrow, holding all the weapons. "What makes you so sure I won't use these against you?"

He chuckled. "The way I see it, you are James Elliot's son, which makes you a good man. I am John Thomas, a man who has made mistakes most of his life. It seems the logical move. I'm glad you don't trust me. It means you're wise, which puts my mind at ease." He looked over at me, tranquil. "Besides, if you do kill me, I will get to see Rachel again."

He held his hand out for me to proceed inside the carriage. I scrutinized him for a moment longer before I finally obliged.

Lily

So many emotions fought for my attention as I sat in the drawing room. I held a piece of embroidery, pretending to be productive, though I only stared out the window, rubbing my fingers over the fabric again and again. I smiled briefly, touching my lips once more, reliving Henry's kiss. Disappointment hit next as I reflected upon his abrupt departure. Disappointment was then trumped by irritation at Henry's callousness towards Jane. How could he have been excited about Lord Elliot's intended? It made me furious.

"May I join you?" I looked up at hearing Jane's hushed voice. She leaned against the doorway, attempting to wear a pleasant expression for my sake. It made me even more angry that she had to try and look happy. It took everything in me not to huff indignantly, my anger resurfacing toward Lord Elliot tenfold.

Instead, I plastered a pleasant look on my own face. "Of course." As much as I was furious with the earl, part of me wanted to tell Jane to fight for Lord Elliot. Perhaps she could persuade him to choose her. But what was the use in that if it would just break her heart further if he didn't? The other part of me wanted to tell Jane to forget about Lord Elliot altogether and focus on Mr. Ashby.

"How was your time with Mr. Ashby this morning?" I asked as she took a seat next to me. I could think of nothing else to say.

She gave a flat smile. "It was well enough. He was kind and attentive—"

"And handsome," I interjected, as if my statement would somehow make her feel better. "And he plans to take you riding tomorrow afternoon as well," I said, with an encouraging smile. I hated feeling useless in a situation like this. I wanted Mr. Ashby to come in and sweep Jane off her feet, then watch Lord Elliot crumble, realizing he gave up the best thing he ever had.

"He *is* handsome," Jane said, clearly an act to remind herself more than anyone. I knew exactly what she was thinking. *He's not Lord Elliot.* It was exactly what I would be thinking if Henry was suddenly out of my grasp.

A knock sounded at the door and David, our butler, walked in.

"Good afternoon," he said, dipping his head. "This has just arrived for you, miss." He brought a letter forward and handed it to me. Jane looked at me curiously. There was no name on it.

"Pray it's not from Mr. Johnson," I said, feigning exasperation. In truth, it was most likely from Henry. What would Jane think now if she found out about him? "I'll open it later," I said, breathing out a dramatic sigh. "I'm not ready for more of Mr. Johnson's antics just yet."

She looked at me suspiciously, then resumed her look of emptiness. I wanted to cheer her up somehow.

I rested my hand on Jane's. "Let's go for a ride. I don't think I can bear to just sit here for the remainder of the day."

"It's almost four o-clock," Jane countered.

"Then we will go for only a short time, and be back in time for dinner." I gave her a hopeful smile.

Jane looked out the window and nodded. "I believe a ride will do me good."

"Perfect." I was relieved that she accepted my offer. I wanted to feel useful somehow. "I'll get changed and meet you here shortly." I stood up quickly, moving to the door, letter in hand. I wanted to read it and get outside where I could escape the feeling that time was standing still.

Jane held her position, looking out the window. Would she even move from her place and go riding with me? Or would she simply sit there, lifeless and empty?

I couldn't bear to see her this way. Holding in an angry sigh, I left the drawing room, praying she would be ready by the time I returned. I all but ran up the stairs to my room, shutting the door behind me, then ripped the letter open.

Lily,

I hope you will not be angry with me.
I am leaving for London immediately. I
thought we would have more time.
When I see you next, I will no longer be
Henry. I hope you will forgive me.
I'll not stop thinking of you.

My heart tore as I read the letter over and over again. I had been counting on finding out Henry's identity tomorrow. I had no idea when I would see him in London. I tried to calm myself, but the more I tried, the more it left room for questions and doubt. It was the essence of Henry: mystery, with no end in sight.

The hope of knowing the truth, of almost discovering him fully, to then have it ripped from my grasp—I paced my room as the worst sorts of thoughts entered my mind. What if he had lied about everything? What if we could never be together? What if I never saw him again?

It was too much. My head swam and my breath quickened. I stared at the words on the page over and over until I could bear it no longer. He was gone. Crushing the paper between my fingers, I threw the letter inside the low burning flames of my hearth. I quickly wiped away a tear that threatened to spill over as I watched the page slowly become engulfed with fire. Perhaps I was overreacting, but I couldn't help but feel despair. I should have been more careful. I knew it was dangerous involving my heart, and yet I didn't listen.

A shaky breath left my lungs as I contemplated the mess I was in. I quickly changed and ran down to the drawing room. Jane was still sitting exactly where I had left her.

"Are you coming, Jane?" I asked, not caring to hide my unraveling emotions. She slowly stood, though she hadn't changed into her riding habit, and walked toward me, moving through the motions of a task without being present to understand what was happening. A ride was exactly what we needed. That, and a perfect wishing leaf.

Charles

John Thomas's carriage rolled on. After the first half hour or so of Henry's father staring out the window, he fell asleep. Eventually, I diverted my own eyes away from him toward the window, watching the countryside pass me by. A few hours elapsed before John woke. I looked at my pocket watch.

"It's nearly seven," I said, evenly.

John nodded. "Lord Elliot, we will need to stop at some point to rest the horses and sleep."

I leaned back on the seat. "We will come upon the Boar's Head soon. We can lodge there for the night and begin again tomorrow morning."

"We'll leave early," he said, nodding his head in agreement. He looked out the window again.

"How is Henry?" I finally asked, realizing that at this point he possibly knew more information about Henry's plans then even I did.

"Ironically, Lord Elliot, I wanted to ask you the same question. I hadn't seen my son for fifteen years until this morning." He continued to stare out the window. "However, I do believe he is excited to claim the money I have been working hard to save for him these past fifteen years. He is hopeful he can convince Jane Mason to accept him with it."

"How ironic." I shook my head at such a paradox—The only reason Jane wouldn't accept Henry was because she believed him to be engaged to another woman. Henry thought she wouldn't have him due to his lack of fortune. Henry would be speaking with Jane right now if I had only caught him in time.

"What's ironic?" John asked.

"I'll keep it to myself for now." I still didn't trust him.

John raised his eyebrows and smiled. "There must be a good story behind it all." He looked on before the corner of his mouth turned up. "The two of you are close, you and Henry." His smile appeared grateful.

My next words came out with a tone of protectiveness. "We are." I let my words fill the carriage before I spoke again. "Mr. Thomas, I would like to hear for myself the things you discussed with Henry today. I consider him my brother . . . more than that, even. He is the other half of me; the better one of the two, I might add. Henry is even more Elliot than I am. He puts on a good show, even when life is unbearable, and he trusts easily. Needless to say, I'm somewhat skeptical of your sudden interest to help him."

He nodded his head, breathing in deeply. "I understand. I hoped I would only have to retell this once, but it appears as though God intends for me to unburden myself further."

He was quiet for a time before he finally relayed a painful story. One filled with despicable acts, one after another. He shed tears through most of it. He spoke of his controlling nature over his wife. Of his jealousy toward my father and eventually Henry. He spoke of his violence and how he loathed himself and my father to the point of madness. By the time his story concluded, I felt as though I had aged. An even deeper respect blossomed in my heart for my own mother and father. I felt a deeper respect for Henry, and surprisingly for this man, John Thomas.

I respected the difficult decision he made to let Henry live with us and be raised by my parents, the very people he had despised for so long. I still didn't trust him fully, but I found that I did trust him more than I had, and was able to relax somewhat. He didn't try to hide any part of his terrible past. He gave me details that he could have easily omitted. He painted himself in the worst light and told each detail exactly as it was—not to mention the fact that he did it all while I had possession of his pistol.

"I never did have the chance to apologize to your mother and father for my despicable behavior," he said at the conclusion of his story. "I never had the chance to thank them for loving my wife and son so fully." He breathed out. "Your parents' deaths came as a shock to me. The news of each one affected me deeply. Your parents were truly remarkable." He looked up at me. "I won't let another opportunity pass me by while it presents itself. So I would like to thank you, Lord Elliot, for being there for my son. For being his brother, and for sharing your parents with him. Thank you for being an Elliot."

31

MUSTACHE

Lawrence

November 14, 1816
Later that night
One day of disguise remaining

It was approaching nine o'clock when we neared the Boar's Head, an inn located halfway between London and Wilton. Though we wished to push our journey through the night, our horses needed rest.

I looked over at Henry. "I'll go inside and get everything situated. You should hide until then. We'll find a clever way to sneak you in once everything is settled; I don't want word spreading that 'Lord Elliot' is traveling to London."

Henry nodded then pointed out the window. "I'll wait for you near those trees."

A burly man stood behind the counter as I entered. The few gentlemen present in the open room were scattered about at various tables, heads bowed over bowls placed in front of them. The smell of stew wafted from the room and the kitchen behind the counter.

I needed to act the part of servant, not butler. "Evenin', sir," I said as I approached the counter, slouching slightly.

"Evenin'," the man returned with a gruff voice. He had a no-nonsense look about him. "You lookin' for lodgings this evenin'?" he asked.

I nodded. "Two beds. The man I'm attendin' to this evenin' don't do well in carriages. He was sick for most of it and would like his food brought to 'is room." It had been too long since I'd assumed the role of someone else. James would have been proud. I had always been better at impersonations than he was. James's forte was picking pockets.

"Very well," the innkeeper said. "I'll have some stew brought to your room within the next quarter hour." The innkeeper handed me a key.

"Thank you," I said hastily, snatching the keys from his hand. I turned and walked out the door, finding Henry hidden where I left him.

"I feel like a fugitive, slinking in dark corners," Henry mused.

"Better a fugitive than a corpse," I quipped back. "Not many people are in the parlor. If I carry my trunk on my shoulder, you can walk just on the other side and your face will be hidden from the innkeeper's view. We will walk swiftly and hope that no other guests see you."

Henry lifted an eyebrow, impressed. "Very well, Lawrence. You lead the way."

Our plan went without a hitch, and Henry went unnoticed. I set Henry's trunk on the floor in our room then gestured to the bed nearest the window. "Lie down and turn your head toward the window. I don't want anyone to see your face when they bring our food up. I need to collect the rest of our things. I'll be quick."

Henry grinned. "As always, you've thought of everything."

Once each detail was taken care of, I returned to our room to find Henry still lying down facing the opposite wall.

I shut the door and locked it, placing my trunk on the bed, then unlatched it and flipped the top open. It revealed a sleek, black, medium-sized box.

"You can turn around for now, sir," I said as I pulled the box from my trunk and put it on top of a small table. I smiled as I eased the lid open, exposing the contents inside: a newspaper clipping and missive containing the wax seal of a goldfinch.

Henry

I couldn't believe what I was seeing.

After setting aside a newspaper clipping and a letter of some sort, Lawrence brought out a fake, dark mustache, followed by three others in various shades and styles. His hands carefully reached back inside and brought four different wigs forward, followed by a few pairs of spectacles.

"Lawrence, what, exactly, is all this?" I laughed. "Are you a butler by day and a spy by night?"

Lawrence grinned. "Wouldn't that be something?" He looked at his collection fondly then turned to me.

"During James's first season in London, he was approached by the Goldfinch Society."

"The Goldfinch Society?" I narrowed my eyes.

Lawrence nodded. "They are not an organization you can simply find on your own. *They* approach *you* if they want your help. As I was saying, they approached James during his first season. They were working to find a murderer, Etienne Dupont, but they needed more eyes. They asked James if he would help them. He agreed, adding that he would only accept if I could join as well.

"When James asked for my help, I couldn't turn down the opportunity. In those days, I wasn't butler of Wilton Manor. I was James's valet, making it easier for me to accompany him around London. We didn't know any of the identities of the gentlemen we

worked with. We would receive coded messages, explaining where
to meet for our training. Disguised men would teach us how to work
covertly, then leave us information on how to contact them." He smiled
at me. "Where do you think James learned to make things disappear? I,
on the other hand, was more efficient at impersonations."

"Eventually they brought James and me our own disguises—two
each." He gestured to the objects in front of him, smiling nostalgically.
"They instructed us to be careful with how often we used each one.
James and I practiced different ways to walk and talk—carry ourselves
with our various identities." Lawrence closed his eyes and smiled,
reliving the moments again.

"After two months of investigating the French murderer,
Etienne Dupont, James and I made contact with him. He let us in as
acquaintances and was very . . . unhinged. A chameleon of sorts: Able
to act whatever part he wished. He was an aristocrat, killing for the
sport of it. James and I exploited him, though it certainly wasn't easy.
Right before the end, Etienne Dupont discovered our true identities
and there was a fight. It really is a good story, but I'll save the details for
another time."

He raised his eyebrows mysteriously. "Ultimately, he was accused
of murder. Due to his lineage, they didn't hang him, but sentenced him
to life in prison. He is still being held in London, at Newgate prison, to
this day."

"Why have I never heard this story before?" I asked in
bewilderment. Even in death Papa was reminding me that there was no
one quite like him. It was akin to hearing some fantastical story made
up for children.

Lawrence chuckled. "James didn't want you and Charles getting
any ideas. He met Elizabeth during all the excitement and recognized
it wasn't the sort of life he wanted to be tied up in while raising a
family. We no longer participated in helping the Goldfinch Society
after Etienne was apprehended, but we have stayed in contact with
them. They are helping me here in London while investigating James's
murder. They, too, are grieved about his death."

"And what are we going to use these disguises for now?" I asked.

"Tomorrow morning you will leave this inn dressed as someone else. I won't change my appearance until we are near London. The innkeeper has already seen me."

"And what will we be doing in disguise?" I notched an eyebrow.

"We will be paying a few gentlemen some visits," Lawrence said.

I clasped my hands together, chuckling. "Do you think it will matter if I wear this disguise while I claim my father's money?"

Lawrence shook his head, a corner of his mouth turned up. "You will leave this inn disguised and arrive in London as such, until you resume your identity as Henry Thomas. I will help you switch back and forth."

A wide grin spread across my face, shaking my head at Lawrence. "I can't wait to see the look on Charles's face when he sees you wearing—this." I picked up a brown mustache that curled at the ends and a wig with brown, wavy hair.

Lawrence smiled. "As a matter of fact, good sir, those are reserved specifically for you."

Charles

It was dark when we arrived at an inn called the Boar's Head, halfway between Wilton and London.

"Lord Elliot, I assume you don't want your presence to be known here. Would you like me to speak with the innkeeper to secure a room for you?" John asked.

I didn't want John's help, but I recognized the need for it. I nodded. "Very well. Will you ask for my food to be brought up, and find out which room mine will be from the outside?"

John nodded then quit the carriage, walking inside without further questions. I waited for a time before the carriage door opened once more. John held out his hand. "Here is the key to your room. Second floor, third window in from the left, facing the back stables." He paused for a moment, then muttered to himself, "Or was it the second window in?"

I gave him a flat stare. I intended to climb in through the window. I needed to know *exactly* which one it was.

I handed the key back to him. "Unlock my door and open the window once you get inside."

His eyes widened when he finally understood my meaning. "I'm sure there is a better way for you to get into your room unseen," he said. "I would hate for us to go through all this trouble just for you to die falling from a window."

"I have no intention of dying, Mr. Thomas. Will you open the window or not?"

John shook his head in frustration then looked toward the windows on the second floor before he trudged away with my key.

I pulled myself into my room from the *third* window to the left once it was opened. The climb wasn't terrible, though there were a few tough places to navigate.

"Here's your key," John said, placing it on top of a small table next to a bowl of soup that had already been brought in. "I took the liberty of directing the innkeeper to where your things were to be placed."

It was then that I noticed my father's rifle and my dueling swords. They too had been placed inside, alongside my trunk. If John wanted me dead, he'd had every opportunity to make it happen while I was climbing through the window. No one knew that we were traveling together, and no one would have been the wiser.

"I have taken a room next door, my lord. If there is a disturbance I should be able to hear it. I suggest we get to sleep presently so we can leave early tomorrow morning." He began shutting my door on the way out. Just before it closed, he poked his head back in. "Don't forget to lock yourself in," he added. I nodded before the door clicked shut behind him.

I reflected on everything I'd just discovered about John Thomas. He certainly had a complicated history—but it appeared as though he had every intention of helping Henry and me. Perhaps I could trust him after all.

Henry

Boar's Head Inn
November 15, 1816
Early the next morning
Last full day of disguise

It was early when I woke. The sky was still pitch black, and only the sound of the early morning stagecoach could be heard. Lawrence was shuffling around in the dark room.

"What's the hour?" I asked, voice gravelly.

"It's nearing half past four." Lawrence struck some tinder and lit a lantern. "I suggest we prepare for the remainder of our journey."

I, too, was eager to reach London. I pushed the blankets off and sat up, placing my feet on the cold, wood floor. I walked toward my trunk and proceeded to dress as Lawrence opened the lid to his box once more and pulled the items from it.

"Come sit." Lawrence put the lantern at the table and pulled a small chair out for me. Once I was settled, he held the four different mustaches above my lip one at a time, scrutinizing me, then finally nodded as if he'd found the right one. He repeated the same process for the wigs then pulled a shallow, wide-based bottle from the box, along with a small brush with fine hairs. He released the stopper from the bottle then dipped his brush inside. When he pressed it above my upper lip, it was wet and sticky. I scrunched my face up at the feeling against my skin.

"Are you ready?" he asked with a grin.

I smirked, rubbing my fingers over my chin. "So long as you don't ruin this face," I hadn't shaved the day before, and I could already feel the coarse stubble forming. I was surprised at how much I enjoyed being clean shaven—I would never admit it to Charles, but the look was growing on me.

"Do your worst," I finally said to Lawrence.

"Very good, sir," he said, a mischievous grin in tow.

Charles

A quiet knock sounded on my door as I was drifting into wakefulness. I could hear the early morning coach departing; it must have been somewhere between half past four and five.

The knock sounded again. Stalking to the door, I cracked it open. John appeared on the other side, dressed and ready to go, holding up a lantern.

"It's time." His voice was low and tired.

I let out a tired sigh. "I need to change. I'll be down by the carriage in fifteen minutes."

He nodded. "I'll give the order to have your things brought down. I'll be waiting in the coach."

"Thank you, Mr. Thomas." My thanks came out before I could stop myself. One side of his mouth turned up at my first kind utterance—I saw Henry's mannerism in it. Then he silently turned from the door and walked down the hallway.

I shut the door and quickly changed, then opened the window and looked down. It was always easier climbing up than it was making the descent. My eyes peered right, then left, assessing the best way to proceed. To the right, near the next window over, was a large, thick vine that coiled itself around a vertical beam. It was my best option. I stood on my window ledge and reached until my hand rested securely on the wooden pole. I pulled myself from the window to the beam and grasped for part of the vine, testing its strength. It wasn't strong enough to hold my weight entirely, but it helped me stay put as I looked around. I grasped the foliage in one hand while I looked down. There was a small overhang of brick protruding from the wall a little way down. If I could just—My right foot slipped and planted itself against the outer wall with a loud thud. I prayed the noise was louder from the outside than it was from the inside.

Henry

As Lawrence handed me some spectacles to wear we heard a *THUD* against the wall near the window. Lawrence and I looked at one another.

"What the Devil?" I muttered. I took hold of the lantern and unlatched the glass panes, pushing them open, a breeze filtering in. A tall man clung to the side of the wall, making his way down from the next room over. The man's face snapped up to me, and I did a double take as his face came into focus.

It was Charles.

Charles

The window from the next room over suddenly swung open. A man with a long, curled mustache, full, long beard, round spectacles, and hair parted down the middle of his head peered out at me, lantern in hand. I squinted at him in the darkness.

He did a double take as he saw me, then chuckled. "I say, good sir," he said with a foppish voice, "once you are done washing the windows, might you fix the draft from this blasted room?" His voice was familiar;

it felt as though I had met him before.

I didn't know what to say.

He smirked. "If you come inside now, good fellow, I won't have to ring for the innkeeper's wife." A corner of his mouth turned up before he said, "No? Oh well, no matter if you can't. I'll just ring for her now."

Surely the innkeeper's wife would find me out here if she came to inspect the drafty window. I would certainly be in trouble then.

"I'll fix your draft," I said irritably. I grabbed the wooden frame of his window and pulled myself inside. The man gave me a grin, making me feel as though I had been left out of a joke. Movement sounded just behind him, notifying me that someone else waited in the room. The figure approached until his face came into the lantern's range.

"Lawrence?" I said in confusion.

"My lord?" Lawrence sounded just as confused as I was. I turned to the other man, who was shaking with laughter.

"Henry?" I asked, completely bewildered.

"I know," he said, laughing. "You didn't think this face could become even more dashing than it already was."

He stroked his long beard. It was terrible. I didn't even recognize him with the spectacles and his hair parted down the middle that way. In fact, it didn't look like his hair at all.

"Might I ask what this is all about?" I finally asked.

"Certainly," Henry said. "Once Lawrence has had his fun." Henry steered me over to an open trunk where he and Lawrence immediately held three mustaches up to my face, looking at me intently.

"Henry, I need to tell you something," I said.

"In a moment," Lawrence said, shoving a pipe in my mouth. "Keep this pipe between your lips, my lord. Even if you aren't smoking, it will alter the way your mouth looks."

Henry shoved his hands in his pockets as he watched Lawrence go to work. "It's a shame Miss Lily can't see you now." Henry's mouth twitched upward with amusement as Lawrence brushed a sticky substance over my actual mustache and attached something to it.

Henry continued, "I'm half tempted to ride back to Wilton now.

Perhaps my new look will change Jane's mind and she will marry me tomorrow morning."

I opened my mouth to tell Henry the exciting news about the eldest Miss Mason when I faltered at the words he'd just stated. They ignited a thought I hadn't yet considered: If I told him the news now, he might rush back to Miss Mason immediately. I needed him in London with me to finish what we started so we could avenge Papa and be safe to live our lives with the women we loved.

The Mason sisters would arrive in London within a few days anyway. If I waited until we arrived in London to give Henry the news, he likely wouldn't make it to Wilton in time before Jane had already departed.

I shut my mouth and continued considering my options.

"Now, what were you going to tell me?" Henry asked, taking the pipe out of my mouth.

I stared at him for a moment, debating. "It can wait."

Henry

I held the lantern close to Charles's face and simpered. He wore a thick mustache that framed his lips all the way down, hanging near his chin, bringing to mind the image of a walrus. The color blended well with the color of his natural beard.

Lawrence placed a wig on Charles that was a few shades lighter than his natural hair color—not so much lighter that it wasn't believable, but light enough that it altered his appearance. The hair went just below Charles's shoulders, giving Charles a look of being unkempt. I couldn't help but laugh. Charles would die if he saw his reflection. He always prided himself on being well groomed and clean. Charles gave me a flat look, but I detected a smile beneath the surface.

As Lawrence continued modifying Charles's appearance, he retold the story of his adventure apprehending Etienne Dupont with James during their younger days. He handed Charles a set of round spectacles similar to mine, though the lenses were larger. Once Lawrence was finished, I couldn't recognize Charles.

Lawrence brought out one more trunk and opened it, revealing a few short, shabby-looking top hats. They weren't the current style, but they were not so out of date to make us stand out.

Last, he brought forward two worn-looking coats to match. Charles traded out his coat for the one Lawrence handed him, removing two pistols and a knife from inside his pockets. Lawrence and I gave him a questioning look.

"Ah, yes," he said, holding one of the pistols out to me. "This one belongs to you." Then he pulled out a sheathed knife, adding, "And so does this." After handing me the knife, he put the second pistol inside a pocket of the ragged jacket he now wore. I didn't recognize either of the weapons he handed me, but I took them and placed them in my own coat.

"I believe you're ready," Lawrence finally said to us both. He turned to Charles. "When you traveled, did you pass anyone on the road in the open chaise that would have recognized you? Was the journey suitable?"

"I didn't take the old chaise," Charles said. He had a funny look about him.

Lawrence knit his eyebrows. "Surely you didn't bring the main carriage?"

Charles Grinned. "Certainly not." He was clearly enjoying this game.

"The stage coach would be an even worse idea, my lord, and I don't take you as an idiot. How did you get here?"

Charles held a hand out toward the door. "I believe we are wasting precious time. I suggest we head off. And I suggest we take *my* carriage." Charles paused. "Come to think of it, Henry, I believe it's actually *your* carriage."

Yes, Charles was definitely enjoying his little game of secrecy. He grabbed one of the loaded trunks and walked out the door. Lawrence and I looked at each other in confused silence, then quickly shut the other trunks and carried them out after Charles.

Lawrence

It was no use trying to push down my smile as I watched Charles and Henry in their new disguises. It was too comical. We neared a modest but comfortable-looking private carriage that I had never seen. A coachman took our trunks and loaded them, except for the sleek box I carried for my disguise.

I knit my eyebrows in curiosity as Charles opened the door and motioned for us to step inside. How did Charles come by such a thing? Henry entered the carriage first, followed by Charles. I entered last and was surprised to find a vaguely familiar-looking gentleman already seated, looking bewildered at the three unknown men entering his compartment.

"Father?" Henry finally said as he got a good look at the man already seated.

The man did a double take at Henry, staring for a while before he finally chuckled, "Henry?" He then turned to Charles, trying to hide a grin. "Ah, Lord Elliot, it appears as though I misunderstood your meaning when you stated your need to change."

This gentleman was none other than Henry's father, John Thomas. I had only ever seen him once or twice before he was no longer welcome in the Elliot home.

"Mr. Thomas," I said as I nodded my head curtly. Clearly Henry and Charles both trusted this man. Charles's opinion should have been sufficient enough for me, since he didn't trust easily—but I still planned to watch him like a hawk.

"Lawrence, I believe," he said, nodding respectfully in my

direction. I was surprised he remembered me.

Charles gave a look of mock disappointment. "And here I thought we would have to make introductions and fill people in. But since we all seem to know one another, I suggest we start making plans."

Noticing my hesitation, Charles gave me a reassuring look, sending the message that we could trust John. I still felt reluctant, but Charles was right; we did need to formulate a plan.

Once I related details for the old Elliot carriage to be returned to Wilton Manor, I entered John's conveyance once more and rapped my fist a few times against the carriage roof. Its lurch forward made me sway, practically dumping me into Charles's lap, before I took a seat, irritated that a butler would be seen in such a fashion. James would have found it humorous.

Charles looked at each of us without skipping a beat. "I believe the first two items we need to address are that of the physician and his apprentice, following which we need to find out who would sell poison in London." He turned to John, adding, "We will fill you in once we assign tasks. Here's what I propose." Turning to Henry, he continued, "Once your affairs are in order, and you have signed all the necessary documents to secure your future with Miss Mason, we will make a visit to the physician and his apprentice. We need to speak with the apprentice alone to discover whose report the physician falsified.

"When we have accomplished this, we need to seek out Robert Graves and his uncle. They no longer work together, but they may each know something that the other doesn't. We need to find out if either of them sells poison, or if they know *who* would sell such a thing.

"Finally, if we are able to find any solid evidence from those two courses of action, we will approach Arthur Brown. We have to be able to ensure his family's safety before asking him to reveal the identity of the other man he heard behind his shop. I believe he knows who threatened my father that night.

"Once we have all the information, we will take it to the Bow Street Runners. There is a chance we may also need to pay our little bird friend a visit," Charles said, looking at Henry.

"It might not hurt to pay Jacob Hughes and Alexander Campbell a visit as well," Henry added.

I glanced at John, who tried to keep a smile hidden beneath the surface while watching Henry and Charles feed off each other. He appeared to be soaking in every bit of it as they went back and forth.

Charles grinned. "At that point, we can't leave Frederick out either. If he's unconscious, he can't propose to your Miss Mason."

Henry smiled. "I like the way you think, Charles."

32

REPORT

Jane

Wilton
November 15, 1816
Later that day
Last full day of disguise

Alice pinned my curls up. I didn't look in the mirror; I would see only emptiness. Trying not to be consumed with thoughts of losing Charles was exhausting. The memory of his kiss tormented me relentlessly. My heart cursed me for not staying just a moment longer with him beneath the tree—as if that small moment would have somehow made all the difference.

I took in a deep breath and tried to think about Mr. Ashby as I made my way down the stairs and into the drawing room. I reminded myself of all his admirable qualities, telling myself I could someday feel something for him. I looked out the window at the falling leaves, realizing that I was more like Charles now; I saw the beauty in the falling leaves, but they meant something different for me than they

used to: a constant reminder of what I could never have. Mr. Ashby
arrived near ten o'clock to take me riding. Lily said she wasn't in the
mood for an outing, so it was only the two of us and Alice. Mr. Ashby
and I rode side by side.

"There is a place over here that I would like to explore," Mr. Ashby
said, pointing to a group of trees I had never explored. I nodded and he
led the way, Alice following at a distance.

Eventually, Mr. Ashby dismounted his horse and approached me.
He lifted his hand, taking mine, then helped me down. I waited to feel
something at his close proximity, but nothing came. He offered his
arm to me, and my heart protested as I threaded mine through his,
remembering my walk with Lord Elliot in a similar manner.

We strolled in silence for a moment before he said, "Miss Mason—
Jane. We have known each other for a number of years now."

"Indeed, Mr. Ashby. We have." I swallowed, understanding what
was most likely to follow—He'd just used my Christian name.

It felt like a betrayal, allowing another gentleman to call me Jane—
as if my name somehow belonged to Lord Elliot now. The truth was
that I didn't want any other man to call me Jane. I knew it would only
disappoint me, as no one else could say it the way he did.

Mr. Ashby smiled but his eyes held uncertainty. "Jane—" he
said again. I was right. His utterance of my name fell completely flat
compared to when Charles said it.

Mr. Ashby looked at me curiously. "Forgive me for being blunt, but
you seem distant."

"I apologize." I looked down, unsure of what else to say.

"It is not my intention to make you ill at ease," he said, waiting for
me to look at him. I was afraid of what he might find if I did meet his
gaze for even a moment. But he was stubborn and waited until I could
no longer ignore his request. I finally obliged.

He gave me a warm look. "I have been fond of you for some time."
The warmth beneath his gaze turned into an apprehensive smile. "I
know you've had your aims set high for years now, and I am nothing
worth mentioning when it comes to title, rank, or fortune. I have kept
my distance due to this fact and it's my own fault for doing nothing

until now." He slowly took my hand. My heart raced, flooding with fear that he might propose. I didn't know what I would do if he did. Mr. Ashby was a wonderful sort of gentleman, but my heart belonged to another.

He continued to hold my hand as he spoke. "When I sat by you at dinner the other evening, I felt as though something had changed in you, compared to our interactions from past years. It made me wonder if I might have a chance. I was completely taken by the sincerity of your smile and eyes, and hoped that perhaps they were meant for me."

He studied my face. "I am realizing now, however, that they may have been intended for someone else." He gave me a knowing look. "I had a mind to propose, but I sense a deep-rooted sadness in you."

I didn't know what to say.

He stepped closer to me. "Perhaps I could have won your heart at some point if I had tried sooner. But I feel as though your heart already belongs to another. And no amount of this," he slowly lifted his hand wrapped around mine and gave me a knowing grin, "will fix it."

I was relieved that I wouldn't have to consider a proposal from him right at this moment, but I also felt hopeless knowing he could read my feelings so easily. Why couldn't my heart prefer Mr. Ashby? It would make life so much simpler.

He slowly released my hand then added, "If your heart opens once more, and Lord Elliot no longer holds it, you know where to find me." He smiled. "Now, I would like to think that we are at least friends." He offered me his arm once more and we walked together. "Will you not confide in me the reason behind your sadness? It is clear to me that Lord Elliot shares your feelings. He made it very obvious the other evening."

"Mr. Ashby." I hesitated. "I feel odd speaking about this with you, especially when you have been so sincere about your feelings. I do not wish to cause you unnecessary pain."

"I assure you I am quite safe," he said kindly. "I would feel better if I could help you somehow."

I exhaled slowly. "Lord Elliot does love me, I believe. But he is intended to marry someone else. I believe he will be announcing his engagement very soon."

Mr. Ashby stopped walking and looked over at me. "Do you love him? Answer honestly and without reservation. I am fond of you, yes, but you will not break my heart by saying the words." It was peculiar having this conversation with another man.

My next words came out quiet. "I do love him," I finally confessed. "I love him to the point of pain."

"Then tell him," he said. "I wish I hadn't waited so long with you. I was afraid you would look down upon my lack of fortune, so I held back. Now I will have peace knowing that I did at least try. But you, Miss Mason," he shook his head. "This will haunt you forever if you don't tell him."

He was right, and yet... I sighed. "I don't know if my heart could bear it if I say the words and he still rejects me."

Mr. Ashby nodded sympathetically. "There is that possibility." The corner of his mouth turned up. "And if it does happen, I'll be here."

William Ashby really was a gentleman of the best sort. I doubted that I would ever be able to get over Charles, even for all of Mr. Ashby's goodness. But I had to admit that the lady who ended up holding Mr. Ashby's heart would be a lucky woman indeed. And his words gave me courage knowing that if Charles did reject my feelings for him, Mr. Ashby would at least be here to comfort me.

"Thank you, Mr. Ashby. You have given me courage and hope." I gave him a grateful smile as we continued to walk back to the horses.

Lily

The long grass swayed in the meadow as my brothers and I tread paths through it to pass the time.

"Why hasn't Henry come back for seconds yet?" Oliver took a bite of a crisp red apple, munching on it as he said, "I was banking on that second platter of pastries."

"Who's Henry?" Sterling asked.

"You missed all the action," Oliver said with a grin. "He came to do business with Papa the other day, but I found him making cow eyes at Lily, so I gave him up to Cook to see how he would handle her. And he won her over!"

Sterling rolled his eyes. "Like I believe that."

"I'm serious! Ask Lily." Oliver threw his thumb back toward me before he continued praising Henry. "He told Cook he would take her plate of pastries whether she liked it or not. He held his ground and even called her 'madam.' " Oliver raised his eyebrows, as if this was the boldest move anyone could undertake. "In the end she handed him the whole platter and some pudding to go with it."

Sterling's face turned to mine to hear Oliver's tale contradicted.

"It's true," I finally said with a smirk. "Apparently the way to Cook's heart is not sweet words after all." I found that I both loved and hated talking about Henry. It reminded me that I had no clue as to when or even *if* I'd see him again. It was especially hard when I could tell Oliver wanted him to come back too.

"Why hasn't Lord Elliot come back to visit either?" Sterling asked. "He still needs to teach me his magic." Sterling and Oliver weren't helping.

Wilton had always been a refuge for me. Now that I was finally home, all I could think of was returning to London—or better put, Henry. Wilton could no longer be my haven until everything was settled. Despite the fact that we weren't due to return to London for another day, I would ask Jane if we could leave at once.

Jane

I entered the stables feeling determined. I would confront Charles and figure out what to do from there. If he still chose to go through with his engagement, at least I would know I tried.

The lie I continued to feed myself was that I needed to speak with him in order to make a decision one way or another. I pretended it wasn't the fact that I needed to see his grin again, or lose myself in his eyes, if only for a moment. That I just needed to hear his voice one more time; hear him say my name.

As I led Winnie to the mounting block, I found Lily waiting, talking with Stella. She gave me a look of relief when our eyes met.

"Jane, I know we aren't due to leave for another day, but please tell me you want to return to London as soon as possible." She began to pace. "There is someone I must see, and I fear I shall go mad if I have to wait here a moment longer."

I loved Lily's honesty. She was never one to skirt about the issue. Conveniently, I was in the same boat. I steered Winnie to the mounting block and removed myself from the saddle.

"Who must you see so urgently?" I led my horse to her stall.

Lily opened her mouth to speak and floundered for a moment. "I will introduce you to him when we return. Please tell me you want to leave."

"I daresay I couldn't agree with your sentiment more," I finally said, a corner of my mouth pulling into a grin.

"How soon can you be ready to leave?"

"I'll begin packing immediately."

Henry

Before I entered the building to sign everything, Lawrence removed my beard and mustache with a concoction that smelled odd. I waited until fewer people inhabited the street before walking out of the carriage and into the solicitor's office. Fortunately, signing the documents didn't take long at all.

Breathing out a sigh of relief, I sent a silent prayer of thanks heavenward: I was now Henry Thomas, a man with means.

Upon reentering the carriage, I did a double take. Lawrence, a man who usually had graying, short, well-kept hair, was wearing a wig of dark brown pulled into a low ponytail, along with a short, straight, dark mustache. He topped off his disguise with a monocle and an old top hat.

I chuckled. "Lawrence, you've been holding out on us."

He held his face with a look of no nonsense. "To what, exactly, are you referring?" He said the words as if he was bored to death before he gave me a wink.

Once I got a good look at my father I couldn't help but guffaw. "Who dubbed you the feeble old man?"

"Apparently I am the oldest one here," he said, a hint of bitterness in his voice. "By a whole two months." He shot an annoyed look Lawrence's way. I bit down another laugh. He wore a wig of graying white that came down in thin, wispy strands. Graying eyebrows had been seamlessly attached over his normal ones, and he wore a white, scraggly beard and sparse-looking mustache. A walking cane leaned against the bench next to my father, and he wore an old, torn coat with a few missing buttons. Upon closer inspection, it appeared as though Lawrence had glued a few bumps to his skin as well. He looked terrible.

The moment I sat down, Lawrence went to work placing my disguise back on.

I clapped my hands together then rubbed them in excitement, looking at Charles. "What are we waiting for? We have an apprentice to interrogate." I swiped the cane resting against the bench next to my father and pounded the top of the carriage until it lurched forward.

Charles looked over at my father. "Last week I overheard a man, Doctor Fairhurst, speaking with his apprentice. I have recently discovered that this apprentice's name is Mr. Jones. Mr. Jones accused Doctor Fairhurst of falsifying more than one report, one of which included a death with clear signs of poison, but was written up as natural causes."

I shook my head, angry all over again that someone would poison Papa. Charles's attention then turned to me. "The only way we can speak with Mr. Jones effectively is if Doctor Fairhurst is away from the establishment. As such, you and I will need to arrange a later time if the doctor is present."

I nodded. "Understood."

Charles gestured to my father and Lawrence next. "We will need the two of you to stand guard outside in case Doctor Fairhurst returns unexpectedly. Henry and I will need to be given a signal if his carriage approaches. If all goes according to plan, the doctor will know nothing of our visit."

Lawrence and my father looked at each other hesitantly, clearly uneasy about the thought of working together. A corner of my mouth twitched up, imagining their attempt at a cordial conversation without Charles and me. Eventually they swallowed their uncertainty and nodded in agreement.

"Good," Charles said. "Henry, you and I will exit the carriage first. One of us will send you both a signal if the physician is out." He pointed between Lawrence and my father. "We will give it to you by putting our hands behind our back and holding up four fingers."

"Why not three fingers?" I asked, simply to annoy Charles. "If it's you, me, and the apprentice, that's three people." I held up my fingers to emphasize my point.

"It doesn't matter how many fingers we hold up," Charles snapped.

"Oh good," I said with a smirk. "Then I'll hold up three."

Charles shook his head, holding back a grin beneath his annoyance. It was good to see that Miss Lily had been cracking his shell.

Charles continued, "If the physician is away initially, but returns prematurely, the two of you must alert us by knocking on the back room. Henry and I will leave through a back window at that point." We all nodded in agreement.

The carriage came to a stop in front of an older building at the end of a secluded street.

"Are you ready for your performance?" I teased, smiling at Charles. It was humorous to see Charles looking so unkempt . . . until I remembered my own appearance and stopped smiling.

We crossed the street toward the old building, worn and disheveled with peeling paint. A small, wooden sign nailed just off the side of the door read "Doctor Fairhurst, Physician." Just before I knocked, Charles stopped me.

"I have news for you. I wanted to tell you sooner, but we've had an audience." I didn't know if I should feel excited or worried about the fact that he wished to tell me in private.

I let out a slow apprehensive breath. "What is it?" I finally asked.

"Jane Mason believes you are engaged to another woman." He gave me a grin as if it was marvelous news. "She won't have you because she believes you will be marrying someone else, not because she believes you to be penniless."

A flood of emotions filled me when his words solidified in my mind.

Charles continued. "I believe she may have heard part of our conversation out in the garden. But she only heard the part about 'Lord Elliot being intended for someone else.' "

A weight lifted off of my chest and I smiled. "Did you set her straight?"

Charles opened his mouth slightly as if he was going to speak, closed it, then opened it again. "No. I actually ran Apollo harder than ever to inform you of the news so you could sweep the lady off her feet yourself, but you were already gone." He gave me a look as if it were all somehow my fault.

"So she still believes at this point that I lured her to me all while I was engaged to another woman in secret?" I was mortified.

"I would say that sums it up," Charles said with a smirk.

"And it didn't even cross your mind to clarify that point before you left for London?"

Charles's stare was hard and his next words dripped with sarcasm. "You're welcome for the happy news."

"Forgive me if I'm not leaping for joy, Charles." I returned his sardonic tone. "But Mr. Ashby may be doing his utmost to ensnare Jane at this very moment, all while she has every reason to believe that I am a despicable gentleman." I couldn't believe Charles hadn't even considered this. I was grateful that she hadn't dismissed me because of my lack of money, but now I had to wonder if she despised me.

Her words from the other night played through my head. It was no wonder she was so insistent on leaving me. She probably thought I wanted her for a mistress. I groaned inwardly at the thought.

It was hard to act normal. I was so angry that Charles hadn't considered such a thing. I knew he meant well, but if he'd only said something to Miss Lily, or talked with Jane once he realized I had left for London, I wouldn't be in this predicament.

"She returns to London tomorrow, Henry," Charles said defensively. "I highly doubt she will run away with Mr. Ashby this very day and marry him."

I shook my head. "Let's get this over with so we can both smooth this mess over as soon as possible."

"Agreed," Charles said irritably, pounding firmly on the door. A moment later the door cracked open ever so slightly, revealing a spindly housekeeper. She eyed Charles and me skeptically, taking in our shabby appearances. When Charles spoke, his tone and posture held authority. "Hello, madam. Is the physician, Doctor Fairhurst, in?" She looked back and forth between us, looking uneasy at our imposing height. Clearly, Charles's approach was intimidating her.

She swallowed. "I'm sorry, sirs, but you missed him by an hour or so. Only Mr. Jones, his apprentice, is available at the moment." It was obvious by her tone that she mistrusted us. It was time for a gentler approach, and perhaps a touch of flattery.

"Mrs.," I said with a kind tone. "I can see that you take your work seriously. Doctor Fairhurst is lucky to have you." She smiled at the recognition and seemed to relax a little. "May we speak with the apprentice, Mr. Jones?" I added, giving her a winning smile while placing my hands behind my back to hold up three fingers for Lawrence and my father. The housekeeper nodded her head and opened the door fully, allowing us to step inside the small entryway. Old bowed stairs led up on the right side, looking as though they may collapse during their next use. To the left was a dark, narrow hallway.

"Come this way," the housekeeper said as she led us down the unlit passage. It smelled of old, decaying wood, and the floorboards creaked as we traipsed over them.

"I'll do the talking," I whispered to Charles under my breath. "This might take some coaxing, and based on your performance with the housekeeper just now, I believe the task should be left to me."

Either Charles didn't hear me, or he pretended not to. We made our way to a door at the end of the enclosed corridor. The housekeeper knocked, then poked her head inside.

"Some gentlemen are here to see you," she said to someone beyond, before opening the door and gesturing for us to enter the room. As we emerged, I noticed that the window on the back wall was small. It would be a tight fit for Charles and I to squeeze through if the physician came back early. A young man with dark hair and blue eyes greeted us.

"Please have a seat," he said, gesturing to some chairs across from his desk.

The housekeeper left, shutting the door behind her.

"How can I help you?" He looked between the two of us. I opened my mouth to speak, but Charles beat me to it.

"Mr. Jones," Charles spoke with a deep, rumbling tone. The way he presented himself was intimidating with those two words alone. I shook my head at his stubbornness. Was he to make himself as imposing as possible due to what I had just said in the hallway?

As Charles said his next line, he rose slowly from his chair, his tall, broad frame appearing even larger from my seated position. "We have reason to believe that you may have been an accomplice in the murder of the late Lord Elliot." He stared at Mr. Jones. I held back my look of shock. Why was he trying to harass this man, when we knew he was innocent? We needed to get information from Mr. Jones, not scare him into a corner. Perhaps Charles thought he could frighten this man into submission.

Mr. Jones's eyes widened in surprise, but he was otherwise unaltered. "If that is the case, gentlemen, then I must respectfully ask you to leave unless you have a Bow Street Runner with you. I have had no part in such a thing, and I will not speak to you further unless I'm forced."

I pulled Charles down to his seat and gave him a look, hopefully conveying that he'd better not utter another word.

"Mr. Jones," I said with a confident but affable tone, "you must forgive my colleague, Nicholas Wimblebopper. He is hasty and headstrong." I felt Charles's heel crush my foot at the ridiculous surname I'd just given him. I held back a grunt and offered Mr. Jones a reassuring look before I continued.

"You are not suspected of murdering the late Earl of Wiltshire. Rather, the man by which you are apprenticed is suspected of withholding evidence, or better put, falsifying a report as to his cause of death." I hoped our information was right. We would hit another dead-end if not.

Mr. Jones held perfectly still, keeping his thoughts to himself. We were putting him in a precarious position. If Doctor Fairhurst found out that Mr. Jones had divulged information, it would certainly lead to the end of his apprenticeship. He needed to feel as though his only option was to tell the truth.

"We have evidence that the earl has been poisoned," I lied. "If we bring this evidence forward, it will reflect poorly upon Doctor Fairhurst and anything attached to him thereby, including you as his apprentice."

"So you have come to blackmail or threaten me in exchange for silence on the matter?" His expression didn't change.

A corner of my mouth turned up at the irony of his statement. "Certainly not, good fellow. Quite the opposite, in fact. We would like to give you a chance to come forward with the evidence yourself before we expose Doctor Fairhurst.

"If you come forward with the information, he will be put under investigation. You, on the other hand, will still be free to practice. Society wants a doctor they can trust. They will see you as the man who did right, even when it threatened your very position. People will start seeking you out, and you'll move from apprentice to physician overnight."

Mr. Jones gave us a skeptical look. "What do you get out of this arrangement?"

"Peace of mind," I smiled. "It will ease my conscience knowing that a good physician is on the streets of London instead of a crook who can be bought off."

Mr. Jones gave me a suspicious look . . . he didn't believe me.

Charles shook his head at my attempt to butter up the apprentice before he spoke. "We have an interest in the case of the late Lord Elliot's death." He still spoke with his deep, authoritative voice, but he wasn't nearly as intimidating as he had been at our entrance.

"Although we do have evidence that will not look favorably upon Doctor Fairhurst and his establishment, it would greatly add to our case if you brought your evidence forward beforehand. We do benefit, Mr. Jones. But not at the expense of anyone else.

"We are giving you a chance to be something better than the doctor was. Show London what a real physician looks like. Though my colleague Samuel Shortstacker's sentiment may sound unconvincing, there are people we care about in London. It truly would give us peace of mind knowing an honest man is seeing to the health of those we love."

I refrained from crushing Charles's foot behind the desk at the name he dubbed me. Of course the word "short" would be in there. But it appeared we were getting somewhere with Mr. Jones, so I kept myself still. We waited as he looked down at the desk, considering the information we had just given him.

"What do you need from me?" he finally asked.

"May we see the report for Lord Elliot's death? And will you state that Doctor Fairhurst falsified the report to an official? We will also need you to bring any further reports falsified by Doctor Fairhurst to a Bow Street Runner."

He nodded, finally confirming our suspicions. "I'll do it this very day. It has weighed heavily on my mind since he falsified James Elliot's report. It disgusts me that I work with a man who is supposed to help others, but only picks and chooses when he will be honest." He stood from his chair.

I rose too before asking, "Do you know why the doctor would have done such a thing?"

"Money," was his response.

"Do you know who would pay him to do it?" I asked.

Mr. Jones shook his head. "I wish I did. But Doctor Fairhurst keeps his secrets close." He walked to the door. "I must retrieve his reports upstairs. I'll be quick."

He opened the door quietly, then closed it behind him with even more care.

Lawrence

John and I waited near the corner of the building, trying to appear as though we were having a casual conversation. I couldn't remember the last time I felt so out of place. As I stood by John, watching and waiting, I hadn't the faintest idea what to say.

I was always the butler at the door who knew exactly which words to use: "Let me take your hat, sir"; "It's good to see you again"; "Please be seated; he will be with you shortly." But what was there to say to John Thomas? "So, you tried to kill Henry, did you?" "What was it like when James took your entire household staff?" "Would you like to see the pistol in my coat pocket?"

"Do you like to fish?" John's voice penetrated the unbearable silence. He clasped his hands together nervously. No sooner had he done this than he placed them inside his pockets, swishing them back and forth for only a moment, and then pulled them out again and held them behind his back. Clearly he felt just as awkward as I did.

"I do like to fish," I responded, keeping my hands behind my back like a good butler, even though I wanted to fidget.

John nodded his head. I waited for him to respond but nothing came. He puffed out his cheeks in small breaths as if he was thinking about what else to say. His scraggly fake mustache moved haphazardly as he did so.

"Do *you* like fishing, sir?" I finally asked back.

"No, not really."

"I see."

The silence returned. It took everything in me not to make an excuse as to why I needed to wait somewhere else. John scratched the side of his head, as if he simply didn't know what else to do. And so we stood in front of each other for the next half hour, trying to look as though we were having a pleasant conversation, all while saying very little and hoping Charles and Henry would hurry up.

It startled me when John finally spoke again. "Can Henry sing? His Mother had the most beautiful voice."

I couldn't help but chuckle. "No, sir. Henry can't carry a tune, he has no sense of rhythm, and he has one volume only . . . loud."

John chuckled as well, rubbing his fingers over his forehead in embarrassment. "It sounds familiar. I guess he did get something from me after all. Tell me more about him."

I wasn't sure what to say. I still didn't know John very well and I didn't want to tell him anything that Henry would rather keep to himself. But John looked so eager, and both Henry and Charles seemed to trust him.

"There's not a kinder soul than Henry. Ironically, there seems to be no one who enjoys pestering Charles so much either."

John smiled, hanging on to every word. A memory of Henry suddenly came to my mind.

"On one particular occasion," I started, "the late earl was hosting a large dinner party. Charles and Henry were visiting on holiday from Cambridge. Lady Elliot fussed over both of their appearances until they were both looking their very best. Unfortunately, she had their hair done the exact same way and had them dressed in some new suits that were matching. Once she was satisfied, those sixteen year-old boys looked so identical that everyone, including myself, was having a hard time keeping them straight.

"Usually they sat by each other at dinner, but this time they made an exception and seated themselves on opposite ends of the table, strategically placing themselves so they wouldn't have to compete for the girls' attention. Within no time, Henry had every girl near him smiling and giggling until one of the girls sitting right next to him accidentally spilled her soup onto her lap. She was close to tears. To assuage her mortification, Henry purposely spilled his entire soup and drink in his lap. After Henry soiled his outfit, he made a point of stating that *he* was Lord Elliot.

"Charles had no idea about Henry's ruse until the evening wore on and the girls were talking and laughing about the young Lord Elliot spilling his soup and drink into his lap. The next part of the story was told to me like this:

"Charles confronted Henry and said, 'You'd better explain yourself.'

" 'Explain what?'

" 'Explain how "Lord Elliot" spilled his soup and drink in his lap when he was on the other end of the table.'

"Henry patted Charles on his back and said, 'That is rather bad luck. You always were a little clumsy.' "

John and I chuckled together as I finished the story.

I looked over at the house. "It's been a pleasure to watch your son grow. I don't know what any of us would have done without him."

The sound of an approaching carriage suddenly filled my ears.

"Do you hear that?" John said, turning his head with mine toward the noise.

A carriage wasn't yet visible, but if we waited too long, and it was in fact the physician, he'd see us standing near the porch before long. We hid ourselves behind the corner of the establishment before we peered back toward the isolated street at the corner where it bled into a busier road. Sure enough, a small carriage turned onto the street and approached.

Charles

Mr. Jones entered the room again carrying a wooden box. He placed it on the desk with a heavy thud. The box had clearly survived a great ordeal in its life; it appeared as though the wood was scarred by years of travel and misuse. With how worn and stripped the latches were, I was surprised they held. The lock on the front was cast iron, though I questioned whether the patina of age was purely from the lock's make, or from the treatment it had received over the years. Mr. Jones pulled out a key and looked at it for a moment. His next actions would be pivotal one way or another. He breathed in slowly, then gave us a nod of resolve and placed the key inside the lock.

As he twisted the key, it stuck as if the lock was hesitant to give up its contents. Jerking it hard, the lock finally fell loose, allowing him to open the creaking box.

"We will need to do a bit of digging," Mr. Jones said as he fingered through the first few sheets of parchment, then pulled the entire stack out from its prison. "But nothing is to leave its order; is that understood?"

"Understood," Henry and I repeated in unison.

Mr. Jones thumbed down the stack, muttering dates to himself as he glanced at the top corner of each document then at the clock. He finally parted a large section of the papers and placed them on a cleared area of his desk.

"Remind me when the late Earl of Wiltshire died." Mr. Jones moved quickly to his stack inside the box once more.

"The sixth of May," Henry said as I did.

Mr. Jones nodded as he continued his furious pace. "Doctor Fairhurst will be home soon." He glanced at a clock on the desk again. "But we are just about there." He pulled another stack swiftly from the pile and handed it to Henry. "Place this stack next to the other one. Be sure it's set to the right."

Henry nodded then obliged. Anticipation was beginning to set in as we watched him whittle away at the stack. His muttering became faster and faster. I heard him mumble, "June sixth, fifth, third, second, May—"

We were getting close. I could feel Henry's eagerness increasing with mine.

Mr. Jones continued rambling off numbers until he said, "Sixth! The sixth of May. Right here!" He pulled a few documents out, searching the top of each page for the name scrawled across the top. He finally stopped on one of them.

"James Elliot, Earl of Wiltshire," he read aloud. I leaned forward as he read each syllable, willing myself to keep my hand in place instead of snatching the paper from Mr. Jones's grip as he slowly brought it forward.

Bam! Bam! Bam!

We all jumped as a series of loud knocks sounded against the tiny window.

"He's back," Henry said, looking at the small window on the far wall. He gave me an amused look. "Ladies first." He gestured his arms toward the small rectangular opening we were each supposed to climb through. I would be surprised if a man of regular height and breadth could squeeze through.

Bam! Bam! Bam!

I quickly took the document from Mr. Jones. "Let's button this back up. Will you be able to find the other documents you need later?" I asked Mr. Jones, speaking in haste.

"Yes. I will return to my objective once Doctor Fairhurst leaves this evening."

I nodded and folded up my father's report, placing it inside my pocket. Mr. Jones quickly placed a stack of papers inside the old wooden box, and Henry came with the next pile in hand. I followed with the last stack. Mr. Jones promptly bolted the box and forced the lock in place once more.

"What should I tell the physician when he sees the two of you?" He looked between Henry and me.

Henry proceeded to force the protesting window open then looked back. "You'll not say a word. We were never here. If the housekeeper mentions us, tell the physician we were looking for an apothecary and you sent us on our way. Everything will come to light in due course once you divulge your evidence and we ours."

"According to the rattle at the window just now," I said, picking up the warped wooden box, "I assume you have anywhere between one and five minutes before Doctor Fairhurst walks through the door. Can you manage getting this upstairs and be back before then?"

He put his hands beneath the heavy box then proceeded to pull it toward his chest. "I believe so."

Before I released the box from my grip I held it firm, making eye contact with him. "Thank you for your help, Mr. Jones. You have until the end of tomorrow to bring your evidence to the Bow Street Runners before we reveal ours."

Mr. Jones gave me a quick nod before I let go of the box and he dashed out of the room. Swiftly shutting the door behind the apprentice, I turned and saw Henry sizing up the window. Lawrence and John waited on the other side of the open frame. It was about three to four feet to the ground below the window.

"Best you move out of the way," Henry said to John and Lawrence as he removed his coat and hat and handed them through the window.

I shook my head. No doubt Henry was about to make a hasty move. Sure enough, without warning, he dove headfirst out the window with his hands outstretched in front of him. It would have been an impressive move if the window hadn't caught his sides, resulting in his body being wedged halfway in and halfway out. He shimmied and squirmed from side to side, looking absolutely ridiculous.

"Well done, Henry." A side of my mouth twitched up. "Now we are both stuck in here and we haven't even got the largest part of you out." I looked at his bottom getting nearer the window as his legs kicked to give him momentum forward.

I chuckled and shook my head, looking for some way to shove him through. I searched the room for a stick of some sort when he suddenly surprised me and shimmied through, landing on the other side with an "*oof!*"

I was not about to repeat his method. I would exit with much more *finesse*. I quickly poked my head out the window, finding Henry wiping debris from his clothes.

"Lawrence." I motioned him over then carefully handed him my coat and hat through the window as well. "The document is in one of the outer pockets. Be careful not to lose it."

He nodded, then looked to the door behind me in the room. "You haven't much time, my lord. The physician will be walking in any moment now."

I would be quicker than Henry. I noted that if I angled my torso between the two diagonal corners of the window frame I would have more room. I brought a chair over and stood atop it so I was more level with the window, then crouched down backwards and angled myself with the corners so my feet would touch the ground first. I was making excellent progress and got the largest parts out first.

"See, Henry, that's how it's done," I said as my upper body was just about to come through with the rest of me. Just as I began to release my hold on the window sill, my mustache got hooked on a part of the frame, pulling my upper lip forward.

"Uugh!" I let go of the frame with one of my hands, grabbing the unhooked end of the mustache and trying to pull it free. The glue was pulling on my short facial hair and tugging unpleasantly. My face was practically kissing the window frame. I shuddered just thinking about what Henry might say next at the spectacle.

In response to the very thought, Henry's smug voice said, "It is rather efficient, Charles, though I'm not sure if Miss Mason will like you kissing something other than her." I heard John and Lawrence chuckle behind me. I let go of one hand on the frame to grab the mustache and began to pull. I heard footsteps sounding down the hallway. It may have been Mr. Jones, but I wasn't willing to stick around to find out. I gave one last yank and fell backwards through the window, landing with a hard thud on my behind.

"Not a word, Henry!" I snapped, before he had a chance to tease me further.

Lawrence and John quickly shut the window.

"I wouldn't dream of it." Henry looked at my mustache, trying his hardest not to laugh. It was no use. His shoulders shrugged up and down violently at the attempt.

Loud footsteps sounded in the room Henry and I had just escaped. My eyes met Henry's briefly before we all bolted for the carriage, hurriedly jumping in. I dove in last then slammed the door behind me as the carriage lurched forward.

Lawrence turned toward us and opened his mouth in horror. "Charles!" Lawrence hadn't called me Charles in such a way since I was seventeen. "You've ruined your father's favorite mustache."

My fingers flew to my face. Half of the long, drooping mustache was ripped clean off. The other half must have been inside Mr. Jones's office, dangling like a banner of evidence that Nicholas Wimblebopper and Samuel Shortstacker had been there.

33

DRAUGHT

Henry

London
November 15, 1816
Later that day
Last full day of disguise

L awrence was clearly enjoying himself. "Yes, my lord, it is absolutely necessary."

Now that Charles's mustache was ruined, he needed a new disguise—and Lawrence may have been making Charles pay for splitting Papa's favorite accessory in two. I was impressed that he was able to do it all from the confines of the carriage.

Lord Charles Elliot, Earl of Wiltshire, was now being disguised as the old man. I felt immense satisfaction at seeing the white, wispy hair trail off around Charles's shoulders along with the battered hat atop it. Lawrence then used a polishing brush and a canister of white powder to discolor Charles's already-existing facial hair and eyebrows until they were silvery white in color, just to be sure his natural dark hair wouldn't show through when it was time to put the beard and eyebrows on. He opened another canister of a thick, pasty substance and smeared it on Charles's face, focusing on the lines around the mouth and forehead and the outer corners of the eyes and cheeks—leaving a weathered, old look to the skin in its place.

Last, he pulled out a few different-colored powders and set to work dabbing and smudging. By the time Lawrence was done, Charles's skin looked old and sickly with a slight yellow tint, as if he suffered from a liver complaint. Lawrence opened another jar and brushed the sticky substance on the top of Charles's lip and around his mouth and secured the full beard and mustache. He continued the same process with the old, white, errant eyebrows. Lawrence adorned Charles with a few moles then finally looked satisfied, sitting back to admire how terrible Charles looked. I swallowed down a smile. Charles gave me his old flat stare.

"Careful, Charles," I said, no longer caring to fight my grin. "If you carry that look on your face, everyone will see through your disguise."

Even Lawrence snickered at my comment. Charles stared evenly between Lawrence and me, clearly not amused.

"Lawrence, you will be coming with me this time." Charles's words were clipped and curt.

Lawrence's momentary bout of fun was over. He immediately snapped back into his role as butler. "Very good, my lord."

Charles turned to my father. "John, do you think you can keep your son in line for this next task?"

My father's mouth tugged upward into a grin. "I can't make any promises, my lord. He's got too much Elliot in him."

Charles rolled his eyes at the comment. He pulled out a pocket watch and opened it.

"We have one hour before we need to meet back here. Lawrence and I will visit Robert Graves, and you two will visit his uncle." Charles looked between my father and me. "Don't be late."

My father and I turned the corner, taking the lane ahead. At four past noon, the sun was already beginning to bend shadows across the street at slanted angles. It was a quaint part of London. Not necessarily the most embellished part of town, but neat and clean.

I turned to my father. "Show me the address again."

He lifted the note and my eyes searched the shop just across the lane, pinched between other establishments. A display window took up most of the limited space, with a dark-green door to the left of the window. Above was a burgundy sign with black lettering edged in gold paint. It read:

Graves Remedies

My father noticed it at the same time I did. We crossed the street and approached the door, entering to the warm chime of a bell above our heads. No one greeted us on the shop floor—not the best of omens for making a quick stop. I held back the urge to call out to the space that carried beyond the far side of the wall. Instead I held my tongue and inspected the area, hoping someone would emerge shortly.

The place was well kept and went deeper than it appeared from the outside. Wood-paneled walls were lined with shelves on both sides. Toward the back wall stood a long counter, and to the left of the counter, a small table held a few different products advertising various remedies. The faint scent of licorice root, wood, and spices filled my senses.

Finally, a burly man with a stern face emerged from the back of the shop. He wore a sharp suit accompanied with well-oiled hair and thick sideburns. He was an enigma: his frame was more built for the dockyard than for the intricate work of tinctures and remedies. He approached us with a few heavy steps.

"Good afternoon, gentlemen," he said in a deep, gruff voice as he nodded to us. "We have just developed a new sleeping draught that works better than anything you'll find in London." He looked at us skeptically in our worn hats and coats, as if we were there to make off with his goods. It was time to make things interesting.

"Thank you, sir," I said, taking a shilling out of my pocket and flipping it in the air before I caught it. "We aren't looking for any regular sleeping draught, however. We need something that puts a man to sleep for a very long time." I paused. "A very ... very ... long ... time." I gave the apothecary a knowing look and tapped the side of my nose a couple times as if we were both in on a secret.

"How dare you suggest such a thing!" The man's voice was low and gravelly. "This is a respectable establishment."

I dropped my bargaining chip in my pocket. It sounded with a *ping*, joining more coins below. Perhaps his tongue would loosen if he knew there were more shillings than one to be had for his information.

"I have no doubt of this shop's respectability," I said as I put my hand inside my pocket and jangled the coins. His eyes drew to it despite his best efforts, clearly tempted by what was housed within. "If your shop does not carry what I'm looking for, perhaps you could be so kind as to point me in the right direction."

We locked eyes for a time. I pulled a small handful of shillings out of my pocket then slowly dropped them back in one by one, advertising what could be his if only he spilled his secrets.

We waited in silence until my father finally spoke.

"How much for your sleeping draught, Mr. Graves?" His voice pulled us both from our unblinking war.

"I beg your pardon?" Mr. Graves said, confused.

"You said you have the best sleeping draught London has to offer, did you not?"

"I did," was all Mr. Graves obliged him with.

My father looked at him expectantly. "And am I to pay you for it, or am I to simply take it?" My father gave him a look of amusement.

Mr. Graves looked at my father long and hard before he walked toward a shelf. "I'll show you what I have, but the moment I smell mischief, I throw you out." Mr. Graves made his way toward the small display by the counter, looking back at me suspiciously.

I took my hands out of my pockets so he could see them and sat at a small bench near the window, watching with mild irritation as my father talked on with the gentleman. I wanted to be out of the shop with information sooner rather than later—he was stalling the progress

I had been making. I had a mind to walk over and resume my approach but decided to watch them instead. My father folded his arms and rested his fist beneath his chin as he listened intently to Mr. Graves.

His eyebrows lifted as if he was hearing something truly spectacular when Mr. Graves expounded on the ingredients and the effectiveness of his product. Mr. Graves then took a bottle off the small display table and handed it to my father. It was odd watching this man I had feared for so long as a child interacting in such a congenial way.

It was strange that he was here with us, laughing at Charles's and my jokes and helping in whatever way he could. Odder still was the fact that Charles had driven in a carriage with him from Wilton. I didn't honestly know who John Thomas was, having interacted with him so seldom in my childhood.

As I sat in the moment, observing him, I couldn't help but be grateful for this small display of my father's personality, despite the limited time we had to be back at the carriage with our information.

Mr. Graves led my father next to the shelf on the right side of the shop toward another remedy. My father repeated the process of listening and becoming engrossed in what the apothecary was describing until Mr. Graves's posture eventually became relaxed.

They went on this way for nearly a quarter hour, at which point my father's voice grew quiet. I could no longer hear what they were saying. Mr. Graves's expression slowly turned serious and sympathetic, looking over at me, knitting his eyebrows together, then nodding to my father.

By this time, my father carried three different remedies in his arms. He set them down on the counter near the back and reached in his pocket, taking out some coins, counting them out and placing them in Mr. Graves's palm. The man then turned and walked to the back of the shop. "And what do we have today?" I asked as my father approached me, three bottles in hand.

"Ah, yes." He looked at the remedies in his arms. "I have London's finest sleeping draught, a remedy for aches and pains," he lifted one of the bottles, "and this one is supposed to keep me from falling asleep during the day."

My mouth pulled up to one side. "Don't mix those two up." I

pointed at the sleeping draught, then the one to help him stay awake.

"That could certainly prove problematic," my father said with a grin. "I want Martha to try them. She has a hard time sleeping, which makes her tired during the day. And her joints and bones are giving her grief."

Mr. Graves reemerged, a small piece of parchment in hand. When he spoke, his voice was still gruff but no longer edged with suspicion.

"You could have just said you were investigating the death of the late Lord Elliot and that you believe he was poisoned." He handed me the small paper, an address scrawled across it. "I must warn you though, it isn't a place you want to visit. Rough-looking men stop by every few years giving me this address to hand off to clients looking for things I won't sell. I wouldn't want to cross them—and I don't scare easily."

"Why haven't you reported this to the Bow Street Runners, Mr. Graves?" I asked, grateful for his forthright information.

"Because I don't know who runs the operation. And I don't want a knife to the back if someone gets wind of the fact that it was me that squealed."

I nodded. "I understand. We hope to get to the bottom of this and expose all who are involved. Until then, we will keep your name out of it." I put my hand in my pocket and pulled out two pounds and five shillings, extending them to Mr. Graves.

"I'll not take your money for this, sir." He looked at the money with hungry eyes even as he said it; a true man of business.

"Then perhaps you'll take it in exchange for a sleeping draught," I said. The two pounds and five shillings were well over the price of the bottle, but I wanted to thank Mr. Graves somehow.

"I suppose I'll part ways with it for that amount," he deadpanned.

Charles

Lawrence and I walked down the lane toward our destination. Already, I was receiving looks from passersby. Some looked at me with concern while others glared with disgust.

"There's no point in carrying a cane as an old man if you don't use it," Lawrence muttered under his breath. "I suggest you play your part." I shook my head in irritation but obliged, limping with my left leg.

"Next time, *you* will dress as the old man," I muttered back.

"Very well, my lord." Lawrence was a master at hiding his grin. But I could tell he was enjoying every moment of my discomfort wearing this hideous disguise.

The buildings on this street weren't as glamorous as some of London's other shopping areas. But it was a clean, well-kept part of town. Though it was a petty thought that I'd never admit aloud, I hoped Robert Graves's shop would be run-down and nothing worth mentioning. It was clear to me that he was interested in Lily based on the dinner party last week.

Admittedly, my small bit of jealousy was unwarranted, for I was certain Lily had feelings for me. But I'd never felt the need to secure a lady's affections with some form of competition. I didn't love that Robert was an agreeable gentleman who got Lily to smile, while I had to just sit back and watch from an outside window.

The shops looked like replicas of each other, nothing standing out, as we passed them. Forest-green, tan, black—

An eye-catching royal blue, with lighter-blue railings met my view. I looked down once more at the address, and sure enough, it matched. The sign above gleamed brightly in gilt lettering. It read:

ROBERT'S REMEDIES

The paint looked sharp, freshly applied. There was a storefront window with perfectly cleaned glass and some gold filigree in the corners. Behind was a display of gleaming bottles of all colors and sizes. It was, to my dismay, a very fine looking establishment that stood out across the entire lane.

I assumed my character and limped through the storefront door with Lawrence. There was a clear, bright chime above us, announcing our entry. To my right and left were fine, warm-wood shelves with brass railings. On each shelf were different bottles, tinctures, and droppers. The room had a light floral scent that brought to mind lavender, rose, and cherry blossom. I also caught the aromas of orange and lemon, and an herbal scent in the background, like grass or lemon balm.

I recognized the sound of high laughter deeper into the shop. Several women surrounded an array of small bottles near the back, the congenial smile of Robert Graves meeting each of them. He looked up at Lawrence and me, giving us a welcome nod.

"Please look around," he said. "I'll be with you in just a moment." He turned back toward his female customers.

"I can't choose!" one of the ladies said, holding up two small bottles. "Which scent do you prefer, Mr. Graves?" She smiled at him coyly.

His smile and easy manner held each woman's attention. It was clear they found him handsome. This grated on me even more.

"Both are excellent choices. I wouldn't sell them unless I thought so, miss," he said with a grin.

"Yes, but which one would you prefer to smell on a lady?"

He held up one of the bottles and unstopped it, holding it out for her to smell. She smiled as she took in the aroma. "This one has a light floral scent with combinations of rose and lavender. It also has orange peel and vanilla extract. It's very pleasing, calling to mind spring and summer."

He picked up the other small bottle and unstopped it, wafting it below his nose. "This one is more rich." He handed it back to her and she held it beneath her nose, eyes widening in delight as she took in its fragrance. He smiled at her reaction. "This one has nutmeg and cinnamon, along with extracts of vanilla and cedarwood. It smells mysterious to me, reminding me of autumn and winter. Both are equally alluring in my mind."

She gave an undecided look at the two bottles, trying to figure out which one to choose. She finally let out a sigh of indecision. "I simply must have them both."

Robert Graves smiled then addressed the group of whispering, giggling ladies. "If you have finished collecting your items, I can help you back here." They slowly made their way to a back corner. Some of them held remedies; others held bottles of herbal scents. Money was exchanged, all while smiles were aimed at the handsome shopowner.

Lawrence and I slowly made our way deeper into the shop, making our presence more obvious. Robert's gaze turned from the women to us.

"Excuse me, ladies," he said, approaching us. I could practically feel the women's disappointment as he walked away from them. The one who had taken so long deciding gave Lawrence and me a pointed glare as if we had ruined her entire day. When she got a better look at me she reeled her head back in disgust and hurried toward the door with her party.

"Good afternoon, gentlemen. How can I—" Robert stopped talking when he got a good look at me. "Sir, are you alright? How long have you been suffering from a liver complaint?"

I hadn't seen my reflection since Lawrence changed my appearance. Apparently he'd gone overboard. I stared at Lawrence, hoping to convey my vexation. He couldn't quite hold back his grin this time before he spoke.

"I'm afraid he has been poisoned."

Robert's face snapped to Lawrence. "Poisoned?"

"Yes sir. I believe someone may be sneaking arsenic into his drink."

Robert walked quickly to a shelf and pulled a canister from it. "This is a powder containing turmeric and milk thistle. It's normally used to calm the stomach and help with aches and pains, but it can also help reverse the effects of liver poisoning."

Robert handed Lawrence the bottle.

I did my best to make my voice sound old and feeble. "I know some apothecaries use arsenic for medicinal purposes and for exterminating pests. Do you carry arsenic? We could pay you well for some."

Robert shook his head. "It is true that arsenic has many uses, some of them helpful. But my uncle taught me to use caution with what I supply in my shop. I will never offer arsenic or anything that can be used as poison."

Unfortunately Lily and Henry were right. Robert Graves appeared to be honorable and seemed to care about those who solicited his help.

"Do you know where we could find such products?" I asked. "I would like to find out who supplied the poison."

He shook his head again. "I don't. My uncle, owner of Graves Remedies, has told me to send any inquiries about such things to him so he can 'set them straight.' "

"I see," I said with a frail voice. "I must have misunderstood Jacob Hughes's meaning."

"Jacob Hughes?" He looked at me suspiciously. "You are the second person who has stated that he recommended my services. How are you connected with Mr. Hughes?"

"We had a business arrangement," I lied. "He swindled me and I believe he poisoned me shortly after to keep me quiet. Before he tricked me, however, he stated that you were the best apothecary in London and that I could find anything at Robert's Remedies. I assumed he bought his poison from you based on that comment. Clearly I was mistaken."

"Sir, do you have proof that it was Mr. Hughes who tried to poison you?" He sounded hopeful and truly concerned for my welfare.

"I don't." I leaned heavily on my cane. "But if you know any information that would help me put him where he belongs, I would be much obliged."

"Unfortunately I don't have much." Robert's face showed his disappointment. "I have been giving Jacob Hughes remedies for a foot condition that gives off a strong, foul odor. He asked me to keep it a secret, but under the circumstances I don't mind divulging this information. Aside from that, the only thing I can say is that I hope you can find a way to bring the truth to light. He is a despicable man.

"When I delivered his last order, he wanted me to bring it to an address that was not his usual place. It was a bulk order, and he stated he would be using my product at this other location. We arranged a time to meet, but I had unexpected business and arrived at the address a few hours later than our arranged time. When he opened the door, Jacob had nothing but his trousers about him.

"He was surprised to see me and asked if I could return at a different time. That's when I heard a female voice in the back room. At first I thought he was with a prostitute, but her speech was refined. She was clearly a lady of the upper class. I'm not exactly sure what Jacob is about, but whatever it is, it's no good."

"Do you still have the address?" I asked.

"I believe I wrote it down in my records with his last order. I can copy it for you."

He walked toward his counter near the back and pulled out some papers and a quill. He jotted down the address into the bottom corner of a piece of parchment then tore it away, fanning it for a moment before handing it to me.

"Thank you, Mr. Graves," I said, nodding my head. I reached into my pocket and paid him for the canister to help my 'plagued liver,' then handed him twelve shillings as gratitude for his help.

His face lit up. "Thank you, sir. I've had my eyes on a small gift for a lady, and this is exactly what I need to get it."

"And who is this lady?" I asked, afraid that I already knew the answer.

"Miss Lily Mason." Robert smiled as he said the name, as if he couldn't help himself.

My hand snatched the shillings back as fast as the words left his mouth. He looked at me with confusion.

"On second thought," I said, "honesty is its own reward, wouldn't you say?" I gave him a wink, then began to walk toward the door.

"Thank you for your help, Mr. Graves," I heard Lawrence say behind me. "And my friend is right, honesty is the best reward. Here's *fifteen* shillings for your honesty . . . and for that gift for Miss Mason." I could hear the smile in Lawrence's voice.

"Thank you, sir!"

I continued for the door, not caring to limp, rolling my eyes. Robert Graves could buy Lily a gift. Mine would be better.

We waited for Henry and John at the carriage for only a few minutes before they arrived. We had both been successful in obtaining information. When comparing addresses, we discovered they both resided in the same area of London. We decided to drive by the address Henry acquired first.

As we surveyed the street through the carriage window, near the docks in a run-down, hardened part of town, I found that the address I received from Robert Graves belonged to a dilapidated house directly next to the one that corresponded with the location Robert's uncle gave to Henry. It couldn't be a coincidence.

The two old, decaying houses were set back away from the street, near the water's edge, nearly identical in appearance. A narrow alleyway separated each structure, the buildings leaning into one another. They had been well acquainted with the elements: wood rotting and warped—jutting out at odd angles. I wondered how much longer the buildings would stay upright as they moaned and creaked. Whether the sound was from the docks or the houses themselves, it seemed the two buildings groaned in agony. It was a scene I'd have depicted in a haunting story to scare Henry when we were children.

A small window flickered with dim light in one of the buildings on the main floor. On the floor above, a darkened window, larger in size, loomed in the center. No doors could be seen from the street. They must have faced the docks and the river on the other side.

As the carriage slowly rolled past the houses, I spotted the same young man that had been watching Arthur Brown's shop the day I met with Molly Black; he was clearly keeping an eye on the street in front of the old houses. I quickly averted my eyes as he glanced at our passing coach.

"That's the same young man who was watching Mr. Brown's shop," I said under my breath to my companions. "And the house just next to it is the one Robert Graves found Jacob in. I believe this proves that Mr. Brown is being watched, followed, and possibly threatened by whoever runs this operation. If we can get Mr. Brown to confess the identity of the other man talking with Papa that night, I believe it will confirm Jacob as the murderer." The houses rolled out of view.

"Don't we have enough information at this point to prove it's Jacob?" my brother asked.

"Perhaps. But I would like to ensure he isn't working alone." I thought of Alexander Campbell and Matthew Johnson.

I scratched the itchy white beard attached to my chin. "Lawrence, John." I looked at each of them. "Will you visit Mr. Brown's shop tomorrow? I would like to ensure he meets us at the Woodwards' ball tomorrow evening in order to discuss details without him worrying about being watched at his shop. If he doesn't currently have plans to deliver goods there tomorrow, see to it that he does."

"Yes, my lord," Lawrence nodded.

"And Lawrence." I looked over at him with a flat stare. "I'm not sure what you're about, giving Robert Graves money to buy Lily a gift when I plan to propose first chance I get."

Lawrence looked at me. "Are you certain she wouldn't prefer Robert Graves, my lord? He's not nearly as ill tempered."

"Is this still about that blasted mustache, Lawrence?" I said in disbelief. "I told you I was sorry."

"No, actually, you didn't," Lawrence said with a pointed look.

I understood now. Lawrence was making me pay because I hadn't apologized.

"It was *implied*." I said each word with emphasis.

"But never stated. Even your father knew when to apologize." He averted his gaze to the window.

I hadn't seen Lawrence disappointed in me since I was a teenager; he was usually completely agreeable about everything. How irritating that I now felt guilty about it.

We were all silent. John appeared to be making himself as invisible as possible, scooting into his darkened corner, keeping his eyes glued to the window.

"I'm sorry I ruined my father's favorite mustache, Lawrence," I finally said. I did my best to hide my annoyance.

Lawrence lifted an eyebrow as if I was missing the point. I exhaled and tried again, this time trying to be sincere.

"I'm sorry that due to my actions, you no longer have something that you kept safe all these years. Something you remember my father by and that reminded you of fond times. It was an accident, and if I could change it I would." I let myself feel the words I spoke, even though I hated admitting them.

"Thank you, my lord," Lawrence said genuinely, then added with a smirk, "And next time, I will dress as the old man."

"And next time you won't give young gentlemen money to buy gifts for the woman I plan to marry?" I cocked a brow at Lawrence.

Henry smirked facetiously. "She returns to London tomorrow, Charles. I highly doubt she will run away with Mr. Graves upon arriving and marry him."

It was almost word for word what I had said to Henry about Jane and Mr. Ashby when I hadn't cleared up the truth before leaving to London. I looked over at Henry, annoyance etching its way back into my mood. He wanted an apology too?

"I'm not apologizing, Henry. I left Lily in the middle of a ride to come bring you the happy news, thinking you would still be home. Furthermore, I will not apologize for leaving Wilton in haste to get to the bottom of this." I gestured out the window toward the houses near the dock. "We must avenge Papa. Adding to that, it is the only way you and I can safely live at this point—the only way I can guarantee Lily's and Jane's safety as well. If you and I are not safe in London and it is common knowledge that the Mason sisters hold our hearts, it may put their lives in danger as well. I'm sorry if I didn't think about Mr. Ashby," I snapped. "I already had quite a few things on my mind."

"Now was that so hard?" Henry grinned.

I rolled my eyes. I wouldn't have noticed my "apology" if Henry hadn't pointed it out, as it was meant to be a retort. But I did have to admit that I was sorry that Henry had to wait, knowing what Jane thought of him.

Henry looked at me, sincerity marking his features. "Thank you for rushing off to tell me the good news. And I agree that we must put this to rest. We need to put Jacob and anyone else responsible for Papa's death behind bars before either of us can find peace." The coach was silent as Henry's words sank in. Eventually, a corner of his lips twitched up, holding back a smile of amusement. "And I'm truly sorry that age doesn't suit you, my friend." He broke, chuckling. "Truly, you look terrible."

John chortled in his corner of invisibility, finally breaking. I wasn't amused, though my flat smirk threatened to betray a smile.

The carriage pulled to a stop at an inn, the Blue Lion. It was growing dark and we were all tired and hungry. Lawrence suggested we enter the inn at different times so it didn't appear as though we were traveling together. We each waited a few minutes between each other's entry to the inn, before retrieving our own key. Supper was served on the main floor, and we sat at separate tables, keeping to ourselves as we finished a meat pie and some fruit.

One by one we retired to our bedrooms, waiting for Lawrence's knock.

Mine finally came.

I followed him at a distance, looking over my shoulder to verify no one was watching, then quickly slipped into his room, waiting until Henry and John made their way into the room at separate times.

"I suggest we formulate a plan for tomorrow morning so we don't waste any time," Lawrence said. We all nodded in agreement.

"But first, when do I get this itchy thing off my face?" Henry asked. I was wondering the same thing. There was no way I could sleep in it.

"We will take off our disguises tonight and reapply new ones tomorrow." Lawrence took out his box. "My lord, we will start with you."

I felt immense relief as Lawrence set to work at freeing my face of the itchy paste and fake hair.

I looked over at Henry. "I believe you and I should pay our bird friend a visit first thing tomorrow morning. I would like to find out what he knows and if he has any part in this. I would also like to make it very clear that he isn't to bother Lily anymore."

Henry nodded. "I believe it's also time to make the switch back to our true identities tomorrow evening when we attend the Woodwards' ball." His usual humor was replaced with a look of exhaustion—we were all ready for a good night's rest.

I nodded in agreement. "Let's find out as much as we can before then." I turned to John. "Once you and Lawrence have relayed the information to Arthur Brown tomorrow, will the two of you give all of the facts we have discovered to the Bow Street Runners?"

"Certainly," John said with a nod.

I took in a deep breath. "Let's hope Mr. Jones holds up his end of the bargain."

Lily

London
November 15, 1816
Late that night
Last full day of disguise

The carriage pulled up to the London house, the street dark. I prayed that the letter we sent to our aunt and uncle, informing them of our early return, had traveled ahead of us. We were back a day and a half earlier than we had originally planned.

We had been traveling all day without any breaks, and according to the stagecoach driver, it was nearly eleven o'clock. I was stiff and tired from being seated for so long. Jane and Alice seemed just as sore and exhausted as I was.

Alice stretched her neck and arms as we descended the carriage. "I doubt your letter traveled ahead," she said, yawning. "I'll see to it that everything is brought in and settled. You two get comfortable in your rooms and I'll be up shortly to help you change for bed."

34

RAZOR

Jane

London
November 16, 1816
The next morning

I woke when the sun peeked through my curtains, keeping my eyes shut, though I no longer dreamed. Charles's face was still perfectly in my mind, and I didn't want it to disappear.

Despite my newfound courage, I felt trepidation at what lay ahead, and I was filled with nerves from head to toe. But determination would surely see me through it. I would ask him all the questions I had looming in my mind. *How long had he known his intended? Was it an arrangement of love? Or one of title and wealth? Was it arranged by his father before he died?* I would tell him how I feel. I would tell him that I love him. I would voice my every thought and let him make his choice. Once he made his, I would make mine.

Charles's deceit still stung. Why would he convince me to forfeit my plans with Frederick when he had plans for someone else all along?

I couldn't think about it for too long, or I would never see this through.

A light knock sounded at my door, breaking the image of Charles that I was holding to.

I sighed. "Come in." Aunt Mary poked her head through the open door, a bright smile lighting up her face.

"I'm so glad you've returned early." She closed the door behind her and moved to the end of my bed, taking a seat. "Your uncle and I have been dreadfully bored without you and Lily. We haven't gone to a single social event since you left. Your uncle was very insistent that he have a break while you were away." She raised her brows, musing. "The last two nights, I have fallen asleep before midnight. I worry that if we don't immerse ourselves in some diversions immediately, I'll no longer have the ability to stay awake for London events. I'll become just like your uncle, sleeping anywhere I can rest my eyes." I had missed Aunt Mary, her persistent stream of words and gossip in tow.

I grinned. "And what diversions are there this evening, Aunt?"

"The Woodwards' ball is this evening. I anticipate Lord Fletcher will be attending." She smiled expectantly.

So much had happened in such a small amount of time. Aunt Mary assumed I was still aspiring to catch Frederick. She probably had no idea that Charles had even left London to visit Wilton, since she'd been cooped up since we left.

As if in answer to my thoughts she said, "I wonder why Lord Elliot hasn't been by to visit. I was hoping he would offer some form of distraction for your Uncle Francis and me while you and Lily were away."

"I believe he has been away from London this past week, Aunt." I didn't want her to think he was avoiding them.

Her eyes lit up. "Well, I hope he will be in attendance tonight at the ball, and that he will come visit us shortly."

My heart pounded as I considered the idea. Aunt Mary stood and walked toward the door.

"I'll see you downstairs for breakfast. It's good to have you back, Jane." She smiled once again then closed the door behind her.

Alice came upstairs to help me dress for the morning a few

minutes after Aunt Mary left.

"What would you like to wear this morning, miss?" she asked, opening the wardrobe. She pulled my white morning dress from the wardrobe. "Are you planning on staying at home for the remainder of the day to rest from your tiring journey yesterday?"

She knew me well. Normally this would be exactly what I would do.

"Actually, I would like to go for a walk after breakfast. I will wear my yellow dress."

Alice grinned. "You always look fetching in that dress. Hopefully you'll run into some handsome gentlemen while you're out."

I *did* hope to run into a very particular gentleman today. And I planned to look my best when I did.

As I waited for Alice in the parlor, so we could take a morning stroll, I heard the low hum of two men speaking in hushed voices near the front door. My heart suddenly picked up speed as I heard George's footsteps approach. I tried to steady my breathing, awaiting Charles.

George entered. "Miss Mason, a gentleman is here to see you and wishes to speak with you alone."

Despite my best efforts, my heart hammered faster and harder. It was now or never. I needed to be brave—I needed to ask my questions and hold nothing back.

I stood from my seat. "Thank you, George. You may show him in." My voice sounded stronger than I felt.

George dipped his head and walked out of the parlor as footsteps entered. I pictured Charles's eyes and smile as he walked through—but the eyes and smile of the man who walked in didn't belong to Charles. They belonged to a man who wore a flat, even expression.

"Lord Fletcher!" I said in surprise.

His next words sounded cold and bored as he spoke. "Are you truly surprised to see me?" He raised a questioning brow, piercing me. "I told you I wanted to see you the moment you returned from Wilton."

He walked closer to me, taking my hand. I felt nothing but emptiness as his fingers wrapped around mine. How could I have ever entertained thoughts of spending my life with this dull, dispassionate, cold man?

I swallowed. "Indeed, you did state your desire to see me upon my return from Wilton." I wasn't sure what else to say. My voice was quiet, lacking the confidence it had held moments before. "I'm only surprised by your visit since we weren't planning to return to London until tomorrow."

My mouth went dry and my heart pounded. I wasn't prepared for this conversation.

"And yet here you are," he said with an icy voice, lifting my chin slowly. "Looking more beautiful than ever." His tone held insinuation, as if he knew the exact reason for my extra care in appearance.

I was forced to look into his eyes until I stepped backwards, releasing his hand beneath my face. "You flatter me, Lord Fletcher." I hadn't intended to put a sting behind my words.

"I want to do more than flatter you, Jane." It was the first time he'd used my Christian name. His tone eluded that he felt betrayed. His cold stare said it all. He knew. Somehow he knew I was in love with Charles.

"I desire to make you my wife."

The words were a pit in my stomach. I didn't know what to say. I was out of time. He took my hand again and pulled something from his pocket. My heart was caught in my throat as he opened a small box, a ring inside. He removed the ring.

"If I could take you to the altar this very moment I would do it," he said quietly. "But I will settle for next week."

His words sent panic throughout my entire being. "Lord Fletcher, I have given you no answer."

"What answer is there to give?" He gave me a straight look. "You have led me to believe that you would embrace such an opportunity."

I felt sick. I knew he wouldn't take this easily, but he was making it even harder than I'd anticipated.

I looked up at Frederick. "There was a time when I welcomed such a proposal. But I don't love you. Nor do you love me." I took in a shaky breath. "And I need to love and be loved."

Frederick's mouth was taught, in a flat line. "You may not love me, Jane, but I have always loved you. You have no title or connections. I am the son of a duke. Our alliance would not benefit my family in any way. Why else would I want you to be my wife if not for the fact that I love you?"

His words surprised me, made me pause. He had been so plain about his views on love—that it was for silly people with no self-control. He had even told me that he'd never fallen in love. But as I watched him standing there, holding a ring, telling me he loved me, I wondered if perhaps he did. It would be so much easier if it were true.

I waited, trying to feel something—But it was no use. I knew what it felt like to be loved, to be adored and cherished. To be held in a man's arms and feel him breathe in relief knowing I'm close to him. To feel his very heart beat for mine and groan in agony when we parted.

Frederick did not love me.

He couldn't love me the way I needed to be loved even if he tried. And I could never love him. I could love only one man: The man I searched for even when I knew he wasn't there. The man who could pull a smile from my lips and a wish from my heart. The one with eyes that lured, lips that tormented, and words that pierced me to the core.

I held Frederick's gaze.

No, he could never love me, and I could never love him. He knew it the moment our eyes met, for he clenched a fist over the ring and threw it back into the box.

Guilt settled in. "I'm sorry, Lord Fletcher," I said remorsefully. I hoped he wouldn't be too angry. I'd heard he could have a temper, though I had never seen it aimed at me.

He looked into my eyes, coldness filling their depths. "It appears as though he has stolen something from me once again." He shoved his ring box inside his pocket then pulled me into his arms forcefully.

"Stop," I cried, pushing away from him. He didn't stop until his face was close to mine.

"When he leaves your heart to bleed," he whispered, "I'll be waiting." He kissed my cheek then released me, storming out.

Henry

This time *I* was the old man. I had been feeling rather left out—I couldn't let Charles and my father have all the fun. I insisted it was my turn, and Lawrence was all too happy to oblige.

Now, Charles and I stood in our disguises on the doorstep of a small apartment, meant for one gentleman alone to dwell, without any staff. I double checked the address then rapped loudly on the door. I could hear someone scurrying about on the other side, the sound of objects being moved quickly, most likely being tidied up.

I looked over at Charles. "Apparently he wasn't expecting us." I grinned, then hunched over on my cane.

Charles's mouth twitched up on one side. "I'm certain he'll be thrilled to see—"

The doorknob twisted, the door cracking open a pinch. A short figure with thin lips stood on the other end. He would have only been able to see me and my old, stooped, appearance from his vantage point. Charles was still hidden from his view.

"May I help you?" he asked, putting his nose up at my shabby attire.

"I have some questions, Mr. Johnson," I said with a feeble, wobbly voice. "And a little bird told me you were the man with the answers."

He looked at me condescendingly. "I'm busy at the moment." He dismissed me altogether, closing the door. I quickly slipped my foot inside, stopping it from shutting, then easily forced it open, straightening up until I towered over him. He stared up at me, confused.

"It can wait," I said with a deep, clear voice.

Matthew stepped back, his eyes finding Charles next, who suddenly emerged. Mr. Johnson masked his fear well, but I could see it all the same.

Charles shut the door behind us. "Isn't this cozy?" he said with a deep rumbling tone that lacked any sort of friendliness.

I looked around at the small apartment that housed a single room with a small kitchen, table, chair, fireplace, and bed. Figurines of birds made out of metal, wood, and even glass were displayed about the place. Watercolors of the winged creatures in mid-flight scattered the walls.

I walked over to a small glass bird sitting atop a wooden beam above the fireplace: A shrike.

"Tell me, Mr. Johnson, what kind of bird is this?" I held the bird near the burning fireplace, watching the light reflect off the polished surface.

He looked back and forth between Charles and me, looking less confident than before.

"What is it you want?" he finally said.

"You are a shrike." I examined the small glass bird once more before putting it back on the wooden beam. "Or so Lord Elliot has told us." I gave him an even stare.

His eyebrows creased upon hearing the name. "Lord Elliot? Are you here on his behalf?"

"Perhaps," Charles said, taking a few steps closer to Matthew. "Or perhaps we would simply like to understand why you enjoy sending dead birds in boxes to gentlemen you've only just met."

Matthew reeled his head back in horror.

"Indeed," I said, backing up Charles' statement. "Lord Elliot received a sparrowhawk, a bird that closely resembles a cuckoo, with a large spike through its chest, mere days after you likened him to a cuckoo and you to a shrike."

Matthew opened his mouth in anger. "How dare you accuse me of something so disgusting. I would never do such a thing!" He actually looked offended. "I am only ever kind to fowl species. I would certainly never injure one of my feathered friends nor desecrate its body in such a disgusting way."

Charles and I looked at one another, eyebrows raised. Of course he wasn't offended about being accused of sending such a message to a gentleman as much as he was about the fact that a bird had been harmed and marred.

I looked around Matthew's room once more and realized that he didn't actually have a single live or stuffed bird. Not even a feather about the place. Only figurines, pictures, and a few open books with images.

"Are you denying any knowledge of, or connection with this event?" I asked, lifting an eyebrow.

"Indeed I am!" Matthew said insistently.

"Then how will you explain your story to the Bow Street Runners when we show them the evidence, along with statements from two other witnesses besides Lord Elliot claiming that you made the comparisons between you and Lord Elliot and the scene that portrays such a description?" Charles asked.

We didn't really have evidence, since Charles had thrown the box in the fire in his anger, but it was the right question to ask. For the first time since we arrived, Matthew Johnson seemed to grasp the gravity of what this could mean for him.

"This has nothing to do with me," Matthew said, putting his hands in the air defensively. "It is possible that others may also think of Lord Elliot as a cuckoo." He said it as if this should be obvious to anyone. "Just the other day I was talking with Mr. Campbell about the similarities between Lord Elliot and a cuckoo, as well as the likeness between myself and a shrike. He found it to be quite clever and agreed that it was a perfect comparison."

Charles's and my eyes snapped back to Matthew at the mention of Mr. Campbell.

"Was Mr. Campbell the only one listening to your comparison?" I asked.

"Certainly not. A good number of Mr. Campbell's friends were in the circle as well, agreeing with my depictions," he emphasized.

"Could you name them?" Charles asked, pulling out a piece of parchment.

"I will list the faces I remember, though I'm sure I will forget some of them, as there were many." He squinted his eyes in thought. "There was Luke Blakely," he opened his fingers, counting them off. "Preston Stone, Collin Pembridge, Oliver Bradshaw, Jacob Hughes—"

"Jacob Hughes?" I said, interrupting him.

"Yes, and a few more gentlemen. Richard Barton, Timothy Caldwell, Lord—"

"That will do," Charles said, cutting him off. Charles and I gave each other another look of understanding. Matthew had not sent the dead bird, though it appeared he had planted the idea. It had been either Jacob Hughes or Alexander Campbell. Which meant that one or both of them knew about our disguises, if the message on the lid of the box had been any indicator.

"Do you mean to harm Lord Elliot?" Charles asked.

"You should ask if Lord Elliot means to harm *me*," Matthew sneered. "He is endeavoring to snatch my Golden Eagle from me."

Charles balled his fists, as though he was barely holding himself back from knocking Matthew to the ground.

Charles articulated his next words with a quiet chill that would have brought even the boldest of men to waver. "Let me make something *very* clear." He loomed over Matthew, giving him a dangerous glare. "Lily Mason has stated that she rejects your attention toward her."

Matthew swallowed.

Charles continued, "If you antagonize her again, I will make every effort to ensure you regret it."

Silence filled the small apartment. Matthew actually looked terrified.

"Well!" I said, clapping my hands together cheerfully. "It was certainly a pleasure." I bit down a grin as Matthew glared at me. I dipped my head in his direction before turning, opening the door, and exiting with Charles on my heels.

A few hours later Charles and I were inside the carriage, removing our disguises the way Lawrence had shown us. It was a relief removing the itchy wig, facial hair, and eyebrows. We put our accessories back in the box that Lawrence left behind, then I banged on the top of the carriage three times before it lurched forward.

The plan was to drop me by the London house, no longer under the guise of Charles, where I was to ready myself for the Woodwards' ball. I only had a few days' worth of stubble on my face, and my hair still looked exactly like Charles's, but it would have to do. We decided I would carry a pistol with me wherever I went in case I ran into any trouble, and that I would not drink anything the staff gave me.

Charles would take the carriage to Truefitt & Hill's barbershop, where he would resume his former look as Lord Elliot. He would then return to the London house and we would send the carriage to pick up Lawrence and John.

The carriage came to a stop in front of the London house. I stepped down and onto the cobblestone path, putting my right hand in my pocket on instinct. A coin rested inside that wasn't there moments before. I pulled tuppence out and looked back at Charles, his mouth curved up on one side.

"Welcome back, Henry Thomas," he said, pulling the carriage door to a close. Soon we would look nearly identical again, save for the few days' worth of stubble on my face. The carriage lurched forward, leaving me with nothing to do but walk inside.

Lawrence wasn't there to greet me, but a young man I recognized noticed my entrance. He was no more than seventeen, with dirty-blond hair and blue eyes. He looked surprised to see me then nodded his head in my direction.

"Good afternoon, Lord Elliot," he said. "We weren't expecting your arrival today."

"Mr. Thomas, actually," I said with a wink. "Lord Elliot will arrive shortly."

I didn't wait for a response. I found my way upstairs, walked into my room, and closed the door, locking it behind me. I passed the mirror above my wash basin and paused as I peered into the glass.

I examined the reflection looking back. The same dark-brown eyes stared back at me as usual, but I wasn't the old Henry Thomas, nor was I Lord Elliot. So much had changed. I rubbed my fingers against the scratchy surface of my chin, already missing the look and feel of a clean shave.

I looked to my right at a small desk and chair in the corner: the reason I had come up here. I opened the desk and pulled from it a piece of parchment, an inkwell, and a pen. I needed to make sense of my thoughts and plans, and put them to paper. I dipped my pen in the ink before writing my four new favorite characters . . .

Jane,

Jane

The old bouquet from Charles that sat on my dressing table was wilted by now—not the best of omens. I studied them as Lily went to work on my hair, insisting that she do it tonight. I didn't need to tell her my desire to look my very best. She understood perfectly without a single word being exchanged.

She placed a curl in one direction, tilted her head as she looked at my reflection, then put it somewhere else and repeated the process until she was satisfied. I slowly watched myself transform. She pinned the front pieces of my curls back then to the side in big, arching curves, followed by a single, fine ringlet to fall in front of my ear on the left side. The rest she styled with most of my ringlets pinned to the left side, draping over my shoulder.

She used the jeweled hairpins again, placing them throughout my auburn locks until they gleamed in the candlelight.

"And as the last finishing touch." She opened the small drawer in front of me. I knew what it held inside before she pulled it out. As she withdrew it from its place, the dark blue ribbon glistened in the candlelight.

She curled and weaved it through until the blue stream formed the same shapes as my hair. She looked at my complexion. Based on past experience, I knew she was contemplating whether or not to pinch the skin near my cheekbones for a blushed look.

"You don't need it tonight," she said. "Your cheeks are already rosy. You look absolutely perfect." She stood back and admired her work. "If Lord Elliot has any sense, he'll forfeit this arrangement with his 'intended.' "

I stared at my reflection, taking in a slow, steady breath. It was now or never.

Lily walked to my wardrobe and pulled it open. "Only one dress will do this evening." She pulled the deep-blue dress out and brought it to me.

I nodded in agreement—I needed to be bold tonight.

Lily

I walked out of Jane's room. She looked different this evening—not because of her hair or her deep-blue dress, or any physical description I could place, for that matter. She was wearing every piece of her heart out in the open to be taken or rejected, and she looked all the more beautiful for it. I took comfort in knowing that if Lord Elliot still went through with his plan to marry his intended, at least he would be tortured by her presence . . . how could he not be?

I entered my room and sat at my dressing table. Alice had already curled my hair, leaving the front pieces straight on my orders. Now I needed to arrange it in a way that would make Henry unable to resist me. I shoved away the knot forming in my stomach along with the whispering thoughts that I could never be with him.

I draped the front pieces of my hair so they loosely framed the front of my face, then carefully pinned them back. I gently pulled a few delicate curls forward until they fell near my temples. The rest of my curls I took one at a time, pinning them halfway up the strand at the back of my head, forming a voluminous halo of waving loops and curls. It was similar to other styles I had done in the past, but it was looser and held more volume, framing my face and eyes perfectly.

I heard my door open and watched Alice walk in.

"Are you ready for me, miss?" she asked.

I smiled. "Perfect timing. I was just about to call you in. Could you help me place these jewels in the back of my hair?"

She nodded, approaching. "You look especially lovely this evening, miss. I fancy the gentlemen will be lining up for a dance." She gently slid the crystalline pins into my halo of curls.

I only wanted one man to line up tonight. I didn't know what I would do if Henry didn't come. I couldn't think about it now.

"There," Alice said as she placed the last one. "I can't wait to hear all about the evening."

Alice helped me into my dark green dress then dismissed herself. I peered into the full-length mirror, pinched my cheeks, and bit down on my lips for good measure. This was my best.

All that was left now was nerves. Taking in a shaky breath, I reminded myself of the objective for the evening. In a few hours' time, I would lay it all out for Henry to take or leave. If he continued to hold secrets, I would walk away forever. One way or another, tonight would change everything.

Lawrence

No bell sounded as John and I entered the shop, Arthur & Co. The same rough-looking man that had been keeping a watch at the houses near the docks waited just outside the establishment, watching those who entered and left. John noticed him as well and glanced at me, raising an eyebrow of suspicion.

It seemed intentional that this shop carried no bell—removed for the sake of those spying, in case they needed to enter undetected. John and I walked to the counter and stood behind two older women. Besides the two ladies, we were the only ones present. Mr. Brown helped them with their purchases then greeted us.

"How can I help you gentlemen today?" he asked. I remembered the item Charles told me to ask for to give us privacy in the back room.

"I'm in search of a new penknife." I gave Mr. Brown a cordial smile.

I heard the shop door open and shut behind me, announcing the departure of the two women.

Arthur's eyes swept to the window, no doubt finding the young man keeping watch just outside the building. Mr. Brown waited a moment before he said, "Right this way." He extended his arm out, gesturing toward an archway on the far wall. He led us through to the back of his shop.

Once inside the back room, he pulled a box from one of the shelves and placed it on top of a small table just below. An assortment of penknives was stacked neatly side by side, displaying their unique patterns and designs.

"Mr. Brown," John said quietly. "We have come with information on behalf of Lord Elliot." He reached into his coat pocket and pulled out the small piece of parchment with the details of the meeting place for this evening.

"Put it away," Arthur quietly hissed. "He may come in at any moment, and they've been checking my pockets and mail as of the last week."

John quickly put it back inside his coat.

"Who is checking your pockets and mail?" I asked.

Mr. Brown squeezed his mouth shut. "I shouldn't have said as much."

I gave him a reassuring look. "We are already aware that your shop is being watched and that you are being tailed. Lord Elliot believes he can offer you and your family protection. We would like to meet you this evening at the Woodwards' ball at the northwest side near the servants' quarters to explain everything. There is a small gazebo tucked behind a large tree. Are you familiar with the area I'm describing?"

"I am, sir," he nodded, shifting anxiously.

"Be there at half past nine. Upon approaching the gazebo, you will say, 'Excuse me, I seem to be lost. Could you please point me in the right direction?' We will respond with the phrase, 'We are all a little lost.'"

Arthur looked nervous. "I haven't anything to deliver there this evening."

John gave Mr. Brown a grin. "Oh, but you will."

I nodded in agreement, pulling a bag of Charles's coins from my coat, allotted specifically for this purpose. "Indeed you will," I said with a smile.

John and I quickly chose a few items to be delivered in bulk to the Woodwards' estate this evening, then we each picked out a penknife. While we were paying Mr. Brown at the counter, the door quietly opened. I wanted to look back to see if it was the man watching the shop, but held my ground, continuing our business as usual. Mr. Brown kept his eyes on his task of counting out the money.

"Thank you for your purchase, gentlemen. I'll have the order delivered to the Woodwards' this evening as described. Is there anything else I can help you with?"

I recognized our cue to leave. "No, sir. That is all." I dipped my hat at Mr. Brown and turned to leave, John following suit.

The gruff-looking young man eyed us as we left.

Charles

I stood in front of Truefitt & Hill's barbershop window, rubbing my thick, short beard. I hated admitting it, but I was going to miss this look. Part of me worried about whether Lily would like how I looked if it came off. More than that, I wondered if she would still have interest in me as Lord Elliot.

Lily was unlike anyone I had ever met. She didn't care about wealth or position. How ironic that in all my years of meeting women in society, I feared they only ever saw me for my title and wealth—and now that I had found a woman I'd completely fallen in love with, who brought me back to life, I worried that she wouldn't have me *because* of my title and wealth. Not because she hated such things, but because she knew me as a man with neither—and more than money, she loved the heart of a person. And the heart she had been drawn to was mine as Henry Thomas. Would she still want me as Lord Elliot?

She loved purely and openly without holding back or hiding. I saw it in the way she interacted with her sister and brothers. I loved Lily's loyalty to her family and her Wilton origins, despite her newfound wealth. I loved Lily for her strength. She never backed down from anything, absolutely fearless. And she never stopped surprising me. She held my heart completely. I looked at my nearly transparent reflection in the glass window of the shop one last time, steeled myself, mourning the close of this adventure, and walked in.

"Good afternoon," a tall, slender man greeted me. "Are you here for a shave? Or a trim?"

"Both," I said, with a confidence I didn't feel.

"Very good, sir. If you'll follow me this way." He ushered me toward a tall, wooden chair with a bowed footrest placed in front. I'd intentionally chosen to come at a time that was less busy. Thankfully the shop was empty, a rare occurrence for a barber in London. I sat and made myself comfortable, leaning back as best I could in the rigid seat.

"What type of shave are you looking for today?" the man asked.

"A full shave."

"And for the hair?"

I showed him with my fingers how short I wanted it cut on the sides and the top.

He nodded then set to work, lathering soap on my chin, jaw, and upper lip. I hadn't fully shaved in ten weeks.

As he took the first swipe of his razor down my cheek, I took a deep breath and let it out. He wiped the instrument on a towel across his arm. With each smooth descent of the blade I felt the finality of becoming Lord Elliot once more. The weight of my role as earl crept in as each trail was meticulously carved by the barber until there was nothing left. A familiar hardness settled in my heart as I touched the smooth surface of my jaw and chin—an old friend returning to his place now that these weeks were over. Dread filled me as my fingers continued to graze across my cheeks.

How had my father done it? How had he kept a smile all those years while carrying this weight? How had he laughed so easily and found the magic in everything?

The barber put his razor down on the small table next to me and replaced it with some shears. I felt the scissors cut the first section of hair and watched as the dark strands fell in front of me.

Mama's beautiful, long dark hair came to memory at the sight, her rich-brown eyes and smile in tow—The warm embrace that always greeted me when she entered the room. *That* was how my father had borne the weight with a smile. He had Mama.

Lily's expressive green eyes flashed through my mind. Her animated smile, and her open heart. What if I wasn't the man she'd fallen in love with? What if she wanted me as Henry Thomas, not Charles Elliot?

Panic set my heart to race. Would Lily have me? Would I close my heart again?

The scissors came together once more, cutting away more of Henry. I shut my eyes and tried to calm myself. As I did so I was transported to the recesses of my mind, to a memory stored away, forgotten.

An angelic voice spoke. "Look at me, Charles."

I was staring at my hands, reflecting on the boredom I had felt the night before at the Barringtons' ball.

Mama's eyes were glossy as they looked at mine. I didn't know it at the time, but in a fortnight she would contract an illness that would take her life.

"I have missed you," she said, eyes welling with tears.

"I haven't been gone so long, Mama," I said. "I've been back a fortnight now, and Henry and I visited only three months ago."

She pressed her lips together, trying to hold back emotion. "You've been gone longer than three months," she said, a tear forming in the corner of her eye. "It's been almost two years since I've seen you pull a prank with Henry. You only smile when absolutely necessary, and then it's either marked with annoyance, or it's subdued."

She brushed a finger at her tear. "Anna Wells couldn't keep her eyes off you last night, and all you had in return for her was a cold stare."

"I know she couldn't keep her eyes off me," I said with annoyance. "She's a title seeker and only wants me for my wealth and station."

Mama shook her head. "She was besotted with you, but you hadn't the eyes or heart to see it."

"No one will ever see me as anything but a lord, an earl, wealth, station, class, a title."

"That's how *you* see yourself," she said. "I see my son, Charles, who used to tease and laugh. My boy who has grown into a tall, handsome young man, who has a heart that is ready to listen and be loved if he could only open it once more."

I shook my head. "I don't think I will ever see myself that way again, Mama."

Another tear escaped her eyes. "Open your heart, Charles. Open your eyes!" My eyes flew open as the barber combed sections of my hair in the back. I quickly brushed away the moisture collecting in the corners of my eyes as I recalled my mother's words, grateful that the man holding the scissors was behind me.

"Open your heart," she had said. Lily had opened my heart when I was Henry. Could I truly return to my old life and still stay the same as I had been the last two weeks?

The shears closed once more, severing another part of my life with them. But this time *I* decided what would fall away. I let my walls drop as the scissors made more hair tumble to the floor. I let my boredom leave me with the next cut. Irritability, evasiveness, no-nonsense, distrust; each left when the blades came together, relieving me of what I had let my life become as earl.

By the time he finished, I had rid myself of "Lord Elliot."

He led me to a mirror to inspect his work. I looked at my shaved jaw and chin, my old hairstyle back in place. I was no longer Henry Thomas or the lord, the earl. I was no longer wealth, station, class, or title.

I was the son of James and Elizabeth, who could tease and laugh. I was the boy who had grown into a man, tall and handsome with a heart ready to listen and love. I was Charles Elliot, and my eyes and heart were open.

I looked in the mirror again, nodding my head to the barber. It was done exactly as I had requested. Henry and I looked the same again.

I paid the barber for his services, adding a generous amount of extra coin for his skill, then pulled the door open, stepping out into the cool air.

I wasn't looking forward to the Woodwards' ball this evening. It would be my first in the last two weeks without Lily. It would be my first as Charles Elliot. I would have to endure the ladies and their schemes. I would have to smile like Henry did, and wish all the while that I could have even a glimpse of Lily.

But despite my dread at entering society once more, I felt a sense of determination to see my father's murderer behind bars once and for all. Tonight would be pivotal—I could feel it.

Clouds loomed above, casting a gray hue overhead. I rubbed my smooth chin again, realizing how much colder my face felt without the covering of hair.

Instinctively, I reached into my coat pocket and pulled out a slightly warped metal ring. I held it between my fingers and grinned as I remembered Lily's obstinance that first night we met. I let out a slow breath, remembering the kiss we shared just the other day.

I put the ring back inside its holding place. As soon as Lily returned, I would propose . . . and then I would let my beard grow out again.

35

GAZEBO

Henry

London
November 16, 1816
Later that evening

Charles sat across from me in the library with the door closed so we could speak privately. He looked different again—He looked like me.

I was envious of Charles's smooth jaw and chin. It felt suffocating going back to this old life of mine—a life I had left only two weeks previous, before Jane.

She would be traveling back to London by now. They would return sometime tomorrow, and I would be waiting when she arrived. I would make it up to her somehow. Even if Mr. Ashby made his move and she turned her sights to him, or if she decided to go back to Frederick, I would find a way to win her back. I had to.

"Are you sure you don't want to be Lord Elliot for just one more night?" Charles asked with a smirk, interrupting my thoughts. "I don't know if I'm ready for society just yet."

I chuckled. "And miss out on the rare opportunity to watch you smile and pretend to be my version of Lord Elliot for an entire evening? It's my turn to have a break from the title seekers and gossips." The truth was, I couldn't stand the thought of being at a ball without Jane. It would be torture to dance with other ladies without her presence. I would far rather observe from the window for once.

"Fine. But you can't let Jacob or Mr. Campbell out of your sight," Charles warned. "If they are inside, I will find a way to speak with them. If they are outside, that is your territory."

"I wouldn't have it any other way," I smiled, remembering how good it felt to knock Jacob to the ground at the Morgans' ball.

Footsteps sounded before Lawrence and my father opened the library door.

"Finally!" I said, clapping my hands together.

"Is everything in order with Mr. Brown and the Bow Street Runners?" Charles asked, turning to Lawrence.

"Indeed, my lord." Lawrence said, dipping his head. "Arthur Brown will be at the meeting place tonight at half past nine to meet John and me. I am prepared to recite the words you and I went over last night, but I do believe it would mean more coming from you, my lord."

"If everything goes according to plan, I will be there at the arranged time." Charles checked his pocket watch, then added, "It appears as though we are almost out of time now. Only five minutes remain before we must leave.

I turned to my father. "What did the Bow Street Runners say?"

"They said Mr. Jones dropped by earlier today with a few reports that had been falsified. When we gave them our information they stated that an investigation would be started immediately. They are concerned for your safety, Lord Elliot." My father nodded to Charles, then looked back at me and added, "As well as yours, Henry. They recommend you retire from London for a few days until they can get to the bottom of everything."

Charles's lips formed a line of stubbornness. "I intend to have everything buttoned up tonight. Lily returns to London tomorrow and

I have every intention of proposing when she arrives." I wholeheartedly agreed with my brother's plan.

My father breathed in slowly then exhaled. "Then it appears we have a busy night ahead of us."

I nodded. "Indeed we do. But if we can resolve everything by the end of tonight it will be worth it. We can finally put these events to rest."

"Well said, sir." Lawrence stared at the ground, almost reverential. It dawned on me just how hard all of this must have been for Lawrence: Losing his best friend—knowing Papa would still be here if it weren't for the act of murder. Lawrence cleared his throat. "If the plan tonight is to leave no stone unturned, I suggest John and I bring each of your dueling swords tonight to the ball in case either of you run into any trouble."

Thank goodness we had Lawrence to think of everything.

Charles

The four of us left the confines of the carriage when we arrived at the Woodwards' estate.

"Good luck," Henry said to Lawrence and John.

"Be on your guard," John cautioned, looking between Henry and me.

Lawrence looked resolute. "Let's find out what Jacob Hughes and Alexander Campbell have been up to and get the information we need from Mr. Brown. By this time tomorrow, we should have enough evidence for a trial. Hopefully enough that the murderer can be detained in jail until the assizes commence next month. At the very least it should keep you from harm, my lord, since it would certainly seal the killer's fate if you suddenly died."

It still didn't solve the dilemma of keeping those I loved safe, but it would have to do for now. I could always marry Lily quickly, if she would have me, and leave the country until the trial was over. I would bring Henry and Jane with me to ensure their safety as well. For now, we needed to complete the puzzle in order to start the trial.

Henry nodded. "We'll meet you and Mr. Brown when we are finished interrogating Jacob and Mr. Campbell."

"Do you have your pocket watch for the time?" Lawrence asked Henry.

I grinned as Henry looked down to find his pocket watch missing. I pulled it out of my own pocket and began twirling it the way he had the first night of our disguise.

Henry shook his head at my mischief then pulled my own pocket watch from his jacket.

I smirked. "Touché. Let's see if we can work our magic this evening to uncover the truth."

John and Lawrence excused themselves before circling around back, heading to Mr. Brown's meeting place.

Henry pulled his hand out of his right coat pocket, revealing tuppence. His eyes studied the coin I had snuck in his pocket minutes earlier. "For Papa," he said, rubbing his thumb over it.

I reached into my own pocket, finding a similar coin.

"For Papa," I agreed.

I headed for the main entrance once we parted ways, while Henry skirted the edges of the estate from the outside.

Lawrence

John and I waited in silence beneath the gazebo as we listened for Arthur Brown's footsteps, dueling swords at our hips in case we needed them.

"Do you think he will come?" John whispered.

I held up a finger for him to be quiet. I didn't want to answer his question. Mr. Brown simply *had* to come in order for this to work, and

I would accept nothing less. John's impatience was grating at my own insecurities about this plan. I wasn't used to being around someone my age who voiced all my fears out loud. It made it harder to be the ever calm butler.

John shuffled quietly. "Is it possible he isn't aware of the exact location and is lost?"

"No," I said simply. "Arthur Brown is familiar with these estates; he makes large deliveries on a regular basis. I told him to meet us on the northwest side near the servants' quarters, inside the small gazebo tucked behind a large tree. There is no other location that would meet that description. If he doesn't come, it's for another reason. We must wait and be patient."

John raised his pocket watch near a small lantern in his hand. "He's a quarter of an hour late."

I sighed and whispered back, "And we will wait until the night is over or until Charles and Henry come for us."

As if on cue, quiet footsteps sounded behind the large tree. John must have heard it too, for his lantern suddenly went dark and he became still as a statue. I held my breath, waiting for a silhouette to emerge from beyond the trunk.

Eventually a portly frame poked around the tree. "Excuse me, I seem to be lost. Could you please point me in the right direction?" Mr. Brown's voice came out in a whisper.

I relaxed slightly. "We are all a little lost."

Arthur let out a breath and looked behind him before he came to meet us.

"Thank you for meeting us here, Mr. Brown," I said in a calming voice. "Lord Elliot is detained currently, but we hope he will be here shortly."

Arthur stood motionless. "I can't stay away too long."

"I understand," I said. "Lord Elliot has tasked me with relaying this information in the event he couldn't make it personally. He wishes to offer you and your family protection until we have successfully solved the case of the late Lord Elliot's murder. He has offered his estate in Wilton for your family to stay in until that time. We will shut the shop down for a short time, using the guise that you are traveling with your wife and children. We will spread mixed rumors about your whereabouts, each leading to nowhere. We can leave tonight if you wish."

Mr. Brown breathed out a shaky breath. I couldn't tell if it was in relief, fear, or a combination of both.

"That is very generous of Lord Elliot." His voice cracked, overcome by emotion. "But I can't go through with it. My house is being watched. There is no way we would get my family out safely. My wife and children have no idea of any of this."

"Who is doing this to you, Mr. Brown? Who killed James Elliot?" My voice held authority, the way Charles's often did.

"I can't. I've already said too much. If the murderer is discovered, the men who watch my house and shop will kill my family."

I shook my head. "Then why did you write to Lord Elliot and give him information in the first place?"

"Only *my* life was being threatened at that time. I hoped Lord Elliot could solve it on his own somehow with a small nudge and help me out of my own bind. But after Lord Elliot entered my shop the next day, I was watched even closer. My mail was opened before I received it. A man came into my shop when I was alone and threatened my family if the killer was discovered. They make sure I won't forget.

"The men watching my shop have started coming inside, asking my customers questions about their business with me. One of these men talked with my youngest son, who is only ten, in the street, only to catch my eye with a menacing grin, his hand on the hilt of a knife at his hip all the while. I've already risked too much. I can't risk more."

"Mr. Brown, I have contacts here in London that have already observed the men watching your house. My friends are confident they can overpower them. We could have a carriage ready to take your family straight to Wilton, and you could breathe easily in as little as twenty-four hours knowing your family is safe. We wouldn't write or send any letters to you directly, so nothing could be traced back to you. We would come back to Wilton once everything is secure. And if we still felt you weren't safe, we would send you to John Thomas's house."

I gestured to John, hoping he wouldn't berate me for volunteering his home without his consent.

John nodded his head before speaking. "Mr. Brown, I know it is a risk. But you are living the same risk every day by staying in London, doing nothing. Do you honestly believe these men won't eventually tire of watching your family? What will happen when they receive new orders? Do you think they will just leave you alone when that time comes? After you've seen their faces and know their identities? You know as well as I do that they will dispose of any possible evidence." He looked at Mr. Brown long and hard, then continued with more urgency. "You have a hard choice to make, Mr. Brown. But your family will not be safe in London regardless of how you slice it. If you want to act, it must be tonight."

Silence filled the air as clouds rolled over the moonlit sky, dimming the small amount of light we had.

Arthur paced back and forth, his breath quickening. We waited patiently for him to come to a decision. His legs finally stopped moving.

He inhaled deeply. "I'll go through with it."

"You are wise and brave, sir," John said.

I nodded in agreement with John's assessment. And now it was time for the name we needed in order to close this mystery for good.

My view fell to Mr. Brown in the darkness. "Now sir, who killed James Elliot?"

Charles

Upon entering the ballroom, I was already irritable as a group of ladies smiled demurely at me, fanning themselves. I inwardly rolled my eyes but remembered to put a congenial look on my face, as Henry had done, while acting the part of *Lord Elliot*.

I put a charming smile on my face and dipped my head in their direction, reminding myself to shoot Henry later for putting me in this predicament. They gave each other excited glances as I did so.

I walked away as quickly as I could politely manage, eyes darting between guests, seeking out Jacob and Mr. Campbell. The sooner I got this over with, the sooner I could leave.

As I examined the room, Frederick's familiar flat expression found mine. For once he held a look other than sheer boredom. He looked angry. I was absolutely delighted about it. I dipped my head in his direction, knowing it would irritate him further, before I continued scanning the room.

I saw Mr. Campbell first. He wasn't hard to miss in his vibrant green suit, a gold and purple striped vest beneath. I shook my head at his ridiculous attire, remembering Lily's story of his arrogance. It would be a miracle if I could interrogate him without punching his face, which appeared to be held in place by his large cravat. He was talking with someone, but my view was blocked by another gentleman. I walked a few more paces until I had a clear view. Mr. Campbell was speaking with Jacob. They were speaking quietly by the looks of it, watching the room shiftily as people passed by.

My luck couldn't have been better. I weaved a path along the wall toward them, keeping my eyes on their faces. Not watching my surroundings, I bumped into a gentleman.

"I beg your pardon," I said as I turned to acknowledge my fault. He had already moved along, giving me a clear view to the opposite side of the ballroom. I stopped in my tracks.

Dark hair glimmered on the other side of the dance floor. A silky, dark-green dress the same color as her eyes gleamed as she moved in place, looking about the room. I couldn't look away from her. Lily was always stunning—tonight she was a temptress. Her keen eyes were searching the guests with determination as she pursed her lips in frustration. I spotted Mr. Graves a short distance away admiring her visage. I looked back at the two men speaking. I would certainly interrogate Jacob and Alexander . . . the moment I was done speaking to Lily. I immediately changed course and weaved my way through the crowd of men and women toward her.

Lily

Henry was nowhere to be seen. I knew it was too early to despair, but I began to panic, constantly attempting to push off the thought that I might never see him again. Jane and Aunt Mary were across the room visiting with Marianne Morgan while I stood by Uncle Francis who was engaged for once in a conversation with some gentlemen.

As my eyes found Jane across the room, I found that she wasn't paying attention to the conversation in front of her. Instead, her eyes were locked onto someone moving across the floor. My eyes followed her line of sight until they found Lord Elliot. He was making his way toward me. Our eyes made contact briefly before I looked away. He looked different somehow, but I couldn't put my finger on it exactly.

Good, I thought. *I can confront him now about Jane.* I continued searching the room for Henry until Lord Elliot was right in front of me. I didn't look at him directly. I was too angry with him to acknowledge his presence fully.

I looked at his cravat when I spoke. "A word, Lord Elliot." My voice didn't hold warmth or friendliness.

I saw him smirk out of the corner of my eye but I still didn't look at him. Couples began making their way to the dance floor. He was silent but put his arm out for me to take.

Fine, I thought, irritated but determined. I would interrogate him while we danced.

Henry

It took almost ten minutes to find the ideal window to peer through to watch the guests. As I looked through the glass, Alexander Campbell, now sporting a ridiculous bright-green outfit, was the first person I spotted. Jacob Hughes was next to him. They stood close together near the far wall, speaking so their mouths barely moved. Their eyes watched the guests carefully, as if they couldn't afford to let anyone overhear their words.

My eyes searched for Charles next. A dance was in full swing.

"Lord Elliot?" a voice purred behind me.

"What ever are you doing?" another woman said in an overly sweet tone.

As I turned around, the eager faces of three women greeted me: Miss Elwell, Miss Barton, and an older woman I could only assume was Miss Barton's mother.

I wasn't about to waste time and explain that I was Henry Thomas. I played along for the time being. Besides, it would give me something to laugh at when they walked in the ballroom and met the real Lord Elliot inside.

They looked at me expectantly.

"I am simply observing these splendid windowpanes," I said with a smile. "I find them fascinating." They were very ordinary. "Miss Elwell, don't you find them absolutely delightful?"

"I've always found glass exquisite, regardless of what form it takes," she said silkily.

"Oh, me too!" Miss Barton cooed. It was hard to keep a straight face when she looked at me longingly, as if we shared a special bond due to our similar taste in glass. Charles was going to detest these two title seekers. It made me grin just thinking about it. As amusing as this thought and conversation was, I needed to get back to my post in case

Charles needed me. I would most likely have to find a new window now or break our plans and just go inside the ballroom and help Charles from there. I was sick of wasting time.

I dipped my head in their direction. "If you ladies will excuse me, I must return to the merriment." I took a step to leave but Amelia stepped in front of me.

"I hope we will see you inside, Lord Elliot. It will be positively dull without you." She fluttered her lashes and looked up at me coyly. She wanted me to ask her for a dance and it was the fastest method for her to leave me alone.

"Certainly, Miss Elwell. You and Miss Barton must save a dance for me." Their faces lit up and Amelia swayed to the side, allowing me to pass. Once they could no longer see me, I shook my head in annoyance. My feet took each step a little faster than the last, bringing me closer to the entrance of the Woodwards' estate. I felt an itching sensation to run, as if I was missing something. I knew it was most likely nerves from trying to finish everything up this evening, but my pace continued to pick up nonetheless.

Lily

Lord Elliot and I lined up across from each other, but I still didn't meet his eyes. Instead, I continued searching the room for Henry. If he didn't come by the end of the hour I would beg Uncle Francis to take me out to the gardens to see if he was outside.

The music began and we bowed. When we came together, my breath caught and my eyes flashed to Lord Elliot's for a split second as he pulled me in closer than usual. I quickly looked away. The earl had never looked at me in that way or danced with me like this.

"Lord Elliot," I began, putting more distance between us. "You told me you are acquainted with Henry Thomas. I'm tired of these games.

He said he would tell me his identity in Wilton, but he left abruptly. Where is he?"

He didn't answer. I still didn't meet his gaze but not for the same reason as before. The look he had given me moments before felt intimate—I didn't want to see it again.

After more silence, I rallied my courage. "I want to know what your intentions are toward Jane. Is it true you are engaged?" My voice was accusatory.

Our hands fell away and I circled around another gentleman before I came back to him, still avoiding his eyes. I could tell he was watching me all the while. This time when we came together, he pulled me even closer.

My breath hitched in surprise and my eyes flew to his. "Lord Elliot, I don't know what you—"

"Not Lord Elliot," he said, finally speaking to me.

I gasped as his voice echoed inside me. His eyes held mine. They were Henry's eyes.

"Henry?" I asked, my heart pulsing as he looked at me with intensity. The room fell away and my only thought was of him.

He grinned, shaking his head. "Not Henry." His arm slowly tightened around my waist as if he couldn't help himself.

I was silent as I studied him. "Charles," I finally said. My voice came out quiet as I spoke his real name.

He breathed in as if he had been waiting an age to hear it. His eyes showed his relief.

How could I have never considered this? I had known from the first time I saw Henry and Lord Elliot in the shop that they looked alike—but I had never realized how identical they were until this moment. I thought Henry was simply working undercover for Lord Elliot. In my wildest dreams, I would have never thought they'd traded places.

"Lily," he said quietly, a mischievous glint in his eye. "Was your goal to drive me mad tonight?" His eyes dropped to my lips. "Your intent is either madness or torture."

Our kiss from the other day flashed through my mind. My heart sped up as his eyes returned to mine with hunger. His fingers trailed my wrist before we separated again. This time my eyes followed his until we came back together.

"My only intent was to draw you out of your hiding place." I looked at his clean shaven jaw, hair shorter than before. "But it appears you were hiding in plain sight," I said with a smirk.

"Are you disappointed?" he asked, holding me close as he swept me through the steps. I wanted to take him away to the garden outside, to ask all of my questions. I wanted him to whisper in my ear that he loved me—to kiss me again. My eyes found his lips. I remembered his question. *Was I disappointed?*

"I'm only surprised . . . Charles." I said his name, trying it out again. The intimate nature of saying Lord Elliot's Christian name sounded foreign to my ears.

My eyes returned to his. I could feel that he was barely holding himself back from pulling me into him even further.

He released me again as the dance required it, my heart pounding stronger with each step. The look in his eyes changed further with each pace we took away from each other until it appeared as though something inside of him snapped. As we came together again, he didn't hold back. He drew me to him.

"Lily," he said near my ear as if he was truly in torment. He held me close with one arm while his other hand held mine. Something small and shiny glinted between his finger and thumb. I caught sight of my ring just as he slowly pulled my left hand to his lips, placing a tender kiss on top. My breath sped up as he slowly move my fingers toward the ring until he slid it onto my ring finger. As I looked at my ring on my left hand, my heart exploded at the implication and intimate gesture.

His hand gently slid beneath my chin, coaxing me to look into his eyes. They consumed mine with an unyielding trance.

"Lily," he breathed. "I love you to the point of madness. I cannot bear the thought of being parted from you again." His eyes went back and forth between mine. "Please say you'll have me."

His thumb lightly traced the corner of my mouth, the way he had done before, eyes burning with intensity before they looked down at my lips.

Charles bent down to close the distance.

My eyes closed, no other thoughts besides Henry . . . Charles.

Jane! My eyes flew open and I gasped just as Charles was about to kiss me.

"What is it?" he asked with concern.

"Jane! She has no idea." Realization entered Charles's features. How could I have gotten so carried away? My head flew to where I had seen Jane last. We had an audience. Every eye in the room was on us, including Jane's.

She shook her head as our eyes met, wearing a haunted, betrayed expression. My heart plummeted as I realized what she was thinking.

Her chest rose and fell rapidly. She looked as though she might collapse where she stood.

Then she turned and ran out of the ballroom toward the gardens.

Jane

My feet were unstable as I staggered through the crowd, pushing through the high-browed faces looking down on me. I couldn't breathe. I needed to escape, leave this place forever. I understood now. Lord Elliot was intended for another woman— my sister. How could she betray me so deeply? Her secrecy of the past two weeks suddenly made sense. But how could she encourage me to pursue Lord Elliot? There was no reason to any of it.

I pushed through the doors leading out to the garden then continued to flee as far away from the ballroom as possible. My heart tore as the image of Charles holding Lily flashed through my mind. I heaved in pain as I replayed him placing the ring on her finger and pulling her face close to kiss her. My thoughts screamed in my head, urging me to wake up from this terrible nightmare, but it was no use.

It was worse than a nightmare. It was my entire world upended—my heart torn and bleeding by the two people I loved most, without the balm of ever waking up.

Lily

As Jane fled from the dance floor, the ceiling seemed to come crashing down. I saw the pain, the betrayal on her face. Charles still walked me through the dance steps.

I couldn't speak for a moment as I stared after her. My thoughts finally snapped into place. "Charles! Where is Henry?" I asked frantically.

Jane was already out of the ballroom, and I watched as Mr. Hughes slipped out after her.

"Not Mr. Hughes!" I cried, remembering how he had already tried to take advantage of her. Panic filled every fiber of my being, and I pulled away from Charles's arms, though he didn't let me go completely. "Mr. Hughes is going after Jane. You need to find Henry now!"

Charles's eyes finally flicked to the door, concern for Jane entering his features.

"Stay here." He kissed my cheek and fled the dance floor to find Henry. I took no care for the roomful of eyes staring at me in mortification before I parted the throng of men and women and ran after Jane.

36

CARRIAGE

Henry

When I finally entered the ballroom, people were whispering to one another. Looks of astonishment and mortification circled each woman's face, and several were covering their mouths. Every single person in the room was staring at the back wall that led to the garden as if something monumental had just occurred.

A lady eventually saw me and put her nose up. She whispered to another woman next to her and they both stared at me in abhorrence. Slowly more heads turned toward me with similar expressions. One lady I had danced with at one point looked at me, tears in her eyes, giving the impression that I had broken her heart.

I looked around for Charles. He was nowhere to be seen. Jacob and Mr. Campbell were gone as well.

I stepped through the crowd full of appalled men and women, hearing snippets of their whispers. "He practically kissed Miss Lily on the dance floor. Did you really not see?"

Another girl I had called on at one point cried on her father's shoulder. "I fancied myself in love with him, Papa," she said. I made the mistake of making eye contact with her father as I passed by. His face contorted in a look of rage when our eyes met. If his look was any indicator, he might possibly shoot me on the spot.

What had Charles done?

Jane

I ran through the garden without a thought of where I was going, weaving myself in as far as I could so no one would find me.

"Jane!" I heard Lily's voice piercing the air. She sounded frantic. I turned in the opposite direction of her voice, tears streaming down my cheeks. My name echoed again in the darkness.

I would leave London immediately and head straight for Wilton. I would walk to Aunt Mary and Uncle Francis's house then take the stagecoach home before Lily arrived. I would beg Alice to come with me. I could never face Charles or Lily again.

"Jane, please!"

I heard Lily's voice grow farther away.

I would ask William Ashby to have me, or even Frederick. Perhaps Mr. Ashby would take me as I was, knowing I was in love with Lord Elliot. Maybe I could turn my heart slowly and love Mr. Ashby someday. Or perhaps Frederick would take me abroad, and I could go years without seeing Lily and Charles.

I turned in the direction that would lead me up the side of the house and toward the front when I heard footsteps behind me. I turned quickly, preparing myself for what I would say if Lily or Charles tried to stop me.

"Leave me be!" I cried before a figure emerged out of the shadows.

"Fancy meeting you here." Mr. Hughes's smug face appeared in the darkness. For once in his life he didn't seem to be drunk, though he was panting. Realization dawned: He had followed me out of the ballroom.

He walked toward me, a fierce look crossing his features. I knew exactly what he intended to do. He was going to have his way with me once and for all—not only because he was a shameless rake, but because he wanted to make me pay for wounding his pride at our last meeting. Though Mr. Hughes was not considered a strong man compared to other gentlemen, he was certainly stronger than I was. I knew from experience that there was no escaping him once he had a hold of me.

I prayed that I could outrun his pursuit as I turned and darted away from him. I sped toward the front of the house as fast as I could. If I could get close enough to the entrance, I could call for help. Perhaps someone would defend me.

I was close to breaking around the corner of the house, but it was no use. I heard his movements before I felt his hands close around my arm. I screamed as loud as I could but he quickly clapped a hand over my mouth, holding me tight from behind.

"One more scream from you and I'll not hesitate to render you unconscious," he hissed in my ear, pulling me closer. He turned me around to face him, his eyes taunting me to push the limits. He dropped the hand covering my mouth, gripping me tight to him so I couldn't flee. He brought his face close. I cried quietly in desperation as I leaned my head away from him.

"There will be time for that later," he said with a twisted smile. "For now, I'll behave if you do. If you make a public scene, so will I. And if I make a public scene," he looked at my lips, "there will be no question about your reputation when I'm done."

I swallowed in disgust as his eyes wandered over me suggestively.

My options had me pinned against a wall either way. If I went with him, he was sure to take advantage of me without anyone around to help. If I yelled for help, he would ruin my reputation with an audience. I needed more time to think; more time meant I needed to cooperate for now. Perhaps I could somehow outsmart him.

"Come on." He jerked me away from the house. I didn't struggle enough for him to lash out, but I didn't come easily either. I pushed back just enough to slow our pace as much as I could, legs shaking, afraid of what awaited me as we got farther from the house.

"Stop stalling." He yanked me hard, putting me off balance. I tripped over my own feet, taking a tumble to the ground. He grabbed me angrily and pulled me back up, gripping me painfully.

I didn't struggle against him anymore. I walked at a medium pace, without resisting. His firm hold on my wrist didn't ease up as we made our way to a large tree, far from prying eyes. A carriage waited below, two horses tied up to a thick branch.

Mr. Hughes pulled the door open. "Get in."

My heart pounded in fear. I looked at him with pleading eyes.

"Please, Mr. Hughes. I can give you money if you'll leave me be." It was all I could offer him.

"It's tempting," he said sarcastically. "But not tempting enough." He stepped toward me. Seeing no other choice but to climb in, I reluctantly stepped in the carriage. He shut the door once I was inside and walked toward the horses. I couldn't believe my luck—perhaps I'd be able to sneak out while he readied the carriage. I grabbed for the handle of the door but my hand fell through the place it should have been. I looked closely. The handles had been broken off from within the coach. My heart sank as I realized I was locked inside. Only someone from the outside could free me now.

A stab of pain pierced my heart when I remembered the last time I had been saved from Mr. Hughes. I then relived the night in Wilton when Charles had kissed me and made me believe he loved me. The way he held me close as if I was everything in the world to him. How could he look at me like that and look at Lily the same way? Why didn't she tell me? I wrapped my arms around myself as my heart ached, and screamed, and wished it had never discovered Charles Elliot.

Lily

Darkness surrounded me as I darted into the chilled night air after my sister.

"Jane!" I yelled as my feet fell quickly upon the stone walkways of the garden. I looked left, then right as I ran through the tall shrubs. "Jane!"

Tears filled my eyes as the look on her face kept running through my mind. "Jane, please!"

I weaved deeper through the garden before I stopped in place, listening and watching for movement or any sign of Jane. The clouds rolled slowly in front of the moon that had lent a small semblance of light, making it even harder to see.

I started as I heard distant footsteps to my left. I walked further down the path of tall shrubs then turned the corner and hurried toward the sound.

"Jane?" I said as I approached a figure in the darkness. But it wasn't Jane.

Charles, shrouded in the darkness of the night, took my hand and led me off the path. He put his arms around me and held me tight . . . a little too tight. "You're hurting me. What are you—

"You shouldn't have rejected me."

I gasped as Mr. Campbell's familiar pompous cadence filled my ears. I tried to push away from him but he held me firm. Just as I opened my mouth to yell out for help, he gagged me with a dirty cloth, spun me around, and tied the fabric tight around the base of my head. I thrashed my hands behind me as he did so, hitting and scratching the side of his face. He grabbed both my hands next and forced them behind my back, tying them tight. I heaved in fear and anger as he pulled me further into the garden. I buckled my knees, dropping to the ground so he would have to drag me to get anywhere.

He cursed and pulled a pistol out from his coat pocket, holding it to my back.

"Get. Up." He pressed the pistol against me. I tried to tell him I would shoot him with his own gun once I got out of this, but only muffled murmurs came from behind the gag.

He cocked the hammer back when I didn't immediately oblige. A chill ran down my spine. I finally stood, though I glared at him with all the venom I could possess.

"I don't want any more trouble, Miss Mason. You will come without a struggle, or I will take whatever means necessary to ensure you obey."

I gave him another cold, furious glare, but I walked when he pulled me along this time. As he guided us toward the parked carriages, I prayed someone would notice us or at least question what we were doing. But we didn't see a single soul in the dark.

We passed wheel after wheel, Mr. Campbell forcing me along, the barrel of his gun never leaving my back. We finally came upon a carriage secluded from the others. Horses were already drawn and tied as if he had planned all along to leave in haste. He opened the door quietly.

"Get in," he hissed in my ear.

A rustling was suddenly heard nearby. I turned toward the sound. A lantern emerged from a nearby tree, surrounded by low bushes. The light cast a faint glow, revealing Matthew Johnson's face leaning over a small shrub. He didn't notice us.

"Not a sound," Mr. Campbell whispered in my ear. The cold metal gun pressed harder into my back.

"There you are, my friends," Mr. Johnson muttered in a quiet, soothing voice, staring through the bushes at the base of the tree.

I tried willing him with my mind to face us, but it was no use. He was engrossed in whatever he was looking at.

"And here's more for your babies tomorrow." Mr. Johnson sprinkled something about the bushes and smiled in delight as the bushes shook.

"Such luck to find you out here," he cooed to whatever was hiding below. He reached a hand down and rummaged around for a moment before bringing it close to the lantern, revealing a baby quail.

"Your family is late migrating south." He spoke to it as if it were his dearest friend in the world. "Have no fear," he said. "I'll return with shelter. Or perhaps you can all come home with me and wait out the winter. We will be cozy in my quarters." He lowered his hand back into the bush, but the action must have startled the other quail, for a line of birds ran out from underneath the bush toward us.

"Don't run!" he called back to them with a saddened voice, holding up his lantern in our direction. Mr. Johnson finally noticed us in the lantern's light. He looked at the gag in my mouth and his eyes widened in shock.

"Miss Mason?" he asked in horror.

Mr. Campbell shifted the gun until it was pointed at my chest and barked at me, "Get in now or I'll throw you off the docks when we arrive!"

I could tell he was losing his nerve now that Mr. Johnson had spotted us. I didn't want to press my luck. I turned to enter the coach when the pistol fired into the night. I looked down at my chest and gasped in horror. Mr. Campbell shoved me inside and shut the door.

Henry

I stared at the men and women, and anger raged in my chest as I put the pieces together. Charles had dropped our plans to practically kiss Lily on the dance floor. My heart thudded harder as I realized that if Lily was here, so was Jane. I scoured the room in anticipation for her familiar eyes.

I spotted Jane's Aunt Mary. She looked horrified as she continued to look toward the back garden. Our eyes finally met across the room. She wore a look of confusion as I immediately strode over to her.

"What's happened?" I asked the moment she was in earshot. "Where is Jane?"

"You tell me, Lord Elliot," she said with a clipped tone. Everyone's eyes were on us.

"I'm not Lord Elliot," I finally said.

She looked at me with disappointment, not buying my claim. Her next words came out short and mocking. "Lord Elliot, I applaud you for your disregard of the rules entirely. You have completely ruined Jane's and Lily's—"

"Henry!" Charles's voice carried from the doors leading out to the garden.

The entire room broke into a frenzy of gasps and mutters as they took in both of our appearances. Charles ran to me.

Aunt Mary looked at Charles and then at me, her eyes wide. "I believe you have some explaining to do," she said, aghast.

"In a moment, Mrs. Mason." I rushed toward Charles.

"Where have you been?" Charles hissed, accusatory.

"What have *you* done?" I seethed. "Is Jane here?"

"Yes," Charles said with a mixture of emotion. "At least she was, until she ran into the garden."

"She thought you were me," I said, already angry as the words left my mouth.

"Yes." He had the sense to look apologetic before adding, "Now Jane and Lily are both gone and neither Mr. Campbell nor Jacob Hughes are anywhere to be found."

I wanted to knock Charles to the ground. This was all his fault. But there wasn't time for that now.

I turned back to Aunt Mary. "Where is your husband?"

"He's in the garden looking for Jane and Lily." She looked bewildered.

"Mrs. Mason, listen to me very carefully. Jane and Lily are both in danger. Can you find your husband immediately and leave to find the Bow Street Runners?" I handed her the addresses to the run-down houses near the docks, as well as to Jacob's house and Mr. Campbell's apartment. "We need them to search each address as soon as possible. I have written out instructions of what we need. All you need to do is ensure that these papers are handed to the Bow Street Runners directly."

"What's all this about?" Mary said, putting a hand to her chest in panic.

"I don't have time to explain right now. But you must find your husband this very minute and do as I've instructed."

She snatched the paper out of my hand and pointed at Charles. "If my nieces are harmed in any way, I'm holding you responsible."

"I'll hold myself responsible," Charles responded remorsefully.

Without further argument, Mary ran out of the ballroom toward the back garden.

"Where have you searched?" I asked Charles, getting to the point.

"The entire back garden." Charles shoved his hands through his hair anxiously. "I'll kill Jacob and Mr. Campbell."

"And then I'll kill you," I said, unable to control my anger.

"Gladly." Charles looked at me, full of self-loathing. "And then I'll shoot you for not being at your post."

"We can punch this out later," I retorted. "Let's search the front of the house and the carriages."

The guests parted, staring wide-eyed at us as we bolted for the door. We ran side by side, stride for stride, until we broke through the doorway.

Just as our feet landed in the entryway a sound rang out into the air, plunging my heart into ice.

A pistol was fired.

Lily

Mr. Campbell shot me. I wasn't able to catch my fall with my hands tied behind my back when he shoved me inside the carriage, and I landed hard on my shoulder. My heart sped up as I lay there on the floor. How long would it take before I lost consciousness?

A few breaths later, and a good look at my chest lent me clarity. I hadn't been shot. Scrambling around with my hands tied behind my back, I finally tucked my knees up under my stomach and eased myself up off the floor. The carriage began moving before I was able to fully get to my feet. It rocked and swayed, making it difficult to find my footing. After righting myself, I found my balance and collapsed into the seat, looking out the window.

I searched in the darkness for Mr. Johnson, finally spotting him. He darted toward the entrance of the house, lantern still in hand. I let out a breath of relief that Mr. Campbell's shot had missed its target.

Matthew turned around for a brief moment as he ran, facing me—

I gasped as another shot was fired. This time Matthew tumbled to the ground, his arms splaying out. His lantern went black as it rolled on its side. My stomach wrenched and I cried out into the cloth in my mouth as the image ran through my mind of him bleeding out on the cobblestones, all in the attempt to help me. Matthew Johnson had just been shot . . . and now I had no hope of rescue.

The carriage tore out onto a main street and sped off through the night. I didn't have time to cry or fall into panic just now. I looked around the interior of the coach, assessing my options of escape. It wasn't enough that my hands were tied behind my back; the handles were also broken off, locking me inside. I shifted around, looking for anything that could be used as a weapon or that could help me cut through the rope around my hands.

Nothing.

I hit my back against the seat in frustration and yelled out against the gag.

Tears fell from my eyes as I thought about everything that had happened in the last half hour. How was it possible that less than an hour earlier, Henry—no, Charles—was dancing with me, proposing?

Charles! My stomach lurched. Everything suddenly made sense. Mr. Campbell had me hostage; Mr. Hughes had slipped out after Jane. This entire thing was an elaborate plan to trap Charles and Henry . . . and Jane and I were the bait.

Lawrence

My heart pounded in my ears as I waited for Arthur Brown to say the name. Was it Jacob Hughes or Alexander Campbell? He shuffled in place. I could understand his hesitancy—He had kept this information safe for months now. But the time for secrecy was over. It was time for Mr. Brown to speak—to reveal the identity of the man who had threatened Lord Elliot so many months ago.

"Who is responsible for all this?" I asked, losing my patience.

"There isn't just one man," Arthur Brown finally said, breathing out. "So much is involved."

"So Jacob Hughes and Alexander Campbell are working together?" I asked. It was as we feared.

BANG!

My heart stopped as a shot rang out into the night. I stopped talking, holding my breath. It came from the direction of the carriages not too far from where we stood.

Without another word, I ran toward the sound. I prayed that Charles and Henry were alright. I could hear John's and Mr. Brown's quick footfalls behind me.

BANG!

Charles

Henry and I sprinted through the entryway. A second shot sounded, sending my heart through my chest, my legs driving me faster. I didn't let my mind settle on what the gunshot could mean. If they hurt Lily . . .

We threw the doors open and burst into the dark, chilled air just as a carriage pulled onto the street and charged off.

I yelled out, watching helplessly. We needed our horses immediately, but they were stabled up a short distance away from the carriages—We'd never get to them in time to catch the speeding coach.

"Come on!" Henry barked as he charged for the stables. We passed several carriages when my foot connected with something that rolled and clanged: a darkened lantern. I stopped, realizing a man's body laid lifeless on the cobblestones just ahead. Henry saw it too. He let out a conflicted breath. We didn't have time for this. We needed to move fast. Every second that passed was a second the carriage got farther away.

Matthew Johnson laid sprawled out, face down.

He groaned as we quickly turned him over; He wasn't dead.

"What happened?" Henry urged.

"Mr. Campbell has my Golden Eagle," Matthew gasped, clutching his hands to his chest as if it hurt to breathe. "Her hands are tied behind her back, and she's gagged. He just threw her into the carriage and tore off. I didn't see where they were going, but he was holding a pistol to her back last I saw her."

My heart stopped. "There were two blasts! Did he shoot her?"

"I can't be sure. But I think the first one was aimed at me. He missed, but the second one hit."

I patted my hands around his chest, quickly surveying the damage. There was no blood I could see or feel, but he still held his chest as if it hurt.

Henry quickly pulled Matthew's hands away, revealing a large, heavy, metal pin attached to his lapel. It had most likely resembled a bird before a bullet was lodged inside. I pulled the pin from his suit to ensure the bullet hadn't gone through.

"Well, Mr. Johnson," Henry said, looking at it. "In this case, your fowl friend has saved your life."

"And has made me hallucinate," he said dramatically. "My vision is distorted. I see two of you."

"You'll be fine," I said, moving to stand.

"Wait!" Matthew pulled my arm. "Tell my Golden Eagle I tried to save her." He held up the large, heavy pin and added, "Give this to her as a sign of my bravery."

I rolled my eyes. "She will never be your Golden Eagle, Mr. Johnson, but I will give it to her all the same."

"Thank you, Lord Elliot," he said sincerely. "I'm grateful to you, even if you are a cuckoo, stealing my nest and my eagle." Henry rolled his eyes this time. Clearly Mr. Johnson was just fine.

Henry stood quickly. "Where should we search first? Mr. Campbell's apartment, Jacob's house, or the docks?"

"I don't know. They could be anywhere," I said helplessly.

Mr. Johnson inserted himself into the conversation, making his voice sound more weak and ragged than before. "I don't know where they are exactly." He coughed. "But Mr. Campbell said he would throw Miss Mason off the docks once they got there."

I had never been so grateful to have Mr. Johnson around in my entire life.

"Thank you, Mr. Johnson!" I said, already beginning to run toward the stables. "Thank you!"

With a disfigured bird pin in hand, I raced toward the stables, Henry at my side. When we finally arrived, we didn't stop for air, though my lungs burned. Two stable hands approached us in the dimly lit space as we entered.

"We need to leave this very moment!" I ordered.

Henry and I began to untie Apollo and Spartan. The stable hands understood our urgency and went about taking the horses from us to saddle them quickly.

I almost argued, but knew they would be faster at the task.

"Charles! Henry!" Lawrence's heaving voice called before he ran into the dimly lit barn. "Thank goodness!"

John and Mr. Brown followed closely behind.

"We heard the gunshots," John panted.

I looked at my horse then back at Lawrence. "We must leave this very moment. The Mason sisters have been taken by Jacob and Mr. Campbell to the docks."

"What of my family's safety?" Mr. Brown asked frantically.

I nodded to Lawrence. "It must all be done tonight. I have a feeling we are up against more than we originally thought. If anything goes beyond tonight I can't guarantee anyone's safety. Take Mr. Brown with you now and secure his family. Reach out to the Goldfinch Society. Notify the Bow Street Runners. Do what you must, but have Mr. Brown and his family out of London by tonight."

"Very good, my lord. It will be done." Lawrence turned to the shop owner. "Now, Mr. Brown, we must get you back. We need the element of surprise on our side."

Mr. Brown cleared his throat, taken by emotion. "Thank you, Lord Elliot."

I stopped my pacing and looked up at the shopkeeper. "I'm grateful to be able to lend a hand to any friend of my father's. And have no fear, Mr. Brown—we will bring Jacob Hughes and Alexander Campbell to justice."

37

PISTOL

Jane

The carriage rolled to a stop, the ever present question of what came next looming over me like a black shroud threatening a violent storm. I peered out the window, unable to distinguish much of my surroundings, the moon still covered by clouds. What little I could make out were two haphazard structures silhouetted against a river.

My breath shook in and out as footsteps approached. During the ride over, I had checked every possible place in the carriage for a weapon but found nothing. Realizing I was out of options, I reached up into my hair and pulled a pin from one of my curls, slipping it between my fingers.

The door rattled before it swung open, revealing Mr. Hughes. I wanted to cower away from him, but held firm, unwilling to show my fear—if I could help it.

He extended his hand out to me in mockery, as if he were a gentleman escorting a lady.

When I didn't budge, he twisted his smile, holding up a long, thin piece of fabric.

He pulled it tight, making a snapping noise. "Would you like me to tie you up, or would you like to cooperate?"

Cooperation was my safest move for now. I placed my hand in his, knowing I had to wait for the right instant to use my pin. I allowed him to help me down, steeling myself.

He cocked an eyebrow when I came willingly. "Perhaps you've come to your senses after all," His eyes swept over me.

He yanked me to him, but I didn't resist . . . not yet. I needed to wait for him to lower his guard. His grip lessened slightly and he gave me a surprised look as I came without a fight.

I gripped the pin, waiting.

He released his hold on me with his other hand, lowering his guard. This was my moment. I made a fist, putting my hairpin between my fingers so it protruded out like a spike. In a swift motion, my fist connected with his face. The force hurt my hand, but it did the trick. He let go of me, cursing as his hand flew to his cheek. I turned to run but he was too quick—he grabbed my dress and jerked me back.

"You'll regret that," he fumed. He whipped me around to face him, pinning my arms behind me with his hands until it hurt. A trickle of blood ran down his jaw.

"And now you have nowhere to go," he sneered. He looked at my lips. I had lost. I was out of options. Fear seized me as he began to lower his face to mine.

"What is the meaning of this?" Before Jacob could kiss me, I heard a familiar voice echo in the darkness. Frederick's voice had never sounded sweeter than it did just then. My eyes leapt to my rescuer dismounting his horse. He didn't even bother to tie it up as he ran to me.

Mr. Hughes released my arms. "I can explain." He raised his hands in the air, and I shoved him away, running to Frederick. In no time I was in his protective embrace. I cried with relief.

"I heard what happened," he said. "What did he do to you?"

"Other than being forceful and threatening me, he hasn't done anything," I said with a shaky breath.

His arms held me closer. "Good." He lifted my face upward. "That's my job." He pressed his lips forcefully against mine. I tried to pull my head away but his hands came up behind me and firmly held my head in place. His kiss had no passion to it—only a statement of the power he had over me. I slapped him forcefully, but he only laughed, grabbing my hand so I was even more helpless.

"I like you this way, Jane." His voice held a suggestive tone I had never heard. It made my skin crawl.

Frederick was stronger than Mr. Hughes; my attempts to pull myself free seemed even more futile.

His eyes flicked to Mr. Hughes. "Where is our collateral?"

"Alexander was just behind me when I took Miss Mason," Mr. Hughes said. He lifted an eyebrow. "She's a fiery one." He nodded toward me then looked at me with a twisted smile.

"Don't worry." Frederick grinned mirthlessly. "Once I've had my way with her, she's all yours."

My heart stopped as the words left his mouth. "Please don't do this," I begged. "What do you want?"

He gave me a calculated smirk. "You'll find out soon enough." He pulled me toward one of the run-down houses, taking no care with how fast he forced me along or how hard he dug his fingers into my arms.

Henry

My eyes flicked to the stable hand saddling Spartan. They were moving quicker than I would have, but each second that passed was a second that Jane was with Jacob Hughes.

"If Jacob touches Jane . . . " I trailed off.

Mr. Brown shook his head, resignation written on his face. "Mr. Hughes and Mr. Campbell are only part of this scheme. They are pawns in a bigger man's game."

"Mr. Brown," Charles said, his eyes darting from his horse to the shopkeeper, "answer me once and for all. Who was the man you heard threatening my father before he died?"

Mr. Brown exhaled, afraid to reveal the secret he had been carrying for so long. "It was Lord Fletcher."

Everything went still as his words hung in the air.

Mr. Brown continued. "I don't know why he killed the late earl, but he discovered me lurking near their conversation. Once your father died, Lord Fletcher came into my shop and threatened me personally. He has men that work for him. Men he pays well. He holds the cards, and no one can disrupt what he wants."

I gritted my teeth. "We'll see about that." I turned to my father. "Will you find Frederick's father, the Duke of Hastingwood? He should be here at the ball tonight. Bring him to the docks."

"I'll do it immediately." My father grabbed the buckle at his hip, loosening the strap that held my sword. "You'll need this." He moved quickly, passing it over to me.

Lawrence did the same, handing his to Charles.

"Do you still have your pistols?" John asked us. We nodded. "And your knives?" We patted our coats and answered that we did at the same time.

My father looked at us both with pride. "Then Godspeed." He strode over to another stable hand. "Will you please ready His Grace's carriage immediately?"

The stable hand nodded then ran into action while my father took off toward the house. Only a few seconds more and the horses would be ready.

"Boys."

I turned to see Lawrence. He hadn't called us boys since we were really young. His eyes pricked. "Show Lord Fletcher what happens when he plays with fire. Show him what an Elliot is made of. And above all else, make sure you return to tell me all about it."

The stable hands finished at the same time, as if they had been racing. They stood up straight, Charles and I mounting Apollo and Spartan faster than ever before.

"Good luck, Lawrence." I tossed him a familiar coin astride my horse before I dug my heels into Spartan and flicked the reins. He took off without hesitation.

Charles called out to his horse, close behind. Within a few seconds, Apollo moved beside Spartan until they were running at a furious pace, neck and neck.

Jane

Frederick stood behind me and pushed me toward the house, holding my hands together behind my back. I tried to squirm free, but it was no use. I knew screaming would be pointless. I let my knees buckle so he would have to drag me, but it backfired—he pulled me back into his chest.

"I didn't know you felt this way, Jane," he whispered suggestively in my ear.

My stomach writhed. "Why are you doing this?" I cried again. I pulled away from him and finally twisted one of my hands out of his grip. I turned to slap him again, but he caught my hand just before it met his face.

He looked at me flatly. "You can slap me all you want. It won't change anything. But the more you slap me, the more I'll make you pay for it. Do you understand? You are no match for my strength, and I will get what I want."

I swallowed.

"Now, walk into the house or I'll make you do it in whatever fashion I please."

I obeyed for the time being, worried I might actually empty my stomach on the ground if he tried anything further just now.

Frederick forced me inside the pitch-dark house then bolted the door behind us. He led me into the room then let me go. I couldn't even see my hand in front of my face. I thought about darting for the door, but I didn't dare move for fear of running into something. His footsteps sounded away from me until a dim lantern ignited. Frederick picked it up from off a circular table for two, illuminating a small space in the darkness. There was a stove on the same wall as the door. A wooden chair was set facing a small window on the opposite side.

"Have a seat," he said in mock kindness, gesturing toward the window. Before I had time to run for the door, he stood in front of it, then walked in my direction, lantern in hand, backing me against the opposing wall, next to the window.

"I insist," he said with a calculating tone. He raised the lantern against the wall, just above my shoulder. The light contrasted with the shadows of his face, making his cheekbones appear sharp as flint, the hollows of his eyes black as coal. He planted his other hand on the wall next to my other shoulder, trapping me. An icy chill ran down my spine. He lowered his voice.

"You need to see what's at stake."

My breath shook in and out at his soulless, twisted grin, making me wonder how I had never seen the monster beneath his veil of cold boredom. He released his hand holding the lantern from the wall and gestured to the chair once more. I slowly moved toward it, searching for anything I could use as a weapon in the dimly lit room.

I found nothing obvious.

"Now," he said quietly as he followed me. "Just watch." He forced my shoulders down, making me sit in the chair, facing the window.

He knelt beside me. "What I want," he whispered in my ear, "is to marry you." My breath stole away. To think I had been considering it not even an hour ago. "Not because I love you," he sneered. "Though I do love the way you look." He forced my chin toward him, but I pulled my face away.

"My father has given me until the end of the year to find a bride; otherwise, he will disinherit me. He has not only specified that I am to be married, but he has ordered it must be to a woman who is kind, who has sense, and a fair amount of money to her name. He believes that only such a woman would be able to change my 'despicable nature.'

"He approves of you, Jane, despite the fact that you have no title or rank. He believes I'm up to 'disgraceful things,' though he can't prove it. He thinks a wife would magically cure me, the idiot—as if everyone finds love the way he has with my mother.

"I tried to do it the right way, but you fell for a man who was a wolf in sheep's clothing instead." Pain struck my heart as I was reminded of Lord Elliot's treachery. "And now I have no other option but to take what I need by force."

"Why would I ever marry you after this?" I hissed.

The rumbling of carriage wheels was heard in the darkness. He spoke in my ear. "Don't move, Jane, or I promise you'll regret it. Just watch."

I waited for now, biding my time.

The carriage rolled to a stop in front of the house. A man atop the carriage grabbed a lantern at his side. The light illuminated Mr. Campbell's features. He stepped down and opened the coach door, holding the lantern high. He stepped inside for a moment then pulled someone out.

Lily

The carriage door swung open with a creak. Mr. Campbell's face came into view as he held a lantern high. Before I had time to think, he climbed inside and grabbed my arm forcefully, pulling me from the interior.

"It really is a shame you didn't just fall for me the way most women do," he said arrogantly as he forced me out. "You really are a pretty thing." His eyes scanned me as he held his pistol toward my chest.

When I got out of this I would personally burn down his apartment, starting with his hideous suits. We stared each other down for a moment, each of us glaring at the other.

"Just in time." An oily voice came from the darkness as a figure appeared. It belonged to Mr. Hughes.

"Where's Jane?" I tried to yell through the fabric in my mouth, but only muffled nonsense came out. I shook with anger.

"What's that?" Mr. Hughes asked, coming to stand right in front of me. He cocked an eyebrow. "She really is just as alluring as her sister."

I stomped as hard as I could on his foot. Unfortunately it didn't carry much weight. My ballroom slippers were no match for his dress shoes.

Mr. Hughes smirked. "I see she has Jane's spirit as well. I wonder whose lips are softer."

I backed away from him as he grabbed for me.

"Don't touch my prize," Mr. Campbell said. "She's mine."

Mr. Hughes turned to Mr. Campbell. "You'll learn soon enough that we share everything." He patted Mr. Campbell's cheek in a mocking way.

Mr. Campbell swatted Mr. Hughes's hand off then shoved him.

It was now or never. I darted away as fast as I could, but I only made it a few steps before Mr. Campbell gripped my arm and yanked me back.

"Don't make me use this, Miss Mason." He waved the gun in the air. "I'd rather have a wife with all of her limbs." A wife? What did that have to do with murdering Charles and Henry? Mr. Campbell looked over at Jacob. "We might have a problem. Just before I threw Miss Lily in the carriage at the Woodwards' ball, we were spotted by Matthew Johnson."

"And?" Jacob folded his arms.

"And now if he squeals, my reputation is on the line."

"You didn't dispose of him?" Mr. Hughes seethed.

"I shot him and he went down, but I was driving the carriage when it happened. I'm not sure if he died from the blast or not."

"It's your problem, not mine." Mr. Hughes talked to Mr. Campbell as if he was some sort of child in training.

"It might be everyone's problem," Mr. Campbell muttered under his breath.

"What do you mean?" Mr. Hughes's eyes narrowed.

"Miss Lily was being difficult. I told her if she didn't get in the carriage I would throw her off the docks."

"And you announced it in front of Matthew Johnson?" Mr. Hughes looked furious. "You idiot!" How was it that these two men, who had no brains, could plot something so elaborate?

Mr. Hughes stalked off to one of the shabby houses and pounded on the door. "We need backup!" he yelled.

I couldn't hear the words on the other end. Only a deep, tired, raspy voice.

My breath halted as I felt Mr. Campbell's eyes on me.

"Do you promise not to scream if I take that out of your mouth?" He looked at the gag.

I nodded my head in hopes that he would actually do it. "Very well. You have one chance. If you scream, it goes back in immediately. But I can no longer stand looking at you with that disgusting thing in your mouth."

I inwardly rolled my eyes. Of course Mr. Campbell would take it off only because it made me less attractive.

Jane

My hand flew to my mouth, dread overtaking me. Lily stumbled out of the carriage with a gag in place, hands tied behind her back. Mr. Campbell held a pistol to her. She gave him a look of loathing.

She was collateral.

So many emotions boiled beneath the surface as I looked at Lily in such a state. I was horrified and furious that Frederick would do such a thing. I felt betrayed by Lily's and Charles's actions. Sad that our sisterly bond didn't mean as much to her as it did to me. I felt a need to protect her, loyal despite her deceit. Love, pain, fear, resentment.

"Now listen carefully," Frederick said. I flinched away from him as he ran a finger down my neck. "You will marry me within the week. If you refuse, you will no longer have a sister."

I couldn't breathe.

"If you tell her about our arrangement or try to sneak her out of the country, I will have her hunted down and killed. In addition to that, I will slaughter your entire family. Do you understand?"

My heart raced with panic.

Frederick's next words were cold and quiet. "If I have any luck, I'll kill Henry too."

My head was swimming. I— "Henry?" I asked in confusion.

"I believe you call him Charles," Frederick said in my ear, his voice taut with loathing.

"What do you mean?"

"I mean that Lord Elliot has a shadow, Henry Thomas. An identical shadow. A brother of sorts, though, as I understand it, they are only loosely related. The way I understand it, you fell for a penniless, titleless liar. Henry has been claiming to be Lord Elliot since he made an appearance in London. The real Lord Elliot wasn't at any public events until tonight."

"You're a liar."

"Oh, yes. But not about this. Only Henry Thomas sings like an out-of-tune trombone to that magnitude. I recognized their disguise the night of your aunt's dinner party."

My mind exploded. The man with the beard that looked just like Charles at the autumn celebration quickly flashed through my mind. I had all but forgotten about him. So he wasn't a figment of my imagination after all. He was Lord Elliot. And Charles wasn't Charles at all. Everything began to click. 'Loved and penniless.' The reason 'Lord Elliot' would suddenly be engaged to another woman ... Lily.

Somehow she must have met the real Lord Elliot when he was disguised. Perhaps she didn't even know his real identity until tonight. And now ...

My eyes welled. I shouldn't have run. "This is all my fault," I breathed out. A tear fell from my cheek.

"Such a sweet sentiment," Frederick said mockingly, his fingers trailing up my cheek and towards my hair. I pushed them away, unable to stomach his touch, despite knowing my resistance would likely make him behave worse.

He let out a twisted chuckle of amusement. "You can take the blame if it makes you feel better. But it wouldn't have mattered. Jacob and Alexander were planning to hold up your carriage at gunpoint with masks on your way home. They were instructed to shoot your aunt and uncle if they put up a fight. Mr. Campbell and I were going to be the knights in shining armor to 'rescue' you both after you were brought here. You just sped things up a bit for us and took your aunt and uncle out of the equation."

I looked back at Lily outside. I was so relieved that she was innocent in all of this. She didn't mean to hurt me. She didn't betray me. And Charles *did* love me. Or rather, Henry did.

As I watched Lily, Mr. Hughes approached her, making me feel even more frantic to get her away from him.

"Lord Fletcher, I will cooperate. Just let Lily go and don't hurt Henry. You can gain nothing from it." I tried to say the words as if they were a business negotiation, but they came out with desperation instead.

His lips lurked at my ear. I pulled my head away but he pulled it back toward him so I couldn't move.

"You *will* cooperate," he whispered menacingly. "And I plan to take every measure tonight to ensure you don't run, and that you marry me within the week. If there is even the slightest possibility that you are carrying my child, and your family's life is on the line, you would have nowhere to turn but me."

My heart lurched in my throat. "Lord Fletcher, I will marry you within the week to save my sister. Anything else is unnecessary."

"But it's absolutely necessary. No one will have you once you're ruined, except for Henry, of course. This leads us to why he cannot live. I can't have him running off with you just before the wedding."

"You will never get away with it. I won't sit by and do nothing while you plot to kill him."

"Then you will lose Henry *and* your family."

"You would have nothing more to hold over me at that point."

"And you would have no one left to love."

"One day it will catch up to you and you'll waste away in a prison cell," I spat, surprised at how even and icy my voice sounded when I felt like falling apart on the inside. I stared back out the window. Mr. Hughes and Mr. Campbell were arguing about something.

"Now that you know what's at stake, we'd better not waste any more time," Frederick said. "Besides, I haven't had my way with a woman for a few days now."

A disgusting feeling crawled over me. "A few days? You sleep with prostitutes?" It didn't surprise me, really, after everything I had just discovered about Frederick, but it still made me sick.

"Prostitutes?" He tsked. "My father believes me to be despicable, but I wouldn't stoop *that* low. I run an operation here. Prostitution is all well and good for the average man, but men of high breeding want a woman of high class and breeding in their bed. Not some wretch from the street." He said the words as if it was something abhorrent. "I'm not Jacob. I won't sleep with just anyone. I arrange, anonymously of course, for men and women of the upper class to meet here in secret. Jacob and I get our fair share of the action, as well as some spare change for arranging everything. The women get paid a portion of the money so they have more than enough to keep them coming back."

How could he have fooled society so well? He was the son of a duke. He was supposed to represent all things moral and good. I couldn't believe he had set up a prostitution house for London's elite. His bored expression began to make more sense—only the most vile things in life held any pleasure or enjoyment for him.

"You're disgusting," I seethed. "Eventually your father will discover the truth."

"As long as he doesn't find out before my next birthday, it won't really matter. My father's will states that by my twenty-fifth birthday I'm legally able to inherit everything if my father passes unexpectedly. In about five months, I plan to kill him myself."

My breath drew in quickly. "You would kill your own father?"

"Correction, Jane: I *will* kill my father once the time is right. It wouldn't be so different from poisoning James Elliot."

"James Elliot?" Would his words ever stop shocking me?

"Indeed. He was on to my business. I don't know how he found out about our little operation, but he told me I had better come clean or he would expose me. I had him followed until I knew exactly how and when to administer poison to his drink. I have eyes anywhere and everywhere." He put his lips to my ear, whispering, "so I'll know if you talk."

"You plan to have me followed."

"Would you expect anything less?"

"So my life is to become a nightmare," I said, despair consuming me.

"That depends on how you look at it." He pulled me suddenly from my chair and in one swift movement bound my hands behind my back, tying them tight with a piece of fabric. I tried to pull away with everything I had, but it was no use. The lantern suddenly went out and he let me go. My breath heaved in the darkness, no longer able to see.

"Let Lily go!" I yelled.

"I can't do that." Frederick's voice penetrated the black room. It was worse not knowing where he was.

"Let's talk this through," I pleaded.

"There is nothing to talk over. Mr. Campbell is destitute and he needs someone with a large dowry to pay his debts. It's how I'm paying him for bringing your sister here tonight for me."

"She will never go along with it!"

"I might also add that you are collateral for her. If she refuses to go through with it, or if she speaks to anyone of her arrangement, you will be killed."

"Then I die either way! Either you kill me or you kill those I love. I won't go through with this unless you let Lily go." I stepped backward, feeling the wall press against my bound hands. I still couldn't see anything, so I quietly slid away from Frederick's voice. Perhaps I could find the door and open it somehow.

"You would prefer your sister to be a corpse over being married to Mr. Campbell?" Frederick's voice came closer. I decided not to speak. There was no way he could see me in the darkness, and I didn't want to give away my whereabouts.

I held my breath and he chuckled. "Oh Jane, you really are fun." His voice got closer. "But we don't have time for fun right now." His arm suddenly snaked around me.

I gasped. Somehow he could see in this darkness—as if he was more at home in this unlit space than he was in the light.

"Lord Fletcher, please. I'll do what you want, just let us go."

"You'll do what I want regardless." His arm restricted me further. I tried to twist my hands free from their knot, but it was no use. My breath came in and out rapidly as he held me tight with one arm. I twisted and squirmed. He grabbed my jaw with his hand so I would hold still. I did the only thing I could think of. I bit his hand as hard as I could. He cursed and loosened his grip, allowing me to pull out of his hold and race toward the door—Frederick jerked me back again then wove his arms through both of mine from the front so I was facing him. I tried twisting my hands again but the tie around them wouldn't budge.

"I underestimated you, Jane," he said with angry pleasure.

A loud pounding came at the door.

"Open up!" It was Mr. Hughes's voice.

Frederick yelled out with a growl of fury before he released me and pulled me toward the door.

He threw it open.

The thought to yell Lily's name crossed my mind, but it would do no good. She was gagged and wouldn't be able to yell back.

"This is not what we arranged!" Frederick barked at Mr. Hughes.

"I understand, but we have a problem." Mr. Hughes held a lantern up on the other side. "You may need to have your rendezvous elsewhere. Alexander just told me that Matthew Johnson spotted him forcing Miss Lily into the carriage at the Woodwards' ball before he left. He shot Mr. Johnson, but he's not sure if the impact killed him. Regardless, I think we should be ready for anything. Apparently Alexander practically advertised our location and Mr. Johnson overhead."

My heart pulsed with hope, though I doubted anyone would find our exact location.

"I'm working with idiots!" Frederick hissed.

Mr. Hughes scowled. "I've done everything you asked tonight. I didn't even touch your woman."

"You're still an idiot! I told you not to interrupt me for anything. Go knock next door and tell them you need backup. Then stand guard. His face looked truly evil in the dim light. He planned to have his carnal desires no matter the cost. He proceeded to slam the door but Mr. Hughes put his foot inside, stopping it just before it closed.

"I already knocked. They are all watching Mr. Brown's family and the shop. Jim is at his post, but he's sick with a bad fever and can't get up. What if someone notifies the Bow Street Runners and we are all caught here?"

"They would have to search every house by the docks," Frederick retorted.

"Yes, but what if they get lucky? I know you were looking forward to this part of your game, but are you really willing to lose this entire operation for it? We can take them to an inn and finish our work there. We will have them home by tomorrow."

Frederick gave Mr. Hughes an icy look. "You don't think rumors would spread and get back to my father about Lord Fletcher taking a woman to an inn? I need her home by tonight so my father doesn't suspect," Frederick hissed.

"Then ruin her another day. She knows her sister's life is at stake. She wouldn't flee now."

The distant sound of beating hooves against cobblestone suddenly came into earshot. It was getting louder as if the rider was on a desperate mission.

Mr. Hughes raised an eyebrow at Frederick as if to say, "I told you."

"Find my pistol and my sword now!" Frederick barked.

Mr. Hughes ran into the house while Frederick pulled me outside.

"It appears we are going for a little ride," Frederick's icy voice said in my ear.

Lily

Mr. Campbell held the gun to my back as he untied my gag. I breathed in relief as he removed it. I thought about yelling Jane's name, but I felt the time wasn't right.

His next words came out in a snooty tone. "That looks better," he leered.

"Mr. Campbell, where is my sister?"

"To put it plainly, Miss Mason, your sister is inside one of these houses being held hostage." He said the words importantly. "Now walk." He held the gun to my back, gesturing to the small alleyway between the two dilapidated structures.

"You plan to trap Henry and Lord Elliot in the house to murder them?" I needed to find out as much as possible so I could try and warn them if they arrived. I moved as slowly as I could without angering him too much.

He scoffed. "It's meant to trap *you*."

"What do you mean?" I stopped walking and looked back at him in the darkness.

He forced me forward, now almost at the alleyway.

"If you don't agree to marry me, your sister will no longer breathe."

I gritted my teeth. "And what exactly would that accomplish?"

"I thought that would be fairly obvious." He put his nose up as if he were speaking to a simpleton.

"I didn't realize that marrying me or threatening Jane's life would improve your odds of killing Lord Elliot."

"I have no intention of killing Lord Elliot." He narrowed his eyes as if I'd truly gone mad. "I need your dowry to settle my gambling debts."

"Then what are Mr. Hughes's intentions with Jane?"

"Jacob is easy to please. He's an imbecile. As long as he's promised good wine and a woman, he will do just about anything."

My stomach writhed in disgust, panic seizing me as I realized Jane was most likely Mr. Hughes's payment for the night once I was coerced into this union. If only I could somehow turn them against each other.

"Take me to see Jane *now*, or I won't go through with this. How do I know you aren't bluffing?"

We reached the dark alleyway. He pressed me forward slowly until we were in the center of its dark walls.

"All in good time, Miss Mason. Lord Fletcher said he would murder me if I were to interrupt him while he's—" He stopped talking mid-sentence as though he had just spilled the greatest secret of all.

"Lord Fletcher?"

"No. I didn't mean to say Lord Fletcher. I meant to say Mr. Hughes."

"But Mr. Hughes is not inside with Jane. He was out here when we arrived." A chill ran down my arms. What if it had been Frederick all along?

Frederick was cold and calculating. He came across as bored and stuffy, but he also struck me as devious and cunning as well. My next words came out with an icy tone.

"Why does Lord Fletcher need Jane?"

"I never meant to say Lord Fletcher." He was getting flustered, an expression I had never seen from him. He was truly terrified. I needed to get under his skin even more—but not to the point of him using his gun.

"Very well, Mr. Campbell. But I will have you know that as of right now, you and Mr. Hughes are suspected for the murder of the late Lord Elliot. If it truly wasn't you who did it, then I would start talking."

"You're bluffing." Mr. Campbell tried to use his arrogant tone again but he had already given himself away. He was afraid of Frederick.

I had to think on my toes. "Very well. Don't believe me. But new evidence has come forth—I'm surprised you haven't heard the gossip circulating. You threatened the late Lord Elliot at White's only weeks before his death, and Mr. Hughes is next in line to inherit the Elliot legacy. It appears as though you and Mr. Hughes are well acquainted, putting you both in line as cohorts in crime. Even if you somehow found a way to marry me, my money wouldn't keep you from the hangman's noose."

"Keep your mouth shut, Miss Mason, or I'll gag you again." Mr. Campbell sounded furious, but there was also a touch of fear behind it.

"You may gag me again, Mr. Campbell, but I'm only looking out for your welfare. I believe Lord Fletcher is setting you and Mr. Hughes up."

"Stop talking about Lord Fletcher. He has nothing to do with this. This has everything to do with the fact that I tend to ruin you tonight and make sure that you understand that if you say a word to anyone, I will have your sister killed in front of you."

His threats angered me beyond anything I could contain. I wouldn't stand for his bullying. Not when he threatened Jane. I gave him a biting glare.

"I might believe your words if you were Lord Fletcher, or if you had the means to back it up. But you just told me yourself that you have no money. Therefore, you couldn't possibly pay someone to hunt my sister down. Perhaps you would try it yourself, but you wouldn't know where to start. I do have money, however, Mr. Campbell. I could find men to hunt *you* down, after which I could kill you myself in whatever way pleased me for threatening my sister.

"I don't take you as a complete idiot, however, Mr. Campbell. I believe your threats bear weight. I believe someone with money is supporting you. It could be Mr. Hughes, but I don't know that he is wealthy enough for this—and even you just stated that he hasn't the capacity to do anything besides drink and steal women's virtue. So listen to me when I say this. Lord Fletcher is setting you up. And I believe he intends to kill Charles Elliot and pin it on you and Mr. Hughes so that he can breathe easier knowing that the finger couldn't possibly ever point to him."

"That's enough!" Mr. Campbell brought the gag back out.

I shrugged my shoulders. "Fine. There is a simple way to figure all of this out, but you're right. If my fortune-seeking husband-to-be is hanged or goes to prison right after we are married, it will simply make my life easier." I opened my mouth for him to place the gag back inside.

He yelled out in fury. "Why can't you just be like every other woman?"

"First," I gave him an annoyed look, "I don't believe any two women are the same. Not even Jane and me. Second, I have no intention to stop talking, so you might as well put the gag back in my mouth."

He threw it to the ground angrily. It was a confirmation. Frederick was inside with Jane.

"Let me speak with Lord Fletcher," I said mechanically. "You can hide somewhere and listen to our conversation. I will tell Lord Fletcher that I can't believe he is friends with men who are suspected of murder. We will see what he says. If he decides to defend you and claims that you are both innocent, then clearly I'm wrong. But what if I'm right? What if he states that it was his plan all along? Wouldn't you like to know what you're up against?"

"I don't know." His voice shook uncertainly.

"What does he need my sister for? It may solve the puzzle."

"His plans are his own."

I cocked an eyebrow. "I see. He keeps you and Mr. Hughes in the dark, while he knows every single move you two will make."

He gritted his teeth. "That's not what I said."

"You didn't have to."

Mr. Campbell would most likely shut down my plan to speak with Frederick, but I had accomplished my task. The seed of doubt began to percolate in Mr.Campbell's mind. He didn't fully trust Frederick any longer.

"I don't want any more words from you, Miss Mas—"

Mr. Campbell stopped talking. An echoing of hooves against cobblestones suddenly filled the air. It was getting louder, as if the riders were on an urgent mission. Hope sprouted throughout me. Perhaps Matthew Johnson had come through after all.

38

KNIFE

Jane

Frederick let out another angry breath as the clop of horse hooves grew in volume. Any minute now the cavalry would be upon us.

Now that we were out of the house, my eyes could see clearly; the moonlight revealed the docks at the water's edge and Mr. Hughes's carriage parked close to the street. Mr. Hughes scurried outside, holding out Frederick's dueling sword.

"Where is my pistol?" Frederick barked.

"I couldn't find it," Mr. Hughes quipped back.

Frederick yelled out with a growl. "Hold her!" He shoved me toward Mr. Hughes, snatching the sword from his hand, then walked back inside. "I'll find it myself, you worthless dog!"

Mr. Hughes scowled at Frederick but gladly took me from him, twisting his arms through mine and forcing me into a tight grip. If only I could turn them against each other.

"Mr. Hughes," I said quietly, trying my best to give my voice an air of politeness. It made me squirm inside, but it was the only thing I could think of that might help me. He could easily outmaneuver me, leaving only my wits to use—and *they* would only possibly work.

I continued. "Why is it that Lord Fletcher will take me for a bride, and Mr. Campbell will take my sister? Do you not get anything? It seems unfair. After all, you did all the work of capturing me. Do you not want a wealthy bride?" I didn't try to lay it on thick. I stated it as a matter of fact.

He didn't answer.

"I believe Lord Fletcher is trying to swindle you," I said, smirking as if I pitied him.

"I know your tricks," he said, looking at me. "You have always despised me. If you could get away from me you would do it in a heartbeat." He gave me a hard stare, but his lips curved up ever so slightly, clearly liking the attention.

"You're very astute, Mr. Hughes. I absolutely detest you, and I *would* run if I had the chance. But I don't think Lord Fletcher values your genius enough. If only he consulted you more, I believe you would run into less setbacks. You certainly bring something unique to the table." I studied his expression. He was definitely enjoying my "compliments."

I continued in a hushed tone so Frederick wouldn't hear if he emerged unexpectedly. "And despite the fact that I do despise you, and that I would run if I had the chance, I would certainly pick you as a husband over Lord Fletcher. I believe you are slightly less evil than he is. And less . . . imposing. Besides, Lord Fletcher treats no one with respect. Especially you, his most loyal friend who has always done his bidding. He always orders you around.

"You are the brains of this whole operation. You captured me, you figured out a way to make me come to your carriage without too much of a fight, and you didn't even need to use a gag or bind my hands the way Mr. Campbell did with my sister. Though you are no gentleman by any means, you were kind enough to lead me to your carriage without hurting me or holding a gun to my back." My words were absolutely ridiculous. But if it worked to turn Mr. Hughes against his friends, it was worth it.

He looked at me skeptically, but I could tell I was boosting his ego.

"I would be careful with what you say about Lord Fletcher," he said. "I will not betray him. He has been a loyal friend to me."

"Perhaps." I shrugged. "But does he ever do anything for you that doesn't benefit him?"

"We each benefit equally." He was defending Frederick's position, but I could see the cracks slowly forming.

"And yet you are responsible to capture me for Lord Fletcher, and find his sword and gun for him without so much as a thank you?" I raised my brows. "Last I checked, that's not an equal benefit. He may be your superior in title and rank, but that's as far as I would take the description."

"Are you stating that I'm superior to Lord Fletcher and Mr. Campbell?" he asked flatly.

"Are you not?"

He gave me an even stare before a small smile formed on his lips. "Perhaps I am." He looked at me as if he was finally being seen for his admirable qualities. It was hard not to shake my head and roll my eyes.

"You are a smart man, Mr. Hughes. You're an excellent judge of character. I have always despised you, and you saw it immediately. I have never liked you, nor could I ever love you. But I would certainly love you more than I could ever love Lord Fletcher."

He went rigid with surprise, as if I had given him the biggest compliment in the world.

I shrugged my shoulders. "I'm just surprised that a man as smart as you isn't fighting for Lily or me. As my husband, you would have no obligation to me. I am very wealthy and—"

Frederick's footsteps were approaching from inside. My time was up. He threw the door open from inside, his face livid.

"Get back in there, and don't come back out until you have my gun!" Frederick shouted, his sword now attached to his hip.

"I'm not the one who lost it," Mr. Hughes quipped.

"But you'll be the one who gets a bullet to the chest if you don't find it!"

Frederick was proving every word I had just fed Mr. Hughes. And there I saw it, a spark of rebellion in Mr. Hughes's eyes. I had planted a seed. I hoped it wouldn't come back to bite Lily or me.

Frederick took three long strides toward us and tore me from Mr.

Hughes.

"What are you waiting for?" Frederick barked.

Mr. Hughes gave him a steely look before storming back inside the house.

Frederick took my arm and jerked me toward him, making me fall as he pulled me along. He let out an angry breath and forcefully yanked me to my feet.

"I want none of your antics just now." He dug his fingers into my back.

"You're hurting me!" I shouted.

"Jane!" Lily's voice called out with hope in the darkness. My eyes filled with tears at the sound of her familiar voice.

"Lily!" I yelled back, unable to see her.

Frederick forced me along the small yard, his eyes on Mr Hughes's carriage. I couldn't let him take me inside. It was my last fight before Frederick would have full control. I fell again, this time on purpose, trying anything to slow him down.

Frederick growled and lifted me by my hair at the base of my neck. Fear touched every single part of my body as he looked at me with rage.

"I know what you're doing," he snarled. "You'll pay for it this time!" He raised his fist high. I had never been struck, let alone by a man. I closed my eyes and flinched, waiting for the impact.

BANG!

"Lily!" I screamed, remembering Mr. Campbell's gun. My eyes flew open. But Lily was nowhere to be seen—instead, I saw a tall, broad figure riding atop a large, dark horse, a pistol raised toward the sky. My heart pounded faster and faster. I was afraid to hope, but it had to be him. I knew his presence better than anything in the world.

Without seeing his face, I knew he was enraged. Without being close to him, I knew his heart hammered as loud and strong as mine did. I knew he was ready to kill. And now I knew his name was Henry.

Henry

Smoke billowed around me as I fired my gun into the air. I clenched my jaw as I looked at the outline of a man that resembled Frederick, his fist still raised in the air to strike the woman I loved more than life itself. Everything fell still. Jane was looking at me. I couldn't see her features in the darkness, but I knew it was her. It was her silhouette, her heart calling for mine.

I wasn't sure if she would want to see me after what Charles had pulled in the ballroom—which only drove me further. I needed to see her. I needed to hear her speak. I quickly dismounted Spartan, keeping my eyes on Jane as I ran forward. If Frederick harmed her in any way, I would make him pay for it . . . slowly.

As I dashed toward them, Frederick forced Jane's back into his chest, snaking an arm around her waist, so I couldn't attack him without hurting her, then began walking backward as fast as he could to a carriage a short distance away. He fumbled for something in his pocket with his other hand. I ran faster. I was so close.

Jane's features slowly came into view along with Frederick's. His fingers moved quickly in his coat pocket for something as his back pressed against the carriage. He was trapped now. I reached for Jane just as Frederick pulled a knife from his coat and held it to Jane's throat.

"Don't move or I'll cut her," he said with an icy voice. I froze, my hand close to her—the smallest movement away. But it was too risky. His blade was too close to her throat.

It was agony. Her eyes were locked onto mine, begging me to save her. To pull her to me. My heart erupted at the expression.

Her lips parted, breath escaping rapidly as if she had waited a lifetime to see me again. I could see it plain as day. Somehow she still loved me. She didn't despise me.

"Henry," she whispered into the darkness.

My heart ached as Jane said my name . . . my real name.

I would kill Frederick.

My eyes moved to his. "Only a coward would put a knife to a lady's throat," I seethed.

"At least I'm not an imposter," Frederick sneered back.

"Let Jane go and I might not prolong the torture as I kill you."

"Actually, Jane is coming with me." Frederick coiled his arm tighter around her waist from behind and pulled her closer. He moved the knife slowly up her neck, grazing her skin until he held it beneath her chin.

My breath quickened in anger at the way he held her and the way he threatened her. Jane's eyes filled with tears as she looked at me, mirroring my pain.

I gritted my teeth. "Are you too much of a coward to fight me, Frederick?"

"Why would I fight you when I don't have to?" Frederick asked with a twisted grin. "Jane is mine whether you like it or not." He moved the knife from under her chin back to her neck while his other hand moved her hair away from her shoulder. He slid his finger up her shoulder then up her neck. flaunting that neither Jane nor I had any control of the situation. I barely managed to keep from lunging toward him. He moved his mouth toward her neck as he watched me.

Tears welled in Jane's eyes as his lips moved closer to her skin. She thought Frederick had already won.

Something inside of me snapped as Frederick's lips almost touched her and her tears fell. I needed him to loosen his grip on the knife for only a moment before I could—

It happened. He lowered the knife slightly from her throat. In one swift move, I grabbed his hand and pried it away from Jane's neck. When his eyes found mine, I knew what he saw. I was ready to kill him. He saw the rage, the fierce anger to end his life. And for once, I saw fear enter his soul.

Jane

If I thought Frederick was strong, it was nothing compared to Henry. Henry pried Frederick's hand away from my neck. Once the knife was free from my throat I pulled away from Frederick and slid out of his reach. Frederick took his other hand, his back against the carriage, and grappled with the dagger while Henry pulled his left arm back and lunged his fist into Frederick's face.

Frederick dropped the knife and staggered to the side, dropping to the ground. Henry picked up the blade and put it in his pocket before he grabbed Frederick by the shirt and pulled him up.

I was frozen watching Henry.

He immediately punched Frederick again, this time in the stomach, twice. Frederick fell to his knees, clutching his abdomen. Henry hooked his fist to Frederick's chin from underneath, then followed it up with a blow square on the nose, knocking Frederick to the ground. He made a grunting noise, but didn't move immediately.

Henry's eyes jumped to mine as he breathed in and out rapidly. He looked hesitant, as if he was afraid this moment might not be real, though determination was written on every inch of his face. I wanted to reach for him, but my hands were still tied behind my back. He took three quick strides toward me then turned me and held where my wrists were bound. The fabric rubbed against a blade until it broke free. He quickly sheathed and pocketed the knife.

"Jane," he breathed out in relief as I turned to face him. His arms enveloped me, holding me tenderly.

As Frederick moaned and writhed on the ground, Henry reluctantly let me go, then turned, urgently leading me to his horse. "I'm going to help you mount Spartan. I need you to get as far away from here as you can!"

"Henry, wait!" I exclaimed as he put his hands about my waist, ready to lift me to the saddle.

I brought my hand toward his face. "Come with me. Let's find Lily and leave."

His hand rose to mine, lacing our fingers as he gently pressed the back of my hand to his cheek, moving it slowly down to his lips. Emotion rose to my heart as he looked at me the way I remembered. I was everything to him. He loved me. Tears pricked my eyes as he brought me close.

"I can't come with you, Jane. I have to finish this."

He looked a few yards away to where Frederick was trying to pick himself off the ground. Frederick let out an angry, ragged breath, attempting to stand, but not yet able to manage it.

Henry guided me behind him, shielding me from Frederick, in case he unexpectedly advanced.

My next words came out frantic. "Henry, come with me. Please! If we go now and find Lily, you don't have to fight him." I took his hand in mine. "He's a lunatic. He told me he killed James Elliot, and that he plans to kill his own father after his next birthday."

Henry stiffened at my words. I kept going. "Please," I begged as fresh tears began to form in my eyes. "He boasts about the training his father has paid for, that he can best any man." I pulled on him but he was completely immovable.

"When I tell you to run, Jane, I need you to go, immediately." He said the words with unyielding finality. "Frederick knows I'll do anything to keep you from harm. If you are close to me, he will have the advantage. Take Spartan, and don't go after your sister on your own. Charles will protect her."

"But Lord Elliot is outnumbered. Mr. Campbell and Mr. Hughes are both still out there."

"Yes, and you could become a bargaining piece for either of them and make it harder for Charles to retrieve her safely." His face was anxious and firm. "If you run after your sister, I will not be able to focus."

I looked at Henry's dark horse blending in with the night. Spartan stood at the ready, a loyal advocate.

My fingers reached for Henry's face as I stepped around to his side.

I guided his face to look at me until our eyes met.

"I'm not leaving you again," I whispered. "Would you leave me?"

He let out a pained breath and looked at me hopelessly. "I could never leave you, Jane." His words melted me. "But Frederick will certainly run me through if you're here at my side. And I'm not leaving until this is finished." He took his spare hand and lightly traced my cheek. "If I know you are safe, Frederick doesn't stand a chance."

Frederick's teeth were bared in fury as his eyes moved to Henry's hand on my face and he finally stood, leaning on the carriage for support. He wiped blood from his nose and snarled, pulling off his coat, jaw clenched. He threw his jacket to the ground, slowly drawing his sword, though he still didn't advance at that moment, catching his breath.

Before I could argue further, Henry took my waist in his hands and lifted me into the saddle.

Henry removed his own coat then moved to unbutton and cast aside his vest, leaving only his loose white shirt. He looked absolutely formidable as he deftly drew a sword at his hip.

Despite Henry's powerful presence, a crippling fear consumed me.

Frederick took a step toward us and then another until he was running, yelling out in fury.

"I don't want you anywhere near our blades," Henry said, looking up at me on his horse. Panic edged his voice. "Run!"

I didn't wait any longer. I flicked the reins, leading Spartan away quickly. Henry was right. I would only make things worse if I stayed close. I stopped a few paces away, watching their every move. Frederick watched my retreat, and for a moment, I wondered if he would follow me. I held fast to the reins, ready to charge at Frederick if it was warranted.

Lily

As the sound of horse hooves came closer, Mr. Campbell began to panic, his hand shaking as he held his gun. It was no longer the time for me to push my luck.

"Not a sound from you, or I will shoot whoever is coming." His voice quivered as much as his gun did.

"You're hurting me!" Jane's voice suddenly filled the air from somewhere around the back of one of the houses.

"Jane!" I yelled, despite knowing I was pushing my luck with Mr. Campbell's nerves.

"Lily!" she called back. She sounded relieved as she said my name. Tears pricked my eyes. She didn't sound bitter despite the fact that she thought I betrayed her. If only I could speak to her and tell her the truth of everything.

"Quiet!" Mr. Campbell hissed with a terrified voice.

We waited in the black of the alleyway, holding perfectly still. Each beat of my heart was an eternity, each breath agony, as I waited for something. Anything.

Mr. Campbell suddenly gasped from behind me and let go of me. I didn't wait to see why he released me. I ran toward the back of the alley toward where I had heard Jane's voice. Perhaps I would be able to find something to free my hands with. I had only taken a few steps before fingers grabbed me from behind. I began to scream out but a hand clapped over my mouth.

"I'll have none of that," came an oily voice behind me. It wasn't Mr. Campbell, but Mr. Hughes. I attempted to bite his fingers but he moved them out of the way as I bit down.

"I like a little fight," he whispered. Terror ran through me as he pinned me against a wall.

"If you scream when I release my hand, I'll make things interesting very quickly." He took his hand away from my mouth as he revealed a knife, tipped in blood.

I was suddenly missing Mr. Campbell's approach.

Mr. Campbell! My eyes darted in the darkness until I made out his figure, lying on the ground moaning. What had Mr. Hughes done? My eyes flicked to the knife in his hand once more, understanding dawning.

"What do you want with me?" I asked. "Do you have gambling debts too that you need a wealthy lady to pay?"

"No. I just don't think it's fair that Mr. Campbell gets a rich wife and I'm stuck with nothing. I know Lord Fletcher won't let me have your sister, but I think you are just as . . . " His finger trailed up my spine. "Delicious."

I was going to be sick.

"Mr. Hughes, don't touch me," I spat.

He leaned in toward my ear. "I'll do what I want—"

The gallop of the horses grew louder until it was upon us.

BANG!

I gasped, turning my face toward the carriage. A man held a gun in the air, looking to the side of the house.

I opened my mouth to call out, but Mr. Hughes's hand flew over my mouth again. He gagged me next before I could do anything else. It wasn't much of a fight with my hands already tied behind my back.

He hissed out an angry breath as he looked out at the rider enveloped in billowing smoke from the gunfire. Another man jumped from his horse, hurtling to the ground by Mr. Campbell's carriage.

Charles! I tried to scream out, but no sound carried against the obtrusion in my mouth.

Mr. Hughes didn't even try to pull me along. He grabbed me roughly and flung me over his shoulder. It wasn't easy for him. He lumbered about as if he'd never done a day of work in his life, but eventually stumbled out of the alleyway. I considered kicking and squirming, but if I somehow wiggled my way off, I had no hands to break my fall. Mr. Hughes walked as fast as he could toward the back of the house. I prayed that Charles would find me in time.

I held my breath, apprehensive, as Mr. Hughes wobbled, walking up the few creaking back porch steps to one of the houses and quietly opened the door.

It seemed the perfect place to make some noise. I suddenly lashed out, trying to connect my foot with the door. It worked, though I wasn't sure it was loud enough for anyone to hear. Mr. Hughes ran inside and bolted the door, trapping me inside with him.

Charles

I flung myself from Apollo as soon as we arrived. Henry was already approaching a man that looked like Frederick, who was about to strike Miss Mason with his fist. Lily was nowhere to be seen.

My heart pounded as my eyes searched in the darkness. I considered calling out to her, but I didn't want to give away my position in case I needed the element of surprise. I ran around back to one of the houses, keeping my eyes and ears peeled for the smallest movement, the smallest sound. A thump sounded near the opposite house. I ran swiftly past the wall and adjoining alley, but as the decaying steps of the other worn structure came into my sights, the door slammed then bolted shut.

I cursed under my breath, reminding myself not to yell out and give my position away. The two small windows that ran the perimeter of the main floor were locked, though it wouldn't have mattered since I wouldn't have been able to fit through them. I arched my head back, finding a large window on the second floor. Removing my coat and vest, I detached my sword, and hid it beneath the back steps. I reached into my coat pockets and snatched my sheathed knife and pistol, securing them inside the pockets of my breeches. I paused as something else clunked to the ground. It was Mr. Johnson's heavy metal bird pin. I didn't have time to fit it in my pocket. Every second counted.

I threw my coat and vest beneath the stairs then turned, leaving the bird pin behind. I took two steps forward—then immediately darted back, snatched up the metal pin, for it seemed a lucky omen, and forced it inside my pocket as I ran around to the front of the house. Looking up once more at the large window on the second floor . . . I climbed.

Lily

I breathed frantically against my gag as Mr. Hughes lumbered through the pitch-black space. He moved deeper through the room, heaving loudly with each step, then ascended stairs that croaked beneath our weight. I closed my eyes, despite the darkness, wondering if he might fall backward while carrying me. Eventually he reached the top of the staircase and walked straight several paces forward. My eyes still hadn't adjusted, but my foot grazed a door frame. We had just entered another room.

He walked another few steps until suddenly, he collapsed. I gasped, waiting to hit the ground. Instead, I was met with a thick mattress. Mr. Hughes landed right next to me, panting. I kicked him away from me as hard as I could. He grappled with my foot, but I kicked again as hard as I could, and this time I struck his face. I heard him hit something from behind, cursing loudly. With violent speed, I rolled over and got to my feet.

I wanted to run, but still couldn't see. My breath shuddered in and out as I walked slowly through the darkness. I had no idea where I was or where the stairs began, and the last thing I wanted to do in a moment like this was take a tumble down the stairs. I finally made contact with a wall and quietly put my back to it, following it carefully. If only I could put my hands in front of me, but they were still tied tightly behind my back.

Mr. Hughes scrambled around in the darkness, no doubt

looking for me. I tried to control my breathing so it wouldn't give me away.

All went quiet.

My heart pounded faster. I didn't dare move. I heard shifting right next to me, and then the air was pulled from my lungs as I heard the wall being scraped by something that sounded like a knife. Any second now he would find me. I thought about moving, but he would only hear me, and I knew running blindly wouldn't be helpful either. My breath shook out as his hand grazed over me. I couldn't breathe. Fear seized me, my legs unable to move, glued in place.

He chuckled as tears burned my eyes.

He brought his mouth close to my ear. "You're going to regret that."

Just as he pried me away from the wall, throwing me toward the mattress, a gun fired and glass shattered from somewhere on the upper floor.

Mr. Hughes gripped my arm tight, his fingers digging in until I could barely hold back from whimpering.

"If you push me, I'll put a dagger in my cousin's back, right in front of you."

I tried to yell out to Charles, knowing it would be no use. Only muffled murmuring came out through the gag.

He seethed quietly at my muttering. "Very well, have it your way. You can be the bait." He let go of me suddenly and slunk away. I couldn't see well enough to notice what direction he went.

Though Mr. Hughes was no match for Charles's strength and skill, he clearly knew his way around this dark, creaking hideout. Adding to that, he was quiet and had no conscience.

Charles

I was grateful for the old wood that made up this rotting structure. Boards jutted out at odd angles from the wear of age and moist air, making it easy to find grips as I scaled the outer wall. I climbed at a frenzied pace, feeling that each second, each breath mattered. Time was my enemy, and it already had the lead.

I breathed heavily, fearing what horrors awaited Lily. I was halfway up the wall when a loud thud sounded from the upper floor, followed by some rummaging and banging around. I let out an angry shout and climbed even faster, my eyes on a window just above and to the right. I moved myself upward, climbing until I was just above the window. I didn't wait to see if I could pull it open. I pulled the pistol from my pocket while I held tight to the wall with my other hand. Without hesitating, I cocked it back and pulled the trigger. Glass rained down below as I gripped the wall tightly and kicked the remaining pieces of glass away from the frame. Now standing on the ledge, I jumped inside. A shroud of blackness surrounded me on every side, taunting my every sense.

I waited for my eyes to adjust, listening carefully for any movement. Whoever was inside wanted to remain hidden until the right moment. Once again, I thought about calling out to Lily. But I knew Lily. If she was able, she would have warned me.

I gritted my teeth in frustration—My eyes were taking far too long to adjust. Throwing caution to the wind, I moved along the wall as quietly as I could, putting a hand out in front of me.

My fingers soon met the corner of another wall. I followed it at a quicker pace, feeling a consuming desperation to find Lily. I shoved away the nagging thoughts that flew through my mind of her possible fate. I refused to consider any of them. The wall stretched on for what felt an eternity until my hand found a door frame. My eyes were finally beginning to adjust, though I still felt mostly blind. I peered inside the doorway, making sure to keep myself hidden. What awaited me halted my breath, made me pause. There, in the faint glow of a small window stood a subdued silhouette in the middle of the room. I could tell by the height and delicate outline that it was Lily. But why was she standing in the middle of the room making no sound? Where was her captor? I crept inside, making certain to draw no sound. She was facing me but I couldn't see her expression. I didn't know if she could detect my presence in this sea of shadow.

I still didn't dare call out to her. Instead, I eased forward, afraid to believe she was really in front of me. It was unnerving to see her so still. I finally stretched out my hand and touched her arm. Her breath caught but it was muffled.

"Lily," I breathed out quietly.

She began shaking her head back and forth and making muffled murmurs. I finally realized she was gagged and her hands were tied behind her back. I quickly reached for my knife and moved around her, carefully cutting away the ties at her hands, then untied the bind around her mouth.

She turned to me frantically and held tight to my shirt, trembling.

"He's in here with us," her shaking voice whispered. "I'm the bait."

I wanted to put Lily behind me to ensure her safety, but I didn't know if someone was lurking beyond in the blackness. I held her close to me with one arm, my knife outstretched with the other. She wasn't safe anywhere. We were sitting ducks in the middle of a pond of shadow, waiting to be fired upon.

Lily

Charles held me close. I had never felt more relieved and more anxious at feeling his touch. I wanted to crumble in his arms and cry. What I wouldn't give to be with him on the dance floor again and hear him say that he loved me.

My eyes had finally adjusted enough that I could make out the door frame and the stairs just beyond. I needed to leave—run from Charles so he could protect us both. Mr. Hughes would either bolt after me or he would advance on Charles. Either way, Charles was safer without me to protect. It was the only way he would make it out alive. If I could somehow find a lantern downstairs, Mr. Hughes wouldn't stand a chance.

Before I could talk myself out of it, I moved out of Charles's protective shield.

"Stop Mr. Hughes, then find me downstairs," I whispered.

"Lily," he whispered back urgently. My breath shook but I didn't give in. I ran for the stairs as quickly as I could.

Charles

Lily tore herself from my grip and darted for the stairs before I understood what was happening. I called for her then remembered that I was a standing target and that Lily needed my protection. I crouched low on instinct. Jacob would most likely attack me before he ran after Lily. He would have a much harder time seeing me if I was low to the ground.

Just as I crouched low I heard him advance toward me. I dove toward the sound, hoping to knock him off his feet. We made contact and he stumbled forward, though he didn't completely lose his footing. I watched his faint silhouette charge for the door after Lily. As much as I wanted to run my dagger through his heart right then and there, I knew I needed to wait for the Bow Street Runners. We needed answers.

I quickly jumped to my feet and ran for the door, pulling him backward. As he turned around to face me, the outline of a knife in his hand barreled downward toward me. I grabbed his wrist just in time, stopping the blade from piercing my chest. Once I had a hold of his wrist, it was not a fair fight—I had all the advantage. I pried his hand away easily, then yanked it toward the floor, slamming my foot down on his fingers. He wailed out in pain, dropping the blade. His hunched shoulders made it easy for me to drive my knee into his stomach, immediately followed by a series of blows to the face with my fist. He bowled over to the ground and moaned in pain. It would hopefully be enough until the Bow Street Runners showed up. I grabbed his knife and ran out the door, slamming it behind me as I bolted for the stairs. I would leave no more chances for Lily to be taken again by someone else.

Just as I reached the bottom stair, a lantern illuminated the room below. Lily held it up until my face could be seen. She breathed out in relief.

"Charles," she whispered.

Warmth and relief poured over me as she placed the lantern on a small table and took quick strides toward me.

I discarded Jacob's knife, tossing it to the stove, as I closed the gap and pulled her close. It took everything in me not to sweep her up into my arms and carry her to my horse immediately, flying far from this black hole.

"Where is Jacob?" Her voice still trembled slightly.

"He won't be coming down for some time. And I closed the door, so if he leaves, we will hear it open first. Now we just wait for the Bow Street Runners to arrive."

"No, we need to find Jane now and leave immediately," Lily said urgently, pulling my hand toward the door.

"Henry is taking care of Jane."

"But Lord Fletcher is with her," she said frantically.

I chuckled. "Henry is more than capable of handling Lord Fletcher." I slowly brought her back into my embrace. "Henry is going to try to get him to talk. We can't interrupt just now or it could ruin all our plans. I need Lord Fletcher, Jacob, and Mr. Campbell in jail tonight."

"Mr. Campbell might not be going. I think Jacob stabbed him."

Lily leaned against my shoulder. She had been through quite the ordeal in just a few hours. Her intelligence and bravery always amazed me.

I pulled her closer and held her to me for what felt like minutes until her trembling finally subsided.

Eventually, she lifted her face away from my shoulder and looked up at me. Even in the dim light of the lantern's glow her eyes were hypnotic. She reached her hand up to my cheek and traced her fingers along my skin. I closed my eyes then turned my head, pressing a light kiss to her wrist before opening my eyes again.

"You shaved." The corner of her lips turned up, revealing her dimple.

I had been dying to see that expression since I had left her in Wilton. Her fingers then trailed the sides of my hair.

She smirked. "And you cut your hair."

"Do you like it?" I asked, unable to hide my self-consciousness.

Lily's arms wrapped slowly behind my neck. "I don't believe you could do anything to your appearance that I wouldn't like."

I pulled her close again until the side of her face rested against mine. I let out a breath of contentment at her nearness. She held herself close. After a time, I felt her soft lips press to my cheek before she spoke in a hushed tone.

"I do hope that eventually I'll see your old look again." I could hear the flirtatious grin in her voice. "But I do really like this look too."

My arms tightened around her instinctively. I could feel her heart racing against mine.

She brushed her lips a little further down my cheek and lightly kissed it again. She was tantalizing, drawing in every part of me.

I turned my face toward where she kissed me, my lips drawn to hers. She held her breath as if my nearness made it hard for her to breathe. I slowly drew myself forward until our lips were only inches apart. She let out a sigh as I trailed the back of my fingers down her cheek, continuing down to her neck. She closed her eyes, letting the moment take her. Once her eyes opened again, I knew it was over. Her desire for me was as palpable as mine was for her.

She closed the distance, finding my lips with hers. They were even sweeter than I remembered: soft, pure, and perfect. Our lips moved together slowly as I shifted my hands to her hair. I hungered for her touch more than ever now that she knew who I really was. My shirt gathered in her fingers as she slowly moved her hands up over my chest.

My heart hammered loudly against her every move. My fingers clung more deeply to her hair as my kiss deepened. She didn't pull back even when her hair began to fall from their pins.

I needed to stop. Lily still wasn't safe. But when she kissed me this way and pulled herself to me as if she could never have enough, it was impossible to find the will to end it.

Lily

If Charles's first kiss had been hard to pull away from, this was something else entirely. He kissed me with such feeling that I had no thought for anything else. I was completely swept away by it. His lips were slow and tender while he caressed me as if I was something divine. His fingers were buried in my hair until one by one each curl fell away from its captor, trailing down my back and shoulders.

I was completely consumed.

Charles

As Lily's hair fell around her, I knew I was in trouble. Her lips fell away from mine, my fingers still entwined in her hair. I drank in her eyes—her lips. I needed to stop now before I could no longer control myself.

If only she hadn't worn this dress and been so . . . Lily. I promised myself I would only taste one more kiss. But I knew it was a lie the moment I pulled her lips to mine again. I untangled my fingers from the dark locks that surrounded them. Her smooth dress slid through my fingers next as I moved them about her waist. Our passion was consuming us both.

A creak sounded from the stairs. Reality doused me like a cold shower of rain. Lily heard it too. My eyes opened as hers did. Our breath came out in heavy waves as we still clung to each other.

First, I would kill Jacob for ending mine and Lily's kiss. Then, after they took him to jail, I'd thank him for giving me the clarity I needed to save this moment with her for another time.

Lily and I waited silently for another noise but nothing came. Every heartbeat and breath felt an eternity, and sounded even louder. My eyes didn't leave the stairs.

"I need you to hide," I said under my breath in Lily's ear.

Her head turned toward the kitchen, scanning the small table and stove. Nothing would keep her unseen in that small space. Her face then turned toward a door frame that led to a back room, tucked away behind the stairs. I looked at her for a brief moment and nodded before my eyes returned to the stairs.

I reluctantly let her go, heart still pounding from the way she moved me. She was only a few steps away from me when I heard the clicking sound of a pistol, ready to be fired.

"If you move, I shoot." Jacob's voice came out of the darkness of the stairway. The lantern didn't illuminate those parts beyond the lower steps—he could see me, but I could not see him.

Lily froze, looking over at me. Terror filled her eyes. I wanted to reach for her but I knew it could be the last thing I did.

"I really did enjoy that little demonstration," Jacob said with an oily voice. "I didn't realize you had a passionate side, cousin." I could hear his twisted smile in his next words. "And now I have seen the sort of untamed passion Miss Mason possesses. I can't wait to discover it for myself."

My blood boiled at his implication. Hands resting at my side, I could feel the knife, bird pin, and pistol inside my pockets. Unfortunately I had already fired my pistol and it was now useless. If I reached for my knife, Jacob would pull the trigger.

"What do you want?" I finally asked.

"And here I thought you were the smart one," Jacob said.

"Do you want money?" I asked.

"I get money either way," Jacob said. "If I shoot you, I inherit your wealth and everything with it. After that, I will marry Miss Mason and have even more wealth. On the other hand, if I decide *not* to shoot you, I will take Miss Mason as my bride anyway."

"And what makes you think I would let you marry Miss Mason?" It was difficult not to snarl as the words came out of my mouth.

"I know you, Charles. You are stuffy and arrogant, and all you care about is your title and station. Lily is a ruined woman. You won't want her now. Before you made it to the house, I had my way with her. She is already mine." I felt sick. If Jacob had truly forced himself upon Lily I would never forgive myself.

"I will love Lily the same regardless of what you have done!" I seethed.

"Jacob's a liar," Lily spat. "He has done nothing to me."

"You must not value my cousin's life." Jacob twisted a grin at Lily, coming down the steps slowly as he held the gun's position aimed at my chest. "Once a bullet is lodged in his heart, you will have nowhere to go." His finger began to tighten on the trigger.

"If you shoot him, you will be hanged!" Lily heaved.

"Only if I'm caught. And you already know what will happen if you squeal. But in case you've already forgotten, you will no longer have your sister or family if you talk." Jacob smiled as if he was relishing the thought.

"It doesn't matter," Lily said, trying to calm her voice. "An investigation has already opened for the murder of the late Lord Elliot, and you are the lead suspect. If Charles Elliot is killed in the middle of the investigation, all evidence points to you. You will be imprisoned immediately for killing an earl, and you will hang within the month."

Lily had always displayed a gift of getting her point across. If Jacob's look of shock was any indicator, she had succeeded again. I cocked my eyebrow at him. "It's true."

"You're bluffing," Jacob said angrily.

"Are we?" I asked.

"Then it appears that I hang either way," Jacob fumed. "I might as well take you with me."

"Or," Lily said, putting her hands up, walking carefully toward Jacob, "you could leave now. Take a boat or ferry and leave this place. Let Lord Fletcher take the fall for everything, since he is the one that actually killed the earl. You can walk a free man."

Jacob gritted his teeth. "Charles would never let me run without seeing that I am put away eventually for capturing you."

"It's true," I said. "But it's the only chance you have. If you kill me, you hang. If you don't kill me, but wait around, you will still hang. The Bow Street Runners are on their way as we speak."

"Or," Jacob hissed, "you are both liars and I can take it all."

"And are you willing to take that risk, cousin?" I said the last word with disgust.

Jacob clenched his teeth.

Lily

It was all I could do to hold my ground. I wanted to run between Charles and Mr. Hughes. His finger tightened on the trigger once more.

"Mr. Hughes! Put your gun down now, or I won't come with you!" My voice was frantic.

He notched his brows. "What do you mean?"

"How else can I spell it out?" I said derisively. "If you put down your gun, I will come with you."

"I would rather just shoot him and force you along," he said with a suggestive smile. Something snapped inside me at that moment, making my next words come out icy and quiet.

"Then let me make myself very clear, Mr. Hughes. If you shoot him, I will kill you myself when you least expect it."

He opened his mouth to remind me of his threats for my family but I cut him off.

"You will go to prison if you kill him. I will not hesitate to speak about what you have done. You can threaten my family's safety, but I, too, have money. I can hire my own muscle to protect those I love, or have them flee the country. But if you shoot that man . . . " I pointed to Charles, "I will already be dead. And I will make it my mission to haunt you for the rest of your short, miserable life."

"And what will you do if you go with me?" he asked, clearly not convinced that I would do anything different.

"I will most likely flee, or kill you another way," I said matter of factly. "You are not bright, Mr. Hughes, nor are you strong. You are often drunk, and I doubt you will become sober for the rest of your life simply for the fear that I may either escape or put a knife in your back."

He was getting angry at my condescending remarks. Good. I just needed him to lower his pistol a little farther.

His hand lowered even more as his eyes shifted to me.

Charles slowly reached inside his pocket, then stopped moving his hand when Mr. Hughes's eyes moved back to him. But his gun was off of its aim and he was losing patience.

"It seems that either way I die. I might as well take one of you with me," he sneered as he looked at Charles. "Best I put my bullet where it does the most damage, cousin."

In one swift movement, Mr. Hughes aimed his gun at me.

I gasped and clutched my chest as an explosion of sound echoed in the small space. My ears rang and everything moved slowly. As my eyes found Charles, his hand released a knife. It rotated in the air until it found its place in Mr. Hughes's heart. He dropped the pistol and staggered backward, pulling out the knife. Red liquid pooled through his vest as he looked down, an oddly shaped piece of metal protruding from his wrist.

It made no sense.

At first my breath came in and out quickly. Everything moved at an odd angle, the room swaying. A white, foggy haze enveloped the room right before the floor came up to meet me and everything went black.

39

DOCK

Jane

My breath halted, heart dropping, as Henry moved in powerful strides toward Frederick, whose sword came down for the first strike. Henry's blade came up to block before he shoved Frederick.

A bead of water marked my cheek, followed by another. I turned my face heavenward, the sky a covering of formidable clouds, rolling over the moon and stars. A tense breath left me as I gripped the reins.

Blood pulsed in my ears, a deafening surge, as I fixed my eyes on Henry, sword at the ready. I didn't know what sort of training he had received, or if he was skilled with the blade. But I knew Frederick was quick and ruthless.

I tensed as Frederick swung from above once more, coming down hard. Henry parried it with confidence, making Frederick grit his teeth and strike with a series of slashes back and forth. My breath caught each time their swords clashed, though Henry moved through the attacks with ease.

More drops of water fell from above until the whole sky plunged its tears to the earth below, making Henry's shirt cling to his skin. My eyes were drawn to his torso and back as his sword clashed against Frederick's again and again.

Not only were his blows powerful, with arms seemingly sculpted from marble, but his stance was strong. Water dripped from his hair as he moved the blade deftly, born to wield it. Frederick may have received the finest training England had to offer, but Henry was something else entirely. And the look on his face stole my breath. He was completely enraged. He was raw, masculine power.

As their swords connected again with force, the rain fell in droves. Henry blocked Frederick's attacks as they came in crossing patterns. After my initial panic dissipated, and I continued to watch them closely, it seemed that Henry was holding back. The fury on his face stated that he was barely able to keep himself from running Frederick through. What was he waiting for?

A slight movement caught the corner of my eye: Three men hiding behind Mr. Hughes's carriage. They watched, waited.

Henry finally spoke. "I assume you are tired of me stealing everything from you." He raised a brow, intentionally antagonizing Frederick.

"You have stolen nothing from me!" Frederick barked. "Jane will be mine whether you've captured her heart or not."

"Idle threats," Henry said, grinning. "The lady ultimately gets to choose."

"She will have a hard time choosing you once you are dead."

Their blades clashed again, and I finally understood why Henry was holding back. He wanted Frederick to confess in front of these men.

"Would you really kill me, Lord Fletcher?" Henry asked.

"I *will* kill you—no one will even bat an eye. You're not even an Elliot. The world won't shed a tear when I rid it of poor, penniless, Henry Thomas." He spat on the ground. "I will take Jane and she will pay for what she's put me through tonight. You can be assured that when I have my way with her, it will be forceful and thorough."

Henry almost lost his composure. He gritted his teeth and dealt Frederick a blow that he was barely able to deflect.

On Frederick's next swing, however, Henry barely blocked the move in time. Frederick grinned and immediately began a series of fast blows. Henry was breathing quickly and brought his sword up just in time with each collision. My stomach knotted—His strength was wearing out. I thought about charging into the middle of their fight with Spartan, but it could do more damage than good. Despite Henry's exhaustion, he taunted Frederick.

"You're a lot of talk, Lord Fletcher." Henry's breath came out even quicker than before. "But you and I both know that you don't have the stomach to end someone's life."

A quiet gasp escaped me as Frederick swung his sword out from the side. Henry moved slowly, blocking it at the very last moment. The force sent Henry to the ground.

"Henry!" I yelled, frantic. He looked at me for a split second and Frederick flicked his sword, cutting Henry's arm. My heart plummeted, breath catching in my throat.

Frederick gave a twisted smile as he pointed his sword at Henry's throat. "You think I don't have it in me to end your life? Frederick chuckled and spoke with an icy tone. "Unlike you, I'm not afraid to get my hands dirty."

"You say it as if you already have blood on your hands. And yet I still don't believe it," Henry retorted defiantly.

"I do have blood on my hands, and I intend to have more, starting with you—followed by my father, as soon as I'm eligible to take my inheritance. And before you question whether I would do it or not, I might ask how you think James Elliot suddenly died."

"You can't take credit for killing a man that died of an illness," Henry scoffed.

"I can if it was an illness from poison." Frederick moved his lips up over his teeth in a barbaric, snarling smile.

"So you killed my father in the shadows, as the coward you are?" Henry seethed.

"Don't worry, I won't make the same mistake with you."

"No," I breathed as Frederick pulled his sword back to make his final move. I closed my eyes just as metal clashed against metal. My eyes flew open to Henry batting Frederick's sword aside with his own, then quickly jumping to his feet. Henry no longer breathed rapidly.

A hard line was etched in his lips and he looked as rigid as stone. In three swift strokes, Henry disarmed his foe, his sword now pointing at Frederick's throat.

Had Henry intentionally let Frederick have the upper hand in order to obtain his confession? Frederick growled out at Henry, lunging. In a flash, Henry flicked his wrist, cutting Frederick's cheek, before moving his sword once more to Frederick's throat. Frederick bellowed in pain as his hand flew to the mark on his face that would brand him forever.

Henry's jaw tensed. "That's for my father."

The men behind the carriage walked toward Henry, each one bearing a uniform. The largest of the three men spoke in a deep, rumbling voice.

"Lord Fletcher, you will be held at Newgate Prison until you are tried for the murder of the late James Elliot, Earl of Wiltshire."

Frederick tried to pick up his sword again but Henry flicked his wrist once more, making an identical mark on the other side of Frederick's cheek.

"And that one is for Jane," Henry said with a clenched smile. "I suggest you remain still."

As a man in uniform put Frederick in handcuffs, Henry moved to walk toward me then stopped, turning back to Frederick. "You were only wrong about one thing, *my lord.*" Henry used Frederick's title with a mocking tone. "I do have it in me to end your life. I would just rather see you pay for your crimes."

Charles

I caught Lily as she collapsed to the floor.

"Lily!" I cried out, gently placing her limp body on the ground. My heart hammered as I searched for a wound. It was too dark to see well. Her breath came out low and shallow.

"Lily, Can you hear me?"

She still didn't respond. My heart roared, lungs iron as I cradled her and rushed to the back room, placing her on a bed.

I darted back out to the table and snatched the lantern, returning to her side. The lantern illuminated her frame, but I couldn't immediately find blood. She looked pale in the dim light.

"Lily, please wake up." I lightly shook her, fear seizing my heart. "Wake up!" I put my ear to her heart—but my own heart hammered loudly in my ears, deafening any other noise. I cursed out with a shaky breath, taking her hand in mine. Her fingers were freezing.

She suddenly took in a labored breath and her fingers moved against mine.

"Lily?" She stirred again and gave an airy groan. I leaned over her and felt her shudder as her breath started coming in and out normally. I let out a breath I'd been holding and shoved a hand through my hair, my heart still pounding furiously.

She tried to speak but her words came out slurred and muffled until her eyes opened slowly and settled on mine.

She looked at me for a long moment, confused, then smiled and reached up, brushing her fingers through my hair.

"Am I dreaming, Henry?" Hearing her voice after such a moment was like breaking the water's surface and taking in air after drowning.

A guttural exhale escaped me, leaving my entire body jittery but relieved. I leaned over and placed the lantern on a small table next to the bed then smiled, drinking in her eyes.

"Not Henry." I took both her hands and kissed each of her fingers, lingering on the one that currently held her ring.

Her forehead creased and her eyes searched mine until they filled with a remembrance of the night's events. She gasped and attempted to sit up. "Where is Mr. Hughes?"

I took her shoulders and eased her back down onto the bed, worried about her sitting up too quickly.

"He's . . . in the other room. And he will be staying there until somebody moves him out."

Her eyes settled on our intertwined fingers. "The last thing I remember was Mr. Hughes firing a gun on me. He pulled a knife out of his chest and there was . . . a lot of . . . blood . . . " She began to go limp again.

"No, no, no, no . . . " I carefully propped her up, beginning to understand. Lily hadn't been shot—she had passed out at the sight of Jacob's blood.

She groaned again. "My head is spinning."

I kissed her cheek, sighing with gratitude that she was alright. "Here." I helped her move to a sitting position before I sat against the head rest next to her, then carefully guided her to me until her back was resting against my chest. She let her head lean back against my shoulder before I rested my head on top of hers and breathed in her light floral scent.

"Lily, do you normally faint at the sight of blood?" I finally asked.

"No," she said with some defiance, then paused, questioning herself. "Mm . . . Perhaps. I have never seen blood of that magnitude before, or in those circumstances. But now that I think of it, I did feel off-kilter once when I saw Oliver with a bloody nose. But I only got a glimpse of it before I bolted."

"Well, don't think about it too much," I chuckled, moving her hair away from her shoulder, lightly stroking my fingers against her skin. I closed my eyes at the warmth that flowed through her now.

"Charles, was something metal sticking out of Mr. Hughes's wrist?"

I pulled her closer to me as I thought about the metal bird pin. It was the reason she sat here breathing against me.

"There was." I kissed the top of her head. "I believe we may have to invite Matthew Johnson to our wedding."

She reared her head back. Her next words came out quiet and somber. "Mr. Johnson was shot."

"Mr. Johnson was very lucky," I countered.

"So he didn't die from the shot Mr. Campbell fired?" she asked.

"No."

She breathed out in relief, then looked up at me. "What does any of that have to do with the metal object I saw in Mr. Hughes's wrist?"

"Well, if you must know, Matthew asked me to give you that

particular item. It was a heavy pin that had been in the shape of a bird before Mr. Campbell put a bullet inside it. But it saved Matthew's life, and he was able to tell us where you'd gone because of it. He asked me to give it to you and say, in his exact words, 'Tell my Golden Eagle I tried to save her. Give this to her as a sign of my bravery.' "

Lily chuckled. "Poor Mr. Johnson; ever the romantic." She turned her body into me so I now cradled her. "And how did my souvenir end up with Mr. Hughes?"

I was unable to speak the words just then. I was still trying to push away the image of Lily's lifeless body in my arms.

I buried my face in her hair and breathed in her scent to remind myself that she was still here. "When Jacob turned his pistol on you, I grabbed the first thing in my pocket and threw it at his gun. It connected with his wrist instead, and I thought it threw off his aim. I immediately hurled my knife at his heart next, but then you lost consciousness." My next words came out ragged. "I thought the worst."

She held perfectly still as I leaned in and kissed her head. She nuzzled her face into my shirt, then raised her fingertips to my face. I closed my eyes as she trailed them along my cheek and temple and up through the side of my hair. I felt her hair shift against my arm as she sat up, bringing her face closer to mine.

She tenderly kissed my cheek. "How long do we have before the Bow Street Runners show up?"

"Any minute now, if they aren't already here."

She kissed my cheek again right next to my lips. "And how much do you care about my reputation?" She was teasing me, but also making a very good point. If we were discovered alone in this bedroom, her reputation would certainly be ruined.

"You always have enjoyed tormenting me," I said, turning my lips toward hers. I kissed her ever so gently, this time reminding myself that I loved Lily enough to spare her reputation as much as I could.

"Do you think you can walk now?" I asked, pressing my lips to her dimple.

"Yes. But I would rather just stay here with you."

"Don't tempt me, Lily. Your charms are the reason we are in this entire mess." I slowly helped her up from the bed, making sure she was stable on her feet once they touched the floor.

"We are in this mess because you couldn't wait to propose," she said, smirking.

"Only because you wanted to lure me out." I cocked an eyebrow. "You knew you would drive me mad with all of . . . this." I gestured my hands toward all of her. "And what have I told you about smirking?"

She smiled. "I plan to do it as much as possible if it means you can't stay away."

I smiled back, feeling completely whole. "Good. Now, let's see if Frederick has confessed."

Henry

Frederick roared out in anger like a wild animal. He clenched his teeth, blood dripping down his jaw, as two men in uniforms took his arms and guided him toward Jacob's carriage. I found the piece of fabric that had been used to bind Jane's hands and wrapped it tightly around the cut on my arm. Thankfully, it was nothing serious.

"This isn't over!" Frederick bellowed. "You and Charles will never be safe. I'll make those Mason brats pay! I have this city in the palm of my hand."

The man forcing Frederick into the carriage grinned and said, "We'll see about that, Lord Fletcher." He slammed the coach shut behind Frederick. That in itself was a beautiful irony: Frederick being taken prisoner in the same carriage in which he'd imprisoned Jane.

Jane! I looked over to find Spartan, but he no longer had a rider. I felt her fingers take my hand from behind before I saw her.

I turned and let out a throaty breath, relieved. Water clung to her hair and dress. She must have been freezing. And the beads of water that dripped from her curls and ran down the front of her neck made my pulse race.

I took each of her hands in mine and pressed them against my heart. "Your hands are ice."

A rumbling voice sounded behind me. "It looks like Frederick is still completely worthless." I turned to find Charles smiling, holding Lily's hand as though it were his lifeline.

Lily broke from him and ran to Jane. They embraced, shaking with tears.

I turned to Charles. "I need to speak with Jane alone. Are Jacob and Mr. Campbell—"

"Jacob is dead," Charles said without remorse. "Mr. Campbell was stabbed. I'm not sure if he's dead or not. I'll take care of him and speak with the Bow Street Runners." He gave me a nod and a grin. "Go speak with Miss Mason. There's a secluded dock behind the house."

Charles walked over to Lily and gently held her fingers in his as Jane and Lily talked. They spoke in hushed voices. Jane looked at Charles and then at me, shaking her head in disbelief at our nearly identical appearances.

I moved to her side, unable to keep myself from putting a hand on her back.

Miss Lily looked over at me and smiled in gratitude before she returned her gaze to Charles.

I spoke quietly in Jane's ear. "Might I have a private word?"

Her eyes found mine and she nodded. I offered her my arm, then led her behind the decaying houses toward the dock.

Jane

Moonlight rippled on the water, a gentle rushing sound meeting my ears. As Henry led me out onto the wooden slats, the warmth of his nearness spread throughout me, diffusing every piece of my soul with serenity.

He took my hand in his and turned to face me. "Jane," he said softly, eyes tortured. "What do you think of me?"

I stepped closer, studying his eyes. "Loved and penniless." I breathed out the words, understanding them for what they were. I remembered the way he had kissed me, thinking he could never have me. The way I had torn myself away from his arms that night. His anguish. My heart ached as realization struck: he'd initially believed I wouldn't have him due to his lack of fortune.

Leaning in, I rested the side of my face on his chest then slid my arms around his back. Henry's heart hammered strong and fast. His fingers gently coaxed my face upward until I was looking into his eyes. Even in the darkness they burned. They spoke a hundred words: he loved me; he would die for me; he couldn't live without me.

I committed to memory his every look, his every breath, then sighed. "Why didn't you tell me?" I swept my fingers up along the side of his face and rested them against his cheek. He slowly pressed his hand against mine. The warmth of his strong jaw spread against my palm. He closed his eyes and breathed in.

"I didn't tell you for more than one reason." I absorbed the sound of his voice. Especially while he held me this way.

"What reasons?" I asked.

His eyes moved between mine. "First, I was raised by the Elliots. I consider James and Elizabeth my parents, and Charles my brother. When Charles and I received an anonymous letter that our father was murdered, we decided to switch places to better investigate. Charles is better with facts, and I'm better with people . . . usually." He grinned as a corner of my mouth lifted, remembering our first encounter.

He continued, "Charles and I promised each other we would keep our disguises a secret. Under no circumstances were we to divulge our true identities." He stopped speaking.

"Why else?" I urged, putting the side of my face to his chest again, over his rain-soaked shirt, and listened to his heartbeat. He tightened his arms around me and breathed in, softly resting his head atop mine.

"Aside from keeping our disguise a secret, there were five rules." I could hear his smile through his words. My lips turned up at the sound. "One of them being that we were not to form any romantic attachments." He stopped talking, guiding my face upward once more until our eyes met.

"When I first saw you, Jane, I was struck by your beauty. I was convinced then, as I am convinced now, more than ever, that you are the most beautiful thing I have ever seen. I assumed your beauty would be your downfall.

"But when you put me in my place that evening without holding anything back, you stole a piece of my heart right then and there. You weren't wooed by my smooth words or my 'title.' I truly believed you would never come to tolerate me. It drove me to madness. I wanted to be around you more and more. Your untainted heart stole me even further. I couldn't get you out of my head." He released me with one of his hands and brushed his fingers against my lips. "I have dreamt of you every night since then."

My heart melted at his words. These confessions were too wonderful. He returned his hand to mine, lifting my fingers to his lips.

"At first I thought my heart would eventually have to break when our disguises ended and you would marry Frederick. But I couldn't accept the fact that you could be with such a barbarian. I felt guilty deceiving you, but I justified my actions of pursuing you by telling myself that I simply had to show you why you couldn't be with Frederick. Deep down I knew I was lying to myself. I couldn't stop seeing you. Each interaction left me craving more. I felt desperate to see you each day. After our carriage ride, I knew I was in love with you, and guilt often plagued my conscience.

"But still I kept it a secret from you and from Charles. Each time I saw you I told myself it would be my last. Yet each new day brought a new justification as to why I could see you just one more time." His eyes shifted between mine. "And so you stole my heart completely."

I slowly breathed out, bringing his hand to my heart. "And you stole mine." His eyes followed my every move before he spoke again.

"Which leads me to the final reason I didn't divulge the truth: I was afraid of losing you. You were under the impression that I was Lord Elliot, yet I had nothing to my name. I decided to travel for business in order to earn a living so I would have something to offer you." His need to go away suddenly made sense.

Henry's eyes turned somber. "And then you told me you knew the truth, and that I should know you better than to think I could lure you into such a trap."

I closed my eyes in regret as my painful words came back to haunt me.

"I thought you were engaged to another woman." Pain was etched in my voice. "I was out in the garden when you and Lord Elliot were speaking. The only thing I knew was that 'Lord Elliot' was intended for another. I thought you wanted me as your mistress."

Henry shook his head plaintively. "Jane." His deep, smooth tone sent tingles throughout me. I wanted him to say my name over and over again.

His eyes moved to my lips. "I want to be very clear. I am not engaged to another woman." His fingers glided up my arms until they reached my shoulders. From there, he trailed them upwards until they swept gently up my neck. His touch left tingles throughout my entire body before his hands cupped my face. "And I love you more than anything in this world."

Henry

My world changed forever the first time I laid eyes on Jane Mason. And now she held me more captive than ever before. It was as if she had arranged herself that night with the sole intent to torture me, and now the rain clung to her curls and dress, making her even more tempting. She was finally here with me, letting me reach out and touch her. She admitted that I'd stolen her heart and that she didn't despise me for it—even while she still believed me to be penniless.

My heart swelled, full of wonder: she knew the truth about who I was, and still she held tight to me.

As my fingers trailed from her cheek to her neck, her eyes closed.

When they opened again, they pulled me with their lure of rebellion—their desire to break all the rules. Her fingers moved slowly around my torso until they found my shirt clinging to my back. She drew herself closer then released one of her hands and brought it forward. My breath picked up as her hand moved over my chest and up to my shoulder. Her fingers drew higher, trailing up the back of my hair before lacing around my neck and slowly pulling my face close to hers. I was completely under her spell.

"I love you, Henry," she breathed. I knew the moment she said the words that there was no stopping what came next.

My hand fell to her waist, my other hand found the back of her neck, my fingers burying into her damp hair. Her breath came out with longing, inches from mine, as if she had been waiting an eternity for my nearness. Our time of agony was over.

The water from the docks rippled and shimmered around us as my lips whispered over hers. Her lips were even more divine than memory served. Our kiss was filled with hunger, driving my heart through my chest. My fingers entwined in her damp curls as she clung to my wet shirt. I gently pulled her hair until her head tipped back further, then cradled her head in my hands and trailed my lips down her neck.

She breathed out in satisfaction at my every move. I needed to stop, but when her lips tasted mine again, kissing me with such feeling—I couldn't hold back. I was spellbound by her every move, devoured by the fire that burned through me.

Her fingers traced my neck and my jaw as she kissed me without reserve.

An exhale of satisfaction escaped me as she gently pulled away. I brushed her lips against mine once more, ready to let our passion take over further when something yelled in the back of my mind. I wanted every part of Jane. If I didn't stop now, I didn't know how far I would go. She was too much for me to leave alone if I started again.

"Jane." My voice came out barely above a whisper. I couldn't help but put one more soft kiss to her lips as I held her face in my hands. "I think we had better go back and find your sister."

She let out a contented breath then nodded as I took her hand and coaxed her to turn, her back now against my chest. I wrapped my arms around her from behind, then leaned my head forward and rested the side of my face to hers.

She breathed with satisfaction. "Henry." She said my name as if it was the most splendid word she knew.

I closed my eyes as she said it, then kissed her cheek softly. "Jane." She made a brief humming sound of contentment, as though she could hear me say it a thousand times over.

"We need to get you dry," I finally said.

She turned back around to face me, resting her fingers over my heart as I pulled her close. A sheepish look crossed her face.

I grinned, cocking my head. "If you don't tell me what that look is for then I'll simply have to guess." I quoted her verbatim from when she caught me watching her on our first walk together.

She opened her mouth to speak, then closed it again quickly, smiling timidly. I chuckled at her expression. "Tell me."

She waited a moment before she finally spoke. "I was only thinking that you should probably get dry too . . . but I rather like this look on you." She looked down at my chest bashfully. She finally dared a look at me again, looking absolutely adorable with her shy but daring expression. "And I believe you are now in *my* debt for putting me through so much unnecessary heartache."

I smiled as I put my hand over hers. I loved the turn this conversation was taking. I wanted to be in Jane's debt for the rest of my life. I trailed my fingers beneath her chin until she was looking directly at me.

"And what do you want, Jane?"

"Aside from plenty of kisses . . . " I could see her searching for the right words, and for the nerve to say them.

It was hard not to kiss her right then. Her timidness was so charming that a part of me didn't want her to say what she was holding back just yet—but my curiosity got the better of me.

I grinned. "Do I need to pry it from you?"

"I think you owe me a fencing demonstration," she finally said. "Preferably one in the rain."

I chuckled, gratified that she enjoyed watching me. And I was even more pleased to hear that the attraction I felt for Jane was reciprocated. It was maddening sometimes how much I was taken with the way Jane moved and looked.

I held my grin, speaking quietly. "Or I could just remove my shirt when I fence. We can't always predict the weather, after all."

Even in the darkness her cheeks flushed. She swallowed as if the very idea was scandalous, but all too tempting at the same time. It was exactly the reaction I was hoping to get.

I couldn't help but chuckle.

She swatted my arm. "Stop teasing me." She tried to put on a serious face, but she couldn't manage it. Her smile leaked through.

I smiled and brushed my lips against her forehead, bringing her close again. "You would miss my teasing if I stopped."

She looked up at me and smiled warmly, reaching her fingers toward the front of my hair, still damp from the rain. She pushed it away from my face.

"Would I?" She looked at me again with her eyes of rebellion that always contradicted her perfect poise. It never failed to make my heart skip at least a few beats.

She rested her head on my shoulder and laced her hands together behind my back. My arms tightened around her further.

"Can I see you tomorrow, Jane?" I asked softly as I soaked in every beat of her heart next to mine.

She sighed with contentment. "And the day after that?"

"And the day after that." I grinned, feeling completely whole. My heart was overflowing. Jane loved me.

We stayed that way for a while, holding each other close, warm despite the wet and the cold. Eventually the sound of carriage wheels against cobblestones grew in volume.

"That's most likely your aunt and uncle." I closed my eyes and placed my cheek on top of her head. "I need to get you back."

"What time will you call tomorrow?" Clearly she was just as disappointed about leaving me tonight as I was about letting her go.

"I'll come as early as I can break away."

"Promise?" She looked up at me.

I smiled. "Always."

Jane

I was finally having my moment with Henry and now it had to end. The chill of the night air against my wet dress set in as he moved away from me. I quickly began to shiver.

Henry looked at me with concern. "Let's find my coat."

I nodded. I could tell it took everything in him not to put his arms around me again, but he did take one of my arms and wrap it through his, leading me toward the front. When we reached the place near Mr. Hughes's carriage, he picked his coat up from the wet ground and shook the water from the outside. His hands moved against the interior before he exhaled in relief. "It's dry." He wrapped it around my shoulders, and I immediately felt warm and safe. His coat smelled like him—like wood and soap. I pulled it around me further and breathed in his clean, masculine scent.

"Jane!" Aunt Mary's voice rang out before I turned and saw her running toward me, a few yards away. I smiled as she flung her arms around me, crying as I hugged her back.

"Were you hurt, Jane? Lord Elliot told me everything. That fiend, Lord Fletcher! And I can't believe how much Lord Elliot and Mr. Thomas—"

Henry stepped up to my side just then, taking my fingers in his hand. Aunt Mary stopped talking as she looked at him and smiled. "Tell me, Mr. Thomas, is Lord Elliot as charming as you are? I daresay you had us all swooning in your presence."

Henry laughed. "You flatter me, Mrs. Mason. But Charles is definitely not half as charming as I am." He gave her a wink.

"I'm sure he's not. Though I hear he has a deal more money than you do."

"Aunt!" I gasped at her rudeness.

"Oh Jane, you have enough fortune for the both of you. I was simply stating the facts."

Henry grinned. "A very true fact."

Aunt Mary clapped her hands together. "You and Lord Elliot must come for dinner tomorrow." She said it as a statement that couldn't be refused.

"I would be delighted. But only if you get Miss Mason home immediately. She has been caught out in the rain and I don't want her to catch cold."

Aunt Mary looked at me with concern. "Absolutely. We will leave this very minute. Come, Jane." Henry reluctantly released my fingers as Mary pulled me along. I looked back at Henry as I walked away.

His eyes said it all: He already missed me.

Henry

The ache already began to set in as Jane walked away from me. I knew I would see her tomorrow, and yet, I already missed the feeling of her safely tucked away against me.

Her aunt and uncle escorted her into the carriage. Charles stood near the carriage with Lily and reluctantly released her hand as she followed Jane inside. He looked the way I felt: heartsick at her distance, no matter how small that distance was.

The Masons' conveyance rolled forward. My gaze stayed fixed on the black windows for as long as it could until the carriage passed out of my view. The darkness inside the coach made it impossible for me to see within. Even so, I felt Jane's eyes watching me back.

Charles looked over at me. For the first time in a long time, I felt that he was the very reflection of me inside and out—the way it had been when we were young. At that moment, we didn't only look the same, but our thoughts mirrored one another's, his smile mirroring mine, a sign of our gratitude for the victory we'd won in uncovering the truth about Papa's death and finding justice.

A Bow Street Runner approached Charles, and they made their way toward the alleyway between the two houses, most likely to retrieve Mr. Campbell. As they neared the lane, the Duke of Hastingwood's carriage rolled to a stop in front of the docks.

For the first time, I considered what this would mean for Frederick's father. His son had not only confessed to murdering James, but was also found covertly operating an upper-class prostitution organization. On top of that, Frederick had openly admitted that he planned to kill the duke, his own father. I felt for His Grace's plight as he stepped out of the carriage, my father stepping down behind him. A Bow Street Runner greeted the duke slowly and respectfully, speaking with a hushed voice. I wasn't able to make out their words. Frederick's father simply nodded his head, a grim expression on his face.

In the end, he walked to the carriage window, peered inside at his son, put his hand against the window as if to reach out, then walked away slowly. His shoulders drooped, bearing the weight of his world, now completely upended.

My father opened the duke's carriage door as he slowly approached and put a hand on the duke's shoulder. My father's eyes shone with true sympathy as he looked at a man who would lose his son forever. The duke nodded thanks to my father then entered his carriage.

I couldn't help but reflect on the nature of the world and humankind itself as the duke's carriage rolled away. I reflected on my father, John Thomas. A man who was a violent drunk as a young husband and father. A man who broke his wife's heart and tried to kill his eight-year-old son. In blood, I was John Thomas's son. And yet I felt inclined to none of those tendencies myself. I was raised by a man that wasn't my true father—James Elliot—but I was arguably more like him than even his own son was.

Frederick was raised by a respectable father and mother, a duke and duchess no less. He had anything and everything he could have ever needed or wanted, and turned out nothing like his own flesh and blood.

Although station and circumstance often shapes and molds a man, it was clear to me in that moment that we each carve our own path.

And as I stood there and watched, a silent figure in the darkness, I thanked God for the angels He sent to help me along my own journey. For my mother, who was the only light in my world of darkness before she died. For Katie, who cared for me and saved me from my father, even when it risked her own life.

I thanked Him for James and Elizabeth, the parents who raised me and loved me as their own. For Charles, my brother; Lawrence, my mentor. My own father, John, who could have taken me back, but who loved me enough to let me become an Elliot instead. I thanked Him for Jane, the woman who brought light into my world. The one who completed me.

And as I raised my eyes to the cloud-covered sky, blanketing the world in blackness, I soaked up all the goodness my life had brought up to that moment, marveling that God had been so good to me.

My father slowly made his way toward me until he stood at my side.

"She's proud, Henry," he said as he looked up at the sky. "Your mother's proud of the man you've become."

I put a firm hand to his shoulder. "She's proud of the men we've *both* become."

From the corner of my eye, I watched his head move down as if he doubted my words. I looked over at him until he looked my way. We were silent, but I nodded my head, standing by my statement, until he finally nodded his head in return, eyes wet.

"She's proud," he echoed quietly to himself as we both returned our gaze to the sky. We were silent for a time as we watched the clouds shift, rolling off the moon and a small patch of stars, revealing more light.

My father finally sighed peacefully then looked over at Spartan and Apollo. "I've just realized I have no way home."

"I could always help you off the dock," I said, raising a corner of my mouth.

He looked over at the water, grinning. "And how would you do that?"

I smiled. "Well, I figure you're getting pretty old. You might need a little push."

He laughed. "What makes you think I would be the one ending up in the water?" He raised an eyebrow with a look of challenge.

I chuckled. "Touché."

We did need to find a way for my father to get home, though. As if our minds were in sync, we glanced over at Mr. Campbell's carriage then looked at each other, clearly thinking the same thing.

I nodded my head at the same time he did.

"That will do it," he said, nodding with enthusiasm.

"Indeed," was all I said before he strode over to the horse-drawn carriage, jumped up to the driver's bench with an athletic ability that surprised me for a man his age, and took hold of the reins.

"I'll see you in Wilton." The corner of his mouth turned up. "Don't wait too long before you come visit with Miss Mason. Martha will want to meet her."

I nodded, unable to hide my smile as he flicked the reins and rolled away.

Charles

Moonlight reflected off the river as the water passed slowly under the wooden slats of the dock, Henry standing at the very edge. I approached him from behind and slapped a hand on his back before standing at his side, looking out at the water.

"It's good to be back," I said, breathing out.

Henry looked over at me. "I thought you said you weren't ready for society just yet. Why the sudden change of heart?"

I shook my head. Of course that's where his thoughts would go. "You *would* think about society."

"Charles, Lord Elliot will have to deal with society."

"I'm not referring to 'being back' in that way."

Henry's brow creased as he looked at me in confusion before understanding dawned on his features. *I* was back.

He nodded his head then clapped a hand against my shoulder. "It's good to have you back." His face didn't hold his usual humor as he looked at me. "Charles, I never understood the weight you've had to carry as Lord Elliot. In many ways I feel as though I've passed years this last fortnight. I still don't understand your burdens fully, but I've had a small taste of it. I hope you will let me share your load."

I was truly touched by the sentiment. And I *had* seen obligation and worry weigh heavily on Henry these last two weeks, even if they weren't the same burdens I had to face as earl.

"It *is* a heavy burden to carry," I breathed out. "But I've never expressed my gratitude for the way you let the troubles of life roll off you. I appreciate the way you take life with a smile even when it's impossible to do so. After Mama died, it was you that kept her spirit alive. You kept us all together. I will help you in that effort from now on. It shouldn't only be up to you."

Henry gave me a grateful smile and nod before we both looked up at the sky. He eventually broke the silence. "What's the state of Mr. Campbell?"

"He's alive, though barely. He lost a lot of blood. Only time will tell his fate. For now, the Bow Street Runners will see to it that he receives medical attention. But he will be looked after in a cell for the time being."

Henry nodded his head. "Good." We stood in silence for a time before I let out a frustrated breath.

"I can't help but feel that Papa died for nothing. I hate realizing that he would still be here with us if it weren't for Frederick. I keep wondering if he would still be alive if we had simply gone to London with him . . . "

"I've been thinking similar thoughts." Henry looked over at me before he smiled sadly. "He would have loved Jane and Lily."

"And they would have loved him."

"And yet," Henry said with quiet respect, "if he hadn't died, we would have never traded places. You would have never met Lily in the circumstances you did, and you would have never even given her a second thought."

I almost pushed him off the dock. "I would have noticed Lily," I objected.

"Perhaps," he said, raising an eyebrow. "But you would have labeled her as a title seeker if she had shown any interest. And she most likely wouldn't have liked you and your stuffy attitude."

I hated it when Henry was right.

"And what about you?" I asked. "You would have still pursued Jane."

Henry shook his head. "Being 'Lord Elliot' gave me a certain confidence I don't normally possess. I wouldn't have dared pursue Jane if she thought I was simply penniless Henry Thomas." He inhaled then blew the air back out. "I'm not suggesting that if I could go back and save Papa I wouldn't. Or that I would trade his life for what we have now. I do believe we would have somehow found a way to Jane and Lily even if he were still here."

I looked over at Henry as he looked out at the water. Even from my vantage point I could see that his eyes were glistening. I admired that about Henry—he wasn't ashamed of his emotions.

He continued. "We can't change the past, Charles. But I can see that even in death, Papa is still using his magic."

I quickly brushed away moisture at the corners of my eyes as we stood silent at the water's edge. Henry was right. In a strange way, Papa had given me Lily. Just like he had given Jane to Henry.

I reached in my pocket, revealing tuppence.

Henry went to reach in his pocket until he realized he wasn't wearing his coat.

I grinned and pulled out another coin, tossing it to him. He caught it with ease then rubbed his thumb over the familiar metal circle as I did the same. Then, as if we both had a part of the same brain, we tossed them into the river, sending luck back to Papa as he watched down on us from heaven.

We were silent for several minutes. A peace entered my soul that hadn't been there for a long time.

"I do believe Papa is happier where he is," Henry said. "He was never the same without Mama."

I nodded. "I'm understanding that sentiment more and more."

"As am I." Henry looked at me. "And it really is great to have you back, Charles. We are the same again."

I grinned. "I'm still one inch taller."

With a sudden shove from Henry, my feet teetered to the edge of the dock. I tried to correct my footing, but it was too late—I fell from the wooden slats in a massive splash. When I resurfaced from the icy water, Henry was laughing.

"You can keep your inch," he said, chuckling, as he turned to walk back to Spartan.

I dove to the dock and grabbed his ankle, pulling hard. He flailed his arms about but stayed grounded.

"Nice try," he said with a grin. "But I'm too—" I grabbed his other leg and yanked him into the water. This time I was laughing when he resurfaced.

He punched my arm. "I still hit harder than you."

"At least I don't sound like a dying cow when I sing."

"Good luck convincing London of that." Henry gave me a winning smile, raising his eyebrows, then added, "And I'll always be more charming than you . . . just ask Aunt Mary."

We pulled ourselves out of the water and made our way toward Spartan and Apollo, water sloshing from our clothing and shoes.

Henry's stomach suddenly growled. "Do you think it's too late for Mrs. Caldwell to whip something up?"

"Will you eat all the cake?" I asked with a smirk.

"Be fair, Charles. I always leave you a little."

40

BRAID

Lily

London
November 16, 1816
That same night

After a soothing bath, Alice helped me into a thick nightgown that had been hanging by the fire. It swallowed me up in its warmth. A smile tugged at my lips as I breathed in the clean scent of linen. Alice led me to my dressing table and began brushing my hair. The familiar movements made it impossible to keep my eyes open.

My body was at war with my mind. I wanted to collapse on the bed and never move again. My shoulders and back ached from being thrown into Mr. Campbell's carriage, and every muscle in my body was spent from the tension of Mr. Hughes's threats.

My mind, however, was ablaze, replaying scenes from the night. It would be a miracle if sleep would find me in the end. More than anything, I wanted to speak with Jane. I wanted there to be no more secrets between us.

A quiet rapping came at the door. Alice stopped her brushing as

Jane poked her head through. She was already in a warm nightgown of her own, a braid neatly woven down her back.

"Alice." Jane gave a warm smile. "I'd like a moment to speak with Lily in private."

Alice returned the smile. "Of course, miss." She dipped a curtsy and placed the brush on the table before dismissing herself.

I watched Jane through the mirror as she approached me. When I was little, I sometimes wondered if my sister was an angel in disguise. Tonight I was reminded of the thought: She glowed.

Picking up the brush, Jane moved it through my hair in a slow, methodical rhythm, the way she did when we were little.

The corners of Jane's mouth turned up as her eyes found mine in the reflection. "I guess I was wrong. You'll be a countess, not a fairy." I smiled as I remembered the story she'd always told me when she used to braid my hair. She parted my hair into three sections and began weaving it into a braid down my back.

I looked down at my hands. "It really should be you, Jane. I'm not well suited for high-class society."

Jane grinned as she came to the end of the braid. Her fingers moved to the small drawer in front of me and she pulled it open, selecting a fabric tie before she continued speaking. "Henry helped me remember the things I really want. No title or any amount of wealth would make me happy. I only wanted them so that my family wouldn't be looked down upon."

I was filled with tender feelings for my sister's untarnished heart—for her ability to love and forgive so easily, despite the fact that she would not get a title and would now marry a man with little to no means.

Jane carefully wound the fabric piece around the end of my hair and tied it in a knot. "It is ironic; I was aiming for a title and wealth while you have always cared little about such things, and only wanted to be loved. Neither of us got exactly what we expected. But in the end, we both got what we wanted. My desires simply shifted after meeting Henry. How could I help it?" She laughed lightly, then added, "And you're wrong. I think you are very well suited to be a countess . . . even if you did sneak out to the garden alone on the night of the duchess's ball." Jane raised her eyebrow and smirked.

I covered my eyes before offering her a sheepish grin. "I wanted to tell you! But you were already so upset about the way I left Mr. Campbell on the dance floor and hid from Mr. Johnson. I was afraid you would never let me see Henry—" I paused, shaking my head. "Not Henry; Lord Elliot. This is going to be really confusing," I said with a chuckle.

She grinned back at me. "Yes, it is. And you're right, I would have done my best to make you stop seeing a man unchaperoned, Lord Elliot or not." She set the brush down and walked over to my bed, making herself comfortable on the mattress. I smiled and followed suit, sitting beside her.

"No more secrets," I said, feeling a weight lift from my chest.

"No more secrets," Jane agreed. "Now, tell me how you met Lord Elliot. And don't leave anything out."

Lily

London
November 17, 1816
The next evening

The sound of wheels against cobblestones grew until it stopped in front of the house. Jane and I looked at one another as we sat on the sofa, mirroring each other's nervous excitement.

Aunt Mary appeared, Uncle Francis at her side. She paced to the window, peering out. "They're here," she said with anxious enthusiasm before she took a seat on the sofa next to us. She fidgeted with her hands. "Everyone act natural."

Jane smiled at Aunt Mary's reaction. "Don't trouble yourself, Aunt. You're already acquainted with Mr. Thomas. And you met Lord Elliot last night."

"Yes, but I wasn't very cordial with Lord Elliot in the ballroom."

I knew I should stay put, but I couldn't help myself. I stood and walked over to the window. Just as I parted the curtains, Charles looked at me from the street as if he knew I would be waiting. His lips turned up into a smile.

I mirrored his expression. "You can tell Lord Elliot just how intimidating he is now, Aunt; he's about to come inside."

"Lily, come away from the window. They'll see you!" Aunt Mary said it as if it was the most scandalous thing in the world.

I gave Charles another smile until I realized Mr. Thomas was watching us. Mr. Thomas gave me a grin then looked at Charles, muttering something close to his ear, raising his eyebrows. I chuckled as Charles grinned and shoved his friend. Letting the curtain fall back in place, I took my seat next to Jane, trying my best not to smile like an idiot.

George's voice could be heard greeting our guests. Jane's hand wrapped around mine for a second and she gave my fingers a squeeze in anticipation. I squeezed back.

George appeared at the doorway of the parlor. "Mr. Thomas and Lord Elliot to see you."

We stood. The two gentlemen entered, looking more alike and yet more different than ever before. They both had a smooth jaw and chin from a clean shave. Their hair was styled the same way. But when they entered, I knew exactly which one was Charles. Perhaps it was the way his eyes rested on mine immediately after entering the room. Perhaps it was his heart that I recognized. Regardless, I knew it was him, and I couldn't look away.

Aunt Mary began the conversation in a formal tone. "Lord Elliot, Mr. Thomas, I'm honored you accepted my invitation to dine this evening." I was still trying to get used to the idea that Henry was actually Charles—the Earl of Wiltshire. Watching Aunt Mary speak with him this way made it feel more significant than before. This was a man that received respect and represented authority wherever he went. Before today, he had just been Henry. Now, he was Lord Elliot.

He dipped his head toward Aunt Mary with a straight back, giving off a formal, stiff air. I remembered our first meeting, and his rigid, unyielding arrogance. I wondered how he would act now that he was back in his role as the earl.

"Mrs. Mason," he said. Did each person in the room, including myself, lean in, waiting to see what he would say and do next?

His smile finally appeared. "I can't thank you enough for inviting us." It felt as though everyone in the room audibly sighed in relief of his approval . . . except for Mr. Thomas, who only had eyes for one thing: Jane.

As we walked to the dining room, Charles strode alongside Aunt Mary and Uncle Francis. He was putting their minds at ease, and despite the fact that I wanted his attention, I was grateful for his consideration of my relatives.

Mr. Thomas slowly made his way toward Jane. He discreetly took her fingers in his for just a moment, while no one was looking, as if he couldn't help himself. Before he released her hand, Jane looked over at him, warmth radiating from her entire being. I smiled at the sweet gesture.

"Good evening, Miss Mason." The deep, rumbling voice that I'd been waiting to hear all evening suddenly sounded just behind me.

I turned to find Charles offering me his arm, a small grin tugging at his lips.

"Good evening, Lord Elliot." I couldn't hold back my smile as I threaded my arm through his.

He leaned his head down toward me as we walked into the dining room. "I really do insist that you call me Charles." As I turned my head to face him, he winked at me.

I smirked. "I have been calling you Henry these past two weeks, my lord. What makes you think I'll start calling you Charles now?"

"Miss Mason, what have I told you about smirking?" He looked at the corner of my mouth and smiled.

"Lord Elliot, what have I told you about calling me Miss Mason?"

He raised an eyebrow. "You haven't told me anything about calling you Miss Mason." It was rather silly that his use of my formal name was making my heart go haywire just now. I was used to meeting Charles in dark corners and shrubs, only ever in secret. Now he was here as Lord Elliot, escorting me into dinner with nothing to hide. He was everything he was before. But now I was rediscovering him all over again.

How was it possible that I could feel shy in his presence now, when just the night before I was kissing him without reservation? The thought brought heat to my cheeks and I had to look away from his penetrating gaze.

He chuckled softly then leaned close to my ear. "What *have* you told me about calling you Miss Mason?"

Charles would have to wait for my answer, for we were out of time to speak privately. As we entered the dining room, Charles pulled a chair out for me then took a seat next to me. He leaned in one last time, speaking quietly so only I could hear.

"You're off the hook for now, Lily, but I'll want to know later."

I bit back a smile. I loved leaving Charles in suspense.

"Now I must ask, Lord Elliot," Aunt Mary began. "Are we to expect any more disguises from you and Mr. Thomas?"

Charles smirked. "If you ever suspect us of being in disguise, you can always ask for a song."

Mr. Thomas rolled his eyes.

Aunt Mary chuckled. "Then I insist that you favor us with a song, my lord, so that we will be able to distinguish the difference."

Mr. Thomas grimaced. "The difference, Mrs. Mason, is that one will sound like music, while the other will sound more like—"

"A herd of cattle," Charles finished, trying his best to hide his smile. "Loud, excruciating on the ears, and painfully difficult to wrangle in."

"True," Mr. Thomas chuckled. "But I can still pin you to the ground, last I checked."

"That was two years ago," Charles said, pinning his friend with a stare.

"Yes, and you haven't heard me sing since Cambridge." Mr. Thomas was barely holding back a smile.

Jane was biting back a smile of her own before she said, "Then I insist you sing

for us again tonight, Mr. Thomas." He looked at her with alarm, then relaxed when he noticed her teasing smile.

Mr. Thomas looked over at Charles. "I have to let Lord Elliot stand out occasionally. Unless you would like me to outshine you tonight with a song?"

"No!" Charles didn't even try to hide his mortification at the very thought of watching his brother sing.

Aunt Mary laughed, enjoying their banter.

The rest of the meal played out with lively conversation. Even Uncle Francis chimed in occasionally. My heart was full as I watched Jane smile and laugh without reserve.

My stomach suddenly flipped as I felt Charles's fingers brush against my hand, resting in my lap. His eyes were fixed on me. He looked at me intently as he traced his fingers against mine. He stopped on the finger that held my ring and slowly spun it around my finger until it came free. He slowly withdrew his hand from mine and returned his gaze to the conversation.

My pulse quickened as the feeling of his touch lingered on my skin. It was then that I realized I was holding a small piece of parchment. I did my best to hide the smile that was threatening to peek out. Tilting the small piece of paper, I read the words beneath the table.

You will recognize your moment when it presents itself. Be ready.

They were the exact words he had given to me in the shop the day after our first meeting. I looked at him again, but he only smiled and pretended to be interested in the conversation at the table.

His fingers brushed mine again, this time leaving something cold and metallic in the palm of my hand. I smiled as I glanced at the familiar form of tuppence inside: for luck.

Charles suddenly stood from the table and walked over to Aunt Mary, whispering something in her ear. She looked at me and grinned, then nodded her head to him.

My heart pounded faster and faster as his eyes met mine, determined.

The table went quiet and I could feel that all eyes were on us. Once Charles reached my chair, he leaned down near my ear.

"Might I have a private word, Miss Mason?" He put his hand out for me to take. I looked up, my insides stirring. His eyes, confident and resolute, summoned me to come. I took in a breath as my heart continued to hammer, then put my hand in his and slowly rose from my seat as he coaxed me toward him. Why was I so nervous? Breathing became a contradiction: I had to remind myself to do it all while it sped up at an alarming pace.

His eyes didn't leave mine. He threaded my arm through his then led me away from the table.

"Breathe, Lily," he muttered, a corner of his lips turning up. We stepped out of the dining room, finally alone. Once we were out of sight from our party, Charles turned me toward him until we were facing each other.

He brought my fingers to his lips then led me by the hand to the library where a small lantern was already burning. Its light cast a faint glow about the room. Charles led us inside then quietly shut the door behind me. I had been alone with Charles on multiple occasions, but I had a feeling this time would change everything. I knew what was coming, and although it was everything I wanted, I was terrified.

"Now that we are alone," he began.

It was happening. My breath quickened. I couldn't meet Charles's gaze.

"I've been dying to ask . . . "

I held my breath.

"What *have* you told me about calling you Miss Mason?"

My eyes shot to his.

He was holding back a laugh.

"Did you really bring me in here just to ask that?" I said, annoyed that I was worked up for nothing.

Charles grinned. "Just answer the question."

I smirked. "Answer mine first."

He smiled. "Are you always this stubborn?"

"Do you really need to ask?" I cocked an eyebrow.

His hand found my waist, slowly pulling me in close before he traced his finger over my dimple, eyes moving to the spot. My mind went completely blank.

He repeated his question. "What have you told me about calling you Miss Mason?"

My breath fluttered in. "That isn't fair," I protested weakly, as his lips found their way to the place he was looking.

"Neither is the way you keep me in suspense," he said quietly as he kissed my cheek. His lips grazed my ear. "Now answer my question, and I'll answer yours."

I wanted to continue arguing my point, but Charles had me completely disarmed.

I breathed out in resignation. "I told you that although I do prefer Lily, I rather enjoy hearing you call me Miss Mason from time to time."

Charles chuckled. "You've never said such a thing." He brought me even closer.

I smiled. "I *did* tell you."

"When?"

"Just now." I raised my eyebrow, daring him to challenge me.

He shook his head and breathed out a laugh. "You like it when I call you Miss Mason?" His eyes moved back and forth between mine.

My heart skipped. "I do."

His hand slowly moved to his pocket, pulling out a thin metal band, holding it up to the dim light. It was my ring: old, warped, and tarnished with age.

He flicked the ring up and over into his other hand, catching it with ease. A smile tugged at the corner of my mouth as I anticipated what would happen next. He opened the fingers of his other hand slowly, one by one. The ring was nowhere to be seen.

His eyes ignited with resolve. "And, Miss Mason." His fingers closed quickly and came together, something new appearing between his thumb and finger that sparkled and gleamed in the dim light. "How do you feel about the name Lady Elliot?"

My breath caught as my eyes fell upon the ring. Small, elegant diamonds formed a thin almond-shaped cluster. The band and casing around the diamonds was gold.

I had no words.

"Lily." Charles's deep voice rumbled. "For many years now, my life has been a prison. There was nothing that held excitement, love, passion, or even surprise for me. You woke me up that first night we met." His lips turned up on one side. "I haven't laughed or smiled so much in six years . . . perhaps longer."

I bit my lip, moisture pricking my eyes. I felt as though the sun was weaving its way through my heart.

Charles's eyes simmered. "You stole my heart almost immediately with your wit and heart and stubbornness, and I can't bear the thought of life without you."

He took my left hand in his and raised it to his lips, tenderly kissing each finger. My breath quickened and my heart sped as he slowly lowered my hand, then slid the smooth band onto my ring finger.

Charles's voice turned achingly tender. "Lily Mason, will you take me as yours? In sickness and in health? To have and to hold?" He lightly brushed my cheek with his lips then placed a kiss next to my ear. "Will you marry me?" he whispered.

My entire being pulsed with joy. Charles would be mine and I would be his. I didn't expect tears to well in my eyes, but they came anyway.

He pulled away from my ear until his face was close to mine, taking in my eyes.

I wrapped my arms around him as he leaned his face closer to mine. "I love you," I said. A tear streamed down my cheek as my lips found his. He pulled me closer and I felt as though our hearts were one. He held my face gently and kissed me tenderly until I felt my heart would burst.

"I love you, Lily," he whispered. Then after a pause, he added, "And just to be clear, are you saying 'Yes, I will marry you' with that kiss? Because I swear if you are teasing me in a moment like this—"

I laughed. "I am!"

"You are teasing me? Or you are saying yes?"

I kissed the corner of his smile, finding it hard to believe that I was lucky enough to capture his heart.

"Yes. I will marry you." I slowly pulled his lips to mine. He exhaled as my lips parted from his, as if he had needed to hear those exact words.

I slowly kissed him again, moving my hand with my ring to his cheek. "I want to spend the rest of my life with you, Charles Elliot."

The look he gave me took my breath away. It was his heart worn on the outside. It was joy, love, desire, relief.

And it was all for me.

Lawrence

London
November 18, 1816
One day later

Charles and Henry watched as I broke the seal of a goldfinch insignia pressed into wax. It had just arrived from a man disguised as a mail carrier. I began to read aloud:

"Greetings brother,"

I let out a breath of relief then looked up from my page at Charles's and Henry's expectant faces. "It's the opening code used to state that a mission was successful." I continued to read.

"The infant has arrived ahead of

Schedule. Mother and baby are well."

I translated the message once again. "Arthur Brown and his family arrived at Wilton Manor ahead of schedule safely." Henry nodded, eyebrows raised.

"We are eager for you to meet your newest nephew.

Write soon."

I looked up once more. "Mr. Brown is anxious to receive information."

Charles cocked an eyebrow. "I'm impressed, Lawrence. When do we get to meet the Goldfinch Society?"

Lawrence grinned. "If they want you to meet them, they will find you, my lord."

Henry folded his arms. "When can we leave for Wilton?" Charles and Henry had just received news that Jane and Lily were sent home to Wilton immediately on their mother's orders due to the scandal with Lord Fletcher.

"I believe we can make it back to Wilton by Saturday," I said, looking between Charles and Henry. "It should give us enough time to button up any loose ends with the Bow Street Runners and travel back."

41

TREE

Jane

Wilton
November 23, 1816
Five days later

An entire week had passed since I'd seen Henry.
My parents received word of mine and Lily's capture at the Woodwards' ball and demanded that Lily and I return to Wilton immediately. We'd received their letter the day after Lord Elliot proposed to Lily, and the stagecoach was loaded with our belongings, Lily and me in tow, that next morning.

Each day that passed brought new hope that this would be the day that I would finally hear news of Henry's arrival. And now that I held a letter in my hand, sitting on the garden bench, I had to read it over and over again to make sure it was real. I smiled as I memorized Henry's writing.

Jane,

I would address the letter to "my dearest Jane," but I cherish your name more than any other word. Any other description would only lessen its significance.

Lord Elliot and I have almost concluded our work with the Bow Street Runners. The moment everything is completed we will return to Wilton. I imagine we should arrive on Saturday.

Until then, try not to fall in love with Mr. Ashby.

All my love,

Henry

I chuckled as I read the part about falling in love with Mr. Ashby. Only Henry would write something like that. I read it one more time, beaming at the thought that I might see Henry today. Old practical Jane sounded in my mind, trying her best to convince me that Henry may not arrive today after all—that it would be better if I didn't get my hopes up. But it was no use. I was already smiling and hoping like a lovesick schoolgirl.

I was grateful to discover, upon entering the drawing room, that my hope was not in vain.

"Jane, there you are!" Mama's voice was excited and a little frantic. She was holding a letter. "We've just been invited to dine at Wilton Manor." She gave me a smile. "I assume Mr. Thomas will be there as well."

Mama had taken the news well when we explained to her that the man she thought was Lord Elliot, was actually Henry Thomas—and that the man she thought was Henry Thomas, was in fact, Lord Elliot.

In the end, the only thing either of my parents were disappointed about was the fact that we had all left for London so quickly after the autumn celebration. They were convinced we could have avoided the entire scandal with Lord Fletcher and Mr. Hughes if we had just stayed put and communicated better with Henry and Charles. They were right of course, but there was no changing it now.

Lily suddenly appeared in the doorway, smiling without reserve. Even from the doorway I could see her ring sparkle.

"When can we leave for Wilton Manor?" Lily asked, barely keeping a handle on her excitement. "Can we go now?"

Mama chuckled. "You aren't even dressed to dine, Lily."

Lily smirked and looked at me. "Jane, do you think as a countess I can start a new fashion trend that women can wear the same dress all day, no matter the occasion?"

I chuckled. "I would certainly love to see you try."

Lily cocked an eyebrow at me. "Well until then, I think we should drive Mr. Thomas absolutely mad tonight. It does make me feel so accomplished when I've worked my magic on your hair and he can't keep his eyes off you." She took my arm and nudged her head toward the stairs, a mischievous grin in tow. "I have just the thing for tonight."

Mama's brows raised as she looked at Lily. "Should I be concerned?"

"Of course," Lily said with a wink, leading me to the upper floor.

I wasn't sure about Lily's idea for my hair. It fell down my shoulders and back in loose curls. She draped a large part of my curls to one side without securing any of them. There wasn't a single pin, ribbon, or jewel in my hair.

"Lily, are you sure about this?" I asked. I looked completely undone. Like a free spirit with rebellion at its helm.

Lily smiled. "Come to think of it, your reservations are valid. Perhaps I don't want to watch Henry kiss you the second he sees you."

I rolled my eyes.

"Trust me." She tried to hide her smile, but it peeked through. She walked to my wardrobe and pulled out a cream-colored evening dress. It was elegant, but simple. She laid it out on the bed. "Only this will do tonight."

As we rolled up to the Elliots' estate, I let out a breath that I'd been holding, feeling relieved and nervous at the same time.

Sterling helped me out of the carriage. "Tell Henry he'd better not give me a reason to punch him in the face." A corner of his mouth turned up, then he helped Lily down. It warmed my heart to see Sterling take on a protective role.

"Don't worry, son," Papa said. "I'll shoot him first if he tries anything." He gave me a wink then offered Mama his arm.

Oliver jumped from the carriage, swatting Sterling's hand away. "Well I won't punch him if he teaches me his magic." His tone was serious.

Oliver then offered Lily his arm like a regular gentleman. She looped her arm through his dramatically and they began walking in, gliding theatrically.

Sterling looked at me. "Are you nervous?"

I cocked my head. "When did you become so observant?"

He smiled and offered me his arm. "I'm not completely blind, sis." We slowly made our way toward the entrance of Wilton Manor.

"Apparently not," I said with a smile.

He sighed. "Do you think you'll ever catch frogs and snakes with us again?"

I stopped walking and looked at him, surprised by the turn in our conversation. He had grown so much since Papa came into wealth. Sadly, I hadn't noticed until Lily and I had returned to Wilton for the autumn celebration. It had happened so slowly. As I looked at him, I realized that this was the last piece of his childhood before he went away to Eton.

"Are *you* nervous, Sterling?" I asked.

He looked at the ground, then back up at me. "I just don't want to change. I don't want to wake up one day and realize I don't want to catch frogs anymore. Or that I would rather be with society over pulling a prank with Oliver."

"Like *I* did?"

He looked away from my eyes. His reaction didn't surprise me. I knew that his fears were an extension of what he saw happen to me.

It did sting a little, realizing how much I had changed—how much I had missed at home while I was away at London, and how much I had missed the past few years, even when I *was* home.

"I'll make you a deal," I finally said. "Tomorrow, you, Oliver, Lily, and I will catch as many frogs as we can carry, and we will sneak them into Henry's and Lord Elliot's beds." I smiled. "And later, if ever you forget your family, or if you forget this moment, I will help you remember."

Sterling's mouth turned up and his eyes returned to mine. "Promise?"

I smiled. "Always." Henry was already rubbing off on me.

"In that case, future Mrs. Thomas, I'd best get you inside." He grinned, straightening up, then held his arm out for me to take once more.

I took it and we walked in as if we were royalty, trying our best to keep straight faces.

Lily was right about my hair, as usual. When I walked into the dining room, Henry's eyes found me immediately. He stopped talking with Papa mid-sentence as if his mind had gone completely blank. His eyes studied me before he remembered himself. He cocked an eyebrow at me as if I was in trouble for making him lose his words, then turned back to Papa.

"I'm sorry, Mr. Mason, what was I saying?" It wasn't long before Henry's eyes found mine again—apparently he couldn't help himself.

Sterling laughed quietly next to me at Henry's response. "Good luck," he said, releasing my arm.

I looked over at Lily, her brows raised in delight as if to say "I told you so." Charles stood behind her, his fingers entwined with hers. He was smirking and shaking his head at Henry's inability to have a regular conversation with my father.

Eventually, Papa lowered his voice in Henry's direction. "You seem a little distracted, Mr. Thomas. Perhaps we could continue this conversation another time." He gave Henry a knowing look and a nod, then walked toward Mama.

Henry didn't wait before he walked over to me. His hand reached out to take mine but stopped, most likely remembering that we had an audience. Lily and Charles could hold hands because they were engaged. Henry and I . . . were not.

"Jane." His voice rolled over me like mist, leaving tingles in its wake. "I have a question for you."

I couldn't think as he looked at me with his penetrating stare. Seconds passed before I realized he was waiting for me to say something. "And what is that?"

"Was our carriage ride more than suitable?"

I laughed, grateful to release the tension building inside me. "I told you it was."

"Well I don't feel it was adequate. Will you allow me to take you for another one?"

I smiled. "I will as long as you promise not to take me back too early this time."

He looked at me with a mischievous grin. "I can agree to those terms." He held his hand out.

I looked at him with confusion. "Right this moment?"

"Don't worry, I brought your chaperone," he said quietly. "Alice is waiting by the carriage. And I already spoke with your father about it. He told me to tell you that he will not shoot me . . . this time."

I deadpanned. "How comforting."

"Indeed." He looked at my hair rippling over the side of my face as if he could barely contain himself from bringing me close.

"Shall we?" he spoke barely above a whisper, gesturing toward the door.

As we made our way outside toward the open chaise, the sun was setting. It cast a glow over the landscape, the crimson leaves ablaze.

Alice sat up front with the coachman. She smiled when our eyes met, then returned her gaze forward in typical Alice form, giving Henry and me a chance to have some privacy.

Henry handed me up then took his seat right next to me, his warmth reminding me that he wasn't simply a figment of my imagination. Light poured over the transport, bathing us in the last rays of sun amidst the chilly November air. He took my hand in his and brushed his fingers against mine, driving a sense of excitement and contentment into my heart. We rolled on for a time, then deviated from the main road until eventually the carriage came to a stop. We were surrounded by trees, but I didn't recognize our exact location.

"We're here." Henry's voice was quiet as he spoke next to me. He helped me down then shrugged out of his coat, wrapping it around my arms. Though it was still light enough to see, the sun was sinking below the horizon.

Alice moved from the carriage next, a handsome graying gentleman with a confident presence helping her down. Alice quickly averted her eyes from his as he helped her from the carriage.

Henry looked over at the man and smiled before he addressed me. "Miss Mason, may I introduce you to Lawrence?" He gestured to the newcomer. "He's family."

Lawrence nodded politely. "I'm also butler of Wilton Manor."

I smiled. "I'm delighted to meet anyone associated with Henry."

Henry gestured to me next. "Lawrence, this is Miss Mason?" I curtsied.

Lawrence grinned. "I can see why Henry is so smitten." His voice was kind. "It's a pleasure to finally meet you."

Henry rubbed his hands together, looking at Lawrence. "Is everything ready?"

"Indeed, sir."

Henry smiled then offered me his arm. "Do you mind if we take a small detour on foot?"

"I would expect nothing less." I took his arm and followed as he led me through a thicket of trees. It opened up to a small patch of meadow, then was enclosed by more trees. This pattern repeated itself a few times until we came to the back side of a glen that looked vaguely familiar. As we neared from this side, I slowly recognized the place better than any in the world. It was mine and Lily's wishing tree. And now my tree was set up with a blanket beneath it, along with some lanterns placed on the ground and in the low-hanging branches.

I looked over at Henry, mouth open in disbelief. He was already watching me, waiting for my reaction. I smiled and grabbed his hand, pulling him toward the blanket. Lawrence and Alice lingered behind. Despite the fact that the sun was below the horizon, there was still a bit of light left in the sky for us to find the perfect leaf. Henry guided me next to the tree then sat on the blanket with his back against the trunk. He motioned for me to sit next to him and I obliged. His arms slowly entwined around me and he shifted until my back was against his chest. He breathed out with contentment, pulling me closer until he brushed the side of his face against mine. I breathed in with satisfaction knowing that I would never have to leave Henry again.

"Now," he said quietly in my ear. "Where is our perfect leaf?"

My head tipped back on his shoulder as I looked skyward to the branches. And there I saw it. It was big, and yellow, and perfect. I guided my finger to point to it.

"I see it." Henry smiled, kissing my cheek.

"Now we just have to watch it until it falls."

"What if I would rather watch you?"

I smiled. "Then your wish won't come true."

"And what if I have everything I could ever wish for right here?" He took my hand in his and raised it to his lips, kissing the top of my hand.

"Then there was no point in me finding the perfect leaf." The corner of my mouth twisted up.

"Unless I'm not enough for *you*. I'll never be able to buy you all the dresses in the world."

"As long as there is food on the table."

"Speaking of food." Henry kissed my cheek once more then released his arms from around my waist.

I sighed as he let go of me, wishing he would just stay put. He slowly stood up, then disappeared behind my view. Upon his return, he carried a candelabra with three long candlesticks inside. He lit each candle with a nearby lantern and set the candelabra on a small board atop the blanket. He came to where I sat and took my hand, helping me up, then gestured for me to sit in front of the candles. I obliged and he joined, taking a seat right next to me.

Lawrence and Alice appeared, carrying various items. Alice placed a bottle of wine on the board next to the candles, along with two elegant glasses. Lawrence came up behind her, carrying a large basket. He set it down carefully, then extracted two plates and placed them in front of us, followed by utensils. It was curious. The setup appeared to be a picnic, and yet they were bringing out items used for fine dining.

"What is this, Henry?" Candlelight danced on his features as he watched Lawrence set out the items. He looked leisurely without his coat, leaning back on his palms. My eyes moved over him, reminding me of our first picnic.

He grinned, eyes watching mine. "You can't look at me like that right now, Jane."

My cheeks warmed at being caught.

He smiled as I blushed. "And to answer your question, I didn't think it fair to rob you of a splendid meal at Wilton Manor. So I brought it to you. And don't tell Lawrence I told you this," he said loudly so his friend could hear, "but if he wasn't a butler, he would most likely be a hermit living in the woods, surviving on his bare instincts alone."

"You flatter me, sir," Lawrence said, the corner of his mouth twitching up.

Henry smiled, but not in jest. Deep appreciation etched his features. "Lawrence has been out here for hours, performing tasks that no regular servant would undertake."

I looked at Lawrence, truly touched that he would make such an effort to help Henry make this evening special. The butler gave me a smile as our eyes met, then turned his attention back to his work.

"Lawrence," I said, a small grin in tow. "If ever you decide to become a hermit, I will be the first to visit."

"So long as you don't bring any sociable creatures with you." He gestured his head toward Henry. "And don't tell Henry I told you this, but if he wasn't so annoyingly persistent, he would still somehow be annoyingly persistent."

I laughed.

"That laugh will cost you your spoon, Jane." Henry raised his eyebrow as Alice handed us each a spoon. Just as I grabbed mine,

Henry quickly slipped it from my grasp and made it disappear. Even as I shook my head and rolled my eyes, a smile betrayed me. Alice grinned at our teasing then moved away from us. Lawrence handed us each a bowl of steaming liquid, then straightened up as he moved toward Alice. "Hermit or not, I can't take all the credit for this evening," he said, looking over at her.

I grinned. "Alice, have you been helping Lawrence?"

"Only a little, miss," she said quietly, trying to hide a smile.

Henry smirked. "Lawrence needs someone to keep him in line. I thought Alice would be perfect for the task."

Lawrence grinned, taking several covered pots out of the basket with Alice's help.

"Thank you," Henry said, nodding to both of them. "Now, Lawrence, if you would be so kind as to take Alice to one of your fires to warm her hands, I would be most obliged."

"Very good, sir," Lawrence said, holding his arm out for Alice to take. She looked at me, eyes wide, unsure what to do. I nodded my encouragement. She slowly took his arm then he led her away, until they were no longer in sight.

Henry chuckled and I couldn't help but join in. "I didn't take you as a matchmaker, Mr. Thomas," I teased.

"Nor did I." He smiled. "I simply needed help and knew no one could perform the task as well as Lawrence could. And you needed a chaperone." He brought his hand forward and made my spoon reappear. "Or better stated, *I* need someone to keep me in line." He smirked as he handed over the spoon.

I took at it and grinned. "I have some tricks of my own coming your way." I was barely holding back a laugh as I contemplated putting as many frogs as Sterling and I could muster into his bed.

"Do you, now?"

"How much do you like frogs?" I asked.

His forehead creased in confusion. "Frogs?"

"Yes, frogs."

"Are you asking me how much I like them as a pet? Or if I like how they taste?"

I couldn't help but laugh. "Both." I leaned back on my hands again.

He looked at my lips as I laughed. "Jane, I don't think we will ever be able to eat if you keep distracting me."

"That would truly be a shame after all the work Lawrence and Alice have put into this."

Henry's hand brushed against mine as he leaned back, mirroring my posture.

"Indeed it would." I could still feel Henry's eyes on me. I knew that once I turned my face toward him, his lips would be a breath away from mine . . . which was exactly what I wanted.

As my face slowly turned toward him, his eyes moved over my face, my hair, my lips.

My stomach leapt as he moved closer, gently closing the distance. His lips moved so gently against mine making me completely breathless when he pulled away. Small currents pulsed throughout me until I felt as though my heart would light on fire.

He kissed me once more, softly, before exhaling regretfully. "We really do need to eat before this gets cold." I slowly nodded, feeling completely disoriented.

I shrugged out of Henry's coat and laid it behind me as he handed me the soup. He opened the wine, pouring us each a small amount. I tried the soup first. The savory broth was soothing and warm with a perfect blend of vegetables and meat. I hadn't realized how hungry I was until I started eating.

The wax from the candles spilled over as we moved through the courses. Henry ate faster than I did then told me old stories and recited poetry until I was finished. I loved the sound of his voice; I wanted it near me always. His arm occasionally brushed against mine as we sat side by side.

Eventually it was silent and Alice and Lawrence were still out of view. I turned my gaze to Henry's, his eyes reflecting the candlelight. My own burning desire for him ignited until it consumed me completely.

Turning toward him, I knelt until we were facing each other. He looked at my hair again and then my lips, still leaning back on his hands. He reached one of them out to me and trailed it behind my neck. I rested my hand on his chest, his heart hammering stronger than ever, before I moved my fingers up to his face and kissed his cheek. He closed his eyes and moved his fingers through my hair. My lips moved over until they were only inches away from his. He opened his eyes slowly, looking at me with intensity. He breathed out with longing as my lips brushed against his, and then I kissed him. As my lips tasted his, I leaned against him, lost in the intoxication of his very presence until he slowly lowered his back to the blanket, his fingers entwined in my hair. My heart leaned over his and he pulled me close, kissing me in a way that was achingly tender.

"Jane," he finally breathed.

My heart hammered louder than his voice carried. He slowly sat up, his lips finding mine again, this time tracing my neck with his fingers as he did so. His lips remained slow and gentle, moving with such feeling, each touch deliberate.

He slowly trailed kisses down my cheek until his lips brushed against my neck.

His next words came out quiet and gravelly. "It's not living, to have this constant ache in my heart when you're away from me."

I closed my eyes as he said the words.

"I yearn for you, the one who makes me whole, and long to hold you in my arms forever." His lips pressed just below my ear.

My eyes filled with moisture at the remembrance of his words from the last time we stood under this tree.

He breathed out. "I dream of you, the one I love, by night, and crave to have you next to me when I wake."

When I opened my eyes, his were completely ablaze as he watched me. He slowly stood and took my hand, guiding me up toward him. His eyes and lips had me completely ensnared in the soft flicker of the lanterns surrounding us. He led me to the edge of the blanket, against the tree. A few lanterns hung from the branches, granting us more light.

We stood in the exact place where he kissed me the first time, but this time was very different. He looked at my eyes as if they consumed him as much as his consumed me.

He gently brushed his fingers over my shoulder and reached inside his pocket before he spoke again.

"You haunt my every waking thought. And I still never imagine your eyes exactly right."

He slowly moved one of his legs out behind him until he was kneeling down on one knee.

I moved my hand over my mouth as I suddenly realized what was happening. I was so taken with his words and gestures that my mind hadn't cued me properly.

"Jane, will you put me out of misery and take me as I am? A man who is desperately in love with you?"

He held his hand out in front of me, holding a beautiful ring between his finger and thumb. My breath caught as I noticed it sparkle in the lantern light.

"Will you marry me?" he asked, holding his breath.

My heart pounded as his words echoed throughout me. I looked up at the branches of the trees and watched the perfect leaf fall slowly to the earth below. Tears pricked my eyes. I couldn't speak for the emotion that clung to my throat. I nodded my head then let out a breath of joy as tears streamed down my cheeks.

Henry sighed in relief then took my left hand in his. He slid the ring on my finger then kissed the top of my hand before he drew me close to him and gently wiped a tear from my cheek.

"Do you know what your tears do to me, Jane?"

I shook my head, smiling. "No, but I have the rest of my life to find out."

He wrapped his arms around me tighter as I rested the side of my face over his heart. My hand splayed over his arm and I finally had a good look at the ring. Four small diamonds clustered brilliantly on a shining golden band—a rare thing, especially for those who weren't part of the aristocracy.

"Henry," I said as I looked at it. "I don't need diamonds."

He kissed the top of my head. "But I wanted you to have them."

His fingers slowly lifted my face until I was looking at him. "I will never be as wealthy as Lord Elliot. But my father, John Thomas, has left me his house, and a large sum of money." He smiled. "And I will continue to make money in order to leave a legacy for you and our children. So you can be loved *and* wealthy."

"I will love you regardless of how much money you have."

"And I love you more than anything in this world." He lowered his lips to mine and kissed me slowly again.

His face eventually pulled away from mine, brushing my hair away from my shoulder, shaking his head. "One thing is for certain, we will need better chaperones than Lawrence and Alice until we are married."

"And then I can have you all to myself?" I smiled.

"And then *I* can have *you* all to myself." He repeated my words with a grin.

"Promise?" I stood on my tiptoes and kissed his cheek.

He took my hand in his and held it to his heart. "Always."

EPILOGUE

Frederick

Newgate Prison
December 29, 1816
Approximately one month later

A guard led me through damp stone halls, my hands chained together. Iron bars passed us one by one as we made our way down the dark, musky passageway, ceiling hanging low. He led me to the last door then pulled out a large, black key. Another prisoner already waited in the cell, watching us. He was an unearthly creature with unyielding eyes and an icy stare. His hair was long and wavy, dingy and gray.

The guard shoved the key inside and turned it with effort, the old lock finally relenting and coming free. Groaning with age, the door was pushed open. The guard released my chains then pushed me into the already inhabited cell, forcing the creaking bars to their original position. The iron door clanged shut, reverberating with a deafening finality as the lock was secured.

"Enjoy your stay, Lord Fletcher," the guard said with a mocking tone. "I'm sure Etienne Dupont will keep you company." He chortled then gave the unkempt prisoner a stare.

I glared at the guard as he walked away. I'd kill him too, once I was free from this stinking, rotting hole. A life sentence to this miserable existence meant nothing to me. I would find a way out.

"I'll kill you, Henry," I murmured under my breath as I clenched the bars of my cell. "I'll kill you and Jane slowly and make you watch as I put a dagger through Charles Elliot."

"Deed you say... Elliot?"

I flinched as a smooth, eerie voice spoke in my ear, heavy with a French accent. I hadn't heard his approach. I turned swiftly and grabbed him by his shirt, slamming his back against the bars. "Don't sneak up on me again, or I promise it'll be the last thing you do," I snarled.

He gave me a chilled look as he lifted an eyebrow and tsked. "You shouldn't have done zat." He gave me a twisted smile as he lingered on his words. Ice traveled up my spine at the way he looked at me—as if he could kill me at any moment, without me ever being the wiser.

I wouldn't let him see how unhinged he made me feel. I roughly released him, but his twisted smile didn't cease.

"How many people do you sink I have killed?" he spoke slowly. "Do you... sink I will kill you... only if someone pays me?" He curled his lips over his teeth, baring them in an animalistic way.

I continued to glare at him icily.

"I will kill you for free if it suits me." He opened his mouth and snapped his jaw shut, making a clicking sound with his teeth.

"You will not touch me if you wish to breathe," I growled.

"Zen it appears... zat we will never get our... revenge." His pale blue eyes were wild as he said the words.

"Revenge?" I asked evenly.

He grinned. His lips stirred in a creeping motion, as if every move he made was the essence that made up a nightmare.

Without warning, his hand shot to my jaw. He dug his fingers on either side of my cheeks, clawing the scabs that had formed from Henry's sword. I gritted my teeth and threw a punch from the side but before I made it very far, he jammed the fingers of his other hand into my windpipe, taking away my very breath. I coughed, but he didn't release my jaw.

His grip tightened on my cheeks and his teeth bared. "Now," he said with his eerily smooth voice, "tell me about zis… Charles Elliot… And I sink… perhaps we will be good friends." His smile twisted again as I clutched my throat and heaved at the pain of breathing in and out.

Lawrence

Wilton
December 31, 1816
Two days later

The entire building was full. I sat on the front pew as Henry and Charles took Jane and Lily by the hand over the altar. There weren't two happier couples in this world than the ones standing before the onlookers. If only James and Elizabeth could have been here to witness such an idyllic moment.

I smiled and shook my head as Charles and Henry took their vows. If they could have had it their way, they would have taken Lily and Jane to the altar the second the ladies had agreed to the union and would have invited no one.

Henry's father, seated to my left, quickly brushed a tear away as Henry took his vows.

Katie nudged my arm on my right. "I've never seen them look so content," she whispered with a grin.

"Nor I," I said, smiling.

"Lord and Lady Elliot would be pleased."

I nodded then looked over at the small bundle in her arms. She cradled her baby so he was looking out toward the two couples.

"Take note, little James," she said quietly to her baby before she leaned into her husband, Stephen, on her other side. He wrapped an arm around her as the couples kissed across the altar.

It was a perfect wedding.

Robert Graves

Lord Elliot was a lucky man indeed. Miss Lily Mason was always stunning; today she was a vision in her white dress. She smiled at the lucky devil as they stood at the altar. I never stood a chance competing with the Earl of Wiltshire.

I wouldn't have come to the wedding, but Lord Elliot had invited me personally. He said he was grateful for the help I gave his friends when they came to my shop inquiring about arsenic. When I asked Lord Elliot how his friend with the liver complaint was faring, he chuckled and didn't respond.

I couldn't claim a broken heart. It wasn't as if Miss Lily and I had even courted. But if there was a woman that would have easily stolen my heart, she would have been the one to do it. Social conventions were not her concern. She was spontaneous and positively delightful.

A man exhaled next to me with a conflicted breath. I looked over at him, wondering if he was pining for Miss Lily as well. But he wasn't looking at her. His eyes were directed toward her sister. Miss Jane Mason and her groom were also standing at the altar, hand in hand.

I looked over at the poor fellow next to me. "I could be wrong," I said quietly, "but I don't believe Miss Mason will notice you, even if you keep looking at her that way."

His head jerked in my direction, as if he had forgotten he was in the middle of a wedding ceremony. He knit his eyebrows together. "Looking at her what way?"

"How long have you known Miss Mason?" I asked.

"Quite a few years," he said.

I felt for him. I'd only known Miss Lily for a few weeks. I had only danced with her and sat by her at dinner once.

"I would tell you that there is always a chance to win her over," I said, smirking as I looked at Miss Mason and Mr. Thomas. "But we both know that would be a lie."

The man chuckled quietly. "You sure know how to cheer up a man." He extended his hand out to me. "William Ashby," he said, barely above a whisper. We were beginning to get looks for talking during the ceremony.

I shook his hand and spoke even quieter. "Robert Graves."

My eyes returned to Miss Lily. She promised to honor her marriage and then her lips parted and Lord Elliot kissed her. I couldn't help but let out a breath as I wondered what it would feel like to be in his place.

William chuckled next to me. "Perhaps if you sigh a little louder, Lady Elliot will come give you a kiss as well."

"I'm not sighing," I scowled as I rose to my feet with the guests. Miss Lily and Lord Elliot walked out of the church hand in hand. It was done.

Mr. Thomas offered Miss Mason his arm as they followed the first couple down the aisle. Miss Mason didn't even notice William as she was escorted out; she had eyes only for Mr. Thomas.

We followed the crowd outside where people cheered and threw rice as Lord Elliot and Henry Thomas helped their brides into an open carriage. Lord Elliot didn't mind taking full advantage of the chilly weather, wrapping his arm around his new wife and pulling her close. She looked up at him, smiling, then bit her bottom lip as if she couldn't help herself. He kissed her again.

"Don't worry," William said, barely holding back a grin. "I'll catch you if you swoon."

"Are you still here?" I asked, annoyed that I couldn't enjoy—or rather, imagine this moment differently—in peace.

"Yes. And now that the eldest Miss Mason is married, you can let me cry on your shoulder."

I grinned and handed him my business card. "I have a remedy for that."

He pocketed the card and chuckled. "You have a remedy for a broken heart, do you?"

I nodded. "Indeed. My shop usually has at least one woman roaming its shelves."

William laughed.

William Ashby

Wilton
November 2, 1817
Almost one year later

I held the letter in my hand and read it again, just to be sure I hadn't misunderstood. The sender was from His Grace, Andrew Fletcher, Duke of Hastingwood.

As my next in line to inherit, you are hereby summoned to Hastingwood Manor. We will receive you in six week's time.

There is much to discuss. I await your response,

Hastingwood.

I knew we were loosely related, but last I checked, there were seven or eight men in line before me. I wanted no association with the Fletchers—especially after the rumors about what Frederick had attempted with Jane.

I thought of Jane. It was true that she hadn't truly broken my heart. She didn't have the chance. Or I didn't, depending on how you looked at it. Her wedding had taken place almost a year ago, and I was thankful that I no longer thought of her.

I looked at the letter in my hand again and let out an uneasy breath.

This complicated things.

Charles

Wilton
November 7, 1817
Five days later

I looked in the mirror and rubbed my fingers over my short, well-trimmed beard. It was nice to be back. It would be interesting to see if Henry had decided to keep his face clean shaven or grow out his beard again. He had been gone with Jane for almost a year now on business and a small tour abroad. Lily and I had returned from our own journey only a week previous.

Lily was dying to see her sister, and although I would never admit it out loud, I couldn't wait to see my brother.

My heart jumped as slender fingers wrapped around my torso from behind. She rested her head on my back then pressed her lips where she rested. I slowly took her hands in mine and brought her to stand in front of me. Her beauty radiated from the inside, then overflowed to every part of her. I loved her more than life itself.

I rested my arms around her waist as she placed hers behind my neck. "Are you excited to see Jane?" I kissed her softly.

She smiled. "I *am* excited to see Jane." She kissed me this time, leaving me hungry for more.

"There should be a rule about you staying out of my bedchamber before company arrives." I pulled her closer.

She gave me a look of mischief then kissed just below my ear. "I'm sure we have some time before they get here."

I shook my head at her ability to completely upend me in a matter of seconds.

"I don't just want *some* time, Lily."

She smirked. "My apologies, Lord Elliot; you'll have to wait until later."

"Not if you keep looking at me like that."

She grinned and kissed me one more time, making sure to leave me completely breathless before she walked out in a slow, sultry way.

I shook my head as I realized she would never stop casting her spells.

Henry

Wilton
November 7, 1817
Earlier that morning

It was autumn when I held my entire world. The rustle of leaves touched my window outside as she laid in my arms and softly breathed, the linens and blankets keeping us warm. I knew we needed to get ready, but I didn't want to wake her.

"You tell me when you're ready," I whispered.

Eyes still closed, she slowly moved her head from off my chest and pressed a kiss to the base of my neck. Her hair cascaded over my shoulder as she returned her head to where it had been. I breathed in slowly and wrapped my arms tighter around her loose nightgown. She looked like a goddess with her wavy auburn hair flowing around her, too divine for this world.

"*I* don't mind if you're never ready," I said quietly. "But your sister will probably murder me."

Mornings with my wife were a favorite of mine. I loved watching her sleep peacefully as the darkness slowly shifted to light.

Jane sighed, then propped her elbow up next to me and rested her head on her hand. Her eyes greeted mine for the first time that morning. There wasn't a sight I loved more.

"Lily is probably still asleep," she said with a tired grin.

"Perhaps." I pressed a soft kiss to her lips. It was our first morning in the house since we had returned from our tour.

"Just a while longer," Jane said, kissing me once before she laid her head back down against my shoulder. I kissed her forehead then brushed my fingers through her hair, wondering how in the world I was lucky enough to have this angel.

"As long as it takes," I said, bringing her closer.

The sun peeked through the clouds as Jane and I rode in the carriage, side by side. I intertwined my fingers with hers and raised the back of her hand to my lips. My father and Martha sat across from us, both pretending they weren't watching us.

"Martha, you look lovely today," Jane said, smiling. Martha was now in her seventies, a good twenty years older than my father, and she was treated like a mother and grandmother in her older age.

Martha smiled back. "Thank you, my dear." She reached over and took Jane's other hand, squeezing it. "You and Henry have brought so much excitement in the house today, I think it's making me feel younger."

My father chuckled. "Martha, you'll outlive us all."

"Only to keep you in line." She tried not to grin.

I smirked. "Jane will keep us all in line. Except for when she sneaks frogs in your bed."

Jane laughed. "Next time it'll be snakes."

"So long as they stay out of my bed," my father said with a grin.

Charles and Lily were waiting for us when we pulled up. Lily ran to the carriage before it stopped. The second Jane stepped down, they threw their arms around each other and embraced while they laughed.

"It's been so long," Lily sighed, tears already escaping her eyes.

Jane squeezed Lily tight. "I've missed you." She quickly brushed away a tear of her own and then they laughed once more. "What mischief have you been up to?"

Lily grinned. "Mostly working my magic with Alice's hair to see if I can break Lawrence."

Jane laughed. "Lily! You can't be a countess and do the lady's maid's hair."

She smirked. "Why ever not?"

I smiled as I watched Lily and Jane laugh back and forth. As I stepped out of the carriage and helped Martha down, Charles walked over. I smiled as I got a good look at his face. I slapped a hand on his shoulder and laughed. "It appears the squirrel is staying." I eyed his beard.

He stroked it with his finger and thumb. "It had to." He smirked. "In order to give you a sporting chance." He gestured to me. "It appears that you're having trouble growing the squirrel now."

"It really is a mystery," I said, grinning. "It just doesn't want to grow back."

I had missed Charles these past eleven months, not that I would ever admit it out loud. Up to the point we both married, we hadn't gone anywhere or done anything without each other.

Jane and Lily walked over to join us. I turned to my sister-in-law. "Tell me, Lady Elliot. How many times did your husband cry because I was away?"

Charles rolled his eyes.

"At least twice a day," Lily said with a smirk. Charles grabbed her hand and pulled her into him until his arms were completely surrounding her in a vice grip so she couldn't move. She laughed and squirmed, trying to get free.

"Sorry, Lady Elliot," Charles said next to her ear. "You've been caught giving away treasonous information."

Charles looked up at me. "I was only crying that you weren't staying away longer."

I grinned. "The feeling is mutual."

Jane smiled. "Is that why you told me stories about your brother at least five times a day?"

I poked Jane's side and she gasped. I gave her a wicked smile—I had recently discovered that she was ticklish. Her eyes got big as she realized what was about to happen.

I shook my head. "My own wife, conspiring with the enemy."

She ran before I had a chance to grab her hand. I gave her a small head start before I ran after her. I had her in three strides. I hadn't even attempted to tickle her and she was already curling up in a ball with anticipation. I couldn't help but laugh, wrapping my arms around her and kissing the top of her head.

"You're getting off the hook this time, Mrs. Thomas. But only if you promise to help me put snakes in Charles's bed."

Lily laughed at my comment to Jane, remembering their sibling game of loading mine and Charles's beds with as many frogs as they could the day after I proposed to Jane.

A new voice approached. "Will you at least make sure they are done shedding their skin beforehand?" Lawrence joined our circle.

"Lawrence!" I couldn't help but embrace him, slapping his back.

He smiled. "It's good to see you too, Henry." He looked at Jane for a moment. "And it's good to see that you are keeping your husband in line." He winked at my wife as I moved back to her and wrapped my arms around her from behind. She smiled.

Martha shook her head and rolled her eyes. "I'm going inside. All of this sentimental stuff is turning me soft. And I can't keep the deadness off if I turn soft."

We all laughed as Martha stalked inside.

It was autumn when I held my entire world. She was wrapped in my arms while we laughed with the people we loved most. She rested her arms over mine and leaned her head back against me. And as our laughs fell away, we all looked at one another.

And *we* breathed it in. All of it.

THE END

Charles, Henry, and Lawrence will return in Crimson Snow to solve another mystery with William Ashby and Robert Graves

PLEASE LEAVE REVIEWS

AMAZON

GOODREADS

ACKNOWLEDGEMENTS

It is a miracle this book happened. I'm not a good writer by nature—I was actually only ever barely passable in school. I failed at my one creative writing project in high school, then washed my hands of it, more than happy to never pick it up again. Little did I know that a year ago, October 2023, I would write a book. Miracles need to be recognized by their source—their heavenly source. I can only attribute it to my Maker, my Heavenly Father. I have been reminded multiple times through this project that this is not a natural gift of mine, that it was a gift that was given to me and that I had better take care with how I use it. This book wouldn't be possible without Him.

Second, I couldn't have done it without an amazing support group. My husband, Chris, has listened to me talk non-stop about this book and has helped me through my blocks. I couldn't have done it without him. My daughters have been so patient with me as I've been torn between being a homeschool mom, and working on this long, taxing project. So, thank you family, for loving me through arduous road we have all walked this last year.

Third, Chalyce Peck practically held my hand through the marketing part of my releasing my first edition. Oh Chalyce, what would I do without you? Her emails and texts come through late into the night when I knew she could have been sleeping. She has been such a cheerleader for me and has made the nitty gritty somehow exciting. Thank you, Chalyce!

Fourth, Ashlyn Pells for doing the original editing for my first edition, and Ruth Owen for editing my second edition. Both ladies did a phenomenal job with each edition.

Fifth, although you should never judge a book by its cover, who doesn't? Emily Bourne @naturalbournephotography made my vision come to life when I launched my first edition. If you haven't seen my original cover, you should check it out. I'm so grateful for her late nights, for her search for dry ice and fog machines to make the fog look just right. She really put her heart and soul into my original cover, and it showed. Now, for all the other people who have cheered me on that I couldn't have done this without. My sister Michelle, who gave helpful feedback at the very beginning when I was only four chapters in and reminded me that it's impossible to hate Henry—so Jane had better have a really good reason not to like him. My mom, who read as much as she could even when her eyesight didn't allow it. My cousin Aubrie, who has been one of my biggest cheerleaders, staying up late reading my book. My sister Nicole, who read the whole book in three days instead of taking care of other important tasks. Sarah Lontine, who reminded me that Jane and Henry's relationship needed to be an enemies-to-lovers trope, or at least have a bumpy beginning. Bryn Webb, another cheerleader for me. My cousin Rachel… with the sexy ankles, who read my work when it wasn't quite completed and then had to stop and wait for me to finish, helping me fix the problems in the middle. Ruth Owen, who helped me fine-tune my first three chapters that I just hated in the beginning. My first writing group, Utah Wordsmith, who helped me see things I'd never even considered.

Last, I have to mention my oldest daughter, Jane, who has been my number one fan. What would I do without my Jane?

ABOUT THE AUTHOR

JANA L PERKINS is a romance writer who is devoted to giving her readers a sweeping experience that leaves them wanting more. A mother of three, Jana homeschools her daughters. She believes that education is essential for every mind, young and old, and should be explored in many different ways. When Jana isn't writing or teaching her children, she enjoys taking long walks with her husband, playing with her dogs, and trying new things.

You can support Jana L Perkins by leaving reviews. You can also sign up for her Newsletter through her website at https://www.thecrimsonarchives.com/newsletteremail

www.ingramcontent.com/pod-product-compliance
Lightning Source LLC
Chambersburg PA
CBHW020642110726
47901CB00001B/21